The Sword of the Lady

"Well written. Stirling has the ability to make the commonplace exciting and to dribble out the information needed to complete the tapestry of understanding . . . a good tale."
—SFRevu

"Absolutely stunning work [that] proves again why people say that Stirling is the best postapocalyptic writer today. There are enough twists and turns to keep fans of the series happy."
—Bitten by Books

"A thrilling, action-packed, and suspenseful quest narrative that takes place in a vividly described postapocalyptic world."
—Romantic Times

The Scourge of God

"Vivid. . . . Stirling eloquently describes a devastated, mystical world that will appeal to fans of traditional fantasy as well as postapocalyptic SF." —Publishers Weekly (starred review)

"Stirling is a perfect master of keep-them-up-all-night pacing, possibly the best in American SF, quite capable of sweeping readers all the way to the end." —Booklist (starred review)

"I liked this book. . . . Stirling is a master of world building. This series has gone a long way from its point of departure, but still keeps a horde of fans wanting more." —SFRevu

"Fans will remain enthralled. . . . The tale is filled with action, strong characters in conflict, vivid descriptions of a battered, dying land trying to come back to life two-plus decades since the Change, and a great cliff-hanging climax."
—Midwest Book Review

"Stirling has crafted a complex follow-up to The Sunrise Lands that vividly describes the political landscape. . . . Rudi's character is satisfyingly multifaceted, deeply troubled by his visions as he searches for answers at the risk of his life in a world gone awry." —Monsters and Critics

continued . . .

The Sunrise Lands

"Combines vigorous military adventure with cleverly packaged political idealism.... Stirling's narrative deftly balances sharply contrasting ideologies.... The thought-provoking and engaging storytelling should please Stirling's many fans."
—*Publishers Weekly*

"Brilliant action." —*Booklist*

"Fast-paced." —*Futures Mystery Anthology Magazine*

"Stirling has his world firmly in hand.... All those who were on board for *Dies the Fire*, *The Protector's War*, and *A Meeting at Corvallis* should jump on this ride as well."
—*Contra Costa Times*

"A master of speculative fiction and alternate history, Stirling delivers another chapter in an epic of survival and rebirth."
—*Library Journal*

A Meeting at Corvallis

"[A] richly realized story of swordplay and intrigue."
—*Entertainment Weekly*

"Stirling concludes his alternative-history trilogy in high style.... [The story] resembles one of the cavalry charges the novel describes—gorgeous, stirring, and gathering such earth-pounding momentum that it's difficult to resist."
—*Publishers Weekly*

"A fascinating glimpse into a future transformed by the lack of easy solutions to both human and technological dilemmas."
—*Library Journal*

"Grand and resonant ... exciting and suspenseful.... Blending elements of Arthurian and Tolkienesque romance with down-in-the-muck details of birth and death, farming and herding, building and politicking, Stirling manages to fashion a narrative that acknowledges that humanity is a creature of both soul and body, heart and mind, lust and sacrifice, much in the manner of Poul Anderson.... Stirling has blazed a clear comet trail across his postapocalyptic landscape that illuminates both the best and the worst of which our species is capable." —Science Fiction Weekly

"The ensuing maze of intrigue, diplomacy, and battle (with a wonderful variety of weapons ingeniously exploiting archaic technology) comes up to Stirling's highest standards for pacing, world building, action, and strong characterizations, particularly of women ... a major work by an authentic master of alternate history." —*Booklist* (starred review)

The Sword of the Lady

A NOVEL OF THE CHANGE

S. M. STIRLING

A ROC BOOK

ROC

Published by New American Library, a division of
Penguin Group (USA) Inc., 375 Hudson Street,
New York, New York 10014, USA
Penguin Group (Canada), 90 Eglinton Avenue East, Suite 700, Toronto,
Ontario M4P 2Y3, Canada (a division of Pearson Penguin Canada Inc.)
Penguin Books Ltd., 80 Strand, London WC2R 0RL, England
Penguin Ireland, 25 St. Stephen's Green, Dublin 2,
Ireland (a division of Penguin Books Ltd.)
Penguin Group (Australia), 250 Camberwell Road, Camberwell, Victoria 3124,
Australia (a division of Pearson Australia Group Pty. Ltd.)
Penguin Books India Pvt. Ltd., 11 Community Centre, Panchsheel Park,
New Delhi - 110 017, India
Penguin Group (NZ), 67 Apollo Drive, Rosedale, North Shore 0632,
New Zealand (a division of Pearson New Zealand Ltd.)
Penguin Books (South Africa) (Pty.) Ltd., 24 Sturdee Avenue,
Rosebank, Johannesburg 2196, South Africa

Penguin Books Ltd., Registered Offices:
80 Strand, London WC2R 0RL, England

Published by Roc, an imprint of New American Library, a division of Penguin
Group (USA) Inc. Previously published in a Roc hardcover edition.

First Roc Mass Market Printing, September 2010
10 9 8 7 6 5 4 3 2 1

Copyright © Steven M. Stirling, 2009
Map by Cortney Skinner
All rights reserved

 REGISTERED TRADEMARK—MARCA REGISTRADA

Printed in the United States of America

ACKNOWLEDGMENTS

The saga continues and grows—for a solitary business, you need a lot of help!

Thanks to my friends who are also first readers:

To Steve Brady, for assistance with dialects and British background, and also natural history of all sorts.

Thanks also to Kier Salmon, for once again helping with the beautiful complexities of the Old Religion, and with local details for Oregon. And for further use of BD!

To Diana L. Paxson, for help and advice (amounting to virtual collaboration in the Norrheim chapters), and for writing the beautiful "Westria" books, among many others. If you liked the Change novels, you'll probably enjoy the hell out of the Westria books—I certainly did, and they were one of the inspirations for this series; and her *Essential Asatru* and recommendation of *Our Troth* were extremely helpful . . . and fascinating reading.

To Dale Price, for help with Catholic organization, theology and praxis; and for his entertaining blog, Dyspeptic Mutterings, which can be read at http://dprice.blogspot.com.

To Brenda Sutton, for multitudinous advice.

To Will Sanders, for putting me in stitches with Princess Yumping Yimminy; read his excellent mystery "Smoke" for his take on this—unbelievably—real-life character.

To Melinda Snodgrass, Daniel Abraham, Sage Walker, Emily Mah, Terry England, George R.R. Martin, Walter

Jon Williams, Vic Milan, Jan Stirling and Ian Tregellis of Critical Mass, for constant help and advice as the book was under construction.

Thanks to John Miller, good friend, writer and scholar, for many useful discussions, for lending me some great books, and for some really, really cool old movies. And to Gail Gerstner-Miller, ditto. Also the steak pie recipe was delicious.

Special thanks to Heather Alexander, bard and balladeer, for permission to use the lyrics from her beautiful songs, which can be—and should be!—ordered at www.heatherlands.com. Run, do not walk, to do so.

Thanks again to William Pint and Felicia Dale, for permission to use their music, which can be found at www.pintndale.com, and should be by anyone with an ear and saltwater in their veins.

Lyrics of "The Trawling Trade" are used by kind permission of the writer, John Conolly, who also wrote the folk classic "Fiddler's Green" (further details on myspace.com/johnconolly).

And to Three Weird Sisters—Gwen Knighton, Mary Crowell, Brenda Sutton, and Teresa Powell—whose alternately funny and beautiful music can be found at http://www.threeweirdsisters.com.

And to Heather Dale for permission to quote the lyrics of her songs, whose beautiful (and strangely appropriate!) music can be found at www.HeatherDale.com, and is highly recommended. The lyrics are wonderful and the tunes make it even better.

Thanks to S. J. "Sooj" Tucker for permission to use the lyrics of her beautiful songs, which can be found at www.skinnywhitechick.com, and should be.

The "ancestral epic" in Chapter Seventeen is actually

the opening paragraph of *The Broken Sword*, a fantasy classic by Poul Anderson. Go out and get it!

Much overdue thanks to Russell Galen, my agent, who has been an invaluable help and friend for a decade now. By a stunning noncoincidence, my career has shot up like a sapling in this period. We make a good team; not only is he smart as a whip on the business side, but his advice on literary matters and on the conjunction between the two has been spot-on.

All mistakes, infelicities and errors are of course my own.

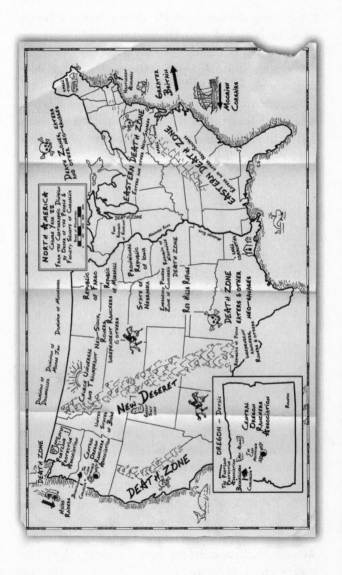

CHAPTER ONE

"Shining pearl within the crimson sky,
Guide me in the coming night
Perfect seed within the humble husk,
Ground my feet in soil so I may rise
Patient leaf within the endless pool
Calm me when the torrent falls
Gentle wind within the slanting grass
Bear me ever on until I rest—"

Rudi Mackenzie and Edain hadn't been singing the hymn; more of a breathy whisper, though it rang loud in their minds as the moon rose enormous on the horizon, and they'd come down here below the lip of the valley where there was more cover for the rite. Rudi stopped instantly when a stick snapped. The warm sense of communion ghosted away like dust in a desert, and he sank down behind the tangle of wild rose in a motion that was swift but smooth rather than a catch-the-eye jerk.

Five paces to his right and a little behind him Edain Aylward Mackenzie did the same; his great shaggy half-mastiff bitch Garbh vanished even more completely, belly to the ground, ears cocked and only her black nose moving as it wrinkled. The air wasn't moving enough to carry scent any distance, but her blocky barrel-shaped head seemed to split as the thin black lips drew back silently from her long yellow fangs.

The other half of her was probably wolf.

Both men listened hunter-fashion, with their whole bodies: not straining, but opening themselves to the summer twilight, letting sound and sight and smells and the movement of air on skin flow in until you *knew*. The evening hush was strong and the hot thick air hazy along the ridge where they lay above the river valley, full of rank odors of flowers and greenery and warm earth damp from yesterday's thunderstorm. Sweat trickled down Rudi's flanks beneath the brigantine torso-armor he wore, a corselet of little steel plates riveted between two layers of soft green leather. Something with too many legs bit the back of his left knee below the kilt and above the sock-hose, adding to the prickling itches. The coarse sandy grain of the leather on the riser grip of his longbow drank moisture from the palm of his left hand, growing damp but not slippery, which was the point.

The steep fall of ground to the river below was a patchy almost-forest. Single stands or clumps of mature pre-Change burr oak and shagbark hickory, black walnut and sugar maple reared above teardrop-shaped surrounds of saplings, where they'd rolled their seed downslope in the decades since the State foresters had stopped coming to prune and tend. The new growth ranged from fresh sprouts to fair-sized trees as old as Rudi, but the canopy wasn't tall or closely spaced enough to shade out the undergrowth yet, and a dense understory of weeds and scrub was just past its summer prime.

The open spaces were brushy meadow scattered with white pasture thistle and Queen Anne's lace, and thickets of four-foot-tall Gaura, its pink flowers a wash of fading color as the deeper scarlet of its leaves turned black with sunset. The faint sweet scent of it became stronger with crushed stems and petals; as the sun dropped lower behind him he could see the tops of the plants swaying in little jerks in half a dozen spots. Once . . . a moment's stillness . . . twice . . . again . . . another pause . . .

And there's no wind, Rudi thought grimly, as his mouth went dry.

He was only twenty-three, but he'd seen enough violent death to know how easily it could happen to him—know in body and blood, as well as his head. He kept his breaths long and deep and slow to help loosen the tightness in gut and crotch and slow the pounding of blood that were the instinctive response to a sudden deadly threat. Half of transcending fear was making the flesh serve the spirit's need, instead of letting it command you. And breathing deep could give you a little extra endurance at need. Not much, but every bit counted at the narrow passage. His eyes stayed fixed on the vegetation, and the off-and-on course of the small betraying motions.

Men crawling on their bellies then, moving a bit at a time and pausing in between. Men or wolves or wild dogs, they all know that trick, but I'd be betting the first.

Here in the Wild Lands men would most likely attack him on sight, and they'd likely be faster than he afoot, over ground they knew. He glanced over to where Edain waited, a movement of eyes more than head, and got a very slight nod.

That meant both agreement that they were undetected so far and *waiting on you, Chief.* Here and now that was both a burden and a comfort; the call was his, but you couldn't ask for a better man than Edain to have your back for all he was just turned twenty. Rudi moved his right-hand fingers, thumb to each as if counting on them, then turned it palm-up and lifted it a bit, a combination of gestures that meant *how many?* in Clan war-Sign. Edain's answer was a tiny shrug; he didn't have any real idea either.

So . . . no less than six, possibly about thirty if they're very good. And they haven't seen us yet. It's someone else who's the expected guest at the feast, and them laying the table and knocking out the bung of the barrel of red salt ale. Someone coming by the track down there along the river; the position they're in will be invisible from down by the water's edge.

The ambush was being set with real skill; he doubted most Mackenzie warriors could have done it better, or even Dúnedain Rangers. He kept his breathing slow and quiet and deep, and his body motionless with a silent wariness that was coiled rather than stiff, ready to explode off the ground if he must. Nothing moved but his eyes, and he flicked them back and forth; a steady fixed gaze was oddly noticeable to the one you were staring at, like brushing a feather over the nape of the neck.

If it *was* only six or so savages then he and Edain could probably handle them, not taking into account whoever they were planning on ambushing. The two Mackenzies would have the advantage of surprise, height, good purpose-made armor and weapons rather than crude makeshifts, and skills none of the wild-men could match.

But there's also the matter of the rights and wrongs of the thing, so.

The ones walking into this ambush might be men of deep-dyed wickedness for all he knew, and meeting their fate; this wasn't his territory, and he wasn't one to draw the blade on strangers lightly.

On the other hand, I need friends here—or at least al-

lies. I've no time to spare; the lives of my friends depend on it. And at seventh and last, fights are usually about us and them, not rights and wrongs. Needs must when the Fates drive.

Half in prayer: *And if this deed must return on the doer, let it fall on me; it's my decision, and Edain but follows his chieftain. This is a burden I took up with the sword.*

A warrior's cold appraisal took over. They could certainly shoot at least three or four each before the enemy came close enough for handstrokes, perhaps more if there were many targets. If it was thirty of them . . . that was a different matter altogether.

There was a certain brute simplicity to the arithmetic of war. Thirty men weren't fifteen times stronger than two.

More like forty or fifty times stronger, he thought unhappily. *The advantage grows as the square of the difference, other things being equal.*

Nor was there any absolute certainty of safety whatever when men fought to kill. Sheer luck was involved; if your eye was in the place where a random arrow wanted to go, then it was off to the Summerlands willy-nilly. He hadn't come all the way from the Willamette in Oregon to die in a little skirmish two-thirds of the way to his goal. Too much depended on him.

Their horses were behind and above them, in the strip of fire-scarred brushy woods where the open prairie met the valley, all loose-tethered, except his mare Epona who was guarding them. He made a low chittering sound between his teeth, something that melded into the natural buzz and twitter and creak of the wilds. That would keep her quiet, even if she scented another horse or heard it neigh. The problem was that it wouldn't mean anything to Edain's horse or the pack beast, who were . . .

Not more than average bright, even for horses. I love horses but Epona aside . . .

He was glad he'd done so a minute later, when the dull thud-and-clop of hooves sounded on the broken asphalt and dirt of the roadway that followed the Illinois River below. Four men rode into sight, with as many more packhorses on leading reins—there were bundles over their backs, and from the look of them and the trail of flies those held butchered game carcasses strapped up in the hides. Between them and Rudi the brush moved again, and he thought he caught the glint of edged metal through the gloaming of the summer evening. Someone was being a little overeager, or had forgotten to dip the blade of his spear in mud.

Ambush, sure and I had the right of it, Rudi thought. *They're concentrating on the road down there, and with the sun at their backs to blind anyone looking their way. The which means they can't see me and Edain easily either, of course.*

From what he'd heard in Iowa the only dwellers here were vicious savages, descendants of city folk who'd lived through the first Change years by eating each other, worse and worse as you went farther east. That had been Ingolf's opinion too, and Ingolf Vogeler had made his living off salvage expeditions into the dead cities for many years. Journeying halfway across the continent with him had taught Rudi that the man from Wisconsin was usually a good judge.

On the other hand, Edain and I cannot haul all those wagons of treasure to the Mississippi alone, Rudi mused. *From the way things have gone this past week, we can't even get* close *to them without help from the folk hereabouts.*

He ducked lower and thoughtfully picked up his sallet helm and set it on his head, with the visor slid up along the low steel dome and locked in place and the sponge and felt lining pressing firmly around brow and temples and the back of his skull. Then he reached over his shoulder to his quiver for a shaft to set on his string. Edain did the same with his open-faced helmet, nocked one arrow and eased out three more from his quiver, holding them between one finger and his bow, a trick for rapid shooting. If they were careful there was little chance the ambushers would notice, and it was well to be ready. Also the dull matt-green surface of the steel was less conspicuous than the raw metallic brightness of his shoulder-length red-blond mane, or even the sun-streaked oak brown of Edain's curly mop.

And haul those wagons to Iowa I must, since that is the price demanded to release Matti. And Ingolf and all my friends and kin by that . . .

Right now he had to keep his mind cool. Thinking *mad tyrant* of Anthony Heasleroad would just make him rage, though the very Gods knew it was accurate.

. . . by that . . . eccentric gentleman . . . the Bossman of Iowa. Will there ever be a chance with less risk? Even trying to back away might spook the ones hiding there. And what better, quicker introduction to the men they mean to kill than a rescue? If I must work with cannibals or the children of such, I will.

After all, if you got too choosey about people's ancestors . . .

Were the Gael not once headhunters who burned men alive as sacrifices? Did the English not come to these lands with fire and massacre? And was not my anamchara Matti's father a monster to turn a man's stomach, sure?

Decision jelled. With his free hand he reached down and picked up a clod of soil, touching it to his lips in silent prayer for an instant: *Earth must be fed.* To take life was to accept your own death's part in the world, and the gesture acknowledged it. Edain copied the motion, and they both set their fingers to the strings of their longbows.

The horsemen riding unaware into the trap down the road below were stripped to the waist in the muggy heat, regardless of the mosquitoes that were beginning to whine. Even at a hundred yards and through the gloaming he could see that three of them carried long spears tipped with ground-down butcher knives, and they all had a clutch of javelins slung over their backs as well in something like a big quiver. Then the still air shifted and a little breeze cuffed at leaf and twig around him, cooling the sweat that stuck strands of his hair to the back of his neck beneath the flare of the helm. The horses tossed their heads at the scent of their own kind; one nickered, and was answered by an equine snort from behind the two Mackenzies.

Rudi came smoothly to his feet, as swiftly as if he and the animal had practiced the signal together.

"Ambush!" he shouted, his trained voice throwing the sound from deep in his chest. *"Trap! In the brush above you!"*

The scrub exploded with armed men, screams and ragged figures and the ugly sheen of spearheads; many-more than he'd thought there would be, but it was too late to undo his decision. They wavered for a moment, caught between the foemen they had expected to take unawares and the strangers above them.

Closer to thirty than to six of them. More like forty, the Dagda club them dead! went through him in a flickering instant. *I do hope the men they wanted to kill can take some of the weight!*

"Morrigú!" Rudi screamed, to rivet their attention. *"Morrigú!"*

He called on the Crow Goddess as he drew and shot, for She was the one whose feathered host fed on the fruits of battle, the Dark Mother who had sent Raven to claim him in the *nemed* while he was still a child. Edain simply howled, the cry of the Wolf that was his sept totem, and then their voices rose together in the racking banshee shriek of the Clan's battle-yell.

One of the ambushers had a short stiff bow of some sort ready, and he had the presence of mind to turn and aim at the tall figure on the slope above. Rudi had already started to draw Mackenzie-style past the angle of his jaw as he called the warning, shoulders and gut and hips as much as arms in the force that bent the great stave of yellow yew-wood, but Edain was a fractional second ahead of him.

The cloth yard shaft snapped out as he let the string roll off his fingertips and lash at the bracer on his left forearm. The range was short, and his war-bow drew well over a hundred pounds. The arrow was a blurred streak in the dimness and then a *crack* of parting bone before the enemy archer flipped backward with the gray-goose fletching standing up like a brutal exclamation point from his face. Edain's shaft hadn't missed either; it went through the man's torso in a double splash, breaking ribs going in and coming out, then struck the next man behind in the stomach and stayed there. Rudi's hand flicked to the quiver again and again, nock-draw-aim-loose in the deadly fast ripple Mackenzies were taught from child-hood, three seconds for an arrow. They were both shooting wherever a telltale shape or motion betrayed the obvious threat of an enemy archer.

Some sort of leader grabbed ambushers and pushed them towards the pair of clansmen as he yelped an order in a yammering dialect. It cut off in a gurgling scream as Edain shifted aim and sent an arrow through his throat. A score of the wild-men came uphill at the Mackenzies in a bounding rush, while as manymore boiled down towards the river; they must have thought there were more than two new foemen, fooled by shock and the eye-watering brightness that lingered behind him and the shower of cloth yard arrows stabbing down at them.

"Left, mine!" Rudi called sharply as the foe came on in a yelling mob, then spread out into a rough line.

The enemy must have had some concept of archery; they knew that they had to get across the killing ground as fast as they might. They had no idea at all of what the west-country longbow could do in skilled hands, from the way they came straight on regardless with their shields up instead of dodging to and fro as they charged. And they were about to learn.

Snap. Snap.

The waxed linen of the bowstrings struck their leather bracers with a light whapping sound, and the arrows blurred out with a *whirrrt* of cloven air. A man dropped from each end of the attackers' rough formation, with the flat punching smack of arrowheads striking flesh loud enough to hear.

Snap. Snap. Snap. Snap.

Four more men died in eight seconds, three instantly and one screaming and thrashing as a cedarwood shaft hammered through shield and arm and chest before it lodged in his spine. Then the rest were upon him, snarling shouting hairy faces vaguely seen as they labored up the hillside as if from a well of darkness, weapons reaching for his life. He tossed aside the bow and swept out his longsword in a hiss of steel on greased wood and leather. The other hand stripped the little buckler from its clip on the scabbard.

He was the second-ranked archer in the Clan Mackenzie, who were a people of the bow. But Rudi had never met his own equal with the sword since he got his full growth, not anywhere in his travels. Not yet. Everything slowed, sound burring deeper, vision fading except for faces, hands, weapons; he felt light and easy, his motions flowing like water over rocks in a mountain torrent.

I'm dead if I let them get around me and settle themselves, he knew. *And I must keep their eyes on me and away from Edain. He has my back.*

Existence was a dance through the purple dusk, lines precise as those scribed with compass and surveyor's strings linking blade to target. It was *ríastrad*, the battle-madness of the warrior Goddess whose scythe reaped men. He charged, shrieking, clearing the bush ahead of him with a long lunging stride; a yard of layer-forged steel in his fist and the eerie keening scream of the Mackenzies on his lips. A rust-pitted spearhead ground down from one blade of a pair of garden shears went over his right shoulder as he ducked beneath a thrust, and he struck with the buckler as it did.

The soup-plate shape of the metal shield cracked into a face covered in a black beard that crawled with lice, hard enough to make bone crumble and throw the wild-man backward to roll downslope in a tangle of limbs. With the weight of his armor added in there were better than two hundred pounds behind the blow, and the man wouldn't be getting up again. The twinge from the old wound in his right shoulder was distant, unimportant except to remind him of how the infected arrow had weakened it a little.

In the same instant the blade in his left hand flicked out, the point driving through a throat and past it with scarcely a tug. Behind it a spray of droplets hung in the air for a second, black in the dying light.

There was a wisssst-*thud* behind him and an earsplitting scream, as an arrow struck and lodged in bone; more hissed past to strike, one close enough for the fletching to brush the skin of his neck in passing. The *first*-ranked archer in the Clan was in back of him, twice winner of the Silver Arrow at the Lughnasadh Games and a hunter of beasts and men. Then another cry of horrified pain, beneath a roaring growl; Garbh was at work protecting her master as he shot, darting in to slash at a hamstring and then close her great jaws on the man's face as he fell, jerking him back and forth as she worried at what her long fangs held.

The twisted gorgon mask of Rudi's face made a man stumble back in midattack. And die an instant later in a galvanic convulsion as the sword point flicked into and out of his eye faster than a frog's tongue licking up a passing insect on the wing, punching through the thin bone and into the brain.

Another time, and the grating, crunching sensation that flowed up his hand and arm might come back to leave him sweating and clenched in some moment of peace. Now it was only a slight tug on his wrist as he wrenched the sword free and sliced down a spear shaft in a motion that left a long curl of wood flying free with the wielder's fingers.

A thunder of hooves, and Epona was there, her eyes white and rolling, her great slab teeth bared as she bugled a challenge. One of the wild-men looked around just in time to see her milling forehooves come down on him like steel-shod warhammers, and threw up his arms in a gesture as futile as his scream. The remaining attackers crowded forward towards Rudi, half attacking him, half fleeing her. A thought flickered through some remote corner of his mind:

There are people who think horses can't be dangerous because they eat grass.

A stab as precise as a surgeon's scalpel in over the collarbone, and a man collapsed with the great mass of arteries above the heart severed. The withdrawal turned into a smashing backhand chop that sent a spearhead pinwheeling away into the evening with half a foot of shaft still attached. He slid forward in a smooth savage rush; the man made one futile jabbing motion with the stub before Rudi cracked the pommel of his sword into the temple and drove bone-splinters into his brain.

Get in close, he thought/knew.

He leapt over the hocking swing of a blade that had probably started life as some sort of hedging tool and was near enough to the weapon westerners called a billhook. It hissed beneath his boots, and one of the wild-men screamed as it struck *his* leg, as much in rage as pain. Rudi kicked as he landed, a solid heel-strike to the billman's knee; something gave under the boot with a grisly snapping, crunching sound.

Ignore that one, he's out of it.

He pushed off the impact, using it to swing himself around, the longsword slashing horizontally as he spun.

Get close, get close . . .

Too close for anyone to draw a spear back for a stab, and himself a whirling screaming striking blur that left death and ululating agony in its wake as the melee stumbled across the hillside's uncertain footing. Edges and clubs grated and banged on his helmet, thumped into his brigandine, hard enough to leave bruises he'd feel later, if he lived—they were striking at the head and body from instinct, unused to dealing with real armor and not knowing how vulnerable they were to his ironclad violence.

If I had full war-harness on and a knight's shield I could take the lot of them!

But he didn't, and it could only be seconds until sharp metal hit something unprotected and vital, throat or limbs; he couldn't block a dozen men, couldn't kill them all. There wasn't *time*—

An ax looped towards his neck. Rudi's buckler deflected it with a *crang*, and his sword licked down on the man's arm above the elbow. The edge cracked into bone and through it with an ugly thump that jarred up the weapon and into his arm and shoulder. The man spun away, staring at the bleeding stump and then sitting down to die. Startled as the blood spurted over her fetlocks, Epona stopped stamping a body into rags of flesh and bone-splinter and reared to pound her hooves into him instead.

Rudi recovered with desperate speed and a spray of leaves and twigs beneath his boots, but the next man was poised with his spear cocked back to thrust into Rudi's face, the lunge already beginning . . .

. . . and he froze, with an expression of intense surprise on his features for an instant, as a wet red point appeared through his chest. Then he went flaccid and collapsed at the Mackenzie's feet. Behind him a horseman swerved his mount and snatched another javelin out of the hide bucket slung over his back, throwing it with a whoop. The shadowed woods were alive for an instant with leaping fleeing men, throwing aside their weapons to run with heedless speed and crashing through the thickets as the horsemen they'd ambushed harried them on.

Rudi thrust the point of his sword into the earth as a support, leaning with his mouth open to suck in the air his lungs craved despite the raw stinks it bore. His other arm went around Epona's neck as she nuzzled him, the sweet grassy-musky scent of her breath and sweat strong in his nostrils as he panted. The wave of rage that had filled his veins and nerves like liquid fire cooled, leaving his skin rippling with a sudden cold and his body full of a leaden weakness.

Suddenly half a dozen minor cuts stung like itching fire, above the duller ache of wrenched and battered muscle. For a moment he was not sure if the gathering darkness was natural, or the product of a body driven beyond its limits. Fighting was the hardest labor in the world. He was young and very strong and in hard condition, but his body still tried to shake like an overworked horse, and he had to swallow again and again with a paper-dry mouth to keep the heaves from starting. His trainers back home, Mackenzies and Bearkillers and Association knights alike, had warned him that he pushed himself too hard.

So had Master Hao in Chenrezi Monastery, in the Valley of the Sun, where they'd taken refuge last winter from blizzards and pursuers; he'd been more specific about it, too:

There is a deep inner well that the body can tap, a store of great strength, and of great speed. Most never reach it; and of those who do, most only when uttermost need breaks down the barriers. A few by long training in the inner disciplines. But you, Raven-man, you can open that gate by wishing it so; it is in your nature. Be cautious with this gift! The merciful Buddha buried this deep within us for a reason! It is the last reserve against extremity. You shorten your life a little each time you draw from it.

The problem being, of course, that having your skull

dished in or six inches of steel shoved through your gut shortened life by much more than a little. He was very good with a blade, but nobody was good enough to deal with fighting many against one, unless something took him beyond himself. His skin quivered again. And you didn't feel the fear until afterwards, some place in the mind knowing how it would be when the edged metal grated through your eye sockets and the world went black—

There's a place beyond the Gate, and we return, he thought, not for the first time. *But not to this life. Death is a forgetting, whether it comes in terror like a tiger hunting in the night, or as the gentle Mother whose last gift is an end to pain. I'm not through being Rudi Mackenzie yet! Yet neither were these ready, who had their own purposes and needs. Dread Lord, Keeper-of-Laws, be gentle with those torn untimely from the world of men; and me also when my hour is come.*

He'd straightened when the three horsemen returned from their pursuit, and was wiping his blade on a swatch of rags torn from a body; Edain stood ready with another arrow on the string, discreetly pointed down and not drawn . . . yet. Garbh was glaring at his heel, tongue licking her reddened muzzle, ready for a leap to take a man out of the saddle. Epona abandoned a rear as Rudi grabbed at her hackamore with his free hand—you didn't use a bit on her—and she prepared to tolerate the men as she did those around him when he asked it of her.

Three. They lost a man, then. All of them wounded, but none very badly.

She tossed her head and whickered a little disdainfully at the strangers' mounts; they were all shorter than her seventeen hands of sleek black height, and none had her long-limbed grace. Their harness was crude, simple pad saddles and pre-Change bridles patched and repaired with bits and pieces of this and that. The Mackenzie chieftain waited with the sword still drawn, ready to strike if the three were inclined to add him to the larder.

"Owe you one, west-men," their leader said to Rudi, dismounting and extending a hand to them both in turn.

Ah. They can tell we're from west across the Mississippi. From the gear, most likely. Though probably not quite how far west.

"I'm Jake sunna Jake, n' these are my bros Tuk n' Samul." His smile revealed several missing teeth. "We runs with the Southside Freedom Fighters. I'm the big man a' Southside. Youze save our asses."

Rudi thrust his sword into the earth and took the man's hand, as callused as his own and very strong for his size. Probably *big man* meant something like *chief.* The native of the Wild Lands was several inches shorter than his own six-two, and failed to match Edain's five-nine by a finger or so; he was wiry-slender, with a sparse young black beard and hair haggled off below his ears and eyes so crow-colored that the pupil disappeared in the iris.

The dark olive face was scarred and weathered, but he judged the man was about his own twenty-three years, give or take. His short pants of crudely tanned and worse-sewn rabbit skins were held up by a broad belt with a buckle of salvaged metal; his weapons were a knife and a hatchet, besides his javelins, and all but the wooden shafts of the throwing spears looked to be of pre-Change make.

His eyes were shrewd as he took in Edain's bow, and he nodded at the peace gesture as the archer returned his arrow to the quiver. They went a little wider as he looked around and realized how many of the enemy had long gray fletched shafts in their bodies, and how far away

some of them were; both were obvious as the younger
Mackenzie went about the grisly but essential task of re-
trieving intact arrows and the heads of the broken ones.
It was also obvious how easily they'd smashed through
crude armor—leather studded with bits of metal, wooden
shields surfaced with salvaged STOP signs and similar
makeshifts for the most part, though one body wore a
modern mail shirt stolen or bartered from the other shore
of the Mississippi.

That hadn't helped its wearer either, though it made
it harder to get the arrow out undamaged.

"Kin I zee?" he said. "Thass new."

Edain shook his head wordlessly as he grasped an
arrow delicately with both sets of forefinger-and-thumb
and pulled. He didn't like letting strangers touch his
longbow—that one had been a special gift from his father, Aylward the Archer, the old man's personal war-
bow that he'd set aside when he could no longer bend
it. Rudi bent to retrieve his own and let the other man
try it. Jake grunted incredulously; his arms were knotted
with hard lean muscle, but they quivered and shook and
he abandoned the effort before the string was halfway
to his jaw. Drawing the great war-bow wasn't just a
matter of raw strength, though it needed that too. You
had to have the knack, and that came from long and
constant training—Mackenzies started their children at
age six or so.

Edain slipped his own weapon into the carrying loops
beside his quiver, cleaned his hands on a tuft of grass and
pointed to the bow riding behind one of the horsemen's
saddles with a crook-fingered *let me have that* gesture.
The rider hesitated for a moment, then handed it down.

"Fiberglass," the young Mackenzie archer said, at the
feel of the stave.

That meant it was pre-Change, and lucky not to have aged and cracked into uselessness. The stuff the old world had confusingly called *plastic* mostly didn't rot, but it lost strength and suppleness unpredictably. Then he bent it with one contemptuous finger on the string before handing it back.

"Twenty, twenty-five pounds draw. Nobbut a toy for little children, and feeble children at that, sure."

Most warriors were proud of their gear. Rudi could see the man begin to bridle before he looked around and spat in reluctant agreement.

Jake pushed a body over on its back with his foot.

"Knifers," he said, pointing a bare toe at two long-healed zigzag scars on the dead man's cheek like parallel thunderbolts, evidently some tribal mark. "Shig-man's boys, all three bunches got together fer dis. Bettuh we git outta here."

One of the others snorted. "Runs allem till dark-dark aftah dis comin'."

They'll still be running at sundown tomorrow, Rudi translated mentally.

Jake shrugged. "Mays they come back. Tuk, Samul, git gowin."

The other two Southsiders had a family resemblance to their leader, save that one was naturally dark brown of skin with tight-curled hair and broader features and the other pale blond. The ragged blankets all three had thrown over their saddle bows were probably their only other garments, and their bare feet were broad, callused enough that they likely went so always unless the weather was freezing. As the leader spoke, his companions were collecting any weapons worth having and making sure of the enemy wounded.

Rudi grimaced slightly to himself. That was sometimes

needful, but never pleasant—much harder than killing in the white-hot savagery of battle. He noticed with relief that the wild-men were going about it with a rough mercy, taking care to make the final stroke as quick as possible. The sounds of agony died down into an echoing silence.

"Youze got free of our turf," Jake went on to the Mackenzie clansmen. "Come Southside fires anytime y' want, sit down 'nd put a hand in the pot like a Freedom Fighter stud."

Rudi had to strain for a moment to understand the words through a thick accent, harsh and slurred and nasal at the same time, that turned *these* into *deeze* and *are* into *ur*.

"My thanks to you, Jake son of Jake," he said, slowly and clearly. "My name's Rudi Mackenzie, of the Clan Mackenzie; my sept totem is Raven. This is my blade-brother and sworn man Edain Aylward Mackenzie, called the Archer, of the Wolf sept. And you saved my life with that last spear-cast, as well, so I'm thinkin' we're even, so."

From his frown Jake found Rudi's lilt—stronger than most in Clan Mackenzie and the product of Juniper Mackenzie's own County Mayo accent—hard to follow as well. One of his tribesmen brought up a horse with a dead man across it.

"Thass our bro Murdy. The bastards killed him," Jake said. To the air: "You don't haunt us none, spook-Murdy, 'cause we got 'em for y'!"

The others in the Southsider party added more to the same effect. Rudi nodded approval; it was a warrior's duty to avenge his comrades, and a kinsman's too.

"And speaking of duties, now that we have time . . ."

He and Edain each bent to one of the bodies of the slain foemen, touched blood to a finger and that to his

forehead. Then they faced the west and he murmured
with raised hands:

"To Your black-wing host we dedicate the harvest of
this unplowed field, Morrigú, Lady of the Ravens. Dread
Lord of Death and Resurrection, Guardians of the Western Gate, guide the souls of these our foemen to the
Lands of Summer where no evil comes and all hurts are
healed. Goddess Mother-of-all, gentle and strong,
through whose Cauldron we are all reborn, witness that
we killed these Your children from need and duty, not
wantonness, knowing that for us also the hour of the
spear shall come, soon or late. For Earth must be fed."

"So mote it be," Edain finished.

They exchanged a glance and a slight nod. Rudi could
tell the other Mackenzie was adding the same silent
observation:

*And return these rotters in better condition for their
next go-round on the Wheel, once they've spent some time
with You.*

Jake gave Rudi a sharp look. "Hey, that's a good saying word t' keep spooks down . . . You two aren't part'a
those bastards from Iowa, are you? You sure don't sound
like 'em and they pray to the Jesus-man."

It took Rudi a moment to realize what *doze bassids*
meant; he made a mental effort to switch sounds and fill
in the missing parts of speech.

"No, that I am not," he said. "We're from the Far
West, from the lands of sunset, where we follow the Star
Goddess, Who is also Earth the Mother, and Her consort
the Sun Lord."

Well, some of us do, he thought.

"I came to Iowa with my friends on a journey eastward—" *To the farthest East, to the lands of sunrise, to seek
a sword seen in visions.* That *might perhaps be a wee bit*

complicated to discuss right now. Also the way the Prophet's men pursue us.

"—and the Bossman's men set on us and took them captive."

Which oversimplifies a bit, but is true in the essence.

"He holds them hostage, until I return with a treasure—wagons left on a road north of here, just past a ruined town. The fall of . . . three years ago now."

Jake's brows went up; it was visible, in the light of moon and stars.

"Those? We know 'em. Nothing worth taking there. We checked. Not cloth or saddles or blades or nothing. Wagons too big for us, so we left 'em. Mebbe haunts there, mebbe bad spook luck."

Rudi shrugged and smiled. "They're what he wants, nonetheless. And I've been trying to get to them, and not be killed by everyone I meet."

"Talk about it later," Jake said. He glanced up at the sky, obviously judging distance and time by the stars. "We gotta get Murdy away fore we bury him. Otherwise the Knifers, they'll track and dig him up and eat his heart 'n balls."

The dark young man, Tuk, spat on one of the bodies. "Bassids. Eaters. Monssers."

"Monssers?" Rudi asked, as they collected Edain's mount and the pack animal with their gear.

The living men mounted and headed westward along the river. Fireflies flickered across the waters, and a cool wet breath came from the river's surface. Rudi took a deep lungful, glad to be away from most of the stink of blood and opened bodies, though Murdy and the game on the packhorses—a white-tail, an elk and a feral cow—weren't all that fragrant either. Something hooted in the woods;

they all stiffened, and then relaxed when experienced ears told them it was a real bird. Tuk continued:

"Yeah, monssers, like the ones who chased our pamaws—"

Ancestors, Rudi realized, as they crossed the river where a fallen bridge broke the current and made a ford.

"—outta Chi-town in the Bad Time. They were just littles, but they was clean, our pamaws. Clean!"

In fact Jake and his friends were a fair bit ranker than the wet heat of summer here demanded, and their ill-cured clothes and harness smelled worse, not to mention the spatters of sticky drying blood that they ignored, despite the river being close at hand. Jake explained for the stranger as Rudi quickly bent and scooped up water and sand in passing to rub his hands free of the sticky mass that threatened to gum his fingers together. He could finish the job later, and take care of his sword—even the finest metal got nicks when you slammed it through bone.

"Didn't eat nobody, even when they had to kill 'em anyhow to keep their own asses off the cookfire. Not even once. The Knifers, they still eats man-meat sometimes. Even when they don't hafta. Think it makes 'em spook-strong."

Pride of ancestry rang in his voice, and Rudi gave a little sigh of relief. That spared him the necessity of explaining what was *geasa* to him, taboo.

And that story would help account for how crude their gear is, Rudi thought. *If their parents were mostly children . . . teenagers at most . . . themselves. And how much their speech has changed. And if this man is chief, none of the pamaws survived much longer than it took their own children to be three-quarters grown. He's no older than me, I think.*

From what he'd heard, most of the folk of the old world had been utterly helpless when the Change came and the machines stopped, countryfolk and farmers only a little less than townsmen. In some places enough skills had been found or pieced together to build life new on old foundations; the Clan Mackenzie had been luckier than most, since many of its founders had been lovers of the ancient arts. Close to the great cities it had been worst of all. There tens of millions were left without food or water; everything went down in a doomed scramble to keep alive an hour at a time, and plague ran through the surging masses like wildfire through dry grass.

From the Mississippi to the east coast, where the cities had been thickest, little remained but bands like these—and Rudi seemed to have been fortunate indeed in the ones he met.

Luck of that sort is only to be expected, if you're fated to dree a hero's weird, he thought with an inward grin, half at himself, half defiant mockery at the Powers. *It's one of the compensations for the fear and danger and general misery and the prospect of an early death. You're lucky until you aren't, so to say.*

"They was all littles, the pamaws, 'cept old Jake, he was my pa, and Tuk 'n Samul's," Jake said. "He brought everyone out and hid 'em till the New Year. He was a good one, old Jake the sailor man. Dead a long time now, though; he's a good spook"—

Spirit-guardian, Rudi translated mentally.

—"for all of us Southside studs n' bitches."

Men and women, his mind added.

It was going to be a strain talking, until he learned a bit of this dialect. He'd heard many on his trip across the continent, but none quite so strange except those that weren't English at all.

They stayed in the river valley for the most part, working their way south and slightly west, despite the deep dark under the trees that blocked most of the moonlight. A little reflected from the rippling surface of the Illinois, enough to use if you were very careful, and if the horses were sure-footed. They rode on the verge of the broken pavement to spare their feet, with only the sound of the hooves to mark their passage. Rudi guessed that the Southsider camp was down by the riverbank, and wasn't surprised; it would be easier all round, with firewood close to hand, drinking water, cover from prying eyes, and shelter—the higher land around here was mostly open tallgrass prairie.

Epona tossed her head up and snorted. Rudi inhaled deeply; that was the smell of fires and cooking, and the sweetish-rank smell of a camp not strictly kept, wastes and old food and raw hides curing with brains and piss. Evidently nobody had told these folk about using oak tanbark, despite it being all about them. Garbh growled at a chorus of yelping, barking mongrels, until Edain called her sharply to heel. Three more of the Southsider men stepped out from behind trees . . .

No, Rudi thought, looking at the faces and naked torsos behind the spearheads. *One of them is a Southsider woman . . .*

. . . and leveled their weapons, before crying greetings to Jake, and wailing at the sight of dead Murdy. More came swarming out to pelt them with questions and beat the curs off with sticks and feet; about three score of all ages, and they walked in a crowd around the horses until they passed a tiger's skull on a pole and reached the fires and the rough corral.

Say a hundred of them in all, half children. Three more-or-less grown women for every two men, or thereabouts, Rudi thought, making a warrior's quick estimate.

Nobody was much older than his new friend Jake; he doubted more than a handful had been born at the time of the Change.

High casualties?

The mob gazed gape-jawed at Rudi and Edain in their strange gear, pointing and gabbling in a way Mackenzies would think rude. Rudi sat his great black horse with long-limbed grace, the bright red-gold hair falling to his shoulders and his sharp-cut high-cheeked face smiling. Edain was less easy, his strong square face blank; he wouldn't ask Rudi *are you sure?* with strangers about . . .

None of the Southsiders matched Rudi's height, and none had his companion's breadth of shoulder or barrel chest. *Not a prepossessing lot, but truly friendly, I think.*

Rudi winked at a naked toddler with a huge mop of frizzy hair; she ducked behind her mother, herself a girl of no more than sixteen years who cradled a baby on her hip.

"Let these studs have room!" Jake called. "They saves our asses, truth! An' lay on eats! We got Murdy to bury, an' our new friends to show our right n' good ways!"

When the mob surged back towards the camp Jake went on quietly:

"And when we've had the eats, you can tell me more of that story of yours. We don't like the Iowa motherfuckers or their bossman at *all.* Shoved our pamaws back into this shit with their pitchforks. Keep us here still."

Rudi nodded gravely; Edain thawed a little, since he too had little use for Iowa's ruler and liked the whole place less than the older Mackenzie. The Iowa folk *had* closed the Mississippi bridges in the chaotic months after the Change and patrolled the western shore . . . or they'd have been buried beneath the tidal wave of refugees heading west from Chicago and the other lakeside cities, and north from Saint Louis.

Though now they've more land than they can till, he thought, remembering pasture where fields had once been, and at that more grass than the cattle could eat down. *They could change their policy, if they would, and both would benefit by it.*

There was a hungry smile in Jake's words: "Anyone's got a hate against that Bossman bastard, he's got a word to say here."

"Sure, and I'd not weep if he were to be done an injury," Rudi said. "He's not the worst ruler I've ever met, but he's far from the best—and not the smartest, either, that he is not."

The smartest of rulers? A toss-up between my mother and Matti's, that would be; the one wise and good, the other wise and wicked.

He realized with a start that he missed Mathilda's mother; missed her counsel, and her peculiar way of looking at the world. They'd always gotten on well enough, even when he'd been her husband's captive during the War of the Eye, but then again you never really knew where you stood with the Spider of the Silver Tower. He *did* know she loved Mathilda . . .

I've never really understood her, otherwise. She's a bad person, really, but she's raised Matti to be a good one, and she was always kind to me, even when she pushed me hard to learn and grow. She's done great evil, but great good also, if more from policy than inclination; and I think that the good will long outlive her, while the evil will mostly vanish . . . start to vanish, at least . . . when Matti takes the throne of

Portland and rules the Association. And the more I travel, the more I realize I've learned from her, those months every year I lived in the Regent's Household—things I never could have learned at home. Mother has true wisdom, but it's not all the wisdom there is. What she stands for is good, but some things can't be seen from where she stands.

And that was something he could only realize at a distance from them both; as if the knowledge unfolded with the weight of their personalities removed for a while, letting it open like a flower from the bud.

And at home I would never have realized what I knew, he mused, looking westward to where stars shone over the treetops.

Nor learned what I have from others on this journey. Am I journeying to the east, then, or do I travel towards myself? When I meet the man I am becoming . . .

"Who will Rudi Mackenzie be in himself?" he mused. "Will those I know, know me still?"

One thing I do know: I'll rescue Matti for her own sweet sake . . . but even if she wasn't dear to me, I'd be downright terrified of failing Lady Sandra Arminger!

CHAPTER TWO

The Lord High Chancellor and the Grand Constable of the PPA rode side by side through the harvested field, with their hawks on their wrists and the attendants at a discreet distance behind. A covey of pheasants exploded from the ground ahead of their horses in a cracking flutter of wings.

Both the Associates were in what Portlander fashion decreed for gentlemen engaged in rural pleasures on a summer's day; turned-down thigh boots with the golden spurs of knighthood on the heels, doeskin breeches, baggy-sleeved linen shirts beneath long T-tunics cinched by broad sword belts of studded and tooled leather, and wraparound sunglasses in gilded frames.

Embroidered heraldic shields on their chests showed their arms. Those of Chancellor Conrad Renfrew—also Count of Odell—were sable, a snow-topped mountain argent on vert; it echoed the towering perfect cone of Mt. Hood, just visible as a tiny silver spike on the eastern horizon. Baroness Tiphaine d'Ath bore sable, a delta over a V argent; she wore a discreet livery badge at the brow of her hat as well, her own arms quartered with Sandra Arminger's in token of vassalage.

"Your turn," the Count of Odell said, nodding towards the pheasants skimming over the ground.

"Thanks, Conrad," Tiphaine said.

This was one of the Five Great Fields of her manor of Montinore, and the three hundred acres of brown-blond wheat stubble with clover pushing up below provided plenty of cover. The ring of hawthorn hedge and wide-spaced poplars around it were full of good places for nesting, and even conscientious gleaners didn't get all the fallen grain that attracted quarry.

"Three gets you five that cock pheasant makes it to the hedge," the older noble said.

The big black-gray peregrine on her wrist crouched and bated with a bristle of feathers as she slipped free the hood, and a faint sweet ring from the silver bells on its bewit-straps as the talons closed and relaxed in anticipation. It knew what the sudden coming of the light meant. Then its mad slit-pupil yellow eyes flared dark as they fixed themselves on the prey; she could feel the strength of its grip on her wrist through the thick leather of the glove.

"Done," Tiphaine replied. "Go for it, Riot Grrrl."

She tossed the arm up in a quick throwing arc and the bird flung itself skyward, soaring upward in a widening gyre with a harsh *skri-skri-skri*. The wind of long graceful wings was cool on her cheek and neck for an instant, in the mild dry warmth of a Willamette summer's day.

The covey's alarm suddenly turned panic-stricken as the incarnate shadow of deep ancestral fear fell across them; they scattered, spattering away like water popping on a hot griddle. Frenzied, the male pheasant tried to outrace the circling doom rather than going for cover, his long tail feathers streaming as he strove for height.

"Stop taking the air, you idiot," the Count of Odell said sourly. "She's twice as fast as you are!"

Tiphaine watched the dance of life and death in the cloudless blue above with eyes the color of moonlit glaciers, and smiled with a very slight curve of the lips. It made everything seem more intense for a moment, from the feel of the great muscles moving between her thighs to the smells of equine sweat and oiled leather, sweet crushed clover and dry dusty earth.

"That's a lovely falcon you've got there," Conrad said, following the flight of the peregrine. "And she's going to cost *me* some money, dammit. Alaskan?"

She nodded. "Aleutian."

"Must have cost *you*," he said.

Trade was sparse from those remote islands, and had to run the gauntlet of Haida pirates in the Queen Charlottes and the Inland Passage. Only the most expensive luxury goods could bear the costs.

"Worth it," she replied. "Northern birds always fly better, especially in yarak."

The Association nobles reined in and watched the falcon climb; the bird sitting hooded on Conrad Renfrew's wrist was a big dark brown mews-bred Harris Hawk with chestnut shoulders and white banding on the base and tip of its tail. It had already taken two rabbits and a duck today. Despite which . . .

It's hardly falconry at all with a Harris, Tiphaine thought.

She privately considered that species to be like Irish setters with feathers and talons. Unlike pretty well all other birds of prey they were social hunters, coursing in flocks in the wild, and they were affectionate to their handlers in ways other breeds just weren't. That and the ease with which they could be bred in captivity made them favorites.

They do everything but lick your hand and lift a leg to pee.

"You've got a good eye for a falcon," he admitted.

"I always did identify with predators. Back before the Change"—

Conrad had been over thirty then; she'd been fourteen. They'd both survived the first Change Year when the vast majority of the human race had not, but the experience divided as much as it linked them. His generation were of the old world; those a few years younger than she were Changelings. She hung between—

"my bedroom was plastered with pictures of hawks and wolves and tigers and leopards."

The Count of Odell's hideously scarred face quirked in a smile. "Isn't it usually horses with girls that age?"

"Usually. I preferred things with fangs or claws or both."

"Why am I not surprised, *Lady Death*?" he said, using the common pun on her title.

"Well, I had a Melissa Etheridge poster on the wall too."

"Who . . . oh, she was a musician, right? I think I've heard you do some of her stuff now and then."

"Right. Serious crush on her at the time."

That had been an eventful spring. She'd turned fourteen in January, met Katrina Georges in February when the other girl transferred to Binnsmeade Middle School, won a medal at the Oakridge gymnastics meet at the beginning of March, and then on the seventeenth the world had ended, at 6:15 p.m. Pacific Time.

Birthday, first love, victory, then the laws of nature Change while you're on a camping trip. Killed my first man five days later and couldn't believe how easy it was. But I do miss CDs and my Walkman sometimes. Calling for the minstrel just isn't the same.

The thought was odd; it had been a long time since she remembered the Change much, or thought of herself as Collette Rutherton rather than the name Sandra had chosen for her when she became an Associate of the PPA. Conrad's generation always had one mental foot planted in the old world, however hard they tried to pull it out or deny it; hers remembered it, but as though seen faded through multiple panes of glass . . . except on the rare occasions when it came flooding back to make the *now* seem like a mad dream for an instant.

To those a few years younger, the Changelings, it was a fable.

And I envy them that. Envy them and fear it a little. Even Delia . . . I love her but I don't understand her sometimes. The kids are even worse. They don't just take this world we've made naturally. They think but they don't think about thinking *the way I do sometimes and Conrad and Sandra and the other oldsters do all the time. The Changelings . . . it's like they're in a dream. So am I, but I know it. They never wake up or know they're dreaming.*

"Ah," Tiphaine said, pulling off her tinted glasses and shading her eyes with the hand that held them.

A second later Conrad pushed his mirrorshades up onto the bald dome of his head and muttered something under his breath—probably *damn* as the falcon selected the cock pheasant's gaudy gold-and-green plumage for its target.

The peregrine stooped out of the sun, folding its wings and turning itself into a blurred streak of purpose. There was a faint *thud* from the air above, a puff of feathers against the bright afternoon sky.

"She binds!" Tiphaine said, and didn't add: *I win*.

The two birds spun groundward locked together by the attacker's talons. They struck with a thump on the wheat stubble not far away; the peregrine shrieked its triumph and its rage, mantling and darting its ripping beak downward with cruel precision. Everyone cantered over and pulled up; the falconer dismounted and whirled his feathered lure on the end of its cord with a rattling humm. The bird cocked an eye at it and jumped, then consented to be hooded again and fed from the hand. Varlets picked up the pheasant and added it to the basket, giving the neck a quick twist to make sure.

"That's enough for verisimilitude," Conrad said with a sigh. "Duty calls, and so does lunch."

Tiphaine nodded and turned her horse. They heeled their mounts into a faster pace, towards the little un-walled pavilion where the others waited. Conrad looked around at the stubble field.

"Nice work," he said. "You can hardly see where the individual strips are."

Montinore manor operated on the usual PPA system; the peasant families each held scattered strips in all of the Five Fields, and the crops—winter wheat, spring oats and roots like turnips or potatoes, grass and clover for fodder—were rotated through the fields in turn. Back in the early days the semi-communal arrangement had let a few real farmers supervise hordes of refugee suburbanites who'd never before done anything more rural than curse the dandelions in their lawns. Nowadays it made it easy for the manor lord to exact his share of the crop and labor service on the demesne.

Tiphaine shrugged. "I've got good reeves on my estates and a first-rate seneschal," she said. "And Delia keeps *them* from dipping into the till while I'm away, which is too often. I *like* living here, and to hell with Portland and Castle Todenangst. I'm sick of spending my days in armor; being Sandra's assassin and duelist was fun, but Grand Constable is just work. Damn the Prophet, damn the United States of Boise, and damn this war too."

"Now you know why I was so glad to unload the job on *you*." Conrad shrugged in turn. "Be glad you've got a nice defensive war you can really get your teeth into. We'd likely be fighting about now even if Boise and Corwin hadn't gotten big eyes. Sandra hasn't had us spend the last decade and change building castles and saving up money and training troops for nothing."

Tiphaine sighed. "You're right, of course. She's not any less ambitious than Norman was, just a hell of a lot more patient and sneaky. Oh, well, she's the sovereign."

"Until Mathilda comes of age," Conrad said, and grinned like the ornament on a cathedral waterspout. "*That's* going to be interesting."

"Then it'll be the Changelings' turn. I suspect by then a lot of things will be different."

They drew rein near the pavilion, under the branches of the great garry oak that shaded it; Tiphaine returned the salute of the Guard captain with a curt nod and a lift of her riding crop.

"Sir Lothair."

He wore half-armor like the two-score mounted crossbowmen, and a peaked Montero cap with a long curling feather at one side, what she'd have called a Robin Hood hat in her youth. The dozen lancers nearby were in full fig, armored cap-a-pie on barded destriers, blazing steel statues with their visors down and eyes invisible behind the narrow vision slits. The men-at-arms would be feeling like buns in a bake oven right now, combined with a sauna. She'd experienced it often enough, and would again unless the enemy were civilized enough to fight only in cool weather.

Though oddly enough, when the weather's really cold, full armor doesn't give you any warmth at all.

"My lady Grand Constable," he said after a moment's scrutiny for form's sake. "My lord Chancellor. You are recognized and may pass."

Grooms took the horses as they dismounted, and the hunt servants brought up their count of pheasant and duck, quail and rabbit, for the semiritual inspection.

They are, indeed, very dead, Tiphaine thought with a trace of whimsy as she looked at the limp, bloodied forms and prodded one with a gloved finger. *And someone should eat them very soon in this warm weather.*

She went on aloud as Conrad handed his hawk and perching glove to his falconer: "The game to good Father Mendoza, with my compliments."

She nodded towards the steeple of the village church a mile westward across the great common field, rising above trees and red-tiled roofs, with the Coast Range green-blue beyond it. They'd give the parish priest, his household and some of the ill or indigent a couple of good dinners.

Slyly: "And tell him that my lord the Count of Odell has graciously donated five rose nobles for the almshouse fund."

"Gold? I didn't say anything about 'three gets you five' in *gold*," Conrad said, alarmed; that was a month's wage for a mounted man-at-arms.

"Even for someone who started out as an accountant you are *such* a cheapskate, Conrad. You've got the whole Hood River Valley in your fief, for God's sake. And two toll bridges. And a chartered town to tax. I'm a lowly baroness with a few manors. Show some class."

She stripped off her gauntlet and held it out. He unwillingly dropped the little dime-sized coins inside; she folded the long cuff over and into the wrist, then tossed it into the game basket.

"Go," she said.

The varlet gulped thankfully and jogged away. Listening to the higher nobility exchanging badinage wasn't comfortable for someone that low on the food chain, though it would probably make excellent gossip at the village taverns, crowded as they were with the entourages of the visitors.

The pavilion was Sandra's, and hence in exquisite taste—heavy oiled silk striped white and blue on a hidden framework of galvanized poles. Bullion tassels all around the edges were woven with glass strips that chimed lightly when they touched. Rugs covered the ground, glowing with designs of flowers and vines in wine red and green and blue. A light folding table and chairs of carved reddish wood stood within; it was quite private, and even the men-at-arms and crossbowmen of the Protector's Guard were at a discreet distance.

Tiphaine removed her round roll-brimmed noble's hat with the broad trailing tail and joined Conrad in two elaborate leg-and-hand-flourish bows to the pair of noblewomen within. One was Delia de Stafford, blue-eyed and black-haired and delicately beautiful and thirty to her own thirty-eight, and dressed in a daring new mode she'd pioneered for semiformal occasions away from court. It was based on what commoner women wore; a long light under-tunic and knee-length over-tunic, but with gauzy silks and lots of lace making it a fantasy in white and lavender instead of utilitarian plainness. A belt of old woven gold held a jewel-hilted ceremonial dagger to show that she was an Associate, and the equally symbolic ring of silver keys that marked her as Chatelaine of Barony d'Ath.

The other was Sandra Arminger, Lady Regent of the PPA, in a conservative pearl gray and white cotte-hardi and a silk headdress confined in a net of platinum and diamonds. To her Tiphaine and Conrad added a bend of the right knee that touched the carpet for an instant.

Although technically I should curtsey, she thought. *It looks ridiculous in pants, though.*

"My liege lady and Regent," she said. And: "My lady Delia."

"If you two are finally finished slaughtering harmless birds and quite small animals we can get to work," Sandra Arminger said.

She folded the *Weekly Trumpet* she'd been reading—it was turned either to the crossword puzzle or to an article headlined: "Feudalism: God's Will Or Just Common Sense?"—and tossed the newspaper on top of two illustrated magazines, *Tournaments Illuminated* and *The Associate's Town and Castle Journal*. Then she extended her hand to both of them in turn for the ritual kiss of homage.

"The social cover story for this is a bit of hawking," Conrad of Odell pointed out. "It helps to actually *do* some hawking."

Tiphaine nodded, standing hipshot at catlike ease with her left hand on the hilt of her longsword. A falconry party was something you could invite only chosen people to, without offending anyone—or at least without giving them formal reason to be offended, as exclusion from a Council meeting would. Even if everyone *knew* it was really a political conclave before the Council.

"Though we'll miss the boar hunting this year, with the war," she said with a sigh, looking westward.

Montinore village was in the foreground, just across the road and railway that led south to Newburg; beyond that was the white manor house, the fields and hilly vineyards and orchards of her demesne, and then the stark square tower and walls of Castle Ath on its height, ferroconcrete covered in pale stucco, like a fortress in a picture book with banners streaming from the turrets.

After that started the great forests of the Coast Range, mile after mile of quiet umber shade. She thought of the quick belling of hounds through the glades in the chill October air, and the quarry at bay beneath a half-fallen fir tree . . .

"Fighting with pigs?" Sandra said, sipping at a glass of scented herbal tisane that tinkled with ice. "In freezing mud? While it's *raining*? This is *recreation*?"

"It's not quite as much fun as hot sweaty sex," Conrad acknowledged. "But in the right season you can do it more often, or at least for longer."

"Speak for yourself, Odell," Tiphaine said with an expression that had the shadow of a wolf's grin behind it. "Not all of us have your limitations."

Delia smothered a chuckle, and Sandra sighed.

"Children, children. Oh, sit down, Tiph," she went on, tucking a lock of graying brown hair back under her wimple. "You *do* tend to . . . loom over one."

"My lady Regent is . . . a dimensionally challenged person," Tiphaine said; Sandra was five-two, and still slight in her fifty-fourth year. "I was fourteen when you took me and Kat into the Household and I was *already* taller than you. I can't *help* looming."

"You can't help being a big blond horse of a woman,

you mean, d'Ath," Conrad said. "That's why you'd never have made it to the Olympics."

She nodded, although she had a whipcord-and-steel length of limb that made her look quite slender at first glance. The Olympics had been her dream before the Change, but . . .

But in fact I was already too tall and still growing. Gymnasts were all munchkins, like muscular little steroidal pixies. I'd have ended up a Phys Ed teacher or a girls' basketball coach or something. Or, maybe *if I'd switched to track and field—*

"Whereas I just cast a welcome shade," Conrad continued smugly, slapping dust off his blocky torso.

His chair creaked a little as he sat. The Chancellor of the Portland Protective Association was no taller than Tiphaine—around five-ten—but he'd always been shaped like a fireplug made of bone and muscle. Now that he was past fifty and not taking the field anymore he'd added some solid flesh to that, and he grunted with relief as he sat, running one spatulate hand over the shaven dome of his bullet-shaped head.

"That's one way of saying *I'm getting fat*, Odell."

Tiphaine sat with more than her usual leopard grace and crossed ankle over knee. Conrad grunted again as he reached to take a handful of shelled hazelnuts and walnuts from a Venetian glass bowl on the table, salvage from some museum.

"You too shall be in your fifties sometime, my lady Grand Constable," he said, tossing one of the nutmeats into his mouth. "In precisely twelve years, in fact."

"Possibly, my lord Chancellor," Tiphaine said. *In the unlikely event someone doesn't kill me first.* "But I don't think the years shall *weigh* quite so *heavily* on me as they do on you."

Conrad's facial nightmare of thick white keloid scars made his laugh even more alarming than that gravelly sound would have been otherwise. A steward with a white tabard and ivory baton made a gesture, and two pages brought trays from the other—much plainer—tent twenty yards away. They set out a platter of sandwiches, petit fours, and chilled pinot grigio wine with seltzer and waited, demure in their black livery of silk hose and pour-point jackets embroidered with the d'Ath arms, curl-toed shoes of gilded leather cutwork and fezlike brimless hats.

"Your sons make such charming and efficient pages, Lady Delia," Sandra Arminger said. "With such large, pink, shell-like, quivering ears."

Delia took the hint: "Lioncel, Diomede," she said, and made a graceful gesture.

The boys—blond Lioncel was twelve, dark Diomede two years younger—bowed in unison and walked backward until the distance was outside easy hearing, even with keen young ears. Tiphaine took a sandwich. The PPA's liege lady Sandra and Tiphaine's lady-in-waiting and chatelaine Delia—*My girlfriend-for-the-last-fourteen-years Delia*, Tiphaine thought, with a familiar flicker of resentment at the necessity for discretion. *Best not to get out of the habit of being careful, though*—shared a liking for dainty little things on manchet bread with the crusts cut off and some parsley on the side; in this case potted shrimp in aspic, deviled ham with minced sweet Walla Walla onions, or cucumber. Since this *was* Tiphaine's own personal fief, there were also some substantial examples of bacon, lettuce, and tomato with mayo on sourdough. She smiled a little as she bit into one, savoring the smoky taste of the apple-cured meat and fresh, melting-ripe tomatoes and almost-warm crusty bread.

"What's the joke, darling?" Delia asked.

They'd been together since Kat died in the Protector's War, and she knew that slight curve of Tiphaine's lips was the equivalent of a grin or even a chortle.

The baroness shrugged, swallowed, blotted her lips with a linen napkin and said: "A pleasant memory. The only pleasant memory our unlamented pseudo-Pope Leo ever gave me, but it made up for all the rest."

These days the local branch of the reunified Church was just annoying to someone like her, guarded by rank and powerful patronage. She pretended to be a good Catholic with sardonic relish and with gritted teeth the clergy pretended to believe her; Delia did the same, and was a secret witch to boot and High Priestess of a coven. But Norman Arminger had been *literally* medieval on the subject of gay people, as on much else, and his psychopathic pet "Pope" Leo had been worse.

About the time her husband died Sandra Arminger had found out that the *real* Catholic Church had survived—a remnant had fled dying Rome behind the halberds of the Swiss Guard and ended up in the little Umbrian hill town of Badia, still their HQ—and that they'd managed to call a conclave to elect an equally real Pope. To lay the groundwork for reunion the Lady Regent had delegated schismatic Leo's tragic, timely and officially accidental demise to Tiphaine, who'd been her wetwork specialist of choice back then.

"One sane Pope half the world away by sailing ship is much less trouble than a deranged one right next door," Sandra acknowledged. "We needed our own Church immediately after the Change, but by that time Leo was . . . a problem."

Tiphaine's smile grew a little wider. Sandra was fond of an old Russian saying: *When a man causes you a prob-*

lem, remember: no man, no problem. The recollection of the look on his starved-eagle ascetic face when he saw her step silently from behind an arras in his private chambers and hold up the hypodermic . . .

I smiled then, too, she thought, happily nostalgic. *That was a good day. We did a lot of housecleaning around then.*

"Ah, if tombstones were only honest—how many would read *died of being an inconvenience to the powerful,*" Conrad said genially.

He was obviously following at least some of her thoughts; Delia winced slightly, for the same reason. She was a gentle soul.

"It's not as if it was a personal impulse," Tiphaine said, mildly defensive. "As the Lady Regent said, the man needed killing."

"And you certainly didn't leave muddy footprints all over the place," Conrad said admiringly. "Very neat. Until just now I actually thought there was an outside chance it was really natural causes."

"I don't screw up. And I had a *lettre de cachet* with me just in case, anyway," she pointed out.

Sandra smiled, with a faraway reminiscent expression of her own:

"*The bearer has done what has been done by my authority, and for the good of the State.* I always *loved* actually writing that . . . milady."

"Tiph never had one stolen by a dashing Gascon musketeer, either," the Count of Odell said. "And God knows she had enough of them pass through her hands—or did you just use the first and not bother having a fresh one made up for every job, d'Ath?"

"No, a new letter every time. I've still got all the old ones, stamped *canceled* in red ink."

"You're joking, right?"

Delia shuddered and rolled her eyes. "No, she isn't. A whole *file* of them, all on parchment and all tied up with ribbons."

"That's sort of sick, you know?" the Count of Odell laughed.

"We all have our hobbies, Conrad," Tiphaine said, pouring herself a glass of the fizzy white wine, and taking a sip that tasted of flowers and almonds and oranges. "The Regent has her cats. You and Lady Odell are always on about those roses of yours. Delia loves babies."

Sandra turned to Delia and asked politely: "And how is little Heuradys?"

The younger woman brightened. "Teething, poor lamb, my lady. But"—she caught Tiphaine's eye and abbreviated the details to—"still cute as a button."

"Oh, cute as a puppy," Tiphaine agreed. "She's going to be fair, like Lioncel."

And this is the last *one!*

Three was a smallish family these days, and Delia had wanted to try again for another daughter to balance the set, but . . .

We're retiring that turkey baster, if I have anything to say about it! Which admittedly I may not.

"However, babies are much harder to housebreak," she finished. "Plus puppies don't need to be found dowries or fiefs when they grow up."

"And on that note," Sandra said more seriously. "What do you make of the situation? Not the details—the larger picture."

As always she was in combinations of gray and white, with silver gilt buttons down the sleeves and bodice of her cotte-hardi. A Persian kitten rested in a small basket on her lap, and dodged a paw out at the dangling trails of the wimple now and then.

"The enemy are still not pressing us very hard," she added, reaching in a hand and running a finger down its head; the little beast turned on its back and began to wrestle with the digit as she tickled its stomach. "I expected them to be more aggressive."

"The dance starts soon," Tiphaine said, and went into the details.

Conrad nodded agreement when she'd finished. "It's a persisting strategy. Subtle, for an alliance. The sum total of a whole lot of little fights is more predictable than one or two big ones where luck and generalship can overcome the odds."

Unlike the older noble, Tiphaine reached for a second sandwich. *Benefits of an active metabolism,* she thought, as she marshaled reports and observations in her mind. *Perks of running around wearing sixty pounds of steel half the time. Also good food makes me feel less pessimistic.*

Sandra pursed her lips and tapped a finger on them. "I'm surprised our enemies are being so . . . farsighted. They're both young men—Prophet Sethaz is barely thirty, and General-President Martin Thurston of Boise is younger still. In my experience, patience isn't a quality of which men that age show any great fund."

"Sethaz is . . . I'm not sure if he's altogether human," Tiphaine said. "He's certainly mad and I wouldn't rule out the stories of demonic possession."

Conrad grunted agreement. Sandra raised one elegant brow; her brown eyes were a little surprised.

"*Et tu,* Tiphaine?"

"I've had too much contact with the CUT to doubt that something very strange is going on out there in the

Valley of Paradise," she said. "Strange and . . . unpleasant. You taught me to evaluate the evidence, my lady, not reject it because it conflicted with my assumptions. And you heard about Lady Astrid's headache?"

Sandra's brow went up. "That was *supernatural?*" she said.

Conrad snorted. "Damned straight it was. I've seen Tiph draw, spin a hundred and eighty degrees, cut a dragonfly in half on the wing, sheath the blade and be back where she started in about a second," he said. "Astrid's just as good."

"Just as *fast*, certainly," Tiphaine said with hard-won professional detachment.

The *Hiril Dúnedain* had killed her lover Katrina during the Protector's War in the course of the botched first attempt to get Mathilda back from the Mackenzies. Tiphaine didn't dwell on the memory; it was too stressful.

"Stress" is mostly the result of not being allowed to kill some asshole you really want to slice and dice.

"*Something* is going on," Conrad said grimly. "And I lost my belief in the absolute reign of impersonal natural laws about twenty-four years ago. There's something else at work in the universe. And it doesn't seem to like us much."

"A point," Sandra said reluctantly.

She was that rarity these days, an atheist to the core, a complete materialist and rationalist. Tiphaine had been one herself, until recently, though they were both pious enough in public. As Sandra said, God was a myth but *religion* was as real as rocks and far more useful to rulers.

Now I'm . . . not sure anymore, Tiphaine thought. *I'm still not sure about God, that is, but the devil is starting to*

*look awfully convincing. I'm going to have to have a talk
with Delia about aligning with some protective spook or
other. Even if I'd rather pull out my own toenails with my
teeth.*

She went on aloud, her voice coolly neutral:

"And Thurston is just too smart for comfort. He *is*
having riverboats built in Pendleton, with the locals and
the CUT supplying materials. Sethaz lets him do that—
the Cutters have those religious taboos about machinery.
But as long as we hold the castles and walled cities along
the Columbia we can strike north or south at the flank of
any invader and we have superior water transport for our
logistics."

"Clear enough, then. Let's not get bogged down in
military details at this point," Sandra said. "I leave that to
you, my lady Grand Constable, and to the Chancellor.
What's the state of morale, Conrad?" she went on.

The thick-bodied man looked at the wineglass in his
hand and said grudgingly: "Uneven. The older nobles are
being effusively loyal—and will stay that way as long as
we keep the enemy outside our boundaries. If they get
inside and it looks profitable to start cutting deals . . ."

He shrugged, and Tiphaine mentally followed suit.
Norman Arminger had built a feudal kingdom, albeit a
strong one; his personal obsession had been the eleventh-
century Norman duchy and its offshoots. Homegrown
varieties of neo-feudalism without the PPA's elaborate
organization and terminology . . .

Or our spiffy boots and radical-cool costumes, she
thought.

. . . were certainly common in other areas of the continent, and evidently overseas as well. But.

*But while loyalty is the great feudal virtue, unfortu-
nately treachery is the corresponding vice*, Tiphaine thought;

history had been a compulsory subject in Sandra's Household. *And the older generation had to* learn *about loyalty, while treachery was something they already knew very, very well indeed. All those gangers . . .*

Sandra had never pretended to be any sort of soldier, and generally didn't try to joggle her subordinate's elbows—unlike her husband's practice. At politics, however . . .

"I've looked over the list of tenants-in-chief you want to summon to the muster," the Lady Regent went on. "It's approved, with the following modifications."

She reached into an attaché case on the ground beside her and slid the typewritten schedules to them. Tiphaine took hers and her eyebrows went up. Tenants-in-chief held their land directly from the Throne on payment of mesne tithes—a share of their income—and service of knights, men-at-arms and foot soldiers of set number and equipment on demand. Part of the Grand Constable's job was to see the troops were ready and call them up at need. The total numbers here were the same as her recommendations for the opening stages of the campaigning season, but some of those summoned were awkwardly placed.

Then she smiled thinly as the reasoning sprang out at her. The initial levies of House Stavarov, the Counts of Chehalis up near Puget Sound, were summoned for the war in the east and the rally point at Walla Walla—the Counts themselves, their menie of household knights and paid men-at-arms, spearmen and crossbowmen, their castle garrisons, their subinfeudiated vassals and *their* menies. The third string, the peasant militia and town levies, were detached for service under the Warden of the Coast March against the nuisance-verging-on-threat of Haida raiders. Which meant . . .

Conrad spoke first. "Ah . . . Uriah the Hittite, my lady?"

If there's anyone who would change sides when a Cutter army arrived in front of his castle gates, it's Count Piotr Alexevitch Stavarov.

"I've nearly killed Piotr at least three times," Tiphaine said meditatively. "Isn't there a saying that it's the things you *didn't* do that you regret at the end of your life?"

And Conrad's not looking too upset. He had that run-in with Piotr during the Protector's War, when the idiot got half his command killed trying to rush a bunch of Mackenzies head-on. There's still bad blood there.

"No, no," Sandra said. "I'm not telling you to *get* them killed. We need every man, from what you and Lady d'Ath say. But if men *must* die, why not men from the menie of County Chehalis? They do their duty, and the Stavarovs are weakened."

She held two small, beautifully manicured hands out palm up and mimicked a balance, raising first one and then the other. The Grand Constable nodded.

"I can make the adjustments easily enough, my lady," she said. "The logistics are a little more difficult, but not enough to matter."

"The younger nobles are eager for a fight," Conrad went on, and Tiphaine nodded silent agreement.

"Ordinary people are . . . frightened, my lady Regent," Delia said, a frown on her oval face as she joined the conversation.

She'd been a miller's daughter here in Montinore village before she met Tiphaine. When it came to how the commons thought, she had a better instinctive grasp than any of them, despite all the Regent's spies. Sandra and Conrad Renfrew had been founders of the Association, of course, and Tiphaine had been *raised* as an Associate. Delia went on:

"They're nearly as frightened of having the Throne weakened and the nobles unrestrained if we lose as they are of Boise and the CUT. What's helping a lot is the stories and songs about Princess Mathilda and Rudi and the rest, particularly with the younger people."

She was near-as-no-matter a Changeling, too, which helped. Tiphaine had noticed that the older generation tended to *miss* things, and she did too, albeit less often.

"Ah, yes," Sandra murmured, with a secret smile. "How helpful of dear Juniper to compose and spread them. Between her and the Church preaching a holy war, we're well covered on the propaganda front."

I've never seen you so openly furious as you were when you found out Mathilda had scooted off east with Rudi, Tiphaine thought. *I actually had to talk you out of sending the army haring off eastward to drag her back. But trust the Spider of the Silver Tower to adjust and see the advantages!*

"My lady, I think you're underestimating the impact of these . . . songs . . . that are going the rounds," Tiphaine warned. "As Delia said, the same technique is more effective nowadays, since so manymore are Changelings. Yes, it's convenient right now—but it will have political consequences after the war too, provided we win, that is. Ignoring Mackenzie propaganda hurt us badly in the Protector's War."

Sandra frowned; she'd known her husband's weaknesses, but—

But then she actually loved him, Tiphaine thought; she'd hated Norman Arminger herself, and feared him as she feared few men. *Loved him despite his screwing everything that moved and shaking what didn't, and his general skankiness. Leaving aside the mass murder and so forth; that was just business, though he enjoyed it.*

"The latest . . . this vision of the Virgin telling Father Ignatius to look after Mathilda . . ." Sandra said. "I like that one very much indeed. It makes anyone who challenges her rights a *blasphemer*. And the cream of the jest is that Ignatius probably believes it himself—everyone knows the Order of the Shield of St. Benedict is outside our influence. Mt. Angel is cool to the Protectorate at best. They fought us in the war, after all."

"The Princess was already popular," Delia said. "Everyone who met her liked her. The commons love her. They . . . ah . . ."

"Look forward to her rule." Sandra nodded, with a wry twist to her mouth.

Tiphaine could read her thought: *And they'll never love me.*

Respect and fear, yes; the smarter ones realized how she held the barons in check; but love, no. Too many memories of the early days remained raw, among the ordinary people. And for different reasons, among the Associates as well. Norman Arminger had taken Machiavelli's dictum that it was better for a ruler to be feared than loved rather literally.

"This . . . this quest thing . . . it's made her more like an icon," Delia continued. She hesitated again. "Rudi too. The Sword of the Lady . . . it's not just the people who follow the Old Religion. The rest think of the Virgin, you see? And Ignatius' vision added to that. They think Rudi is the hero who returns, the one who comes back to save his people when the evil day arrives and things look their worst."

Sandra chuckled, a gurgling sound that made her cool brown eyes warm for a moment.

"Certainly dear Rudi has all the qualifications for a legendary hero. He's very *young*, and he's very *handsome*, and he's very *strong*, and he's very *brave*, and he's very . . . not stupid."

For some reason Conrad thought that was funny too, though she couldn't see why: it was all true. He sobered quickly, though.

"It's good that the stories are perking the ordinary people up," he said. "Even with our allies, we can't win this war just with the nobility and their retainers; it's going to be too big for the Associates to handle. But what happens . . . well, my lady, what happens if Rudi and Mathilda *don't* show up?"

Sandra was very quiet for a moment. "If Mathilda is killed? Then it's all rather moot." Softly: "What have I worked for, if not for her?"

CHAPTER THREE

"So, you're *really* a princess?" Kate Heasleroad said, her pink young face wide-eyed and guileless. "I mean, they *call* you that?"

"Yes, I'm entitled Princess and styled Your Highness at home; my mother's the Lady Regent," Mathilda Arminger explained to the Bossman's consort.

She must be at least twenty, she thought. *And I'm only two years older, but it feels like more. I think she led a sheltered life. Until recently, at least.*

Aloud: "But I inherit through my father, Lord Norman Arminger, whose only child I am. He was our first sovereign lord; Lord Protector of the Portland Protective Association. He was a knight before the Change, of course, in the Society, as well as a great scholar of the old ways at the university."

The other woman made a fascinated sound and inclined her head towards a painfully young man in a military uniform that involved a good deal of braid and a gold lanyard.

"Something for me and the Princess, please, Lieutenant."

"At once, Mrs. Heasleroad!"

The aide sprang away towards the buffet and the bar.

It's all just homelike enough to make me homesick but not enough to comfort, Mathilda thought, as she schooled her face to friendly interest. *Not that it's hard to be friendly. It's brief acquaintance, but I find I do like Kate.*

A burbling surf of conversation rose to the carved plaster of the ceiling two stories above; more guests leaned on the balustrade that ringed the reception room. Heels clicked on the marble tiles and on the curving staircase that linked the levels. The Bossman's household troops—they called them the State Police—stood at attention along the walls amid framed pictures and half-columns, their burnished mail-shirts and helms glittering in the brilliance of the incandescent mantles of the gaslights, along with the crowd's crystal and gold and diamonds, fine cloth and polished leather. Open French doors brought an occasional waft of cooler air from the gardens, and the scents of roses and cut grass, along with the odd suicide-bent moth.

"So everyone says *your Highness*?" Kate said, returning to the subject that fascinated her.

"Yes," Mathilda Arminger said, with a practiced smile; there were people at home obsessed with protocol too.

Quite a few of them, in fact.

The aide came back and she took a plate of what her mother called *faculty fodder* for some obscure pre-Change reason; little pieces of toast with shaved ham and pungent cheese, or bits of pickled fish, or tiny sausages and capers and pâté or peppers and sweet corn. A glass of some fizzy drink called sarsaparilla came with it.

"I'm not Princess Regnant or Lady Protector yet, of course, not until I'm twenty-six. Then I'll be styled *Your Majesty.*"

Kate laughed. "And everyone will have to go down on their knees?"

"Only one, until then. And only at ceremonies, of course—receiving homage, bestowing fiefs, that sort of thing. We're less formal most of the time."

"Is there a book of rules or something?"

"Well, the College of Heralds have their lists . . . but really, if you grow up around it . . . it's all sort of natural."

"It sounds like fun, really. Like a costume party!"

Not if it's your life, Mathilda thought. *Mother complains about it sometimes. Of course, for her before the Change it* was *a game. Sometimes I think it still is and she can't help it. People that old . . . it's as if they were always* watching themselves live *their lives instead of just living them and being themselves. Weird.*

An inspiration came to her: "You're a princess too, my dear Kate."

At the other woman's laugh she went on: "No, truly. You're the lawful consort of a ruling prince, after all . . . unless it would be more accurate to call him a King? In which case you'd be Queen, of course, and your *children* would be Princes and Princesses."

"There's only little Tommie so far," Kate said. For a moment her face was soft with love, and went from strikingly pretty to beautiful. "And he's *my* Prince!"

"Then you're *definitely* a Princess, at the very least."

She made a dismissive gesture, but Mathilda could see the corners of her mouth turn up in pleasure; she could also see half a dozen others in the big room noting the exchange as they milled around. The biggest knot was around Anthony Heasleroad, of course, the Bossman of Iowa—Governor and President Pro Tem, formally, but that was the word everyone used in ordinary speech. She could just hear him saying:

". . . keep the great agricultural industry of Iowa in responsible, experienced hands for the common good of Farmer and Evacuee alike . . ."

His voice held the same booming sententiousness most barons at home would use when talking about mesne tithes and heraldry and the idleness of the peasants. Like Mathilda and Rudi he'd been born in the first Change Year, but he looked older to her. Part of that was the fact that he also looked like the statue of an athlete that had been covered in an inch of soft tallow and left in the hot sun until it began to sag a little.

Though I may be prejudiced, Mathilda thought. *And he also looks like a man who trusts nobody, including the men who guard his sleep. They say Mom's that way but she isn't: she always said paranoia was as stupid as gullibility, and just as likely to kill you.*

Kate was tall and willowy; her neck and fingers and piled dark hair sparkled with some truly impressive and not too gaudy jewelry, offset by the simply cut but obviously new blue silk of her knee-length dress. That had probably cost more. Jewelry could be salvaged, but silk had to be imported around the world over trade routes just beginning to function again.

And unlike her demented spouse, she seems amiable enough. Not the brightest candle in the chandelier, but good-hearted.

"Oh, it's bad enough being married to the Governor, much less being a, um, Queen!" Kate said. "I swear, I didn't expect everyone to be always *asking* for things before I married Tony! That was before his father died and he became Bossman, of course."

"Ah, well, that is a drawback of being close to a sovereign," Mathilda said.

She forced herself not to give an incredulous snort; what *else* would a ruler's consort or heir await? That was one reason she'd enjoyed her yearly stay with the Mackenzies so much after the Protector's War—there on the Clan's land she was just Rudi's friend Mathilda.

What did you expect when you married the ruler here, Kate? she thought but did not say. *Gossiping with the other goodwives at the village bakery while your husband digs the garden or sits in the tavern with his cronies over a mug of beer?*

Instead she turned to take a *real* drink off a tray; it was something sweet but potent in a glass like a cone on a stem, with a little cherry on top. For the first time in her life, she understood the temptation that made some people drink to excess. It wasn't so much a matter of drowning sorrows as of untangling the knot of fear that curdled under her breastbone. Or at least putting a slight glassy layer between her and it.

There wasn't anything she could *do* about the fear—she was here, the guards wouldn't let her leave, Rudi was in hideous danger across the river among the savages with only Edain at his side, poor Ingolf was in a dungeon, and most of the rest of her friends were hiding God-knew-where in this vast alien city, even dear kindly Father Ignatius was away so that she couldn't confess or receive the Sacraments . . .

But God does *know where each is, as He sees every sparrow. Mary pierced with sorrows, watch over the ones I love! And especially Rudi. Everything depends on him. And I miss him so much.*

"And sometimes I wish I was back on father's farm—"

Kate went on; she probably felt freer to speak with a stranger than with most of her courtiers.

Farm . . . ah, she means a barony, Mathilda translated; they'd kept the old words here, but a tract one family could work with machines before the Change needed scores or hundreds now, with the landholder as lord. *A manor, a knight's-fee, at least.*

"—instead of all this. I like a party, but they're all the *same* and there are so *many* of them. And a lot of the people aren't really here for the fun."

"I get the same feeling at balls and tournaments," Mathilda said.

Sometimes. As Mom says, they're our working time. If God calls you to a station, you have to do your best, whether it's peasant or Princess. With princes and nobles, socializing is a big part of the business of ruling. Things that come up formally at councils really get settled first while you're feasting or hawking or hunting or dancing a pavane.

"This is a fine country," Kate said softly after a moment. "We Iowans have so much more than anyone else. Our parents were so lucky! Why do people have to quarrel and fight each other for more?"

Mathilda bowed her head slightly, honoring the sentiment if not the thought.

"Why indeed?" she said. "But that seems to be the way people are, a lot of them. It's a ruler's duty to keep their quarrels from spilling too much blood."

And to lead in war so that the realm's strength is a single blade of power in a skilled hand, she thought unhappily. *But in the west, we have no single ruler to fight the Prophet. The Meeting is well enough but it's a council and never gets anything done quickly. Most of the time it's much better at stopping things than doing them.*

The thought carked at her. Her own duty . . .

But the rest of the Meeting realms will never accept an Arminger. The Protector's War showed that. They don't hate and fear me the way they did Father, but they would if they thought I wanted to be overlord. And our nobles wouldn't accept anyone—

A thought made her eyes go wide.

But the Association would *accept the man who brought back the Sword of the Lady and led them to victory—it could just as well be the Virgin who's the Lady as some pagan goddess, after all. Not accept him as Lord Protector in Portland, but as . . . what did the ancient Gael call it, an Ard Ri, a High King over all the realms. And they most certainly would accept it if by my marrying that man they could have their own Lord Protector's blood on the throne in another generation . . .*

The thought passed through her mind in an instant, but her blood leapt at an image of Rudi beside her and a cheering host of Associates and Mackenzies, Bearkillers and Corvallans and manymore below crying him hail. Her heart beat even harder at the thought of him leading her to a bride's bower. How Rudi would love that, and hate the idea of a crown! And how well he'd do at both . . .

But right now he's over there in the wilderness and I'm a prisoner in everything but name, and likely to lose my head if my attention strays. Concentrate, woman!

Kate had sighed and nodded, looking around.

"There are always people who won't live peacefully, like the Heuisinks. Why, why, when we have all this?"

Candles burned on the tables whose snowy linen held the buffet; the aide brought them a second set of hand-sized plates, this time with garlicky meatballs on toothpicks and little skewers of hot spicy grilled chicken and tiny, tender vegetables. Some of the guests plowed stolidly through cold meats and breads and salads and dishes of spiced pickled fish or nibbled on candied fruits, while others punished the wet bar and grew red-faced and expansive or brooded in corners.

"It scares me sometimes," the Bossman's wife said softly. Then in an undertone, but fiercely: "And people are always flattering Anthony, and, and telling him anything he wants to hear. It's like water dripping on iron!"

Mathilda turned away diplomatically, watching the crowd as Kate stammered and flushed and then cast her a grateful look for letting the matter drop. Younger men and women flirted; serious-looking ones in middle age stood in small circles, holding drinks and talking politics and business . . . or possibly just gossiping. A chamber group of musicians tootled away at something soothing in a corner, and the air smelled of fine food, wine, perfume, warm linen and wool, a little of sweat and perfume, and strongly of expensive beeswax candles.

Like the feast before the High Council meets, Mathilda thought.

If you mentally substituted colorful modern tunics and hose and cotte-hardis for the drab, antique Iowan costumes, and tabards for the servants' white coats and bow ties. The occasional lidded glances were easy enough to catch, and the way factions avoided each other accidentally-on-purpose. She'd grown up in a real court, after all, where her own frowns or smiles could set feuds going. Granted, it was the court run by her mother—her father had been killed in the Protector's War when she was ten—but the Lady Regent had known how to do things. She'd been in the Society before the Change, where the knowledge of such things was kept alive. Iowa was large, and rich, and far more populous than any of the realms around the Columbia and Willamette, or even all of them together . . .

More than two and a half million people! A hundred and twenty thousand just in this one city!

. . . but in some ways it was a bit old-fashioned. A good many of the older men here were actually wearing suits with jacket and tie, for example, or military uniforms based on those of the old American republic. Though more favored the bib overalls and billed feedstore cap that were a gentleman's garb in Iowa, the mark of a Farmer or Sheriff, which was what they called knights and barons.

And they're running a court, but doing it badly, as if they were stumbling through an unfamiliar dance, or like children in a catechism class with a half-literate teacher. What they really need is someone to tell them how to do it properly!

"That dress looks absolutely gorgeous," Kate went on, brightening once more. "What's it called again?"

"A cotte-hardi. There's an arcane terminology for every bit of it—this headdress is a wrapped wimple, for instance."

"Beautiful!" she said. "Those carved rose-crystal buttons down the front and sleeves, and the lace! I've never seen such fine needlework, either."

"Well, Mother *does* have the best. But right from the beginning my parents went looking for craftspeople—they were thinking ahead."

She flicked her wrist, and the ivory leaves of her long-handled fan opened out to make a tracery of tiny figures that showed children dancing around a maypole.

"By now we have a lot of fine makers, for practical things and for beautiful ones as well. And not just in my mother's Household. This was a present from a friend, Lady Delia de Stafford."

"Lovely!" Kate said, taking it for a moment and holding it up against a light.

She hesitated and then went on: "But . . . isn't that dress . . . well, isn't it all a bit cumbersome?"

Mathilda laughed. "It certainly is if you don't have a lady-in-waiting and a couple of maidservants to help you on and off with it," she said. "Which I suspect was part of the point—that's why it's a noblewoman's style."

At home she wore male dress as often as her special status let her get away with it, and hated the constriction of the court fashion's buttoned sleeves and bodice and the way you couldn't lift your arms above your shoulders, and the long full skirts and the wrapped headdress, though even that was better than the tall cone-shaped ones. The two tunics and shift of commoner female costume were much more comfortable and less confining, but noblewomen could get away with that in only the most casual settings.

She'd have just chucked the clothes chest, herself—God and His Mother knew that they'd lost most of the gear they'd started out with in Bend at one emergency or another, which had included everything from battle and headlong flight to million-strong stampedes of mad buffalo. Now she was glad she hadn't insisted; it made her feel a little less frightened and homesick, and it emphasized that she wasn't *officially* just a prisoner here.

And the warm browns and golds of the silk and embroidery *did* complement her seal-brown hair and hazel eyes and warm light olive complexion. She wasn't beautiful; her features took after her father's, too bold and a little irregular, but she knew she could be striking.

And I have to uphold the Portland Protective Associa-

tion's honor here. These Iowans think everyone else is a monkey from the wilds, or at best a hick.

"You look enchanting, your Highness," Odard Liu said.

He came up to them, a middle-sized young man, black-haired and olive-umber of skin, slim and elegant in parti-colored hose and curl-toed shoes with little silver bells, trailing dagged sleeves and hood with tippets and gold-link belt, his slanted blue eyes amused and his lute over his back, troubadour fashion.

Some of the younger local gentry trailed after him, looking fascinated; the more so when he made an elaborate leg-bow and hand-flourish to both women, the long tail of his round flat nobleman's hat fluttering and sweeping the floor as he drew it through the complex measure.

"And your Majesty is also enchanting in her own person, if I may be so bold," he went on to Kate Heasleroad. "Your lord is to be envied for his wealth and power, but not least for the jeweled beauty of his consort."

Everyone loves flattery, but keep in mind that when people deal with royalty they lay it on with a trowel, Mathilda's mother had told her once. *Your friend Odard at least does it with some style.*

He'd also clung to the box with their last Court outfits inside like grim death, even when they were starving in that cave in the Rockies wondering if they'd have to eat the horses while the blizzards howled outside. He'd laid out gold here to have his gear repaired, too—and hers, to be sure.

"But though Iowa is rich and mighty, I say that only in Portland do we know how to praise fair ladies."

Odard brought his lute around and strummed. His fingers teased out a stately tune, one of his own.

Oh, no! Mathilda thought. *Not that one!*

The chamber group had fallen silent. His smile was half warm and half a teasing pleasure in her embarrassment as he sang a chorus in a pleasant tenor:

"So let the Hall ring for the Light of the North!
For the Princess Mathilda—the Light of the North!"

"Odard, I *still* haven't forgiven you for composing that," she said, and rapped his knuckles with her fan.

He grinned unrepentantly as he shook the hand and then went on: "I was just telling these good fellows about the High Tournament of the Association."

"Great stuff!" one of them said enthusiastically. "We have Reserve drills and National Guard muster days at the county fairs, but nothing that fancy. It sounds like a hell of a lot of fun!"

"Not when you're smacked right off your horse and knocked silly and you throw up inside a closed helm and they have to unharness you with bolt cutters," Mathilda said with feeling. "*Or* when a horse breaks something and screams until they put it down. I always hate that part."

"Girls compete?" Kate said, interested.

"The Princess is a special case, to be sure," Odard said smoothly. "And of course the current Grand Constable of the Association—Lady Tiphaine, Baroness d'Ath. Apart from them, no, not very often. Though one young lady is always crowned Queen of Love and Beauty by the winner."

Mathilda choked back a gurgling laugh. Two years ago Tiphaine d'Ath *had* won, and the Grand Constable had ridden up to the stands and dropped the crown from the point of her lance into the lap of her lady-in-waiting Delia de Stafford. At which the local bishop had nearly choked on the blessing, since everyone knew about Tiphaine and Delia.

That was wicked *of her. Funny, yes, but wicked.*

Though nobody spoke about it, unless they wanted to face Baroness d'Ath in a duel, which wasn't anything a sane human being would do unless they were tired of life. Mathilda sighed a little, struck by sudden homesickness.

In the unlikely event that I *ever win a tournament—*

She knew herself to be fair to middling at best despite a lifetime's coaching by experts, without the supernal speed and skill that d'Ath used to compensate for men's greater raw strength.

—I'm going to crown myself *Queen of Love and Beauty and nobody else! Or maybe I could crown Rudi* King *of Love and Beauty . . . all the warrior saints witness he's beautiful . . .*

Odard went on, diplomatically ignoring her sudden flush:

"I'm surprised you don't have tournaments here . . . weren't there any Society people in Iowa? In most places which survived at all they did very well."

A new voice broke in: "Oh, there were some here in Des Moines. Dad said he found them very useful as instructors, the craftsmen and the fighters at least—the rest were . . . sort of flaky. He didn't want anything to do with all that ceremonial they liked so much."

Mathilda concealed a start. That was the Bossman, just breaking away from the people she *didn't* want him talking to—the emissaries from Corwin in Montana, the redrobed and shaven-skulled priest of the Church Universal and Triumphant, and the hard-eyed officer of the Sword of the Prophet who'd been pursuing them ever since they left Oregon. Anthony Heasleroad saw her glare at them and motioned them away. Being here on sufferance themselves they went, not without glares of their own.

"Dad always said you could afford to have people curse you in private, but not laugh."

Pride stiffened Mathilda's spine, and she sank in the formal curtsey her tutors had drilled into her in girlhood. When she spoke her voice was cool courtesy:

"I'm sure your father was a very able man, my lord Bossman," she said. "But so was mine; Portland lives, when all the other great cities on the West Coast died. And I assure you *nobody* laughed when he was styled *Majesty* or *my lord*. Not more than once, at least. Your Majesty."

Then Mathilda saw the glitter in his pale eyes. There was something not quite *right* there.

"You say that word 'Majesty' with such *conviction*," Heasleroad said. "I could get used to it . . . if people said it the way you do. And if I was *sure* you're not trying to disrespect me."

Mathilda met his eyes. *If he says* kill her, *the guardsmen will cut me down*, she thought. *You can see it in their eyes; most of them would do* anything *he said*.

There was a slight hush around them; even Kate stiffened, until the Bossman chuckled and nodded. People relaxed, and the bubble of silence collapsed inward again.

She felt a slight trickle of sweat down her spine, more than the heavy clothing and sticky-warm night warranted, and sipped at the sweet strong liquor again. *That* wouldn't have happened at the Palace at home, or Castle Todenangst. Sandra Arminger killed when she had to, with the cool dispassion of a housewife selecting a chicken. But not from spite or for the pleasure of it.

Darling, people should be afraid of the ruler's power,

she'd said to her daughter. *They shouldn't live in terror of the Throne's whims—that can make men willing to kill even if it means dying, just to end the uncertainty. The surest way to drive a dog dangerously crazy is to punish and reward unpredictably, and people aren't that much different.*

An intense longing for that cool quiet voice filled her, and their evenings together in the Silver Tower, talking or listening to the minstrel or playing chess or just sitting together reading . . .

I even miss Mom's damned Persian cats shedding all over me! I'm even looking forward to how mad she's going to be at me for running away with Rudi on the quest!

A little to her right Odard slid his right hand away from his left sleeve. She wasn't surprised that he'd managed to get a knife and conceal it. But she was suddenly, shockingly aware that he'd been ready to attack Heasleroad if he ordered her cut down. One thing desperate times did was show you who your friends really were. She'd had her doubts about Odard before they left home.

And I really *doubted it when he said he loved me. Now I'm not so sure. Which is . . . messy. I don't love him that way . . . do I? More like a brother.*

"Your family were Society people, then?" Iowa's Bossman said to the baron of Gervais.

"Ah . . . not exactly, my lord Bossman," Odard said cautiously. "My father Edward Liu was a freelance man-at-arms before the Change, and gained the golden spurs afterward. He rose high in the Lord Protector's service and was ennobled and granted Barony Gervais to hold as tenant-in-chief, for his loyalty and valor."

Mathilda winced slightly behind a polite smile and nod. Her father Norman Arminger *had* been in the Soci-

ety for Creative Anachronism, but not all his first followers had been of its Households. A lot of them had been
like Odard's father Eddie Liu—freelancers, bandits,
mercenaries—what they called gangsters back before the
Change, or Mafiya like old Alexi Stavarov with his reptile
eyes.

Dad had to use what was to hand, she told herself. *The
others didn't understand what had to be done, that so many
had to die if anyone at all was to live. Yes, Dad wanted
power. What conqueror or founder of a dynasty hasn't? But
if he hadn't gotten it, Portland would have been like Seattle
or LA, nothing but bones and ruins and wilderness.*

Instead there were hundreds of thousands of people in
the Association's territories in the Columbia Valley, villages and towns, the living fields that fed humankind, the
churches and proud castles . . .

*Even Eddie Liu wasn't that bad. He was always nice to
me, at least.*

"But my mother *was* of a Society household," Odard
said. "And of course both the Princess' parents were, and
they gave a lead to things. The Lord Protector was a very
great man, and his lady has ruled us with justice and wisdom since his death."

And your *mother has lethally pissed* my *mother off,
Odard,* Mathilda thought. *She's been intriguing with the
CUT. You know and I know Mother . . . the Lady Regent . . .
will have her head for it.*

That wasn't a metaphor; it meant an appointment with
a wooden block and a man in a black hood with a very
large ax, the latter a privilege reserved for the execution
of those of noble blood. Ordinary people just hung by
the neck.

Where does that put you, Odard? I know you're loyal to

me here and now, *but a mother is a mother. When we get back . . .*

"And that . . . Rudi fellow?" Heasleroad said.

"His mother was . . . is . . . a bard," she said.

Mathilda fought down a smile as she remembered how indignant Lady Juniper had gotten when a teenaged Mathilda Arminger thoughtlessly suggested that being The Mackenzie was more dignified for one of noble blood than busking.

Chiefing it is as dignified as pumping out a cesspit, the which is needful work too, she'd said indignantly. *And I'm of the blood of plain dirt farmers and workingmen. A bard I was and a bard I shall be until the Hunter comes for me, and I will make music in the Lands of Summer for the simple joy of it!*

Then she'd sung—a beautiful a cappella piece that ended:

"I ha' harpit you up to the Gods' own thrones,
I ha' harpit your midmost soul in three;
I ha' harpit you down to Anwyn's dell,
And ye would make a Chief of me?"

The smile was in Mathilda's voice for a moment as she went on:

"Lady Juniper Mackenzie, *the* Mackenzie of the Clan Mackenzie. There was a war . . . her forces captured me during a raid. Then my father's took me back and captured Rudi, and then the Bear Lord and the Lord Protector fought between their armies and killed each other—it's a very long complicated story."

Not least because the various sides tell different versions and I'm not altogether sure which one is true, if any, even though I was there myself for part of it. I was too young to know a lot of what went on.

Aloud: "After the Protector's War Rudi and I spent time with each other's peoples every year as part of the peace settlement, so we were raised together a lot of the time. We're, umm, very good friends."

"Extraordinary," the Bossman said. "My mother used to read me stories like that—Richard the Lionheart, Robin Hood . . ."

"I always sympathized with the Sheriff of Nottingham, myself, my lord," Odard said. He raised his hands with a charming grin. "After all, he was on the side of law and order."

"Rudi's a . . . very able man, too," Mathilda said. "I'm sure he'll get your wagons back, your Majesty."

The glitter came back. "He'd better."

The bossman moved away, and Kate began chattering about something inconsequential. Mathilda smiled and nodded, keeping mental track in case she should say something, without really listening—another skill she'd learned at court.

The problem is that I sort of recognize the way he looked at me—besides the mad whimsy that might order me killed on an impulse. Lord Piotr de Chehalis did too, once—and his interest in a woman starts at the eyebrows and stops above the knees, she thought, remembering a polite discussion of the latest ballad of courtly love that had turned into a brief wrestling match in an alcove.

I didn't enjoy convincing him he wasn't as irresistibly attractive as the fifth brandy told him he was—

Which she'd done via a ringing slap across the chops that left him bleeding from lips cut against his own teeth, no maidenly restraint *there*. She wasn't as strong as the burly blond noble, but she'd trained to the sword all her life and there had been plenty of power behind the blow. He'd taken it in silence, bowed, turned and left, not being suicidal enough to draw on her or strike back even when drunk—that had been in Castle Todenangst, the heart of House Arminger's power.

And besides the Protector's Guard ready to come at the first call, Tiphaine d'Ath had been in the next room. The Grand Constable would have cut him to pleading, sobbing ribbons on the dueling field and then stood watching him bleed to death by inches, her head cocked slightly to one side and that chilly little smile on her lips. The thought made Mathilda shiver a little even now. Even with nothing said those iceberg-colored eyes had narrowed a little and followed Piotr as he stalked out. Pursing her lips while her left hand's fingers moved like graceful cables of living steel on the long hilt of her sword, and her right turned a hothouse rose beneath her nose.

Tiphaine *liked* killing people who annoyed her, men particularly; and she'd been as protective of Mathilda as a mother cat with a kitten as far back as the heir to the throne of Portland could remember. It was rather like having a friendly tiger running tame in the house; you could forget the nature of the beast except that every now and then the claws slid free for a moment.

Piotr never spoke to me again except formally, which pleased me well enough. And it would be very, very reassuring to have Baroness d'Ath here now. Or to be back in Todenangst. Or anywhere I wasn't in Anthony Heasleroad's power.

But the only rescue she was likely to get was one she or her friends came up with themselves.

Mary pierced with sorrows, pagan though he is, Rudi was also born of woman. Help him! Help us all!

DES MOINES
CAPITAL, PROVISIONAL REPUBLIC OF IOWA
BOSSMAN'S COMPOUND
SEPTEMBER 5, CHANGE YEAR 24/2022 AD

"At least I'm not hanging up by my thumbs," Ingolf Vogeler said to himself, looking up at the gray cracked concrete of the cell's roof and breathing the smells of iron and old sweat and piss and less pleasant things. "Or being hammered with lead-lined hoses. Or being strung up *and* hammered. Yet. Rudi's got a couple more days before the month is up."

It was too dark now to read the graffiti. He'd spent several days tracing the opinions of a generation of prisoners about the Heasleroads, father and son. The standard of literacy had gone down but the sentiments were pretty uniform—and he agreed with every one of them. He'd been tempted to add his own, at length. He'd been born a Sheriff's son back home in the Free Republic of Richland and sat through schooling every winter until he was fourteen or so, his family being masters of broad acres and able to spare his labor without hardship.

But it was always *possible* that it would make things worse. Venting was a luxury he could only afford if he gave up every scrap of hope, and he couldn't do that. For Mary's sake if not his own, and for the others.

"Here's my plan!" someone screamed in a cell down the row. *"Just listen! First we catch the rats and train them and then—"*

"Shut up!" half a dozen others bellowed, until the madman drifted off into grumbles and then snores.

"Fucking politicals!" one of the other voices yelled, and gave the bars of his cell a rattling kick before he lay down again. "Fucking loonies, every goddamned one of you!"

The common prisoners were genuinely angry. Sleep was the only real escape from the State Prison, at least for the hard-cases who made it to this pen inside the perimeter wall of Des Moines' inner citadel. The other ways out led to places that were even worse. The main punishment for offenses against the—permanent—Emergency Regulations was life at hard labor. Which only meant four or five years in the salvage gangs or quarries or in the mines grubbing out coal, or a miserable decade if you were rented out as a part of a convict chain gang. The Heasleroads thought capital punishment was wasteful, save in exceptional cases. And far too merciful.

Anthony will probably make an exception for me, if Rudi doesn't get those wagons to the bridge on time. Or maybe even if he does.

The close confinement here was a compliment, in a way; it meant they were taking his capacity to do harm seriously, even if they didn't believe it had been a Cutter spy who'd betrayed him and Vogeler's Villains when they were nearly back to the Mississippi with the plunder of Boston's galleries. Here the Church Universal and Triumphant was a barely noticed oddity somewhere far, far out west, beyond Nebraska and the ranchers and the Sioux. He'd learned better, painfully . . .

And Rudi's quite a guy, but he's not going to pull four Conestoga wagons two hundred miles by himself. Or even with that damned spooky black mare of his, and Edain to help. And even if he did, I somehow doubt Tony Heasleroad will pay up on the bet. Though Rudi may actually have a better chance at it than I would. The Villains just cut their way through and back—he doesn't have any blood feuds among the wild-men.

"Back in goddamned Iowa," he muttered, with a quirk of the lips. "Nothing's gone right since I took that Boston job from Tony H."

He sighed, remembering one place near Boston. It had a four-story internal courtyard with a mosaic floor and a marble throne in it, still dimly lit by the great pyramidal glass roof at the top, unbroken by some miracle. The galleries around it had held some things that had riveted him, even in that place of hideous peril; paintings, carved wood, a curious statue with its hand upraised in blessing and an infinite compassion in the ancient stone face. Treasures and wonders beyond knowing lying doomed behind dusty glass, looming up out of the darkness as their lanterns passed, then fading into oblivion. They'd had a list to salvage, but it was a fraction of that one single treasure house.

And if we're lucky, the stuff we did *get is still in those steel boxes on the wagons.*

The keepers had solidly boarded the doors and windows to preserve their charges, before they went off to meet their deaths. He'd admired that at the time, and the more so as he saw what was within. There had been this wall of stained glass like nothing he'd seen in all his life, far too large and fragile to take . . .

I got to see that. It came all the way from Europe! And I met Mary. That *was better than right. Hmmm. Unless meeting the one woman you want to settle down with just makes* this *worse? Giving you more to regret, you betcha.*

He'd set up an exercise program when they put him in this cell, which for a wonder he had to himself—except for the miniature inmates in the cornshuck mattress. The sit-ups and chin-ups and push-ups and running in place ought to have left him tired enough to sleep easily, but the stinks and snores from the other cells kept him wakeful.

Now he lay on his back with his hands behind his head, a tall powerfully built man just short of thirty, with a pleasant battered face and a nose that had healed a little crooked long ago after an encounter with the blunt end of a Sioux tomahawk, brown hair and short-cropped beard, and dark blue eyes now half closed. He was barefoot, and his trousers and undershirt were getting a little gamy, but he'd known worse conditions—as a hired soldier in a free company, and then as a salvager leading a gang working the dead cities.

Memories drifted through his mind on the verge of sleep. His home, Readstown, the day he'd left with the volunteers who were going to fight the short glorious war against the Sioux, turning to watch petals from the blossoming apple orchards blowing like frothing white mist down towards the river. Mountain-tall towers in Chicago, scorched and leaning against each other like drunken giants long asleep, with their feet in swirls of lake water running in whitecaps through rivers that had once been streets. Dawn breaking up like thunder out of the Atlantic—he'd been one of the few men from the civilized lands to see that, since the Change. That weird little village on Nantucket, and the even weirder . . . place . . . that shared the island with those refugees out of time. Mary's one bright blue eye laughing at him, as she reached for him with long-fingered slender hands.

Mountains rearing above the half-built bulk of the Temple in Corwin . . .

He awoke with a shudder; he'd been back *there* for a moment. His chest heaved under a film of sweat, and he called up something they'd taught him in the Valley of the Sun this last winter, in the Monastery of Chenrezi—a mandala, and a chant. The patterned figure began to turn, drawing his mind into its depths, and heart and breath slowed.

Heels beat a staccato on the concrete, hobnails grating. A bright Coleman lantern showed, and then the man carrying it as he turned the corner. None of the other occupants complained, even if they felt inclined; the man wore the harness and uniform of the State Police, not the turnkeys. They were the Bossman's personal retainers, and widely—and justly—feared. And this one had Captain's bars on the shoulders of his plain mail shirt; he carried a cloth-wrapped bundle as well.

Edgar Denson, by God! Ingolf thought, with a sudden prickle. *Come to kill me in person? Possibly. Though he'd probably have brought a crossbow if he had that in mind.*

The State Policeman kicked a three-legged stool over and sat, one foot sweeping the scabbard of his shete aside as he did. The distance was close enough for easy conversation—but just beyond reach if Ingolf lunged against the bars. He was bigger than the policeman, and at least ten years younger, since Denson had to be with a couple of years either side of forty.

He's a tough son of a bitch, but I could take him one on one. Somehow I don't think that's going to happen.

"You know, you're a pain in the ass," Denson said conversationally, leaning forward with his palms on his knees. "Ordinarily I'd think you should have been 'killed while resisting arrest.' Or 'while trying to escape.'"

Urrrk! Ingolf thought.

That was *not* what you wanted to hear from a high officer of the all-powerful secret police and general Brute Squad.

"Anthony Heasleroad would have been sort of annoyed if you'd killed me before anyone asked questions," Ingolf pointed out, his voice carefully neutral. "He wanted to find out what happened to four wagons full of salvaged artwork."

There was a flicker of respect in the other man's cold

gray eyes, and he ran a hand over his close-cropped gray-ing blond hair.

"Yeah, there is that . . . especially since he really be-lieves you about his man Kuttner being a spy and finking you out to the Cutters."

"He *does*?" Ingolf said, keeping his voice from squeak-ing by an effort of will.

"Yeah. You know, a lot of people think Tony is just a stupid, crazy spoiled brat. They're only about half right, and only about half the time."

"If he believes Kuttner was a spy and ratted me and my Villains out, *why am I here?*" Ingolf ground out, clutching at the bars to burn the rage out of his muscles. "Why aren't the *Cutters* in here?"

Denson grinned, a remarkably evil expression. "I didn't say he wasn't crazy. I didn't say he wasn't a spoiled brat. I just said he wasn't stupid . . . when he bothers to think."

"What would he say if he heard you voicing that opin-ion?" Ingolf asked, forcing calm on himself.

Because it might *be the sort of confidence you get killed for hearing.*

"He'd laugh, like he did when I told him to his face. He thinks it's funny. It is, when you look at it right. I need him just as much as he needs me, and the way I need him means I do all the work and he gets all the fun. I've told him that, too."

"Must be a refreshing change, someone telling him what they really think."

"Hell, he's had people lying to him to get stuff all his life, and like I said, he's *not* stupid. He's gotten pretty good sensing it. And then there are all the people who swear they think he's a devil of a good fellow, and he knows better than to believe *that* . . . So he realized Kuttner was stringing him; he just didn't realize it was more than the usual get-on-the-gravy-train stuff."

A slight wince. "And it makes me and the Staties look bad; *we* didn't figure him for a plant, either."

For a moment Ingolf wondered what it must be like to *be* Bossman Anthony Heasleroad, Governor and President Pro Tem, the wealthiest and most powerful man on the North American continent. He felt one corner of his mouth quirk up involuntarily in an emotion uncomfortably hanging somewhere between pity and schadenfreude.

"Yah, he must be about the loneliest man on earth," he mused.

Denson shrugged. "Kate actually *loves* the fat, ugly bastard, poor girl. God knows why. Oh, yeah, and his son loves him too, but Tommie's only eighteen months old. And old Bossman Tom doted on him. Apart from that . . . you said it, Sheriff Vogeler."

"Captain Vogeler, if you have to use something besides my name. I *earned* that. My dad was a Sheriff, but my elder brother inherited the title. The pompous asshole."

Another chuckle. "Vogeler, I'm not surprised you made your hometown too hot to hold you, and your friends are just as bad. That priest who was with you was seen going into the Catholic Cardinal's palace—and it wouldn't be good politics to try to muscle in there, even though I suspect he gets in and out without our noticing, somehow. The other four, the black kid and the three women, haven't been found, and I don't think they're just waiting for you to get the chop. That sensitive spot between my shoulder blades starts getting an arrow-itch every time I go outdoors. And the two we did catch are the Bossman's pets now. They're giving him ideas."

"I thought you State Police were the Bossman's loyal muscle. What do you care what ideas he gets?"

"We are," Denson said, and pulled a pipe out of a case at his belt. "And don't play dumb with me."

To Ingolf's surprise he pulled out the wanderer's battered briar as well and filled and lighted it, before handing it to him through the bars.

"Your two friends in the playing-card costumes are telling the Bossman he should be a King with everyone swearing homage on bended knee. *And* telling Kate Heasleroad that she should be Queen. He likes the idea. So does she, though I think it's mostly the thought of having a crown and a fancy dress like that *Princess . . .*"

"Princess Mathilda."

"Yeah, Mathilda Arminger . . . has. I said Kate loved Tony. That's pretty good evidence she's not too bright, hey?"

"Tony *is* King, near as no matter, Denson," Ingolf pointed out. "That's the way they think out west, anyway—Mathilda's and Odard's bunch of them, at least. They're nuts for that knights-and-castles stuff. Some of the castles are pretty damned impressive, too; not as big as Des Moines, but high. And you wouldn't want to meet their heavy cavalry in a bad mood, believe you me."

"No shit. Actually it all sounds pretty workable. Not *all* that different from the way we do things, but more . . . polished. More regularized, you know, sort of as if a lot of the kinks and rough spots had been worked out."

Ingolf nodded; he'd had the same thought, when he was west of the Cascades. If you subtracted the castles and coats of arms, the Association's territories had the same setup as most parts of the Midwest; refugees from the cities and their children—grandkids too, just lately— working for landowners, the landowners owing allegiance to bigger landowners who managed the local defenses, and all of them to an overboss. Although the Farmers and Sheriffs in Richland—his own homeland in what had been southern Wisconsin—were a lot less high-and-mighty about it than here in Iowa, and the Bossman of the Free Republic was a lot closer to first among equals than either of the Heasleroads, father *or* son.

"But a King doesn't have quite as much need for the State Police," Denson said, smiling like a shark. "The only reason we haven't done anything about 'em is those Cutters from Montana. *They've* been telling Tony the Bossman should be a fucking *God*. Provided he follows the—what do they call that funny-farm fake Bible of theirs?"

"The Dictations. And the Book of Dzur. That's how *they* run things, which I've seen firsthand," Ingolf said.

Along with some other things I'm not going to mention, because you'd think I was crazy. And being a prisoner in Corwin . . . you do *go crazy. I don't think I realized how much until I began to recover, in Chenrezi Monastery.*

"But I think they have their own Prophet in mind for the job, and nobody else," he said aloud.

"That's about what I thought," Denson said. "Besides, that everyone-is-dirt-beneath-your-feet and soulless-min-ions-of-the-Nephilim stuff is just *far* too tempting. I'm all for the Bossman's authority, but let's not get ridiculous."

He produced a silver flask from his belt and took a nip. Without looking around he also lashed out with one foot, and connected with a set of fingers that were gripping the bars of the next cell at the sight of the liquor. The hairy face behind them jerked backward, swearing—quietly—and disappeared.

"Which sort of presents me with a problem," he said. "They've also been telling the Bossman that you and your friends should all get the chop, soonest."

"That's the sort of advice Tony Heasleroad usually listens to," Ingolf said sourly.

There was a certain freedom in his position. Denson's confiding mood confirmed it; the man was probably talking more freely to him than he could to anyone else, because he didn't expect one Ingolf Vogeler to be around very much longer. One way or another. Though he wondered at his letting the other prisoners eavesdrop.

Ah, he thought. *He wants to judge my reactions before he risks letting me out of the cage even for an instant, even at the end of a catchpole.*

"I get it," Ingolf said, snapping his fingers with a look of sardonically exaggerated surprise. "You're going to sit there and tell me all your evil plans before you kill me."

"Christ, no, I saw that movie before the Change," Denson said genially.

He extended the flask—cautiously, at arm's length, so that Ingolf could just reach it but not the other man's hand. It was peach brandy, well-aged, smooth and sweet, and went well with—at least temporary—relief.

"Ah, that's sippin' liquor," Ingolf said. To himself: *Phew. He needs me for something. Needs me alive.*

"Thanks."

"You're welcome," Denson said, taking it back. "No, when *I'm* going to kill someone I just kill them, fast and quiet. Dead men don't figure a way to turn the tables on you."

Ingolf felt an unwelcome stab of emotion; it took him a moment to recognize it as hope. That made the inside of his head itch.

Careful, he told himself as his breath caught involuntarily. *You can't afford to get muddleheaded.*

"So I figure I need to get that hard-ass Graber and even more that lunatic they call a High Seeker out of town, and hopefully your bunch too. You can all go off and kill each other somewhere else, and we can get on with life. Tony will be annoyed, but he'll get over it when he finds some new toys. If I had you all chopped against his orders, he might . . . probably would . . . start thinking of *me* as a threat."

"And that wouldn't do. He might get antsy."

"Oh, you've got no idea. Our boy has a well-developed sense of self-preservation."

"The Corwinites probably have plans of their own," Ingolf said.

"Yeah. The other guy usually does, the dirty bastard." Apropos of nothing, Denson went on: "You're not old enough to remember the Change, are you?"

"Nope," Ingolf said. "Not really. I remember the flash of light and the headache, but not much before that and not much more after, not for years. I wasn't even six then."

"Yeah, I can't remember much of when I was six either." Denson nodded.

"I *do* remember how scared everyone was."

"Yes," Denson said; the flask halted for a moment halfway to his lips, then came down again. "I was old enough to *know*."

When he went on his eyes were locked on nothing, on a vision that gave them a haunted bleakness Ingolf recognized. He'd grown up seeing it in his father, and the other adults.

"People are always saying how lucky Iowa was. It didn't feel that way then. The whole world had just dropped out from under our feet. If the fucking *laws of nature* can change on you, what can you count on? Most people were . . . you know how a cow or a pig looks when you hit it on the head with the hammer, just before you cut its throat?"

Ingolf nodded at the familiar image; the only people who didn't know that were those too exalted to ever slaughter their own food or so poor they didn't eat meat, both small minorities in this part of the world. Denson snorted at the automatic agreement.

"Yeah, you're a Changeling, all right. Back then, even here in Iowa most people *didn't* know how that looked, 'cause they'd never seen an animal butchered unless they worked in a slaughterhouse. Even *farmers* hadn't. Hell, *I* hadn't."

"Whoa," Ingolf said, shocked despite himself.

He'd known things were very different back then, but—

"Not around Readstown. My dad butchered deer; he was a hunter even before the Change. I *do* remember that. And one of my uncles raised pigs and slaughtered them and smoked his own bacon."

"Wisconsin. The Kickapoo country in Wisconsin at that—the *sticks*."

"Yah, we're all ignorant cheeseheads, I've heard that before. You still had it lucky here."

"Everyone says that, because we've got as many people now as before the Change. That's after a generation of everyone breeding like crazy—hell, the kids are even *useful*, now, instead of swallowing a fortune in college tuition. Back around the Change enough people here died that life got real cheap, real fast. Only a few saw what had to be done if we weren't *all* going to die. Get the city people out to the farms, get the farms rerigged to work with hand tools, get tools made, get the food in the silos and such stored before it went bad, get the livestock out of the confinement pens before they died, organize the

Amish as instructors so we could plant a crop that first year . . ."

"Wise people like *you*, I suppose," Ingolf said.

He'd noticed that people who'd been adults before the Change tended to think that they were smarter than their children. When they were actually just more . . .

What was the word? Right, introspective. *Always watching themselves watching themselves watching themselves. Sometimes I wonder why they didn't just disappear up their own assholes.*

Denson grinned. "No. I was sixteen then, scared spitless, but old enough I remember it pretty good. Dad was like some crazy preacher then, spreading the gospel—that drove it into my head good and hard. He was number three or four in the State Police; though he drafted me, soon enough. And Tom Heasleroad, he *really* knew what had to be done, and saw the opportunities, if you know what I mean. Abel Heuisink saw it too, damn him, and he was in the State government like Tom."

"I've met him. We stayed at his place."

"He's no fool, just . . . in his old age he's turned into what they used to call a flaming liberal."

"You mean he's a free spender?" Ingolf said, puzzled; the Heuisinks had struck him as generous even for rich, well-born landholders, but not wasteful.

"Nah. The word's changed meaning—changed back, actually; I looked it up once when I noticed. We could close him down, but he's got supporters. And Anthony likes to have an official opposition . . . keeps all the other groups competing to make sure he doesn't deal them in. Plus he knows Abel isn't a friend of mine, personally, and neither is *your* friend Heuisink Junior. Balance of power stuff."

"Jack doesn't like you either, no. His father worked with your father, though."

"Yup. Holding his nose while he did. Trouble was, they weren't the real bossmen back then. The guys right at the top were sitting around wringing their hands, or putting Band-Aids on gut-stabs, shuffling the deck chairs on the Titanic—"

He paused at Ingolf's look of incomprehension and shrugged, amending the phrase:

"Fiddling while things burned, when we didn't have any time to waste. They couldn't get their heads around what had happened. Not fast enough."

"So Tom Heasleroad and old Abel Heuisink and your dad took over," Ingolf said. "And of course, Tom and your late father just *had* to *keep* running things because the Emergency never quite stopped."

Denson laughed. "Pretty much. Though that bastard Heuisink really *would* turn everything over to the vakis"—which was Iowa slang for *evacuee*, the ex-townsmen and their descendants who were the Farmers' labor force—"which I admit just between me and you wouldn't mean everyone starving to death, not anymore, since these days they know something about working the land, but that's politics."

"But you've put all your money on the Heasleroads, and if they go down, you do too," Ingolf said. "Why haven't you just taken the Bossman's Chair yourself?"

Denson shrugged again. "I'm the boogeyman for Tony, like Dad was for *his* father. The *Bad Cop*," he added, chuckling. "Though with Tom Heasleroad and my father it was more like Bad and Worse. A lot of these Sheriffs and County Commissioners and Guard colonels hate me too much to take my orders directly, but the Heasleroad name still has a lot of chops—we *didn't* all starve, after all, which everyone likes, and the Farmers and Sheriffs are on top of the heap, which they like plenty.

And they like the way the State Police keep order without their having to do the dirty work themselves."

"And the point of this little history lesson is?"

"That I have to *manage* the Heasleroads. Which means I have to keep the wrong people away from Tony; his father was a lot more sensible, but what can you do?"

"Not give him everything he wants just because he wants it?" Ingolf suggested. "That'd turn a saint into a monster, and I'll bet Tony Heasleroad was never a saint."

"Well, maybe. Tom was a lot better Bossman than he was a father, if you ask me; Dad never spoiled *us*. Water under the bridge, though."

"Nice to know I've got a good grasp on the situation, you betcha," Ingolf said. "But why the little confessional? I'm Catholic"—*more or less. Mary isn't, and . . . well, one of us has to convert in the interests of a happy marriage, so*—"but you were Lutheran, I thought."

"That's where getting rid of the Cutters comes in. Or you come in to get rid of them; I always believed in giving men a full briefing before I sent them to do something. You're more likely to get results if your people understand what's going on. That way they can improvise, not just be robots . . . be windup toys, I mean."

Ingolf bit back *I'm no man of yours, Denson*, and the policeman's grin replied: *For this you are, like it or not.*

Aloud Denson went on: "They're staying here because *you* are here, and because that Rudi guy is coming back for you. If he is."

"Ah," Ingolf said, and smiled wolfishly. "I bleed for you. I won't say from where. And Rudi will flap his arms and fly like a duck before he abandons friends. Or anyone he promised to rescue."

"Oh, one of those, is he? That type gets more throats cut than evil bastards like me."

"I'll take Rudi's word for it on who needs fighting," Ingolf said.

Then he blinked to himself. *You know, I really believe that*, he thought. *Life's not dull around Rudi Mackenzie, or safe, but you don't have to worry about him. A man could do a lot worse than be the one who had his back. One way or another he's going to need good men, and not just on this trip.*

He thought of Mary, who was after all the Mackenzie's half sister, and grinned to himself.

And I could do a hell *of a lot worse than be his brother-in-law. Half brother-in-law. Whatever.*

Denson looked at him slit-eyed, evidently distrusting his good cheer.

"You said the Cutters had plans of their own? They do. Evidently they've got a real hard-on for all of you; especially the big redhead, but they want you all dead in the *worst* way, and it's starting to sink in with them that Tony thinks you're too much fun to kill and isn't going to change his mind. Not anytime soon. And then your friend—the big redhead—sent a message, saying he's *gotten* the stuff. The wagons."

"He *did*?" Ingolf almost-squeaked.

Denson laughed. "Yeah. Surprised me no end too. I thought the wild-men would be tanning his hide for a drum over there by now. And that made the Cutters decide they could get you all at one swell foop, if they timed it right."

He nudged the bundle at his feet. It clinked significantly; Ingolf stiffened. He recognized the metallic *shink* sound of chain mail, and the rattle of a boiled-leather scabbard against something hard.

"What they forgot," Denson said, "is that the State Police is a *police* force, not just the . . ."

He grinned like a shark and made an odd gesture with his hands spread and the first two fingers of each crooked.

". . . 'Royal Guard' quote unquote. We're not the fucking *National* Guard, either, just parading around in tin shirts and breaking heads hup-one-two-three-left-right. We find things out. And we've got informants all over the place, including the guest quarters of the Boss-man's House. Those guys should *really* be more careful how they plot where the help can hear. I know all about them now."

"Why not tell the Bossman?" Ingolf asked.

To himself: *You don't know as much about the Church Universal and Triumphant as you think, Denson. But I'm not here to tell you what the monks at Chenrezi told* me.

"That might get rid of the Cutters, though not until they start to bore Tony. It wouldn't get rid of you guys. Tony really *likes* that Arminger chick. Got the hots for her, maybe, and he likes the stories she tells. What I'm going to do is let my problems . . . sort of solve each other. The timing will be close, though. Get moving. You're going to Dubuque."

Ingolf nodded slowly. "So, what's in it for me, Denson?"

"Longevity," the State Policeman said. "And a better view."

He toed the bundle over. Ingolf grabbed it, snaked the awkward length through the bars. There was the padded jacket, the short mail shirt that went over it, the weapons belt with his new shete—what they'd called a *dao* in Chenrezi—and bowie and tomahawk, shield and quiver, bow in the case beside them. He left the kettle helmet looped over the shield and tied down with a raw-hide thong.

"Don't put the ironmongery on right now. Figured you'd want a shower and some strong soap first. And keep the shete wrapped; it might attract attention."

Ingolf nodded reluctantly. He did stamp his feet into the boots; it was amazing how much better they made him feel . . . which was the demoralizing point of taking away prisoner's footwear, of course.

"What about after we get out?" he asked. *If we get out*, he added to himself. "I presume we're not all that welcome in Iowa, so how do we leave?"

"Oh, your friend Tancredo took care of that," Denson said, with a crooked smile. "And wouldn't he just shit if he knew we knew about that ship he rented? Nice little gaff-rigged river pedal-galley."

"What if we get caught in Dubuque?"

"Well, that's where *killed while resisting arrest* could come back into the picture. So don't screw up."

"You're an evil bastard, Denson," Ingolf said. *And now I know you need me, so I can say so. In fact, you'd fit right in with the Corwin people, some of them.* "I think you've got a hole where your conscience should be."

"People say it runs in the family. But we survived the Change without morals when billions died fully equipped with theirs. Plus I'm a *rich, powerful* evil bastard, and most of the other survivors ended up hoeing beans twelve hours every day, and living on cornbread and fatback with some hick farmer kicking their ass. Now follow me."

The sound of the key grating in the lock made Ingolf release a breath he hadn't been conscious of holding; that was when his gut decided that he really was getting out of here—if only into mortal peril. The feel of the blade and the weight of the mail shirt in his hands put his shoulders back, and a swing into his stride. Eyes glittered at them from the cells, reflecting a little of the light of the lantern Denson carried; he cupped a hand around the chimney to blow it out when they reached the steel door and the sections where the gaslights were left on all night.

But at least it's mortal peril I can do something about. The helplessness was the worst part of being locked up.

A squad of Denson's men waited outside the door at the end of the corridor, most of them holding their crossbows at port arms, along with a scared-looking screw Ingolf recognized without affection from his habit of spitting in the prisoners' food before he pushed it through to them, and laughing when they complained. As they passed, Denson jerked a thumb over his shoulder and spoke:

"Don't you men hear the riot?"

"Riot, sir?" the sergeant of the squad said.

"Yeah, the criminal scum are out of their cages and running wild. Go to it, men! I wouldn't be surprised if you had to kill them all to reestablish order."

"Yessir, *that* riot," the sergeant said.

"Stack the bodies in the corridor."

"Yessir."

Then he nudged the turnkey with an elbow; the man was still gaping in thick-witted bewilderment.

"What about this sad sack of shit, Captain?"

"Ah, too bad about the way the prisoners hauled him through the bars and took his keys off his dead, mangled body," Denson said. "Still, it was fucking careless of him to get that close to the cells, right?"

The turnkey blinked in alarm as the words began to penetrate; the sergeant grinned.

"Dead men contradict no tales," he said.

And struck again with his elbow—this time into the man's throat, a quick savage jerk of a blow without warning, and then followed it with a steel-toed boot to the side of the head when the man collapsed. One of his men dragged the body behind the file of troopers as they went through the massive door and then closed it behind them with a clunk and a rattle. Ingolf winced as he and the police captain walked away, and then again. Faint from the cell block he'd shared came the sound of screams, screams and then the deep *tung* of crossbows.

Denson's doing me a big favor, Ingolf thought. *Why doesn't this make me feel as optimistic as it should?*

"Don't sweat it," Denson said, at the gray of his face. "It isn't you, right?"

"Right," Ingolf said tightly.

I've got to live, he thought. *I've even got to let* Denson *help me. Too much depends on this mission coming off. Mary . . . all her friends . . . Christ, I think the* world *may depend on it. I want to have someplace we can go when this is all over.*

CHAPTER FOUR

"A woman had a baby boy
She loved him much and he gave her joy
The Good Folk came and on a whim
They took the boy away with them—"

Edain sang as he worked, loud but tuneful; his voice echoing oddly off the cracked, crumbling concrete of the highway overpass where the Southsiders were camped and over the quiet murmur of voices and clatter of tools. The wild-men had put up screens of woven branches, so not much of the hissing rain outside blew sideways into the sheltered spot. Acrid smoke from their campfires curled upward and hung beneath the arched surface, joining the soot that blackened it—this was one of their regular stops. The goaty smell of wet-but-not-washed humanity, wet dog, half-cured hides and cooking food was strong, under a stronger scent of damp earth and greenery and the silty water of the nearby creek.

"Eggs and crumbs and milk and grain
Bring my baby back again—"

Rudi didn't sing as his hands moved sharp steel across the six-foot length of wood clamped between his booted feet and bare knees. He was a competent journeyman bowyer, as many of the folk of Clan Mackenzie were, but no more than passable compared to Edain. That meant he had to concentrate to get any sort of results, particularly when he didn't have any tools besides knives and a hatchet. Edain's father was a master at the trade—it was one of the reasons he was called Aylward the Archer—and the younger Aylward had grown up as familiar with it as he was with plowing a field or shearing sheep or skinning out a pig or deer.

And to be sure, concentrating makes me worry less. I must get those wagons back to Iowa! But I cannot do it alone, and so I must win the trust of these folk. That takes more than a strong sword-arm!

"There," Rudi said, setting down the blade he'd been using as a drawknife and unlocking his ankles from about the other end of the workpiece.

He took the stave and ran it through his hands. Mountain-grown yew from the Cascades was the finest of all woods for a stick-bow, because the sapwood and heartwood were a natural laminate—strong in tension and compression respectively. This was tough springy hickory, which was a fair second best and abundant here in the east.

"What do you think?" he asked his companion.

Edain laid his piece aside and glanced down the length of trimmed wood; he'd finished two bows and half done another to Rudi's one, as well. His face was wholly intent, lost in the task; Rudi envied him that.

A few of the Southsiders grouped around sighed unhappily when he stopped singing—they were mad for new tunes. The warrior-hunters in the front rank stayed silent, focused as sharp as augers on the making.

"Dad would laugh," Edain said. "Or cry. Cernnunos dancing drunk on Beltane Eve, maybe he'd laugh and *then* he'd cry."

"He'd curse, sure and he would," Rudi said, grinning. "But it'll work, eh?"

"Eh. More or less, more or less, the Huntress willin'."

Rudi had been in and out of the Aylward household down in Dun Fairfax all his life; it was only a half hour's walk from Dun Juniper by the short forest path, and the two young men had been friends ever since a difference of a few years in their ages stopped seeming a chasm. Sam Aylward had been one of Lady Juniper's right-hand men from before Rudi's birth, as well. His son braced the central grip across one knee and slowly bent the stave with his hands braced wide apart on it; muscle bunched on his thick bare arms.

"Sixty-five pounds weight at a thirty-inch draw, near as I can tell without a proper tillering frame. Between sixty and seventy, at least."

That was only a little more than half the draw of their own longbows, but those were designed to punch through plate armor at need, or send a stout bodkin-head shaft three hundred paces and hit hard when it got there. Sixty pounds draw-weight was plenty for even heavy game, boar or bear or tiger, and it would deal with light armor well enough if the range wasn't too great. It was certainly ten times better than anything the Southsiders had had before they came.

"Without proper vises and clamps and drawknives and gouges and . . . and proper bloody *everything*," Edain grumbled. "Hmmm . . . by Lugh of the Many Skills, I think it needs—"

He braced it as Rudi had and took up the knife, holding the blade by the thick back and carefully shaving off a few long dark curls of seasoned wood. Then he repeated the flexing process.

"There!" he said. "Nice balanced draw. Not a bad job, Chief, considering what we've got for the workin' of it."

The wood itself wasn't bad at all; thoroughly dry, at least, and from fair-sized timber that he and Edain had split into proper triangular-section rough blanks along the grain. The Southsiders left billets in sheltered places to season on their rounds; hickory was a fine wood for spearshafts and tool handles as well. Unfortunately that seasoning and hacking some vaguely bow-shaped object out of the results was about the limit of their bowyer skills, and the product was barely worth *that* degree of effort. They didn't even know enough to unstring them when they weren't in use, and so they became worthless in a few months, though they'd grasped the fact fast enough when the clansmen told them.

The simple tapered sticks he and Edain were making had none of the walnut-root risers and polished antler-horn nocks and subtle reflex-deflex curve of Sam Aylward's masterworks, or those of his many pupils. They might have made him laugh or frown, but they did have the true taper and D-shaped cross section, and an arrow-rest of sorts at the right point; they'd boiled a little glue from the hooves of a deer and attached tufts of rabbit fur for the shaft to rest upon, and to fasten the fletching feathers of the arrows.

And all the folk in Jake's band exclaimed in wonder, Rudi thought. *No glue, for the love of the Mother-of-all! The good part of these being so crude is that it only takes about half a day to finish the job, even without proper tools. And anyone handy with a knife and used to working wood can learn to do it. Well enough for rule of thumb, at least, if not to equal a true craftsman. A thousand times better than no bow at all. And it's just the sort of gift they will value the most. It helps them in the long run, not just their present trouble. Help for help . . .*

A young woman came in with a cracked rain poncho of dull yellow plastic over her shoulders, and a lopsided sort-of-woven basket full of greens and roots. She dumped it into one of the big pots that were kept going as long as the camp stayed put, and an older female—all of twenty-five or so, and looking easily forty—stirred them in with a long paddle. Which was fortunate, because it was hard to survive on an all-meat diet and stay healthy, unless you were careful and ate the whole beast.

My hosts know some *of the wholesome plants,* he thought.

But even this far from home and the woods they knew, the two clansmen had been able to show them some new ones, though neither of them had anything like the knowledge of such a loremistress and healer as Aunt Judy. The Southsiders had no inkling whatsoever of which mushrooms were deadly and which were safe, for example, so they shunned them all. Or that you could make acorns edible by grinding the nuts to flour and then leaching out the tannins, which meant that they had no starch that would keep any length of time. Or that—

And to be sure, they aren't *very healthy.*

From the state of their teeth he suspected scurvy was a regular visitor to the Southside Freedom Fighters, come winter; they certainly weren't rotting them out with too much sugar, and there were cases of goiter and terrible scarring from infected cuts. Their carnivore diet would have made them taller and more muscular and less scrawny-tough, too, if they didn't have times of dearth fairly often.

They can make fire with a drill. They can cook what they eat, more or less, which is to say they hold it over the fire or boil it in a pot. And that's all that can be said for their food. They can't make good leather, or any cloth at all, or even the simplest metal tools—what will they do when the last of the salvaged gear is gone? They don't even know how to make salt from a lick! This is no way for human beings to live.

Impatient as he was, he wished he *did* have more time; a month here . . .

I could do more for them in a month. Or a year. Or ten; there's no end to it. I'll do what I can in the days I have, that's all.

He was wearing only his kilt, to keep respect—the Southsiders might be primitive, but they were certainly hardy men—and also to show his scars, for the same reason. Jake sunna Jake handed him the string of hand-twisted sinew, and Rudi whipped the lower end to the bottom notch of the longbow. Then he slipped the other loop upward, and strung the stave Mackenzie-style—bottom tip over his left boot, right thigh over the center. He pressed down with his leg and pushed up with his right hand at the same instant, smooth and steady. Muscle stood out in long swells under the pale skin of his chest and arms like a slow wave of the sea, and the loop at the end of the cord slid into the upper nock.

"There," he said, running a finger down the back to make sure no splinters stood proud in sign of a fault that would snap the wood under strain.

I wish I could glue a strip of rawhide here . . . but if wishes were horses we'd have enough to move those wagons . . . it will do, so.

"It needs to be well greased against the wet, but it will serve you well enough against anything but a knight in full harness on a barded destrier, and it might do for him as well if you were lucky."

"Cool!" Jake said.

Odd, Rudi thought. *I've heard folk in Corvallis use the word that way, or Bearkillers now and then.*

They'd ceremoniously given Jake all the bows, and he'd handed them out in turn to his favored followers—there had been cursing and jostling in plenty too. They'd all seen what the Mackenzie weapons could do, in the fight with the Knifers and in hunting since and they were panting-eager to have something like it themselves.

He handed Jake three arrows he'd also made; the little tribe's notion of fletching was even more sad than their attempts at bowmaking. The heads were ground and crudely hammered from old spoons, but they would do; it had been straight shafts and the delicate, skilled work of fastening the flight feathers that they hadn't mastered. Jake slipped on his bracer and looked around and spotted a dead chestnut fifty yards away, across the thinner grass growing in drifted soil over the old roadway's pavement. He drew with an odd motion, pushing the bow away with his left arm as much as drawing with the right.

Snap.

The shaft stood in the hard wood, buzzing like a malignant bee; the sound was distinct even through the quiet white noise of the rainfall.

Ah, well, the bow's good enough for journeyman work, I'm thinking. There will be more hand shock than I like, a bit of vibration, and quite a surge.

The Southsiders had half a dozen of the pre-Change bows, fiberglass wonders that they couldn't even dream of replacing, and they handed them around often enough that they were mostly reasonable instinctive shots by the time they were full grown. But the weapons had been made in all truth as what Edain had called them in scorn: children's toys. Their draws were light, just enough to be useful for hunting rabbits or birds but nearly worthless for war or bigger game. Good pre-Change arrows were so scarce among them that no man carried more than one or two, with even the enduring plastic feathers growing more and more tattered.

Most of the time they relied on javelins for anything beyond arm's reach. With those they were quite skilled.

"Can you teach us how to make bows like these?" Jake asked. "And arrers?"

Arrows, Rudi thought. *I'm getting the hang of the way they shift the sounds about, so I am.*

"Southsiders need it, Rudi-man. Need it bad."

"That we can, my friend. It's a help to your people, it will be."

Though I can't know how much of a help.

Jake grinned at him, showing gaps in his teeth. Suddenly for an instant Rudi was *elsewhere*, a dizziness that left him no time to even stagger. Jake screamed as he pulled against the bonds that held him to an ancient streetlamp. Wood around his feet smoldered, and ragged figures danced triumph—

Rudi blinked again and shuddered; the Southsider chief was still smiling, so it hadn't been long. Cold sweat lay dank along his sides and under his chin. He'd been raised by Juniper Mackenzie, a High Priestess who walked with the Otherworld, and he'd been touched by it himself more often than most. More, the Old Religion made fewer distinctions between magic and the works of the gods and the stuff of common day than other faiths.

And still visions like that weren't easy to bear, and they'd been getting uncomfortably common on this journey. Not to mention the Powers who'd walked the pathways of his dreams.

I think that was a sight of what would happen if I didn't help these folk, he thought. *The which makes me grateful to Whoever guided my steps here. But it gives my skin the crawls too, so. If a man knew every possible twist and turn his actions might bring to the world, would he dare to act at all? Yet it's also a comfort; I'm not merely using these people for my own needs, urgent as those are.*

Edain sang again as he went back to work on his own piece:

> *"The elfling shrieked and howled and cried*
> *And naught she did would make it bide!*
> *She formed a plan to prove*
> *This elfling child was not her love—"*

Several of the Southsider babies *were* howling and crying now and then, which wasn't surprising. If Rudi had had to endure this damp chill with nothing but a rough rabbit-skin diaper stuffed with moss or leaves *he'd* have cried, even in his mother's arms. When some of the tribe's women began casting thoughtful glances at their infants, Rudi grew a little worried himself.

Surely they couldn't take it literally? *The fey don't* really *do that. Not often, at least.*

He wasn't altogether sure about how the Southsiders *would* take it, though. If you had an empty place in your soul where such things should be, *something* would fill it.

We need tales to make sense of the world.

"Tell's another story, Rudi!" one of the children said, as he took up the next billet of the hickory, spat on a smooth hand-sized rock and began to hone hatchet and knife before he began his work.

The hunters and warriors and women who were gathered around to watch him fashion the longbow murmured agreement. Jake unstrung his new weapon and scooped a little congealed fat out of a dish and began to rub the wood, squatting and looking eager for the tale himself. The Mackenzie had never met folk so poor in story and song and legends, and it moved him to a pity that prickled at his eyes. Without that tapestry of color and words and ritual, what was life but eating and mating, sleeping and moving your bowels? All of them good and necessary things, but not enough; and they themselves needed that framework too, to give them meaning.

It surprised him as well as saddened him. Granted their pamaws had been young, any random group of Mackenzie children today would have known more and handed it down.

Though the Clan's youngsters have had two generations of loremasters by now, he reminded himself.

He remembered long evenings sitting at his mother's feet with the others in the great hall at Dun Juniper, listening to her storyteller's voice weaving music and magic as strong as any she made in the *nemed*, the Sacred Wood. Her hands shaping images and the light of the fires on the god-faces carved amid the rampant vines on the log walls; flame-crowned Brigid and Lugh Longspear of the clever hands, elk-horned Cernnunos, the triple Morrigan and the Dagda with his club, red-bearded Thor and Sif of the golden locks . . .

And the most of our clansfolk's parents and grandparents were probably no better off than these before they became Mackenzies. Before the Change.

First he demonstrated how to measure the proper taper from grip to tip of the bow by the joints of your forefinger, and the length of the stave by multiples of your drawing reach, and how to calculate the proper fist-mele between the belly and the string. A little to his surprise he was better at teaching the bowyer's craft than Edain; the younger clansman knew so much he was impatient with their ignorance.

"Well, then," Rudi said, when he'd reached the working stage. "It's a tale you want, is it now?"

"Yah!"

"You betcha!"

"No shit, dude!"

Ah, he thought, sorting through scores he knew. *Yes, this will speak to them. And there's nothing like telling one of the old stories to put away your own worry and care and fear!*

"Then you work on this one as I showed you, friend Tuk, and I will tell the tale—and correct your work if your hands go wrong. Now, the story! This happened very long ago, you understand, and far away, in a land across the oceans, among my ancestors and yours."

Most of mine, and a lot of yours.

"There was a man named Niall who was born to be King . . . to be the big boss . . . who later came to be called Niall of the Nine Hostages. And once in his youth he was traveling alone through the woods at night as he journeyed back to the hunting lands of his people."

They all shuddered and leaned forward; to be benighted alone was a thing of fear to them.

"He came across a hut, and in the hut was a withered and ancient crone . . . ummmm . . . an ugly old bitch . . . of an ugliness which hurt the eyes to see—but unknown to him she was not just the poor old woman he thought her; she was the Sovereignty of Midhe, the eldest of the Threefold Morrigú, and herself the patron Goddess of that earth."

"I thought you said there was this Lady and her stud who made everything?" someone asked.

"That there is," Rudi said.

His voice was casually confident; he was as sure of that as he was of his own breath and heartbeat.

"One of her, or a lot of her?"

"Both! Her forms are more numerous than the stars! How not, when the stars themselves are but the dust scattered by Her feet as She and the God danced all that is into being?"

Many of them nodded. Nobody had ever told them to prefer either/or to yes/and, nor that it was impossible for something to be one and many at the same time. Which meant it didn't drive them wild.

The way it would say a scholar from Corvallis. Or Father Ignatius.

"Each form She takes, or the Lord, is true; yet each a part of a greater whole. As we put it—"

He paused, then filled his lungs and sang, a hymn his mother had made, the "Farewell to the Sun." As might be expected of his parentage and rearing, at song he was better than fair even by the reckoning of Dun Juniper, where all the Clan's best bards were trained and many outlanders as well. Here Edain was the journeyman to his master craftsman, and his deep baritone filled the cavelike space effortlessly:

> "We know the Sun was Her lover
> As They danced the worlds awake;
> And She lay with His brilliance
> For all Their children's sake.
> Where Her fingers touched the sky
> Silver starfire sprang from nothing!
> And She held Her children fast in Her dreams.

"There was a glory in that forest
As the moonlight glittered down;
And stars shone in the wildwood
When the dew fell to the ground—
Every branch and every blossom;
Every root and every leaf
Drank the tears of the Goddess in the gloaming!

"There came steel, there came cities
Wonders terrible and strange,
But the light from the first-wood
Flickered down until the Change.
And every field, every farmhouse,
Every quiet village street
Knew the tears of the Goddess in the gloaming!

"Now the Sun comes to kiss Her
And She rises from Her bed
They are young—and old—and ageless
Joy that paints the mountains red.
We shall dance in Their twilight
As the forests fall to sleep,
And She whispers in our ears the word remember!"

When he looked back, the Southsiders were rapt; there were tears in some eyes, and some of those were scarred warriors. Back in the Willamette country there was a saying that Mackenzies were a clan, divided into septs, duns, choirs, choruses and soloists, and he was used to praise for his singing from that exacting audience. The Southsiders were more than moved; transported, even.

And sure, you can strike home in a man's soul—or a woman's—more easily by telling them stories that speak to their heart than by making arguments to convince their minds. Listening to stories comes naturally to us. Argument you have to study, like sword-work or archery, however much it seems a part of you once you have it learned. Striking home in their souls is what I need to do the now.

He went on, his voice falling into the storyteller's cadence:

"Now Niall was a great warrior . . . fighter . . . bitchin' tough stud . . . but he had been fostered far from home because of the hatred of his father's second wife, and he was almost a stranger to the land of his birth. Yet the King must be as a husband to the Lady of the land, for he stands in the God's place; as She is the Earth, so also Lugh of the Sun—so that folk and mine call Him—is the rain that brings the soil to life in springtime, and the warmth that ripens the harvest. This crone invited Niall to share her fire and her food, which were poor enough, but he being a man well trained in seemly ways did not refuse the hospitality even when she asked him to lie down on the same pallet as she—"

He told most of it and sang parts—the Southsiders had a few simple catches, as much chanted as sung to nothing more complex than the beat of palms on thighs or sticks on rocks, but they'd never heard trained singers before and they hung on every note, often weeping openly or looking half-tranced.

Well, mother made us a people, and her a bard from her youth. And little enough else they had to do on the long evenings of the Black Months but make music, in the early days. Though we aren't as . . . constant . . . about it as the Rangers, to be sure.

By the time the light faded Rudi and Edain had roughed out three more bows, and guided the best of the Southsider makers through the beginnings of enough more to give all the adult warriors one suited to their strength and their length of arm. He noticed one young fellow with a slight limp sitting by himself, hugging his knees. His eyes stared at nothing and lips moved a little as he repeated the tale of how Niall of the Nine Hostages met the Goddess of Midhe and won Her blessing on his kingship, not by his hero's strength, but by his kindness and pity to one he thought the least and worst of his people.

Driving it into his memory; none of them have their letters here.

A woman was crooning to her own baby Edain's song about the mother and how she tricked the child of the faerie folk into revealing his imposture.

Well, and we've given them that wealth, too, the which nobody can take, Rudi thought. *For what is living, day by day, but living out the story you're in?*

Few stayed up much past dark here, when a burning stick was the best light they had—and that used sparingly, lest it draw enemies. Edain yawned and stretched when he'd emptied his plate the second time, smiling.

"It's cheerful, you are," Rudi said.

"Sure, and I'm glad to do some *work*," Edain replied. "Traveling and adventuring are well enough—the things we've seen and done, Chief!—and fighting, well, you fight when you have to, not when you wish. Hunting's work and play at once. But I miss the dun and the fields."

His eyes grew distant. "Wheat harvest will be over, but there's the soft fruit and the apples and the rest of the orchards, and haying, and soon it'll be time to raise the spuds and get the turnips into the clenches, and put all right for the fall plowing, and there's always the stock. Or going over to Sutterdown and helping with the grapes there. It makes me fair itch a bit to miss it all, not to mention the Sabbats and Esbats and the Wheel of the Year. I'd be glad even to muck out the dairy, and that on a cold wet day in the Black Months, so."

"Now, boyo, that's going far and far!" Rudi laughed.

He was a warrior by trade, though of course he'd done his share of fieldwork and put his hand to this and that, in the smithy most often. Shoveling compacted manure out onto a cart was one particular chore he didn't remember fondly; it made getting in the sheaves or even pig butchering pleasant by comparison. He spoke lightly:

"Dun Fairfax has a fine dairy barn, but I miss sitting in your mother's kitchen more, watching her taking an apple pie out of the oven, and the outrageous fine smell of it, and the taste of it too with a piece of her cheese and a big glass of cold fresh milk."

When he said it he wished the words back; Edain smiled at the half jest, but Rudi could tell he *was* wishing himself back there, at table with his parents and brother and sisters and the rest of the Aylward household.

"But there's some *here* glad enough of your presence," he said teasingly, to break the moment.

It was true, too. Two Southsider girls were standing behind the barrel-chested bowman, one of them winding a lock of her black hair about her finger and both smiling and giggling when he turned to look. They were considerably cleaner than most of their tribe. Edain had whittled them combs and toothbrushes and shown them the use of the Sweet William that bloomed by the creek a little way from here; you could get a good lather out of the roots, which was why it was also known as soapwort.

And the washing of them was a piece of instruction he probably enjoyed more than trying to turn their menfolk into bowyers, Rudi thought.

Between constant toil and weather and one child after

another—so many died, and they didn't seem to have any idea how to prevent conception anyway—the Southsider women aged even faster than their men, but these were a few years younger than Edain.

"Ripe as summer strawberries, they are," Rudi said; one of them looked at him, and pouted when he shook his head, smiling.

"Ah, I'll be off to my blankets, then, Chief," Edain said, brightening considerably as he let himself be led into the shadows with one girl tugging at each hand.

"And to sleep, eventually, eh?" Rudi called with a grin, and Edain threw a laugh over one shoulder.

Theirs were not a bashful folk. Didn't the Charge of the Goddess Herself say "All acts of love and pleasure are My rituals?" Rudi remained by the embers of the fire himself; there had been plenty of those lingering glances cast in his direction, but there weren't so many unattached women here he could be sure of avoiding trouble over it. And he hadn't had the heart for dalliance right now anyway.

What with worry, toil and care. Ah, the merry life of a hero! And it's pure joy to be the Chief, too; well, I've seen that wear on Mother over the years, that I have.

The rest of the little tribe rolled themselves into scraps and tatters of pre-Change cloth or crawled between stiff hides; Jake had a nearly intact sleeping bag, which he drew across the sleeping form of his woman and their two living children. Others huddled together, with leaves as extra insulation and protection from the mosquitoes.

At least they don't have lice, Rudi thought; probably none of their founders had, and they'd been too isolated to pick them up since.

The sentries ghosted out to take up their positions; the rain had faded away into a close damp night, and there

was absolutely nothing wrong with the skill with which
the lookouts vanished into the rustling, buzzing darkness. They'd had to learn *that* well, or die horribly. Jake
fished a drumstick out of the remnants of the perpetual
stew in the communal pot, originally an aluminum trash-
can roughly cut down with the jagged edges hammered
over, and took a meditative bite.

"And now, my friend, you and your folk were to help
me with *my* task?" Rudi said softly. "I wouldn't ask it save
that need drives me; we *must* have those wagons at the
bridge, and soon. The lives of oath-brothers and kin and
one very dear to me rest upon it."

Jake frowned and looked around at his sleeping people. "You helped us plenty," he said. A hesitation. "You
could be the big man here, if you stayed. Plenty of the
bitches would like you, even more than the Archer. You
could show us lots and lots, make us strong. Strong like
your Clan, that you talked about. Show us how to get
right with the spooks, too."

Rudi smiled, but there was real respect in his nod as
well as pity.

*This man may be a savage and pig-ignorant of a thou-
sand things, but he knows that to be a true Chief is to serve
his people's need,* he thought. *And he's realizing how great
their need is, now that he's seen a glimpse of the world outside. He'll give anything he has to aid them, even his own
position.*

"My friend, it's honored I am by your words," he said,
which he found was true. "But I have my own kin and
friends to think of. Also I could not help you as much as
you think. Your people's problem is not only that you
lack skills, but that you are too few, and your enemies too
many."

"Yeah." Jake's fist hit the ground. "There's lotsa

things we could do, if we could settle down an' not run an' hide all the time. Mebbe plant corn, even, like the Iowa men, 'n raise cows instead of just killing them. Fix up houses so's not so many of our littles die in the cold time, learn the making of stuff . . . Can't do that if the Knifers and the Bone Breakers and the Skull Cookers are always up your ass."

Rudi nodded; you couldn't plow and plant if the horizons were always apt to spew out armed men without warning.

"I'll stay until you've men who can make bows," he said gently. "But I must be getting back, you see."

"Yeah," Jake said dully, and crawled under the opened sleeping bag.

Rudi sat for a while watching the fire, his long hands around the scabbard of his sword and his chin resting on one of the crossguards. As he looked into the red-gold glow that wavered over the embers he thought he could see the shape of a sword indeed; the one he and his mother had seen in the *nemed* when Raven came for him, fourteen years ago, after the War of the Eye. The one Ingolf had seen on Nantucket—a great longsword, with a guard like the crescent moon, and a pommel of moon opal held by branching antlers.

Why must it be there? he wondered. *It's hints and visions and parables I've had when I asked why, and the Cutters make war on our people back home with me not there to aid . . . but they also pursue us across mountain and plain and river. Their leaders think this journey is a danger to them.*

"A penny for your thoughts, Chief," Edain said quietly.

Rudi looked over. Edain yawned, but he obviously wasn't going to *sleep* with local company—he was too wolf-wary for that, in the Wild Lands. Instead he was setting his blanket roll in the usual place, not far from Rudi's, with Garbh curled up close by. She'd burrowed down into the dry duff that made up the floor of the overhang, and only tufts of her shaggy hair showed, and an ear that flopped over at the top. Though even asleep she was a better sentry than half a dozen men.

"Of home," Rudi said.

"Ah, that's a thought that steals over a man just before sleep, when he's far away, eh? I can see Dun Fairfax now, and the houses garlanded when we brought in the Queen Sheaf, and my mother standing there to break the first loaf before the altar—"

He stopped. Then with forced cheerfulness: "But it would be Dun Juniper for you, sure, and the gates swinging wide, and a fine set of cheers, and the Chief Herself Herself there to bless you home."

Rudi opened his mouth to say, *Dun Juniper, of course.* But it wasn't his mother's steading that was really in his thoughts, dear though it was, nestled amid the forest edge beneath the Low Cascades. Nor even all the lands of the Clan, the forests and the little villages and their checkerboard fields along the eastern edge of the Willamette . . .

"That too. But there was more to my thoughts, my friend."

Edain's square face looked puzzled, and he scratched at his curly mop of hair. Rudi went on:

"Say we gain this sword on Nantucket, the one Ingolf saw and was told was for me—the Sword of the Lady for the Lady's Sword."

"Ah!" Edain said. "By Ogma the Honey-Tongued, you know, that never occurred to me! They *are* different words."

Rudi nodded and murmured the words of the prophecy his mother had spoken when she held him over the altar in the *nemed* at his Wiccaning at the end of the first Change Year:

> *"Sad winter's child, in this leafless shaw—*
> *Yet be Son, and Lover, and Hornèd Lord!*
> *Guardian of my sacred Wood, and Law—*
> *His people's strength—and the Lady's sword!"*

They weren't a secret. Wiccaning was a public rite, not even limited to Initiates, and rumors had been spreading up and down the Willamette ever since, and through the whole Columbia Valley. For all he knew, they'd reached south of Ashland and up to the Okanogan.

"But who are the people I'm to be the strong right arm of?" he went on.

"The Clan Mackenzie of course, and who else might it be?" Edain said, sounding a little indignant but throttling it down in respect for the sleepers.

"Them to be sure. But them alone? My father, my blood father, was Mike Havel, the Bearkiller lord. Many of my blood kin are there in Larsdalen; Mary and Ritva are my half sisters, which makes Aunt Signe really my aunt, in a sense. And Lady Astrid too, the *Hiril Dúnedain*. And Mathilda is my *anamchara*, my soul sister, and I've spent months every year these last fourteen in the Association lands. You and I fought those Haida raiders there and shed our blood for the folk of County Tillamook. I've studied at Mount Angel and in Corvallis, and Rancher Brown of the CORA is my mother's guest-friend and mine, and I've shared tobacco with the Three Tribes. You see what I'm after saying?"

Edain's brows knotted. "That's a substantial herd of

people you're after being the strength of, Chief. Peoples, you might say, and each of them a different folk with different ways and names for the Gods."

Rudi chuckled a little. His eyes were halfway between turquoise and emerald as he stared into the bed of coals that almost matched the color of his hair. The hot clean scent of burning oak drifted through the dampness of the night air. The shoulder-length mane fell forward, framing the chiseled lines of his face.

"A mix-up it is, and no mistake; a *mispocha* as Aunt Judy would call it. So many peoples and so large a land we don't even have a *name* for them all. The lands or the peoples-together, either one."

"Oregon . . . well, Oregon and Washington and Idaho, I suppose . . ."

Rudi shook his head. "Those are the names of the old world. They've lost their magic, even for our parents, and they never meant much to us; they don't stir men's souls or make music in their hearts anymore, they're not *ours*. It strikes me that we need a new name for the whole of it, a footing that we can build the walls of our dreams upon."

"You could say *the lands of the Corvallis Meeting*," Edain replied. "But that would be just a wee bit cumbersome."

Rudi nodded. Images tumbled through his head. Masked dancers in the streets of Sutterdown on Samhain Eve; the perfect snowpeak of Mt. Hood; the towers of Castle Todenangst rising over green vineyards and wheat fields gold to the harvest; the Columbia flowing like molten silver between high cliffs with hang gliders dancing in the air above; waterfalls like threads tumbling down from green heights in the mountains; the bells of Mt. Angel calling the monks to prayer on their hilltop aerie; trumpets and splintered lances in a tournament beneath the ruins of Portland; a student hangout in Corvallis and the smell of beer and hamburgers and the sound of sharp young voices arguing the whichness of the wherefore; tall ships spreading their white canvas wings off Astoria amid a storm of gulls, and whales sporting in the gray Pacific waters . . .

"Montival," he whispered, and the sound had a . . . *rightness*, like an echo of music heard over the hills by moonlight. "It's called Montival. Though the folk there don't know it yet."

He looked up and saw Edain shape the word silently a few times, then nod and look up with a light kindling in his direct gray gaze.

"Now, that's a name with the blessing of the Powers upon it, Chief! *Montival.* It takes all the names—the Clan and Portland and the Yakima and Corvallis and Bend and the others—and puts them together, without making them any the less each by themselves. And it's *ours*, a Changeling name, not handed down."

Rudi tapped his fingers on the black tooled leather of his sword scabbard. "It does have that sound, eh? And this Sword we're after . . . that could be the symbol for it, do you see? For we go to fetch it through great trials, clansman and Princess and baron, monk and Ranger, and we bring it back through fire and peril to its new home, there to guard the land."

Edain nodded slowly. "The sword of the High King," he said, as if testing the sound.

His words dropped into the noises of the night like a distant horn-call that makes men stop and listen amid the work of field and street.

"The High King of Montival."

Rudi's head came up. A complex shudder went through him; he closed his eyes and shook his head.

"I've no desire for *that*," he said with quiet vehemence. "Tanist of the Mackenzies and Chief in my turn . . . that would be more than enough."

Edain grinned. "Sure, and if you did want it with an eager craving, you'd not be the man for the job, now would you? But I've heard you say to others that the King is the sacrifice that goes consenting."

"If . . . if we *needed* it," Rudi said reluctantly.

"And do we not? To deal with the Cutters, if nothing else."

"There's the Meeting at Corvallis," Rudi noted—but his own tone was defensive, and Edain snorted.

"Which has something in common with a donkey, does it not? And it's not so long ago we fought each other in the War of the Eye, and wouldn't a High King be the one to make sure that doesn't happen again? But better you than me, Chief. All *I* want is to have my own croft and roof-tree someday, and a hearth to sit beside on winter evenings."

He lay back and gathered his blanket roll about him. Rudi shook his head again, then sighed and did likewise. There was much to do; tomorrow they'd get to work.

Though getting people to do what's needful is *part of a Chief's work,* he thought. *And bashing their heads not the best way of doing so, when another's to be had. High King, though . . .*

He shuddered again; bad enough to be Chief, even among a folk who mostly governed themselves. To handle a dozen lands, each as likely as not to quarrel with the others, would be a nightmare all his life long.

But . . . there's a good deal that needs doing, and perhaps a High King could *do it*. More happily: *And such a man would* have *to marry Matti, now wouldn't he? For only as her handfasted man would the Associates accept him.*

His thoughts quieted, and he drifted down into the soft darkness. But the Sword glowed against that velvet, turning as if it fell through stars and shadows, falling out of memory and time towards the hand he stretched up to grasp it.

As if he *remembered* wielding it on a stricken field.

CHAPTER FIVE

"*A vision of the Blessed Virgin?*"

Father Ignatius, priest and knight-brother of the Order of the Shield of St. Benedict, bowed his tonsured head to the Cardinal-Archbishop of Des Moines as the older man looked up from his written report, and put his hands inside the wide sleeves of his coarse monastic robe. The cleric had read it twice before the comment.

"I was honored beyond my worth, Your Eminence," he said, with humility in his voice.

Suddenly his serious young face was lit up from within by a joy that he could feel filling him as candlelight did a glass globe. No detail of the meeting in the cold December mountains above Chenrezi Monastery had left him in the long months since, and neither had the happiness that plucked at his soul like a harpist's fingers at a string.

"What can I do but strive all my life to be worthy of it?" he said, and only stern control kept the tears from his eyes.

The Prince of the Church leaned back in his chair, his crimson-sashed cassock rustling; his short-cropped beard and the little left of his hair were white, and his face lined and seamed beneath the red skullcap. The office was plain, as befitted a man of austerity, but it was large and paneled in smooth dark woods; this was the headquarters of the Church in the whole of the upper Mississippi Valley. The view gave on gardens, and not far away the lime-fueled searchlights of the perimeter wall around the old State Capitol where the Heasleroads now ruled.

"I must either pity your madness, or struggle against the sin of envy," the Cardinal said.

Ignatius felt a flash of resentment at the skepticism he saw in the probing gaze; who was this hesitant old man to doubt him? There was no time for delay!

The Princess I am commanded to guard and serve by the Queen of Angels *is in need of his help, and he* dares *to question me?*

Ignatius had learned discipline in hard schools; as a smallholder's son, and as novice, brother and ordinand at Mt. Angel. Not least he had learned the discipline of the self. He bowed his head a little further; when he raised his face again it was calm, whatever turmoil clenched his soul within. He catalogued the objects within sight, as an aid to self-control. A prie-dieu stood in one corner, and a fine crucifix on the wall behind the desk between two tall open windows, and a photograph—post-Change—of the late Pope on the mahogany surface.

Ignatius met those eyes for an instant, the haunted indomitable gaze of a survivor who had seen a world die and flinched from nothing as he worked to build anew from the rubble. Then he raised his own eyes for a long moment to the Man upon the Cross, and felt a flush of shame.

Forgive me, Lord, and help me put down pride. Always we crucify You, over and over again. Help me find the cour-

age to follow where You lead, to take up my *cross and make of all suffering an offering to You.*

The older man sighed and touched strong stubby fingers to his brow. Then he looked at the documents Ignatius had presented with their seals and ribbons; he flicked one of them aside slightly, with a rustle of stiff official paper.

"You bring glowing recommendations from the head of your Order, and favorable ones from Cardinal-Archbishop Maxwell in Portland; the more favorable for being slightly grudging. As it happens I knew the Cardinal-Archbishop before the Change; we were young men together in Rome for a time. And of course Badia has kept me informed of the founding and growth of your Order. Nor is the vision without precedent even in recent times; there is St. Maximillian Kolbe . . ."

Ignatius nodded gravely; he'd studied that when he was a novice. The Virgin had appeared to Kolbe when he was a boy in Poland about a hundred years ago now, offering him a choice between the red crown of martyrdom and the white of purity. He'd chosen both . . . and been sent to Auschwitz for sheltering Jews in his monastery during the great war of the previous century. And died there when he volunteered his own life in place of a younger man with a family.

The tale was daunting, but strengthening as well. Kolbe had died of thirst and starvation and then poison in that mortal-made antechamber of Hell. And died blessing the men who killed him so slowly and so cruelly, begging them to seek God's forgiveness for their souls before it was too late. *That* was what the Faith could make of a man, or a man make of the Faith.

Can I reach such heights? he asked himself. Then he

looked up once more to the Man of Sorrows. *Dare I do less? Be ye perfect, He commanded.*

The Cardinal went on: "And I do not think you are mad, my son. But I am not altogether sure that you are to be envied. You have received a stupendous honor; but from such men much is demanded."

"Thank you for your trust in me, Father," Ignatius said; his gaze flicked back to the great carved Rood.

The elderly man suddenly smiled. "Yes, yes, there is always that. How dare we decline a burden, when we are called to imitate Him? But *are* you aware of the honor done you? She herself called upon you to be her champion?"

"You shall be my knight, Karl Bergfried," Ignatius said quietly, wonder in his tone. "And . . ."

The worn wise Jewish face, a smile as tender as motherhood itself, and the glimpse of a soul that blazed with a fire of majesty and power like the jeweled radiance at the heart of suns. His hand went to his forehead, remembering the touch of that finger, and the world dissolving in joy.

". . . it is impossible to describe, Father; though I had the tongues of men and of angels."

The Cardinal crossed himself. "This report must be dispatched to the Curia and the Holy Father in Badia by the next courier boat down the Mississippi," he mused. "Both the vision, and the knowledge you have won of the Cutter cult, will be of the greatest value to Holy Mother Church."

Ignatius nodded grimly and signed himself in turn; the skin over his spine and groin crawled at the memory of what he'd seen. Of Kuttner pulling himself up Rudi Mackenzie's sword, laughing between teeth bright with arterial blood and reaching for the living man's throat with dead hands.

"That is not simply heresy and lust for power," he said. "Diabolism is at work. The power of the Enemy is made manifest through Corwin."

"Those who would sell their souls usually find a buyer, to their eternal regret," the Cardinal said; his fingers traced the cross again. "Lord have mercy. Christ have mercy. And we must certainly give you every aid in the Church's gift here."

He sighed. "My only fear is that that may not be as much as you need. We have little secular influence in Iowa, and while God has favored this state in many ways, it is . . ."

The ecclesiastic hesitated slightly. Ignatius recognized the tone: it was the one used when tactful words were made to convey a blunt truth.

". . . not well-governed at present. The factions around Anthony Heasleroad are like a knot of rattlesnakes beneath a rock. We need not obey unjust laws for their own sake, but prudence is also enjoined on us. *As gentle as doves, as wise as serpents*, remember."

"Still, there are many of our flock here who have positions of wealth, power and influence," Ignatius said. "The Heuisinks, for example. We were guests at their estate before we came on to Des Moines, and Ingolf Vogeler is a close friend of the Heuisink heir."

The Cardinal nodded. "But they are not much in favor at court." He shook his head, looking a little bemused for an instant. "How natural that sounds now!"

Ignatius frowned. *Why shouldn't it sound . . . ah, the Cardinal is an elderly man. One must make allowances for those raised before the Change. They had a habit of judging the years they lived as if they were a play or story, rather than taking their roles for granted.*

"In any case, I had no intention of calling on you for physical force, Your Eminence," Ignatius said. "My Order is a militant one, but we are strictly enjoined not to seek secular power or to defy the authorities of any realm except at greatest need. What I principally beg of you is first, information, and then—"

"Ú-Maer, ú-Maer," Ritva Havel murmured fretfully in Sindarin, the special language of the Dúnedain Rangers her Aunt Astrid had founded a few years before she was born. "Not good, not good."

"That place is as bad as the dungeons of Dol Guldur," Mary Havel agreed softly, staring northward from the balcony towards the harsh metallic gleam of Iowa's citadel.

Then beneath her breath: *"Olthon o le, Ingolf."*

Somewhere in there was Ingolf Vogeler, Mary's friend, her companion on the trail since they left the Willamette Valley to cross the Cascades, and for the last six months her lover. Ritva's twin touched one finger lightly to the black patch that covered her left eye socket, a habit she'd acquired since a Cutter sorcerer-priest slashed the eye out of her head in the mountains of eastern Idaho late last year.

They'd been identicals, before Mary lost the eye. It still gave Ritva an absurd pang now and then to realize they couldn't play games with people's heads by switching identities anymore. They'd been doing *that* since about the time they learned to walk. It had been useful in more serious business now and then too. Mary's face showed only a cool intentness, but when Ritva put her hand on her shoulder it was quivering tense.

We've always been able to read each other's souls, Ritva thought. *I've been envying you all this time for winning that game of papers-scissors-rock we had over who'd get a try at Ingolf. Now I don't, sis. At least, I don't if I'd have come to really love him—and we're alike enough I think I would have. It's bad enough knowing he's in there when I just like him as a friend.*

"We *will* rescue you, my beloved."

"You said it, sis," Ritva replied stoutly.

She raised the monocular to her eye and lowered it again. Staring at those smooth granite-sheathed concrete battlements and towers, the multiple welded-beam steel gates, the ranked firing ports for murder machines and flamethrowers, was just too depressing. Even the golden dome of the old State Capitol behind it seemed like a taunt.

Impressive, she thought grudgingly; and she'd seen Castle Todenangst, and the walls of Boise.

Not so much the height, but the circumference. And that's just the ruler's citadel! The ones around the city aren't as high . . . quite . . . but the quantity!

She'd never seen anything on this scale, and the Rangers traveled widely—that was a major reason she and Mary had left Larsdalen and moved in with Aunt Astrid.

Besides the fact that we Dúnedain are just so cool, of course.

"Well, we weren't planning on *bashing* our way in, anyway," Mary said. "As Aunt Astrid says, bashing is *crude.*"

"Uncle John says there's always a place for it."

"John Hordle is six-foot-seven and weighs three hundred and twenty pounds," Mary pointed out. "He carries a sword with a four-foot blade. Of *course* he likes to bash. We're sneaks. That's what's bothering me. I can't think of any way to do *that,* either."

"They've probably paid a lot of attention to security, too," Ritva said, with reluctant thoughtfulness. "These tyrant types generally worry a lot."

And the Heasleroads have been busy as beavers on their citadel for longer than I've been alive, and with all of Iowa to draw on.

There were *millions* of people in the Provisional Republic, nearly as many as there had been in the state before the Change; Ignatius said they had somewhere between a tenth and a fifth of all the human beings left in North America, and on some of its richest land. Usually the places where the Change killed the least had been those that had the fewest to begin with, remote ranching and farming country. More people meant more cities, and above a certain size cities had meant death for themselves and the land around them when the machines stopped.

Portland was a partial exception, but from what she'd heard that was because Norman Arminger and his dreadful consort had managed to get most of the inhabitants to leave, one way or another. Sandra had spread rumors that the State government had answers, or huge stocks of food and medicine, and had her Judas-goat organizers lead scores of thousands southward to die in the plague-ridden refugee camps around Salem. Norman himself had just burned great swaths of the city down, turned off the gravity-flow water system, or had his goon squads prod people out to die at the point of improvised spears.

He'd also hanged the former mayor and chief of police from meathooks outside the building he'd taken for a palace, just to make a point about who was in charge.

Heasleroad Sr. must have been a lot like the Lord Protector Arminger, she thought. *Except that there was so much food here he could keep a lot more population alive to work for him, and fewer people fought him.*

Then she sneezed, not liking the coal smoke that made your eyes water here . . . not that any of them did, being country bred. Des Moines had a great many factories and foundries and furnaces worked by water power or even the low-pressure steam engines that still functioned in the Changed world, and coal came in piled in barges on the river and cars on the horse-drawn railways.

"We *could* cross the Mississippi and join up with Rudi and Edain," she said carefully, when the silence had grown a little uncomfortable.

Usually I know you're not going to do anything stupid and reckless. Smart and reckless, yes . . . but is your judgment still good, sis?

Aloud she went on judiciously: "Get the wagons, get them back to the river, and the Bossman promised Ingolf and Matti and Odard would go free."

Mary Havel sniffed, and tossed her head; the wheat-blond fighting braid bobbed behind her long shapely face.

"And how are we supposed to *find* Rudi there? His trail will be cold, and the Bossman's men are watching all the city gates. Besides which, that assumes the Bossman will *keep* his bargain. Would you care to bet on that?"

"No," Ritva sighed. "We'll have to do something ourselves."

So we have me and Mary, who are the sneakiest of all Rangers, Ritva thought. *There's Father Ignatius . . . well, yes, a man of many skills. There's Virginia Kane, who's . . . oh, well, she's a good enough woman of her hands and she grew up on a ranch, so she's a good rider and shot, but even more out of place in a city than we are. Middling with a*

*blade, even those meatchopper shetes these easterners use.
And there's Fred Thurston, who's just nineteen and a likely
lad, and has connections . . . which would be useful back in
Boise, where his father was President-General, if it weren't
for his brother Martin wanting to kill him because he knows
who assassinated their father. Not much of a storming
party to take a fortress in a foreign land!*

She turned back into the room. They had the top floor
of this . . . place . . . to themselves, which meant four chambers and a narrow hallway, since it was a tall pre-Change
brick house; they used this one as common, she and Ritva
shared another, Ignatius had the third, and Virginia and
Fred had set up together in the last. When the twins turned
away from the balcony, Virginia and Fred were sitting at
the table holding hands and smiling at each other, their
meal forgotten, a brown-haired young woman and a man
of nineteen years with skin the color of old oiled wood and
tight-curled black hair.

Ritva could feel something halfway between grief and
pure pain shoot through Mary. The other Havel sister
closed her eye for an instant, and murmured a prayer of
those Dúnedain who followed the Old Religion:

*"Oh, Lady, You descended through the Dark Gate for
Your lover, and where You danced even evil's self was
pierced to the heart. All life and love is in Your gift. Bring
my man back to me! Lord of the shining mountain, who
loves the warrior's courage and craft, bless my sword that
fights for him!"*

"So mote it be, sis," Ritva said. "Now come on and
eat something. We're going to need our strength."

Fred looked up. "No ideas?"

"Not beyond walking up to the gate and asking them
to put us in the next cell," Ritva admitted as she sat and
reached for the bread knife.

"Anthony Heasleroad is a walking argument against hereditary monarchy," Mary growled.

The two Rangers signed their plates and murmured the Invocation and blessing. Ritva's mouth twisted a little. In a bard's tale fear for your beloved drove out everything else, but she could hear her sister's stomach growling, now that she'd dragged her in and made her notice the body's needs, and she was ravenous.

About to drool down my jerkin, in fact. Well, the Histories agree that a good dinner now and then is an important part of Questing.

"Well, Fred here's a good argument *for* it," Virginia said, in her Wyoming rasp.

Fred Thurston winced; he'd ended up on the run because his elder brother *did* believe in sons following fathers . . . and had killed their sire to avoid inconvenient elections in Boise.

"Dad always said you couldn't hand a country down like a farm," he said.

"Why not?" Ritva said. "It seems to be the way most people have always done it, if you listen to the stories."

"It does seem natural," Mary agreed. "After all . . . most people do what their parents did, don't they? You learn how as you grow up. I mean, we're fighters—so was our father, and our mother. And they were both rulers."

"I just can't see myself as the picture of a Crown Prince," Fred said.

"Sorry, sweetie," Virginia said. "But you *are*, whatever your brother Martin's like. Hell, so are Rudi and Mathilda. Seems to be pretty much a crapshoot, whether you go on who your daddy was or on a show of hands. Or those things they had before the Change, bullets."

"Ballots," Fred said.

"Oh, way I heard it, sometimes it was bullets," Virginia said, and grinned.

She and Fred were both just short of twenty, but her plain strong face looked a little older than her real years to folk raised in the gentle lands west of the Cascades. The winter blizzards and wind-borne dust of summer on the High Plains had taken a little of the life out of her dark brown hair, and started little lines beside her dark blue eyes already.

Remember to use that lanolin stuff, Ritva reminded herself.

The lines showed a little more as the rancher's daughter smiled and went on:

"I won't say anything about me bein' a Princess."

What a sappy smile, Ritva thought, as Fred grinned at her and put his hand over hers again. Virginia's father had been a prominent rancher in the Powder River country, until the Church Universal and Triumphant killed him.

And Princess just means your father was a King, like Mathilda's, or Rudi's and ours, not that you're anything special in and of yourself. Or your father some sort of a sovereign, at least, Ritva thought. *Which Virginia's was, pretty well.*

"In the Histories, it says the Numenoreans handed down the throne to the eldest child—man or woman," she said.

"Well, dip me in dung and fry me crisp, that sounds good to me!" Virginia said.

Fred opened his mouth, looked at the three women, and closed it again.

"We'll probably get some sort of job running a Ranger steading, or something, eventually," Mary added. "Not that Aunt Astrid and Uncle Alleyne would give it to us if we were *stupid* or anything."

"If you're going to have a monarchy at all that's the big problem," Fred said. "I'm still not sure about that. And Kings . . . get flattered all the time."

"Yes, but they expect it," Mary said. "Look at Mathilda—can you imagine anyone putting anything over on *her*?"

"Not easily," he admitted.

"But ordinary people like flattery just as much as Kings, if anyone will give it to them," Ritva said. "I mean, look at all those dreadful people the Corvallans keep electing, who promise them ridiculous things and tell them how smart and superior they are. Well, you've never been to Corvallis, but take my word for it. It's no better when one man is flattering thousands than when thousands are flattering one man."

"Never came at it that way," Fred said thoughtfully. "But you've got a point."

"You Rangers are Numenoreans, then?" Virginia added. "I never got that part straight. I've heard *of* those stories . . . Histories . . . but never read 'em."

"Well, we're descended from Numenoreans," Ritva said. "That's what Dúnedain means—'folk of the west.' And Numenor was in the West. Well, west of Eriador, which was where Europe is now. Of course, things were different then. The Earth was flat, to start with."

Mary's mouth quirked, and she fell back into their habit of finishing sentences for each other: "But that was two Ages of the World ago—at least. So probably *everyone* is descended from them by now."

"Aunt Astrid thinks we're *more* descended from them than most people," Ritva said. "Because the Histories speak to our hearts, you see."

"That's logical. She's very smart and learned," Mary continued.

Ritva nodded. "Of course, some people think she's also crazy."

"Inspired."

"Same thing."

Ritva's heart lifted a little at her sister's smile; it was still a bit bleak, but better than nothing. They began to pass plates around; there was a joint of cold roast pork, potato salad, a dish of eggplant cooked with cheese and onions, a loaf of brown bread still faintly warm, butter and pickles and an apple pie, with little pots of ketchup, mustard and hot sauce; their host wasn't stinting them. The jug of beer was even cold. Des Moines had Stirling-cycle ice machines, so the milk was fresh too; what passed for wine in Iowa was coarse musky stuff not worth the effort of drinking. She cut a slab of the bread and spread the butter; it was soft with the summer night, and almost melted as it sank in.

Mary brooded again as she ate, hardly even noticing the second slice of the really excellent pie, lost enough that Ritva's head came up a full half second before she noticed the light tread on the stairs below.

"Our host," Mary said sourly. *"Orch."*

Ritva sighed and shrugged. Nobody could really object to the term. There weren't any bugs in the mattresses in their rooms, but they were stained, and there was a slight smell, and you could *hear* what went on below; she was fairly sure that a lot of the girls weren't here voluntarily, or at least they cried and drank a lot when they weren't working. Technically the two of them should be burning the place down and setting everyone free; that was a Ranger's oath, to help the helpless and defend the weak, even if what they mostly did for a living was hunt and guard caravans and track down bandits.

*But we have to get the Sword. Key to the Dark Lord and
all that. I judge this host of ours to be a bad man, but one
with some scruples about debt and obligation.*

"Hi," Tancredo said, through the open door, blinking
a little at the uniform stare he got.

He was about the same color as Fred Thurston but
otherwise unalike, a slight wiry man in his thirties with a
ready smile that didn't reach his eyes. Ingolf had done
business with him years before when he ran a salvage
outfit; they both disclaimed friendship.

"OK," he said, leaning against the doorway. "Look,
I owe Ingolf. I owe him money and favors. So I've got
that ship he wanted waiting at the docks in Dubuque. I
don't owe him my life, or my wife and kids' lives, which
is what tangling with Captain Denson of the State Police
would mean. So you're *not* going to do any crazy stunts
from here, or from anyplace I own. Understand? Do
you folks want to get on your way, or not? That's up
to you."

There were vague hulking shapes on the stairway behind him, probably hired muscle. That didn't bother
Ritva; she had a high opinion of her companions, and an
even higher one of herself. The problem was that Tancredo was their only defense against the State Police.
None of them knew their way around Des Moines' enormous dirty warren—and a walled city was a hard place to
get out of.

"Excuse me, my son," a quiet voice said on the stairs.
Father Ignatius beamed at them as he came into view. "I
fear we must move, my children, and quickly. Collect
your gear."

Usually Ritva felt a slight irritation when the Christian
priest called them that, although she liked him well

enough. He was only a few years older himself. And the more so when he assumed an authority only Rudi and Ingolf had in this band, since she was no part of his flock.

This time she beamed back at him.

CHAPTER SIX

A horse whickered. Rudi Mackenzie grinned to himself in the hot prickly darkness. He lay in the big bluestem grass that blocked vision everywhere beyond arm's reach; it was five feet tall hereabouts on this dry-soiled stretch of upland prairie, with dense-packed stems as thick as his little finger ending in a three-lobed end that looked a little like a turkey's foot. The huge mass of dried grass smelled like the hayloft of the Gods, a dusty-sweet mellow odor that only cured grass had, but magnified by the sun-cured expanses that stretched to the horizon on every hand.

He grinned a little wider; about eleven years ago he'd had a very pleasant encounter with a girl named Caitlin in a Dun Mellin stack that smelled a lot like this, while he was there helping with the threshing. She'd been three years older than he, and you never forgot the first time.

And herself as sweet and bouncy as the clover that fine night, the Foam-Born Cyprian's blessings on her for being patient with my boy's clumsiness, he thought.

He'd danced at her handfasting to Bram the Smith four years later, too; pranced and tumbled and leapt and spun with goat horns strapped above his ankles amid the other youths, to lead her and her flower-garlanded maidens to the dun's *nemed*. Nowadays she was a hearth-mistress and High Priestess and a potter growing famous for her slip-glazed ware, and had a pair of little girls as pretty as two young jays and a baby boy at the breast.

And so to business. I'm seeing to their safety, and that of all the Clan's hearth-homes, and more.

He felt alive at the thought, intensely conscious of himself and the moment. These were the things for which he had been made, the deeds that were his very *self*.

Besides which, this should be fun. The stealing part, at least. My totem is Raven, *after all . . . and doesn't that One love to carry things off? More, I'm doing it for Matti and my friends, and it is a relief beyond words to be* moving, *not just persuading and cajoling, the which is needful but drives a man mad!*

The horse nickered again, more urgently, but he wasn't particularly worried that the sleepy guard-riders would be alarmed.

If there's one thing that a herd of any size will always produce, it's that sound; the which is why it's easier to steal forty horses than one. And it tells me everyone's in position.

The night had become dense-dark anyway with the setting of the moon sliver several hours ago. Patches of high cloud ghosted across the sky, hiding the bright Belt of the Goddess, and denser black masses piled to the west with a flicker of distant lightning now and then, too far for even the faintest rumble of thunder. It was three hours past midnight, the time when old men died and sleep was deepest. But it wasn't still. The cicadas were loud here, as loud as he'd ever heard them, and the tall prairie grasses made a peculiar sound not quite like anything he knew, a long *hssssss* that swelled and died away as the ripples passed him by.

It's like the sea, he thought.

He'd heard something a bit like this once while he single-handed a ketch off Newport, the Corvallis sea town, on a day when the Pacific whitecaps marched from the farthest horizon to his boat's bow. A seal had swum alongside for a while, and sometimes heaved itself up for an instant to peer over the gunwale at him with great brown eyes. He'd bowed back gravely, and laughed as it dove away with a flick of the tail that shot cold saltwater into his face and made him nearly luff as he came about on that tack.

Yes, it sounds like waves. And the breeze is picking up.

"I don't like having to rely on the Southsiders, Chief," Edain said quietly—whispering's sibilants carried farther than the tones of ordinary speech. "Sure, and they're good-hearted and brave, but Tamar's favorite team"—his elder half sister was well known as a trainer of oxen— "knows more about the which of the where."

"At sneaking through the dark, they're skilled enough," he replied. "They'd have been dead long ago else."

A glance at the stars to confirm his inner time sense, and then:

"Now."

They both rolled to their feet, their longbows in their hands. The arrows they needed were stuck point down in the sod, and Rudi flicked open the improvised beech-wood firebox with the tip of his bow. Air struck the banked embers within, and they glowed for an instant beneath the covering of white ash with a hot dry smell. He set one of the arrows to the string, and dipped the lump behind the head into the coals; the ball of frayed wild flax soaked in oil flared up immediately. Then Rudi turned and shot, the fire-arrow's point up at a forty-five-degree angle as he sank into the draw inside the bow, using the backside-down posture best for distance work. The ball of flame traced a red line through the night; three more were in the air before it struck.

"And there's a sign that's sayin': *Hurrah, we're here! Tasty and fookin' edible and doing ye the great favor of cookin' ourselves!*" Edain grumbled beneath his rhythmic grunts of effort as he shot.

"Last one!" Rudi said.

Between them they'd sent sixteen flaming missiles westward into a tinderbox fanned by the dry warm wind. The arrows traveled a little less than three hundred yards each to make an arc—they were lighter than a battle shaft, but the bundle of burning matter made them less well balanced and too thick to cut the air efficiently. Now they turned and trotted eastward with the wind at their backs, stooping a little—more than a little, in Rudi's case—to keep the tops of their helms below the level of the grass.

It was surprisingly hard to push through, especially in the dark; the grass itself was thick, and there was a dense understory of knee-high forbs and thistles. Once an ancient tangle of barbed wire caught at his foot, but it was rusted through and crumbled when he tugged. Garbh seemed to have an easier time of it, bounding silently at Edain's side. It was her check and quiet growl that alerted them, an instant before the thud of hooves.

"Ssst!" Edain said; that brought her quivering-silent.

They split to either side and froze, kneeling and laying down their bows. The rider was coming at a trot; he had a short spear in his hand ready to throw, and he was standing in the stirrups and peering at the growing red glow to the west, blinding his own night vision. The two Mackenzies moved like the twin jaws of a spring-steel trap; Edain grabbed the man's foot with both hands and flung it upward. Taken by surprise, the Knifer catapulted to his right as if jerked by elastic cords.

His startled yell broke off at its beginning in a croak; waiting, Rudi grabbed the back of the man's greasy leather tunic, slammed him to the ground with stunning force and struck behind his ear with the blade of his other hand. Then he stepped back with a grimace and picked up his bow again; for one thing he didn't want the man's lice to be able to jump ship. And while it would be easy enough to finish him, perhaps wise . . .

Perhaps he wasn't a bad man, by his own lights; and like as not a woman and her children would mourn him. Now let him live or die as the Powers and his own fate decree.

"Earth must be fed," he murmured.

Edain gentled the horse. He'd been a competent rider when they set out, since the Aylwards had a pair of mounts—unusual affluence for Mackenzies, who usually kept their working stock for plows and wagons and walked or rode bicycles themselves. More than a year of constant travel on horseback and caring for a series of local remounts had made him an expert; he had his plaid wrapped around its head, and was stroking it with one hand and keeping a firm grip on the bridle with the other. Rudi took that over immediately—he wanted the best archer with his bow-hand free. He did take an instant to undo the girths and let the pad saddle and its blanket slide off, and he snorted in silent disgust at the sores and saddle galls beneath.

Sure, and I stand corrected. He was *a bad man, and bad cess to him as he makes accounting to the Guardians of the horse-kind!*

That was illogical; the Southsiders weren't much better. These wild-man tribes didn't really raise horses; they caught mustangs, broke them crudely, and used them until they died. Which wasn't all that long given the general fragility of equines.

An animal that can die because it can't puke needs humankind to look after it. But the Horse Goddess gives Her sons and daughters to be our helpers and our friends, not machinery.

It made him feel a bit better about clouting the Knifer and leaving him in the path of the fire, the more so since he'd given his Freedom Fighter hosts a few pointers on the care and feeding of the beasts.

The horse was getting upset again; the smell of fire was starting to grow. So was the light. He could see a little better now, with red flame licking up like a new sunset. Bits and pieces twisted into the air, drifting up and then followed by others moving faster even as he glanced. Then he could see the tips of flames, redder than his mother's hair, as he first remembered it when she bent over him with the sun behind her turning it to floating copper. Tips of flame, and others skipping ahead where the wind blew it. A crackling roar began to build, not the deep sound wood made burning, but lighter—almost a hissing, like a serpent of fire.

"Like the snakes of Surtr," he said. "Now, this calls for careful judgment; we want the fire to be on our very heels. A moment . . . and another . . . and let's *go*!"

He tossed Edain's plaid back to him and let the horse run—bolt, rather, neighing in panic, which was entirely understandable now that the fire was visible. With any luck at all the guards would just assume that it had thrown its rider. According to the Southsiders, nobody hereabouts used fire arrows—they'd had to have the concept explained to them.

Rudi whistled, two rising notes and one sustained. Epona trotted up like part of the darkness with Edain's roan gelding following, its reins secured to a loop on the big mare's war-saddle. She didn't like coming closer to a fire—she *was* a horse, however unusual—but she did it. The roan followed perforce, despite the way its ears were laid back and its eyes rolling and its body covered in fear-sweat. The reins were strong solid leather, but Epona's dominance over the other beast's dim instinct-driven mind was stronger still.

She *was* the herd mare, and it would take a much closer brush with the fire to generate enough squealing panic to cancel that. His advisors on the gentle art of reaving horses had always used a mounted man to hold the raiders' mounts and bring them up at this point, but Epona could do the job just as well.

"Working just like Red Leaf said it would." Edain grinned, as he unlooped the reins.

Neither man mounted; they turned the horses and loped beside them, holding on to a stirrup leather to smooth their pace. It made running through the thick grass much easier. Epona's breast parted the tall whippy stems, and with a hand linked to her solid weight he could lift himself past obstacles that caught at his boots, bounding along as if each step was off a trampoline.

"Horse-stealing being their national sport, so to say," Rudi replied as his long legs swung along. "The Sioux would be doing this hanging under the horse's belly."

"And that would be showing off, if you ask me, fine folk though they are."

This June past they'd spent some time in a hocoka of

the Lakotas, as guests of Itancan-Chief John Red Leaf. It had been a brief period, if eventful—fights with pursuing troops of the Sword of the Prophet, hunts that included an unexpected little brush with some ex-Texan lions, buffalo stampedes, a sweat lodge ceremony, and another that ended with them being adopted as Strong Raven and Swift Arrow.

But they'd also gotten quite a few stories on the theory and practice of horse theft as the lords of the High Plains managed it these days, it being their pastime and delight. He'd adapted one technique of theirs for this night's work, but a look over his shoulder made him hiss between his teeth. The fire was a *lot* higher than anything you could get up in the short-grass country, and a lot hotter, and it was coming along faster. Faster than they were moving. Unfortunately their Sioux friends had been quite clear that you *didn't* mount up and silhouette yourself against the fire until you absolutely had to.

"That moment being at hand," he muttered to himself, inaudible under the Epona's hoof falls and panting, and the crackling white-noise roar of the flames.

Then shapes moved in the middle distance ahead, horses amid an area of grass trampled down where they'd fed and rolled. The herd was up now, awake and beginning to be frightened from their sounds. The Knifer guards were running from one beast to another, frantically yanking the slipknots on their hobbles free; others already mounted snapped crude whips in their faces to keep them from bolting as soon as they were freed.

They were utterly focused on their work; the seventy mounts here represented years of work, and to lose the herd would be a catastrophe for all their tribe.

The which they deserve, for not leaving the Southsiders in peace. It's not as if they were so crowded here that they need

*to fight each other for land, like two wolf packs in the same
valley. Still, I'm glad I'll be free of them after this night. I
have no wish to be the ogre their mothers frighten children
with.*

The last of the restraints came free as Rudi watched,
and the three men who'd been removing them raced for
their own horses, looking over their shoulders with their
eyes wide in terror. One checked as he ran and opened
his mouth to yell warning as he finally picked out the two
Mackenzies beside their horses.

"Now!" Rudi said.

He grabbed for the bridle of Edain's horse with his
free hand. There was no possibility of sparing these
men.

The other Mackenzie had four arrows out and gripped
between his forefinger and the riser of his bow, and another between his teeth, with most of its length off to his
left. He brought his bow up and shot that one first, almost spitting it onto the string, and then the others in a
ripple of effort so swift and sure that the second had just
struck when the last flew free. The flickering light behind
them was tricky; only three of them hit. One slammed
into the chest of the man who'd seen them; the other two
punched the riders out of their saddles. Then Edain leapt
and scrabbled aboard his mount, cursing as the beast
crabbed sideways between his hand on the reins and its
impulse to run free.

Epona had already started moving. Rudi bent his knees
between one stride and the next and vaulted as he ran,
dropping into the saddle in a way that would have been
painful if his thighs hadn't caught the weight of his body
before his crutch slammed into the leather. His sword
came out, but shadowy figures were already in among the
horses; the last of the Knifer herd guards were down or

had fled. Jake's gap-toothed grin shone a little in the light of the fire.

"Got 'em, Rudi-man!"

"And let's *go*!"

The half dozen best riders of the Southsiders were on either side of the three-score-and-ten horses, whooping and swinging lengths of braided cord. The snapping and the noise kept the panicked horses bunched; Garbh ran at their heels, snapping now and then to keep them focused. They were letting them run southward—exactly what the Knifers' own herdsmen would have done, with a grassfire coming. After a few moments they angled westward as much as they dared; the main camp of their foemen was to the east. And probably dissolving in chaos right now, as everyone scrambled to get out of the fire's way, though they were by a slough with open water even in late summer.

Probably they'd all wade out into it, carrying what they could. The flames were twenty feet high now, dreadfully bright. They raced forward in a flickering wave, a dancing front of red and gold that towered farther yet into the air in a wall of sparks. The roar was like all the hearth fires on the ridge of the world added together, with the forges of the smiths thrown in; he eyed the end of the line of fire to his right, judging just where it would pass.

He also thought he heard screams of rage from the savages behind; it was possible that they'd seen their horses disappearing, not in a scattered spray but in a solid mass of plunging heads and tossing manes. Or they might have heard the whoops of the Southsiders, who were calling pleasantries of their choice; they all had their new bows slung over their backs, worn through loops beside the equally new quivers in the Mackenzie fashion. Rudi grinned and added the keening ululation of the Clan to the chorus.

And just to be polite to the folk who'd taken him in and taught him this plainsman's trick—

"Kye-eee-kye!" he screamed. "Hoo'hay, *hoo'hay*! The sun shines on the hawk and on the quarry!"

"Hand and hand seven!" Jake called to Rudy, pumping a clenched fist with one finger extended towards the Knifer camp.

"Seventy," Rudi replied, and the Big Man of Southside repeated the word several times to lock it in his memory.

He'll know each one of his new herd by its looks and maybe by a name within a few days, the Mackenzie thought. *But he couldn't say the number until I told him. They have forgotten a good deal, his folk!*

The horses ran reckless through the dark until they were out of the fire's path, and some miles to the west of it. Then they slowed, freed to fear for their legs once more. The whole horizon behind them was turning ruddy where the fire spread out into a front miles long, as if the dawn was coming hours early, and the hot dry smell of it was slow to fade. Then the animals began to slow, down from a gallop to a canter and then to a walk as the night drew its cloak about them once more. The riders touched them up again, half a mile at a trot and half at a walk; that was harder as the horses grew calmer and started to resent this interference with their rest, or to notice that there were strange individuals of their own kind among them without a recognized place in their hierarchy.

Prairie fires were dreadful, and they could travel faster than a horse and scorch your lungs out when the flame front passed you, but they were also routine—from what the Southsiders told him they happened every year as soon as the tall grass went dry, started deliberately to spur fresh growth, or by friction or lightning strikes. Beasts and humans both were used to them.

Which is one reason why there's so little mark of man left in this land, he thought. *With fires like that every year, all that could burn has, of that you may be sure.*

As if to illustrate the point a silo loomed out of the darkness ahead; tall as many a castle tower, and as broad, but canted to one side, and the lower part was cracked open where years of fires past had buckled the sheet metal plates away from the frames. Someday soon a strong wind would catch it and send it to the ground; in the end it would be a stain on the soil.

It's a pity we have no metalworker's tools, and no great fund of time, he thought. *We could teach the Southsiders to make proper brigandines. Or at least scale shirts . . .*

Then he snorted quietly to himself. He'd never thought he would catch the teacher's passion—learning had always been his pleasure—but the situation made it tempting. Rudi Mackenzie had known such people all his life; his mother sitting endlessly patient, coaxing out the music within a novice bard's fumbling eagerness; Sam Aylward's callused hand giving him a genial ear-ringing slap on the back of the head when he let his attention wander at the archery butts; Aunt Judy listing the uses of a plant's roots and leaves in a way that made it more a game than a lesson and then holding the blossom up as she said:

And this . . . this the Mother gives us this for pretty, so She can laugh when She sees us smile.

Or even Mathilda passing on her mother's ideas of what it meant to be a King to Fred Thurston, as they rode east.

"But I'm not the best of teachers, even for blade and

bow," he murmured to himself. "Too hasty, I'd have said. Well, to travel is to learn, eh?"

The rest of their party was waiting for them there by the ruin. There were younger men—the Southside Freedom Fighters seemed to account a male ready to fight at about fifteen—and a few bold women, and the youngster with the limp and the strong voice who was the closest thing they had to a bard.

"I'll make this a telling word for you, Jake," he said. "All these horses! Even Old Jake the sailor man never got so many. Jake sunna Jake, big man who hands out bows 'n horses!"

Jake made a gesture of dismissal, but Rudi could see he was pleased at the thought of the praise song. The rest mounted up silently and kept the stolen horses moving; Epona snorted a little. She wasn't as young as she had been, but she could keep *this* pace a lot longer than these scrubby beasts.

"There!" Jake said.

It was nearly dawn now; the hour between dog and wolf, as the saying went, when you could first tell the difference between a black thread and a white. The air wasn't exactly cold, but there was a hint of cool in it as it dried the sweat on Rudi's face and arms, a token that autumn wasn't impossibly far off. The road was a long stretch of open ground in the ocean of the grass; there were trees along it, short scrubby fire-scarred oaks and cottonwoods and sycamores, growing up through cracks in the pale faded asphalt that protected them. The rest of the Southsiders ran shrieking and dancing with glee to meet the warriors, until Jake cursed them imaginatively for nearly spooking the new horses. That made them a little quieter, except for the children and—until thumped—the dogs.

Rudi confined his attention to the wagons. A long breath of relief at the lack of serious damage escaped him as they walked about; only the last one had been thoroughly looted, and that was the one that had carried the expedition's stores. They were all big, even for road vehicles carrying five or six tons each, the rubber-tired steel wheels nearly as tall as Edain, and the hoops of the blackened canvas-covered tilts were nearly twice his height above the roadway. The outsides showed scorch marks—from that fire Ingolf had described, when the Cutters ambushed his men here, and from later ones, but the pavement acted as a firebreak until the swift flame front passed. Someone had cut slits in the canvas on each and pulled out a few of the rectangular steel boxes. The locks had been sledged off; he opened one of them.

"Ah," Edain said behind him, as he pulled out the picture within and propped it against one wheel. "Now that's . . . something, by Brigid of the Bright Mind and Lugh of the Many Skills."

It was a painting, near man-high, and undamaged save for splintering around the frame where it had been tossed roughly back into the box by some wild-man disappointed it wasn't anything useful.

"Now, I wonder who he was?" Rudi murmured after a moment.

A young man, in black clothing a little like what Associates wore, but different in detail; a white ruff stood all around his neck, and the sword he rested one hand on was a rapier with an intricate hilt. The more Rudi looked the more were the intricacies he saw—yet the more it was also a *whole*, a thing in itself. You could see the haughtiness in the heavy-lipped, strong-nosed face, and the way the columns and domes behind focused attention on the figure in the foreground. The glow of rich fabrics brought out the olive of the man's complexion, and the glint off a ruby in his ear . . .

Edain gave a wordless sigh, and Rudi nodded. They came of a folk who respected a skilled maker above all things save courage and loyalty.

"That's something which makes me feel better about doing this," the older Mackenzie said. "I'll never be a friend of Iowa's Bossman, and it may be that he sent Ingolf to fetch this out of nothing but vanity . . . but he'll keep it safe, sure and he will. And his great-grandchildren's subjects will thank him for it."

Edain nodded. "What's that number down there?" he said, indicating the bottom of the frame with the end of his bow.

"A date, in the Christian fashion, from the year their God was born," Rudi said. "The year it was painted, I'd say."

The stocky archer whistled softly; he recognized the system, though Mackenzies of their generation mostly reckoned from the time of the Change.

"More than four centuries ago!" he said.

Jake stood silent, then stooped to peer more closely at the painting as the sun brightened.

"Bitchin' tough stud," he said after a moment. "Some Bossman, right?"

"Right you are," Rudi said, reflecting—not for the first time—that ignorant wasn't the same thing as *stupid*.

"The Iowa-man, he wants this just 'cause it looks good?"

Doubt was in his tone. Rudi replied:

"No. Because having such things of beauty will make others respect him more."

"Yeah. Tha' big-man thinkin'," Jake said with satisfaction. "They rich, in Iowa. Do things for looks good."

"That's one of the better things *about* being rich," Rudi said.

And Matti's mother has scoured the museums and mansions of the west coast for a generation now, he mused. *And Corvallis has too. We Mackenzies and the Bearkillers perhaps a little less, but we've found our share.*

It was still only a fraction of what had been lost; for a moment his soul ached with the thought of it. Then:

"Life is for the living, though. There's never an end to what beauty a maker can summon, and we and our descendants just as well as the ancestors. Let's to work!"

He stowed the painting reverently in the box, and he and Edain heaved it back into place. Then he dismissed it from his mind.

The wagons had been gifted from the Bossman's store, probably from his arsenals, when Anthony Heasleroad hired Ingolf and his company—Vogeler's Villains, they'd been called—for the trip to the east coast, and virtually everything in them was cunningly made of stout fireproof metal. Their beds curved up gently at front and rear, and the bottoms and sides were riveted and caulked sheet steel, able to float like a boat when crossing a ford. Frames within held the crates and boxes with the salvage; the wheels were forged and welded steel, with rims as broad as two palms. A tongue twelve feet long protruded from the front axle of each for the first pair of horses; it ended in a crossbar on which was mounted the chains that ran to the rest of the team.

The horse harness was missing, of course—from what Ingolf said, the Cutters had set a fire to force the Villains to abandon the train; they'd unfastened the horses at the last minute and galloped them clear. Luckily the wagons were built to be controlled by someone riding the front left horse, not by complex arrangements of reins. Unluckily, they needed at least eight pair each; and the horses he had available hadn't been trained for it. Some of them *might* be harness-broke; the wild-men tribes around here did use light two-wheeled carts sometimes, or travois. Most were trained only to the saddle.

And that badly, he thought.

"This is going to be a riding by the nightmare," Edain said cheerfully, looking at the stack of wood and leather the Southsiders had brought along and rubbing his hands. "What I wouldn't give for a proper saddler's workshop now. *Or* a carpenter's. Or even some drills and spoke-shaves, I'm thinkin'."

Badly cured leather, often little more than rawhide; logs and baulks of ash and hickory, and that was the sum of their materials. They'd both *helped* with harness-maker's work and done their own minor repairs in the business of farm and field, but neither of them was what a Mackenzie would call expert at it.

"Well, we'll need . . . call it thirty-two horse collars," Rudi said. "Thank Goibniu Lord of Iron that the trace chains are still sound! We'll make the collars of ash and pad them."

"Another bit to entertain the folk at home, when we can find time to write," Edain said, grinning.

Rudi laughed. "We'll be in Nantucket by the time *that* tale arrives," he said. "They'll be reading what we wrote from Chenrezi Monastery, in the Valley of the Sun, about now. The Luck of the Clan willing, considering how many hands the letters must go through, so."

Edain made an invoking sign with his right hand, then clenched both and worked his arms in an unconscious gesture to loosen the muscles before a heavy task.

"Best we measure the horses, first. Then—"

DUN JUNIPER
CASCADE FOOTHILLS, WESTERN OREGON
SEPTEMBER 6, CHANGE YEAR 24/2022 AD

The packet of letters was thick; the messenger from Bend had come over the old Santiam Pass, and down to Dun Juniper in the western foothills as fast as relays of horses would carry him. Sutterdown was the logical first stop . . . but the man was not just a messenger of the Central Oregon Rancher's Association; he was a retainer of Rancher Brown, an old friend of Juniper Mackenzie. He'd cut across to Dun Juniper, staggered in to lay the saddlebags before her, and then been half carried away to the baths and the guesthouse.

Some of the letters she set aside for forwarding; those from Mary and Ritva Havel, to their mother Signe at the Bearkiller headquarters of Larsdalen, and to the *Hiril Dúnedain*, their commander as Rangers and not so incidentally their aunt Astrid. And of course the sealed report from Father Ignatius to Abbot-Bishop Dmwoski, and Odard Liu's to his mother and to Sandra Arminger up in Portland. She sighed at that.

"Probably a plea for clemency, poor boy," she said; the sympathy in her voice was entirely for the young man.

And if ever anyone deserved an ax across their neck, Mary Liu is the one. A spell in the Summerlands, a talking-to from the Mother, better luck next time . . . She's never forgotten Eddie Liu's death, well deserved as it was. Nor will she give over seeking vengeance while she lives, or pouring poison into poor Odard's ear. He might be something considerable of a man, if he could be kept away from her long enough!

"I doubt Lady Sandra will send Mary Liu to the headsman. Not until Mathilda is safely back in Association territory, and doesn't need Odard's help," her handfasted man Nigel Loring said, in an English accent to the manor born.

"House arrest does seem unusually . . . indecisive . . . for Sandra," Juniper agreed.

Mathilda had done two letters, one to Sandra and one to her, but she laid hers aside to wait until she'd read the missive from her son.

Rudi's was in two parts. One an armsman's report to his Clan Chief, succinct and terse. Even in that there were things that raised her brows: someone else might have discounted the dream vision as a delusion born of the wound fever he'd been suffering while they sheltered in that cave against blizzards and foemen. She did not.

So old One-Eye is taking a hand in this as well, eh? Well, my boy is a hero, right enough, and he a collector of such. But he's not yours yet, Terrible One!

Nor was she surprised to read of the encounters with the Seekers sent from Corwin. Juniper already knew of the Prophet's reckless abuse of the hidden Powers.

Although, knowing, my skin crawls, that it does. Fools! To meddle so with such things! The Threefold Return will be upon them soon or late with a weight like falling mountains . . . but how many will be caught in their web of malevolence first?

The other was a son's to his mother, and it was rambling and warm, and interspersed with tales that brought a smile to her lips, and sketches of places and people done by his *anamchara*, Mathilda, and his half sisters—Rudi could draw a map that looked like a professional's, but that was the limit of his draughtsmanship.

So that's this Abbot Dorje, she thought.

An ageless face, wrinkled and grave, but somehow

with a boy's merriment in the eyes, and a finger raised in half-serious admonishment at the unseen artist.

"I'd like to meet him, sure an' I would," she said aloud.

Her mother's West-Irish Gaeltacht lilt was strong in her voice. She'd long since given it full rein; if her folk were determined to imitate it at least they should have a real model from Achill Island rather than the older generation's vague memories of Hollywood's idea of how an Irishman sounded. Though to the youngsters, what had started as half a jest among their parents or grandparents was simply the way they spoke.

"And he thinks well of Rudi, which is a mark in his favor."

"So does this *Master Hao*," Nigel said.

That sketch was of a face ageless in a different way, hard and square atop a sinewy neck. "Hmmm. That girl *does* have a talent for the pencil. There's a man of his hands, and no mistake, as Sam would say."

Then with a little wonder, and a finger stroking meditatively across the white of his neat mustache:

"Who'd have thought that a Buddhist monastery would end up ruling a lost valley in the wilds of Wyoming? Even if they *were* having a conference in a hotel there when the Change struck."

Juniper grinned a little impishly; it made the laughter lines beside her leaf green eyes suddenly stand out. There were many; she was his junior by more than a decade, but still fifty-four herself this year, and there was nearly as much gray as fox-red now in the hair that fell to her shoulders. There had still been a little yellow in his white mustache when they met, and for that matter some hair on a head now egg bald.

"And who'd have thought that a clan of *Celts* such as ours—" she began.

"Pseudo-Celts, darling, inspired by your charisma."

"—would spring up in Oregon? And the most of it was *their* idea, not mine, the spalpeens!"

"I understand you *did* say they'd have to *live like a Clan, as it was in the old days,*" Nigel observed; that had been nearly a decade before he arrived.

"I just meant we'd have to pull together! The trappings . . ."

She shrugged helplessly. "In any case, stranger things have happened."

"You converting me, for example," Nigel pointed out.

She snorted. "You're as polite to the Lord and Lady as you were to the Church of England—and not one bit more!"

He smiled and spread hands a little spotted with age. "Whatever you say, my dear."

"And it was *whatever you say, Padre,* to the parson, too, eh?"

"Whatever you say, my dear," he replied. "But I assure you my courtesy to the regimental chaplain did not extend *quite* so far as it does with you."

They both chuckled. Then her face grew grave again.

"It's the longest we've ever been apart, my boy and I," Juniper Mackenzie said. "Rudi left April sixteenth of last year. Sixteen months almost to the day."

"And now we know where he's been, old girl," Sir Nigel Loring said, putting his hand over hers.

"And that he was wounded near to death! *And* the arrows were cursed, from the description."

"Infected, at least. *And* we know that he's recovered and well," he went on relentlessly.

She turned her hand and they linked fingers. The mid-day meal was just cleared away, and the two of them were sitting on the dais at the head of the long trestles while those on kitchen duty cleared away the last of it and took up the tables themselves. A lingering smell of it—cold minced mutton pie, salads, steamed cauliflower, cheese and breads and biscuits—remained, and the acrid scent of her rosehip tea. From the outside came the clatter of looms, the rising-falling hum of spinning wheels, the whirr of treadle-driven sewing machines and the rattling clang of a smith's hammer, the neigh of a horse. All the sounds of a working day mixed with talk and laughter and snatches of song, or now and then voices raised in argument.

Though they were at war still the land must be tilled, meals cooked, animals cared for, and tools made.

And weapons, she sighed to herself, remembering Rudi dancing with the blade on the practice field, terrible and beautiful as Lugh come again in splendor and in wrath. *To be sure. That we can't avoid.*

Afternoon sunlight poured in through the windows along the verandah, shafts of it picking out the bright painted carving that ran riot over the smoothed log walls of the Great Hall's interior, vines and leaves and faces from myth and story; the signs of the Quarters were higher, under the rafters nearly fifteen feet above.

The altar over the hearth on the northern wall held her household's images of the Lord and Lady as Brigid with her flame and sheaf, and Lugh with his spear and sun disk; Nigel had made those himself when he was courting her, back during the Protector's War. When he was fresh from England he'd surprised her by how handy he was at all a countryman's tasks and trades, not just the deadly skills he'd mastered in the SAS and the Blues and Royals and after the Change.

Now she looked into the blue eyes in the weathered face that loved hers line for line, and smiled back.

"I'll grant that it's a mercy to learn my son has been wounded *after* he's recovered. This Chenrezi place seems a good one to heal, and to learn."

Her mouth quirked in a smile as she looked at *that* letter. It was signed *Rimpoche Tsewang Dorje,* and she murmured some of it aloud:

"I have spoken often with your son in these months of winter, Juniper Lady, and found in him much strength of mind and body, some wisdom and astonishingly little vanity. We have become friends, he and I."

"Now that is perceptive," Sir Nigel murmured. "I wouldn't have thought Rudi an easy man to get to know, below the surface."

Juniper nodded at him. "Especially perceptive for one of our age, my love. For the Changelings are different from us, do you see."

"I see it every day, rather!"

She shook her head. "Different in a certain way, Nigel. They . . . see the world through different eyes. They *think* differently from us; I love them, but it took me long and long to understand them. To them, what they are here"— she touched her forehead—"is less likely to conflict with what they are *here*." She touched the back of her skull and went on: "Rudi is a hero. The terrible strength of him and the only weakness of it is that he never doubts it. Regrets it, a little, sometimes; but he *is* the role the Gods have thrust upon him."

He nodded slowly. "The Changelings are all a little less prone to self-examination than we were," he acknowledged. "Well, than most of us were. They accept things. I'm more inclined to that than . . . oh, Sam Aylward."

"Ah, and it wasn't only for your looks I married you! Yes, for long and long before the Change people spent more and more of their time examining themselves."

"*Pride and Prejudice*," he said. "Odd that Rudi never liked Austen."

"Yes, he said the people in them are well painted but had far too much time on their hands!" She spread her own hands in a gesture of agreement and resignation. "But he loves the old stories. As do I, but in a different way. He *is* those men. And this I think Abbot Dorje grasps, if not in exactly those words."

She returned to the letter: "*Therefore I say that he shall be the better for the trials he has met and shall meet and I would spare him none of them; for unless a man be tested to the utmost, none may know what hidden weakness lies in him; nor may he know his own strength. On his testing and his strength much will turn. Devils seek to rule men; the Gods give us opportunities to rule ourselves, which is infinitely more difficult, and to assist each other upward through the cycles, which is harder still. I think your son may be equal to this task, when his testing is complete.*"

"Cryptic," Nigel said.

"No, my love. Some things have to be said in such fashion. I like the man's style, sure. And he's shrewd. We owe him a debt, for the rescue and the care of our folk and the help they gave."

"He wasn't entirely disinterested, old girl," Nigel said dryly. "His people are having their problems with the Prophet and the CUT as well."

Their daughters came in—Maude, calm and quiet at fourteen, with hair halfway between brown and dark auburn, and yellow-locked Fiorbhinn, ten and carrying the miniature but quite functional harp that seldom left her; they'd eaten the midday meal with their schoolmates.

Even Maude's preternatural gravity dissolved at the sight of Rudi's letter, and Fiorbhinn squealed openly. They read it over her shoulder, agog.

"Rudi will find the Sword of the Lady and put a stop to the black wickedness of those Cutter folk," Fiorbhinn said decisively.

"He *is* the Lady's Sword," Maude pointed out. "It was Herself who said so, at his Wiccaning!"

Juniper's fingers moved unconsciously as if on strings, while she wove the girl's words into a song she'd been making. How much of the letter to put into it? The earlier ones she'd made of Rudi's journey had already traveled from here to the Protectorate and back, sometimes with changes that surprised her. Then she'd weave them anew . . .

Fiorbhinn's turquoise gaze met hers, and the girl smiled and nodded, knowing what she was about. Maude was solid and good and clever, but fey little True-Sweet was the one who'd inherited the music, running like a tang of wildwood magic in the blood.

Nigel knew as well. "Have you considered what you're doing, Juniper?" he said quietly.

The girls huddled together over the pages she'd allowed them—there were a few things in the letter she didn't want *anyone* else seeing just yet, and a few others not for a child's eyes. They whispered excitedly to each other, reading out the choice bits, gasping when their elder half brother was in peril, Fiorbhinn jumping from foot to foot with excitement at each escape or wonder.

"I'm making him a hero, poor boy!" she said, trying for lightness and failing.

Nigel shook his head. "You're putting his name on everyone's lips from woods-runner cabins south of Ashland to the Okanogan baronies, but that isn't the same thing—he was born to be a hero, I'm afraid, and famous already. What you're doing, my love, is making him everyone's hope in a time of fear—which is to say, you're setting out to sing him onto a throne, if he lives. It's a cruel thing, for a musician to sit and shape a man into a King, like a reed cut and hollowed out to make a flute."

His gaze turned inward for a moment, and then he quoted from a poet they both loved:

> *"And yet half a beast is the great God Pan*
> *To laugh as he sits by the river;*
> *Making a legend out of a man.*
> *The true Gods weep for the loss and the pain*
> *For the reed that will never grow again*
> *As a reed, with the reeds, by the river."*

Juniper sighed and closed her eyes for a second. "I know," she said softly. "And it's a bitter thing to do to a child you love."

"If it's any consolation, my darling, Rudi would do the job very well indeed."

Unwilling, she laughed. "No consolation at all . . . well, not much. But there's no choice in the matter, none at all. I'm a musician, and before that a mother . . . but at seventh and last, I am *Her* priestess, though that road lead through the hard and stony places."

Nigel picked up a letter that bore Edain Aylward's laborious scrawl on its envelope of coarse handmade paper. "I'll send this along to Sam; he's out observing the maneuvers. He'll be pleased at how young Edain's done."

"Proud as punch," Juniper said, grateful for the distraction. "As proud as I am of Rudi, and with near as much reason."

"Proud as punch, but in a very understated way."

"He's English, poor man."

When she was alone in the upper room, Juniper read Mathilda's letter and smiled, as much at the things not said as the words themselves. She murmured those aloud to herself:

"Rudi and I keep thinking how nice it would be if we could just go off together and start a farm, or run an inn, or wrangle caravans. Sometimes I look into his eyes in the evening, watching him watching the fire and thinking, and he'll look up at me and smile and it's like taking a long soak in hot rosewater after a hard day. Does that make any sense? And we're far from home, and lonely, but I really didn't feel *alone* until he was so sick, and we thought he might die. It's not just that we're friends. All the others here are good friends now, even the ones like Fred we've met along the way. It's as if Rudi and I have only now gotten to really know each other—which is funny, since we've been *anamchara* since we were kids, more than half our lives."

Juniper chuckled to herself: "Since we were kids! Says the withered crone of twenty-three!"

Then she continued reading: "Maybe it's that we're so far away from home, and duties, and rank—so that it's just *us* now."

She sat in thought on the bench before her big loom where the brightest lantern hung, turning the paper between her fingers and thinking. Thinking long enough that the flame died down, and she needed to stand and adjust the wick in a smell of scorched linen and oil.

She had loved Sandra Arminger's child as if she were her own—perhaps not *more* than that strange weaver of secrets and hidden plans did, but more warmly, and she believed she'd had some hand in the shaping of a young woman they could both be proud of.

Foster daughter, you were never just a pawn in the game of thrones. How I would delight to see my grandchild in your arms! Friendship, love . . . it's odd how they can tip the one into the other. And Love is a tricksy God, wearing more faces than the stars or the leaves of autumn or the snowflakes in winter, terrible and beautiful, sweet or deadly. Even your evil tuilli *of a father truly loved you, I think; the one wholly good thing he did in all his monstrous, wicked life. What one of Their gifts brings us more joy, or more suffering, than love? Love between you and my son there has always been, since first you came here captive, proud little spitfire that you were! So brave and so lonely, and Rudi was your only friend. But not passion of that sort, not until now . . . though thrown together in desperate peril as you've been . . .*

She stood and went to face the northern wall, where her Book of Shadows stood on its lectern, and her private altar with the blue-mantled figure of the Ever-Changing One crowned with the Triple Moon, and the Horned God dancing in ecstasy amid skyclad worshippers with the panpipes to his lips. She unpinned her plaid and draped it over her hair like a hood; then she made certain signs and murmured invocations and held up her arms with head bowed and palms to the sky.

"You powerful God, You Goddess gentle and strong! You have demanded much of my son and he has never refused You, Lady and Lord. A warrior he is in Your service, and a strong man to ward Your world and folk and law; but he's still the child I bore beneath my heart."

A questioning, like a pressure on her soul. She drew a breath and went on:

"Give him this, at least, on the road You have chosen, the one *he* has chosen to walk willingly with open eyes, consenting to his fate. Let him know the sweet before the bitter. Let him know the arms of a lover who loves him heart-deep, with mind and soul and body. Let him know the gladdest and deepest Mystery; let him see the child of his love born and raised up before Your altar for the naming. *So mote it be.*"

The words were quiet, but they dropped into a silence that echoed; she felt as if a hand had brushed her eyes, and a faint scented warmth elusive as the memory of a dream.

CHAPTER SEVEN

Sunlight blinked off metal far ahead as the road wound downward. His warrior's eye recognized that rippling sparkle: polished mail, perhaps, or lance heads, or helmets. Someone was coming who didn't much care whether anyone spotted him, which meant it was *not* any native dweller in these lands. Hiding was ground into their souls by now, hiding and skulking and the grisly game of stalk and ambush that had killed their parents young.

By what the oldsters say, soldiers all fought like that in the days before the Change, Rudi Mackenzie thought. *Not just bandits and savages, scouts and Rangers. No wonder, when they all had weapons that could kill at a thousand paces like a catapult, and shoot so fast, too! Anyone who could see you could kill you.*

It wasn't like that now. Men who fought with discipline, shoulder to armored shoulder, could plow through those who scattered. Many scorned to conceal themselves at all, thinking it the heart of a fighting man's pride to stand and meet the battle-rush, or to lock shields with their oath-brothers and stride unhesitating towards a line of bright spears in the hands of angry strangers. The Clan were less prickly, but in anything like a pitched battle even Mackenzie longbowmen had to pack pretty tightly together to brew an arrow storm dense enough to stop a charge.

"Whoa!" he said aloud, shifting his balance back, and then reminded himself to pull firmly on the reins; he wasn't on Epona now.

Over his shoulder he called to the woman sitting on the wagon's board:

"Brake!"

The slug of a horse he was riding was both stupid and malicious—either that, or it missed its former Knifer master so much it was grieving-mad.

Which I doubt, he thought with exasperation, while worrying whether the other vehicles would notice in time.

The brake lever locked padded drums against the axles; it was that more than his efforts that made the improvised team stop. He used the slack of the long rein to give the horse a sharp *pop* on the nose as it responded to the halt with its usual attempt to turn its head and bite him on the knee. It took the rebuke as a signal to try and buck, bolt and kick sideways at its teammate in the traces beside it, and it took a few more moments to convince it that was a *bad* idea. The fact that it would break its legs and die if the eight beasts hauling the first wagon were to be thrown into a struggling heap didn't seem to matter to it— probably it was too dim-witted even to fear for its legs, which . . .

"Puts it about on a level with a sheep," he said with disgust. "Except that sheep are usually better natured."

And to be sure, he had to make certain Epona wasn't in view while he rode with the team here. She didn't like it when he rode another horse, even her own get. She *definitely* wouldn't like him riding this crowbait. Horses could be as difficult as people, sometimes. And the thought of trying to put *her* in harness made him shudder. She might or might not have the HorseGoddess for which he'd named her as her dam, but she certainly acted as if she did. In her pride not least.

He grinned, tired but reasonably contented. Horses and their crotchets he'd have to worry about the rest of his life, he supposed, but this part of the journey was about over and with any luck at all he could get back to the *real* quest. The road stretched ahead; he could see the screen of Southsider scouts appearing and disappearing ahead as they fell back towards him.

To his left was about a mile of floodplain, densely wooded but mostly with new growth, here and there a pre-Change tree towering with the height that abundant water and the rich silty soil would endow. Others were dead and gaunt and bleached bone white, killed out when their roots were smothered by the spreading water of renascent swamp. Parts of it were full marsh now; he could smell it, the sweetish-rank scents of black muck and vegetable decay, and see the glints of water where the old levees along the Mississippi had broken. It had probably been cropland before the Change, and very good land at that.

The reeds were brown with the late season, and a few of the velvet sausage shapes of the cattails were beginning to shed white fluff. The leaves of the maples hadn't started to turn, but their green had a faint, almost subliminal hint of yellow to them, and all the trees had a bit of tatter, like a shirt worn until the cuff and tails started to unravel. A string of geese took off as he watched, gusting upward like a spray of black dots before they formed into a V and headed southward. The long slanting rays of afternoon made the great river painful to look at, light breaking and blinking off its rippled surface; despite that the Southsiders trudging along on foot were pointing and peering and exclaiming in delighted wonder, with parents putting their infants up on their shoulders to see. They were nomads, but like most such they'd traveled on a fixed seasonal round in a narrow compass, one that didn't include the Mississippi.

Off to his right was hilly land, the bluffs that edged the floodplain. The rumpled surface had a pelt of old forest, with here and there brick snags through tangled vines and saplings marking where buildings had stood, and brush growing over stands of thick short bluish grass interrupted by sandy spots.

The underbrush had been cleared back about half a bowshot on either side of the road, and the rust-rotted hulks of automobiles and trucks were missing. That meant that they were within the area regularly patrolled by Iowan troops from their beachhead in East Dubuque. Edain came trotting up from farther south, with Garbh at the heel of his horse. *He* was riding the quarterhorse he'd picked up in the Valley of the Sun, in what had once been Wyoming, a decent and civilized beast who didn't even object when the great dog leapt up to sit behind her master.

"Those bearings on the third wagon's rear axle aren't going to last much longer, no matter how much lard we bless 'em with, Chief," he said. "Then we'll be worse off than with an ordinary iron collar and no fancy salvage. But I'm thinking we could—"

His square face had the bullock-stubborn look of a man who was pacing himself by the task, and giving it everything he had.

"Boyo, they have to keep going for another four miles,

or an hour and a bit, so. After that it's Bossman Heasleroad's problem, and none of ours."

Edain blinked and shook his head like a man coming
out of deep sleep. Then he grinned at the Mackenzie
chieftain, and Rudi grinned back.

"Sure, and it seemed like we'd be traveling forever,
didn't it?" he said, and leaned over to clap the younger
man on the shoulder.

"That it did. And not a nice pleasant pilgrimage for
Beltane, either. Fighting, which I do not like, or running,
the which I like even less."

"Is fearr rith maith ná drochsheasamh." Rudi laughed.
"A good run is better than a bad stand."

Edain nodded, then raised a warning fist as Rudi's
mount turned a considering head towards him:

"Keep your teeth to yourself, y' evil-eyed keffle! Forever
and a day, Chief. And the Sword there needing to be
gotten, the which weighs on my mind."

Rudi showed his teeth in what was not quite a smile.
"Do you think it does not for me also? But the quest of
the Sword is only a bit about the finding of the Sword.
It's what we do along the way, too."

Edain blinked at him. "Learning how to travel three
thousand miles, then, would that be it?"

"No, boyo. Learning how to travel three thousand
miles and make an ally against the Cutters every few hundred of those miles. Allies ready to fight with us when we
return. Remember the Lakota? And Chenrezi? And those
guerillas in Deseret?"

The gray eyes widened, and the stocky bowman
slapped himself on the forehead. "Now it's blind I feel!
Well, you're the Chief. High King, perhaps, too."

Rudi pointed a finger at his face. "And the High King's
right-hand man had better learn to think of such things.

It's your wits I'll be needing, Edain Aylward Mackenzie of the Wolf sept, as much as the skill of your eye and hand."

A shout came from ahead. Rudi nodded; he'd expected that about now. Jake and his Southsider warriors jogged back towards the wagon train and the rest of their tribe in no particular order, on either side of a squadron of Iowa cavalry.

The Iowans were in a neat column of twos, with an officer in a plumed helmet at the front and a bannerman with the State flag flying just behind him. They were well mounted on big glossy geldings, and despite the formal stiffness of their formation they also looked tough and alert, unlike some of their comrades he'd seen elsewhere. They all wore coal-scuttle helmets and short-sleeved mail shirts, with heavy curved shetes at their sides and round shields slung over their backs; their four-foot horseman's horn-and-sinew recurve bows were out of the scabbards, and they all had arrows on the string.

And they're notably good horsemen, Rudi thought. *With well-trained mounts. Elite troops.*

The thought was confirmed when the column came to a halt in rippling unison not far away. You needed to use both hands for a saddle bow, which meant you had to control your horse exclusively with legs and balance. Rudi could do it—

On a real horse, not this ambling pot of glue-makings!

—but mostly people with that knack were ranchers or cowboys or Rovers or from the Plains tribes, folk who lived in the saddle from childhood. Iowans were tillers of the earth or town-dwelling merchants and craftsmen as a rule, but these had a different trade.

He slid to the ground and walked forward on the cracked slabs of the roadway, split into uneven segments like the back of a tortoise by a generation's frost heave, glad to be out of the beast's kicking and biting range. His blue-green eyes narrowed as he took in the commander's face beneath the brim of his helmet.

Denson, he thought.

Then they went wide as he saw the big man beside him, the one wearing a kettle helm with a broad brim like a hat's.

"Ingolf!" he shouted. "Ingolf the Wanderer!"

And alive, free and armed, he added to himself, feeling a grin of delight split his face.

"Rudi, you miserable slippery son of a bitch!" the other man called. "Christ, you could fall into a heap of horseshit and come out smelling like a rose with a gold brick in your teeth!"

He slid from his mount as well, and they grasped each other's shoulders, laughing with pleasure; that grip was easier because they were almost of a height, though Ingolf was a bit thicker-built, bull to Rudi's tiger. The other man's weathered face was a little gray under the short-clipped beard, but that was to be expected after weeks of confinement. He fisted the Mackenzie on the arm and stepped back, looking at the wagons with his thumbs hooked into his sword belt.

"By Jesus, I never thought I'd see *these* again. All the way to Boston and back . . ."

His face went cold for an instant, obviously remembering the friends and followers of his who'd died on that trip. Then he shook it off.

"Good work . . . Chief."

"I had help." Rudi shrugged.

"I can see that," Ingolf said, nodding to the Southsiders and shaking hands with Edain. "But you *got* the help."

It was a different tune you were singing when we started out, Rudi thought; there had been a bit of friction when the more experienced man realized the Mackenzie was to be in charge of their group. *But you're an adaptable one, Ingolf Vogeler. And it's glad I am to see you.*

The Iowan commander had dismounted as well. "Charmed the cannibals, I see," he said to Rudi. "No accounting for tastes, either way."

Jake sunna Jake sat his horse to one side, scowling and working his fingers on the shaft of the spear whose butt rested on the toes of his right foot. Rudi had rarely seen a man more ready to kill who wasn't trying to actually do it.

"Ah, Captain Denson, still as much a charmer of a man as ever you were before," Rudi said.

He smiled, and the State Police officer blinked a little; the last time they'd met he'd been seeing Rudi over the bridge into the Wild Lands on a mission meant to fail, and the time before that he'd arrested the Mackenzie, tried to arrest his friends, succeeded in taking Odard and Matti prisoner, and dragged the three of them before Anthony Heasleroad's throne. Rudi's sharp-cut features usually had a half smile about them. It made the expression they wore now more noticeable.

"And it's glad I am to see you again," Rudi said, something cat-playful in his tone. "Very glad to see you again like this."

This being armed, with armed friends at hand, and the Iowan himself within arm's reach. Denson was no fool; he'd seen Rudi before, and refreshed his memory with an expert's quick appraisal of the other man—hands, shoulders, the way he stood and moved.

"Now, Captain Denson, would you be after tellin' me something: you Christians have a proverb, do you not, *Vengeance is Mine, sayeth the Lord*?"

The State Policeman nodded warily. "Yes."

"And you've another to the effect that if a man hits you on one cheek you should turn and let him hit the other, no?"

"Yeah. Your point is?"

Rudi's smile grew a little broader, and his thumb caressed the cross guard of his longsword:

"Well, I'm not a Christian, you see. And we of the Old Religion believe that a man's deeds come back upon him in kind . . . magnified threefold."

"Sorry if I offended," Denson said tightly. "Just doing my job."

"It's to my friend Jake here that you should apologize, Captain Denson," Rudi said. "Because the Southside Freedom Fighters are not cannibals, nor were their ancestors, and because they've helped me regain your Bossman's property. And for the sake of good manners to guests, the which is pleasing to the land spirits while rudeness brings ill luck from the fey."

"Apologize to a *wild-man?*"

There was a genuinely scandalized tone in Denson's voice; that prejudice was no older than Rudi, but it ran deep. The shock of it was enough to knock the man onto his back heel for a moment, mentally.

"When a man's got himself into a pit, the first order of business is to stop digging," Rudi said. "Whether with a shovel or with his tongue. And there's a third reason you should apologize; because you're wearing a sword."

Denson's hand went unconsciously to the hilt of his shete. "What's that got to do with it?"

Rudi smiled. Jake sunna Jake cocked his head to one side, considered the expression, and gave a gap-toothed grin of his own. Ingolf seemed to be wavering between sharing the amusement and looking alarmed, but he also shifted his shoulders a little and casually rested a hand on the strap that held his shield across his back. That might be an idle gesture . . . but it also put him in position to pull it down and slide his arm into the loops quickly. Rudi went on.

"If a man insults another and has no weapon, then he's a coward and beneath contempt, hiding behind his own weakness and the other's honor. But if he does it with steel by his side, it's presumed that he will"—Rudi ran an ostentatious eye over the gray threads in the Iowan's hair—"how did you ancients put it in the old world . . . *walk the walk*, as well as talkin' the talk?"

He didn't draw his sword, or even put his sword hand to the hilt. He did let the thumb of the other press on the guard, enough to start it free of the slight tension of the greased battens lining the scabbard, and let a single thread's-width of the patterned layer-forged blade show.

Denson stared at him for an instant, opened his mouth, then followed Rudi's flick of the eyes and turned to Jake.

"Sorry," he said to the Southsider coolly enough, with a little bow. "No offense meant."

Jake grunted, probably slightly disappointed. Rudi smiled, this time without the edge of menace.

"Graciously said," he said. "Now, let's get your ruler's property to him, eh?"

"I'll meet you at the fort," Denson said, swinging into the saddle and turning his mount; his men followed him, and rocked up to a gallop.

"Imeacht gan teacht ort; titim gan éirí ort," Rudi said in the language of his mother's people. Then he added the English for his companion: "May you leave without returning and fall without rising, addressed to the lovely

darlin' man himself. The which is perhaps a little too close to a curse for comfort, but sometimes things need to be said."

Ingolf let a breath puff out. "We do need *him*," he pointed out. "At least for a while."

Rudi nodded. "But he needs us, or you wouldn't be here, my friend. And he's not the sort of man who sees a friendly approach as anything but weakness."

"Yah, he's the type you have to push back at or get walked on, all right." Suddenly Ingolf chuckled. "And Christ . . . or Manwë and Varda . . . it was good to see *him* backing down. Spending time in his jail warped my perspective a bit, I think."

He swallowed and looked at the wagons. "Thanks, by the way."

"You're heartily welcome, but . . ."

"Yah, Matti and Odard. From what Denson told me they're as safe as anyone could be around Tony Heasleroad."

"Which is not a great and exceeding safeness, so?"

"There's that."

"And I would not put the good Captain Denson above a wee little bit of an exaggeration, if it suited his purposes."

Ingolf nodded. "He's . . . a piece of work, yah. And that collection of gallows bait he runs aren't much better; I've seen plenty of hard men—I've *been* one, a lot of people would say—but most of that crew have got something *missing*, if you ask me."

"And they may regret it," Rudi said grimly. "When a man . . . injures his inner self that way, it's unpleasantly likely that something will come to infect the wound. Something that likes to dwell amid corruption."

Ingolf shrugged and returned to practicality: "Matti

seems to have charmed everyone around the Bossman, though; she and Kate Heasleroad are thick as thieves. And Odard's popular at court too."

"Neither is a surprise," Rudi said. *Though with Odard, it's more of a mask, I think.* "Matti has a gift for being liked; it starts with being likeable, and also with her liking folk who deserve it."

Edain had been leaning on his longbow. Now he nodded after Denson, a considering look in his eye.

"The man's fey," he said. "The shadow of the Hunter's wings is on his face."

There was a moment of confusion—Ingolf seemed to think the word *fey* meant something entirely different from the Clan's use of the term—and then Rudi spoke:

"I hadn't noticed that . . . but strong passion blinds the inner eye, and I confess Edgar Denson makes me regret that the Gael gave up taking heads to nail over the door, the sorrow and the sadness, that he does."

"You hadn't given up chopping them off, that I noticed," Ingolf said dryly.

The two clansmen laughed. "But his deeds are coming back to him, threefold," Edain said. "I could feel it, and I'm not one to see the Dread Lord's mark on a face just because breakfast didn't agree with me."

"That you are not," Rudi agreed. "From your lips to the ears of the Fair Folk, though, that they may send him just precisely the ill luck and black misfortune that he's earned. The man is a waste of living space."

Ingolf looked at the wagons. "You got them moving, all right," he said. "But where *did* you find this collection of crowbait you've got pulling them?"

Rudi laughed. "Thereby hangs a tale. And it was a tale of the Lakota that gave me the idea."

Care seemed to slide from Ingolf's shoulders as well;

he was a few years older than Rudi, but not more than thirty yet.

"During the Sioux War we used to say they could steal your horse and you'd ride on half a mile before you noticed. Guess it's catching, Strong Raven."

"That it is, Iron Bear."

Edain joined the chuckle. "How Dad will grin when he hears about how we got the horses. He's always on about what great raiders the SAS were, before the Change."

"He taught you," Rudi pointed out. "So it's only natural he'll take a bit of the credit."

NEAR DUN LAUREL
CLAN MACKENZIE TERRITORIES
WILLAMETTE VALLEY, OREGON
SEPTEMBER 6, CHANGE YEAR 24/2022 AD

"Advance in skirmish order with fire and movement!"

That bellowed order was faint with distance, but the dunting *huu-huu-hadd-hurrr* bray of the cowhorn trumpet carried more clearly.

The old man leaned silently on his unstrung bow stave and watched the warriors deploy, popping a few blue-black serviceberries from the shrub next to him into his mouth from time to time. Sam Aylward was in his sixties, and had never been more than middle height, though deep-chested and broad in the shoulders; now he stooped a little, and the square tanned Saxon face was gaunt and furrowed, the once earth-brown hair turned gray and white. There was strength yet in the scarred gnarled hands on the yellow yew-wood but they were starting to twist with age, and they were battered with a lifetime of working with animals and weapons and tools, heavy weights of flesh and wood and metal and urgent speed.

He was grateful for the heat of the summer sun sinking into flesh and bone, even as it brought sweat out on his face and flanks; somehow he was cold a lot of the time these days. A deep breath brought a scent of rank greenery and silty mud, windfalls rotting beneath apple orchards gone feral, crushed grass, a few blue lupins still blossoming. Grass heads scratched at his legs below the pleated kilt. This was the time to practice the arts of war, after the grain was in and the stacks thatched and waiting for the threshing, when strong young hands and backs could be spared.

Time to read Edain's letter, too, he thought; he could almost feel the weight of it in his sporran. *The boy's had a bad time. That were cruel hard, not being able to save that girl he met. There's a lesson you have to learn: sometimes you give it everything and nothing works . . . But* he's *all right, and he's been doing a man's work and no mistake. And tonight I can show it to Melissa.*

A slight smile moved his lips at the thought of his son and the prospect of his wife's face. She'd been worried badly, which was natural enough, and spending a lot of time spell casting and trying auguries until Lady Juniper told her once a month was enough.

I've been worried about the boy too. Boy? He snorted. *I've bred and raised me an Aylward fighting man to reckon with! Now stop woolgathering and get back to work, Samkin. They're shaping nicely—and Oak Barstow has them well in hand. He'll be better than his dad at it. More fire in the belly.*

The ground the warriors were using was part of the empty zone that separated Dun Laurel from Dun Carson, far enough out in the flats of the Willamette Valley that the Cascades were a line of blue topped with white in the eastern distance; his own hobbled horse grazed behind him, and John Hordle's thick-bodied warmblood, and his younger son Richard's elderly little cob. The boy—he was fifteen and a bit, still a few years too young for the First Levy—was aggressively red-haired, freckled, and looking at the exercise with naked envy, unconsciously edging forward bit by bit and reaching over his shoulder to finger the arrows in his quiver.

"Dickie," the elder Aylward said mildly, without looking around, and keeping the inward grin out of his voice. "If you don't want to mind the 'orses, you could always be to 'ome helping your mother set up that new loom. Or there's them hurdles that need replacing in the 'ill pen . . ."

A hundred clansfolk were advancing through the burgeoning wilderness. They moved by threes and nines, dodging swiftly from bush to tree to clump of tall grass that nodded like hair blowing in the slow warm wind. The kilts and plaids of the Mackenzie tartan—which here in Oregon was mostly green and dark brown, due to a salvaged load of blankets that first year—made them hard to see; so did the green leather covering their brigandines, and the matt surface of the same color on their open-faced sallet helms. They shot as they came, stopping briefly to bend the long yellow bows and send a gray-fletched arrow whirring downrange before the next dash; shafts thumped home in the man-shaped targets of straw matting bound round posts, or now and then vanished near them.

"Nossir! Sorry, Dad!" Richard Aylward Mackenzie said.

The boy wrenched his eyes from the dance of war, straightened up and chivvied the mounts a little closer together; they responded with lazy good manners.

"Nice to have room for this bit so close to the settlements," John Hordle said, lowering a set of binoculars that looked like toys in his great fist. "Even 'ere in farmin' country."

His rumbling bass held the same slow yokel burr as Sam's, deep English of a south-country village sort. Usually his wasn't as ripe—he was a generation younger, around forty—but he unconsciously fell back into the speech of their shared birthplace as they spoke.

"Moind, with bows you don't 'ave to worry about some git a mile downrange catching one. Still, nice not to be crowded," Sam replied.

The Mackenzies numbered over sixty thousand now, more than half of them born since the Change and more too young to remember much before it, but they weren't short of land—even good land like this, not counting the vast mountain forests to the east on the slopes of the Cascades. There were probably more people about in the rural areas of the Willamette Valley than there had been before the engines died, but they *used* a lot less of the landscape, now that it wasn't machine-cultivated to feed some distant metropolis. Most of the Clan's territory down in the valley flats was like this, kept as a reserve against future growth, and the same was true in the other realms.

"Not much loik the land east of the Cascades, though," Hordle said. "Less cover out there, mostly."

Grazing livestock and dry-season wildfire, deer and elk and sounders of feral swine had kept the scrub and saplings from covering everything here, but the golden summer grass was shaggy and nearly waist high, studded with rosebush and hawthorns gone wild here and there. Scarlet English corn poppies starred the fields with swatches and dots of crimson.

My doing, that, Sam thought, with an inward grin.

He'd helped it along, at least; quietly dumped several score pounds of seed salvaged from garden-supply stores here and there in the first years, and they'd spread far in this agreeable climate and fertile soil. Not that he'd ever admit it, and he cursed the weeds with the best.

Bit of old Blighty, and sod the nuisance they are in the corn. We don't have to squeeze every acre until it squeaks.

There was a stretch of wetland over westward to his right, thick with green cattails and reeds where a field drain had been blocked; most of the birds had fled the noisy humans. Elsewhere the trees that had lined tilled fields or roads before the Change had sent out waves of saplings, poplar and Douglas fir, bigleaf maple and garry oak, the oldest of them of respectable size by now. Another patch of forest marked the site of a farmhouse, snags of tumbled brick showing where the roots gripped and ground away at the old world's works with slow vegetable patience.

More arrows flew; the levies were retreating now, the same stop-shoot-and-dash maneuver. This wasn't the massed volleying by ranks that could darken the sky and smash armies, but a very respectable number of shafts were flicking in their long shallow arcs, blurring through the air.

"Not bad at all," Sam said; in fact he was proud and happy with the performance. "Easier to make summat of 'em than it was in England before the Change. Christ, it'd make you cry, to see some of the things that came into the recruiting offices back then. More like garden slugs on legs than 'uman bein's they was, sometimes. Present company excepted."

The bigger man grunted agreement. "Well, this lot 'aven't spent their lives layin' about watchin' the telly and scarfing crisps."

He smiled reminiscently and went on: "Remember those types they said were cheese and onion flavor? Made from rendered cow 'ooves, I read once."

He leaned on the brass pommel of his sheathed sword as he said it; the weapon was four feet in the blade, with a long double-lobed hilt and a cross guard. It wasn't out-sized beside John Hordle, who was six-foot-seven and broad enough to seem a little squat. In armor he could look overweight, something his great boiled ham of a face might suggest.

"No, it's shoveling muck and hoeing spuds and chopping trees for these, murr loik," Aylward said with satisfaction. "*And* practicing with the bow fraam the toime they're six, naat to mention 'unting. And they don't worry themselves so much as folk did in our day."

"*Your* day, Samkin."

Today Hordle wore a sleeveless linsey-woolsey shirt in the warmth, besides trousers and boots and broad belt and the baldric for slinging the weapon over his back, and you could see that the three-hundred-odd pounds of him had scarcely an ounce of spare flesh. Massive muscle ran and flexed across thick heavy bone on a body the same width from shoulders to waist, with dense auburn furze on the backs of his hands and his arms and great barrel chest. The baldric had a device picked out on it in silver, of a bare tree surrounded by seven stars and topped by a crown.

"Gives a good start," he agreed. "It's the same with most we get for the Dúnedain Rangers. All you 'ave to teach 'em is how to *foight*. And you're roit about their not worryin'. Just take things as they come, which is sommat even sojers came hard to before the Change."

One archer got a little *too* enthusiastic, shooting as he ran without taking time to aim. A bow captain came up behind him and administered a tremendous kick to the man's backside, hard enough to send him forward onto his face with the surprise and shock.

"You've a fine old English discipline goin' 'ere," Hordle said approvingly. "Sir Nigel must approve."

"No, 'e says there are toimes an officer 'as ter be blind," Aylward said. "Take a walk, loik, while the sergeant deals with things. No names, no pack drill."

Hordle nodded. "Funny being one meself—an off'cer, that is. *And* you, Sammy, for all you swore you'd die a sergeant."

Aylward grinned. "Some folk 'ave ancestors. The Lorings go all the way back to Bastard Willie's time—"

"Live up to it, they do," Hordle observed.

"That's so, bless 'em. But you and me, John, we don't *'ave* ancestors. We *are* ancestors, and the kiddies will 'ave to live up to *us*."

"Poor little buggers!" Hordle laughed. "Better them than me."

"But you're king o' the woods, too, eh?" Aylward observed dryly.

Hordle shook his head. "King's roit 'and, p'raps," he said. "Or Prince Consort's. Alleyne allus was better at the strategy side of it. Well, 'e's Sir Nigel's son, and 'e went to Sand'urst, so it stands to reason, dunnit? Still, I'm surprised how you've tamed these wild Irish."

"Wild Irish?" Aylward asked, with a derisive snort. "These synthetic Scots and plastic Paddies? Stage Oirish, more loik, John. I swear if Lady Juniper's last name had been von Hoffenburg they'd 'ave taken to spiked helmets and jackboots that first year; they'd prob'ly have worn lederhosen wi' 'em, too. They're no more Celts than you or me."

Hordle grinned, a slightly alarming expression, and

flicked at a lock of his dark red hair for an instant with one sausagelike finger; the first gray threads showed there this year.

"Speak for yourself, Sam. I don't reckon the Saxons in our stamping grounds scragged all the Early Welsh girls they found when they landed at Gosport Hard and started gettin' antisocial wi' fire and sword. That'ud be proper wasteful."

"It's the way they talk I was thinking of," Sam said. "Saw—'eard—it happen, these twenty years and some. *Oi* was here roight from the beginning, not like you three late arrivals. Drove Lady Juniper fair mad, it did, but they wouldn't stop. I give you the youngsters . . . they just grew up with it, so to say."

"Could have been worse, Samkin. They could have imitated *you* instead of the way 'er Ladyship sounds—"

"—what they *thought* she sounded like, y' rammucky lurden—"

"—I'd 'ave landed here ten years later and found thousands of 'ampshire 'ogs, only talking through their noses loik this."

Hordle finished with an alarmingly accurate impression of someone who'd grown up on General American trying to speak with the accents of a Tillbury villager.

"Says the man who talks sodding *Elvish* most of the time, y' great gallybagger."

The big man winced slightly. "That's Lady Astrid's fault. She were always mad for those tales. Not that I don't loik them myself—and Alleyne liked them even better. Allus did, even when we were lads in Tillbury, back before the Change, and you were drinking my dad's beer at the Pied Merlin and telling us lies about the sojer's life."

"Which is why *he* ended up married to *her*," Sam said. "But your missus is near as bad."

"Oh, no, no, now there you're wrong. She just *loiked* them stories. It's Astrid who took it all for Gospel; Eilir went along with it, and now the youngsters all *believe* it, God 'elp us. Anyway, they were already living in the woods and doin' the 'ole bit when Sir Nigel and Alleyne and I arrived. Doesn't hurt, does it? It's useful, having a language nobody else speaks, like using Sign. Sort of like a regimental badge for us Rangers, too. And we're the next thing to the SAS about these days."

"And you sound a complete pillock when it comes out of your mouth, John."

He sighed and nodded agreement. "You know the worst of it? When I start *thinking* in soddin' Sindarin. Going on sixteen years now I've been in those woods, and everyone *reciting* and *singing* at me about every bloody thing."

Hordle sang, in a deep rumbling bass:

> *"Alack, Lord Hordle!*
> *Woe to the Men of the West*
> *Who get no rest*
> *For there is no bum-wad*
> *In the Silvan crapper!*
> *Nor any yet*
> *In my Flet*
> *No knotted grass*
> *For my ass*
> *In Stardell Hall*
> *Is't there none at all?*
> *Of any stripe?*
> *That we may wipe?"*

Sam chuckled like gravel in a bucket. "Still, they're clever as foxes and they fight 'ard as badgers, so let 'em sing, Oi say."

The big man went on in more normal tones: "*You* don't have to live with it. It's a good thing the missus is deaf and gives me some peace; I'd have done someone an injury, else."

"How's the ear coming?"

"She's foine; the wound's healed up proper. Weren't serious, and she says she never used the ear anyway. Still more of a looker than *I* deserve!"

"How's the other?"

That could only mean Astrid Havel, the *Hiril Dúnedain*, the Lady of the Rangers.

"Lady Astrid? Fine, and lucky with it. The 'eadaches tapered off . . . you know 'ow it is after you get a bad thump on the noggin."

They both knew; you didn't get up from being knocked unconscious and walk away as if from a nap. Blinding headaches for months were a small price to pay. Hordle's fingers played with the hilt of his great blade for a moment; Sam turned his head for an instant and raised one shaggy white eyebrow at Dick, who was leaning forward towards the conversation with his ears almost visibly stretched. The boy went over and began fiddling with his mount's tack.

Hordle lowered his voice a little: "It gave me a fair turn, Sam. That burke in the red robe *caught* Astrid's sword right in the middle of a lunge, caught the flat between his 'ands."

He slapped his palms together to illustrate how.

"Caught it and punched it back into her 'ead. If it hadn't been slippery with some blood on it 'e'd have knocked her brains out. Gospel, Sam; I'm not 'avin' you on."

Sam Aylward whistled through his teeth. He'd seen the *Hiril* fight.

You couldn't *catch her sword like that. John's roit; it's not natural.*

"And the skinny little git who did it had already knocked *me* for a Burton," Hordle said. "One punch under the short ribs and I couldn't move until I got my wind back. One punch through a mail shirt and padding! And I had to chop 'is 'ead off to put him down; he was about to twist Astrid's off like a cook with a chicken. So she's talking about a *real* Dark Lord this time."

"Daft," Sam replied. "But you got out and you took Peters with you, right from his own house. *Astrid's* daft, sure enough, but she's roit fly too, and she does mad things and gets away with them. Of course, you and Alleyne 'elp."

Carl Peters was—had been—Bossman of Pendleton; he was now a "guest" in Castle Todenangst, up in Association territory. Unfortunately his wife had always been the real brains of that partnership, and *she'd* escaped the Dúnedain commando raid with her two sons and was now ruling Pendleton in cooperation with the Prophet of the Church Universal and Triumphant and the President-General of the United States of Boise . . . and playing those uneasy allies off against each other to maintain her own family's power.

"Keep 'er feet on the ground, as it were."

"Samkin . . ." Hordle said unwillingly. "I'm not sure she *is* daft, not about this. The Prophet was in that room, and I saw the bugger, and my bollocks crawled up so high I 'ad lumps on me neck and had to massage them down again with warm oil and cloths later. 'Alf the time I think Astrid's barking mad . . . but the other half I think she may know summat I don't, like this."

"He's certainly a nasty piece of work, our lad Sethaz,"

Sam acknowledged. "I've talked to a few refugees from out east, and Lady Juniper to more."

"No, Norman Arminger was a nasty piece of work. Sethaz is all that and a bit more, believe me."

"Well, I'll let Lady Juniper deal with that side of things, eh? It's 'er job, so to speak. Meanwhile we've got to fight 'im."

John Hordle shook off his mood and grinned again. "We? I thought you were retired, Samkin?"

Sam Aylward snorted. "I'm too old to do much shooting or bashing," he said. "That doesn't mean me brain's gone soft, not yet. Since we lost Chuck at Pendleton I'm advising his boy Oak."

"Good man, Chuck. Good sojer, for all that he came late to it. He'll be missed."

Aylward nodded. He'd been First Armsman—in charge of training and leading the war levy—for the Clan from the beginning, when it was just a few dozen people; Juniper Mackenzie had found him trapped and dying of thirst near her cabin when the first Change Year was young, fruit of an early retirement and unlucky hunting trip financed by an unexpected legacy. Chuck Barstow had been his second for most of that time, a man ten years younger who'd been one of her coven before the Change and a Society fighter. He'd taken the top job after the Englishman got too stiff and slow for field command, in this age when a general had to match the stamina of twenty-year-olds on the march, and fight with his own hands now and then too.

"Good farmer as well, for all 'e came late to that, too," Aylward said.

Chuck had been a municipal gardener in Eugene by trade. Sam Aylward had been brought up on the poorest and most backward little farm in Hampshire himself, a joke and scandal to the neighborhood. They'd been *organic* when it just meant you couldn't afford anything better, not that you got premium prices from fancy restaurants and a pat on the head from the Prince of Wales. Until the land was sold out from under his father's feet to be a stockbroker's toy and the younger Aylward took the Queen's Shilling just in time for the Falklands War.

A thousand years of farming Aylwards, and I thought Dad would be the last. But what he taught me turned out to be as useful after the Change as fifteen years in the SAS, or even making bows as a hobby. All the more so as we couldn't afford the latest gear.

The exercise had ended; the Mackenzie warriors were collecting arrows or sitting crouched on their hams or leaning on their longbows or sparring with shortsword and buckler. The bow captains and commanders grouped around the standard of the antlers and crescent moon; a discussion was going on there—Mackenzie-style, which involved a lot of arm waving and raised voices. A tall fair man ended it by listing things that hadn't satisfied him.

"And by the Powers, you'll do it all over again, or my name isn't Oak Barstow Mackenzie and my totem isn't Wolf!" he finished.

"Oak did well getting the Mackenzies out at Pendleton, after Chuck died. I talked it over with Eric Larsson. But it's still bloody silly to name yourself after a tree," Hordle grumbled.

"Says the man whose kiddies are called *Beregond* and *Iorlas*," Sam commented dryly.

"Well, they'd have felt left out in Mithrilwood, loik, if we'd called them Tom and Bert," Hordle said defensively.

"We'll be sending a thousand archers east next week," Aylward said soberly. "They're about ready, I think."

"They'll be welcome," Hordle said. His thumb ran along the guard of his sword again. "Welcome and no mistake. We're stretched thin."

"Not as thin as Rudi and my Edain and their lot, wherever they are by now," Sam said quietly.

"Roit, Samkin. But thin enough. Thin enough."

CHAPTER EIGHT

"It was so *good* to receive the Sacraments again," Mathilda said. "It always makes me feel less . . . less muddled. Like looking from the top of a castle tower, after you've been in a crowded street."

"I agree," Odard replied; sincerely, she thought.

Though I was never really sure, before.

After all, an Association nobleman more or less *had* to be respectably pious in public at least, or face serious political problems; so did most at court who wanted the Princess Mathilda's favor, as opposed to her mother's.

But I think this trip has been good for Odard. A sigh. *I wish Mother would take more care for her soul . . . and I like Lady Delia, but . . . no, think about that later.*

"And it was homelike, in a way, even if they don't use as much Latin here," he said musingly. "I never thought I could be so homesick. I'll never call Castle Gervais *dull* again, if you know what I mean, your Highness."

"I do, Odard." She put a hand on his shoulder for a moment. "I asked Lady Sandra to be merciful, for my sake."

"Thank you," he said, and wretchedness broke through

his composure. "I *told* Mother . . . but she's actually *guilty*. And intriguing with the CUT isn't just politics, even treasonous politics. I know that now."

She gave the shoulder a squeeze and then turned her attention aside for a moment to let him gather himself; Odard would be bitterly ashamed of losing self-control.

They walked together through the drowsy evening warmth of the grounds, amid a sweet smell of cut grass and roses and a faint trace of incense that was still stronger than the city scents from beyond the low perimeter wall. The air lacked much of the heavy coal-smoke stink of Des Moines, at least; they burned the stuff here, but there were far fewer factories and foundries.

The State Police were discreetly spaced around the outer edge of the cathedral grounds; beyond them were the low hills of the city proper, with few buildings of any height—there evidently hadn't been many high-rises, and those few had long since been torn down for their metal. The low buildings of honest brick gave Dubuque an oddly modern look, like a post-Change settlement.

The cathedral itself reminded her of some back home; not the flamboyant Cypriot Gothic traceries that were so fashionable now that there were resources to spare for such work, but pre-Change types. It was a solid redbrick cruciform structure with a white stone front and square tower and plain windows. And the seat of an archbishop-ric, but the service had been modest, with only two parish priests officiating.

She felt a little guilty at effectively commandeering the place, but not much; she *did* have an extraordinary need. Confessing to a stranger who didn't know the context of her life had been a bit of a trial after having her own chaplain for so long, and then Father Ignatius, but . . .

Helpful, in a way. I had to organize my thoughts. And

He is no respecter of persons; it's probably good for me. And it was a relief to light a candle in thanks. Rudi made it! And Edain too, of course.

Sometimes, not very often but sometimes, receiving the Host was like opening herself to all creation in a blaze of fire that consumed and warmed at the same time. At others, she had to make herself properly reverent by an act of will. Today had been neither.

It was more like being a soldier in the garrison of a besieged castle, and getting a clap on the shoulder from his liege-lord as he walked the battlements. She struggled to control a smile. *And I'll be seeing Rudi again soon, soon!*

A white marble statue of the Virgin stood nearby, beneath a willow tree. A Benedictine in the simple belted black robe and scapular of that Order was there, kneeling; he rose and turned his hooded head towards them.

"I'm sorry, brother, we didn't mean to interrupt your—"

She stopped abruptly. A jolt ran through her, and she forced back an exclamation of joy as she recognized the dark face and slightly tilted eyes.

"Softly, my children," Father Ignatius said; his smile was warm beneath the shadow of the cloth, but brief. "Walk with me."

The two Associates were in local costume, bib overalls for Odard and a simple dress for her; there was nothing strange about two gentlefolk talking with a religious. The Church was very strong in this city, apparently an old tradition reinforced since the Change. Ignatius told his rosary with his left hand as they walked . . . possibly because he didn't have a sword hilt there right now, though he did have a dagger; that was formally part of the ordinary Benedictine habit anyway.

"You and the others can come out of hiding now,

Father," Mathilda said happily. "Rudi has the wagons! They're almost here—just across the river. He found some tribe of wild-men and convinced them to help him. God and His mother witness, nobody else could have done it!"

"Certainly I couldn't," Odard said ruefully. "You know, he makes one feel . . . inadequate, sometimes. If he wasn't so damned likeable I'd dislike him."

Ignatius chuckled dryly. "My daughter, my lord Gervais, Rudi Mackenzie is indeed a *very able young man*, as I understand you informed your . . . host. But what is your impression of the Bossman himself? You have seen a good deal of him; I know him only by reputation."

"Oh," she said. "I thought it would all be over now . . ."

Wishful thinking always lies in wait! she reminded herself; that was one of her mother's sayings. After a moment's careful thought she went on:

"He reminds me of my lord the Count of Chehalis."

"Oh, that is *so* true," Odard said. "An excellent comparison. And I know Piotr a lot better than you do, your Highness. We're friends, sort of."

"No accounting for tastes," Mathilda said dryly.

"Politics." The young noble shrugged. "As much of a friend as a mere baron can be with the son of a Count. The man's a damnable snob, among other things. Passable swordsman, useful with a boar spear and good with horses, and a lousy poet. He's no fool, either, not really, except that he's lazy—lazy between the ears, in which he does resemble Lord . . . Bossman Anthony strongly. But by God, can Piotr *drink*!"

Aloud she went on: "Only Lord . . . Bossman . . . Anthony is even worse than Piotr, because he's had *nobody* to tell him he can't have whatever he wants. I think . . .

I think he was too much indulged as a child. His mother died when he was young, too, and evidently his father had a succession of lemans who flattered him when they didn't ignore him altogether, and none of them bore children."

Ignatius nodded. "That is what my superiors here have informed me as well. That makes it . . . uncertain . . . that he will carry out his undertaking to release us all. It was originally meant as a mocking joke. Accordingly it would not be safe to reveal ourselves yet, even leaving the minions of the Corwinite cult out of consideration."

"Yes," Mathilda said. "Looking at it objectively."

"In fact, we have some information concerning the Cutters' plans," Ignatius said. "From Edgar Denson, of all people."

Odard's brow went up. "And he revealed it?"

"To Ingolf."

"For his own purposes," Mathilda guessed; there were plenty of men like Denson around court at home.

"Indeed, my child." Ignatius nodded.

No surprise to him either, Mathilda thought. *A knight-brother trains in politics.*

"Denson intends to use the Cutters' own eagerness to kill us as a tool to reinforce his influence with the Boss-man," Ignatius amplified. "He evidently fears that it isn't as unassailable as he would like people to think."

"Nobody who has to depend on Anthony is in an unassailable position," Odard said.

Mathilda nodded. "Including Anthony. I think he doesn't know himself what he's going to do from moment to moment, or whether his boredom is going to overcome his good sense."

"This is a man not used to being thwarted in anything," Ignatius said. "I have been . . . very concerned at you being so much in his company."

"Yes," Mathilda said again, unhappily.

I can't very well haul off and give the man what he deserves, though it hasn't gotten past the odd wandering hand. Yet.

"I know what you mean," she replied aloud. "So far I've just let all his hints fly over my innocent head. But I've also become good friends with Kate Heasleroad. And he *does* value Kate's good opinion of him. That restrains him, as much as anything does. He's intelligent enough to realize she's the only person he knows who wouldn't drop him— or murder him—if he weren't ruler."

Ignatius nodded. "That was well and wisely done, my child," he observed. "Both for reasons of prudence, and for itself as a kindness."

Mathilda shrugged. "She has all the drawbacks of *my* position back home, and none of the advantages. Plus she's stuck married to a man I wouldn't have if he were the only male left in creation, and she's extremely lonely. I was sorry for her. And she's not as stupid as . . . well, as I thought at first, though she's no genius either. Just very . . . inexperienced."

The priest nodded. "And I hear that my lord of Gervais has made friends as well."

"A few, Father," Odard said. "Even the Bossman . . . although I don't think he really *has* friends. But I amuse him and he likes hearing about the Association; I've never met anyone so fundamentally bored. He's fairly confident I don't want anything from him in the way of gold or land or offices, too, which must be a relief."

For once I sympathize with him, Mathilda thought; she'd had *far* too many people maneuvering for favor around her all her life, or at least as much of it as she could remember.

"Excellent," Ignatius said. "However, the *enemy* is also aware that there is a good chance that the Bossman *will* let us go . . . and even that he may let us go and keep them, or at least keep them for long enough that our trail will be cold. Therefore they will strike. And soon."

"The Bossman and his guests are well guarded," Odard said.

"From mortal enemies," Ignatius warned. "But remember the fight when you were rescued after the battle at Wendell, Princess."

Mathilda did, and shuddered. "They have a High Seeker of the Corwinite cult with them," she said.

"They do," the warrior-monk replied grimly. "And while the CUT are deluded fools, they speak truth when they say their prayers are answered. They simply don't realize by *what*."

"I could wish Heaven were a little more proactive on *our* behalf, Father," Odard said.

The priest looked at him for a long moment and then shook his head.

"No, my son, you do not. It is precisely the difference between *our* Lord and *theirs* that we are given *help*, while they are treated like puppets and tools."

Mathilda nodded. "What can we do about it? I mean, apart from cutting them into little bits. That seems to work—but we were lucky, and Mary and Ritva were lucky too."

"If luck you call it," Odard said.

They all quirked a shared smile. Dúnedain were not the only ones to read the Histories. She loved them herself; they were far more alive than the chronicles of the world just before the Change, and who knew how much truth had gone into their fashioning, since the distant morning of the world? Perhaps as much as the *Chanson de Roland* or the *Morte d'Arthur* or the "Ballad of Bowie Gizzardsbane"; nothing in the Quest of the Ring seemed as impossible as firebombs that could destroy cities, or talking by invisible waves. But the Rangers were so *literal* about it.

Then after a hesitation the soldier-monk went on:

"There is something you should know; I have permission to tell it now. Something that happened while we were in Chenrezi Monastery. I was alone in the woods on the mountainside, just before Christmas. And as I prayed—"

He told the story. Mathilda felt her eyes growing wider and wider. Ignatius was fervent, yes—you didn't become a warrior-monk of Mt. Angel without a real vocation, much less be ordained priest as well. But—

"Are you *sure*, Father?" she asked; her eyes flicked to the statue of the Virgin.

I don't doubt that you *believe it. So that's why you've been so protective since then!*

"Very, my child," Ignatius said flatly.

He handed her a note. She opened it; the Cardinal-Archbishop of Des Moines' seal was at the bottom, with a brief note in a scholar's hand that was also slightly shaky, probably with age:

I believe that Friar Ignatius has indeed been granted the vision he reports.

Mathilda blinked. *I wouldn't have disbelieved Ignatius anyway.*

He was closer to her than Father Matthew now, though she'd known her old confessor since childhood. Having a Prince of the Church confirm it did help, though.

Which means . . . She felt her heart almost stop, and her voice stuttered a little when she got her breath back:

"But . . . but I'm not that important! The Queen of Angels *in person* told you to guard and guide *me*?"

Astonishingly, Ignatius grinned. "My daughter, how important you are is something that Heaven evidently knows better than you! Doesn't He watch over the fall of a sparrow? And are you surprised that the Mother of God is wiser than Mathilda Arminger?"

Odard laughed and licked a finger, miming making a tally in the air.

"He's got you there, your Highness."

After a moment she snorted unwillingly. "Yes, he has."

"You are a human soul, and all are precious to God, whether Princess or peasant," Ignatius said gravely. "But it was strongly implied that some great purpose is served *through* you. More than your position as heir to the throne, or your role as mother of the next Lord Protector. There is something that *you* are to accomplish."

It was terrifying and glorious at the same time. She closed her eyes for an instant, taking a long deep breath, then gave the knight-brother a glance from under a raised eyebrow:

"And *you*, Father, are apparently important enough that the Lady of Sorrows drops by to tell you that you're her champion!"

The priest sighed and put his shapely, muscular hands in the sleeves of his robe, lowering his eyes for a moment. Sometimes it was irritating when clerics assumed humility, as if they used meekness as a form of rhetorical jujitsu. Ignatius didn't do that, which made it all the more effective; suddenly she felt a little ashamed at twitting him that way.

"My children, that troubles me more than I can say. I hope I am willing to take the martyr's crown of glory, if that is the will of God. But I am not so lost in vanity and pride that I *wish* for it. Even Our Lord asked that the cup pass from him. Consider the implications."

She did, and felt herself quail. Only heretics thought that Heaven's favor meant things were going to go well for you in a worldly sense—her tutors had gotten *that* lesson well home to her, starting with the example of what happened to Christ Himself. The Lord tried those He most loved; the strongest steel came from the hottest fire. The cross you were given to carry up to Heaven's gate would be just exactly as heavy as you could bear by your uttermost effort plus the essential freely offered Grace, neither more nor less. Still . . .

"If *she* says that this quest is vital, then there's really no choice," Mathilda said. "Not that there was anyway; I couldn't desert Rudi. I'm not going to turn back regardless."

"But the Queen of Heaven also told me something else," Ignatius said.

She blinked a little at his smile; he was an undemonstrative man, but for an instant there was happiness in his face that sang despite the matter-of-fact tone:

"You will be tested beyond what you can bear, unless you throw yourself upon Him and His love. In them is strength beyond all the deceits and wickedness you have seen; strength to put them behind you."

He cleared his throat. "I will do my best, your Highness."

"And so will I," Mathilda said.

"And so will I," Odard added. Then, lightly but with an undertone of wonder: "Somewhat to my own surprise."

*   *   *

"As you commanded, my lord," Rudi said with a bow and a sweep of his hand towards the piled cargo.

"Well, yes, yes, it seems to be mostly here," the Boss-man said, flicking aside the trailing dagged sleeves of his new tunic.

And he does that rather badly, Rudi thought absently. *It takes a deal of practice to wear Association court dress gracefully. I wonder if he realizes what he's letting himself in for? I could always eventually escape back to Dun Juniper, and the merciful simplicity of a kilt!*

Anthony Heasleroad paced down the line of pictures with the bells on the upturned toes of his giltwork shoes jingling. A clerk walked behind him, checking off items on a clipboard compiled from museum catalogues of the old world. Some of the paintings were stacked three or four deep, with the finest on the outside. Other treasures besides stood on the lids of the crates that had held them, with wisps of the hay padding still drifting about; cups of carved alabaster, jewels, icons that were themselves jewels of paint and gold leaf, ancient hand-copied books on parchment opened to display the faded glories of their illuminated capitals, worked Church vessels of precious metals, a lotus blossom wrought from ancient ivory in a style as alien as it was beautiful . . .

"Nearly all of the items on the list. My lord," Edgar Denson added hastily, and then: "Your Majesty."

Rudi Mackenzie kept his face politely blank. Evidently there had been changes in the court etiquette of Iowa, since he'd left.

And to be sure, I have a fair idea whose ideas those ideas were!

Kate Heasleroad was wearing a fair imitation of Mathilda's cotte-hardi. Some of her ladies-in-waiting were in less skillful ones; they looked a little out of place in the Dubuque City Hall's plain whitewashed assembly chambers, as much as their floral perfumes did among its faint smell of old lamp oil and harsh soap. The city itself seemed to be ruled partly by an elected Council, all of them present in their best old-fashioned clothing and looking extremely nervous, which wasn't unreasonable at all in the presence of their—

Whimsical, Rudi thought. *Sure, and whimsical is the best way to think of it.*

—whimsical ruler. The Emergency Coordinator of the city looked only slightly less so, and that because he was at court in Des Moines more often.

Rudi caught Matti's eye as he went briefly down on one knee; the courtesy might have been to Iowa's ruler . . . or to her.

The which is no substitute for a hug and a kiss, he thought. *But as close as we can come. For now.*

The impulse sparkled in his eyes, and he could see she sensed it; her smile held a reproof as warm as the wind in a blossoming orchard, and as full of a delicate promise.

He'd had enough time to get his good kilt and plaid out of their baggage, and his ruffled shirt and short silver-buttoned Montrose jacket and raven-plumed Scots bonnet. For some reason she was in the male version of Portlander court dress tonight: tight hose, tooled shoes with upcurled toes sporting little silver bells, brown velvet tunic with long dagged sleeves dropping down from the elbows and the Lidless Eye of her house on the breast in rubies and jet, jewels on her belt and dagger hilt. That she and Odard were armed was a good sign in itself.

Her face stayed grave, but with her eyes on him he was

suddenly acutely conscious of his own appearance in a way that was rare for him.

Good work, he mouthed silently, shifting his eyes from her to Iowa's ruler to show what he meant.

"And you got the savages to haul them back?" the Bossman said.

"Yes, my lord," Rudi said, and gave a brief—and colorful—account of his interruption of the Knifer ambush and the horse-stealing expedition that followed.

"Ah, I wish I'd been there!" Anthony Heasleroad said, his face animated.

"I've no doubt you'd have been like a lion in battle, your Majesty," Rudi said.

And a roar of laughter at this point would be less than diplomatic, so, he thought. *There's an element of truth to it, lions being cats, and so probably more concerned with food, sleep and fornication than heroism.*

Being diplomatic—lying credibly—was part of being a courtier or ruler, and there were certain things you just didn't say to a strange overlord.

I wouldn't trust you on latrine detail, much less a raid was one of them.

He recalled Aunt Judy remarking that a mind healer was in much the same position as a courtier, having to think carefully before talking: for example you'd rarely hear one say *Brigid come in splendor, no* wonder *your mother never loved you*!

Not aloud, no matter how hard she thought it.

Heasleroad nodded to the clerk: "See that they're packed up and sent to the House in Des Moines immediately. We can settle where to put them later."

"Your Majesty, why not a public exhibition?" Denson said. "That's what we originally planned."

"Yes, yes," the Bossman said.

Then he brightened, taken out of his usual peevish boredom:

"We could have it on my birthday. That'll leave a month and a half for getting ready. We could have a public feast, with pigs and oxen roasted in the streets, and a parade, and square dancing, and then the viewing. And . . . and we could have a, a revision of titles at the same time. Governor is so old-fashioned and Bossman . . . Bossman is a bit *rustic*."

"That would be an excellent idea, my lord," Denson said.

A pained smile hid an expression that disagreed violently with his words; he shot Mathilda a venomous glance before he went on:

"Perhaps we could have festivities every year on that day . . . a different theme every year. This year it could be . . . *the Majesty of the Heasleroads, God's plan for Iowa*."

"Good!" Heasleroad said. "See to the details, Edgar. Now—" he looked at the city council and clapped his hands together. "What about dinner?"

As they walked away towards the banqueting hall, Rudi looked over his shoulder; the State Police officer's face showed naked irritation for an instant.

A wise king doesn't show disrespect to his lords, Rudi thought. *Matti's mother is polite even when she's going to kill one of hers; as she says, the cost of courtesy is low and the return often very high indeed. You've much to learn if you'd keep your dynasty safe, my lord Anthony.*

He fell in beside Mathilda. "Not the time to ask for leave to depart?" he said quietly.

"No," she said. "Time to watch for an opportunity, then bolt. Better to ask forgiveness than seek permission."

A troubled smile. "And we'd better not spend too

much time together. The Bossman is, ummm, not a very reasonable man."

He's a spoiled baby in a man's body, Rudi thought, with a snort.

Then he nodded and drifted away, which the local informality made easy. For all Matti's brief lessons and the Bossman's apparent enthusiasm, the Iowans hadn't yet got to the point where courtiers went to dinner in pairs carefully graded by rank, preceded by musicians blowing trumpets and heralds shouting out titles.

The which I always found either amusing or irritating, when I was in Association territory, he thought.

The hall they entered was probably used for something else most of the time; there were basketball hoops at each end, mostly hidden by colorful bunting, and the walls were covered by flags and banners, the floor by rich but mismatched carpets. The banquet itself was as elaborate as an anxious city could make it, with a blaze of expensive wax candles in silver holders, snowy linen and fine china and cutlery, crystal bowls full of flowers and fruit. Carvers were at work, their stations in the center of the square of tables bearing roast pigs and smoking quarters of beef, racks of glazed ribs, roast turkeys and ducks, pheasants and chickens and grouse in the splendor of their crisp golden skins, stuffed baked fish as long as a tall man's leg . . .

A stream of platters with made dishes came out from the kitchens. Rudi sat willingly enough, six positions down from Kate Heasleroad's left hand and eight from Mathilda on the Bossman's right. At least he'd get a good dinner out of this. Ingolf was tactfully absent . . . and had other work to do, to be sure. If Edgar Denson's plan was to work, they needed a bit of extra muscle, beyond what the Southsiders could provide; and Edain would have to lead *them*, he being the one they knew best after Rudi himself.

And after the Southside Freedom Fighters' idea of cooking, this will be very welcome, indeed. Brigid Sheaf-Mistress, how long it's been since I tasted vegetables or bread!

He tore open a warm roll from one of the baskets and buttered it, the rich yeasty scent of the interior filling his mouth with a rush of hunger-spit; he had to swallow before he could bite into it, for fear of drooling down his good plaid. He followed it with a selection of salad, boiled new potatoes left alone in their own perfection, then a little beef in a cream and herb sauce.

There was an added spice to the food, as well. Right down at the other end of the head table were the red-robed High Seeker from Corwin, and Major Graber of the Sword of the Prophet in the rough blue uniform his service wore beneath armor. The server there was setting out slices from the haunch of a suckling pig, but from their glares neither of the Church Universal and Triumphant's men was going to enjoy his food.

Rudi looked at the emptied plate before him, added two slices of roast pork with crackling and mashed potatoes and steamed beets, and covered the meat and potatoes with gravy before happily lifting a forkful to his mouth. It was good honest food, fine materials well prepared, if a little blander than the cooks at Dun Juniper would have made it—no herb crust on the meat, for starters, or chives and minced onion with the potatoes. And nothing like the complicated cooking Portland's nobility favored, where art warred with indigestion.

He chewed blissfully, looking at the Cutters again and nodding good cheer, raising his wineglass to them. Was it his imagination, or did wisps of steam float over the High Seeker's head?

"*Is deacair a bheith ag feadail agus ag ithe mine,*" he murmured, sipping the indifferent vintage.

A plump Farmer next to him stopped putting butter on his broccoli and looked at him.

"What's that?" he said.

"A saying of my mother's people: *It's hard to whistle and eat at the same time,*" Rudi replied, and got a blank look and uncertain smile. "And harder still to swallow when your gut is so tight with rage it aches. Bad for your digestion, that is; bad for your nerves; even worse for your disposition."

And to be sure, it was better to eat before a fight, within reason, for the bit of added endurance. A prickling ran along the back of his neck as Graber narrowed his cold eyes; even without Ingolf's warnings he would have suspected that if Bossman proved cooperative about the quest departing, the Cutters would not.

Indeed not. So, eat, but not too much, he thought, waving aside a second round of the serving platter and taking a slice of sour-cherry pie instead.

The Gods were at play tonight, and he one of the pieces they moved on Their board. He dropped a scoop of the ice cream on the pie.

Something sweet, for quick energy. It wouldn't do to be heavy and slow.

"Right, listen up," Ingolf Vogeler said.

He looked over the men his friend Jack Heuisink had brought from the family estate, Victrix Farm.

Well, there's Jack. He doesn't look like he's let himself rust.

The heir to Victrix was in his midtwenties, a little shorter than Ingolf—just under six feet—but broad-shouldered and slim-hipped, with cropped dark red hair and a broad snub-nosed face, moving like a lynx. The dozen Heuisink retainers grouped around him in the dimness of the empty warehouse amid the ghostly smells of pine tar and fermented soy and freight more nameless, faces underlit by the blue flame of the alcohol lantern he'd put on an upturned barrel.

The household troops were from Victrix Farm's National Guard Security Detail; what they called "deputies" back around his own home in the Free Republic of Richland.

And they actually look as if they'll be useful, not just glorified muscle for keeping the vakis in line, he thought, tapping his sword hand thoughtfully on the plate vambrace on his left forearm.

Jack was a few years younger than the man from Wisconsin; about Rudi's age, in fact. They'd met when he ran away to join Vogeler's Villains up north in the Republic of Marshall during the Sioux War, and he'd spent more than a year with the free company Ingolf commanded in that . . .

Fucked Up Beyond All Recognition exercise in futile butchery and pointless destruction, which ended with the survivors on both sides right where they started, just poorer and less numerous and occasionally missing important body parts, Ingolf thought.

It wasn't the only war Ingolf had fought in that finished that way, either; about par for the course, in fact. That was one reason he'd gotten out of the hired-soldier business.

But it was sure educational, if you survived. Real educational.

It had given Jack actual combat experience, and the Heuisinks' men were notably tougher-looking than the general run of their kind in Iowa, and almost certainly better trained; their coal-scuttle helmets and mail shirts were carefully browned, and their horse bows and long cavalry shetes looked like they'd seen use. Either Jack had worked them hard, or the Heuisinks had hired men who'd seen border duty beforehand, or both. Probably both.

Most important, none of them looked too nervous, just serious and paying careful attention; one was stolidly finishing a ham-and-cheese sandwich and licking a stray squirt of mustard off his fingers as he waited. All of them had given Ingolf a quick professional appraisal; a few had nodded in sober recognition when they met his eyes. Not of who he was, but of what.

And if they are nervous, it's because they're not used to cities, not because it's their first fight, Ingolf thought.

Aloud: "Jack, you're in tactical command."

And they know you, so they're less likely to run screaming if something real bad happens.

"Come fast when I call," he finished aloud.

Jack nodded; he raised his voice a little when he replied and came to attention and saluted smartly:

"Yes, sir, Captain Vogeler!"

One of his eyes drooped a little in a wink as Vogeler returned the gesture. None of these men knew Ingolf from Adam except possibly in Jack's war stories, but they'd grown up around the Heuisinks. None of them were going to be much impressed by the fact that he'd been a paid soldier and salvager all his adult life; they *certainly* wouldn't give a damn about his birth into a Sheriff's family in the wilds of Wisconsin, which was desolate dirt-faced yokeldom's native land to an Iowan. Deference by the master's son and heir would make them a lot more likely to do what Ingolf told them, which could be crucial.

Christ, I wish I had my old Villains with me, he thought.

Not for the first time, and only partly because they'd all been close comrades whom he missed bitterly even now; that had come from years of serving together, and they'd all known what they were doing and known each other's capacities.

Or I wish that we were doing this with just Rudi's bunch. Yah, yah, there's only ten of us, but at least we've been in hairy situations together, and I can be sure they're all first-class. These guys are strangers, except for Jack. And when I did know him he was a wild youngster, not a married man with kids. Hope he hasn't changed too much.

Worrying about the mission as a whole kept him from worrying about Mary, too. She was up there on the roof-tops right now. Or possibly on her way back already, depending when the Cutters made their move.

Goddamn Edgar Denson and his plan. What was it Doc Pham used to say when someone got too fancy?

The Readstown physician had doubled as a teacher in the hamlet's school and director of their amateur theatricals. When the stage directions got complex he'd say—

"Too many notes, Herr Mozart." That about describes it.

Denson was smart, no two ways about that. But he wasn't a soldier, not really; he was an intriguer and politician who did some fighting now and then. Certainly not one who'd had years of firsthand experience of how easy it was for the wheels to come *off* a plan when it met the one the other guy was driving.

Your enemy always has a plan too, the swine. That's why we call them "the enemy."

"Thanks again," he said to Jack, as they shook hands one last time before they buckled their gear.

The other man's hand lacked much of the little finger

and the tip of the next; he'd gotten that putting it between a Sioux tomahawk and Ingolf's face.

"Hell, Captain, you saved my life a lot more often than
I saved yours, back when. Mainly because you knew what
you were doing and I didn't."

Ingolf shrugged. "It was my job. But you've got family responsibilities now, Jack."

The Iowan cinched his sword belt and shrugged to
settle it on his hips; he was wearing a jointed two-piece
breastplate and flexible tassets to protect his thighs. Iowa
had the best metalworkers in this part of the world, and
his family could afford the finest.

"That's really why I'm here," Jack replied. "My kids
are going to be around for the next sixty years, God willing, and by then they'll have grandkids. These Cutters . . .
they may not get to Iowa soon, but if they aren't stopped
now they'll be here in force *someday*."

Ingolf nodded. "Christ, Jack, why aren't there more
who can see that?"

Jack grinned. "You're expecting people to be *sensible*
now, Captain? How you've changed!"

"Point. I wish Mary and Ritva would get back here,"
he said. "What's going on out there?"

Ritva Havel raised her head, slowly, leaving just her eyes
above the ridge of the roof and brought the night glasses
to them; beside her Mary used a monocular.

Their heads and most of their faces were covered by a
knitted cap of wool made in the irregular very dark taupe
color that faded into an urban background better than
black. It was full night—the moon was down—and from
above the gaslights at the corners of the streets hid more
than they revealed, killing much of her night sight no

matter how carefully Ritva squinted and looked aside. The building where the Cutters were quartered was unlit . . . which was significant in itself.

She took a deep breath, feeling her blood pump and senses extend themselves outward. It wasn't particularly nice air in itself—this town burned coal too, like most in Iowa, and it was heavy with wet and still too warm for comfort. Sweat trickled and ran down her flanks, making the coarse dark linsey-woolsey and supple leather of her Dúnedain working garb cling and chafe.

But at least I'm doing *something instead of sitting and worrying!* she thought. *Real Ranger work.*

The door opened. There was only a moment's gleam of muted light, noticeable because it caught at the edges of honed steel. The Cutters' armor was partly metal, but mostly lacquered leather the color of dried blood, not very conspicuous in the dark. They came out in disciplined silence, with only a very slight clatter of harness and bootheels on pavement. A rough count showed forty or fifty; not all the survivors of the troop Graber and the Cutter magus had brought east with them, but well over half.

And unless Denson lied to us, about now he'll—

A brighter light flickered and then steadied. Edgar Denson of the State Police strolled forward, half a dozen of his men behind him, their shetes drawn. According to the *plan* he'd insisted on he was going to hold the Corwinites in conversation for a few moments, enough for the two Dúnedain to flit back and put the rest into motion. She wouldn't put it past him to have some elaborate triple cross in mind, but so far, so good.

She glanced aside and met her sister's one eye above the face-covering mask-hood. Their thoughts ran in perfect harmony:

Just a moment more, to make sure Mr. Denson is doing what he promised.

"Halt," the Iowan said to the Cutter party. "Care to explain why you're all out at night, and armed?"

Graber was in the lead, but the red-robed Seeker pushed past him before he could do more than clap his hand to the hilt of his blade.

"I—see—you," the Cutter priest said.

Fingers of icy slime caressed her at the sound. Memories cracked open like a too-fresh scab, although it had been a year since that encounter in the snow-thick forests of the Teton slopes. It wasn't fear that made her want to flee the Cutter priest's presence, exactly. More an elemental *disgust*. This was something that shouldn't be in the world, and it made everything around her suddenly seem alien, alien and slightly decayed. Some part of her expected to smell rot from her own flesh.

"What?" Denson said.

"I—see—you," the Prophet's man said again, staring into his eyes.

The voice sounded *suffused*, as if it was swollen with freight beyond what words could bear, as if meaning itself would tear apart at the weight and leave words to rattle empty through human skulls.

"You—are—mine. Eternally. For—a—beginning."

Ritva could hear Mary's breath hiss out, a slight sound in the night. It had been a Seeker who cut the eye out of her face. And Ritva who killed him, which had been like a battle in a bad dream, against an opponent who wouldn't *die*. Denson had courage. He cleared his throat, but when he spoke his voice was calm and sardonic.

"Hey, don't you guys know voodoo only works on people who *believe* in it?"

The Seeker laughed. There was no joy in the sound;

listening to it made you doubt the *possibility* of joy for a second. But there was considerable satisfaction.

"Does your sword only cut those with faith in it?" he said, in tones more human. "You have pledged and taken the fruits. Now all is demanded."

Sorta human, Ritva thought. *Sorta-kinda*.

Denson bristled. "I never took anything from you!"

The laugh sounded again, and Ritva fought an impulse to drop the glasses and jam the heels of her hands over her ears.

"We have no need to *buy* men's souls. You *give* yourselves to Us. And you have listened to our counsel for a very long time."

"Fuck you, you lunatic!"

The Seeker shrugged. "What is that you wear around your waist, man?" he asked.

"It's what I use to hold up my pants and for my shete, when I'm not pointing it at some asshole I've suddenly decided needs killing," the secret policeman said, his voice gone hard.

He waggled the long curved horseman's weapon, the point rising until the razor-edged six inches on the back of the blade hovered near the Cutter's throat.

"You may have lost the concept out in Montana along with regular baths and brushing your teeth, but it's called a *belt* in this part of the world," he went on. "Anymore questions about civilized fashions?"

"You lie," the High Seeker said casually. "It isn't a belt; it is a giant rattlesnake. What a fool you are, to wear a deadly serpent around your body!"

Denson started to laugh himself. Then Ritva saw his face shift, as one hand dropped to his midriff. He gave a single high shriek and dropped his sword. He struck convulsively at himself before the steel rang on the pavement, scrabbling and pounding . . . and then pitched to the ground, twitching. Her own breath caught as she saw his purple, distended face and the foam on his lips. Then her throat clenched tighter still, as her eyes dropped to his right hand.

It bled, where the palm was pierced by the loosened pin of his belt buckle.

"Thiach iluuvea gail, Heru Denson," Mary observed, dropping back into Sindarin.

"No, he isn't very bright. Wasn't."

"He wouldn't listen to us, and now look what it got him. And us."

"And there goes our crucial delay. Well, maybe Denson's retainers will attack them—"

The men behind Denson wavered, got a good look at their commander, then threw away their weapons and took to their heels. From the sounds they were making, the State Police troopers didn't intend to stop until they hit the Mississippi—or Nebraska, if that street led west. She very much doubted they planned to stop and inform the authorities of what had happened . . . not that anyone would believe them in time if they did.

I don't know if I believe it myself, she thought in some corner of her mind. *There are stranger things in the Histories, but this is the Fifth Age of the World. Or maybe the Sixth!*

All the Cutters except the Seeker formed into a column, quick-timing down the night-empty street in a harsh clatter of leather and hobnails on pavement. The Corwinite priest stayed a moment and raised his arm until it pointed at the two Dúnedain, where they *should* have been invisible in the blackness.

"There—is—no—escape—for—one—they—have— touched."

Mary nodded. "Uh-oh," she said, very softly.

"I know what *uh-oh* means," Ritva replied. "It means *we're fucked*."

A tile grated under a foot behind them, where the grapnel holding their climbing rope was hooked into the roof's gutter.

"*Kill,*" the High Seeker said.

Then he turned and walked after the troopers of the Sword of the Prophet. The two Dúnedain whirled, as the trio of men swung up onto the edge of the roof. Curved knives gleamed in their hands, and the moonlight glittered from the steel and from eyes empty of humanity. Those eyes blinked in perfect unison. They weren't Seekers, just Corwinite soldiers of the Sword, but something of the red-robed magus was there in those blank faces. A nullity that was less than emptiness, one that hungered for existence and hated it at the same time.

It's as if they're contagious, *somehow.*

Ritva had a sudden flash of memory. Long ago she'd been on her belly behind a fallen fir tree in the mountains east of Mithrilwood, watching a pair of scrub jays feeding their nestlings. Something had made her turn her head, and a rattlesnake as long as her forearm had been there, behind the same sun-warmed log. It had turned its long patterned head and looked into her eyes. Looking into the eyes of the Church Universal and Triumphant's men was like that . . .

Except that she had a feeling that if their eyes stayed locked long enough the same reptile gaze would be on both ends.

"Varda and Manwë aid me!" Ritva said. Then: "*Im suu ei thiach men!*"

Sweat suddenly drenched her, but she felt better: *I fart in your general direction* might not be as dignified as a call on the Lord and Lady, but it helped.

Beside her Mary was still, motionless with something beyond Ranger training, as if she was once more in the Seeker's grip as she had been that day the eye was cut out of her head. The bow in Ritva's hands came up. If she had thought about the action it would have stopped, but she forced her mind *not* to consider it. Ten thousand hours of practice had graven the movement into brain and bone and muscle, as much as breathing or walking. There was the slightest creak, as yew and horn and sinew bent and flexed and stretched.

"Kill," they whispered through identical smiles, their voices overlapping so that the sound was a sibilant blur: "Kill/kill/kill/*Kkkiiiillll*."

And attacked. Their movements were jerky, but perfect and unerring on the irregular surface of the curved tiles. Behind them *something* moved, planes of shining jet that receded into infinity, as if constructs greater than worlds *squeezed* down to interact with the tiny space of the planet, of this rooftop in one place and time. The soot-covered laurel-leaf arrowhead touched the cutout through the riser of her recurve, right above the black-gloved knuckle of her left hand. The fingers on the bowstring seemed locked, but she breathed out and let the waxed linen cord roll off the pads.

Snap.

The string lashed at the bracer on the inside of her left forearm. Achingly slow, the arrow began its flight; she could see the way the fletching rippled, and how the slight curve in the fashion the feathers were set to the cedarwood made the whole spin as it flew. She *couldn't* be seeing it move; the distance was less than thirty feet, and the shaft would be traveling at two hundred feet per second. In this darkness it should be a blurred streak at most.

The central attacker's body flexed loosely as the point approached, as if he was moving backward even before it struck. When it did he swayed like a whip being snapped, and looked down for an instant at the narrow thirty-inch shaft transfixing him just beside the breastbone.

He's not going to stop, Ritva knew.

Then he did, but the fixed smile on his face did not alter as blood runneled out his nose and hung in threads from his lips.

"Not—yet—to—rule—so—many," he said. *"Soon. We—will—be—abroad—and—loose."*

And collapsed forward. The others continued their herky-jerky advance. Ritva bounded back frantically, her soft elf-boots gripping at the roof ridge as she dropped her bow and the longsword hissed out in the two-handed grip.

"Lacho Calad!" she cried.

There was a wheeze of relief in it too, for Mary was moving as well, the ball and hook whirling on the ends of the length of fine chain she unwrapped from her waist.

"Drego Morn!"

Her sister completed the Ranger war cry. *Flame Light! Flee Night!*

CHAPTER NINE

"Sure, and I don't think your Majesty should be unguarded," Rudi said, shifting uneasily with the prickling feeling along his spine.

Kate Heasleroad came back into the room at that instant, and Rudi breathed a sigh of relief, at least in the privacy of his mind. Her husband looked at her with annoyance, as if he'd been hoping she'd stay in the nursery. And he'd been dropping very pointed hints that Odard and the Mackenzie should leave, once his genuine interest in the conversation about heraldry had died.

And not *hinting that Matti should leave,* Rudi noted. *Sure, and it will be a great inconvenience if I must snap the man's neck after all the trouble we've gone to, conciliating him. Still, better than leaving it for Matti to do. Hmmm. Given surprise we could* probably *cut our way to the docks . . .*

"Tommie's sleeping soundly now, darling," Kate said. "Annette's with him."

These rooms were part of the Emergency Coordinator's chambers; in the terms Matti's people used, where the Count of Dubuque usually had his apartments, that worthy being turned out now for his liege-lord's convenience.

Or his lord's convenience and his own inconvenience, he thought wryly, nodding pleasantly at Kate.

One of the ways Sandra Arminger dealt with difficult vassals or ones she suspected of disloyalty was to *visit* them. With the whole court in train, until the hospitality drove them to the brink of bankruptcy, swallowing the resources that might otherwise be spent seditiously. The best part of that jest was that they couldn't do anything but profess delight at the honor and spend on feasts, tournaments and entertainers as if money were water. Juniper Mackenzie had been heard to say that Sandra knew more ways of killing a cat than drowning it in a bucket of cream.

Rudi didn't think Anthony was bright enough to come up with that idea on his own, but . . .

But it is interesting to see that another ruler could stumble on something of the sort by accident. I'll have to be keeping that in mind, if Edain is determined I'm to be High King.

He tried to make the thought light, as if it was a joke, but he had a sinking feeling that was what the Powers—some of them, at least—really had in mind.

And I was afraid of the burden of being Chief of the Mackenzies alone! Hmmmm, though. A High King of Montival would have *to visit about much of the time, wouldn't he? With so many different peoples, and them separated by wilderness and of such different customs and Gods and laws, he'd have to show himself. But not so as to be a burden . . . unless there was some bad and wicked person of note that called for it . . . later, later.*

"And a charming young lad your Tommie is," Rudi said, with a smile that was sincere enough.

Children that age usually were, like puppies or kittens; it was how they made people put up with the nuisance and hard work they entailed. Rudi hoped the boy would have a more normal childhood than his father, and come out of it more of a man—not to mention more of a ruler.

Kate Heasleroad smiled back at him, almost involuntarily; at least Tommie would have *her*.

Behind her Matti mouthed: *You're being* charming *again, dammit!*

Rudi's eldest half sister Eilir was deaf; he'd learned lipreading from her, and it was a useful skill whether you could hear or no.

The Coordinator's quarters were elegant, in a cool style of pastel fabrics and muted colors and blond wood that was not at all the Bossman's usual taste, judging by what he remembered of the throne room in the State Capitol; the modifications that had turned this whole second floor into one were skillful, arched ways linking large rooms.

"And for his sake as well as your own, you should have more guards about you," Rudi said.

"There are plenty of guards," the Bossman said.

He waved a hand and knocked over a glass on the side table beside him. A servant stepped forward noiselessly and swept it away, mopping up the spilled wine and vanishing again.

Rudi had lived several months a year in Portland and Castle Todenangst and other holds of the Protectorate for much of his boyhood and youth; he was used to personal service, if not overfond of it. But while lowly household folk in Portland's territories were sometimes treated roughly by their lords, they weren't expected to be invis-

ible. Their presence was part of an Associate's consequence.

This self-effacement put his teeth on edge for some
reason. It was as if they were trying to mimic the vanished
machinery of the ancient world, that produced the fruits
of work without human hands and will.

Aloud he went on: "To be sure, but the guards are not
here within arm's reach. A dozen yards away can be far
too far, if you take my meaning, my lord. I don't think
those men from Corwin are to be trusted."

"I don't *trust* anyone," the Bossman said, his voice
careless and a little slurred.

*The which is probably true, and makes you as helpless as
a babe. The whole secret of the thing being to know who you
can* trust, *as well as who you* cannot.

"And I don't like having men in iron shirts clanking
about in the same room. Besides, this place is secure," the
Iowan went on.

There was something to that. The windows facing out
a story over the street were broad, intact pre-Change
plate glass panels that ran on grooves set in little wheels,
but the wrought-iron scrollwork over them was more recent. It was ornamental, flowing designs of vines and
flowers, but it also gave no space wider than a man's arm,
without blocking too much of the light in daytime, and
it was set very solidly indeed into steel plates bolted
around the openings.

All the windows in this building were like that, except
the ones on the ground floor; they'd been bricked in until
they were narrow slits, and there was nothing on that
level but storage and guardrooms, workshops and kitchens and armories. It wasn't quite a fortress, but it would
do fine against a rioting mob, particularly with people

shooting crossbows through the openings at anyone on the ground outside.

The Bossman's voice was slurred and his plump face was flushed and sweaty, despite the coolness of the damp air that came through the open panels.

"Always guards," he said, and there was suddenly a wistful note in his voice. "Gotta have 'em. Must be nice not to have to, like you guys. Just going where you want, doing what you please."

"Oh, sometimes I'd have been glad of a few guards," Rudi said cheerfully. "And there are drawbacks to being footloose and fancy-free, your Majesty. Why, I remember—"

Thock.

The sound was faint, but Rudi recognized it instantly; an arrowhead or crossbow-bolt striking in bone. The breath hissed out between his teeth; that was *not* part of the plan. The Cutters should have been *stopped* outside, with Rudi's friends—and the Heuisinks, Ingolf's allies— doing the stopping and the State Police swooping down to halt the brawl. Then the Bossman would wash his hands of them and expel both . . .

Something went wrong, Rudi thought, as his hand went to the hilt of a sword that wasn't there. *But as Sir Nigel says, something always does. Or as Sam Aylward puts it, sodding pear-shaped is the shape to expect.*

"Your Majesty, I think you'd better call those guards of yours," he said quietly, but his voice was pitched to the level of command. "Call them *now*."

Anthony Heasleroad was no fool; Rudi had reluctantly come to that conclusion some time ago.

But if those who had the raising of him had set out to ruin him, they could have done no better. If I was a Christian, I'd attribute it to the sins of the fathers. Or if I were a Buddhist like the good Rimpoche Dorje, I'd conclude he must have been a monster *in some previous life.*

He watched the warning sink through layers of drink-fuddled incomprehension, and then through a gauze of arrogance deeper still.

"Butler!" the Bossman called.

Then as Rudi began to move: "What the hell are you doing, you red-haired beanpole?"

A long scream came from below, where the stairs gave on the main hall. Then a shattering clash of steel on steel, and the sharp hard banging of blades on the leather of shields, and a war cry that made his lips peel back from his teeth:

"Cut! Cut! *Cut!*"

And another scream: not of pain this time, but of horror, an animal cry of disgust rising into the squeal a rabbit gave when the talons closed on it. Rudi leapt to the door and struck it with his shoulder. There was no time for subtlety now. It crashed open, and revealed a man falling backward with his arms flailing; he met another at the head of the stairs and both tumbled down them.

Rudi's hand moved with blurring speed, sweeping their swords out of the rack the guardsmen had been standing sentinel over and leaping back in a ten-foot bound from a standing start. By then Odard and Mathilda were by the door themselves, slamming it shut again and shooting home the bar; the baron of Gervais whirled a heavy chair over and jammed the top home beneath the brackets. Anthony Heasleroad was looking at them blank-faced, then with a dawning suspicion.

The bundle of weapons in Rudi's hands included the Bossman's shete. It had a good deal of silver and niello filigree on the sheath, and jewels set in the guard, but the blade was steel as good as any Rudi had ever seen. He tossed the weapon at the Iowan ruler, still in the scabbard. The heavyset young man gripped it clumsily, staggered back into his chair and rose again, drawing the weapon with a flick of the wrist that showed some skill.

Though I'd swear he lacks the endurance to use it for more than one or two strokes. But at least it'll convince him faster than words that we're *not out to kill him.*

"What's the meaning of this?" he said as Rudi followed the throw by handing the two Portlanders their blades, then raised his voice: "Guards! *Guards!*"

The sound of fighting had died away, far faster than it should have; the sudden coppery smell of blood was shockingly strong. The prickling along Rudi's spine intensified, and his scalp crept, as if his hair was trying to bristle as did a lion's mane before battle. Everything looked normal, but he could feel *gaps* about him, as if bits and pieces of the world were vanishing from the edge of sight, only to reappear when his eyes moved in that direction.

I've felt something a little like this, he thought. *On Samhain, and in some of the rites.*

Not often, and never so strongly. He was no great loremaster, for all that the Otherworld had touched his life often. He knew little more than any Initiate.

But this feels wrong, *so it does. Someone is using Art, but without any thought for the order of the world, or the Law of Threefold Return. That will fall upon him in the end, but before then what evil may it do!*

"The guards—" he began.

A crash came from the door. That barrier wasn't the massive fortress-style portals that closed the exterior of the building. Carved panels splintered under the blows of heavy blades—at this moment you remembered that the shete had started out as a chopping tool a mere generation before. The steel flicked through in glimpses of brightness against dark oiled ornamental walnut. When the upper panel was a sagging mass of splinters a man's helmeted head completed the ruin, *butting* through the remains.

Heasleroad cried out in relief. "Captain Butler! What is going—"

The guardsman looked at him, smiling through the gashes the splinters had cut in his flesh; one eye leaked clear matter down his cheek, running in thick threads through the red of blood.

"Kill," he said, his grinning teeth wet. *"Kill—them—all. Kill—"*

"Happy to oblige," Odard de Gervais snarled, and struck.

He was a man of middling size, but strong and very quick. The longsword blurred down in a silver arc; there was a heavy wet sound, and underneath it a crack of parting bone.

"Haro!" he shouted, and then the war cry of his House: "Face Gervais, *face death!*"

The head sagged free, held by only a shred of flesh. Blood spurted out into the room, but for one long instant the body's hands scrabbled beside the severed neck, trying to enlarge the hole through the broken wood. Then it went limp, and other hands pulled it back.

A billhook smashed through; Odard cut again, but this time the blade skidded with a shower of sparks off a sheath of steel wire wound around the wooden shaft behind the business end of the polearm. The weapon jerked back and then probed at him, thrust two-handed with a savage, skillful snap. He skipped back just in time, or a little later than that; the sharp point of the spike touched his breast, and a dark stain spread on the colorful cloth of the jupon.

"Here!" Mathilda cried.

She tossed him a shield; there were two, done up for Anthony Heasleroad's amusement in the Lidless Eye of the Armingers, with the baton of cadency across one, and the *mon* symbol of the House of Liu—the Chinese ideograph for *Poland*, for his father's mother, silver on red on black on the other. There hadn't been any reason to make the shields genuine, but there hadn't been any reason not to, either, and Mathilda had taken full advantage of the Bossman's expense account.

So these were the real article, elongated triangles four feet from rounded point to curved top, made of plywood and bullhide and covered in thin sheet metal, with the padded loops on the inside parallel to the length.

"Bless your foresight, Matti!" Rudi said. "Flank me— not in plain sight of the door!"

The two Associates took up the stance Portlander men-at-arms used for fighting on foot; left fist at chin height, which put the upper edge of the shield just under the eyes and the point at shin level, and swords over their heads with the hilts forward. Rudi had no protection but the little buckler clipped to the side of his longsword's sheath. He took that in his hand, some part of him wishing they had all their fighting gear at hand; with a western knight's head-to-toe panoply the three of them could hold the doorway in turn, and only be badly hurt by accident.

You fight with what you have, when you have to, he thought.

Rudi crouched and duckwalked towards the door, keeping below the level that could be seen through the ruins of the upper panel; it wasn't easy to stay low when you stood six-two in your stocking feet. The billhook pulled back, and pulled a chunk of the splintered wood free with the curved hook on its rear.

The Bossman of Iowa moved forward, with the shete in his hand.

"*Get back, you fool!*" Rudi barked.

Even then there was some remote corner of his mind that felt a relief at the frank words, like the bursting of a boil.

"*There's nothing you can do here! Look to your woman and your son!*"

Kate Heasleroad added her voice to his; a little to Rudi's surprise it wasn't shrill with fear at all. She was in the far corner of the room near the entrance to the nursery corridor, with an upturned table sheltering her and her own body between the edged metal and the path to her child. Her eyes were wide with fear and her fair skin turned milk pale, but it was controlled fear, and she kept them fixed on the doorway to follow the action there. Her husband's face was crimson, flushed with rage as much as with drink.

So he's no coward, Rudi thought. *What a time to develop the virtues!*

Mathilda acted where Rudi couldn't; she leapt forward just as a bow snapped on the landing outside, and threw herself in front of the Iowan. There was a hard *crack* as the point punched into her shield. It hit at a slant, penetrating shallowly and giving a malignant whine as vibration damped itself in metal and wood. She hit the Bossman under the short ribs with the pommel of her sword to stun resistance, threw him back with an expert heave of shoulders and legs, and used the motion to whirl herself back out of the line of fire. Only then did she snap the arrowhead off with another blow of the hilt, and the inch or two of shaft that had followed it through the shield.

"Haro, *Portland*!" she cried in a valkyr shout as she took stance again. *"Holy Mary for Portland!"*

Two more arrows plowed through the space she'd vacated; they went over Rudi's head with a vicious *whissst* of cloven air like angry yellow-jacket wasps, and slammed into the wall to stand quivering. Rudi came off the floor in a long lunge in the instant they blurred past, leg and arm in perfect line and the blade of the longsword lashing out into the hole in the broken door. The point drove home in meat and bone, and a bill clattered through the broken wood to lie spinning on the floor.

Hands gripped the blade of his sword, naked flesh against the metal. He stripped it backward with a wrench, and fingers fell away from the edge of the layer-forged steel. Another bill rammed close, probing for his life as the wielder crowded among the figures thronging the landing.

"Morrigú!" Rudi screamed.

It was half war cry, half desperate appeal. He was used to fighting brave men, but not those who cared for wounds and pain and death no more than so many windup automatons.

"Morrigú! Come to me, Dark Mother! I am the Lady's Sword!"

The Crow Goddess had sent Raven to him long ago; not in dream and vision, but in the light of common day. He bore the mark of the bird's flint-hard beak in the small scar between his brows. That pain had been brief. It flared again for an instant. Then what filled him was agony and fire, ecstasy beyond bearing, joy and horror at once. The world vanished and reappeared with jeweled clarity, and he *understood*. Every beat of his heart linked him to all that was, and he *saw* those threads.

He dropped the buckler and his hand closed on the bill's shaft behind the head, wrenched it free, slammed it back so that the butt cap cracked a skull. His sword thrust back and forth like the needle in a treadle-worked sewing machine. There was no rage behind the strokes, only a love that encompassed even the snarling faces behind the weapons that reached for him, a vast piteous determination.

Dark wings beat above his head, their drumbeat the death of suns, the wind of their passage a surge of fire like surf on a shore whose sand was stars. Flames circled a single Eye. The sword moved, and men died; others crowded forward, blades lashing at him and weapons beating at the hinges of the door. Planes of black light shattered. He screamed, and the cry was the soul of grief from the Mother of All at the pain of Her children, a boiling ocean of sorrow and rage.

"Lord, have mercy. Christ, have mercy," Ignatius whispered, and crossed himself.

His hands and balance halted the horse before his mind was aware of the need, and calmed the beast's skittishness at the harsh overwhelming iron stink of blood. The rear entrance to the Emergency Coordinator's residence had been well guarded; the men wore the mail shirts and coal-scuttle helmets of the State Police, and the door on its massive hinges was panels of solid steel strapped and forge welded and riveted together into something that even a battering ram could only have dented.

The Order of the Shield sent its knight-brothers where they were needed to succor the afflicted and rescue the weak; he had seen terrible things many times in his nearly thirty years of life, and he was just old enough to remember a little of the first year after the Change. This . . .

"How did they die?" Virginia Kane whispered.

"They killed themselves," Frederick Thurston said; his voice was shocked into a machine flatness. "Or each other."

He pointed with his saber towards one pair locked together; it shouldn't have been physically possible for two men to choke one another to death that way, but the swollen purple faces and bulging eyes were unmistakable. And the same *smile* was on their faces, the same as all the others.

Ignatius mastered himself and swung down, his armor clanking. He was in the full knight's gear of knee-length chain hauberk, coif and visored helm, plate greaves and vambraces, armored gauntlets on his hands and steel sabatons protecting his feet. The well-trained destrier stood stock-still as he dropped the reins, though its eyes rolled piteously and shivers went over its black coat. One young man still lived despite the wounds that leaked blood over chest and belly and groin; his hand was locked around a chain that held a silver crucifix, and his eyes moved towards the priest.

"What happened here, my son?" Ignatius said, going down on one knee in the sticky redness that covered the asphalt.

"*He* . . . came," the young man gasped. "*He* . . . came."

Ignatius nodded. *Now I know where the Corwinite diabolist is,* he thought grimly. *Trying the rear entrance. But first—*

"What did he do?"

The dying man's face jerked, and he began to sob; not with the pain, but as a lonely child might.

"He showed me myself," he whimpered, then began to thrash. *"He showed me myself!* Oh, God, I'll die *and I'll have to see him again—"*

Ignatius leaned forward, and locked the wounded man's eyes with his, pouring his will through the joined gaze.

"He lied, child of God. *No* sin is beyond forgiveness if you accept Christ's mercy. Throw yourself upon His love."

The priest felt *something* flow out of him . . . or through him, for it left him stronger, not weaker. A measure of sanity returned to the other's face for a moment; he slumped, and whispered slowly:

"Bless . . . me . . . Father . . . for I have sinned."

Aloud he spoke the words as the boy died. Within himself, silently, he added: *Lady pierced with sorrows, this man too was born of woman. Intercede for him, I beg. And for us all, now and at the hour of our deaths.*

Then he stood, looking up at the blank wall as he drew his sword and pulled on the leather strap to slide the kite-shaped shield around and onto his left arm. There were narrow windows running up the brick wall, one per flight, but they were covered with grills bolted to the frames. The ends of the bars curved outward in sharp points.

"They've gone through here just a moment ago, but they barred it behind them. We'll have to go around to the front of the building," he said crisply. "And pray we're in time."

"No, we won't!" Virginia shouted.

She snatched the lariat free from her saddle bow and brought her horse around in a broad circle across the street and down a little. The silver spreader-weight flashed in the faint, distant light of the gas lamps as she whirled it overhead, and the nimble quarterhorse sprang off its hindquarters and came pounding down the pavement at a gallop that struck sparks from concrete and echoed off the blank walls in rattling blows of sound. Frederick ducked in the saddle as it flew over his head, and then the loop settled over the bars of the first-story grill as she sped past.

A heavy *whunk* sound came, a whipcrack *snap* as the tough braided bison hide came rigid as a steel rod, and with it a scream of equine protest as the horse was thrown back on its haunches by the shock transmitted through the lariat snubbed around the high horn of the Western saddle—for a moment Ignatius felt a cold stab of fear that the beast would be flipped backward on its rider and crush her against the unyielding pavement.

Then there came a scream of shearing metal from above him; the half ton of fast-moving horse and rider had snapped the bolts that held the grid across. Ignatius ducked again as the buckled, twisted metal fell to the ground and landed with a nauseatingly soft sound on one of the murdered State Police troopers.

"Too small," Ignatius said, his eyes on the gap; a little light leaked out of it, as if there was a lamp several stories higher. "Without taking off my armor, at least."

"Not for me!" Virginia said.

She brought the horse up the stairs; it snorted and picked its way between the bodies with its ears laid back, but stood obedient with its forehooves on the topmost. The young woman from Skywater Ranch put her bowie knife between her teeth, kicked her feet out of the tapadero-enclosed stirrups, vaulted up to stand on the saddle and then jumped. Her gloved hands caught the frame of the window; for a moment she hung with her high-heeled riding boots kicking, and then she eeled her way through the narrow opening.

"Help her! God, gods, somebody, help her!" Frederick muttered.

His face went stiff as a yell came through the window; a man's voice shouting in alarm, and then in pain; and overriding it Virginia's wild cry:

"Skywater forever! Yippie-kye-ey, motherfucker!"

"Get ready!" Ignatius said crisply.

Frederick tumbled out of the saddle and reached for an arrow. Ignatius poised, light on the balls of his feet despite the sixty pounds of gear and fifteen of shield, blade ready over his head. There was a metallic clanking as the door swung wide, and the woman catapulted backward out of it—she'd pushed it open with a thrust of her shoulders, and turned the motion into a controlled tumble head-over-heels as a shete lunged for her.

Snap. An arrow from Frederick's bow flashed by, and then a *crack* as it slammed into and through the overlapping plates of metal-rimmed lacquered leather that covered the Cutter's chest. His face went slack and he fell forward, the weapon spinning away. Another was on his heels, heavy curved blade raised and round shield up.

"Jesu-Maria!" Ignatius shouted from deep in his chest, and sprang forward crabwise, left shoulder tucked into the curve of the long western shield.

His met the smaller round plainsman's model blazoned with the rayed sun of the Church Universal and Triumphant. There was a hard thudding impact, and he grunted as his own weight and momentum overbore the other man's charge. That rocked the soldier of the Sword of the Prophet back staggering on his heels, and the warrior-cleric's blade came down. His lips drew back from his teeth as he felt the edge cleave leather and then flesh.

God forgive him, he thought as he wrenched it back with furious urgency. *And me.*

"Back me!" he called to the others as he pushed through the door.

He came in crouching a little so that the shield covered him from eyes to shin; he left the visor locked up for better vision in the dimness, but there was no part of him not covered except the narrow space between shield-rim and eyes.

"I lead. I've got the gear for this!"

The two youngsters followed, arrows on the strings of their powerful recurve bows. The stairwell was dark, but not absolute blackness. It showed the shadowed outlines of two more Corwinites rushing down at him, and the faint light caught blue on the honed edges of their blades.

"Cut! Cut! *Cut!*"

"Jesu-Maria!"

"Skywater!"

Then Thurston's bellow; some distant corner of Ignatius' mind made a silent *tsk* sound:

"Ho la, Odhinn!"

More feet were pounding on the metal treads above, the heavy ringing sounds of boots with iron heel plates and metal-strapped toes.

We're not enough, not with only three, Ignatius knew; he knew also that they must try anyway. *Where are our friends?*

"Can we kill 'em?" Jake sunna Jake asked. *"Please?"*

Beyond him on the crest of a roofline two dark figures came to their feet and gestured urgently. They used the broad gestures of Battle-Sign, which was common to Mackenzies and Dúnedain: *Come quickly.*

Edain Aylward Mackenzie swallowed; the folk from

the west—*from Montival*, he thought—had taught the Southsiders some of the formulas of courtesy, but this *please* wasn't quite the sort of usage they'd had in mind.

The Chief said not to hurt any of the town folk if I could help it. Now, can I help it, or not?

The mob gathered ahead of him wasn't large, only a hundred or so, though it loomed larger than you'd think in the darkened street and filled it from side to side—that cramped feeling was one reason he didn't like cities. A milling churning mass of dark clothes and pale faces with a babble of voices in the harsh clipped Iowan dialect. An ugly sense of menace, almost a scent, musky and raw, beneath the horse piss and coal smoke of the city.

And the herd of strangers was between him and where he was supposed to go to help the Chief and his comrades. Down this street to the end, past a church, and to the big building on the square. It was past time he got there, too; something had gone wrong.

"Rudi-man says Iowa fuckers 're friends," Jake added, his tone growing more dubious still. "Dese're no friends."

"Bíonn gach duine go lách go dtéann bó ina gharrai," Edain muttered.

That was something he'd picked up from Lady Juniper when she'd come to judge a dispute over straying livestock between his Dun Fairfax and the folk of Dun Carson that had almost come to blows.

"Wha thayt?" the Southsider said.

"That everyone's a friend. Until *your* cow wanders into *their* garden," he said.

And I understand what Rudi meant. We can't afford to make these Iowans think of us as enemies, or bloodthirsty savages. That's the politics of it. The Chief's in danger— that's what I know of it.

"And this is the Chief's business, not mine, deciding such matters," he muttered to himself. "Or King's business."

He knew more about cities than the Southsiders did—it would be hard to know less—but he didn't like them beyond a day's visit or so, even a small and friendly one like Sutterdown, half a day's walk west of Dun Fairfax. Much less this alien monstrosity. The townsmen had sticks—not proper quarterstaves, but heavy enough to give a shrewd knock—and a few had knives; one or two carried short broad chopping swords, what these eastern-ers called footman's shetes.

More than one had picked up rocks or bits of broken concrete or bricks. A ragged figure knocked a bottle against a building's wall as he watched, and held the jagged stump in one fist. All of which was well enough for a brawl, but if he had to fight he was going to *fight*.

Behind him and Jake the grown men—and the odd woman—of the Southside Freedom Fighters fingered their new hickory bows. Some of them were fidgeting, feeling penned in by the three-story brick buildings to either side, or by the distant glow of a gaslight at a corner and the constant grumbling mumble of wheels and hooves and Gods-knew-what that never seemed to stop here. Others grinned at the city folk, an expression that would have frightened the urbanites more if they'd known the wild-men better.

Raising his voice: "You good people should give us the road, that you should. We want no trouble, our quarrel isn't with you Iowa folk, but we're ready to shed blood if we must."

One of the locals turned to the rest of the mob. "Re-member what the Seeker said! The Prophet raises the lifestreams of his followers! The poor 'n lowly are his and he'll reward them."

"Oh, sod all, that tears it," Edain said. "The Cutters have been at 'em."

I'm a peaceable man, sure and I am.

His father had gotten any inclination to brawling for its own sake out of him early, on one memorable occasion with a whistling bow stave on the shoulders and the observation that any young gallybagger in his family who wanted hard knocks could get them at home without bothering the neighbors.

But Da taught me never to back down when a fight was needful, so. The Chief needs me, and these Southside lads are depending on me to see them through, and those townsmen there are getting themselves into a real fight, whether they expected that or not.

The thought made sweat break out on his brow; not the fighting, but the responsibility.

"And these fucks brought *Eaters* into Dubuque!" the Church Universal and Triumphant's convert said. "Eaters! Chicago scum!"

Behind the Mackenzie a snarl went through the tribesmen, as much felt as heard. The Southsiders *really* didn't like being called Eaters, which was unsurprising since they'd spent their entire lives fighting those who deserved the name. Also in their legends Chicago was a lost paradise where their ancestors had been demigods, not to be mentioned with disrespect.

We'll have to go through them, and no holds barred, Edain decided. *They asked for it, and by Lugh of the Long Spear and the Morrigan's black host, we'll give it them.*

And there was a certain relief to the thought. He *was* a peaceable man, but fighting was something he knew how to do. Talking with a bunch of strangers wasn't.

"Yes, you can kill them," he said.

The Southsiders surprised him by falling into ranks as they'd been taught; given how little time there had been for instruction and how their blood was up he'd expected a pell-mell rush. They set arrows to their strings and waited. Then one started a chant; it made him start to hear it in their slurred speech rather than the Clan's lilt, but there was a raw menace to the sound in the shadowed, crowded night. It came like a breath of mountain and forest, the wildwood come stealing home into the walled town:

"We are the point—
We are the edge—
We are the wolves that Hecate fed!

"We are the bow—
We are the shaft—
We are the bolts that Hecate cast!"

"Wholly together . . ." He whipped an arrow out of his own quiver and drew past the angle of his jaw. ". . . let the gray geese fly . . . *shoot!*"

Thirty bows snapped. The whistling sound of the arrows' passage was oddly magnified by the buildings on either side. The light was bad, and the Southsiders weren't even middling archers yet by his exacting standards. Against a bunched, unarmored target less than a second's arrow flight away it didn't matter much. A score of men went down, screaming and thrashing and clawing at the iron and wood piercing them, or silent and still.

"Again! *Shoot!*"

Another volley. Many of the townsmen turned to run, but the long shafts slashed down out of the darkness at them, the arrowheads glinting at the last second as the honed edges of the triangular broadheads caught the light.

"At them!" Edain shouted.

The Southsiders swarmed forward, throwing down their bows and sweeping out knife and hatchet. They had no order at this yet or formal training to the blade; but they had a dreadful bounding agility, and each aided the other in a unison like a pack of wolves slashing at an elk. Their catamount screeching echoed from the buildings; it was actually much like the Mackenzie battle yell. After a moment the only sound from the Dubuque men was panic flight, or the moans and cries of their hurt.

"Leave their wounded!" Edain snapped; he'd stayed back and shot, something he didn't trust anyone else here to do in this dim light and when friend and foe were at close quarters. "No need to finish them."

One knifeman ignored him, jerking up the chin of an Iowan trying to crawl away and preparing to cut his throat. Edain tossed him backward with a snatch and grab—he wasn't more than average height, but his shoulders and arms were broad and thick—and cuffed him silly with a forehand and backhand slap. The man almost lunged at him, but then the mad light died out of his eyes and he grinned sheepishly despite the blood running from his nose and lips, abashed as a child caught with his hand in the nut jar.

"Get your bows and follow me!" Edain snapped. "We've work to do yet."

"Screw this," Ingolf Vogeler said. "It's too long—we have to get going."

Jack Heuisink hissed between clenched teeth. "Leading a band of armed men to the place the Bossman's staying isn't real healthy," he pointed out. "Particularly as the Heuisinks and the Heasleroads aren't what you'd call friendly. *Unless* there's already an attack."

"*Something's* gone wrong, Jack—"

He stopped as a knock came at one of the warehouse windows: *tap*, then *tap-tap*, then *tap*.

Three strides took him there. When he opened it a face was hanging there upside down. All he could see besides the dark cap was the strip of skin across the eyes . . . and one of those was missing.

"Denson's dead and the Cutters are headed for the Bossman's quarters," Mary Havel said. "They'll be there before you. Hurry! Edain and the Southsiders and Ignatius and Fred and Virginia are on their way."

The last of the State Police troopers who'd *turned* went down in a thrashing tangle on the floor as Rudi landed a drawing cut behind one knee; Odard made a quick downward smash with the lower point of his shield, and the curved metal rim hit bone with an ugly crunching sound. Mathilda covered Rudi for a moment with hers, and a spear point scored across the surface, leaving a bright scratch through the paint that covered its metal sheath. The impact rocked her back; she had to use shield and sword in a blur of movement as two more thrust at her unarmored body.

When men fought with no regard at all for their lives, they died quickly . . . but the last of them had forced Rudi back into the room. An unarmored man couldn't just slug it out; he needed room to take advantage of his height and quickness.

Two soldiers of the Sword of the Prophet shoved through in that instant, too quickly for any of the westerners to stop them. *They* weren't berserkers of any sort, and they were in good armor, their round shields up under their eyes. Rudi leapt forward again; he could feel the ache in his muscles and the hard straining as his lungs sucked in air, but the *ríastrad* that was the gift of the Crow Goddess made it seem distant, unimportant. His body would serve his need, until it dropped dead. A shield's frame cracked under the edge of his sword, and the arm beneath it broke, but then he had to whirl and parry a cut at his leg. He gave back, and more men crowded in—

One of the little pauses that happened in most close-quarters fights fell; the three from the west stood together, panting. Rudi recognized Major Graber, the man who'd been after them since Idaho.

The hard blue eyes met his. "If you give up now, I can promise you all a quick death," he said. "But only if you surrender *now*, before the High Seeker comes."

Rudi's mouth quirked; he'd spared the Sword officer's life once.

And this is my thanks? he thought whimsically. *And the jest of it is, it* is *a gesture of grace, so. He might not be such a bastard of a man at all, were he born and reared elsewhere.*

"I'll be thanking you, but declining nonetheless," Rudi said, his voice detached and amused. "If you want us, come and take us and pay the price of it."

Graber's tuft of chin-beard moved very slightly as he gave a brief unsurprised nod, and there was a quirk to the corner of his mouth as he slid the spiked helmet back on his head.

"Kill these three," he said. "Take the Iowa ruler and his woman and the child alive if you can. They'll be useful as hostages."

"Wait!" Rudi heard.

Another man pushed through the door—and the soldiers of the Sword of the Prophet, men who would bite through their own tongues and die at a command, leapt aside to let him. His head was shaven, and a robe the color of old dried blood covered him; a shete was in his hand, but that was the least of the menace that surrounded him.

It was the eyes you saw. Ordinary brownish-green eyes, that were somehow windows into negation, to the bottom of all things where despair itself had drained to lie dead, dust and bones.

"I—see—you," he said, his head tilted at an odd angle, and even to one caught up in the battle-fury of the Goddess the words struck chill. *"Son—of—Bear—Son—of—Raven."*

"And I you, ill-wreaker," Rudi said quietly. "You shall not pass while I live, or harm those I love."

"We—are—abroad—and—loose—and—will—not—be—put—back," the High Seeker of the Church Universal and Triumphant said. *"You—cannot—stand—against—us—without—It."*

Something struck Rudi then, impalpable but with a wave of torment that made him feel his bones crack and grind against themselves until only seared powder was left. He grunted and flexed backward, as if a fist had hit him between the eyes. Then Raven's mark on his brow flared again, a good white pain that cut through the sick agony.

"Lady of the Crows, fold me in Your wings!" he choked. "Lugh of the Sun—"

His head cleared enough for him to remember something else. Master Hao's hard dry voice, in a practice field on the mountainside above Chenrezi monastery, in the

Valley of the Sun. Words as crisp and strong as the bronze bell ringing from below:

But the hand is not the weapon—the mind *is the weapon, and the hand only its extension. Discipline your mind!*

As he had then he turned his will into a dart, and *thrust*. The Cutter priest threw up his arms and howled, a sound that stunned the ears and made even his own followers stagger. Then they hurled themselves forward, shetes raised to kill, and there was only the dance of blades.

I'm about to die.

Mathilda Arminger had time for that one thought. Her blade stopped the stroke of a Cutter's shete, but force of impact almost tore the longsword from her numb hand. Her broken shield turned another, just enough that the flat rather than the edge slammed into her un-protected ribs. It might have broken bones even if she'd been wearing a hauberk and padding; now she *heard* bone crack through her own flesh, and spikes of pain lanced through her chest as she tried to breathe. The shield arm dropped strengthless, steel scored her sword arm, and she fell backward against the wall with an ear-ringing thump of head against stucco and slid downward.

Odard flung himself between her and the rising steel. His shield was tattered and split; the edge cracked down through the wood and leather, into his arm. He shrieked, but in the same motion he stabbed the broken stump of his sword into a face. The man reeled backward and Odard went to his knees, his right hand scrabbling at his belt for the dagger. Another Cutter wrenched his broad-tipped blade out of Anthony Heasleroad's belly and kicked his body aside.

Beyond him she saw Rudi moving like quicksilver, whirling and striking as he fought his way towards them, and as the mist of pain and fuddlement darkened her eyes he seemed limned in fire, a winged shape that danced like spears of lightning amid dark thunderclouds. Then someone else was beside her.

"Jesu-Maria!" Ignatius shouted, and struck.

The man who'd been about to kill her fell backward, trailing blood. The priest's voice rang thunder deep; Mathilda felt it resonate through her aching bones, as she slumped against the wall with the force of the blow that had felled her still buzzing through her head and down her limbs in spikes of agony. A taste like brass and sulfur filled her mouth, and her breath came rapid through a dry throat. Odard crouched at her feet, swaying on one knee with his ruined shield propped against his shoulder.

"On my right hand Michael! On my left hand Uriel!"

The soldier-monk's sword and shield swung in beautiful unison, leaving trails of silver light to her dazzled eyes. Ignatius shouted again, over the slithering crash of steel, the dull ugly sound of a blade in flesh, and the panting snarls of his opponents:

"Before me Raphael! Behind me Gabriel!"

There was anger in that shout, but no rage; instead a happiness that was fierce and joyous at the same time. It was as if the *spirit* of anger filled him, pure and hot and infinitely clean.

As if this was the thing that anger was *for*.

The Cutter in the dried-blood robe came through the press, throwing his followers to either side in his eagerness. *Murk* moved with him to Mathilda's aching eyes;

not darkness that hid him from sight, but something of which darkness was merely a symbol—a whirling chaos that hummed with power but was somehow decayed, as if he were a window to a place where even the stuff of matter itself perished in an endless denial of possibility.

"*I—see—you*," he said, in syllables of burning ash.

The battle ceased for an instant that stretched. Rudi used it to step to the warrior-cleric's side. The Cutter magus looked from one of them to the other with a grin of hatred.

"And I see you," Ignatius said into the panting silence. "Go back, Hollow Man, to the nothingness that waits for you; for you have chosen it."

"*You* are nothing!" the High Seeker rasped. "A bag of bones and slime and dung, a worm that feeds on sunlight and turns it to shit!"

Ignatius smiled. "I am *her* knight, and through her the servant of the Most High, a *miles* of Christ; in His name I command you, not mine. From the bottom of my heart I pity you. Repent! Even for you there can still be mercy. Go back!"

The Cutter howled; Mathilda felt an almost irresistible impulse to beat her own head open on the wall behind her. Only weakness and the thought that *that* face and voice might be waiting for her on the other side of death stopped her. The curved shete leapt at Ignatius, and his sword met it. Sparks flew through the air, and she smelled brimstone and lightning.

"*On my right hand Michael! On my left hand Uriel! Before me Raphael! Behind me Gabriel!*"

Rudi struck as well, and the shadow of a great scythe seemed to move with the sword: "*Morrigú!*"

As the monk shouted, Mathilda's vision blurred. Men fought, but it seemed to her that the two between her and the enemy struggled with a heaving roil rather than another human. Or as if the Cutter was the shadow of a man, a skin sack around a mass of coiling tendrils, behind a gaping scream of agony. Shapes stretched about the knight-brother of the Order as well; were they wings vaster than the Earth could contain, or were they blazing wheels, or a swirling cloud of flashing eyes?

And beyond them a blue-mantled figure whose hands stretched down, touching Ignatius on his forehead and the cross guard of the sword he gripped, a power blazing into flesh and steel. And behind them all a radiance that was terror and longing all in one, that shone through her bones as if they were wisps of air—

"Retreat!" a voice called.

"No!" the Corwinite magus in the red robe—bloody in truth now—screamed. "We are too close!"

Even then Mathilda could sense how a trace of humanity had returned to the voice; there was human evil in it now, bloodlust and a furious anger at being balked, as if the Presence that had ridden him was too exhausted to maintain its grip. When he howled as Graber grabbed him by the shoulders and wrestled him back it was merely shrill.

"High Seeker! Now, or we die without fulfilling the mission. They're hitting us from both sides down there in the street and those whores in black are shooting from the roofs! Brave men are dying to buy us time to try again later. *Now!*"

The Sword of the Prophet's commander gestured, and three men rushed Ignatius and Rudi. The rest backed, then turned and fled, hustling the suddenly limp and half-conscious form of the High Seeker between them. Fred and Virginia shot in unison, and the last man through pitched forward with arrows through the backplate of his armor standing up like masts from a ship.

From below came the sounds of battle, war cries, and a high screeching like so many great cats. Then Rudi was beside her, slamming his notched sword point-first in the floorboards and easing the wrecked shield off her injured arm while Ignatius bound it up with the sterilized bandage from his belt pouch. She almost fainted at the wave of pain, then forced awareness back; more voices were shouting, and others burst through the shattered door, Edain and Ingolf at their head.

"Are you all right, *anamchara* mine?" Rudi said, his arm holding her against his shoulder.

Blood was spattered across his face, some of it his own, but the wildness was fading from it, leaving only the warm blue-green gaze that had been in her life so long.

"No," she said. "But I will be now."

CHAPTER TEN

"He's . . . dead," Kate Heasleroad said numbly.

"Yes, he is, Kate. You can grieve later. You have to *do* things! Now!"

Mathilda Arminger spoke firmly. The pain in her arm and ribs was like white ice playing up into her shoulder, but she kept the bandaged limb hugged against her aching side. The bandages were wet—the priest said she needed stitches—but she could attend to that later; there weren't any bone spikes prodding into her lungs, for all that each movement of her chest was like breathing in molten lead.

If I move very carefully, I'll be all right.

The younger woman's eyes were blank as she repeated: "He's . . . *dead*. Tony's *dead*."

She began to rock back and forth, moaning. Mathilda suppressed an impulse to bury her hands in her hair and shriek in frustration. The urge to slap the other woman across the face was even stronger but she repressed it, even when Rudi raised one palm and mimed the action.

"That only works in stories," she said decisively.

"Well, we'd better do *something*, *anamchara* mine. The wheels are going to come off the wagon here, and soon. The Bossman dead, Denson dead . . . If we don't just run for the docks they'll be looking for someone to blame . . ."

"I know what to do, and I'm not going to leave Kate without help now of all times. I owe her. *Get* this place in order, would you, Rudi? I'll be right back."

The nursery was down a corridor and through a pair of light swinging doors; she put one foot ahead of the other, with a determination that brought beads of sweat to her face. It had room for more than one infant, and the walls had an attractive modern mural of animals and flowers. That showed clearly, for the wall-mounted gaslights had been turned up. The boy rested on his back in a padded crib, dressed in a pink jumpsuit and looking up at a mobile of cutout cats and dogs and birds, taking an occasional dab at it with one chubby paw. The noise had woken him, but he wasn't frightened yet. Kate had said that he was a good baby.

The children of the Coordinator of Dubuque were elsewhere tonight, probably to their parents' eventual intense relief, but there was a sadness to the scattered toys—wooden blocks, a beautiful pre-Change doll with blond hair, a rocking horse with a carefully repaired stirrup. The nurse was a middle-aged woman in a print dress; she stood before Tommie Heasleroad's crib with an aluminum baseball bat clenched in her hands and an expression of wild determination on her rather horsy face.

That grew greater as she took in the newcomer's alien—and blood-spattered—clothes and disheveled hair. Mathilda paused for an instant to take a necessary deep breath and pitch absolute confidence into her voice. The nursemaid deserved it if possible, rather than having the boy taken from her—she was obviously ready to sell her life for his.

And it wouldn't do to bleed all over him, Mathilda thought for an instant of half-crazed humor before she spoke:

"Your mistress needs her son with her. It's quite safe now, but you must *bring* him to her."

She turned, and the nurse scooped up the child and followed . . . although she kept the bat in one hand.

Mother was right. Just act as if there's absolutely no doubt you'll be obeyed, and chances are you will *be. The more so when people are frightened.*

It had been only moments, but the room was in order when she returned, if you didn't count the pooled blood, and white-faced servants were stumbling to clean that up with cloths and mops. The bodies of the dead Cutters and guardsmen had been carried away; Anthony Heasleroad had been laid out, his body covered with something that had probably started as an embroidered tablecloth, and his eyes closed. Mary and Ritva were there too, looking the worse for wear. Mary had a bruise that would cover a full half of her face and was talking in Sign, leaning against Ingolf as she did and squinting as the swelling nearly closed her one good eye:

They had a ship waiting. Left a small rearguard and got away—heading south. It's Chaos and Old Night out there now, Rudi.

Rudi stood at the top of the stairs, and Father Ignatius at the base; between them they limited the men allowed up to a few of the most important, the ones who came with armed retinues at their backs, and a doctor with her black leather case. The doctor set to work, but the potentates milled around, taking in the dead Bossman with exclamations of horror or in more than one case with blank, calculating expressions while turning to look at each other. A few seemed nauseous; well, the stink *was* bad, particularly if you hadn't seen many battlefields.

Kate looked up from her fugue when the nursemaid held out her child. She snatched the boy; he whimpered, but then she controlled herself and turning her clutch into a firm comforting grip.

Seize the moment, Mathilda thought, and bent to put her good hand on Kate's shoulder, willing strength down it.

"Kate!" she said. "Your husband's dead but your son lives. You must act for him, and act *now*."

"What . . . what should I do?"

The edge of hysteria drained out of her voice in the course of the sentence, and she straightened.

"You must summon your affinity . . ." Mathilda said, and saw blank incomprehension. "Your vassals and liegemen . . . oh, Mother of God, your *supporters*, Kate. The ones who'll rally to your son and have fighting men behind *them*. The ones who owe land and office to your family!"

"But I'm not . . . I'm just . . ."

"You're the mother of the heir, unless you let him be dispossessed," she said. "Think of *him* and you can do it."

"I don't know what I'd say!"

"I'll help. I remember what Mother did, after my father was killed in the Protector's War. Just for starters—"

ST. RAPHAEL'S CATHEDRAL
CHARTERED CITY OF DUBUQUE
PROVISIONAL REPUBLIC OF IOWA
SEPTEMBER 25, CHANGE YEAR 24/2022 AD

"Christ on a crutch," Abel Heuisink said, his voice pawky-dry as the gathering before the cathedral doors massed and waited in a murmuring churn. "Thanks so very much. Because of *you*, Kate's going to pull it off. So we get more Heasleroads."

Rudi grinned at the look of grudging respect the elder Heuisink shot towards Mathilda, where she stood three steps down from the hastily erected dais, bright in the court dress of an Association princess. He took a deep breath of the crisp autumn air, enjoying even the pull and itch of his wounds as they continued their healing. None were serious . . . and the feeling meant he was alive, alive on a bright fall day with years yet before him. The best part about a fight was surviving it . . . until you didn't, of course.

Doesn't miss a trick, my Matti! he thought. *And Kate's a more apt pupil than I'd have thought.*

"Don't blame me," Rudi said. "Sure, and it's Mathilda who managed the politics, for the most part, with Odard next. They both learned it in the Lady Regent's school."

"Lady Regent?"

"Mathilda's mother, Lady Sandra, Regent of the Portland Protective Association."

"Yeah, you mentioned her. She's good at politics, this Lady Sandra?"

"Oh, you have *no* idea, my friend. At the game of thrones, there's none like her in all the world."

You couldn't quite call the chair that had been set out on the dais a throne; but with its massive size and glowing inlays of jewels and rare woods and semiprecious stones, you couldn't quite say it wasn't, either. The morning sun made it blaze and sparkle; careful hands had buffed and polished away the patina of age that it had kept all the way to the museum in Boston, and from there westward in Ingolf Vogeler's caravan.

"Tell me, sir," he said to the Iowan. "Do you and your friends . . . your faction . . . this Progressive Party . . . have enough troops to put down all the other factions here without civil war, and the black shame and grief of it?"

"No, dammit," Abel said; this time the frustration in his voice was bleak and bitter. "And if it starts it would be a civil war with about five sides, some of whom would make Tony look like the second coming of Thomas Jefferson."

Who . . . ah, Rudi thought.

He'd learned some of the history of the old Americans, though he'd preferred George Washington, himself—more of a man of deeds and less a creature of words.

The Iowan went on: "And it would go on until every county in the State was a country, and fighting all the others. Tony's father knew about divide and rule, you *betcha*. That's why Tony lasted as long as he did—even with old Tom gone, and even when most people knew how useless Tony was, nobody could agree on who'd take over, and how."

A slight smell of incense from the funeral mass lingered, under the autumnal smells of burning leaves and cut grass and the wild silty smell of the river not far distant. The Cardinal-Archbishop of Des Moines was here, and he wasn't quite adding his blessing to the proceedings . . . but then again, you couldn't say he wasn't either, and he was in full fig of vestments and miter and crozier. Father Ignatius stood just behind his right shoulder, in plain Benedictine robes, but leaning forward occasionally to murmur a word in his ear, to the evident frustration of his own entourage.

"Then isn't a compromise that spares this rich land from death and burning a good thing?" Rudi asked. "You've been long at peace, and I've seen war; an ugly thing, and a war of brothers is uglier yet. Not the ugliest of all things, true, but to be avoided if you can do so with honor."

Troops stood in double columns, down on either side of the strip of red carpet that led to the cathedral's doors. Half were State Police, looking professional and tough in their polished mail but rather subdued beneath the stiff discipline; the ruler they'd upheld and the commander they'd hated and feared and adored both gone at once.

The other half were Farmers' and Sheriffs' retainers, more motley in their gear but solemn with the occasion, and with Jack Heuisink and Ingolf Vogeler at either end to bully-damn them into order; the fact that the younger man was on crutches seemed to make it easier for him if anything.

Behind the dais stood Jake sunna Jake and *his* followers. Rudi suppressed a chuckle at the sight; Edain had managed to get them into kilts of something quite similar to the Mackenzie tartan, at which they'd been wildly enthusiastic, and reasonable body armor, which they liked even better, and civilized barbers had shave faces and trim hair, which they'd liked very little. He'd even found flat Scots-style bonnets. They leaned on their hickory longbows, grinning like so many timber wolves contemplating a flock of sheep. Their pose wasn't even the rough Clan approximation of standing to attention, but they were quiet enough—they were hunters, after all.

Abel sighed. "I've been compromising since the Change for just that reason. Because I had to do it. It would be nice to get my own way for once—and I'm *right*, goddammit. We should be a democracy again, before people forget that there was such a thing."

A roll of drums and a blare of trumpets sounded. Kate Heasleroad came through the doors of the cathedral, from where she had stood vigil before her husband's coffin. With her was the nursemaid, and in her arms young Tommie, quiet but with his face wet with uncomprehending tears.

And he'll never know his father, Rudi thought with a pang.

He'd met his own blood-sire quite a few times, but not enough to *know* him; there had always been the matter of Signe Havel, Mike's wife, and he hadn't been officially acknowledged as the Bear Lord's son until after the man's death.

Still, all things considered, little Tommie's orphaning may be for the best; even love can ruin you, if it's done wrongly, a difficult feat but one his father would certainly have pulled off. I was lucky. A boy could do far worse than have the story of Mike Havel to pattern himself on, and the living Nigel Loring to show him daily what it is to be a man. Not to mention the likes of Chuck Barstow and Sam Aylward.

"Legends change, Colonel Heuisink," Rudi said to his companion. "One will do as well as another, as long as people—the lords and the folk both—hold to them truly, love the story they tell and try to live rightly by them. It's when people *betray* the dreams they have together that they bring real sorrow upon a land."

Heuisink gave him a long look. "Yeah, legends change. But you youngsters . . . especially *you* youngsters, you and your friends, make me wonder. Like I wonder about my sons, but more so."

Kate wasn't quite dressed in a cotte-hardi either, or wearing a crown, though she'd wanted to. Mathilda had talked her out of that; both would be too alien here, for now. But her long gown and the tiara in her hair were stately enough, and the expression on her face was stern and remote as she looked out over the crowd.

And the half of being a Queen is to look like a Queen. For what is rank, but people's belief that you hold it?

"Wonder what?" Rudi said.

"About living by our legends. People have always done that. The trouble with you"—he smiled wryly—"the trouble with the younger generation, is that they're living *in* legends. Being eaten by them, maybe. Does that make you more human than we oldsters were, or less? Certainly it makes you different. It's like you don't live by them, you live them out. Act them out, without noticing you do. You don't . . . talk to yourselves inside your heads as much as we did."

Rudi frowned, then nodded with slow respect. "You're not the first I've heard say something of the sort," he replied thoughtfully. "But few have put it so neatly. To be frank, from my side it seems that you of the ancient world often hardly lived at all, just watched yourself living."

They stared at each other in perfect mutual incomprehension for a moment. Then Rudi grinned.

"Mostly it's: *And you Changelings are weird, the lot of you!*" he said.

Heuisink laughed ruefully. The arc of open garden before the great church held several hundred prominent Sheriffs and wealthy or influential Farmers, mayors and National Guard commanders; men of consequence from all over the Provisional Republic, summoned by the semaphore-telegraph net, and brought here as fast as light railcars could travel—which was forty miles an hour or even better, with relays working the pedals. Beyond the fence and a line of spearmen the hill and the streets beyond were crowded with the burghers and commons of Dubuque—sleek traders and brokers and shipowners, solid shopkeepers and skilled craftsmen, ragged day laborers who had nothing to sell but the strength of their arms.

Kate waited for a long second, just long enough for quiet to fall, and not quite long enough for the murmurs to grow again. Then she raised a hand; the bugles blew once more, and the warriors beat blades on their shields, or stamped the steel-shod butts of their weapons down on the pavement, or flourished their bows. When the harsh martial noise stopped, the silence could have been cut with a knife.

"Sheriffs, Farmers and people of the Provisional Republic of Iowa," she said into it. "Anthony Heasleroad, my husband, your Bossman, is dead. Murdered by foreigners who he gave hospitality as his guests, murdered on Iowan land by agents of the cultist madman of Corwin. Will you let this stand? *Will we let our leader be murdered by savages from Montana?* Will Iowa, proud Iowa, our home, the last home of American civilization, let this stand? *Can they do this to us?*"

"Oh, now that's clever," Rudi murmured softly. "You are your mother's daughter, Matti; I wouldn't have thought of it so quickly, perhaps. *Us* is a powerful word, and it's a sorry excuse for a man who isn't moved by the pull of shared blood. It's no accident we of humankind took wolves to share our hearths and work and to guard our children, for we too are creatures of the pack."

The surprised grumble from the audience turned into a sudden roar:

"No! No! No!"

Abel Heuisink's generation-long feud with the Boss-man's family was forgotten for a moment as he shouted with the others. Fists rammed into the air, and the soldiers shouted with the rest, landholders' retainers and State Police together, until their officers cursed and cuffed them into quiet. The men of note took longer to subside, and the vast crowd of ordinary folk beyond longer still; *their* voices were like a great beast's snarl in a nighted forest.

Rudi felt a little prickle up his spine at the sound. He kept a tactful silence himself; he was a foreigner here too, and he judged the temper of the time not overly friendly to outsiders.

"What do we say to these murderers? What is our answer?" Kate called.

"War!" a voice called, and others joined it: *"War! War!"*

Abel Heuisink started and half turned. A little way beyond amid the notables was a knot of younger men, the sons and in a few instances the grandsons of the old-sters around them—Odard Liu in the midst of them, and the closest to him all the men he'd made his cronies. They had started the call, but others took it up.

"War! War! War!" The chant spread, and then the commons joined in, like a thousandfold echo of Pacific surf upon basalt cliffs:

"WAR! WAR! WAR!"

Rudi blinked a little in surprise when the hoarse bellow cut off at Kate's gesture, quiet rippling out from the dais to the edge of sight. She turned and held out her arms, and the nursemaid set her son in them.

"My boy's father is dead," she said. "And all the promise of a new generation that went with him, a generation born since the Change and tempered in these times of trial."

Rudi grinned to himself. He hadn't come across a single land in his travels where the younger generation weren't itching to take over from their elders, the more so because they were impatient with habits of mind born before the Change. A few of the notables were past sixty, like Abel Heuisink, but most were a generation or so younger and accompanied by grown children who were learning the family business of ruling at first hand by example and observation the way most trades were passed on now. Those were the ones shouting the loudest . . .

The crowd of townsfolk beyond were mostly those who'd been born since the old world died, or at least didn't remember it well.

Kate went on: "But his son lives—named for the man who saved us all when the Change came. Gentlemen, Sheriffs, Farmers and people of our great Provisional Republic, I cannot protect my son alone."

She held the boy over her head in a sudden gesture.

"I need your help. Will you promise that help? Can I depend on you? Will you give me the wisdom of your counsel, the strength of your arms, the courage of your loyal hearts?"

The bellow that answered her was enough to make the glass in the cathedral's great windows rattle audibly. Glancing aside Rudi could see doubt on many faces, but others shone, exalted . . . and even the doubters were looking around them and reckoning odds, and then mostly joining in. A corner of his mouth twisted up.

Matti's mother *had* used that tactic shamelessly among the Associates in the months that followed Norman Arminger's death at the end of the War of the Eye, trotting her daughter around like an icon. She hadn't been the only one to use the method in those days, either. Sandra had employed more vivid words than those Mathilda was putting in Kate's mouth, but even then the Associates had been used to the *concept* of dynastic loyalty. These Iowans had to be led gently, into things they felt already but had no set form of words to express.

"Farmers, Sheriffs, and people; I will do nothing unconstitutional. The Assembly and the State Senate must be consulted. But will you swear, here and now, to uphold my son's rights against this enemy from beyond our borders?"

Which makes no sense if you think about it—the only threat to young Tommie's *position right now is from his fellow countrymen—but few of these folk are thinking much right now,* Rudi knew. *And by the time they might, they'll be committed. She's made her son, vengeance for his father and the insulted dignity and honor of Iowa one and the same thing. And that honor their own.*

The people bellowed approval. So did some of the notables, particularly the younger ones. The rest took it up with a half-second's lag.

Kate Heasleroad glared at Abel Heuisink as he pushed his son's wheelchair through the door. The conference room was large; the long oval of the mahogany table was enough for a score of seats, but it stretched beyond that to tall windows that showed the hilly streets of Dubuque and a glimpse of the Mississippi beyond that. A pot on a sideboard gave off the rich smell of real coffee, only slightly cut with chicory, and a tray of pastries rested beside it; the scent mingled with city smoke and the cut grass of the lawn outside. Nobody had bothered with the amenities yet. The former Bossman's wife hadn't even sat down, and her guards bristled behind her.

"You're not taking what belongs to my son, Colonel!" she snapped.

The elder Heuisink shrugged. "I *can't* take what you think belongs to your son, Kate," he said. "You just fixed it that way, you and your friends."

Rudi kept his face calm, but there was a grin behind it at the expression on the face of the Bossman's widow. Then it turned shrewd; she stared at the spare seamed face of the older man, and she nodded slowly. The armed men behind her relaxed infinitesimally, sensing that it wouldn't come to blades and blood on the parquet floor, not just yet. Some of the politicians did too, and others looked at each other in puzzlement.

"Thank *him* for pointing it out," he went on, and nodded to Rudi. "Though I like to think I'd have thought of it. But that might have taken too long, and a day's a long time in politics. Especially politics conducted with sharp pointed things."

"You're serious," she said. "But you've been an enemy of ours *forever*. Matti said you would be reasonable, but—"

"I was an opponent, not an enemy, but leave that aside. *Iowa* has an enemy now, and we can't afford to fight among ourselves. I didn't kill your husband, Kate. I tried as hard as I could to stop it. Hell, Jack here got himself busted up fighting *for* you, remember."

The younger Heuisink nodded, then winced and touched his bandages; the splinted leg was outstretched on a support rigged to the pre-Change wheelchair. Kate looked at Mathilda, who stood cradling her bandaged arm and tight-strapped ribs. The very slight nod she got seemed to relax her a little further.

"That's true, Colonel . . . Abel," she said. "What do you have to propose?"

"A coalition, and you as . . ."

This time the elder Heuisink looked at Mathilda himself.

"Kate will be Regent until her son's majority," Mathilda Arminger said. "I'm familiar with arrangements like that. A Regency with you, Colonel Heuisink as . . . well, might as well call it Chancellor. And offices and honors divided between your factions . . . parties, you call them . . . according to a mutually satisfactory plan. Or equally unsatisfactory plan; there isn't enough land and offices to satisfy all the claimants, and never will be. With a war coming, you're going to need your unity."

Young Tom Jr. murmured and turned in his mother's arms. She stood and handed him to his nursemaid. "Take him away, Annette," she said. "It's time for his nap and we have business to discuss."

"So we've got a war on our hands," the elder Heuisink said, several hours later. "At least it isn't a civil war."

Mellow evening light came through tall windows. He passed a cup of the coffee to Rudi; they were alone in the room now.

Rudi shrugged, sipping at it and nibbling a cookie rich with walnuts. Sitting in a room full of politicians and helping keep their mutual fears, hatreds and spiteful greeds from boiling over was work, just as sure as skinning a cow or pitching sheaves onto a wagon.

Unfortunately it didn't give you the *honest* weariness that real labor did. His stomach felt sour, and the muscles of his neck stiff and tense, in addition to the fading but still sharp pain of bruises and cuts.

"Not this year, I think," he said. "It's too close to winter."

The Iowan landholder nodded; the season of mud was coming, and the blizzards after that. Iowa's railroads and roads were vastly better than most, but that could do only so much for moving and supplying armies inside the Provisional Republic's boundaries, and nothing outside them.

And besides which, the preparations to build *an army will take time. But not an hour of* my *time here in Iowa and over the river has been wasted, mad though it drove me to stay when the Sword calls ahead. For now I've found allies here, and powerful ones with armies at their commands, bound to me by both honor and policy. When I return, those bonds will be iron chains for the curbing of Corwin and the Cutters.*

The Mackenzie went on aloud:

"And Corwin's domains are far away, though they may move local allies against you. But next year, almost certainly, in my judgment. Fortunately it'll be a war against a foreign foe, not amongst yourselves, and Iowa is very strong."

"Not as strong as you might think," Heuisink said grimly. "Tom Heasleroad was always more concerned with a possible coup than he was with making the National Guard . . . the army . . . effective. The units are understrength and scattered, and a lot of the officers are more concerned with lining their pockets than anything else. Plus the National Guard Reserve—the farm militia— is a joke and a bad joke at that, on most of the Farms. Barely even police, much less soldiers."

Rudi blinked. "That's, ummm, less clever than I'd have expected, from the man's reputation, which was that he was no fool, whatever else his failings. *Ni neart go cur le chéile.*"

At the older man's puzzled look he rendered the Gaelic into English:

"No unity, no strength."

"No, it was very clever indeed," Abel Heuisink said. "From Tom's point of view, if not the whole State's. He was always most worried that someone would do to him what he and John Denson . . . and I, I was in on it too, let's be honest . . . did to the Governor right after the Change. Killed him and took over, no point in weasling about it."

Rudi looked at him. "But that was necessary, wasn't it?"

"I thought so. Tom too, but he *wanted* to do it and I was reluctant. But do it once, and get away with it, and there's always the chance someone else will give it a try. For reasons they think are good. Possibly just a little worse than the ones *you* had. And after that another, and another, until it's just for whatever they can grab, for no better reason than they think they've got a tougher bunch of thugs. We did what we had to do, but we broke things doing it. Broke barriers."

Rudi nodded. "And that's another reason you should keep your promise to Kate . . . to the Regent," he said. "Not that I doubt your honor, Colonel. But for the good of your land, too. Iowa *is* strong . . . if it can learn to use that strength, the which requires years of good lordship. And while I wouldn't wish a war for the purpose, still fighting one together against outsiders who deserve it can be a powerful bond."

Heuisink looked a little surprised, and the Mackenzie went on:

"Men will bow to a naked sword; but that makes your back feel very naked too, and everyone has to sleep sometime. They need a story as well, a story that tells them the ruler has a *right* to rule, and tells the ruler *how* to rule: by right, and not by whim."

"Well, Tony certainly didn't know that one."

"No, he didn't . . . and you'll notice that he's become somewhat dead the now. Such a tale is no fancy; it's as needful as air if men are to live together as men, not like crabs in a bucket devouring each other. The which is not a good thing! You may not like the House of Heasleroad, sir, but here they are. They did bring Iowa through the Change. And *this* Heasleroad heir is very young indeed, and need have no feud with you, you and yours being guiltless of his father's death. If you're Chancellor, and his mother the Regent is your friend, you'll have a hand in the shaping of him. And of this land."

The pouched blue eyes were shrewd as they regarded him. "You're young but no young fool, are you, Mr. Mackenzie?"

Rudi grinned. "No, that I am not. I'm young, but I'm learning, so! Modesty's a vice I leave to Christians."

"And if I'm prime minister, Chancellor, whatever . . . I *can* make some changes. There are too many of Tony's men in power to get rid of them without a civil war—I told Kate the truth about that—but with a *real* war in prospect, we'll need reforms whether they like it or not. We'll have to have the common people on our side, not just following orders."

"We . . . all of the Prophet's enemies . . . will need that strength," Rudi said. "Iowa's neighbors will listen to *you*, Colonel Heuisink; you have the reputation of an honorable man. And the Seven Council Fires of the Sioux will, as well."

"They will with you vouching for me," Heuisink said.

"You're the one who got adopted by them . . . Strong Raven! I wish you weren't leaving us; it'd go better with you in person than in a letter."

"The which is also my wish," Rudi said. "That I was staying just long enough to then go west again with an army at my back to help my folk! But the Sword of the Lady is still waiting for me on Nantucket; nor am I truly the Lady's Sword until I hold it. We have more than armies to fight, sir. We have to deal with—"

"Principalities and powers," Heuisink said, and shivered very slightly.

He crossed himself, and Rudi drew the Pentagram.

MISSISSIPPI RIVER
SCHOONER HAMMERDOWN
NORTH OF DUBUQUE
SEPTEMBER 28, CHANGE YEAR 24/2022 AD

Mathilda waved wistfully as the spires and towers and curtain wall of the Iowan city fell out of sight around a bend of the river. Their shadows fell long across the deck, with the morning sun at their backs. A propeller ship went by in the other direction, the crew chanting at the pedals belowdecks, and fishing boats were out like a flock of gulls. Rudi stood with his hand on the cool metal frame of the schooner's bow catapult, his legs flexing as the ship nosed across the swell, content with the slap of water on the hull, the manifold thrum of wind through the rigging and the groan and creak and squeal of the wooden fabric beneath them.

"I'll miss Kate," she said after a while. "Her husband was a complete bastard, but *she* was . . . is . . . a good friend. A good woman. I don't know how she could have loved him, but she did."

"*Acushla,* if women didn't have bad taste in men and weren't prone to fall in love with right bastards now and then, it's certain, sure and completely beyond question that humankind would have died out long ago."

Mathilda snorted. "Things would have been a lot harder for us without her. She's really getting a grip on things there, too."

Rudi nodded; he'd had the same impression. "And now that she's hatching from her egg, the which you had a hand in, I suspect she'll be a very bad enemy to her foes, as well as a good friend to us. It's important work you did there, work which may decide battles in our favor in a year or two, and perhaps turn the course of the war."

She leaned against him with a sigh, and he put his arm around her shoulders—careful of her wounds—and his chin on her hair, enjoying the clean summery smell of it.

The sun was fairly warm as the morning went on, just comfortable despite the stiff breeze that fluttered the edges of his kilt and plaid, and snatched at his bonnet and shoulder-length hair. The ship heeled as the two triangular sails behind them thuttered and then cracked taut, smooth lovely geometric curves up the white-pine masts. The craft was rigged fore and aft, handy for the confined waters of even a giant river, and ninety feet at the waterline. A little spray came over the bowsprit and touched his face where they stood on the foredeck.

The use of the ship was a gift from the new Regent and Chancellor of the Provisional Republic. She was big enough to take the party, their best horses, and all the Southsiders.

The whole tribe of which are now a pain in the arse of cosmic dimensions, he thought. *But we couldn't leave them there, not even at someplace friendly like the Heuisink's estate. Too many old angers, and they'd be too afraid and bewildered and cramped, too likely for it to end in blood if they felt deserted. At least they're hardy sorts, and not settled folk. They're all used to moving about in dangerous country in all seasons.*

It wasn't something he could get too irritated about now. They were finally *moving*, and quickly—as much north as east, right now, granted, but on their way again, and soon they'd turn eastward up the Wisconsin River.

I can't say our stay in Iowa was wasted time, either. We've made a strong friend, and Corwin and its Prophet an enemy.

And Mathilda was a pleasant warm solidity against his side, as well, the dearer for their separation. The blue-gray surface of the Mississippi slid by, the wooded bluffs on both sides streaked with gold and red and brown as the trees turned, above marshes clamorous with duck and goose and teal, where reeds had gone brown and spilled their white floating seed onto the air. That air smelled of wet and silt, tar and canvas and warm wood. And, faint and exciting, a hint of the wildwood.

Mathilda grinned up at him. "No more prairies!" she said. "No more bug on a plate. No more walking and walking and riding and riding and nothing *changes*."

He laughed. "You took the thought from my mind, darlin'," he said. "Now, just put some high mountains on that eastern horizon, turn this river westward, sow the forest with some Douglas fir, and it would be downright homelike, eh?"

"Just like Montival?" she said.

Rudi's answering grin was wry. There was a yearning in the tone beneath the joke, and he knew his heart as well would leap when he saw the cone of Mt. Hood again, or sailed down the Columbia past waterfalls veining the cliffs in silver, or felt the soft autumn rains that dimpled the Willamette between willow-clad banks.

"That name . . . I think a kindly Power whispered it to me. It has a ring to it, does it not? For our home is all mountain and valley, and it's beautiful . . . which the name is too, you see? Though Edain liked it even more than I."

"I think it does have a ring to it," she said. "We've all been talking about it and we *all* like it. It's . . . it's *true*. The name the land was waiting for."

There was something in her voice . . . He looked down sharply, and her bold-featured face was smiling in a way that had a disconcerting hint of her mother's expression when she'd just maneuvered someone exactly where she wanted them—or was about to castle in a game of chess. The more so as she stepped out from beneath his arm.

He turned, and all the companions of his journey were there, with Jake sunna Jake as well. Edain was grinning like Garbh; most of the others were solemn; Mathilda's face had turned serious as well.

"You've been conspiring behind my back!" he said, half-angry, half-amused.

Mathilda wasn't in court dress today, of course, but the badge of the Eye was on the shoulder of her sheepskin jacket. She tapped it, and grew less grave for an instant.

"Conspiring? *Hel*lo! *House Arminger*, Rudi!"

Then she drew her sword with her good arm, and carefully so as not to stress her healing ribs beneath the bandages. They all did, and raised the blades; Rudi felt himself struck speechless as the ship's crew looked on curiously.

"Hail!" Mathilda cried, her voice proud as an ocean of

lions. "Hail . . . Artos! *Hail, Artos the First, High King of Montival!*"

The others shouted it with her—some of them a little awkwardly, but just as loud; a red-tailed hawk that had been circling low took flight and soared upward into the blue dome of the sky.

He waited until the sound died, and set his hands on his sword belt.

"Is it that you've all gone barking mad the now?" he said sharply. "Here we are a thousand miles and more from home—yes, from Montival—and it's a *king* you would make of me?"

"I think God wants you to be a king, R—Artos, not just us," Mathilda said calmly. "And that's why the Sword is waiting for you to bring it back."

"You're many of you heirs to rulers, but none of you rulers—well, Jake is, and Odard's of age but he's a vassal, not a sovereign himself. It's our parents that should make any such choice, not us!"

"Or the head of my Order, for me, technically," Ignatius said. "Particularly since he's my temporal ruler as well as my Father in God. But I have prayed for guidance, and . . . I think that this is right; even righteous. Against the dark Power that possesses Corwin, God would raise a bulwark of the Light."

"I don't even believe in your version of the divine!" Rudi protested.

Ignatius smiled with polite, invincible certainty. "That is a great pity. But nevertheless, He believes in *you* . . . your Majesty. And He is thrifty, and uses what comes to hand. I have that on the *best* authority."

Ingolf shrugged. "I'm not even an heir, just a younger son," he said. "But yah, who cares what the old geezers think? Here, there, or anywhere? We're all Changelings, or close enough—and this world's going to be ours soon. If it isn't going to end up belonging to the Cutters," he added. "Which is what this crazy trip is all about, you betcha."

"Aunt Astrid will *love* it," Mary said with conviction, and Ritva nodded vigorously. "And Mom . . . well, Signe's reasonable. When she has to be. When it's official Bear-killer business. Sorta reasonable, mostly."

"*I'm* for it," Frederick said, his brown young face grave. "Dad wanted the country united again, and tried all his life, but the bits and pieces went their own way in spite of everything he could do. My brother Martin . . . he just wants to take it all, hammer it flat, and kill anyone who gets in his way. It's time to try something else, something that lets them all be different but puts them together as well. I know you, Rudi, and if anyone can do it, you can. I'd rather be your, umm, vassal, and follow you to victory than fail all by myself."

Virginia Kane grinned and took his arm. "I think you're the boy to put a branding iron on the Cutters' ass, your exalted majesticalness," she said cheerfully. "*And* serve up their Rocky Mountain Oysters on a plate. They killed my father and ran me off my family's ranch; I want 'em dead *bad*. Plus it just needs doing and they just need killing. Besides, Fred's my man. I go where he does, and his fights are mine too."

"You'd have made a great Chief for the Clan," Edain said. "You'll do even better as High King, with Maude or Fiorbhinn to manage at home, they're likely lasses. It'd be rank foolishness to deny it."

Mathilda nodded vigorously. "We can do the formali-ties at home, later, when you've got the Sword. But we *are* the future. Nearly everyone our age back home will want it; they already know *about* you, and the prophecy. And you're *our* King, our Changeling King. Artos."

"Don't—" he began, then choked off: *Don't call me that!*

It is my name, he thought. *Granted it's my Craft name, but it was my own mother that gave it to me in the nemed, and her inspired and making prophecy the while. That's when I was called the Lady's Sword, too.*

A prickling ran down his spine, and a feeling as if a wind were tickling his neck . . . the wind of hovering wings. If it were to be done, he supposed this was the sort of place it *would* be done; far from home, and on his way into deadly peril. The Powers would have their jokes . . . and he had promised more than once to walk the path They set, though it led through the hard and stony places. Images flashed through his mind; Raven's eyes looking into his, this moment . . . and a stricken field of battle where men roared his name as he bore a sword like a wind of flame.

"I . . ." he began, and then fell silent again.

I have been walking that path perhaps . . . since my birth? Since the day Mother held me over the altar in the Sacred Wood? Perhaps only since I was old enough to know it, he thought. *I am the sacrifice that goes consenting.*

Mathilda's shining eyes twisted at his heart. All *she* saw at this moment was him returning in glory and victory, and herself at his side, to rule together. She *was* her mother's daughter, and her father's for that matter; kingcraft was in her blood. Not to mention that if he was High King, many of the religious obstacles to a marriage could be set aside—there were ample precedents for that in the long history of her faith.

And yet if that comes to pass, and all you wish for is granted us . . . even then, anamchara *mine, still the day will come when I know that the King must die so his folk may live. On that day I will leave you, be the parting never so bitter. I have it on the best of authority—from a God, if not* your *God—that it will be before I grow old. Mine is the blood that renews the land. Well, let us hope that day's not today, or soon; and let us see that it is not shed in vain. In the meantime we have time, which can be lived in every moment.*

"Is this truly what you want?" he asked softly—his eyes were locked on Mathilda's warm brown gaze, but his voice included the others.

For answer they thrust their blades into the air again; the young sun broke in a blinding glitter from the honed edges.

"Hail, Artos!" And from Mathilda and Odard and Ignatius: *"Vivat Artos Rex! Vivat Artos Rex! Vivat!"*

The shout woke something in him—something he wasn't sure of, stronger than a jolt of brandy or the battle fury of *riastrad*. He wasn't a man hungry for power, but there was so much that needed to be *done* and which only a King could do. Defeat for the Cutters, first and foremost, but much else beside.

Power for its own sake I do not desire. But a craftsman's urge to set things right . . . that is in me, and there's no doubt of it.

"I ask you again," he said, and now he looked from face to face. "Don't do this unless you are *sure*. For there's no going back. And keep this in mind. If I am to be a King, then by Earth, by Sky, I will be *King* indeed. For such is our land's need, that's beyond disputing. I won't spare myself in serving that need. I won't spare you, either, my friends."

"Hail, Artos! Hail, High King of Montival!"

"So mote it be," he said quietly, and the words fell into the world with a weight like bells cast from bronze.

Silence fell again, broken only by the sounds of ship

and river and wind, and the long *ssshs*-click! of swords being sheathed. Then Mathilda came forward and went carefully to her knees before him, her hands lying palm-to-palm before her.

Rudi took them between his; they were warm and strong but almost vanished in his long-fingered clasp. She spoke proudly, looking him full in the face. The words were half familiar, but not exactly the formula her folk used, or his, or the Dúnedain, or the Bearkillers. They must have talked it over between themselves . . .

There go my people, he thought, remembering a saying his mother was fond of. *I must hurry to catch up with them, for I am their leader.*

Mathilda's voice rang:

"Here in the sight of God and all men I, Mathilda, daughter of Norman, daughter of Sandra, of the House of Arminger and in my person heir of Portland by right of blood, do swear fealty and service as vassal to the High King of Montival and take him as my overlord; in peace to serve with aid and counsel, in war with sword and goods and life, in my waking and my sleeping, in my living and my dying, with heart and hand and all Earthly worship; until death release me, or the world end. So witness God the Father, and Son, and Holy Spirit, and the Blessed Virgin who is Portland's patroness and mine."

Rudi swallowed, but his voice was firm as he answered:

"And this oath do I hear and swear in turn: I, Rudi Mackenzie of the Clan Mackenzie"—the slightest hesitation—"also called Artos, son of Michael, son of Juniper; son of Bear, son of Raven, and High King of Montival to be. I will not forget your oath, or fail to reward that which is given: fealty with love, valor with honor, loyalty with good lordship, oath-breaking with vengeance. This I swear by the Earth below me, by the Sky above, by the Water that is my blood, and by the Fire that is my life, and by the Lord and Lady and all the Gods of my people. May they witness it."

Mathilda offered her sword; he touched hilt and steel and sheathed it again for her. Then she stood, and they put their hands on each other's shoulders and exchanged the kiss of peace on both cheeks. She came to stand at his right, erect, with her eyes bright and glad. Mary stepped forward and knelt in turn and offered her hands, and the others lined up behind her. Rudi took his half sister's palms between his; her single blue eye seemed to wink at him for an instant—but that might just be that it was the only one she had left to blink with.

When she spoke it was entirely solemn:

"In the sight of Manwë Súlimo and Varda Elentári and all of humankind, I, Mary daughter of Michael, daughter of Signe, of the House of the Bear and the fellowship of the Dúnedain Rangers, do swear fealty and service as vassal to the High King of Montival—"

"That delay in Iowa means we can either hole up for the winter, or keep going despite it," Rudi said two days later. "We're far north and going farther, and the winter here will have all the wrath the Crone can muster and the Keeper-of-Laws send."

"Well, I've lived through a fair number of those winters. Snow's easier to travel through than mud," Ingolf said. "Or to travel *over*. It could snow hard as early as Halloween . . . Samhain . . . or even a bit earlier."

The *Hammerdown* was tied up for the evening, with a hawser stretched to the stump of something made of concrete and steel on the eastern shore, eroded and rusted but still strong. The travelers had set up tents ashore there—a little elbow room was very welcome—and Rudi could see, through the slanting windows of the stern cabin, the glow of their fires on the trunks and branches of the great trees that overhung the campsite. It was chilly enough that his jacket and plaid were welcome even in the rather stuffy cabin.

He spooned up another mouthful of an entirely forgettable catfish stew and took a bite from a lump of equally uninteresting corn bread laced with soy meal, his attention focused on the map, a topographic one from a journal of the ancient world called *National Geographic*. Ignatius and Mathilda were there too; the priest paused to turn up one of the lanterns and the blue flame brightened across the aging, fragile paper glued to a backing of new linen cloth.

"The roads are pretty rough, especially past about here," Ingolf went on.

The Readstowner's thick finger came down near his birth home, on the Kickapoo River.

"They already were when I left . . . and hell, that was a while ago, and there's been plenty of frost and heave and floods since. Richland isn't Iowa, and they weren't kept up the same, or the railroads. But once the snow's down hard, you can use sleighs, and skis. A man can go twice, three times as far in a day on skis as he can walking, and carry more of a pack, too, or pull a small sled. We'd make up the time. Stick to the rivers and lakes as much as we could."

Rudi used his spoon as a pointer. "Right east, then?"

"As far as the Great Lakes. Big chunks of 'em freeze hard, especially around the edges, and from what I hear the St. Lawrence freezes solid all the way down to the ocean. We could go that way—less chance of running into hostiles if we stay away from land as much as possible. It's risky, yah, but so is waiting for spring."

"We'd have to wait for freeze-up," Rudi said. "But we do need some time, not least for our wounded to heal fully. Matti and Odard need some rest before they do hard travel again. And to be sure, every time we've taken a break on this journey important things have come of it; not least friends willing to fight the Cutters, when the time comes. That's time well spent, even if it slows us down enough to make me want to run screeching into the woods like a banshee full of brandy."

"I can travel," Mathilda said stoutly. "But . . . yes, I couldn't run or fight well right now."

Ignatius traced the line of the Mississippi southwards from Dubuque.

"And somewhere southward here are what is left of the Cutters, waiting."

"Well south, Father," Mathilda said. "Kate told me that the Iowan river navy patrols well beyond their border, either way, and she and Abel Heuisink will have them looking hard. The Cutters will have to hide; probably they'll have to run their ship up a tributary and abandon it, unless they go so far south they're out of the picture."

"Probably they'll go at least this far," Rudi said, tapping the place where the Ohio joined the Father of Waters. "They'd know that we were thinking of taking the Ohio route."

Everyone nodded. Ingolf shrugged.

"Yah hey, they'd have heard. Tancredo owes me favors and he hid Mary and Ritva and Fred and Virginia. On the other hand, he *is* a pimp. A man who can't be bought doesn't go into that line of work, in my experience."

"They lost about thirty men in Dubuque, killed and left badly wounded," Rudi said thoughtfully. "They'd have eighty left—and a few of their local followers fled with them, to be sure. More than I'd care to meet, if it can be avoided. We were lucky once, but Nike is a fickle Goddess."

"And there is their High Seeker, their adept," Ignatius said. "He has . . . resources. I would not care to meet him again either, except at great need."

Silence fell for a moment. Then Ingolf stretched his thick arms, rubbed one hand across his short-cropped brown beard and spoke:

"The Ohio route's got its problems anyway. Lots of dams and bridges. And then the Appalachians."

Ignatius raised a brow. "I had heard that more survived there than anywhere else in the east."

"Yah, that's the problem, Father. Mostly in the lowlands near the dead cities they're barely human. But there aren't very many of them either. Eaters who got through the first year, well, a lot still died before they could learn how to catch rabbits or deer when people got scarce. Not a lot of their kids lived, either, between starving and the way most of their parents were insane by then. Mind you, with a winnowing like that the ones who did live to grow up are as dangerous as rats—man-sized, really smart rats."

Rudi tapped a thumb on his lips. "Living in the wilds is a thing which requires much skill," he said. "Look at our poor Southsiders and how pig-ignorant they were . . . and they were farther west, and they were *clean*, as they put it."

Ingolf's hand covered what had been West Virginia, eastern Kentucky, southern Ohio and western Pennsylvania.

"Up in the hollers, the back hills where they could hide out from the refugees or fight them off . . ."

"They kept more knowledge?" Ignatius asked. "That accords with what the Church has heard."

Ingolf nodded: "I've talked to a few salvagers who went that way. They grow corn and truck, raise a little stock, and they were mostly hunters before the Change. A few even know how to make cloth or do some smithing. Some of them are decent enough, even if they're mighty standoffish. But then right in the next holler there's maybe a little clot of families that got through the dying time by eating outsiders if not each other, and still like a little BBQ stranger with their grits when they can get it. Or they may kill you for your gear, which means you're just as dead, even if they leave the bodies alone."

"There would be far more of them than there are close to the dead cities, too," Rudi said thoughtfully. "If they farm, and are skillful hunters."

How much food a land produced was always of concern to a warrior; food supplies set the limit on the number of people, hence of fighters.

"A *lot* more, and they've got better weapons and tools, and from what I hear they're . . . not as crazy. You can't just bull through with a troop, the way you can in the lowlands. Parts of northern Wisconsin are pretty much like that too, I'm afraid."

"A choice between evils, so," Rudi said, as his mouth quirked. "It's a wonder and a bemusement to me, so it is, that you find so many who *want* power. If you get it what goes with it? Late nights peering at maps and listening to reports, hard work and harder decisions."

Father Ignatius smiled. "My son, that you feel so makes it much more likely you will use power well."

"And if you don't get the power, other people make

the decisions and you just have to put up with them," Mathilda pointed out.

"To be sure," Rudi said. "And now, my friend, how will we be received at your brother's steading? For it would be the most convenient place to prepare for the next stage if we take that way. And *if* we're welcome."

Ingolf scowled, and his strong worn hands knotted together.

"I'm not sure," he said bluntly. "At worst . . . well, Ed always liked money. Not that he'd lie or cheat for it, but he's . . . tight, and loves a bargain. He'd sell us what we need even if he can't stand the sight of me. Or someone in the neighborhood would. Beyond that I can't say. We were barely speaking to each other when I left, and he'd have stayed up to check that the sun rose in the East if I said it did, but that's a long time ago."

Rudi propped his elbows on either side of the empty bowl, his chin on his thumbs and his lips on his knuckles; red-gold hair fell across his eyes, but he'd memorized the map anyway. Decision jelled.

"We'll go up the Wisconsin, and then the Kickapoo," he said firmly. "We need a base to prepare for the next leg. If your brother's holding is open to us, good; if not him, then another. We've gold enough, but there are preparations we must make. Not least, the Southsiders need every sort of instruction, useful as they are."

Ritva Havel looked over to where Virginia Kane was coldshoeing a horse, with half a dozen Southsiders looking on, and Edain holding the beast's head and soothing it.

"I wish we were on the ship," she said, beneath the *tap . . . tap . . . tap . . .* of the hammer.

Mary shrugged. "We hailed Rudi as High King," she

pointed out. "A King consults who he wants to. Besides, you get a meeting much bigger than four and a leader and you waste too much time talking. Ingolf's smart and so are the others."

Ritva grinned. "You're willing to let him do the talking? Must be love."

"Well, yes, but it hasn't turned my brain to mush, sis," she said.

The Southsider women they'd called drifted in and squatted in front of her, the light of the fire turning their faces ruddy and lying warm on her own back. A few were holding toddlers or nursing babies, which would make her next talk a bit easier. She'd done similar ones with young Rangers . . . but at least they didn't have to be introduced to the concept of *soap*. Not most of them, at least—you got some very odd recruits from little hole-and-cranny parts of the Willamette and the mountains southward towards Ashland and the old California border.

"Now," she said, when they had gathered. "Remember how I told you the Lady's Cauldron is the source of everything?"

At the blank looks, she went on: "The belly of the Big Strong Bitch? It's, ah, like a *pot*. Things come out of it. The whole world, all the people and animals and things."

That brought more nods; they'd gotten that much from the talks on the Old Religion, and they were pathetically grateful for a story that made *sense* of the world as something but malevolence and chaos.

"Well, we're women, you see. So we have a special link to Her. We're Her made manifest in the world. And like her, we can give or withhold the fertility of our, ummm, *pots*."

Frowns of puzzlement. "You mean, tell the studs they can't fuck? They wouldn't like that," one said; she thought it was Jake's woman.

A pause, and the Southsider went on: "*I* wouldn't like that."

Ritva had enough exposure to the tribe's dialect now that she could follow it; her mind translated it into more-or-less standard English. And they'd already modified their way of speech a little in return, though it was complicated by the way they did their best to imitate Rudi and Edain.

"Ah . . . yes, but not just that. We can give or withhold the gift of children because we're sovereign . . . because we have . . . ah, because we can do magic like the Big Strong Bitch."

"You mean spook-stuff so you can fuck and not get littles unless we want?"

"Yes! Exactly!"

That brought an eager babble. The Southsiders lost so many of their children, especially the ones born in the winter, that the thought of spacing them to match the seasons was alluring. From books she'd read in Larsdalen and Stardell Hall, wandering hunters had always done that, even if farmers often didn't. A woman couldn't deal with more than one infant who had to be carried at a time. In this as so much else the Southsiders were worse off than the most primitive human tribes of ancient times.

Eyes went wide as she held up a small coil of copper beads with a dangling silk thread below.

"Now, you see how this looks like the sacred serpent I showed you? What you do is put this—"

*"Like a golden chain, girdling the Earth,
Is the Unseen Hierarchy of the Ascended Lords . . ."*

"High Seeker? Master Dalan?" Major Peter Graber said, as the chanting faded.

He was glad he'd waited until after the evening prayer to talk to the priest; the sun was down beyond the trees in the west, and it would make their conversation more private. The morale of the Sword of the Prophet was like iron, the men were ready to die as they were commanded . . . but even iron had flaws.

And I always liked this time of day, he thought inconsequentially.

The magic blue and green of it, and the slight hush that fell as the breeze died and the birds sang their last, and then the first stars blossoming in the east. Today there was a thin crescent of moon as well, high and ghost-pale southwards. It was a moment when the spirit could fly free. He sighed and returned to the business of the Church . . . which was also the business of the spirit, after all.

The man who called himself High Seeker Dalan had always been a little more solid-seeming than the most of his kind, who usually looked gaunt and scrawny. Right after the fight in Dubuque this one had been like a ghost for days, eating and drinking if you put food in his hands, but otherwise motionless.

Now he just looks like he's dying, instead of already dead, Graber thought.

He fought down resentment at how many of his men *had* died on this trip; he'd crossed the border into the Sioux territories with two hundred effectives. Currently he had eighty-four . . . and that included two men who probably wouldn't recover.

The burden he bears for the Ascended Masters is far higher than mine.

"We must consult," he went on.

A jerky nod. "Yes. Come."

The bitter smoke of the burnt ship drifted this far, but he didn't think the crews of the Iowan warships would pursue; the ruins of Cairo weren't far away, and they'd already had a brush with an Eater band. They'd also shot several deer, fat with autumn, and a wild pig, and the carcasses of the beasts were roasting and stewing with foraged herbs and roots as the leaders talked. He judged the men were cheerful enough, except for the handful of Iowan converts; the Sword of the Prophet was always tasked with the most difficult missions, including the ones where death was almost certain. They knew as well as he that their lifestreams would be bright among the Ascending Hierarchy if they fell in the Church's service.

His stomach rumbled at the smell of the meat, and the scent of wheat cakes cooking on the griddles, but he ignored it; a man of the CUT learned to command the flesh by the power of the *atman*, though only the adepts had the ultimate mastery. The soulless were the slaves of their *Sthula-Sarira*, the gross and merely material body, which meant they were little more than walking corpses. One more sign that their only reason for existence was to serve the True Spirit and the community of believers.

"Hail Maitreya!" he began, when they'd walked a little way from the fires—but well within his perimeter of hidden scouts.

The blessing was always a safe opening gambit with the clergy.

"Master Dalan?" he went on.

"Hail . . . to the Youth of Sixteen Summers."

The priest made the proper reply, his voice starting out rusty, as if he was remembering how to speak.

"We have to decide what to do, High Seeker," Graber said carefully. "Should we try to push through to this Nantucket place and *wait* for the soulless misbelieving sons of the Nephilim? Or should we try to intercept the enemy again?"

They'd tried that and failed repeatedly, though by narrow margins. Graber wasn't particularly disturbed; if you kept trying, eventually you either succeeded or died. He hadn't died yet. The High Seeker's head turned to the north, as if his bruised-looking eyes were probing through the substance of the densely wooded hills.

"They may try to take the northern route," he said. "They will not come up the Ohio, not when we might be waiting for them."

Graber waited. That was a military judgment, and as such it was his to make. As it happened, he agreed. Catching Artos has been like trying to grab an oiled rattlesnake with his bare hands; nearly impossible, and deadly dangerous when you finally did it. And the others with him were nearly as bad. Not least, they all had a damnable talent for getting locals to fight for them.

"Bring me a prisoner," Dalan said.

The officer turned his head and barked a command. Soon two of his troopers frog-marched one of the Eater captives between them. He had his hands tied before him, and a sheathed shete thrust through between his elbows and back; they steered him with it. Graber's nose wrinkled; everyone smelled after a while in the field—this was the first opportunity they'd had to boil water in some time—but the savage was rank even by the standards a soldier learned. Worse than a High Line cowboy in midwinter.

A crude loincloth and the leggings held to it by thongs were his only clothing. For the rest he was an unexceptional man, perhaps in his twenties though looking older with his shaggy hairiness and ground-in dirt; the hair and beard were brown, the eyes a hazel green. Scrawny and not very tall, but that was to be expected.

The High Seeker held up his personal amulet, worn on his left wrist and studded with amethyst, symbol of the Seventh Ray. He murmured something: Graber caught the name of *Djwal Khul*, a great lord of the Ascending Hierarchy who dealt with communication and knowledge.

"Possibilities increase exponentially," the High Seeker said . . . in a normal conversational tone, but as if to himself. "Capacity to affect foam linkages and tap base energy is greater but so is need."

Good that he is not talking to me, Graber thought. *I do not understand and do not wish to. Hail Serapis Bey! I serve the Fourth Ray. The Church also needs those who can deal with the material.*

"But amplification and modulation are necessary. Interaction requires perception. Contaminated. So many possibilities."

He smiled at the prisoner, and the man screeched like some small animal caught in a trapper's toothed steel. His hands went out to grip either side of the captive's face, forcing him to meet his eyes, and the troopers stepped away.

"I . . . see . . . you . . . forever," he said.

The prisoner screamed again, and the guards stepped back farther in involuntary recoil, like men who find themselves clutching something in the dark and feel the wriggling of too many legs. After a moment Dalan screamed back at his victim, in the same pitch of hopeless pain. Graber swallowed as trails of blood started from the corners of the Eater's eyes, trickling like red tears into the scabrous beard, glittering in the firelight. After a time that seemed to last forever Dalan's sound became words:

"Bitch! *Bitch!* Deva, die without dying! You and your he-whore! And the One who sent you!"

He released the prisoner and staggered away, moaning, clenched fists slapping at the sides of his head; yet he was grinning, licking his lips. When the shuddering ceased he straightened.

"They are traveling north. Water. Intention is to the east. I see forests, ice, wolves. Beasts. Beasts. We will pursue. Now it must rest. There is no replacement and it must not be stressed beyond failure point."

The High Seeker turned and lay down on his bedroll, and closed his eyes. What followed did not look like sleep; it was more as if the adept had been *suspended*, somehow. The troopers remained stock-still, because the captive was moving now. Not trying to escape; instead he knelt by a stretch of frost-heaved concrete and began to beat his head against it. The *tock . . . tock . . . tock* sound was like a hammer on hard wood, as regular as a carpenter's. Graber made a gesture with one hand; the man who'd used his shete to control the prisoner stepped forward, set his hand to the hilt and stripped the steel free of the leather. It swung in a brief glinting arc, and there was a final sound—heavier and wetter than bone on stone.

"Get rid of this carrion," Graber snapped. "Vender, Roberts," he went on to his two chief surviving lieutenants. "The maps."

They joined him where he sat on a log; a trooper brought them plates of stew and wheat cakes as they discussed distances and times.

"We'll need horses," Roberts said, tracing the length of what had once been Illinois from south to north. "It's an impossible distance to cover on foot in any useful time."

"It could be done," Graber said; though few men from the High West would think so. "But the tribes around here have some mounts and those in the prairies to the north have more. Say a week to accumulate what we need to start with . . ."

He paused. "What is the date?"

"October first, sir."

"Ah." He smiled, an expression that softened the iron slab-and-angle of his face for an instant.

The other two men looked at him, puzzled. He explained briefly:

"My eldest son's birthday. He will be ten today, in Corwin."

They nodded. "Old enough to begin training in the House of the Prophetic Guard, as we all did, if he's found worthy," Roberts said.

His voice was a little wistful. He had nothing but daughters, and all those were very young.

"He will be. My wives are women of excellent character, and Peter studies hard," Graber said firmly. "Now, if we can acquire two remounts per man, we can begin. The horses will be of low quality."

CHAPTER ELEVEN

"**G**etting close," Ingolf said, rubbing a hand down the neck of his mount. "Soo, Boy, soo," he said to the horse. "You'll get a good feed here, even if you were foaled in Nebraska."

Rudi Mackenzie nodded, tactfully ignoring the slight hoarseness in the other man's voice, as if he were choking back unexpected tears; Ingolf's face was an iron mask locked against a surge of feeling.

A Mackenzie—any who were Changelings, at least— would weep, returning home after so long, Rudi thought. *But customs differ from land to land, and so do the stamp they set on our souls. Wouldn't it be a duller world, if they did not, so?*

It was a bright fall afternoon, comfortable but with an underlying nip to it. This was farm-and-forest country, but you could tell that the North Woods started not so far away, and that the Wheel of the Year was turning towards the Crone's dominion, in a land harsher than Oregon—

Than Montival, he reminded himself; it was growing natural.

As they rode north along the valley of the Kickapoo

from the hamlet at Soldier's Grove the fields had quickly gone back to scrub and saplings, the usual story of more land than the survivors of the Change had means or reason to till when they no longer used machines to feed cities far away. But for the last hour or two the signs of human habitation had grown thicker again, first the chewed look of land used for rough summer grazing, then fields and the odd farmhouse behind its berm and ditch and barbed wire or palisade.

Often there was a wary twinkle of spearheads from the defenses or a fighting platform built atop an old silo, or the sight of livestock being driven up the slope of the land towards the woods; just what you'd expect from sensible folk when scores of armed strangers passed by. That alarm diminished as they went, until men and a few women came out to watch them pass with no more than a little caution . . . and weapons in their hands.

Then Ingolf laughed aloud as they came upon a man-high oak stump not far from the road. It was roughly carved into the shape of a naked big-nosed troll, but despite the crude work you could see a look of ineffable self-satisfaction on its face and in the way its hands folded across a swag belly; from the weathering and moss, it was at least a decade old and perhaps more. In Mackenzie or Bearkiller territory Rudi would have thought it a roadside shrine, but he doubted that was the purpose here and looked a question at the Readstown man.

"I did that," Ingolf said, a chuckle still in his voice. "Well, me and Bert Kuykendall and Carl Heisz and Will Uhe, when we were all about twelve. It's the spitting image of old Bossman Al, Al Clements. He came up from Richland Center that year, doing a tour of his Sheriffs' homeplaces. We snuck out and worked on it after dark, kept it under a pile of brush until the day, and he went right past it and turned . . . what's that color, sort of like purple . . ."

"Puce," Mary Havel put in, sharing her man's good humor.

"Yah, puce. Dad wore out a hickory switch on Bert and Carl and Will, and two more on me for setting a bad example, but it was worth sitting down careful for a while. Surprised Ed didn't have it cut down; he isn't . . . wasn't . . . much of a man for a joke."

"Why didn't your father do just that and take an ax to it, if he was angry, and it annoyed his overlord?"

"He wouldn't give Clements the satisfaction. Never liked the man. I think he laughed about it to himself, despite the merry hell he gave all four of us. Dad was a hard man on his sons, but he expected us to push back at him. Wanted it too, I think."

"Ah, and are you also thinking those three friends of your youth will be there to greet you?" Rudi said.

The smile died. "All dead now. Will put a pitchfork through his foot while he was loading manure that year. He was always a dreamy sort. Got lockjaw, poor bastard."

"A hard passing," Rudi said sympathetically, nodding; they'd had drugs for that in the old days, but . . .

Ingolf shrugged. "What way isn't? Unless someone hits you on the head with an ax when you're not expecting it. Bert and Carl volunteered for the Sioux War and left home with me . . . Bert got an arrow in the eye a couple of weeks later. We weren't even to Marshall yet and he wasn't eighteen when it happened—night attack, just dumb bad luck and our not knowing what the fuck we were doing. Carl was bushwhacked by Eaters in Boston, that last salvage trip east my Villains made. But we collected the head-price for him, and piled the ears on his grave."

Rudi nodded again; he'd have expected no less; Ingolf wasn't a man to let a comrade go unavenged.

"Ritva, Mary," he said. "Ride ahead and see to our welcome."

He reached into his saddlebag and held out a large envelope.

"They'll have had scouts watching, unless Ed's let things slip," Ingolf said. "And odds are someone came ahead when we got off the ship and said who we were and where we were going; they'd have gotten here yesterday, riding fast and switching horses. You can't drag this many people through the countryside tactfully, but nobody's looking too upset over us. They must have some idea who we are."

"To be sure. But I'm thinking it's best to be formal."

"With my brother Ed? Yah, you betcha. Always was a stickler."

The twins reined around; Ritva took the envelope and Mary paused for an instant to reach out and touch Ingolf's hand before she leaned forward and brought her Arab mare, Rochael, up to a canter with a shift of balance.

Rudi waited for another fifteen minutes of travel amid the stuttering clop of scores of hooves, creak of saddle and harness, grind of wheels and the *thud* as one rose and fell over a rock in the roadway, then threw up his clenched right fist. The long caravan came slowly to a halt behind him, with a squeal of brakes and a neighing of horses and curses in two languages and several dialects. There were six big wagons there, and nearly a hundred folk.

It's a migration, not a quest! he thought. *The which is a giant flag to attract attention and an inconvenience, so it is. Finding three pounds of food per head per day . . . it's a lesson in logistics!* Or *a pain in the arse. But the Southsiders will be worth their weight in gold farther east—more than worth it, for the savages don't want to eat gold.*

Then aloud: "We'll await them here. It's . . . polite."

His comrades followed his example as he dismounted, stretching and twisting in relief; it had been a long day in the saddle. Virginia Kane didn't only twist and reach, but frankly rubbed and kneaded her buttocks.

"I got outta condition in Iowa," she said. "*And* on that damn boat. Too much sittin', not enough ridin'."

"I wish you wouldn't do that," Fred Thurston said to her. "It makes me want to do it too."

"What, rub your butt? Why not? We ain't none of us picky about parlor manners, that I noticed. 'Cept Odard, and that's *his* problem."

The baron of Gervais bowed and blew her a kiss, which she answered with a raised finger. Fred grinned and replied:

"No, it makes me want to rub *yours.*"

"Now you're talkin', lover boy!"

She unhitched her lariat from the saddle and swatted him on the backside with the coil.

"Let's go get those remounts bridled and on leading reins; they'll be skittish 'round strange horses. More fun than talking anyhow. 'Specially talkin' to *farmers.*"

She looked around at the valley that held Readstown. "This country's too . . . too crowded with country, you ask me. I feel like I'm stuck in a closet and something's *hidin'* behind them hills and trees."

"You know, Chief, the Rocky Mountains were grand," Edain said, when she'd dropped back.

They stood with the breeze cuffing at their plaids and ruffling the raven feathers in the clasp of his flat bonnet, the tuft of wolf fur in Edain's.

The young man of the Wolf totem went on, with a glance at Virginia over his shoulder where she was roping a skittish piebald:

"And the deserts, and the plains—well, the Lord and Lady made all lands beautiful in their own way, but after a while the flatlands had me feelin' like a bug on a tabletop, and someone about to swat me and say *sorry, little brother* and flick the body off the table with thumb and finger for Garbh to snap up."

The big shaggy beast rose at the sound of her name and butted her head under his hand. He ruffled her ears absently and went on as she grinned and squirmed and leaned against him:

"This now . . . It isn't home, but it's more homelike than most of what we've seen, sure and it is."

"I had the same buglike feeling on the plains, boyo," Rudi said. "It's all where you're raised, I suppose. And this is a delight to the eye, and no mistake."

It *was* a pleasure to look around, and at the same time it sent a lance of pain up under his ribs. There was no alarm now, so Ingolf's thought of scouts and messengers preceding them were probably the truth. He saw folk at work in the fields heaving wicker baskets of potatoes onto a wagon, a shepherd with her dogs, a bow across her back and her crook in her hand amid the dun-white flow of her charges, the people of a farmstead laying fresh shingles on their roofs against the coming winter with the raw wood yellow amid the faded brown of the older layers. The *tack . . . tack . . .* of the hammers sounded, faint with distance.

At home they'd be doing those homely tasks too, and hanging Brigid's crosses from the roof-trees, and making the costumes ready for Samhain . . .

"It's a comely place that bred you, Ingolf, that's a fact," he said.

"It sure is," the older man said quietly, a half smile on his battered, bearded face.

He hadn't seen this land since he left as a boy of nineteen, younger than Edain was now. There was a hungry look in his dark blue eyes as he went on:

"Pretty as I remember, and then some. *Fair is the land, fair to the harvest* . . . I thought about this a lot, in some real bad places. Seeing myself riding up this road, in my head, you know?"

The track their train of jolting wagons had followed up the winding river was dry brown dirt, and deep-rutted where wheels and hooves had churned it during the rains. The old paved road ran down closer to the Kickapoo except where streamside cliffs forced it away, and it looked as if the water had risen and bitten chunks out of it every other season over the past generation, not to mention the locals mining what remained for asphalt. Little was left but patches overrun by vine and shrub and eager sapling.

They were heading more or less northeast, in the strip of cleared land between the river and rolling hills covered in dense forests. The whole area was like that, from where they'd left the ship at the junction of the Kickapoo and the Wisconsin rivers; low wooded ridges rising to table-lands, and valleys between, one opening into another with creeks flowing down them like the veins in a leaf.

That much you could have gotten from a map, Rudi thought.

But not the way mist lay along the twisting river in drifts of soft-edged silver over water that was icy crystal between the tree-clad banks. Nor how the hills were a rumpled crimson and blush-red and yellow-gold shout of sugar maple and oak, basswood and birch and hickory, punctuated here and there by the solid dark green of hemlock and pine, or occasionally a stretch of cinnamon-colored bare sandstone. The cool musty-clean scent of the autumn woods mingled with a little tang of hearth smoke and the mealy richness of damp turned earth, and an occasional pungent waft of manure. The sky was aching-blue above, empty save for the lonely honking of a wedge of geese, a string of black dots drifting southward.

The breeze gusted stronger, and a flight of leaves soared towards them from a lone maple like tumbling coins of ruddy copper or a swirl of butterflies fashioned from flame. Ingolf's lips moved silently for a moment. Then he surprised the Mackenzie by reciting, absently and under his breath, as if to himself:

"Let this be the verse you grave for me:
Here he lies where he long'd to be;
Home is the sailor, home from the sea,
And the hunter home from the hill."

It wasn't a poem Rudi had heard before. Though it was lovely, the clansman still made the sign of the Horns against ill luck with his right hand—down on his thigh where it was out of sight from the other man. He'd be melancholy himself, had his wanderings gone on so long before a return that was no true homecoming, but it wasn't a good idea to speak your own memorial aloud that way.

You never knew when Someone with a whimsical sense of humor was listening.

Well, well, he thought, with a sideways glance at his friend. *And it's often a man will surprise you, even if you've been long on the road with him and fought and hunted and worked side by side, yes, and drunk beer and sung and laughed together times beyond counting.*

"A fine land indeed," he repeated aloud instead. "Even better than your tales of it."

Which was true; Ingolf wasn't clumsy of tongue, but he wasn't a bard either, and the land about Readstown deserved one. This country didn't have the endless fat black earth of Iowa, but there was forest in plenty for game and timber and room for the soul to breathe when you were alone in the wildwood, and fast streams for mills and to delight the eye and ear. Between woods and water was the rolling ground where those of humankind made their own particular and ancient pact with Earth the Mother, one born of sweat and hope, pain and love and a lifetime's striving.

The fields were edged with post and board fences, cultivated in gently curving strips along the contours, signs of the only wealth that was really real. Pastures within had the seared green color that came after the first frosts, somehow more vivid for being a bit faded. They were dotted with plump white-and-black spotted milch cows with full udders swinging as they walked, black Angus or red-coated Herefords like bricks of flesh, and horses that ranged from ponies to huge hairy-hoofed draught beasts. There were ranked orchards where a few late apples still glowed, and sheep grazed beneath the neatly trimmed trees or fat brown pigs rooted and snuffled after windfalls. The potato fields were lumpy-brown, already dug and looking untidy as they always did; others had the blue-green mist over earth plowed and harrowed smooth that marked winter wheat or barley. Sprawling pumpkins on their vines were vivid orange between rustling brown tripods of Indian corn in stubblefields.

Here and there solid stone-and-brick farmhouses stood with smoke trailing from their chimneys and those of the cottages that huddled near them like chicks about their mother. Silos reared tall as castle towers from a distance, and thatched wheat ricks in their yards like conical huts of gold. Tatters of red paint clung to hip-roofed barns now mostly the brown-gray of weathered plank, once or twice the odd curved sheet-metal shapes the old world had used just before the end.

Rudi sighed; there wasn't time to admire the view. Right now the inhabitants should be more his concern.

Ritva and Mary came trotting back along the roadway on their dapple-gray Arabs, giving him the peace sign to show their mission had been successful. With them came a party of a dozen locals mounted on strong cobby-nondescript saddle horses of no particular breed. They rode in a creak of leather and hollow thudding clop of shod hooves on soft dirt, grouped around a middle-aged, brown-bearded man who was . . .

"Ed," Ingolf said quietly, as if to himself. "Still looking constipated full-time, I see."

Edward Vogeler, Rudi thought as the words confirmed his guess.

And he *did* look tight-mouthed; not as if he never smiled, but as if he thought three times before he did.

Ogma, whose words fall sweet on the ear as honey on the tongue, lend me Your eloquence. A quarrel we do not need, so. It's guesting we seek, and open-handed helpfulness.

Rudi gave the group a warrior's swift instinctive once-over as they reined in, soothing Epona's snort with a hand on her neck. Four wore short mail shirts and kettle helmets like bluntly pointed hats with drooping brims. All had long horseman's shetes and bowie knives at their sword belts, with tomahawks thrust through a loop at the rear. Most had quivers and shields on their backs and recurve bows in saddle scabbards at their knees as well. And they looked as if they would no more go riding abroad without the weapons than they would without their rough practical clothes of homespun wool and leather or their shapeless floppy-brimmed hats and battered billed caps.

The Sheriff's household retainers and his kin, Rudi judged, as he saw them give him and his followers the same appraisal, like an image in a mirror. *What they call "deputies" in these lands.*

Not full-time fighting men, but well used to weapons and to working with each other and their lord; probably the core of his war levy, when he called out the land folk, and his right and left hands the rest of the time.

Good practical workmanlike sorts at war, I'd judge, as they would be at felling a tree or hunting a deer or building a house, he thought.

They were big fair men, only half of them old enough to be bearded beyond patchy wisps but nearly all in their full hard-muscled, thick-armed strength; the eyes were light against their weather-beaten tans, hair mostly in various shades of brown and blond and red. Ingolf had told him how this region had been settled by Norski and Deutsch long ago, with a dash of Yankee and Gael, Polaki and Czech and others, all long since melded into a single folk deep-rooted in the land. The way they wore their hair—locks hacked off level with their jaws, beards clipped close—made Rudi suddenly look at his friend again; only now did he realize it was the fashion of his homeland rather than a mere whim.

One of the riders stood out, though he rode towards the rear; he was beardless and ruddy-brown of skin, with high cheeks and long braids confined by a headband, a feather in the band of his broad-brimmed hat and bead-work on the sheath of his bowie. *His* hair had probably been raven black before it went white and gray, and his face was a net of leathery wrinkles. The Indian nodded gravely to Ingolf as the whole party drew rein and raised his hand in a sign of greeting that the wanderer returned.

The youngest of the Readstown men was about sixteen, with hands and feet a little too big for his gangling height. He looked enough like Ingolf to be his son, save for a mop of yellow hair still streaked with summer's faded tow white.

"Uncle Ingolf!" he called, grinning as if to split his freckled face. "Remember how you put me on my first pony?"

Ingolf blinked. "Mark?" he blurted. "Little Markie? Jesus Christ, but you've grown!"

Rudi kept his smile to himself. An exile tended to think that nothing changed in his absence, that home remained like a picture hung on the wall of memory with everything frozen as it was. To think that way below the surface, at least; it would be well to remember that his own homeland was living its own life without him to watch. The thought made his smile die and the longing to ride up the road and see the gates of Dun Juniper even stronger.

"Quiet, son," the leader of the Readstown men said to the youth. "Save it for later. This is man talk."

His voice was gravel-deep and full of the unconscious authority you'd expect in one who wasn't often contradicted in this remote place.

Then, a little awkwardly, leaning forward with his hands on the pommel of his saddle:

"Hello, Ingolf. Good to see you again."

"You too, Ed," Ingolf replied.

There was a moment's silence, and then he added: "How's by you? Looks like the harvest was good."

"Tolerable, around here. Bit of wilt in da alfalfa, lost some sheep to the wolves und a horse with a catamount, but a good year otherwise, so far, touch wood."

Edward Vogeler, Rudi thought, as the man put a finger to the wood battens on the hilt of his shete.

He'd have guessed so even if they'd met on a city street. The older man might have been his comrade's image, if you added on fifteen years, gray streaks in the beard and forty pounds; he still looked bear-strong despite the beginnings of a pot that strained against the silver buttons of his bloodred mackinaw jacket and the way his hair had receded from a high forehead lined with worry marks. The only obvious difference was a straighter nose lacking the scar and kink Ingolf's had, and eyes that were nearer leaf green than dark blue.

"Ah . . ." Ingolf hesitated again; he was a proud man. "Sorry I was such a cast-iron prick when I left, Ed."

He seemed surprised when his brother shrugged slightly and replied:

"When you stomped out, you mean? Runs in the family. All us Vogelers are a bunch of damn stubborn square-heads, yah?"

His voice had the same flat-voweled rasp that Ingolf's did, but stronger, not worn down by exposure to other lands. And with a little more of the singsong undertone, plus a tendency to use *d* instead of *th* at the beginning of words. He swung down from his horse with a grunt and all his party followed; one of the younger men stepped forward to hold the leader's reins.

"You'd be Rudi Mackenzie?" Ingolf's elder brother said, absently fingering a five-pointed star pinned to his coat. "I'm Edward Vogeler, Sheriff of Readstown and head of the local National Guard."

The Sheriff offered his hand and gave one brief flick of the eyes at the other's strange clothing. The second glance was one Rudi recognized as well, taking in his height and length of limb and breadth of shoulder, the muscle and thickness of wrist on his arm where the jacket and linsey-woolsey shirt fell back, the scars on hands and face and the use-worn binding on the hilt of his sword, and the fact that it hung from his right hip. A third glance went to Epona where she stood hipshot with her head over Rudi's right shoulder, nipping at his hair now and then; it had a skilled stockbreeder's grave respect for her lines.

"Rudi Mackenzie of the Clan Mackenzie indeed, Sheriff Vogeler," Rudi said, and inclined his head politely.

He took the strong hard hand, squeezing just enough for mutual respect without foolish games. The calluses reminded him of something Ingolf had said, that Sheriffs hereabouts weren't too proud to put their hand to a plow now and then.

"My sept totem is Raven," Rudi went on. "Tanist by acclamation of the Clan I am, leader of this troop of traveling mountebanks by the inscrutable whim of the Powers, and glad to meet the kinsman of Ingolf. He's been a tried friend and right-hand man to me through battle, storm and wilderness, with a quick sword and wise counsel, from the western mountains to your steading. And soon he'll be my brother-in-law."

The Sheriff of Readstown checked again, his eyes going wide for an instant at his brother's grin and nod and Mary's little wave, then handed Rudi back the letters of introduction he'd sent ahead with his half sisters. They now included one from the new Regency Council of

Iowa, *urgently requesting* all possible help for *our good friend and ally* Rudi Mackenzie.

The Free Republic of Richland *was* free, if he understood the local politics, but they wouldn't want to antagonize mighty Iowa. Richland's independence suited Des Moines because they would rather not annex its problems; its borders with dangerous bandit-haunted wilderness, and what Iowa's ruling powers thought of as the bad example of its looser system of ranks. There was one from the Cardinal-Archbishop too; Ingolf had told him his elder brother was Catholic, and notably pious, and the Sheriff bowed his head as Father Ignatius signed the air in blessing.

So that message from the bishop is just as well. Richland as a whole doesn't care to anger Iowa, but the Bossman of Richland hasn't the power over his nobles . . . his Sheriffs and their Farmers . . . that the Heasleroads have. Or had. And so the Sheriff of Readstown won't necessarily do his Bossman's will. Family feuds can be the worst of all. Nor can I absolutely rely on Ingolf's judgment this time—his brother's feelings might well have festered like an ulcer since he left.

"Well, youse welcome here," the Richlander squire said, hooking his thumbs in his sword belt. "Stay a day, stay a month, stay as long as you damn well please," he went on, in a phrase that was common throughout these lands.

His brows went up as he looked along the length of the wagon train and took in the Southsiders.

"All of you. I'll have to put your men up in the barn lofts, mostly . . ."

Then he saw the Southsider women and children. "Uff da! Your men and, uh, the rest," he added. "I'll spread 'em around a little to my out-farms, if you're here for more than a day or two."

"That's most kind of you, sir," Rudi said.

And I hope none of the ones playing host to my Southsiders are of an excessive delicacy in matters of feeding and washing.

Aloud: "We can pay our way, Sheriff. Sure and we'll also be glad to help with anything that needs doing in the way of work. Or fighting, of course."

Suddenly Edward Vogeler smiled; it looked genuine, if also something he didn't do very often.

"Hell, Mr. Mackenzie, my brother and I parted on bad terms—he's probably told you about it, since he's engaged to your sister."

"Half sister," Mary noted pedantically, sotto voce.

"Ah, and to be sure, that was long ago," Rudi replied diplomatically. "And myself a stranger here."

With better sense than to intrude on a quarrel between close kin, he did not need to add.

"We were both assholes about it, you betcha," Edward Vogeler said bluntly. "But I had less excuse, not being nineteen. A man's *supposed* to think with his dick and his fists at that age. I was already past thirty with a wife and kids."

"Yah, yah, something to that," Ingolf said, after an instant's pause. "Both ways."

"So youse're all my guests while you're here," the Sheriff went on. "You're my brother's friends . . . and from what you say, my in-laws, soon enough."

"I'll accept the hospitality with gratitude," Rudi said. "Though I *will* pay for what we need beyond a normal brief guesting, and what we need to take with us, and for gear and beasts."

"I won't say no to that," Edward Vogeler said, with a firm nod. "Yah hey, got my Farmers und Refugees to think of. We'll dicker on that stuff. We can always buy more supplies in from upstream and down, mostly we swap around here so cash money's always welcome. Gold, that is."

Rudi nodded and moved—almost imperceptibly—back, removing himself from the older man's sphere of attention. It was almost like the hunter's trick of withdrawing into yourself to go unnoticed.

I can tell who he's itching to talk with, and dreading it the same, he thought. *Though he's a man who takes his responsibilities seriously, I think, and would deal with me alone first if it seemed needful; also careful of his dignity, but he's not as pompous about it as I expected, from the little Ingolf's said. Perhaps he's mellowed, perhaps he's on his best behavior now . . . or perhaps an angry young man of nineteen was less of a judge than the Ingolf I've known.*

The Vogeler brothers shook hands in turn, looking into each other's faces. Then the older caught the younger in a quick strong embrace; it was short and stiff on both sides. Edward looked away slightly as he stepped back and cleared his throat before he went on:

"Mom's dead," he said bluntly. "Two years ago almost to the day; it was pretty quick, Doc Pham never did really know what. But she had time to tell me to make it up with you if you ever came back."

"Then we've got no choice," Ingolf said.

A moment's smile. "Yah. Made me promise and threatened to haunt me if I didn't, you know how Mom was."

"Was." Pain flickered across Ingolf's face. "Damn," he said softly. "I wanted to introduce her to Mary. She'd have been glad to see me married and settled. Damn and hell."

Mary Havel stepped to her lover's side and took his arm. Ingolf drew a deep breath and went on:

"Kathy? Alice?" he said, naming his sisters.

"Fine. Both hitched, and their kids—oh, hell, we'll catch up once you're settled in. Aunt Cindy and Wanda and the girls have been cooking up a storm since we got the news and the kitchen's like . . . well, *I've* been staying clear of it after I delivered the meat."

Introductions and busyness took over; it was more than a few minutes before they were under way again through more rolling fields of grain and pasture, truck and orchard, though these were empty of houses. Rudi waited until he had a chance to speak sotto voce himself.

"Well, and you're looking like a man who's been gut-punched, my friend," he said.

Ingolf shook his head. "We spent six months fighting like cats and dogs before I left," he said. "*Just* short of fists, and that only because we were afraid we'd kill each other if we started. I'd forgotten we got on well enough, sometimes, for years before then. And family is family. And . . ."

"And your brother knows this is just a visit, not a homecoming for good and all."

"Yah, yah. There is that. And hell, he's right: we *were* both complete dicks about it after Dad died. I couldn't stand the way he tried to step into Dad's shoes with *me* . . . and he went all Godalmighty about it too . . . but damn and hell, he *was* the Sheriff and he had to show everyone he was bossman here. I guess he was too scared not to be stiff, and he's not the most flexible man in the world anyway."

A deep breath. "Still, I'm glad I didn't show up alone and broke, and glad it's just a visit, too. Maybe we get along better when we don't have to get along, you know what I mean? It'll be . . . interesting to see what else has changed."

"And maybe seeing it's a different place will make it easier for you to leave . . . really leave," Mary said from his other side. "To let it go when you ride away."

Ingolf looked at her and grinned, his worn hard wanderer's face handsome for an instant. "Another reason I love you: you're smart."

Mary sighed with a touch of theater to it. "I'll just have to settle for marrying you strictly for your looks, I'm afraid, *bar melindo*," she said, and they both laughed.

They turned a corner as the road bent elbow-fashion around a clump of woods and could see the . . .

Not quite a town, Rudi thought, looking at the cluster of buildings half a mile away. *Not quite a castle. Not quite a farmstead. Something of all three.*

"Ed's been busy," Ingolf said, after a long moment, standing in the stirrups and shading his eyes with a hand. "About a quarter of that's new. And a lot more of the old ruins were still standing when I left. It's . . . tidier."

Readstown proper was about half the size of most Mackenzie duns, perhaps six-score souls in all, including the dozens of children who came tumbling out, wild with excitement over the newcomers. They kept their noise at a distance, though, and the dogs were notably disciplined; there were only a few growls and barks when they'd been called to heel, despite Garbh's bristling stiff-legged presence. All that was a welcome change from some places they'd stopped on their trek.

There was no curtain wall or palisade around the settlement, not as such, but all the dwellings and workshops at its core had stout fieldstone reinforcement for their first stories, steel shutters with firing slits ready to swing over all the windows, and thick-built covered walkways with loopholes in their walls linking them together into a series of gated courtyards that would be a hard nut to crack.

For anyone without, say, two hundred men and a siege train, Rudi thought. *Give me that many, with mantlets and three or four well-served twenty-four-pounders from Corvallis Ordnance Corporation or the Portland Armory, and I could have it in an afternoon. But they haven't seen war on that scale here. Yet.*

The barns and pens were at some distance, leaving a clear field of fire all around and no shelter for attackers. It was a bit hard to tell what was left over from the old world and what was post-Change; certainly everything had been heavily modified. And more torn down for materials or to get it out of the way, leaving only overgrown foundations and roadways amid small turnout pastures, gardens that included flowers as well as vegetables where lawns had been, and clumps of trees where houses had stood.

At the blank-walled outer face of the largest house of the complex was something he was *sure* was new, once he realized it wasn't a silo. It had that shape, save at the top where crenellations bared teeth at heaven; a squat four-story tower of stone and concrete and girder, with the snout of a catapult showing on a round turntable at one upper edge. A pole bore a plain brown flag marked with a bright orange wedge.

The tower's a good bit younger than Ingolf, or even me, Rudi thought, and murmured a question.

"Yah, Dad built it," Ingolf said. "Used a silo as the shell and built up around it. Finished it the year he died, the year I left. The catapult's dual purpose, you can switch out the throwing trough fast; a thousand yards with bolts, five or six hundred with twelve-pound roundshot or incendiaries. This little four-eyed weedy guy from Richland Center built it. Out of old truck parts mostly, the Bossman sent him 'round to get all the Sheriffs' places up to scratch. All the ones who'd pay. I watched him do it, watched pretty close."

"Hmmm," Rudi said. "Perhaps I was a little hasty in deciding how easily I'd take the place."

Ingolf nodded without taking umbrage; it was the natural thing for someone in their line of work to think about, seeing a defended steading for the first time.

"That gives me an idea," Rudi mused. "Do you think you could put one together?"

Ingolf blinked at him. "If I had the parts, and a smith and a machinist, yah. Why?"

"A thought. Later, later."

Not a real fortress overall, he thought silently. *But ample for the need.*

There was an earth dam and pond to the east where a stream ran down towards the Kickapoo. Two beam-and-plank mills on fieldstone foundations stood there, with big overshot wheels turning merrily. One building gave off the low throbbing notes of millstones grinding flour, and the other a long *rrrrrrrrrr* as a ripsaw went through hard wood; the white water stopped while he glanced that way and the sound died, as someone within closed off the flue gates for the day. Two small churches reared white steeples halfway between there and the hamlet, one Catholic and one Lutheran. A two-story brick building that was probably a schoolhouse for the district stood near them, with an archery range and baseball diamond and football field beside it. Other structures in the distance held the tannery and soap-boiling sheds and similar necessary but smelly trades.

Willing hands bore their animals away to be fed and watered—he had the usual bit of bother convincing Epona that these were friends—and a crowd ushered them through the courtyards. They passed storehouses and weaving sheds, a smithy with its pile of scrap and baskets of charcoal, a combined carpenter's shop and cooperage in a fragrance of sawdust and sap and varnish and glue, a yeasty-smelling brewery and distillery and cider press, the laundry and the clinic, and all the other dependencies of a great man's household. He could feel Edain turning like a hound at a scent as they went by a well-equipped bowyer's workstead, with rows of recurves hanging to dry inside and billets of ashwood ready to be split and smoothed for arrow shafts.

It all seemed well laid out and solidly built, and . . .

Clean, he thought, sniffing. *They're careful of filth here.*

The judgment he made was by a standard no older than he was himself, and a rural one which thought a whiff of horse manure and barn straw perfectly normal, as long as it wasn't allowed too near the supply of drinking water. The verandah of the main house was close enough to the bakery and kitchens for the smell to make his nose twitch with something as familiar as stables and far more welcome; roasting meat and fresh warm loaves, pies baking and dishes more complex making an intriguing medley.

Mathilda gave a little sigh of pleasure at the aroma.

"I don't know whether real food is a relief from trail rations, or just makes it harder to go back," she said. "I can hardly remember what it was like when campfire cuisine was the *exception.*"

"I'm a good camp cook!" Rudi said, smiling at her. "And Father Ignatius is better."

"The operative word is *camp*," Odard observed dryly. "As in, *scorched, raw, stale, monotonous, or all of the above.*"

"You're a *lousy* camp cook yourself, Odard," Mathilda observed.

"I never wanted to learn," he replied. "Why should I? I'm a *baron*, for God's sake. It's not my *job*."

"You're a baron with no servants, just now, or haven't you noticed in all the time we've been on the trail?" Mathilda answered, taking the sting out of it with a smile. "And I'm a Princess without a retinue. Except for you, of course."

"There's nothing better than fresh trout done over a campfire on green sticks," Edain observed, smacking his lips. "Or salmon baked in clay in the embers, with a few 'taters beside them. Good enough for a Beltane feast, that is."

"Trout. Right. And how often have we had *that*?" Odard said dryly.

Edain looked up, counting on his fingers with a thumb. "Four . . . no, I lie, five times."

"In the whole trip. *And* the twins could burn water; their idea of cooking is frying hardtack in the bacon grease, or grilling venison," Odard said. "Virginia is no better when it's her turn—stew, flatbread, fried steak, flatbread, stew, fried steak, flatbread. You say you're tired of steak and stew and flatbread and she looks at you as if she was saying: *you're tired of* food?

"Hey, I can fry chicken too!" Virginia said, glaring at him. "And I can make flapjacks and do beans, or eggs if we could get 'em. Biscuits, if I had an oven. Fred thinks puttin' salt on the roast is fancy cooking; *I'm* lookin' after the kitchen when we're hitched."

"We could leave it all to the Southsider women now," Ritva pointed out sweetly. "They'd be *glad* to burn the water for us."

Everyone shuddered; Rudi wasn't a fastidious man,

but he'd led the effort to get them to stop spitting in the stewpot for luck before calling everyone to eat.

"Mathilda's not bad," he observed. "She set herself to learn, and she did. Dab hand with a pot roast, in fact."

Mathilda nodded and pointed out: "You'd be better at it if *you* set your mind to enjoy it, Odard. Then you could do it the way *you* like. Father Ignatius is a knight-brother of the Order of the Shield, and a scholar, and *he* doesn't think it's beneath his station."

Ignatius smiled and shrugged. "Christ Himself washed the disciples' feet," he said. "He poured them wine and broke bread, too. Should I be more proud than God?"

Odard nodded reluctantly. "Well, when you put it that way, Father . . . though I *still* prefer a real dinner," he said. "With someone else putting it in front of me."

"Then treasure these memories we're about to acquire, to bring out the next time we're huddling against a blizzard and gnawing on hardtack and jerky and glad to get it," Rudi said.

Odard made a face, then turned to the house and swept off his hat as he murmured through a broad smile:

"That's our lady hostess, I should think. Not quite the way that Mother would put in an appearance back at Castle Gervais, but—"

A woman in her forties bustled out of the house, a full-figured blond with a square handsome middle-aged face and her hair piled on top of her head and escaping in wisps. She wore a belted knee-length dress of good green linen with an embroidered hem—about half the women here favored skirts, the other half the same shapeless linsey-woolsey trousers as the men. There were beaded moccasinlike shoes on her feet, and she wore a long apron that had seen recent use close to a stove or chopping-board or both, and there was a smut of flour across her nose. Other women followed her, and a few boys, all carrying trays and tankards.

"Ed!" she said accusingly. "You told me *sunset*! Uff da! *Nothing's* ready yet! Und dere's children—you didn't say there would be children, I'll have to get—"

"Wanda," he said—and suddenly the masterful tones of the Richlander border-lord were apologetic. "They pushed hard from Soldier's Grove, is all. Nobody told *me* about the kids, either. The scouts just counted the fighters."

"Ingolf!" she half shouted, and threw herself down the stairs and into the home-come wanderer's arms. "Mary Mother, you worthless bastard! Not even a *letter* in the last five years! The earth might have swallowed you and then we heard rumors you were dead!"

Ingolf roared and swept her up in a tight embrace, swinging her around effortlessly and leaving her breathless, but not speechless, when he set her down again and said:

"Mary, my sister-in-law Wanda—Wanda, Mary Havel, my intended."

That brought a happy shriek and more embraces. The travelers gave their greetings, and their names and nations; Wanda Vogeler's eyes went a little wide as Odard and Mathilda made their elaborate courtly bows. Wider still as Rudi and Edain put the backs of their clenched fists to their foreheads, stepped back with one foot and bowed in salute to one who was an incarnation of the Mother—whether she knew it or not.

"Merry met to the Mistress of this Hearth and all beneath her roof," the two clansmen said; Jake of the Southsiders made a clumsy copy of the gesture. "By whatever name you know Them, may the blessings of the Mother-of-all and Her Lord be on rick, cot and tree."

She didn't seem to know *what* to make of Mary and Ritva's hand-to-heart gesture and murmur of *Mae Govannen*. She pumped Fred's hand energetically.

"My stars! You *do* take me back, Mr. Thurston!" she said. "I haven't seen a black person since I was a girl in Madison before the Change! And this lady is your intended? Goodness, are those *chaps*? Like Woody in *Toy Story*, oh, Lord, how I loved that movie as a little child! And you'd be the Mr. Mackenzie we heard tell of," she said to Rudi. "And those are your, um, clan?" she said.

Rudi cleared his throat, a little breathless at the rush of words. The Southsiders had learned a great deal beyond and besides how to wear a kilt and plaid, but they were still not the group he'd have chosen to uphold the Clan's reputation—not yet. Not in a display of seemly manners at a feast, at least. For hunting or fighting a skirmish in the woods, he'd be glad to claim them for anyone to see.

"Ah . . . not exactly," he said. "Not just the now; we met upon the way. But they *will* be, if you take my meaning, and they're my people now, their welfare my responsibility."

"Well, they can all use a beer and a snack, I'm sure. Go on, eat! *Und* the beer's our own brewing, *Reinheitsgebot*-style like my grandfather made it."

Rudi grinned. "That we all could use a bite and a brew is no more than the merest truth, and it's a haven of warmth and welcome this is, after so long on the cold hard trail."

He winked and went on: "And yourself the ministering Goddess."

Wanda smiled back at him; he heard Mathilda snort slightly beside him, and read her thought: he was charming the ladies again.

Well, there's nothing wrong with charm, is there, acushla? he thought, a little defensively. *Even our host looks pleased; I suspect he leaves the being a human being side of his existence to his wife . . . well, he could do worse. From the look and sound of her she's good at it.*

The platters were going around. He didn't know if the guest cup and bite were a formal rite here as they would be among his people, but he'd found for thousands of miles of walking and riding eastward that sharing food and drink made you a guest indeed where there was any goodwill at all. The food was some strong pungent soft cheese on wedges of dark dense rye bread, its crust dotted with little nutty seeds and the whole warm from the oven and chewy and richly sour-sweet; there were pastries too, their hot flaky crusts buttery, full of grilled venison and onions and potatoes and a faint tang of herbs.

What Aunt Diana—who'd run Dun Juniper's kitchens since the Change, and a restaurant before that—*would call a Cornish pasty, or nearly,* he thought happily, as the juices flooded his mouth.

The beer was in a mascar, a tall mug lathe-turned from hard maple wood, with foam dribbling over the edges, and—

"Oh, my," Edain said reverently, as he gasped and wiped the back of his other hand across his mouth. "By Goibniu and Braciaca both, and that's *beer*, by the blessin'! My thanks again, hearth-mistress!"

Rudi inhaled the bouquet respectfully himself, and then took a deep draught of the mahogany-colored liquid beneath the white foam. Flavors like chocolate and coffee slid across his tongue, acrid and nearly sweet at the same time, with a cool musty bite.

"My friend Timmy Martins Mackenzie, our brewmaster at Dun Juniper, could do no better and on one or two occasions has done worse," he said, and bowed again. "And more I could not say."

"Come in, then, come in—let's get the children something, and you'll all want good hot baths and soap, and—"

He gratefully surrendered to her bustling efficiency as she organized her household to bear everyone away. They'd be here some time, at least a month, and that was starting to look like a welcome respite.

Perhaps even long enough for letters to get all the way home; they might arrive before Yule.

Thanks to Matti's little conspiracy, *there are things that certain people need to know. And others must be told as well, whether I want to or not. How her mother will take it . . .*

Rudi shuddered.

CITY PALACE

THRONE AVENUE AND ARMINGER STREET

ROYAL CITY OF PORTLAND

PORTLAND PROTECTIVE ASSOCIATION

(FORMERLY THE CENTRAL LIBRARY, AT SW 10TH

AND MORRISON STREETS)

DECEMBER 12, CHANGE YEAR 24/2022 AD

"My lady Regent, the special courier is here."

Sandra Arminger looked up as the door opened; the cat in her lap made a querulous sound and gave her a resentful look as she stopped scratching it under the chin. Outside the tall arched windows of her private presence chamber snow fell, straight down in a windless dark where the occasional street lantern glowed like a blurred smear. Within was the scent of floral sachets and the warmth of the hot-water radiators behind screens of marble fretwork, pale dim elegance of stone and silk and arched wood, the blazing colors of the rugs muted by the low setting of the hissing methane gas lamps.

A little of the chill within her melted at the news but her face remained impassive, framed in its cream-silk wimple bound with steel gray Madras pearls set in platinum mesh.

"Send him in immediately," she said to the gentleman of the chamber whose privilege it was to act as usher. "And send word to the Chancellor and the Grand Constable that they are to attend on me as soon as convenient."

She made a gesture, and a lady-in-waiting motioned the maids to turn up the lights, set out coffee and brandy and little sweet pastries and bowls of nuts on a table whose surface was rare woods and mother-of-pearl and lapis in the shape of peacocks and antelope.

"Now leave me," she said. "Yes, you too, Jehane," she said to her confidential secretary, and the attendants all swept out in a dance of precedence and bobbing curtseys.

And silence fell, though she knew that she had only to raise her voice and someone would be there, as if by magic.

Sometimes that's the hardest thing to take, she thought. *Never really being* alone *anymore. They're always there, listening, watching, may their dear loyal souls fry.*

She'd wanted to be a Queen. The problem was that once you were, it wasn't something you could take off with your clothes. The younger generation didn't seem to have that problem; they weren't playing roles, they *were* their roles. The doors opened again quietly—they were solid steel beneath the soft beauty of the rock-maple veneer, and ponderous—and the stamp and clash of guards coming to attention rang in the corridor without.

Distantly there were voices singing, a chorus of boys practicing in the Great Hall for the festivities of the Twelve
Nights:

"Adeste, fideles
Venite adoremus
Venite, venite
Ad Bethlehem—"

The courier looked as if he was still half-frozen, very
tough and very tired, a lean brown-skinned young man
with his dark hair in the bowl cut and tonsure favored by
most Orders of Roman religious. Apart from that she'd
have judged him to be a cavalryman of some sort, in
anonymous padded leathers half soaked even through the
outer gear he'd shed somewhere and with a strong aroma
of horses and sweat about him. He went to one knee,
took the packet from the glazed-leather case slung over
his shoulder and offered it to her.

The first thing her eyes saw was Mathilda's seal stamped
in a disk of red wax, and a breath she hadn't been conscious of holding sighed out. The heliograph lines had
brought the bare news earlier, of course, and duplicates
would be coming along by safer, slower routes. But actually *seeing* it was something else again.

For a long moment she paused . . . *To be happy*, she
thought. *Simply to be happy. It's a rare feeling.*

Then she read the dates on the outer covering, and
one brow rose on her round, smooth middle-aged face.

"That was quick work," she said. "Where did you
start . . ."

At her inquiring look he amplified: "Friar Matthew,
my lady Regent. A Church courier and of the Order of
the Shield of St. Benedict."

"Where did you start with these, Brother Matthew? And how did they arrive?"

"I was told it came by our equivalents in the East—north from Richland through Marshall and Fargo, and then west through the Dominions—Minnedosa, Moose Jaw, Drumheller. There are intact railways along much of that route, and pedal cars, so it went quickly. I was at my Order's new chapter house on our mission farm at Drumheller, and I carried it on snowshoes and skis over the mountain passes and down to Barony Vernon in the Okanogan country. Then by horse and rail to the Columbia and Portland. I came all the way myself rather than handing it on, as security was of the highest importance."

"Thank you, Brother," she said.

She was conscious of the danger and toil behind the monk's simple words, not to mention the skill a single man needed to stay alive in such country. Most of that route ran through empty wilderness, particularly as far north and east as he'd started; wilderness haunted by tigers and wolves and men who were worse than either, and by the monster storms raving down out of Alaska and the Yukon at this time of year that could bury an unlucky wayfarer twenty feet deep in a day.

"You've brought very good news, and have earned any recompense in reason, Brother Matthew," Sandra said; she had a carefully cultivated reputation for rewarding zeal in her service. "And a good many unreasonable ones."

The monk bowed his head. "I swore both poverty and obedience, my lady. I did nothing beyond my duty."

Sandra smiled. It was always slightly surprising and unsettling to run across a completely incorruptible man. Inconvenient sometimes, but still . . .

"Nevertheless . . . Hmmm. The Order of the Shield

wanted some Crown land north of the demesne of Castle Oroville for mission work. I think that can be arranged. The Cistercians wanted it too, but they can apply for a grant elsewhere."

"Thank you, my lady!"

"Now go. I hope your vows don't preclude a mug of hot cider and a good supper and a warm bed in the Protector's Guard barracks?"

He grinned, and suddenly under the tiredness and stern discipline you could see he'd been a boy not so very long before, and was still younger than her own daughter.

"Not in the least! Thank you, my lady Regent, and I will remember you and the Princess in my prayers."

She waited until he'd left, stumbling slightly with the weariness he could now acknowledge to himself. Certain habits were well ingrained by a lifetime of weaving secrets; only when she was alone again did she use a letter opener to flick off the seals. The original bundle had undoubtedly included material for Stardell Hall in Mithrilwood, Dun Juniper, Mt. Angel and Larsdalen, sent on with someone else beside the polite young monk, but her spies could glean anything that had been left out here in at least three of the four.

And I don't think *any of them have infiltrated to my immediate Household.*

She pulled paper towards her and dipped a fine steel-nibbed pen in the ink, careful to keep the lace at her sleeve off the surface of the sheet. No need to consult a code book; this was one she had thoroughly memorized, a private one she and her daughter shared with nobody and had never written down. Mathilda's report made interesting reading, paced slowly as it was while she transcribed from the cipher. Her eyebrows went up as she read of the doings in Iowa, and then she felt the blood drain from her face as the final scene in the Bossman's quarters unfolded, even as her daughter's bold neat hand reassured her that it had ended well.

"There are times when it's inconvenient to be an atheist," she murmured to herself. "I simply don't have anyone to be thankful *to. My eternal gratitude, O blind and ontologically empty dance of atoms,* just isn't very satisfying, somehow."

Then she smiled, warm and fond, at the younger woman's description of the maneuverings after Anthony Heasleroad's death:

"That's my girl!"

Her eyebrows went higher, and she laughed aloud at her daughter's defiant pride in what she'd gotten the other travelers to do on the deck of the schooner, and Rudi's reaction.

"That *is* my girl," she said, with a glow of pride.

The last brief section was addressed from *Readstown, Free Republic of Richland;* simply that they'd arrived, and had been well received by the local lordling.

"I will report further before we leave; this is probably the last occasion we'll be able to send letters back for some time since we now face a plunge into the wilderness. Duplicates of my dispatches from Dubuque are enclosed and these will go by a different route. All my love, dearest mother and liege-lady, and may God and the Virgin and all the company of Saints hold you and the PPA and all of Montival safe. Mathilda."

When she'd finished her work she sat back and sipped at a cup of coffee, absently pushing aside one of her Persians that was nosing around the little jug of cream on the tray. Another stamp-clash came through the door, and the usher's voice:

"My lord the Count of Odell, High Chancellor of the Association! My lady the Baroness d'Ath, Grand Constable of the Association!"

They made a knee and kissed her extended hand in turn. "Sorry, my lady," Conrad said. "That War Finance Council meeting, you know. I couldn't cut it without offending House Jones and House Gutierrez, even if neither of them can count to eleven without dropping their hose . . . and you did say *convenience.*"

"It's important but not time-constrained," Sandra said. "Better you than me on the War Finance business, Conrad. I know it's important work, but accounting bores me like an auger."

"CPA in good standing," Conrad said cheerfully, slapping his ample stomach; that had been his day job, back when she'd been a faculty wife and they'd both been members of the Society who just *played* at being nobility.

"And I was outside the city wall," Tiphaine said, as she poured them both stiff tots of the Larressingle Armagnac brandy, salvaged from the ruins of Seattle years ago. "Watching our loyal levies squelch and slip and fall on their faces in the mud."

"Read," Sandra said, forestalling the question and pushing her transcript across the table with a forefinger. "It's from Mathilda."

Tiphaine nodded; her ice-colored eyes narrowed slightly in satisfaction. Conrad laughed and swore and slapped his thigh, which was his equivalent. The Grand Constable was in leather riding breeches and slightly muddy thigh-boots and a high-collared, long-sleeved tunic of black wool that looked a little damp; her pale bobbed hair was dark with melted snow. She tucked an owl-shaped pendant she'd taken to wearing into the neck of her tunic, poured her brandy into the coffee—Conrad winced to see the priceless pre-Change French liquor treated so—and sipped while she read.

"You were out drilling troops in *this*?" the Chancellor said; he was in court working dress with the golden chain of office across his bull shoulders and barrel chest.

"Wars don't get called off due to snow and cold and neither should training," she said absently, attention on the writing.

"You've got a general staff and unit commanders for that," Conrad said, in a half-scolding tone; she'd been his second-in-command for years. "I let them do their jobs and I did mine when *I* was Grand Constable."

"Your average man-at-arms has a short attention span and a skull that's iron from ear to ear even without a helm, Conrad. It's necessary to keep reminding them how tough I am. Otherwise I have to kill men occasionally just to make the others pay attention, which creates its own problems. I don't look as repulsively fearsome as you, and I pee in a different position, remember."

Then she tapped her free finger on the dateline of the dispatch. "Barely two months for news from east of the Mississippi. That's very good. We still haven't got what they sent from Iowa."

"We probably won't," Conrad said. "The CUT is clamping down hard on the guerillas in occupied New Deseret, and that's the only way of bridging eastern Idaho unless you go around to the north."

Tiphaine smiled as she read, a hungry expression. Conrad held out his hand wordlessly and she handed him the sheets she'd finished.

"Ah!" he said, skimming rapidly. "Now, *that* looks

promising! Satan's arse, with piles like acorns! Now the CUT has got most of the Midwest lethally mad at them! Corwin has a *genius* for making enemies."

"So did Norman," Sandra said. "And it is *extremely* promising. Iowa is a long way from Montana, but from the description they potentially outweigh the CUT by a very considerable margin."

"The logistics will be murder," Tiphaine said. "But even a small percentage of a big enough sum is still large."

Conrad read the pages as the Grand Constable slid the sheets over to him, occasionally glancing at the rather coarse brown linen-rag paper of the original, then frowned—which turned his scarred face into something even more grotesque.

"Damn, it still hits me sometimes! Two months *is* fast now. I keep remembering FedEx."

Sandra nodded. She'd made a much better adjustment to the Changed world than most adult survivors—her girlhood heroines had been Eleanor of Aquitaine with Catherine de' Medici a close second, and she'd spent a good deal of her time with the Society making believe that she *was* someone like that, even in the old world. And of course being a sovereign and waited on hand and foot eliminated much of the sheer inconvenience of existence without high-energy technologies.

And it still *hits me sometimes too, at moments like this. There are some things that no amount of hand labor can duplicate.*

A decade and a half younger, Tiphaine was untroubled by the look the two shared. Instead she murmured:

"It *is* more convenient now that we're at peace with the Drumhellers. That gives us a route right around the CUT and Boise both. Suitable for intelligence and communications, if not armies, given that the Canadian Rockies are in the way."

Conrad scowled for a moment. "The Dominions are scared of the CUT too; they've got a border with them, or at least Drumheller and Moose Jaw do, and if they've got any sense they'll join in. But I still say we should have held out for more of the Peace River country. It's rich, and it's got a big labor force—"

Sandra went *tsk*. "Which means it is full of contumacious Canuks with bows, Conrad, who really wouldn't appreciate our handing it out in fiefs over their heads."

"We did just that in plenty of other places."

"That was in the first Change Years. We were dealing with terrified hungry refugees who'd do anything for help and had nowhere to turn. It's different now. Things have . . . jelled. In any case, that's for another day, provided that we survive the present war. Read! There's something rather interesting after they left Iowa."

She could tell when he came to the part on the boat.

"They hailed him *High King*?" Conrad of Odell spluttered. His skin turned red under the thick white keloid. "*Mathilda* hailed him as High King of . . . what the hell is Montival?"

"Everything, evidently," Tiphaine d'Ath said crisply. "Everything from here to Idaho, down to California and north to the limits of Association territory, I imagine, at least. Perhaps California too, if we ever get the Westria Project going. Hmmm. Montival is actually not a bad name, now that the old State boundaries are so meaningless."

"Goddammit, she's giving it all away, the—"

Sandra cleared her throat: "Conrad, we're old friends, but I think you're about to say something on the order of *dumb little twat* about my daughter Princess Mathilda, the heir to Portland. Don't. It would be *rude* as well as inaccurate."

"All right, I won't," he said, a tun of a man in black velvet and gold and heraldic colors, with the sweat of anger on his bald dome. He rubbed it with a hand like a spade before mastering himself and going on: "But why, why, *why* did you raise her to be such a . . . such a . . ."

"*Romantic* is the word you're looking for, Conrad," Tiphaine said. "But she's not, really. She's hardheaded enough, in modern terms. Changeling terms. She's just . . . *good*."

The smile grew a little broader. "Not something any of *us* three have to worry about."

"And I raised her to be *that* because I want to build something for her that will last," Sandra said. "Remember what Napoleon said to Talleyrand."

Tiphaine thought for a moment and then nodded. Conrad stopped in midrant and looked at her before he spoke, in the tone used with quotations:

"*Look at the bayonets of my Imperial Guards, how they gleam in serried ranks! With such men, I can do anything!*"

Sandra smiled and completed the anecdote with the diplomat's reply:

"*Yes, sire. You can do anything with such bayonets . . . except sit on them.* Evil has a short half-life, Conrad. Only a man like Norman—and a woman like me—could have built the Association, given what the times were like at the Change. To make it a living thing that survives us all . . . I've found that other methods are necessary. And to really consolidate it needs someone like my Mathilda."

"But she's giving away our sovereignty! Sandra— having the Corvallis Meeting always looking over our shoulders since the Protector's War is bad enough, but *this*!"

Tiphaine sat silent, a considering frown on her face. Sandra stroked the Persian cat on her lap with one hand, and waggled a finger at her Chancellor with the other.

"Conrad, Conrad, Conrad," she said—or almost purred, with the smile of a cat contemplating a mouse squeaking under its paw. "You don't think *I've* gone soft, do you? You're not looking at the big picture!"

"I'm not?" he said.

"Of course not. You're thinking in pre-Change terms."

Sandra held up one soft, well-manicured, not-quite-plump hand; her eyelids drooped in an expression of purely political but still sensual enjoyment.

"Here we have the High King, Rudi—or Artos the First, as his enthusiastic young friends hailed him. When this message gets about, half the nobles in the Association will be crying him hail as well—"

"Three-quarters of those under thirty," Tiphaine put in.

"True. And all the burghers and peasants. All the Clan Mackenzie, of course; though dear Juniper will find some way to feel anguished and guilty about it. Witch Queen or not, you can tell she was raised Irish Catholic! And all the Rangers will *swoon*. Well, not Alleyne Loring or his pet troll Hordle, but certainly Eilir, she's Rudi's half sister after all. And most of all the *Lady* of the Dúnedain."

"They'll start dry-humping and creaming their hose in every *flet*," Tiphaine said, with a slight stark smile. "Astrid particularly, you're right about that, my lady. The demented bitch may get pregnant again just from contemplating the coronation ceremony."

Sandra nodded. "It's precisely the sort of romantic froth they adore. The Bearkillers . . . well, many of them will be enthusiastic too, if not dear Signe. Rudi *is* the son of their precious Bear Lord, after all. And isn't it pleasant to think of Signe striding about kicking the Larsdalen furniture and thinking of how her own dear little lad Mike Jr. should have it, but never will, because he's been done out by his bastard half brother Rudi *again?*"

"The woman can certainly nurse a grudge," Tiphaine said.

You're speaking with unconscious irony, my dear, Sandra thought affectionately, as she nodded agreement to her protégée. *Or as the kettle said to the pot: My, how sadly sooty and grimy is your backside!*

She added aloud in a meditative tone: "I think that she's never really been able to get over that little premarital infidelity of Havel's with Juniper *because* it only happened once. That and Rudi being his spitting image, with three inches and strawberry blond hair added."

"Are you saying that there's nothing we can do to stop this High King of Montival nonsense?" Conrad said.

"*We* couldn't stop it if we tried. But if we throw the Throne's weight *behind* the notion, even the independents like Corvallis and the Yakima League whose rulers don't have any blood link to either the Havels or the Armingers will fall in line. Every single power represented in the Corvallis Meeting. Especially given how frightened they are over the war with Boise and Corwin, and the way the previous messages and all those songs and stories dear Juniper's spread have primed them. If things go well with the war—"

One of Tiphaine's brows raised: Sandra interpreted that as *well, there's deranged optimism for you.* She continued:

"—we might even get Idaho included at the end. That rescue of young Frederick Thurston—splendid mythmaking! It couldn't have been better if it were a lie made up by one of our hired troubadours, and the cream of the jest is that it's *true*."

"Support it?" Conrad goggled. "Why should we? Hell, Sandra, we *created* this country. Did we do it so Juniper's brat could rule all we built up? What . . ."

He paused, and used the most desperate argument. "What would Norman think? Rudi . . . he's damned smart and damned tough and damned likeable with it, but he's the son of the man who *killed* your husband, and his mother was our second-worst enemy all through the wars. You and God and anyone who was within hearing knows I had my arguments with Norman Arminger. But you and he and I *made* the Association."

"Yes. And what did we make, Conrad? A nation? A country?"

"Well—yes."

"Well—no. We made a *feudal kingdom*, Conrad. Which isn't at all the same thing."

He frowned. "That's terminology. Yes, you and I were in the Society, and Norman took it all very seriously but—"

"No, it's *not* just terminology. You're showing your age, Conrad. Think like a feudal noble for a moment, not an executive; think the way the younger generation thinks all the time and you do half the time, for example when you were arranging the marriages of your sons. Think about *family*. If Rudi becomes the High King, he rules Montival—presumably as a loose federation of autonomous realms; that *is* what a High King does, after all, as opposed to an Emperor. The Association territories would be self-governing, but part of Montival."

"That's the problem! Not that I don't like Rudi, but—"

"No, that's not the problem, that's the *solution*, my dear old friend. It's the solution to the problem that I . . . and you . . . and Norman, before the Protector's War . . . have been struggling with since the Change. The problem being that Mike Havel and Juniper and the damned Yakima League and those greed-mongering pedant anachronisms in Corvallis *wouldn't* submit to the Throne. To House Arminger."

"What do you mean?" he said, baffled.

"The High King of Montival must have a *High Queen*. And if she is none other than *my* daughter—and bear in mind that she's also Norman's daughter and only child— then one of her children becomes the High King in turn. Or High Queen regnant, to be sure. Then that means that my grandchild—and Norman's grandchild too, don't forget that part—*rules the whole west side of the continent*, as well as being Lord Protector of the Portland Protective Association. Which is what Norman and I wanted to begin with, and the son of the man who killed him is handing it to us on a golden platter!"

Tiphaine stared at her for a moment. "Ah . . . my lady, how long have you had this in mind? Just as a matter of curiosity."

"Since . . . oh, March 6, 2008."

They both blinked at her, and Tiphaine spoke: "That's . . . the day I brought Mathilda and Rudi back, during the Protector's War. The day we arrived at Castle Todenangst."

Sandra nodded. "Well, of course, I'd had the *beginnings* of the notion before that, as soon as the Mackenzies took Mathilda prisoner and it became obvious how well she and Rudi were getting along. Everyone knows that a dynastic marriage has been . . . mmmm, under consideration for a long time. But that would have been between the heir of the Mackenzies and the heir of Portland— many, many problems. But a *new* kingdom, that's a different matter altogether. Thinking outside the box, as it were."

"You certainly got me and them out of Todenangst fast," Tiphaine said thoughtfully. "I thought it was just to get Rudi out from under Norman's bloodshot eye."

"That too. Dear, dear Norman; he could be so hot-tempered sometimes. But I had to evaluate Rudi personally before it was worth pursuing. Not in detail, of course—the details you always need to improvise as the situation dictates—but in broad outline. And Mathilda *had* to think it was her own idea, which meant it had to *actually be* her own idea. Not difficult, really. Rudi's a delightful boy . . . man, now . . . Intelligent, with quite stunning looks and an embarrassment of talents, and all the charm in the world. And his people *did* insist on Mathilda living with the Mackenzies part of the year, at the peace settlement."

"Where you insisted on Rudi coming and living with *us* part of the year," Conrad said, sounding dazed. "Jesus, that far back?"

"Precisely. To shape him, you see, and also to expose the younger generation of our nobility to him."

Tiphaine burst into laughter; Sandra was slightly surprised. She hadn't seen that happen during business hours more than once or twice in the quarter century they'd known each other. The Grand Constable of the Association went down on one knee and drew her sword, bringing the cross hilt up to her lips in salute.

"Even for you, my liege-lady, that is . . . it's just so fucking *brilliant*!"

Conrad had been standing with his mouth open. He shut it, sat down again, and his gargoyle face split in a grin as he reached for one of the blueberry tarts, absently brushing powdered sugar off his jupon.

"Well, I *will* be damned. I *wasn't* thinking dynastically. And when you do, that's exactly how it looks."

He cupped a hand to his ear. "You hear that? It's old Norman laughing fit to split his mausoleum open."

Sandra sighed, the quiet glee fading from her face.

"And I *still* miss telephones," she said. "Now we know they've arrived safely at this Readstown place. That's the edge of civilization, and they're about to plunge into the unknown. How long will it be before we know what happened there, or later?"

CHAPTER TWELVE

"Ahhhh," Rudi Mackenzie said, and let himself slide blissfully deeper into one of the tubs to which the Readstowners had shown their guests.

"Ahhh, indeed," Odard said happily, sitting up in his own bath and scrubbing at his nails with a small brush. "*Warm* hospitality."

Rudi nodded, with his hair floating around his neck and shoulders.

"Now this, my friends, is an improvement over squatting in a cold creek with your ballocks crawling up, that it is," he said. "Or a cloth and a pan of hot water by a fire with your backside freezing."

"Or just plain dirt and smell," Fred Thurston said. With a wide white grin: "I remember the first time I came back from a three-week field exercise with my Junior ROTC class. My mother said: *How are you?* And I just said: *Mom, I stink.*"

The smile faded; Rudi judged that he was thinking of his father again, or perhaps his mother and sisters, trapped in Boise with an elder brother who'd turned to parricide to make the position of President hereditary. Lawrence Thurston had been about to call real elections. That and the birth of a son to Martin's wife had sealed his fate.

If his mother suspects that Martin killed his father that will be a grim thing indeed, the Mackenzie thought. *Having to treat her son as before, knowing herself watched and every word and glance weighed to see if she suspects.*

He didn't suppose Martin would hurt his own kin without need . . . but he'd shown himself to be a pellucidly ruthless man. By killing his father, and by allying with the Church Universal and Triumphant.

Though that may simply be the arrogance of a young man who thinks he can ride the tiger without ending up inside it.

The thoughts ran on as he lay watching the younger man's misery fade, or at least burrow deeper:

Or does Fred wonder if they believe Martin's tale that he was responsible? That would be an extra twist of the knife in his chest, surely it would. Not likely though, I would say. His mother struck me as a very clever lady indeed. And none too friendly with Martin's wife, who I think has been whispering ambition into his receptive ear for years now.

"This rather reminds me of the baths at Mt. Angel," Ignatius said, after a swift glance at the younger Thurston's face. "The layout is similar."

He's a kindly man, the good Father, Rudi thought. *A gentle one, even. Except when there's a sword in his hand, the which you would not think unless you'd seen him fight. And then he is a thing of terror to anyone on the sharp and pointy end.*

"That it is," he said aloud. "Though not as prayerful, to be sure. It was an interesting thing, the first time I scrubbed my hide with a brother reading Scripture from the lectern."

The Mackenzie heir was a frequent guest at the great fortress-monastery, and had studied there in its famed university and libraries, and its equally famous combat schools. The Clan and the Order were old allies, from the days after the Change, and from the wars against the Association.

"It's *not* much like Castle Todenangst," Odard grinned. "I hear the Silver Tower"—where Sandra Arminger had her private quarters amid the castle-cum-palace—"has baths carved out of whole pink marble blocks, and gold taps."

"Sure, and Mathilda has told me the same," Rudi said, and then had a sudden vision of her naked in such a setting, rising out of the suds . . .

"Even the guest quarters for humble vassals from Gervais had sunken tubs with silver fittings," Odard went on, looking slightly dreamy at the thought. "The Lord Protector and Lady Sandra didn't steal anything but the best when they were looting the decorative features for Todenangst. This is comfortable, though."

Albeit a little different from the way Mackenzies would have handled it. For one thing, the womenfolk were in a separate section, but Rudi was used to that; there were plenty of folk back in the western lands who had such taboos. And the bulk of their party of both sexes were elsewhere, this apparently being the gentlefolk's part of the manor. The tubs were of the old world, enameled cast iron on claw feet and meant for single bathers, but amply sized for his six-foot-two, and the water was gratefully hot and smelled slightly of herbs, aromatic steam rising from the surface and misting on the room's tile floors and walls. There was plenty of it, too, from a big sheet-metal tank with its own wood-fired furnace that also served to keep the room comfortably warm.

"This was part of the fire department, in the old days," Ingolf said, scratching his hairy muscular chest. "Dad started joining the buildings together that first year and moving 'em around. Everyone had to live close. It was still damned cold here in March when the Change came, that's the tag end of winter here. We knew it would be worse come *next* winter and all the old-style furnaces were kaput, and we could only make so many new ones, what with everything else that had to be done. I remember thinking how cool it was to be able to go from place to place inside, you know how kids are. Convenient for playing hide-and-seek in a blizzard, too!"

They all nodded. In the new world that had grown up with them there were few places where a single family could live off by itself, for reasons ranging from defense to the sheer difficulty of heating water, if you wanted something better than hanging a bucket over an open fire. With the aches and stiffness soothed out of him, Rudi's thoughts turned to the next necessity.

"I take it your sister-in-law Wanda is a cook of note?" he said respectfully; that was an occupation honored among Mackenzies, who admired skilled makers of all sorts. "She seemed to be putting her own hand to it, as well."

The which I approve of, he thought.

His mother had always done her share of the chores in Dun Juniper's hall, and seen he'd had experience of scrubbing dishes as well.

Otherwise I might have gotten above myself, with all the time I spent among Association nobles, and they looking down their noses at such.

"Yah. Wanda was a refugee herself—one of the first ones to get here," he said. "Her family were brewers in Madison; she was their only kid. They called it a microbrewery then—God knows why, from the way she talks it was a hell of a lot bigger than the one here."

"Which isn't small," Edain said.

"They were in a city, and lived?" Odard said, slightly surprised; that was a bit unusual, and much more unusual for such to end up with rank and position.

"They left Madison about three days after the Change—they had a big wagon and some horses, some sort of show-off thing brewers did back then. Turned up here . . . I can just remember it, mainly how excited I was . . . about ten days after that. *With* all the equipment they needed to make first-rate beer, sacks of good hop and malting barley seed, some of their workers, and six big draught horses, Clydesdales. You can imagine how popular they were!"

"I find it equally impressive that they arrived here without being robbed," Ignatius observed.

"Just so," Rudi said. "And then she married the heir of Readstown?"

"It was a bit more complicated than that, but yah hey, she did, six years later. She already ran our food supplies when I left besides the brewery, under Mom—not just cooking, you know, the storing and curing and smoking and salting and preserving side of things too."

Rudi nodded gravely; that was a heavy responsibility, when sloppiness or lack of skill could ruin a year's sweating-hard work and condemn an entire settlement to hunger, or at least a diet dull and unhealthful until the new crops came in.

More important still in this land of iron winters, he thought.

"You guys smell a lot better now," a youngster's voice said at the door.

Mark Vogeler came in quickly and closed it against

draughts, leaning against the jamb with his hands in his pockets, elaborately casual but with a barely suppressed excitement. He seemed to have fond memories of Ingolf, and doubtless this was the biggest interruption of the round of seasons and lessons and chores he could remember.

"Hi, Mark," Ingolf replied, and heaved himself out of the tub. "Dinner's on?"

"Pretty soon, Unc' Ingolf, und Mom's chust looking after Jenny a bit before we start."

He has that way of speech his father does, only stronger still, Rudi noticed. *Mother would be interested; she always did like to place a man's accent.*

At Ingolf's look of inquiry the nephew went on: "The youngest. There's . . . well, you know about me, and Dave and Melly—only she wants to be called Melinda-in-full these days. There's um, Ingolf . . . and Sue, and Jenny now too. Jenny's not on solid food yet."

"Ed's been busy," Ingolf said, and the boy blushed a little. "*And* Wanda."

A hesitation, and then the youngster went on: "You really going to marry the pretty lady with the eye patch?"

"Yah, I am."

"Cool!"

Ingolf's grin was rare, but the warmer when it came. "You know, Mark, that's exactly the way I feel about it too!"

"I mean, she's gorgeous and she's got a twin and wears that great stuff und talks dat strange language . . . and I bet she's done all sorts of great things! Real adventures, like you have, Unc', we heard a little about that. Not just hung around home, like . . . well."

"Oh, Christ, don't *you* start getting ideas about running off and having *adventures*, Mark!" Ingolf said. "I did that and ended up in the stupidest damn war since the Change, bar none, for *years*. Sheer dumb luck I didn't get killed for damn-all nothing, like poor Bert Kuykendall. And *he* wasn't more than a couple of years older than you are now when he came running out of his tent and caught an arrow with his eyeball."

The boy flushed and looked a little mutinous; Rudi judged he was at the age when a youngster dreamed of doing the wild deeds for the deeds' own sake, and never considered the price of them, or the desperate need that made men willing to pay it. A chill took him despite the heat of the water.

And how many glad boys like him—on all sides—will lie sightless as a feast for the Dark Mother's scald crows, before this is done? he thought. *How many friendly garths like this will be roofless and burnt, their folk knowing exile and hunger even if they live? The necessity doesn't change the black wickedness of it.*

He rose and took one of the towels that heated on racks beside the boiler, hoarded pre-Change cotton kept for honored guests. The boy looked at him, then did an almost comical double take, *looking* in a way that took in the scars. The expression of awed respect went deeper, as he glanced at all of them in the same light, lingering on the purple weal that marked Odard's left forearm. Now that Rudi thought about it, this *was* a collection of tried fighting men that would impress many a lad.

The more so, I judge, because we're none of us impossibly older than he; Fred and Edain have only four years on him. Mark's on the brink of manhood, and eager for it past bearing. It's well I remember that feeling!

The Mackenzie spoke in a cheerful tone: "My sister Mary has indeed done much, things wild and deadly, but from duty and necessity, not from choice, my young friend," he said.

Then he smiled: "She and Ritva are of the Dúnedain, the Rangers who're sworn to protect the weak and oppressed, and who travel and explore and fight their whole lives long. Which tends not to be all that much of a longness, as it were."

Mark's eyes went wider, and Rudi continued: "It's their trade, a hard and difficult one; that and guarding travelers and hunting bandits and scouting in war. Now, at your age, I also wanted adventures, and I will admit it. Remember though, an adventure is someone else neck-deep in a dung heap, and that far, far away! Until the bards get to work on it."

"Bards?" the youngster said, frowning in puzzlement.

"The songsmiths, the storytellers, you'd say. They can take anything and put a polish on it like hammered gold."

"Says the man who laughed as he rode mad buffalo, jumping from beast to beast, one to the next, with enemies shooting arrows at him the while?" Edain snorted, rubbing his oak-colored curls vigorously with a towel of his own. "And it's a wonder *I* don't have white hair now, from the watching of it: what would I say to Da if I came back without you?"

"That was necessary. They were chasing us," Rudi said quellingly. "The buffalo were the best way to shake the pursuit."

The younger Mackenzie winked at the Readstown boy. "But the Chief, he grinned amidst the million of them while he rode the wild bulls, that he did, while one slip would have meant being hammered to paste."

"Afterwards I remember mostly snorting water out

through my nose, and it half mud from the dust I'd breathed," Rudi said, and threw the wet towel at Edain, who dodged with a laugh of his own.

"And you're all too likely to have a war coming to *you*," he went on to the boy.

Ingolf nodded soberly, but his nephew seemed to feel nothing but excitement at the thought. Rudi shook his head, sighed, and dressed. The two clansmen drew on clean drawers and then pulled their best saffron-dyed linen shirts over their heads, wrapped their kilts and pinned the garments and their plaids with the brooches kept for social occasions, silver wrought in knotwork or intricate running designs of elongated gripping beasts and geometric shapes, studded with turquoise and carnelian.

"Is that the way people dress in . . . in . . ." Mark asked.

"Montival," Rudi supplied. "The some of us do—we of the Clan Mackenzie. It's the style of our ancestors, so, from long before the Change, which our folk remembered after it."

He remembered things his mother and his stepfather Nigel Loring had said, and amended it to:

"More or less the style of some of our ancestors."

"Absurd barbarian fashion," Odard put in as he donned his parti-colored court-style Portlander hose.

That required perching on a stool and gathering it up to the toe and considerable care and effort; Juniper Mackenzie had once told him that the effect had a strong resemblance to what she'd known as *panty hose*, but with even fine bias-cut linen a lot less stretchy and convenient than nylon. The carefully preserved jupon and tunic came out to follow, donned with foppish care.

As the baron of Gervais added a ring and admired the

effect on one hand Rudi reflected that Odard really *enjoyed* dressing up in what Associates insisted on calling *garb*, no matter how uncomfortable, so long as it was rich and sightly. Not being able to do so every day was a real hardship to him, albeit one he bore without too much complaint.

Mathilda was probably putting on her set of the same; she'd left the cotte-hardi in Iowa, observing that once past Wisconsin most of the people they'd be meeting would be either Cutters or cannibals, unable to appreciate a lady's formal dress and all too likely to put her in situations where skirts would be a handicap.

"But I'd guess she's not putting it on just yet," Rudi said aloud. "Have you ever observed, my friends, that a woman may have no more surface area than a man—"

"Distributed differently," Fred Thurston said; he was donning something very close to the green dress uniform of the old American army, with a dark beret on his short wiry hair. "Different in a *good* way."

"Granted, by the Foam-Born! But the same area of skin, do you see? Yet why *cannot* she wash in the amount of time a man finds ample, unless the water is freezing, or has things with fangs in it, so?"

"Or put on a kilt as fast as we do," Edain observed, tucking the little sgian dubh, the *black knife*, into its sheath in his sock-hose. "It's a mystery of the Mother-of-All, that it is."

"Christ, this still fits," Ingolf said, donning his own clothing.

It was a set of blue linen pants with copper rivets, a light roll-necked sweater and a denim jacket dyed with wild indigo. He'd left it all behind when he rode off to the Sioux War, and it had been carefully preserved by his

sister-in-law. More of the fittings were pre-Change salvage than his relatives wore now.

Then he worked his shoulders. "Well . . . the jacket's
a bit tight here. I hadn't quite gotten my full growth
then. It'll do, though. I've got enough range of arm for
getting the beer to mouth-height!"

A soprano voice came from the other side of the door,
a mutter of Sindarin and then:

"Aren't you people ready yet? I'm starving!"

"Harry, I got you those sixty-four acres because you're
my sister's cousin-in-law. People understand that. Now
it's up to *you* to make what you can of it before you start
asking for more favors. People will understand *that*,
too."

Rudi halted, and the others did perforce behind him;
the half-closed door leading to the vestibule let the conversation through only because one side of it was being
conducted at the level of a bad-tempered bellow on Edward Vogeler's part. There was a murmur from the other
man . . .

"No, I'm not going to give you any more County
land," Edward Vogeler said. "*Or* more woodlot rights or
fishing quotas."

Another murmur, and: "Because you can't *work* more
than a tenth-section by yourself!" the Sheriff went on.
"It'll take you years to get that much going, the way it's
grown up in scrub."

Another murmur, and the reply was even louder:

"No! This isn't goddamned Iowa, or Marshall, or even
Ellsworth—I'm not going to tell someone they have to
work for you just because their folks were refugees. Pay

someone if you can, though with what God only knows. Hell, you borrowed all the equipment you've got—mostly from me! Und only one of your kids is old enough yet to do much fieldwork—Mary Mother alone *knows* how Janet's going to make do there on her own without a grown woman to help. Now buckle to und get dat land cleared and be happy I'm letting you off the land tax for four years! If you had any sense, you'd stay and work with your father-in-law and do it bit by bit."

Edward Vogeler was still scowling when Rudi coughed diplomatically and came through the entranceway, but his face relaxed.

"Sorry. Business. Right this way, gentlemen, ladies," he said. "Let's get you all a brew. Unless you'd like wine? We keep some for company."

"Ah . . . no, your beer is of a surpassing excellence, Sheriff," Rudi said. "I'll stick with that."

That has the merit of being true; and it means I need not say that I haven't had a decent glass of wine since we crossed the Rockies, he thought, as everyone else murmured agreement. *Most of them taste as if a fox had peed in the vat with the grapes.*

"Beer we got. Also cider, applejack, cherry brandy, peach brandy, whiskey, and vodka."

The cavernous banquet hall had a floor of polished concrete, and the ceiling above was a simple V of steel rafters and corrugated metal sheets supported by iron pillars, all obviously built before the Change. Their host escorted them through into the great room and jerked his thumb at the row of barrels resting along one wall on X-shaped stands of fragrant pine boards.

"Help yourselves. Gotta run, get some things done first. Mark will show you 'round."

The mugs were old cast glass this time, and sitting in

beds of crushed ice. Rudi decided on a lighter wheat beer, instead of the dark bock he'd had when Wanda greeted them. There were half a dozen types.

And each better than the last, he thought respectfully after his first sip.

"Ice at the end of summer!" Mathilda said, impressed. "We had that at the Palace of course, but—"

Mark Vogeler looked at her oddly, and Rudi didn't think it was just for the Lidless Eye in the heraldic shield on her chest.

"Doesn't it *freeze* out west in . . . in Montival?" he said.

"Several times a year. And we get snow, even down in the valleys sometimes," she said.

"For variety in the endless winter rainfall," Odard said whimsically. "I understand that at least the sun comes out here between October and May. Sometimes. We call that period the *Black Months*, back home."

"You mean . . . the snow doesn't *stay* all winter where you come from?"

Ingolf chuckled. "Mark's looking at you funny for a reason, Matti. Believe me, getting enough ice laid down to last out the summer is *not* a problem here. Wait until you've seen one of our winters."

"We've been known to have some cold weather in the Powder River country," Virginia Kane said, prickly about her homeland on the High Plains.

"Idaho too," Fred Thurston added. "Granted Boise's not as bad as the up-country, or Wyoming."

Ingolf made a gesture that was half acknowledgment, half disagreement.

"You don't get blizzards like ours. It's a lot wetter here than most places out west that aren't on a mountain-side, and it's just as damned cold as it gets in Wyoming,

Virginia. Blizzards here can bury a barn, and they could start any time now, too; Indian Summer's unpredictable."

He drew them both a mug, expertly tapering off the tail of foam, and looked around the hall.

"Ah, bratwash and all the fixings!" he said, with Mary smiling and looping her arm around his waist and enjoying his pleasure. "Damn, this takes me back. I remember the first time we could afford it, when I was about ten. Dad had a big party like this, to celebrate us finally really getting on our feet."

Folk were setting out trestle tables and benches, hauling bright lanterns up to the cross-girders, and wheeling in great wicker bins woven of split oak and full of fragrant warm loaves. The center space held four large hearths made from metal barrels cut lengthwise and full of glowing hardwood coals topped by mesh grills, beneath a broad dismountable smoke hood and metal pipe chimney. Right now big shallow pans were simmering there, with an intense smell of onions and . . .

"Beer?" Father Ignatius said with interest. "Some sort of marinade?"

He sipped at the mug in his fist with evident pleasure; he was a man of studied self-control and moderation, but saw no reason to pretend he wasn't enjoying a beer if he was going to drink it at all.

One reason I like him, Rudi thought. *He's not like some Christian clerics I've met, who act as if they thought the world and all its pleasures were an evil produced by that bad spirit of theirs, rather than the Maker of Stars.*

"Yah," Mark said, obviously happy to enlighten the foreigners. "You simmer the brats . . . that's a sausage—"

"My baptismal name was Bergfried, my son," the

priest said gently, his slightly tilted dark eyes crinkling in amusement. "I've heard of bratwurst. My mother and sisters make very good ones, in fact."

"Oh, sorry, Father. Well, you simmer the brats in beer broth with onions, and then you grill 'em. We'll be starting with that, though."

He nodded to a much larger pot, which Wanda Vogeler was stirring, occasionally taking a sip from the ladle.

"Onion, cheese and beer soup," Ingolf said reverently. "God, that smells just like the recipe Mom used, the one she'd never let anyone write down."

"Yah, Grandma taught Mom, all right. Said she was getting too old to do it herself."

Ingolf nodded, his face somber again for a moment; the news of his mother's death was fresh for him, but his nephew was too young to sustain grief for years. Rudi took a deep sniff: under the cooking smells were others that made him suspect the feasting hall doubled as storage most of the time; he could detect strong hints of something sweet.

"Maple sugar," Ingolf said in reply to his question, as they stood waiting for the trestles to be set up. "We get a *lot* of that and we used to put the barrels and tubs here. That and beer, usually, or that's what we used it for when I was a kid."

"Ingolf," Fred asked thoughtfully as he watched the crowd trickle in; his father had been a general, after all, and besides formal training as an officer he'd grown up around recruitment and logistics. "Just how many people *are* there in Readstown?"

Ingolf looked at him in mild surprise. "When I left? A bit more than a hundred farms that came through; call it, oh, twenty-five hundred people, Farmers and refugees together. That's in the whole Sheriffry of Readstown, not just"—his gesture took in the settlement—"the home-place here; say a hundred-odd here counting kids. Probably more now all up."

"Three thousand six hundred in the Sheriffry," Mark Vogeler said. "We took a count last year. The Bossman wanted to know."

"Is that typical?" the Boisean continued.

"Oh, some are a bit bigger, some a bit smaller," Mark put in, obviously proud of his knowledge—and his country. "We don't have big cities like Iowa, but there are some pretty large towns—Richland Center has three thousand people all by itself. I've been there. God, it's more crowded than I thought any place could be. Half a million in the whole of the Free Republic, if you can *imagine* that many people."

"Hmmmm," Fred said.

Mathilda shaped a soundless whistle. Rudi was impressed himself. Not nearly as many inhabitants as great Iowa, but it was still as many as the PPA had, and half what the United States of Boise or the Cutters could boast; seven or eight times as many as the Clan Mackenzie. And Richland wasn't even the only such bossman-dom in what had been Wisconsin; there was Ellsworth, to the north, and a spattering of independent little villages and counties farther northeast.

"And it seems this land breeds many strong young men," Rudi said thoughtfully. "No doubt it's formidable they would be, should foemen or reivers come this way."

"Right!" Mark said, his chest puffing out slightly. "We Readstowners can muster a battalion of three hundred now for the Free Republic's National Guard."

Or should their Sheriff have a quarrel with the neighbors,

Rudi thought. *From what Ingolf says there was a fair bit of that, at least in his father's time, before things found their balance here.*

Mark went on: "A quarter of them are cavalry. A lot of our guys fought in the Sioux War, or in the trouble we had with Ellsworth, or against outlaws and stuff. Our team won third place in the Guard muster competition at Richland Center this June."

The tables were set up now, and covered with checked cloths; a group with drums and instruments—he recognized a tuba and an accordion—began playing cheerful music with an *oom-pah, oom-pah* beat for a minute or two. That was apparently a signal for everyone to seek their seats; the farm workers and laborers at the lower tables had a guest or two to each family group, and Mark and those of his siblings old enough led Rudi and his immediate followers to the master's table.

The hall was filled with chatter and smiles; even the Southsiders were only mildly nervous despite the strangeness of place, folk and even food—many of them still thought of buttered bread as an exotic treat. The Mackenzie judged the Readstown folk were showing the pleasure to be expected at a break in routine, plus anticipation of the feast and the happiness anyone who lived close to the land felt when the main harvest was in and safely stored.

And local pride that they can afford to guest so many strangers so well, he thought.

Which was pardonable. It *did* show that this was a prosperous community and well run.

"I'm glad it's not Samhain itself," Edain murmured to him as they took their chairs.

Those seemed to be something of a luxury; most of the seating lower down was benches. More benches ran around the outer walls. On them were hollowed pumpkins with candlelight flickering through carved gaptoothed faces, between cooling rows of pies, some pumpkin, others apple, peach, cherry or rhubarb, all grouped around bowls of thick whipped cream sweetened with maple sugar or honey.

A Clan dun might show exactly the same jack-o'-lantern display around this mark on the Wheel of the Year . . . but they both suspected that Readstown didn't take them nearly as seriously as their own folk.

"So am I also glad it's not quite Samhain yet," Rudi said dryly. "Inauspicious it would be, sure and it would."

Every Mackenzie household set an empty place at the Samhain feasts, but that was a symbol of the welcome they extended to the beloved dead who might visit on the day when the Veil was thinnest. The problem was that *other* things might stray into the world of men on such a day; if someone actually came through the door and seated himself he had to be fed and entertained with everything of the best, but matters could get very tense indeed. Such an outsider might be anything—or possessed of such. The world held many beings who were not of humankind, some friendly, some playful in ways heedless of men and their lives and loves and needs, some not friendly at all.

Ingolf Vogeler had come into Sutterdown as just such a stranger on Samhain eve, and deeds bloody and terrible had followed; they were here now because of them.

The head table held the Sheriff and his immediate family, and his chief officers and *their* families—they included the head of his deputies, the field boss and stock boss who managed the Sheriff's own farmland and beasts, the old Ojibwa Indian—Pierre Walks Quiet—who was chief forester and game warden, the fair-haired woman named

Samantha who was housekeeper under the Sheriff's wife, and a few others. Wanda Vogeler hung her apron over the back of her chair and wiped her hands on it before she sat down and beamed at them.

"Everything ready—at last!" she said. "Und Jenny sleeping—at last. Woof! Children! No wonder people get old!"

"There's nothing you ever enjoyed more than laying on a big feed, Wanda," Ingolf said teasingly. "Unless you've changed more than I think."

"Nothing I enjoy more except eating it myself," she said. "And talking while I eat. And dancing afterwards. Both with people who aren't the same ones I see every day, and I know everything they're going to say before they say it."

Her husband cleared his throat and rose. The noise in the hall fell off and then vanished; faces turned towards them, some already chewing on rolls or pieces of cheese from the rounds and blocks and wedges that were set out on cutting boards down the tables, alternating with tubs of butter and jugs of milk, beer and cider.

"Well, folks, you all know my brother Ingolf is back for a visit."

There was a cheer and a ripple of raised mugs; Edward Vogeler looked surprised, and so did Ingolf.

"We all heard how well Ingolf did in the Sioux War," Ed went on. "How the Bossman of Marshall gave him that medal and offered to make him a general."

Rudi and his party looked at Ingolf in surprise; the only tales he'd told them about his part in that conflict had been things comical or tragic, mostly reflecting badly on himself.

"And how his salvage team got all the way to the East Coast after that, chosen by the Bossman of Iowa because he was the best. First people from the Midwest to do *dat* since the Change!"

Family pride rang in his voice as the folk of the steading cheered again. Then he went on:

"With him is his intended and her brother Rudi Mackenzie, the guy he's ramrod for now, who comes all the way from the west coast—that's a first, too! They're our guests here, and so are their people. Let's show them hospitality, and how the Free Republic of Richland, and we Readstowners, treat guests. They've got a priest with them, good Father Ignatius, and I'd like him to lead us in saying grace."

He bowed his head, and Ignatius rose:

"O Christ our God, bless"—he signed himself—"the food and drink of Your servants for You are holy always, now and ever, and forever. As Jacob greeted Esau his brother, may we all be as brothers to one another, in Your love. Amen."

There was a murmur of *Amen* from up and down the tables. Rudi and the others of the Old Religion waited in respectful silence with their heads bowed—courtesy, and also duty to their host—and then signed their plates with the Invoking Pentagram and quietly murmured:

"Harvest Lord who dies for the ripened corn—
Corn Mother who births the fertile field—
Blessed be those who share this bounty;
And Blessed the mortals who toiled with You
Their hands helping Earth to bring forth life."

He didn't think Edward Vogeler noticed what they were about, or perhaps he very thoroughly chose not to. Several others—the housekeeper among them—did, he thought.

A girl carried around a tureen of the soup; Wanda Vogeler wielded the ladle for the table, and Rudi accepted his gratefully. Baskets held half a dozen types of bread—fine white loaves with a crackling glaze, black rye, rich coarse-textured pumpernickel, round rolls with crosses cut in their surface, squares of slightly sweet cornbread. He cut a slice of the rye because it was rare at home and wielded the spoon with gratitude. The soup had a deep savory smoky richness that was just what you needed after a day's hard work in brisk fall weather.

The bratwurst were sizzling on the grills, and a team split crusty rolls, buttered them and set out mustard and sauerkraut and sautéed onions to go with them. Rudi took several when they were borne around. His brows went up a little as others pulled back the cloths on tubs of honey-glazed chicken breasts and steaks kissed with garlic, pork chops, racks of ribs and skewers of venison and lamb and onions ready to go on the coals, and it became apparent that the brats were merely the introduction.

My Southsiders will be happy, he thought; they had a carnivore's idea of food.

Then the vegetable dishes came in, on wheeled trolleys.

"Yah hey, scalloped potatoes with bacon," Ingolf said, rubbing his hands as a heavy ceramic pot was lifted to the table and plopped on an oakwood coaster; it bubbled under its brown-gold topping of grated cheddar. "My favorite!"

"Topped with cheese," Mary Havel said. "It's *good* cheese, all of it . . . but . . . don't you ever get tired of cheese here?"

Ingolf grinned at her. "Tired of *food*?" he said.

*   *   *

Edward Vogeler called this his study. They seated themselves in big comfortable chairs around a table of polished
dark wood; a desk stood in the shadows of a corner, and
books lined the walls. Rudi had a chance for a quick
glance at them. You could tell a good deal about a man
by what he chose to read. These seemed mainly practical—
tomes on agriculture and stockbreeding, war and building and metalworking, along with rows of account
books.

A few were recent titles, their printing and binding less
machine-perfect—one read *Salvaging Gears For Millwork*,
and another *Modern Body Armor*.

And up in a corner were a few tales he recognized, well
read but looking dusty and neglected now: *Joris of the
Rock*, one of Mathilda's favorites and her mother's before
her, and *Sir Guillaume*, by Donan Coyle, one of his own
beloved since boyhood that he'd been given by Sir Nigel.
He suspected those had been Ingolf's, along with the
Tarzan and the *Wizard of Oz* series.

Wanda bustled in behind them and set out a tray with
a pot of hot comfrey-chicory so-called coffee and oatmeal
cookies rich with walnuts and raisins. Then, a little to
Rudi's surprise, she seated herself near her husband, taking up a half-finished sweater from a basket and setting
to work. A white-bibbed black cat took up station beneath her chair, occasionally darting a paw at the skein of
wool as it jerked upward to the click of the knitting
needles.

"Drink?" the Sheriff asked. "We do a good applejack,
if I say so myself. Und I do."

Rudi accepted his with a murmur of thanks. It was a
comfortable room, smelling of polish, old tobacco smoke

and leather and lit by good alcohol lanterns, with a couple of comely if worn rugs on the floor. A brick fireplace held a pleasant crackle of burning oak. On the mantelpiece above it were two black-bordered photographs: one of a thin hard-faced woman in late middle age, and another of a man who looked enough like the Vogeler brothers to be their father and probably was. Unlike the woman's it was a pre-Change piece, with sharp edges and bright colors; he wore dark glasses, a khaki shirt and an odd peaked cap, with a metal star on his breast that Rudi recognized.

The master of Readstown stuffed a briar pipe as his guests settled in, and Ingolf did likewise. They grew tobacco here and were proud of the product.

A habit I do not admire, Rudi thought, coughing a little.

Smoking was rare in the far west, and he wasn't sorry for it; he'd never used the weed himself, save as an aid to ceremony among folk to whom it was sacred. But it would be tactless to protest a man's diversions under his own roof, and impious as well. After all, every home was a little world in itself, with its own customs and guardian spirits, whether it was a crofter's cot or a manor like this.

Instead he sipped at the excellent apple brandy and tried not to feel too bloated. Those had been the best sausages he'd ever eaten, but even an hour of vigorous square dancing and polkas afterwards hadn't worked most of the feast off.

The others here to talk business were Father Ignatius and Mathilda. Rudi thought the Sheriff had been a little surprised when they'd automatically included her.

And I am somewhat surprised that the Sheriff brought Pierre Walks Quiet in on things right away, he mused, nodding to the old Indian. *Even if he does manage the Sheriffry's forests and game, the which is a position of importance and honor.*

"They aren't kidding when they say *Princess*, Ed," Ingolf said, with an inclination of his head towards Mathilda. "Her family runs half the country out there beyond the Rockies—most of what used to be Washington and part of Oregon too. She stands to inherit it. Only child."

Mathilda nodded with regal courtesy. "And parts of British Columbia, my l—Sheriff. None of it's nearly as densely populated as your country here in the Midwest, of course."

"And Rudi's relatives run most of the rest, one way or another."

The older Vogeler nodded. "I've heard a little," he said. "That there was a bunch of King Arthur stuff out there, at least."

"That would be Rudi," Mathilda said; her smile was half rueful and all charming. "His . . . other . . . name is *Artos*. It's quite famous, in the west."

"Yah. News travels so slow these days, und it gets twisted. All sorts of wild stories."

"And Fred's the son of the President of Boise."

"The black kid?" Ed asked, surprise in his tone.

"Yah, yah. Though his elder brother is running it now. They're . . . not friends. He's OK. The brother isn't."

Ed's face twisted a little for an instant, and Ingolf cleared his throat and explained the others, starting with Virginia and the twins. His brother's eyebrows went up, turning his high forehead into a mass of corrugations.

"You've gotten quite a collection together, Mr. Mackenzie," he said. "And you're all heading east?" he said.

Rudi nodded. "To Nantucket itself. Ingolf has been there—"

The Sheriff's eyes went wide and he stared at his brother with the pipe halfway to his mouth for a full fifteen seconds, before puffing it to a moment's glow and then trickling smoke out his nose.

"I always thought you were crazy as much as you were brave," he said bluntly. "I knew you'd gotten to the Atlantic, to Boston . . . but *Nantucket?* That's where the Change started. Remember? Dad was watching TV right then and I was with him. That TV, right there."

He pointed the stem of the pipe at a glass-fronted box; Rudi blinked at it, recognizing it from ones he'd seen, though mostly in abandoned ruins. He shook his head a little; his host had seemed so at home that it was a bit of a shock to realize he'd been a man grown at the Change, or nearly. Enough so that he kept this bit of junk around.

"Nah, I was asleep, remember?" Ingolf said.

"You came down crying."

"I did?" Ingolf asked, shaking his head. "Damn, you know, that's completely gone. But Nantucket . . . yah, I remember that *damn* well. Even if I was off my head a lot while I was there. Spookiest damn place I've ever seen, and that includes Corwin."

The elder Vogeler brother crossed himself. "God might not like people sticking their noses in there. You know . . . like poking around Noah's Ark."

"My son," Father Ignatius said, "God works through human beings. Even miracles only open possibilities to us, to act *as* human beings in this world. We have excellent evidence that something of overwhelming importance awaits us on Nantucket. Holy Mother Church has given Her blessing to this expedition. And the Cutter cult—the Church Universal and Triumphant—"

Ed crossed himself again. "Yah, I know about them, a little," he said. "We've had a few of them through, these last couple of years, preaching. I always told them to keep moving, with a boot to the butt when I had to."

Pierre Walks Quiet spoke. "More of them north of here; I hear stuff from my relatives. They're bad news, bad manitou. Wendigo."

Rudi bit back an exclamation that was mostly sheer irritation.

Is there anyplace they're not *making themselves a nuisance, to be sure?* he thought.

Beneath the annoyance came a small cold crawling sensation down his spine at the word the old man used. His blood-father Mike Havel had been a quarter Anishinabe—his mother's mother had been of the Ojibwa people—and Rudi had heard more than one tale of those sprits of cold and eternal hunger, and how they could possess a man. He remembered dead hands squeezing his throat, and eyes that were like a window into nothingness.

"Yes," he said softly. "Yes, *Wendigo* would be as good a name as any for them. For their adepts, at least, and for the things with which they traffic."

Ignatius continued to the Sheriff: "Then you will know how they are heretics and misleaders of innocent folk. Far worse, we have substantial evidence that they, their inner circle, are diabolists as well. Actual agents of the Adversary."

Ed Vogeler grunted and crossed himself again. "Yah, from what Pete tells me, I'm not completely surprised. He's got a steady head, Pete. Richland gave me a rap on the knuckles . . . hell, young Bill Clements had the nerve to give me a *lecture* on religious toleration, the damn pup."

"I heard Bill was Bossman now," Ingolf said.

"Yah hey, by the time everyone stopped talking after Al Clements died, it was a done deal. I've got no objection; that seems to be the way things are done nowadays and you have to keep up with progress. He's a smart guy even if he really likes to hear himself talk."

"So did Al," Ingolf said. "I remember what he had to say about that stump."

Edward Vogeler grinned for a second. "So do I. Why do you think I kept it around?"

Then he sobered and continued: "It's not that he *likes* these Cutter types—nobody much does, in the Free Republic, no Farmers or Sheriffs at least, nobody who counts. But he doesn't realize . . . Hell, they're not a religion, they're a disease. I put up with all kinds here, we got some strange people settling in after the Change, but not *them*, and if the Bossman doesn't like it he can come up from Richland Center and kiss my hairy Readstown ass. I've got plenty of other Sheriffs would back me up, on general principle. This isn't goddamned Iowa where you need a permit from the Bossman's clerks to visit the outhouse on your own land."

Walks Quiet rolled himself a cigarette and added its tendrils to the haze beneath the rafters.

"Lots of people up north turned Wendigo in the bad time," he said quietly; his eyes looked through the smoke as if he was peering through the veil of years.

Ingolf leaned over under the guise of reaching for a cookie and murmured in Rudi's ear: "That's how Pete lost his family. And why he headed south."

The Indian continued: "Not everyone—there were plenty of people who knew how to hunt, fish, find wild rice, grow stuff like spuds—but plenty, yeah. The land couldn't carry all the people there with nothing coming in, 'specially after we got us some refugees turning up looking for a meal. It's not like down here in the warm places where there was lots of grain and cattle once you got far enough from the cities."

So there were Eaters, Rudi thought. *But not quite so mad and desperate, and with plenty of what my Southsiders would call* clean *settlements in the same territory. That was sparsely peopled land even before the Change, but it's bleak, from what I've read and heard, and what little Mike Havel told.*

The Indian went on: "Nowadays they do pretty good up north, most years, but people remember just exactly how it was the neighbors pulled through. Lots of fights since over that. Preachers telling you it's the way all the big Manitou wanted things to happen, that you're not so bad; they get a hearing up there from some people."

Ed Vogeler stirred his pipe's bowl with a twig. "You planning on taking the northern route down the Lakes and out the St. Lawrence?" he said. "It's been done now and then, but . . . rough way to go. You haven't got all that much time before freeze-up."

"After freeze-up, we thought," Rudi said. "Ingolf says it can be done."

"I always said Ingolf had more balls than sense," the Sheriff said. "Never was a Vogeler didn't have guts, but brains, now . . ."

Ingolf stiffened and flushed a little, then made himself relax with an effort that only an expert eye could see. Rudi thought that Wanda Vogeler *did* detect it; her eyes rolled slightly ceilingward, and she sighed.

But her husband did not, *despite being the man's brother,* he thought. *The tact of a bull buffalo, to be sure.*

Instead of barking a reply, Ingolf tossed back half his applejack and followed it with a sip of the coffee of roasted roots.

"Ed," he said mildly, and set the cup down with careful gentleness. "There's something you're missing."

"What?" the older man said impatiently.

"Yah, yah, when I left Readstown I *did* have more balls than brains. But that was ten . . . no, more . . . years ago. I fought through the whole damn Sioux War as a paid soldier, and other places too, and then I went into salvage work. When I say *salvage* I'm not talking about a trip to Madison for some rebar or leaf springs, either. I've been all the way from the Atlantic to the Pacific and back."

"Yah, we heard, so?"

"And I'm still *alive*, Ed. When hundreds of poor brave dumb fucks I crossed paths with are well and truly dead. Pardon my French, Wanda."

"I've heard the word, Ingolf."

He inclined his head to her and went on to his brother: "I saw them die, and I lived. My balls are doing fine, but my brains took over the thinking job a while ago. Or I would've taken my last trip through an Eater's guts."

After a moment the Sheriff's head moved in a slow nod, and he studied his brother for a full minute, stroking his gray-streaked beard before he spoke.

"Point. But . . . yah hey, it's easier to move on sleds over snow than on the roads the rest of the year, the way they've gotten wrecked. You can haul a lot more weight that way with the same horsepower—that's why we move freight in the winter and do our lumbering then. And yah, yah, da lakes freeze—or at least enough of them does. But man . . . supplies!"

"It's possible," Ingolf said. "Going the southern route

in winter, there's too much mud and wet snow, most of the time—and we're not going to wait until spring. Plus the Cutters had a river-galley waiting for us south of the Iowa border, if we tried to go up the Ohio. There are still just under a hundred of them at least, hard men, and they'll jump us when they can."

"Easier to move the supplies too, it would be," Rudi said. "And the folk, on skis. From what Ingolf tells me, men on skis can travel three or four times as fast as those on foot—faster than men on horseback, unless they had a string of remounts each and left a trail of dead horses."

"Yah," Ed Vogeler said. "As long as you didn't get caught in a storm for three weeks. *Or* run out of fodder for the horses pulling your sleighs. You can't exactly buy hay and oats up there, most places."

"Some places, if you know who to ask. I'll go part way with them," Pete said, and the Sheriff gave him a surprised look.

"Not all the way," the Indian went on. "Got my woman and kids here to think about. And I'm getting too old, not much good in a fight anymore. This is my home, now. But far enough to get 'em started."

"It's your life, Pete," his overlord said. "Hmmm . . . youse could get big sleds built around here, convert your wagons maybe, and enough provender . . ."

He looked over at Wanda. Her square middle-aged face was tight with concern for her brother-in-law.

For him at least, Rudi thought. *And the rest of us too, I think, even on short acquaintance. Mother would like her, I think, even if she talks a good deal. And I notice she's been quiet here.*

"Yah," she said, slowly and unwillingly. "We could

spare a lot." To Rudi: "We keep a three-year rotating stockpile."

"It was two, when I left," Ingolf said.

"Ed's a careful man," his sister-in-law said. "Und it's easier since we've got the stuff for canning and pickling as much as we want now—lots of mason jars and good tight barrels and such. So we're always running down the older part anyway, as we add new. And the out-farms do the same."

"Enough, with some hunting," Pete said. "As far as the midlakes. I don't know much of what comes after, say, Duluth. Just that things get worse the farther east."

Mathilda broke away from the long kiss. "Spare my healing ribs, Rudi! And my reputation."

Rudi ground his teeth silently; she hadn't objected to his hands for quite some time, and the taste of her was upon his lips, along with that of the Sheriff's excellent apple brandy, of which he'd had more than she in the long discussion. It was silent now in the guest quarters, past midnight and all others asleep. Mathilda saw the look despite the dim light of the passageway and smiled a little sadly, patting him on the cheek:

"Waiting like this isn't easy for you, is it, poor lamb? Just you wait until we're married, and you'll never regret the witch-girls again!"

"That I won't!" he said, catching his breath.

Then he drew back a little, his hands on her shoulders. "Matti . . . *anamchara* mine . . . are we betrothed? We haven't said the words."

Her smile died. "Yes. Or at least *I* want us to be."

"And myself also!"

The next kiss was long. He pulled away with difficulty, and remembered Associate custom. From one knee he spoke:

"But some things it's better to say aloud. Mathilda . . . will you marry me, pagan clansman that I am?"

"Yes!"

She caught his head to her, and after a moment he felt a warm drop on it. When he rose, he touched a finger to the track of a tear.

"Why are you weeping, my heart?"

"Because I'm *happy*, you great gangling idiot! Because I can just be Mathilda and happy for an instant, not the Princess."

Then she wrinkled her nose at him. "And yes, I've thought about it carefully—the politics as well. If you *weren't* going to be High King, it would be . . . harder. But I think Mother will approve. And I think the Cardinal-Archbishop will give us a dispensation. That's just bargaining, though. I want *you*."

"And me likewise. Now, when? Tomorrow? Perhaps a week? We've good Father Ignatius here, after all—and my folk have no problem accepting a Christian marriage as valid. We can have a grand celebration when we're home, when the war allows . . . but there's no reason we should be apart the now."

Her hands fell away from him, and the joy in her face faltered—as if the shadows that lay across them in the dim hallway had entered there.

"Rudi . . . we can't get married *here* and *now*."

"Why not?" he said, and grinned. "Besides the delightful prospects it raises, it would be better if you were my heir in law. *Someone* must lead our folk in Montival; and modesty aside, you're the next best choice after me.

For some of it, you're better. I'm not immortal, and we're in just a *wee* bit of danger, you might say."

Her eyes fell. "I . . . I can't marry without Mother's permission, Rudi."

He felt a chill pass over his own happiness. "As you said, she'll be happy enough. For one thing, she cares little for the matter of our different faiths—"

Then he cursed himself as she winced; that was *not* something that Mathilda Arminger liked to remember about her mother.

"—and for another, the kingcraft of the thing will delight her. I wouldn't be surprised if she hadn't had something of the sort in mind!"

Mathilda nodded. "She's mentioned a dynastic marriage before. But . . . I may *think* I'll get her permission, but I'm not *sure* . . ."

"Matti!" He wagged a finger at her. "It's all our lives we've known each other, or nearly. Do you think I can't tell when you're making an excuse? And the same for Cardinal Maxwell!"

"Rudi—" Her voice was half desperate. "Rudi, if I'm your wife, we'll have to *sleep* together."

"And much else!" Rudi said happily.

"I mean . . . it's not really a marriage unless it's consummated!"

"*Acushla*, my thought exactly!"

"You . . . you *man*!" she said, and punched him on the chest; then winced when it jarred her healing arm. "You single-minded tomcat! You—"

He took a step back and raised his hands; it wasn't the first time a woman had said something of the same order to him, but it was a blunt surprise now.

"Matti, darlin' girl, what's the matter?"

"What happens, you idiot, when a man and a woman are together? *Babies!* Why do you call your goddess the *Mother*, Rudi? It's not because she spanks you!"

He opened his mouth, then closed it again. *Yes, there's that* geasa, he thought unhappily. *They think it's wicked to prevent conception. And it's a strong custom. Matti wouldn't break it.*

It was also a real impediment. They were just about to start a journey through some of the deadliest wilderness in the world, and in midwinter at that. They would certainly have to fight at times. Matti was a warrior of considerable skill—no great champion, but well above average for an Associate of her age and easily as good as, say, Odard. But she couldn't swing a sword from behind a yard of pregnant belly.

Or ride quickly, or run and hide, or . . .

She saw his hesitation, and followed the blow with a prodding finger. "And *don't* tell me about the rhythm method. It's good enough for home, but it doesn't *work* all the time."

To be sure not all methods of sharing pleasure lead to babies. But that would require a great deal of willpower. And that particular method is the crux of a marriage, to one of her faith; without it, there's no true handfasting, no matter what the rites and ceremonies. It's the thing that cannot be undone, to them.

"Do you think you're the only one who's tempted?" she said angrily, her voice rising.

She shrugged off his hand as she turned her face to the wall. "Don't *tempt* me, Rudi. It's so . . . it's so *hard* to keep saying no! I don't *want* to! But I have to do what's right."

"It's truly sorry I am," Rudi said soberly.

Truly sorry, and very bewildered. And wishing you were

*a follower of the Old Religion, much more so than I ever
have before.*

She turned back to him and went on more softly:
"Rudi, I can't chance being pregnant in the wilderness. I
just can't. I'm . . . scared of it. And what if . . . Mother
had a very hard time with me. They had to cut! We nearly
both died, and that was with all the doctors in the Protectorate on hand, and Mother couldn't have more
children."

He winced. "Matti, all that is as true as gold. But we're
going to be on this road a *long* time," he said unhappily.
"We've been a year and some months already, and we're
only three-quarters of the way! Matti, having the beauty
of you there is going to be a torment, that it is. We're
betrothed now, not fancy-free."

*And it's extremely awkward I would feel trying to take
back the words. It's "yes" I expected, or perhaps even "no,"
but not "yes, in two years!"*

"I know," she said, and kissed him again. "It's hard
for me too. We'll make an offering of the pain, and when
we're married, it will be all the sweeter for the
memory."

He stared at her. "Ah . . . Matti, I know that makes
perfect sense to you, and as the Gods of my people witness, I respect it. There are many paths to the divine and
they have their own rules; you can see it shining from
Father Ignatius, and he's not the only Christian I've met
who was a holy man for all but the blind to see. But I'm
not a Christian, you know, *anamchara*. My *geasa* are different. Sometimes I don't think you realize quite how
different, for all your time on the Clan's land. And also a
man and a woman are different in that way—"

This time she hit him in the pit of the stomach, where
even a very strong man had no protection. The breath

came out of him in an *ooof*; he wasn't really winded enough to be helpless, but he did have to struggle with his half-paralyzed diaphragm for a moment.

"Rudi, I love you dearly, but sometimes you drive me *crazy!*" she said in a rush. "We'll be married in Portland! When we get there! Now go away and come back when you're . . . you're *civilized*! Tomorrow! When you haven't had so much to drink!"

The door closed; it almost slammed. Rudi clenched one big shapely hand into a fist and cocked it back as if he were going to punch it through the plaster-covered planks of the hallway's wall.

"I drive *you* crazy, woman!" he snarled—softly. "Said the crow to the raven, what an exceeding blackness your feathers have!"

There were times when it was best to just walk away from a quarrel, even if you had *just* the telling word on your tongue—for example, the fact that her father had notoriously leapt on anything female that moved, and shaken most that weren't to see if they were really shamming death, which was where he'd drawn the line. For that matter, Aunt Judy had told him the reason Sandra's delivery of her daughter had been so hard had probably been that Norman Arminger had contracted a case of Aphrodite's Measles from one of his numberless concubines.

Now that I can never say to her. It would be cruel. And perhaps she does know it, and it accounts for some of all this. I'm still angry enough to chew on nails, that I am!

At the end of the corridor he *did* kick the door; luckily it was a heavy thing of beveled oak planks. The pain in his toe made him want to punch the wall again. He stopped the motion with a slight snort of laughter at himself, and looked at the fingers of his right hand, wiggled them and sighed before making as if to kiss them.

"Not so fair and sweet as Mathilda are you," he murmured. "Nor as dear to my heart, nor does the thought of you torment me with fair longings and warm dreams. But darlings, you've never said me no, have you the now?"

He was still trying to curb his thoughts as he took the staircase to his own room three steps at a time, sure-footed as a cat in the darkness.

Discipline your mind, Master Hao said. Easier to do when faced with a deathmongering evil magus than close to the sweet-scented curved warm pleasantness of my Matti! he thought. *And I am* not *a Christian. To me this makes no sense at all!*

He wasn't a sworn virgin either, and hadn't been a virgin of any sort since that pleasant night in Dun Meillin when he was thirteen; nor had he and Mathilda ever formally betrothed . . . Until recently, when it just seemed to have sort of *happened* without any particular day at which you could point, and now he'd gone and made it explicit.

Still, with her eyes upon him twenty-four hours a mortal day, this trip had involved more imitation of monkish chastity than he'd ever desired or practiced. When you were the Chief's son and tall and handsome and had a way with words, he hadn't needed to, given Mackenzie belief and custom. For that matter, according to the Clan's way of looking at things, if she didn't want to lie with him she had no grounds for objecting if he lay with another.

From now on it was going to be far worse, because she *would* object, and most mightily, and by her lights with reason. If they were to be handfasted, he couldn't just disregard any part of her beliefs he didn't happen to like.

I don't know how poor Father Ignatius does it. Or doesn't

do it, so to say. With fidelity after *we're handfasted I have no problem whatsoever; Mathilda's all the woman a man could need, and more. With years of waiting, a great many problems . . . do arise, and arise, and arise, to coin a phrase! And from my time in the Association lands, I know a great many Catholic ladies aren't as stiff-necked about such matters as Mathilda, either. She wouldn't be the darling she is if she weren't sincere, but oh, how I could wish it were otherwise!*

The guest quarters of the Sheriff's house were in a part that was all built post-Change, of honest brick and stone and timber; there were plenty of rooms, since a wealthy landholder and leader had to be able to extend hospitality to many. All the travelers who weren't paired had one to themselves, with empty space besides in between for their gear; his was a story up and around a ninety-degree turn that put him in a different wing. They were all grateful, good friends as they mostly were, privacy and quiet had been in short supply for most of their trip.

He stopped suddenly as he came close; there was a leak of candlelight under the door, and he certainly hadn't left one lit when he went down to dinner—nobody played carelessly with naked flame, if they had any sense at all.

So someone is waiting for me, he thought. *Now, isn't that interesting?*

Right now he'd *almost* welcome a fight. There was no sword at his belt, but he did have his dirk; the ten inches of double-edged killing steel slid into his hand, and he approached with a lightness that most found surprising in a man his size. Some had found it a fatal surprise, and not a floorboard creaked as he ghosted along the edge of the wall where that was least likely. He extended one hand to the knob and then paused.

Assassins didn't usually start to sing as they lay in wait for you, not even very faint and sweet. Like a wisp of melody heard beneath the trees on a spring night that you could scarcely hear and might have imagined. It was a song he recognized too: not precisely a hymn, not quite, but a favorite of his people from their beginnings, and among the witch-folk before.

"So we'll go no more a-roving
So late into the night,
Though the heart be still as loving,
And the moon be still as bright."

Almost without his own will he answered, as quietly:

"For the sword outwears its sheath,
And the soul wears out the breast,
And the heart must pause to breathe,
And love itself must rest!"

Their voices joined as he opened the door:

"For the night was made for loving,
And the day returns too soon;
Yet we'll go no more a-roving,
By the light of the moon!"

The figure lying on his bed didn't seem to be a threat; she didn't look in a mood to fight at all, and the complete lack of clothing was only the first indication. The smile was another; it was Samantha Steward, the housekeeper. He'd thought her a handsome figure of a woman before, lush but taut, with large gray eyes, straight features and long hair so pale it looked white in the candlelight; now he swallowed abruptly to see that mane flung across the brown linen of the sheet and pillowcase.

She made a sign with her fingers; he answered it automatically. Then his own eyes went wider than they'd been already.

"And you're of the Old Religion too?" he said.

"Yah," she replied. "My mom was, in Madison before the Change, and I was only two when she came here at the Change. There's some of us around here, a couple of dozen within a day's ride. We've heard of the Witch-Queen of the West . . . and you're her son!"

Well, and I wasn't expecting it to be that *sort of an advantage, not* this *far from home!* he thought, dazed.

The dirk suddenly embarrassed him, and he sheathed it. "Ah . . . you've not come to discuss religion, I'd surmise, so?"

Her smile grew broader. "What's more reverent than this?" she said, extending her arms. *"All acts of love and pleasure are My rituals."*

Rudi laughed over the blood pounding in his ears. "Oh, now the Powers will have their little jokes with us, lady."

He bowed elaborately. "You are most fair, priestess of Her who blesses us with the joining of spear and cauldron, and my blood leaps at the sight of you, that it does. Nor would I decline the offer to worship Her with you lightly. But of my own will I have taken upon myself a *geasa* that will not allow it, so."

She looked at him, and the smile died. His own grew rueful and he spread his hands, bowing again.

"By Raven who chose me in the *nemed*, I swear it; may She forsake me if I lie."

"Hmmpf!" she said, rolling off the bed and dressing in a long shift, with movements brisk rather than languorous.

Then, when she was clothed, she shrugged. He could see her let anger go as she spoke.

"I'm sorry. That was . . . well, I should have checked, first. The Catholic girl, I suppose? Some of my best friends are Christians, but—"

"We're betrothed," Rudi said. *As of five minutes ago, curse the luck!*

"Oh, I *am* sorry!" she said, obviously embarrassed.

"No apology needed! As I said, were things otherwise . . . I appreciate the compliment, that I do, most sincerely."

"Well, if we can't worship the Goddess together *that* way, there's a favor I would like."

"Ask and you shall receive, fair one!" he said.

"You're an Initiate, of course?"

"Of the third degree; red, white and black are the cords."

"Good! We're having a Sabbat, and I wondered—"

The discussion grew technical. At the last he nodded.

"That will be a fine rite. Not *exactly* as my folk would conduct it—"

"Nor exactly as our coven does," Samantha said. "I like some of the things you tell me about Lady Juniper's way."

"But it feels right to combine them, so." Rudi grinned. "My mother is wont to say that she's *not* the Pope-ess of the Pagans, when others take her word too easily. For Gospel, so to speak!"

Samantha chuckled, and then her voice grew wistful:

"I wish I could meet her. It must be wonderful, where the Old Religion can be so . . . so *open*."

"That it is; but it's like the air—you have to do without for a while to see the value of the thing!"

She laughed, a long uninhibited peal, and he joined her.

"I'll be happy to run a Moon School for your . . . Southsiders, they're called? Sheriff Vogeler won't mind, as long as we're . . . discreet. He's known about us for all my life, after all, and about mother. He's really a gruff old bear, but he's not a bad man. Not a busybody either, not like some I could name."

"My thanks for that, too. It's needful, but I have no time for it. They're a rough tribe, untutored, but good-hearted for the most part. Yet they're barren of things of the Otherworld to a degree I'd not have believed. And where a void exists—"

"*Something* will come to fill it," she said, making a protective sign. "I'll leave you to your sleep then."

Rudi nodded. *Precious little sleep I'll be getting*, he thought.

He showed her to the door, and bowed gracefully over her hand.

"A fond farewell—and skyclad, lady priestess, you are even fairer than one would guess from the comely sight of you clad."

She tweaked his nose with a chuckle and blew out the candle as she turned to go.

"I don't *believe* it!" Mathilda Arminger hissed to herself, her head only a handspan above the top tread of the stairs.

She'd heard the voices and the laughter, but—

"I don't—I won't—"

Her voice choked on tears as she fled for the safety of her room.

CHAPTER THIRTEEN

O dard was strumming at his lute and reciting—perhaps trying out a tune to fit the words; he was a part-time troubadour, after all. Mathilda paused outside the window to listen for a moment, with the crisp leaves crunching beneath her feet.

> *"The hour the grey wings pass*
> *Beyond the mountains*
> *The hour of silence,*
> *When we hear the fountains,*
> *The hour that dreams are brighter*
> *And winds colder,*
> *The hour that young love wakes*
> *On a white shoulder,*
> *Master of the world, the Persian Dawn!*
> *That hour, O Master, shall be bright for thee:*
> *Thy captains chase the morning down the sea!"*

She shook her head and smiled and passed on. Odard tried so *hard* to be a worldly cynic, and then sometimes he spoiled months of labor with a single unguarded moment. It was then she remembered she was three or four years older than he.

"Though I'm really snooping," she murmured to herself, and walked on. "But you know, Odard, you're much more likeable when you're not *trying*."

People waved in friendly fashion as she strolled through the pasture behind the manor, and past the church and school and football field. It was the tag-end of as fine an autumn day as you could wish for, and there probably wouldn't be anymore like it—shirtsleeve weather in the afternoon, and still comfortable in the jerkin she had on, though she was carrying a cloak over her shoulder. The woods beckoned, and there were no reivers in this neighborhood; she had her sword, but that was automatic precaution.

More to the point, I'm not so damned sore *anymore. Amazing what a couple of nights of really good rest will produce! Maybe Rudi's gone for a walk too—haven't seen him or the twins or Ingolf or the others since lunch. It's good to just plain* rest *for a couple of days, too.*

The air was drowsy with autumn, musky with the scent of damp earth and the fallen leaves that rustled softly around her boots. Mathilda sighed, draping the blanket-thick cloak around her shoulders; it had been sultry-warm earlier, but now it was getting on towards full dark, chill enough to raise goose bumps along her strong bare arms. She felt a little tired, but too restless simply to seek supper and bed and sleep, even though she'd walked farther than she intended.

Itchy inside my skin today for some reason, she thought. *Homesick, lonely . . . this is a good place, but it's not my place. I wish I hadn't quarreled with Rudi, if you can call it a quarrel.*

She winced a little. She'd asked if he was sleeping with Samantha, and gotten a blunt *no* and a glare.

It was nothing, anyway, just me being paranoid, but . . .

Indian Summer here in the Kickapoo Valley had a disheveled beauty not quite like anything back home, full of a sadness that was like a recollection of childhood—not the thing itself, not remembering her father swinging her six-year-old self up on his broad shoulders, but somehow the world itself embodying the *feeling* the memory brought. The security she'd felt at his effortless strength, the bitterness not just of loss, but loss of that child's innocent trust.

The leaves were still a mantle of old birch gold and maple crimson, lit at their tops with the last light, but mixed with pines here where the valley floor rose in rolling hills, their needles a dark dense green turning black with the coming of night. Glancing behind, she could see the lights of the Sheriff's manor glinting like flickering stars across rail-fenced fields, and then the pale twisting ribbon of the river. Both dropped out of sight as she followed the trail, hoping it would loop around rather than make her retrace her steps. Now and then she stopped, once when a pair of early-rising raccoons stared at her with an insolence that made her chuckle before they waddled along about their nocturnal day.

Then she heard something, not the normal creak and click and buzz of the woods, but faint and far. The cloak fell free as she went to one knee behind a thicket of blackberry canes with her hand on the hilt of her longsword. She ghosted forward, silent now with long-trained caution and skill. Through a narrow cleft where rock broke through pine duff, then a hollow dell where faded straw-

colored grass stood shaggy amid tall white oaks and hick-
ories and white ash and younger rowans that looked
planted. A broad open space held a fireset, a heap of timber laid crisscross twice a tall man's height amid a circle
of earth that had been beaten bare by feet. An altar stood
there, rough-hewn from a great boulder, with instruments laid upon it, chalice and blade and book, salt and
water.

Her eyes went wide in alarm. And the sound was
stronger, sending a prickle down her spine as she sank
again behind a clump of hornbeam. She knew that music.
The eerie chill of panpipes; a harp playing on the strings
of the listener's mind like mist drifting across forested
hills in the purple dusk of an autumn gloaming; drums
throbbing until it seemed like the pulse of your own
blood in temples and throat and between the thighs.

How could she not recognize it, when she had spent
so much of every year in her youth among the clansfolk
who followed the Old Religion?

The Hymn to Herne the Wild Hunter, she thought. *It's
time for it—the pagans think he rules the cold season, and
grants luck in the hunt.*

But when she was staying at Dun Juniper she'd been
able to keep to her own room and pray before her prie-
dieu when she heard that sound trickle through the
night-haunted woods. Now she couldn't, nor even leave
without the risk of someone spotting the movement; and
these wouldn't be the friends of her childhood, ready to
make allowances. Mathilda turned her eyes away. Then,
inch by inch, they crept back. She watched half against
her will, half with a tightness in her throat that made
breath come hard.

The bonfire waited, in the clearing beyond the tattered
oaks, beneath the moon and great soft stars. The night

was turning crisp, but the two figures that came dancing with torches that made meteor strokes through the darkness were as comfortable in their bare skins as if woodland animals themselves. She recognized Mary and Ritva with a shock of surprise that she knew was foolish—this was their faith, and what matter if they'd found unexpected company for it?

The twins' high clear voices rang:

"Blazing blood on a moonlit night
Firelight glinting, burning bright
We dance and chant and sing delight
Flames, flames, let the Light inspire—
Nothing tames our Sabbat fire!"

One wore only a garland of flowers white and scarlet about her long wheat-blond hair. The other had a delicately beautiful doe-mask over her face, painted leather and twin slender golden spikes over her brows; around her waist and loins were a belt and strap that held a spray of silver bells on either side that dangled against the smooth hard curve of her hips, and a flaunting white deer's tail behind.

"Swirling sparks in a fiery flare
Call to each one of us by name
Igniting passion, staking claims
Couples pair, and it's all fair game
Flames, flames reaching ever higher
Roaring, panting, hissing fire!"

They spiraled inward and then threw the torches high with a last shout, pinwheeling against the sky in a spray of yellow and red sparks.

The dry stacked wood of the fireset was woven with

even more flammable straw and pine needles full of resin; it caught with a roar, a tall pillar of hot gold and molten copper that erupted skyward in a shower of flaming glory. Even at this distance the dry clean scent of it cut through the dew-heavy evening smell of the woods, and the light formed a circle that made darkness more absolute beyond; Mathilda blinked against the dazzle.

Out of those cave-dense shadows came the coven and its guests, in a file of men and another of women, bare-faced or masked as wolf and badger and bear, raven and coyote and cougar and more. A woman led them, fair-haired, heavy of breast and hip, comely with a full woman's beauty; a headband carrying the Triple Moon was around her brows, and a belt around her waist with the Pentagram hanging from a chain to lie below her navel. She recognized the Vogelers' housekeeper, and wondered distantly if they knew what *else* she was.

The coven sang as they came, in voices that held merriment and awe and a husky wildness:

> *"Hunter who tracks outside of time*
> *Guardian Lord of ancient rhyme*
> *Brother Stag in the musky glen*
> *Consort of the Goddess in this woodland den!*
>
> *"Blessèd are we children of the—"*

All of them put their clenched fists to their brows for an instant to mark where their God's horns sprouted, and shouted:

> *"Horned One!*
> *Blessèd are we children of the—*
> *Horned One!"*

The High Priestess stopped before the altar, made reverence and turned. Arms raised, feet spread in the Stance of Power, she let her palms face the ground, then rise to cup the moonlight. Her voice cried in a high chant that called:

"Song and rite, Herne—ours but Thine, Herne!
Bid us dance; let flesh and bone
Wheel around the sacred Stone—
Hieee! Hieee! Herne! Herne! Herne!"

The witches lining the edge of the firelight swayed together, faces inhumanly rapt or blankly hidden by the masks; their voices answered as the swaying turned to a spiraling dance, stately and slow at first but growing faster as she watched to match the beat of the cry:

"Heerrrnnne! Heerrrrrnnne!"

The call went on, and on; she realized that the voices were taking it up in relays. The sustained rise and fall of the sound had a savagery to it, an elemental need, and somehow it *spread*—until it began to ring from the stones beneath her and the sky above and the hills to either side, until her own bones and organs buzzed with it. Her skin tightened until she felt she must burst, as if her very life depended on ripping her clothes away and running to join the celebrants; unconsciously her fingers dug into the thin earth and her body ground against it.

Silence, sudden, jarring, leaving her as breathless-winded as a punch in the gut. The High Priestess spread her arms in welcome, and the coven-folk bent the knee, inclining heads bare but for flowers or grotesquely masked. Then a great voice sang the next verse of the hymn from the circling woods—not far from her. A voice she recognized, but altered as if speaking from some deep well of time, growing as it approached:

"Chant the prayers and work your rite
Burn scented sacred candles day and night
You may leap till dawn to the pounding drums
But you best be ready—"

For a moment the song turned to a huge shout from every one of the worshippers, drowning even the crackle of the need-fire:

"—when the Horned God comes!"

It was Rudi who came, naked save for the great stag mask and spreading antlers, the firelight shining upon the long-limbed grace of his body; in his hand was a tall spear tipped by a flame-shaped bronze head. Mathilda shuddered and bit her lip until the pain cut through the haze that seemed to cloud her eyes and fill her brain. Bending, leaping, strutting in rampant maleness, the figure of Herne turned amid the laughter and the dance, feinting with the spear. Its blade touched some of the revelers in the whirling snakelike chains, metal delicate as a kiss.

"You can wake to the sound of the hunting horn
Dance skyclad in the gathering storm
In Solstice time blood runs to the rod!
It's just the coming—"

Rudi—no, *Artos*—flung his arms high, the blade of the spear glinting like ruddy flame, and as if the gesture had called it forth the worshippers roared:

"—of the Horned God!"

He sprang onto the altar.

"He will call you out, make you sweat
Give you a blessing that you'll never forget
So revel in the chase and let your hot blood run—

"For blessèd are we children—
of the Horned One!
Blessèd are we children—
of the Horned One!"

The Coven answered, swaying forward together, stretching out their hands to the tall shape of the Wild Huntsman:

"We call you forth as we make our way
Waking your power every day
Guide us true in the Hunt this night
And maybe even later—in the Great Rite!"

The masked figure threw back his head and bellowed laughter.

"You can wake to the sound of the hunting horn
Dance skyclad in the gathering storm
So revel in the chase and let your heartbeat run
But you best be ready, pretty-doe one
You best be ready when the Horned God comes!"

The spear lanced out again, as if it were pointing at *her*. It was impossible, but she knew it was true even if Rudi had no idea she was there; and from the point fire seemed to crinkle every tiny hair on her skin.

"He will call you out, make you sweat
Give you a blessing that you'll never forget
So revel in the chase and let your heartbeat run

"For blessèd are we children—
of the Horned One!
Blessèd are we children—
of the Horned One!"

Even then she didn't quite lose control of herself; she eeled backward with a lifetime's skill before she ran blindly, half sobbing. And when folk about the work of the Sheriff's steading stared at her she made herself walk into the lamplight, smile and nod.

Odard looked up in alarm as she came into the chamber the travelers had been given as their common room. His questions died as she sat.

"Just . . . play, would you, Odard? Remind me of home."

"As your Highness commands."

He bowed deeply and sat, taking up the lute. The clear notes rang in the night, drowning all the sounds of the wildwood where it rested like a great feral beast, beyond the walls and laws and rules of men.

"I wish we were *home*," she said at last.

He kept his fingers moving on the lute, and his face averted.

"The problem is, your Highness . . . I think things may be going badly at home, too."

CHAPTER FOURTEEN

Signe Havel cursed quietly beneath her breath, and spat to clear the alkali dust from her mouth. It was futile; the cold morning wind that snapped the dark brown banner with its snarling crimson bear's head beside her blew more back into her face, along with a little dry snow from yesterday's thin fall. The sun was far enough over the horizon now that a squint and the shade of her raised visor did well enough to show the huge rolling landscape that opened out before her. Gray-green sage, a frosting of white snow blown in numberless little crescents against the sides of brown dead bunchgrass, the slightly darker brown of bare soil, aching-blue sky . . .

She was a tall fair woman a little past forty; the face under the raised visor of her sallet helm was still beautiful, in a fashion now slightly harsh. The sixty pounds of Bear-killer cavalry armor—breast- and backplate of articulated steel lames, similar cover for upper arms and thighs, vambraces and greaves—didn't bother her.

It's about the only thing about this cock-up that doesn't *bother me very much indeed,* she thought. *But Mike taught me a long time ago that you have to look positive for the troops.*

She'd kept all her skills up, enough that she wasn't a handicap on a battlefield where command was her primary job, but she hadn't taken the field for years. Most of the time she ran the civil side of Bearkiller affairs from Larsdalen—the core of which had been her family's summer home even before the Change—and left active military leadership to her twin brother, Eric Larsson.

But most of the time we're not scraping the bottom of the barrel and holding on with our fingernails, she thought bleakly.

And then, as she watched the skirmish half a mile away:

I haven't forgotten how to do this. I also haven't forgotten how much I dislike watching men die. Even strangers who've never done me any personal harm; my friends, even less.

It was a chilly winter's day here up on the high sagebrush plains east of the Cascades, which introduced yet another of the discomforts of wearing armor—in summertime she'd have been roasting like a pig after a *blòt* in the suit of articulated plate, and now it made her sweat whenever she was active and then let the moisture in the padding beneath turn dank and greasy-chill as soon as she was still for more than a few moments.

Which right now is the least of my worries.

The enemy had thrown up the earthwork fort beside the old road bridge in less than a day; her own field engineers were lost in professional admiration at how swift and thorough it had been.

Damn them all, Signe thought. *Hella eat them and spit the bones into Ginnun-gagap!*

The foursquare earth walls appeared as if dug by a race of giant prairie dogs, with four low thick towers of prefabricated timbers at the corners, sheathed in steel plates and a broad abatis covered in angle iron and barbed wire. The United States of Boise's flag flew over it; since they considered themselves the United-States-of-America-full-stop they used the Stars and Stripes. Which her husband, Mike Havel, had always considered slightly blasphemous for *any* of the thousand-and-one successor states in the ruins of the world left by the Change.

At least Lawrence Thurston had really believed in restoring the United States. His parricide son, Martin, just wanted to be Emperor, as far as the reports could tell.

The cavalry deployed around it to protect the construction were mostly Pendleton rancher levies, light cavalry armed with bow and slashing-sword, few with any protection beyond a bowl helmet and steerhide jacket. And a platoon's worth of the Sword of the Prophet, elite troops of the Church Universal and Triumphant out of Corwin. Boise's theocratic allies were armored in lacquered leather and chain mail, and unlike the ranchers and their cowboys they used both lance and bow.

Which was supposed to be our Bearkiller A-list's monopoly, she thought. *There aren't as many enemy horses as there were yesterday, when I decided we couldn't take them on. That's because the fort's finished today. Do we get anything by winning this action? But if we just retreat every time they run up a fort, why not surrender right away?*

The Bearkillers had ranchers' retainers with them as well, men and the odd woman from the CORA, the Central Oregon Ranchers' Association. The two forces of light horse were skirmishing, loose knots of horsemen galloping and exchanging arrows that twinkled as they reached the top of their trajectories and plunged downward. Now and then a man would fall, or a horse. A clump of riders would drive in to the rescue, and light broke off the honed edges of the swords as little squads cut and stabbed at each other, saber against shete. One such rescue party got a little too close to the new fortlet, and there was a deep unmusical *tunnnggg-whap!* sound as the heavy truck springs that powered a murder-machine on one of the towers cut loose.

"Shit," she said flatly.

The ball from the six-pounder scorpion was too fast to really see save as a streak until it was nearly to the target. Distance mercifully hid the details, but she thought it smashed a man's head off; certainly he rode on for a dozen paces before toppling. The others exploded outward like a drop of water on a hot greased skillet; one of them paused a second to swing the unhorsed comrade they'd first come for up behind him. The dead man's horse followed the rest of the war band with the stirrups bouncing loose.

"The High One receive him, and the valkyr bring him the mead of heroes," she murmured, and signed the Hammer with her was.

"And that one who rescued his friend is a brave man too," her son Michael Jr. said.

He'd filled out and shot up as he turned sixteen, and though he was taller now he looked more like his father than ever—save that his hair was fine and corn yellow, rather than Mike Havel's coarse black mane. That meant Michael Jr. also looked more like his half brother Rudi, a thought which made her force herself not to scowl; they were both exceptionally handsome young men, straight-nosed, with square dimpled chins and high cheekbones. Mike had the brand of the A-list between his brows, despite his youth. He'd won it by bravery on the field, at the Battle of Pendleton last year, and the privilege of carrying the lance that bore the Bear-head flag.

The lance was perfectly functional. Bearkillers didn't bring empty symbols to a battlefield.

The mounted trumpeter on her other side was also close kin, her twin brother Eric's son Will, and also young for his task. A field-force commander's signaler had to get things *right*. That branch of the family was Catholic; he crossed himself. Both the youngsters wore only mail shirts and leather armguards over their brown uniforms. Not even Bearkiller thoroughness went to the hideous expense of refitting fast-growing teenagers in a new set of plate armor every year. It had to be tailored like a fine suit of clothes.

"Signal *execute retreat*," Signe said.

His brown face was solemn as he raised the trumpet to his lips and blew the six-note call the regulation three times.

"Now let's see if the CORA boys are still fixated on being ornery independent cusses of sure enough cowpokes by goddamn, or whether they've finally learned to do what they're told," she said.

They had; the whole hundred-odd of them started to fall back at a hand gallop, turning in their saddles to shoot. The Pendleton cowboys pursued their outnumbered opponents, yelling and whooping and bunching up, which was almost instinctive in a situation like that. Signe's lips peeled back from her teeth in a she-wolf grin as they approached a certain point and her hand rose. The forces of the realms allied in the Meeting at Corvallis were stretched thin. She had thirty A-list lancers with her, no more, and the lower your numbers the less the margin you had for error.

I don't have any at all.

The retreating CORA riders passed over a low ridge,

and towards a section of sparse grassland dotted with sagebrush that looked no different from a hundred thousand square miles just like it in this part of the continent. The CORA horsemen weren't trying to lead the enemy towards *her*; reckless or not, the pursuit wouldn't come anywhere near the A-listers. Not within charging range of armored lancers on armored horses; not so close that they couldn't disengage on their more lightly burdened mounts and pepper the heavy horse with arrows from a distance.

And . . . yes, one or two of them were starting to look at the ground ahead suspiciously. One stood in his stirrups to shout something. Beside her Will put the instrument to his lips and took a deep breath.

"Wait . . . *now!*"

Her arm chopped downward. Will's bugle call rang out instantly, loud and sweet. The CORA horse-archers split left and right as the sagebrush erupted. A hundred Mackenzies sprang up from where they'd lain prone beneath their war-cloaks since they'd crawled forward in the middle of last night. The cloaks were mottled coarse cloth sewn with loops that held sage and bunchgrass; they fell aside to reveal kilt and plaid . . . and brigandine and helmet and well-stuffed quivers of clothyard shafts fletched in gray-goose feathers.

It was cold *last night. Better them than me!*

A piper was with them, and the harsh, hoarse squeal of the drones wailed out. As it did the long yew bows came up, bent into beautiful shallow curves, and began to snap. Arrows flicked out in a sudden ripple, thirty a second at point-blank range into a bunched target; a target of horses completely unprotected, and of men with nothing more than boiled leather or the odd mail shirt. The charge of the Pendleton men shattered like a glass bottle flung at a castle wall as men and horses went down in a thrashing, screaming tangle, and *now*—

"Sound *charge!*" she called.

The trumpet sang, high and sweet. The A-listers' deep shout of *Hakkaa Palle!* rang out as the lances dipped and the big horses began to move away from her in a mounting rumble of hooves. Tactical doctrine specified a two-deep staggered row for this. Sheer lack of numbers meant a single line.

"Hakkaa Palle! Hack them down!"

They started slower than a ranch-country quarter-horse; sometimes she thought those were crossbred with jackrabbits, and the Bearkiller mounts were carrying the armor of their riders and their own on neck and chest as well. But their long legs were fast enough when they got going . . . and the Pendleton cowboys were too tangled with their own dead and dying to react quickly. The arrow storm stopped as the Bearkillers struck. Five minutes later the enemy were running hard, but by then far fewer of them were able to move.

The CORA horse-archers rallied behind the Macken-zies and slid back around to their right, to the north and as close to the fort as they could get without being back in artillery range. That put them on the flank of any attack by the block of the Sword of the Prophet waiting under the fort's cover.

They weren't moving. It wasn't cowardice.

It's iron discipline, she thought. *Damn. We were supposed to be ahead in* that, *too.*

The Pendleton men still outnumbered the Bearkillers by three to one, even after most of the A-list fighters had speared one enemy out of the saddle in the first onset. That was about as important as fresh eggs outnumbering ball-peen hammers, though; now the backswords were out, armored riders on tall barded horses working in drilled teams. The eastern cowboys stood the melee for moments only, just long enough to look for a way out. Most instinctively broke southward away from the Bearkillers . . . which meant they had to cross the front of the Mackenzies again, as the A-listers left them to the longbowmen.

Even at this distance and over the sound of the "Ravens Pibroch" she could see the grins of the clansfolk, and hear them shouting cheerful bets at each other as they drew and tracked the moving targets and loosed. A superficial acquaintance with Mackenzies could leave you with the impression that they were a friendly, musical, fanciful, harmless people. Signe Havel had been dealing with them almost as long as there had *been* Mackenzies, and she knew that stereotype was about three-quarters right.

The last bit was a *very* bad mistake, though. Lethally bad.

Three more of the enemy squeezed out northward and made straight for her in a triple plume of dust either just trying to get by, or out for some revenge on the party under the enemy banner. They grew swiftly from dollsize to real men on real horses, close enough to see the fixed snarls of terror and rage, the thin reddish beard of one, the bleeding slash along another's cheek.

"Heads up, troopers," she said to her son and nephew, drawing her sword and sliding her round shield onto her arm.

Will slung the trumpet around over his back and pulled the recurve bow out of its saddle scabbard before his left knee; his other hand went back and twitched three arrows out of his quiver, putting one on his string and the other two between a forefinger and the bow stave. They all signaled their horses forward with thighs and balance, walk-trot-canter-gallop; an A-lister usually didn't touch the reins in battle.

Three deep breaths and everything left her mind but the *now*. The cowboys drew closer with shocking speed, strings of foam and slobber running from their horses' jaws. The men were nearly as wild-eyed, their shetes in their hands. None of them had any arrows left in their quivers—most of these cow-country men were fine shots, but the sort of organization that brought ammunition forward during a fight wasn't their long suit. Beside her Mike Jr. was riding with perfect form, shield on arm and lance slanted forward at forty-five degrees, held loosely. The popping fluttering rattle of the flag increased as the wind of their passage cuffed at it.

Will's bow snapped, once, twice, the boy bracing himself up in the stirrups of the heavy war-saddle as he drew and loosed. The cowboy opposite him ducked below the first shaft as it wasp-whined by his face. That put his collarbone right in the path of the next; there was a wet *crack* sound of parting bone audible over the pounding of hooves, and he pitched backward off his horse.

Signe gave her opponent the point, sword extended at the end of her outstretched arm like a lance, but he threw himself to one side just in time. She wrenched her sword up and over to rest behind her back for an instant as they flashed past. *Tunng* and the heavy shete's backhand stroke hit it hard enough for the blow to wrench at her hand, just over the spot where there was a gap between the flare of her sallet helm and the upper edge of the backplate.

Her horse reared and crow-hopped three times on its hind legs as it killed its momentum in response to her signals. It whirled as it came down, eyes bulging, huge yellow chisel-teeth bared as it snapped at the cow pony.

That agile beast had already wheeled and put its master within chopping range; he struck at her three times in fewer than three heartbeats, overarm and forehand and backhand.

Tung. Crack. Tung.

One blow caught on her backsword, one glanced off the surface of her shield, another on the sword, and this time it slid down to hit the guard and numbed her hand again. She had no time to strike back. The man was shrieking as he hewed at her, half her age and quick and *strong . . .*

Then he coughed, looked down at the arrowhead that jutted from his leather coat, coughed again in a spray of red, and slumped away. One high-heeled boot caught in a twisted stirrup as he fell, and the horse moved away dragging him and looking back over its shoulder, dancing sideways until the boot slid off the foot and the body dropped free. Then it galloped away.

Mike Havel had given the Bearkillers many sayings. One was:

Fair fights are for suckers.

Another was:

One for all, and all on one.

"Thanks," she wheezed to Will Larsson, wiping drops of blood off her eyelids with the leather on the palm of one gauntlet. "Been a few years since I did this."

Long enough to forget how it can leave you feeling like a wet dishcloth in a few seconds, she thought, struggling to take steady deep breaths.

"*De nada,*" he replied, his smile white.

He came by the tag naturally; his mother Luanne's mother was Tejano, and Angelica Hutton had been the Outfit's quartermaster-general since that meant cooking dinner personally. His maternal grandfather had been a black horse-breaker from the Texas hills. The combination of that Afro-Anglo-Hispano-Indio mix with Eric's Nordic heritage had given him exotic good looks, bluntly regular full-lipped features, skin the smooth pale light brown of a perfect soda biscuit, eyes midnight blue and hair curling from under the edge of his helmet in locks of darkest yellow.

A look around the Sword of the Prophet were cantering forward a little as her A-listers pursued the fleeing ranchers' men. The A-list lancers reined in at the very fringe of the area covered by the fort's war engines, turned, and cantered back towards her. The Corwinites halted again when the CORA men started lofting arrows at them from extreme range, a bit over two hundred yards with a saddle bow. The survivors of the Pendleton force drew up behind the Prophet's guardsmen—all but a few who kept going east as fast as they could quirt their horses.

"We beat 'em!" Will said.

"Good as we can expect, dammit," she said.

Mike Jr. was out of the saddle, pulling at the shaft of his lance with a foot braced on the body of the man it pierced, looking grim but not too wobbly. The lance was disposable, but the banner had to be retrieved. And bloodstains were nothing new on a Bearkiller battle flag.

This was his second real fight, not his first, she reminded herself.

"Trooper," she said. Mike looked up. "Put something white on the end of that, and ask the enemy commander whether he's interested in a mutual half-hour truce, for each side to retrieve their wounded."

It took an effort to say; the enemy—even the Prophet's fanatics—*usually* respected a flag of truce on the battlefield. About as often as her side did, for the same self-interested reasons. That still meant sending her son into talking distance of men for whom mercy was scarcely even a concept.

I *can't treat Mike any different from the way I would any bannerman*, she told herself.

He grinned at her and saluted crisply. "Yes, ma'am!"

Signe slid her unmarked sword back into the scabbard and rested the palms of her gauntlets on the horn of her saddle for an instant, waiting tensely while her son cantered over the battlefield and picked his way between fallen men and horses. The sun had barely risen at all; the whole affair had taken less than half an hour. Mike waved at her after an instant's conversation with the man beneath Corwin's flag of golden-rayed sun on a bloodred ground before turning and galloping back. She kept her breath of relief behind her lips until he was out of arrow range.

Will used his trumpet again, and the light two-wheel carts came forward to gather the hurt, with medics jumping down to administer first aid. For a moment there was little sound, except the sough of wind and the shrieks and moans and whimpers of humans and horses in pain. That became less, as the wounded animals were put down and the men given morphine.

The Mackenzie commander came up, running afoot with one hand on the stirrup leather of his mounted opposite number from the CORA contingent, the longbow pumping in his left hand.

"Montival's secret weapon strikes again, you might be after sayin'," the grinning leader of the Mackenzie archers said; he was an olive-skinned young man named Beech, after the tree. "We've only a few hurt. They should all make it."

"Stung 'em bad," the rancher said. "We paid for it, but they're busted for now. Bastards won't have as many men to go raiding after our herds next time!"

His name was McGinty, and he had a bullhide breast-plate with his own Bar Z brand pyrographed on the boiled leather. The horsehair plume on his helmet bobbed as he chuckled.

He's younger than me, too. So many are these days. For-ty's not old! Well, forty-two.

That thought marked her age itself. These days, forty *was* fairly well along. Not many people beyond their first youth had survived the generation since the Change; she'd been eighteen then, herself. It was some consola-tion that she looked a lot younger than her age by today's standards, since she didn't pass her days in field labor.

"Get your people heading east to camp," she said to the Mackenzie. "Don't get settled in there, either."

"We're leaving?" he said. "After this fine and glorious thrashing we gave them, and the kicking of their arse so hard their teeth came marching out like little pikemen on parade?"

Signe nodded towards the fort; a century of Boise in-fantry were double-timing out of the gates . . . and they had a fieldpiece with them.

"With that as a base, this isn't a healthy locality," she said grimly. "Move. We'll accompany and the Bar Z men will cover us both. Eat, get your gear packed, get on your bicycles and clear out to the next rally point. And could you get that so-called musician to stop torturing that poor agonized pig?"

"'Tis scarcely war at all without a piper!"

The clansfolk moved in a ground-eating trot that made it easy for the cavalry to hang behind them. The allied force's hasty encampment was four miles up the road—

where another small bridge had spanned a gulch that scored the rolling plain, muddy save for patches of snow now, potentially a torrent. There was no glimpse of the Cascades on the western horizon . . . not quite, unless you used binoculars. Her horse picked its way across the streambed, hooves clotting with temporary boots of black sludge. The Mackenzies took the stretchers with the wounded on their shoulders, cheerfully trudged through the glop themselves, and manhandled the empty ambulance carts over.

They even found energy to *sing*, as they strutted into camp with their piper sounding off, a rollicking tune with a chorus that went:

> *"Gather the sheaves of harvest-time lightly*
> *Many a day will they strengthen our kin;*
> *Gather the sheaves of arrow shafts tightly*
> *Many a battle their feathers will win!*
> *Call the names of the clansmen who've fallen;*
> *Let them be carried like seeds on the wind!"*

The bridge had been as thoroughly destroyed as thermite, metal saws and enthusiastic sledgehammers could manage in the time they'd had.

"That'll delay them," Will said as their mounts surged up the low slope on the other side of the stream.

Rock rattled down as hooves pushed them out of the damp sandy earth. His cousin snorted.

"Yah. Just as long as it takes Thurston's engineers to bring up materials to build a replacement," Mike said. "While they also bring up enough troops to hold us off."

His face turned to her. "Moth—I mean, Ma'am, why aren't *we* bringing up enough force to *stop* this? They're nailing down Highway 20 like someone tacking down a strip of carpet. At this rate, they'll be at the gates of Bend by springtime. After that there's nothing to stop them short of the forts in the passes over the Cascades."

"Trooper, we're not doing that because they're doing something *like* this in half a dozen other places as well. If we put more troops here, they'd push west faster somewhere else."

Greasewood fires were burning under big aluminum kettles cut down from old trash barrels; the smell made spit run into her mouth as her stomach unclenched. Signe swung down from her horse, wondering where several suddenly painful incipient bruises and wrenched joints had come from—except for the ones under her shield arm, and the wrist of her sword hand, which she knew about full well. Military apprentices attended to the Bear-killers' chores, taking the barding off the A-lister horses, packing it on mules, handing out food. They were young men and women of Will and Mike's age, and this was part of their training.

Was this really more exciting when I was campaigning with Mike? she wondered.

She quickly spooned down thick barley-and-mutton soup, gnawing on a tasteless wheatcake with alternate bites from a raw onion and a lump of rocklike cheese that bit back at the inside of her mouth. Then she used the last of the flatbread to mop out the bowl before she tossed it back.

Or am I just getting nostalgic? Nostalgic for a war, of all things. Frigga witness, I was a fucking vegetarian before the Change, and the next thing to a pacifist. Though that didn't last long after I met Mike.

"Was this ever better, Aaron?" she said aloud. "I *remember* it as being . . . fresher back in the War of the Eye, and before that. Not as boring, not as uncomfortable, not as frightening either."

The slim sixtysomething physician didn't look up from his work with splint and bandages, his hands moving with a swift, impersonal gentleness as the man whose leg had been pulped by a war hammer stirred and moaned beneath the drug. He hadn't taken the field lately either, having been the Outfit's chief doctor since before they arrived back in Oregon in the first Change Year. Supposedly his jobs were training and administration.

"No, it was mostly about like this," he said shortly. "You're just remembering being young and hormonally optimistic and in love, and retrospectively you know we won. More or less. So yes, you *are* just getting senile nostalgia. Enjoy the mild case now. It gets steadily worse as age and sagging bits and tits and those wrinkles at the corners of your blue, blue eyes accumulate."

"Fuck you, Aaron," she said, smiling.

"I'm afraid not. You were never *quite* butch enough for me, Signe darling," he replied.

"And they call *me* a superbitch!"

"Unjustly. Women just can't manage bitchery with any style, so I've got you outclassed. Besides, I was always madly jealous, which justifies it."

She laughed; that was a running joke between the two of them, and actually true. Aaron Rothman had been hopelessly in love with Mike Havel too, from the day he'd been rescued from a band of Eaters not long after the Change; not that that unrequited longing had ever kept him from a love life surprisingly varied for their staid little rural community at Larsdalen. He finished off, signaled to the stretcher-bearers and limped over to her—the cannibals had made a start on him by taking his left foot off a few days before the nascent Bearkillers arrived. He was looking over her shoulder.

"Oh, oh, oh," he murmured. "It's our stylishly brutal neofeudal friends, with their banners unfurled."

She turned, and recognized the colorful split-tailed pennant of a high PPA noble at the head of the party coming down from the northwest, almost before the outposts reported it. Her brows went up as she removed her helmet and tucked her armored gauntlets into her sword belt and waited. They went higher as she saw the blazon on the forked pennant and the quartering on the big kite-shaped shields northern knights used—the Portland Protective Association's Lidless Eye with sable, a delta or over a V argent.

The Grand Constable herself, she thought, keeping her lips from showing teeth. *After the loathsome Sandra Machiavelli-in-a-skirt Arminger, my unfavoritest of all our dear Associate allies. A lance of bodyguards, Baroness Tiphaine d'Ath, some hangers-on, and two other nobles. Wait, no, that's a knight-brother of the Order of the Shield of St. Benedict with her. And I know the other guy's face. He's Sir Ivo Marks.*

"*Hell-*o," she murmured. "Ivo is seneschal of Castle Campscapell out east of Walla Walla these days," she said quietly to Aaron. "That's on the front lines, and Boise is pushing hard there. What the hell is he doing back in the West?"

"Lady d'Ath," she said courteously as they drew rein and dismounted, handing the reins to their followers.

"Lady Signe," came the reply in that water-over-ice voice.

The four men-at-arms and eight mounted crossbowmen in half-armor looked as if they'd come far and fast;

so did their horses, despite the short string of remounts and sumpter mules.

D'Ath never shows much sign of wear; you have to give the bitch that.

The knight-brother and Ivo looked like they'd come a lot farther, and they both had the fading bruises and minor cuts that told of a serious fight not long ago. Ivo Marks looked like he'd lost his fight, too; something about the eyes. He was a thick-built man of Tiphaine's age, four years younger than Signe but with his brown hair just beginning to go gray at the temples and starting to recede a bit. There were a few red veins in his cheeks as well.

Brawling thug with a veneer of manners, she thought again. *Typical of that generation of Associates. Not quite a Changeling, but a lot closer than me. At fourteen you're a kid; eighteen is a borderline adult. Or it was. He's not stupid, though.*

"I am Brother Jerome," the warrior-monk said. "Currently assigned as a liaison to the Portland Protective Association forces in the northeast. We have not met, Lady Signe."

Though that didn't matter much. Mt. Angel seemed to have developed some sort of injection-molding process for turning out its knight-brothers a little after the Change. They differed only in complexion, and even that was uniformly weathered. Jerome's bowl-cut tonsured hair was medium brown and his eyes were hazel, and his face was long and lumpy and horselike; the alert stance even when exhausted was the standard, and the expression of mild, calm attention.

"You've been in action?" d'Ath said, looking around and at the spray of blood drops smeared on Signe's face.

The Lady of the Bearkillers bit back: *No, we just had a really rough game of football.*

D'Ath always annoyed her, made her feel halfway between angry and off-balance. Part of it was the personal history. They'd crossed swords a few times during the wars against the Association, and there had been that business in Corvallis where Tiphaine had made them all look like complete idiots just before the final conflict. Part of it was just the woman herself. Signe Havel could be as ruthless as necessary when she had to be, but d'Ath just had something *missing* in there somewhere, as if being a human being day to day was something she did as a conscious decision.

And be honest with yourself, Signe, gay people creep you out a bit, she thought. Then with a glance at Aaron. *No, be even more honest. Gay* men *are restful. Gay* women *creep you out a bit.*

"Skirmish at their latest roadside fort," Signe said aloud. "We beat them, more or less. They pulled out part of their cavalry once their fort was finished so we tried drawing them into an ambush. We inflicted a lot more losses than we took but they can replace theirs and we can't. Technically we won. And then had to retreat. Hurrah."

The Grand Constable nodded. "They can match our numbers everywhere and still keep a central reserve to switch around," she said. "That means they can outnumber us whenever and wherever they feel it's important. It's . . . difficult."

It's a recipe for fucking disaster, Signe thought but did not say. *Unless they start making a lot of big mistakes. Which so far they haven't. Neither have we. Absent idiocy on either side or the Gods taking a hand, numbers win.*

"Well, your castles are holding them up in the Columbia Valley and the Palouse," she said instead. "Which goes a long way to compensate for their numbers."

That had the virtue of being true, as well as complimentary. The only way to hold the Corwin-Boise alliance out if this open plain would be a pitched battle . . . and they'd tried that at Pendleton last year and lost.

D'Ath frowned; if possible, her pale gray eyes grew chillier.

"We need to speak in confidence," she said. "That's why I'm here in person. I'll be moving on to Bend to consult with the CORA leaders next, then back west to stop in Corvallis and Dun Juniper."

Signe nodded. "Did anyone say *stop working*?" she asked the air, and the curious onlookers within eavesdropping range withdrew. "I want us to be ready to pull out of here, soonest!"

Tiphaine looked at the doctor, who showed no sign of retreating with the others.

"Aaron is one of my closest advisors," Signe said. "You can tell him anything you tell me."

Nobody mentioned Will and Mike Jr.; they were family, and learning the family business. Signe looked at the Association commander's followers in turn.

"Armand and Rodard are my squires," Tiphaine said. "And confidential agents. Sir Ivo and Brother Jerome were involved with the matter personally."

She took a deep breath and paused before speaking; Signe was surprised, and felt a trickle of alarm.

What could be upsetting the Ice Dyke of Castle d'Ath?

It wasn't like her to hesitate to spit the truth out, however disagreeable. They'd had as little as possible to do with each other, but she knew that much.

"Castle Campscapell fell six days ago," the Associate said bluntly.

Signe managed to control her impulse to grunt as if belly punched; her sister, Astrid, was operating her Ranger deep-reconnaissance and sabotage teams out of there right now, and her brother, Eric, was backing her up. They'd been running weapons to the Mormon guerillas and harassing enemy logistics in occupied New Deseret, as well. Aaron whistled almost silently.

"That . . . was a very strong keep," Signe said, and glared at Ivo.

Ivo Marks had been a protégé and vassal of d'Ath's since the War of the Eye. Commanding a major castle was a plum job, too. She went on:

"How in hell did that happen? They certainly didn't sit a fucking great army down in front of it for a siege or assault, that I heard of!"

The monk intervened: "A postern gate was opened late at night. By a priest. A joint force of Boisean and Corwinite special forces took the gatehouse, raised the portcullis and let down the drawbridge. They held it long enough for a fast flying column that had approached in stealth to punch through and take the castle as a whole."

Signe's breath hissed out. The gate of a big castle was a mini-fortress in itself. They'd known that the enemy alliance had good special operations troops, but this was a nasty confirmation.

"Bribe?" she said.

Brother Jerome shook his head. "I don't think so. It was a rather elderly Dominican; a harsh man, one of Antipope Leo's appointees, but not a corrupt one. I knew him slightly."

"Why not?" Signe said. "It wouldn't be the first time a priest of your Church caught gold fever. And *knew*? He's joined the majority?"

"No, it would not be the first time a priest was bribed, my lady," the monk said, with that steady courtesy that was more irritating than irritation. "All men are sinners, and priests are men. However, the priest in question then cut off his own testicles and stabbed himself eight times in the belly before he died. And the first enemy through the postern was in a red robe—a High Seeker of the Church Universal and Triumphant. He killed armed men with his hands and they did not resist."

For once the monk's trained calm seemed to waver. "I . . . was there. I saw it. I . . . fought him. Not so much with my sword . . . I have never felt anything like it. Never anything so strong, or so foul. As if I were prisoner in my own mind, and my mind was in Hell. Only by the grace of God was I able to give the alarm and close the inner doors to the bailey long enough for the garrison to arm."

A chill silence fell; they'd all heard the rumors about the Corwinite adepts. Several made the protective signs of their various faiths. Then Ivo spoke, his voice shaking slightly:

"That's all that let any of us escape."

"Ivo got most of the garrison out," Tiphaine said crisply. "Given the initial situation, he did quite well. But that unhinges our position in the western Palouse and it gives the enemy another foothold on the navigable Snake River. It's . . . troubling. We've been counting on our fortifications to even things up."

"If we can't rely on the castles to keep them off the Columbia, what the hell can we do?" Signe said, looking around for a moment as if armies could be conjured from raw need.

One of the squires blurted: "Artos has to return with the Sword. Only that can save Montival!"

"He's right, Mother," Mike Havel Jr. said, before Tiphaine could blast her subordinate for speaking out of turn.

Gray eyes met blue. Tiphaine spoke slowly and reluctantly.

"I have a horrible suspicion that may be correct."

And the Gods alone know what Rudi and the others were doing. Mary, Ritva, is it well with you?

A Bearkiller couldn't show weakness. "It would be a help," she said. "An army or two with it wouldn't hurt either."

FREE REPUBLIC OF RICHLAND

SHERIFFRY OF READSTOWN

(FORMERLY SOUTHWESTERN WISCONSIN)

NATIONAL GUARD DRILL FIELD

OCTOBER 10, CHANGE YEAR 24/2022 AD

Being impatient and not showing it is even more of an unpleasantness than being impatient alone, Rudi thought.

He suppressed an impulse to jig from foot to foot, like a small child in school bursting to ask permission to visit the jakes.

The best cure for it being some sweat. Luckily that also serves our purposes, since we want to be well remembered here. Not just remembered kindly, but remembered well, as folk worthy of respect. Worthy of alliance against a common foe.

He kept a smile on his face as he strode out to the drill field. Partly that was natural to him—he liked most places and most people he met—and partly it was politics.

The which I will never *be able to escape, now, all my life. Fortunately I've been assured that won't be overlong . . .*

Most of the drill field was exactly that: fields, now

reaped and empty of crops, but busy with the local folk. Some of it spilled up into the forested edges of Reads-town, to give a realistic variety of ground. Only parts of it were permanent, like the row of oaken pells—thick posts used as targets for practice with sword and ax. Mathilda and Odard were at a pair of them.

"How's the arm?" he asked.

"Healing," Mathilda said shortly. "Nearly healed. Still hurts a bit, but it needs to be stretched or it'd heal tight."

What's got into her? he thought. Aloud:

"Well, careful while it's still weak, *acushla*—you always did push yourself too hard when you were injured."

She nodded without meeting his eyes and continued the routine she'd started with a light wooden practice blade. This was an overcast day and chilly, but sweat was still running down her face, and doubtless down her flanks beneath the mail hauberk and the padding. He didn't bother repeating the warning to Odard as the baron slammed his own drill sword into the pell again, smashed at it with his shield, set himself and repeated the pattern. The young lord of Gervais worked conscientiously at maintaining his skills at the warrior's craft, but he didn't have Mathilda's driven will and was less likely to overwork.

Over to the archery range . . .

Edain had just lowered his bow after a ripple fire that left the pop-up targets shaped like outlaws and Eaters neatly feathered.

"And how's Aylward the Archer?" Rudi asked.

"Doin' well enough, Chief. Just showing these lads and lasses how it's done, so to speak, and keepin' me hand in."

That got him a chorus of groans and hoots from the

locals; he grinned at them and replied with a mocking gesture. It had taken only a day or so before he couldn't find anyone willing to take a *friendly bet* on a session at the butts. Jake sunna Jake and his Southsiders leaned on their bows and basked in the young Mackenzie's reflected glory. Those bows had been substantially improved; Edain had run joyously amok spending Iowa's gold in Readstown's well-equipped archery shop, and had ordered a set of portable bowyer's tools as well to take with them. They should all be ready before the party left.

The former wild-men had also become noticeably better archers with Edain to instruct and bullyrag them; already they were as good as the average run of the Readstowners.

Rudi took a deep breath of the chilly late-October air laden with the damp smell of fallen leaves and turned earth; it smoked when he exhaled. Then he passed on to the practice circles where the trainees worked with the sword; they were sensibly marked out on sections of irregular pasture, complete with low brush in some or set around trees or big rocks. In his experience, battles rarely took place on neatly level ground raked and rolled for good footing. The Readstown arms master—they called him a Drill Instructor here—gave him a slight wink. They'd already met.

He was a thickset man about ten years older than Rudi and three inches shorter, with hair of dark yellow closer-cropped than most locals and the tip of his nose missing. His father had been a retired Marine noncommissioned man, like Rudi's sire, Mike Havel, and had run a martial arts club and store in Racine before the Change came and set him on a road that ended here. His son had fought in some of the same wars as Ingolf, but returned home to inherit his father's employment and pass on what he'd learned. A scar from the slash that had marred his nose also split a lip and drew a corner of his mouth up into a constant sneer, turning a face not notably lovely to begin with into something most men would blink to see.

"Hello, Mr. Mackenzie," he said.

Then he indicated three big young men in practice gear. That meant mail shirts to the thigh here, and helmets like brimmed hats, with round shields and wooden drill shetes.

"Care to give some of our local boys a bout?" he said, elaborately casual. "I see you're kitted up."

The Mackenzie was wearing his brigandine, plus mail sleeves, mail-clad leather gorget, plate vambraces and greaves, visored sallet helm and breeches beneath his kilt with mail on the outsides. It was all more elaborate than anything Readstowners were likely to have seen before and enough to let him fight like a knight afoot or ahorse, though it gave a bit less protection than a modern suit of articulated plate and weighed slightly more. The gear did have the advantage of being modular, and you could put it on yourself.

"It would be less than a guest's duty should I refuse," Rudi said gravely. "That being the work of the season."

October wasn't exactly the easy time of year here. There wasn't such a thing, amid the thronging tasks of a farming settlement that also made most of what it used and wore. But it was as close as any, with the grain and root crops in, the last hay and silage cut, and stock culling over and the meat steeping in the vats of pickle brine or turning in the smokehouses or freezing amid underground blocks of ice. What was left was the sort of thing that could be attended to anytime, mostly even in the hard dark cold of winter.

That gave time for the arts of war; like any manual skill, they rusted if not used. Their main rival in the fall was hunting. Which also trained you in fighting, and doubly if the quarry were boar or bear or wolf.

"Just a moment, then," he went on, and hung up his sword belt.

He'd had a training sword made up in precisely the length and balance of his longsword, an oak batten around a rod of old rebar, the wood thickly wrapped in wool rags. Now he tossed it up spinning, caught the hilt with a slap of leather on hard callus, and slid the big kite-shaped Association-style shield onto his arm.

"Which one of us first?" the brashest of the young men said.

"All of you at once, I think," Rudi said pleasantly.

He snapped down the visor, and the world shrank to the narrow horizontal bar of the vision slit; by reflex his head began to turn slightly right and left, to make up for the way it cut his peripheral vision. The Readstown youths suddenly looked a little thoughtful as his smiling face disappeared, and left them confronting only the smooth curve of the steel. The visor tapered slightly on the bottom edge in a way that suggested a beak, and its surface and the helm as well were scored and inlaid with niello to hint at raven feathers. A real spray of those black pinions stood up at either temple. Rudi went on:

"Why waste time when we can all fight at once? Ready?"

They spread out uncertainly, looking at each other. Another breath, and he attacked. His face suddenly twisted and the racking Mackenzie shriek burst from him stunning-loud. A crack of shields on shield, the hard *clack* as one blade met another, a dull thud of a blunt wooden point on mail over padded leather and hard stomach muscle, and—

Bonnngk!

The oaken practice sword glanced off a Readstowner's kettle helmet, twisting it half around to break the chin strap and dropping him like a steer hit between the eyes with a sledge. Rudi stepped back and sloped the steel-cored oak lath over his shoulder.

One opponent was down, curled up like a shrimp and giving faint hoarse gasping whoops as he tried to draw breath through a diaphram half paralyzed by a thrust to the pit of the belly; another rolled about with his hands to a head still ringing from the blow that had set his helmet flying with a sound like some dull unmusical bell, and the third was white-faced and shaking from the hard rake across his leg just below his crotch, and from the thought of what it would have meant with live steel—which thought hit more like a *message*, flashed from gut and balls.

"You fellows are far from bad," Rudi said.

His breath was deep but not panting. The world came back in its autumnal bleakness as he flicked the visor back up.

"But you're being too much the gentlemen there. If you're fighting a man three on one, just surround him and flail away, get in more strikes than he can block; even the Sedanta couldn't fight two, as the saying goes. Don't give him a chance to deal with you one at a time."

"Listen to the voice of experience, you lambs still sucking at mommy's tit," said the Readstown arms master.

The three youngsters were all big rangy young men, but a few years shy of twenty. Even in their discomfort they managed to look sheepishly embarrassed. Their fathers were Farmers hereabout, which gave them more time to practice than common folk, and they were well equipped and supposedly well trained. In Rudi's judgment they were on the better side of middling, as far as formal drill was concerned. Certainly they were strong, quick and fearless.

"He doesn't use our moves," one of them complained, when he could stand and speak. "And he's a south-paw."

The arms master's smile was a wonder to see as he crossed his arms on his chest and stared at them; it reminded Rudi of one Sam Aylward had put on when he was fifteen and had done something truly stupid on Dun Juniper's practice field. The kind that made you feel as if you were six and playing at warriors out behind the stable with a rotten stick for a sword and an old fence board for a shield, rather than training for the real thing. When the older man spoke his voice was like a flaying knife:

"Yah hey, if someone attacks you using different moves, or if they're a leftie, you're just going to say you're taking your bat and ball and going home 'cause it ain't *fair*? Christ, Weiss, *I've* known you were a dumb little punk for years, but do you have to show it off in front of strangers?"

Rudi laughed, in friendly wise. "If you travel, you do meet different ways of fighting, the which can be an unpleasant surprise. Surprises can kill you in this trade, for there's no time to think things out when men fight to kill. I had the advantage of you, for I've trained with Ingolf Vogeler for some time now and know the Readstown style. Here, let me show you what happened. Half speed."

He ran them through the moves of the fight. "See, when I sidestepped I put *you* out of line with your shield, and in the way of your friend here so he couldn't strike while I took you out with a lunging thrust, then rammed him off-balance shield-to-shield on the next step."

The DI nodded. "I keep telling you, Weiss, you can

use the shield to *hit* with, not just block. So can the guy you're fighting."

"Then I backhanded this other fine fellow across the head, turned on my heel, and lunged while your friend there was off-balance, which left me with nothing to do but block your other friend with the black hair *so*—"

He mimed letting a shete-cut slide off the blade of his longsword.

"—which in turn left me in position for a quick stab to the inside of the thigh, below the armor and cup. It's a low blow that's often the most effective. A man who blocks strikes to his face and chest well can often be taken with a blow to the thighs or knees or shins—or even a thrust through his foot pinning it to the ground, after which he'll be sadly lacking in nimbleness and no good at a dance at all."

"Christ, you were fast," one of the young men said reverently. "I didn't think a guy your height could move like that. That's why I tried to come in under your guard."

"Well, to be sure, I am very quick," Rudi said.

Modesty was a vice he left to Christians and there was also no point in denying what they'd seen with their own eyes; and while some of it was just the cradle gifts of the fey, more was honestly earned by long hard effort.

"And being both tall and fast is a fine thing. But also, there's the matter of the weapons. Your Eastern shete hits hard, I will not dispute, but it recovers slowly even when held by a strong wrist. Good enough for a melee, where you seldom strike for the same man twice and few men see the blow that kills them, but not for the higher art. Here there's just the four of us, and no interruptions or distractions, of which a battle has more than its share."

The Readstown instructor held out his hand. "Can I see that? What do you call it?"

"A longsword. To be technical, it's a hand-and-a-half, or a bastard longsword. Thirty-six inches in the blade, and the hilt long enough for either a single or two-hand grip. Here, try the steel, it'll give you a better idea than wood."

He picked up his sheathed sword where it rested with the belt wrapped around the scabbard and tossed it over. The Readstowner drew the great cross-hilted blade. His eyes picked out the spots where nicks had been ground out of the layer-forged steel, and he grunted approval of the state of the edge—knife-sharp, but not a vulnerable hair-thin razor edge that would turn on bone, and all the metal covered with a barely perceptible film of neatsfoot oil. He tried it in a few broad sweeping cuts of the type the local blade-style used, feet rustling in the yellow-brown barley stubble, then held the weapon and turned it slowly in a circle from the wrist, and then flicked it back and forth.

"Nice piece of smith work here, you betcha. It's no lighter than a cavalry shete," he said. "But the balance is a lot further back. Just forward of the guard." He tried a thrust. "Bet you could put this right through a mail shirt."

"Yes, with a solid hit. And enough weight behind it and just a wee bit of luck. The blade tapers to a narrow point, as you see, and the tip of it will get inside the first link. Then the edges cut the rings from the inside. Even good riveted mail is much better protection against cuts than thrusts of that sort."

"Like a thin-tipped spear?"

"Precisely, though you won't run a man in a mail hauberk all the way through . . . but inches are enough in the right place, eh?"

"Yah hey, fighting *or* fucking," the man said, to a general laugh.

Then he tossed it up a little, resheathed it and went on shrewdly:

"Bet this thing takes longer to learn well than a shete. Bet *you've* been at it a while; I'd say you're a Changeling. All the way, too, not just mostly like me."

"Probably, though a wise man never stops learning his tools," Rudi acknowledged with respect to the first part of the statement. "And yes, I've been at it since I could walk, more or less, and I was born in the first Change Year. War's my trade, though I've put my hand to other things in plenty."

"Like to fight, do you?"

"No, that I do not," Rudi replied. "I like the art of the thing, and the mastering of the skill, and the testing of the self. A bladesman's skill can be as beautiful as any other. Fighting . . . that you do because it's needful."

"You've won a lot of fights," one of the youngsters said brashly, despite a glare from his instructor when he pushed into the conversation. "What's it like? We've had some brushes with outlaws lately but they just run off if they can't bushwhack you."

Rudi twitched the wooden sword down until its point rested in the dirt and leaned on the hilt. "You've slaughtered beasts, I suppose?" he said calmly.

The teenager nodded; it would be rare for anyone not to have that experience. Anyone except a wealthy dweller in a large city, and such were very rare in the world as it was now. Even a child could help hold the bowl of oatmeal to catch the blood for sausages and black pudding when a carcass was hoisted up to drain.

"Much like that; like butchering a pig, shall we say, they being clever enough to know what you're about, and to fear their death before it comes. Except that you can generally kill a beast cleanly with one blow, since it's not trying to stop you with a weapon of its own, the which is unfortunately rare in a fight. In battle you must often disable before you can put an end to the man; which means you can see the knowledge in their eyes as the last blow falls. Or you must cripple a man and go on to the next, there being no time for mercy."

The instructor nodded vigorously. Rudi continued:

"And animals rarely try to hold the wounds closed, or weep, or scream and call for their mothers because the pain is so bad."

"Oh," the young man said; he and his friends winced.

"And that," the DI said ruthlessly, "would have been *you* three this time."

He pointed to each of them in turn. "Weiss, you'd be bleeding out right now, fast, 'cause that one he gave you would've opened up the big artery inside the crotch. Cartman, you'd be lying flat on your face with blood coming out of your nose and ears waiting for someone to cut your throat. And Andersen, *you'd* have a four-inch stab wound in your gut and after the fever set in you'd be *begging* for someone to finish you. So let's practice some more, hey? Get set, two on one!"

He turned back to Rudi and spoke more quietly as the young men moved off in obedience to his orders:

"They'll do OK, if I can just keep them alive while they get some of the piss and vinegar whacked out of 'em."

Rudi smiled; he liked this man, even on brief acquaintance. "Still, better to have to restrain a noble stallion than prod a reluctant mule."

"Yah, God knows that's true. The timid ones take even more work. These, they're good kids. It's just . . ." A pause. "Trouble's coming, isn't it?"

"It is that. Trouble that follows me and my friends—but even so is just the first wave of a storm of troubles to come."

"Well, shit. I'd better get back to work, then."

Something touched the back of Rudi's hand. It was a snowflake; more fell, and then the wind began to flick them into his face. The young Readstowners stepped back and began to sling their gear.

The instructor gave a smile that would have done credit to a tiger confronted with a crippled cow.

"War isn't going to be called on account of snow!" he barked. "Where do you think you're going?"

Rudi walked over to where his half sisters and Virginia Kane and Fred Thurston had been showing off a little with mounted archery, which was an upper-class style here. Ingolf was leaning against a maple and watching with his arms crossed.

"Standards have gone up since I left," he said. "This bunch are a lot better than I was when I went for a soldier."

"The which is a fortunate thing," Rudi said.

The snowflakes grew larger, and began to stick on his eyebrows.

"What would you say of it?" he asked; Ingolf would be a better judge of weather here.

"Going on to snow hard," he said. "It's early. That means we ought to be able to get going in a week or so."

Rudi nodded. "If I were more eager, ants would crawl out of my nostrils. They're crawling around under my skin, as it is. But again, we've not wasted the time here. I think your brother has come around to our way of thinking about the Cutters."

Ingolf nodded. "Yah. He connected the dots and didn't like the picture. He's going to be sounding out the other Sheriffs and the bigger Farmers about it over the winter too, you betcha."

"So we've accomplished that here." Rudi sighed. "Much as a mad dash would have eased my heart. Do you know the worst of adventuring, my friend?"

Ingolf snorted. "Your Majesty, I could go on all *day* about that."

Rudi shrugged. "It's not so much the hardship or danger. It's the *monotony*. Everyone back home probably thinks it's such a wild and carefree life . . . but it's hard work, and mostly at the same thing. You travel, you fight, you try not to starve, travel some more, fight some more . . . even a pleasant place like this isn't *home*, and it isn't *yours*."

Ingolf chuckled. "Well, you get to see a lot of the country. Granted you do a lot of it bleeding or running or hiding. And sometimes you meet a great girl and she falls for you."

His gaze turned fond as he looked over at Mary; she was putting the cap on her quiver, and paused to blow him a kiss.

The Readstowner went on: "And Mary and I are going to get hitched before we go."

Rudi grinned at that, and put out his hand. They shook, and a grin came over Ingolf's battered face as well. It made him look a good decade younger.

"We're already brothers in battle and camp," Rudi said. "It'll be good to have you formally in the family, so to speak."

"It's not . . . well, it's just a ceremony, but . . . you know."

The rest of the questers came up while they were talking, and Ingolf endured more handshaking and slaps on the back.

"Mary doesn't mind a Catholic service," Ingolf said. "And I thought my folks here would prefer it that way."

Rudi nodded. "You're handfasted when the two of you stand before the folk and say you are. Ceremonies mark a marriage, but they don't *make* it, not to the Old Religion's way of looking at things."

He cocked an eyebrow at Mathilda. "Matti and I have decided we're to be wed, by the way."

Everyone congratulated *them*. He went on. "But we haven't yet decided on a date . . ."

Mathilda looked at him, turned on her heel and stalked back towards the Vogeler manor.

"Now, what was *that* about, for the sake of sweet Brigid Hearth-mistress?" Rudi said, bewildered.

Ritva cleared her throat. "Ah . . . I don't know exactly, big brother. But yesterday she muttered something about witch-boys all being cream-stealing tomcats with their consciences in their balls."

He raised his hands in exasperation and looked from side to side. "What? What? I've been as chaste as Father sworn-to-avoid-it Ignatius the now!"

Virginia laughed, not exactly cruelly, but . . .

"Your Majesticalness, I even believe you. But it ain't *me* you've got to convince!"

Four days later the blizzard howled outside the Vogeler dining room, hard enough to shake the stout walls now and then; it was a second-floor chamber, big enough to seat a score, if not a feast for the whole garth. Today it held all of Rudi's party, the Sheriff and his wife, and what Rudi had come to think of as the Readstown general staff. The windows were good double-glazed ones of pre-

Change manufacture. They rattled a little in the modern frames, and they looked like squares of blackness with ribbons of white spearing at them. It made the glow of the lamps and the flickering coals in the fireplace all the more welcome, and the pleasant lingering smell of the meal.

"And how pleasant it would be, to feast the winter away so, snug and warm, with all the comforts of home," Rudi said. "The which *some* of our party can do."

Jake sunna Jake nodded reluctantly. He also lifted his third wedge of blueberry pie—a quarter of the whole—onto his plate and lathered it with whipped cream; Rudi smiled at his enthusiasm. Until a few months ago none of the Southsiders had ever tasted baked goods, or sweeteners other than wild honey, or dairy of any sort. Some of them didn't like the unfamiliar diet. Jake was not one of them. He'd done justice to the glazed ham, shepherd's pie, glistening panfried potatoes, vegetables, and the better part of two loaves of bread and butter, too. He and his tribe all had the reflexive voracity of those who'd gone hungry often from childhood on, even those who yearned after their old perpetual stew.

And his table manners have become something less roynish, Rudi observed, with some relief. *Even a fork has yielded up its mysteries to the man.*

"'Kay," the Southsider Big Man said, in something that had grown closer to the others' varieties of English. "I kin . . . can . . . go to like have our bitches—um, womenfolks—and littles stay here. They's good ones, here. Southsiders who stay, they can learn plenty till-un we gets here again. And eat good shi . . . good stuff like this alla times, 'n sleep warm, not have lotsa littles die."

Rudi shuddered a little at what a winter in their home range must have been like, with no more arts than they'd had when he met them. Granted central Illinois wasn't as brutal in the Crone's season as the Free Republic of Richland or the territory they were headed for, but it would be bad enough. He also finished his own last forkful of blueberry pie; it had always been one of his favorite dishes, and the berries here were the best he'd ever tasted either fresh or baked or in preserves.

Edward Vogeler nodded gravely, tamping the tobacco in his pipe. "Yah, Jake," he said. "They'll be a help, in fact. Looks like it'll be a hard winter, and an early one."

That was more tactful than usual with the blunt-spoken Sheriff; it was probably also partly true. Even unskilled hands could always be found useful work—if nothing else, they'd free craftsfolk from routine chores like woodchopping. Not to mention the substantial golden sweetener he'd provided to pay for room, board and instruction in arts like weaving and cheesemaking, literacy and frequent baths. If they returned in the spring—

When, he told himself firmly. *When we come back in the spring. I've no choice, now that I've taken oath on it.*

When they returned the Southsider noncombatants would be far closer to something civilized. Enough that founding their own dun in Mackenzie territory would be feasible, with a little more teaching from volunteers there.

To be sure, "Dun Jake" will sound a trifle strange at first!

"And I'm gonna be busy this winter myself," Ed Vogeler said. "It's our visiting season, and we visit hard. There are important men who'll listen to me."

"And women who'll listen to me," his wife put in, a little to his surprise.

He glanced at her and nodded. "You've opened my eyes, Mr. Mackenzie. And Father Ignatius, and all of you.

Ingolf too, of course. These maniacs have to be stopped."

"Good, because to do that we need the *Sword*," Mathilda said, her voice clipped. "We need to get going. The snow's deep enough now. And the sleds are ready."

She shot a glance towards Samantha, whom she seemed to have taken in dislike.

Now, is it more annoying to be suspected of what you have done or what you haven't? She's been intolerable lately, Rudi thought. *The best traveling companion you could want through battle and hardship, and now we've found safe haven for a while, and she's . . . well, I'd ask her if she was under the Moon's domain this week, did I want to enrage her even more!*

"You'd better wait until there's some clear weather," the Sheriff said.

A little reluctantly, Rudi thought. He'd been perfectly honorable, perfectly correct in his hospitality, and once his doubts were overcome full of zeal for their cause—but keeping a party their size fed all winter would be a bit of a strain even for a man of his wealth and power.

"I'll leave you to it," he added.

The other Readstowners made their good nights as well, all except Pierre Walks Quiet and Samantha the housekeeper. She smiled at Jake:

"I'll have a Moon School running for your people too."

He nodded vigorously. "Gotta get good with the spooks, yeah!"

"And here's the list of the last supplies," she said to Rudi, and handed him a paper. "Some things I wasn't sure we could do before you left."

He scanned down it. "Blueberry turnovers?" he said. "Good, I'm sure, but—"

She smiled. "Concentrated food value. And they keep well frozen."

Then she stood, stretched, and said: "And now for the farewell. Farewell to you all!"

They said their good-byes, a little puzzled; those of the Old Religion bowed their heads slightly at her sign of blessing. She extended a hand . . . and Edain, smiling a bit bashfully, took it.

"Some good-byes take longer than others," she said, and pulled him to his feet. "Merry met, merry part, and to all a good night before it's merry met again!"

A ringing silence fell as they left the room.

"Well, well," Ingolf said meditatively. "So *that's* why he's been so carefree lately."

Rudi coughed and decided on another slice of the pie; with ice cream this time.

And that would have been clever, if only I'd thought of it. Keep in mind, High King of Montival—you're not the only one who can be a cunning fellow!

He glanced at Mathilda and raised a brow. She looked back boldly enough, but slowly a blush rose from her neck to her bold-featured olive face, turning it a dusky rose. Then he relented and made a gesture with one hand, one they'd used together since they were children: *It's all right.*

She nodded and looked away. Rudi returned to the pie. *And you'll never know just how* much *I was tempted*, acushla!

CHAPTER FIFTEEN

"You are *sure* the weather will be bad, Master Dalan?" Major Graber of the Sword of the Prophet asked.

The High Seeker smiled. The snow here was falling straight and thick, cutting visibility to a gray blur in the dim sunlight of a winter's afternoon. It gave the air an odd muffled quality, as if everything had been wrapped with thick soft cloths.

"Yes," he said. "The butterfly has beaten its wings. That thunderclap echoes across continents."

Graber nodded. *I do not know what that means, and I do not wish to know.*

"Hail Maitreya!" he said aloud.

The rolling land here was not totally unlike his home; no high mountains, of course, or any open range, but endless conifers a little like the foothill forests. The cold and snowfall didn't bother a man reared in the Bitterroot country and the Valley of Paradise; he had a good buffalo-hide robe over his armor and gambeson, thick wool trousers, and for the rest the Sword of the Prophet were trained to welcome hardship. A true man transcended the material with the stuff of his *atman*.

There had been a village here before the Sword of the Prophet came. Of sorts, patched-up pre-Change houses and sheds built of salvage and scraps of timber; and they had kept most of the buildings that still had roofs intact, so there was shelter and to spare for his men and even for the horses, and food enough for both if they were careful—*he* didn't need to keep seed grain for next year, unlike the former inhabitants. Not enough for the two hundred or so savages who'd drifted in over the past week, but they'd brought their own supplies. Their low domed brushwood shelters stretched in little dribs and drabs through the snowy woods, avoiding the open spaces that had been tilled ground and pasture.

He scowled a little as a scream came from one of their camps. The men of the Sword hadn't killed all the original dwellers, but the newcomers were seeing to that. He'd ever hesitated to do what was necessary, but he didn't do it for sport.

"The storms will continue," Dalan said. "And it will be very cold, much colder than usual for this time of year. Air will flow south from the Pole."

"Good, High Seeker," Graber said. "But they are still likely to bypass us unless we can get the savages—"

"The Bekwa, most of them are called. Those clans have been drifting in here from the east, in the last few years. And there are some of the local clans here now too."

"Get the Bekwa in order, so that we can use them to scout. Surely they are not servants of the Ascending Hierarchy?"

"Some of them are. The missions have reached very far. But the Masters are ever-watchful for all of us, you realize."

"Of course, High Seeker." That was standard

doctrine—all religions had hints of the Truth. "I can't even speak their absurd language, though. And what English they know is hardly better."

"I can speak their language. In more ways than one. Come."

Graber followed him; he made a small gesture with his right hand to keep any of the men from trailing along, thinking his full armor and the fact that he *could* call on his troops enough. He didn't fear the Bekwa, anymore than he would so many rabid dogs—but he wouldn't take chances with a pack of rabid dogs, either. Since he had to work with them, showing fear would be the worst mistake of all. The buildings quickly dropped out of sight in the silent, steady downfall of the snow. There *were* dogs, not mad but vicious enough; they ran barking and snarling at the two Westerners, until Graber thought he would have to draw his shete and beat them aside with the flat.

Then they stopped, staring at Dalan; their bristling fur fell flat. Some whimpered and fled with their tails tucked between their legs. Others fawned on the High Seeker, scattering only when he kicked one. They walked between the shelters of the savages then. Smoke lay in a haze, trickling from cooking fires under little thatched covers, or through holes in the tops of the shelters. It had a bitter tinge, and even in the cold there was a stink that made him wrinkle his nose. The warriors squatted and watched from the entrances of the huts, or from cruder lean-tos, following the two outsiders in silence. Some were Injun; others looked like white men. They all had something of the same feral menace, eyes staring from under falls of tangled or braided hair.

Not quite complete *savages*, he thought. *Not like the Eaters we saw in Illinois closer to the dead cities. They should be useful, if they don't kill and roast us all.*

What wool clothing they had was tattered enough, probably looted, but they had well-tanned leather gear of their own making, and their weapons—hatchets, knives, spears, short recurve bows—were reasonably well fashioned when they weren't salvage. Nor did they look so starved and rickety . . . though some of them grinned at him with blackened teeth filed to points. After a few minutes they passed out of the encampment, and then came to a circle of the domed huts set about with poles bearing the standards of the tribes gathered here—one had the rayed Sun of the CUT; others included the withered worm-eaten head of a wolf, and several skulls.

"Watch here," Dalan said to the Sword officer. "This struggle will not be on the gross physical plane . . . but I may need protection."

Struggle? Graber thought.

His only outward reply was an inclination of the head. Slowly, men came out of the huts; men and a pair of women. Graber scowled at them—they were wearing trousers—but much service among unbelievers had hardened him to the sight of things forbidden. To be honest, the CUT hadn't yet managed to purge even the homeland of such wickedness. Some of the newcomers looked hostile; one or two bowed to Master Dalan in fellowship. All were oddly dressed, with strings of beads, clusters of feathers, the feet of eagles, gear more arcane, or the tanned heads of animals worn as caps.

Several produced small drums and began to beat them with bone hammers, the sound falling flat and distanced among the snow: dum-dum-*dum*, dum-dum-*dum* . . .

There were a dozen of them in all. They began to dance, a swaying shuffling circle, in and out and around, through the screen of drifting flakes. He blinked as Dalan joined them, turning in place in the center with his arms stretched skyward.

Shamans, the Sword commander realized. *They're making magic.*

He shuddered; that was unclean, by the CUT's teaching. Master Dalan must have dispensation from the Prophet himself—of course, what the adepts among the Seekers did wasn't *magic*, strictly speaking; it was powers conferred by the Secret Masters. The dance grew wilder, feet stamping and leaping. Then slower, barely moving at all. At last all squatted and knelt, the circle facing inward towards Dalan. Graber realized with a start that his heartbeat was running in time with the drums, and with a wrenching effort of will that made the sweat run down his flanks and his belly twist with nausea he forced himself to break that rhythm.

Hail Serapis Bey! he told himself, chanting the mantra inwardly as he'd been taught in the House, until calm gradually returned. *Hail Serapis Bey! The Fourth Ray is with me. Hail Serapis Bey!*

When he could focus on the world again he almost started and drew his shete; there were men around him, wrapped in bulky fur coats against the growing cold and the endless snow. A little older than the other Bekwa warriors, and better dressed, all with weapons in their hands.

War chiefs, he thought, noting the array of scars—from the look of them, fighting infection wasn't among their skills. *Waiting for . . . whatever Dalan is doing.*

Some of the chiefs had torches with them, soaked with pine resin. The flames shed a ruddy tinge over the motionless circle, hissing as snowflakes fell into them. The drumbeat stilled at last. One of the drummers seemed to yawn . . . until the gape grew impossibly wide. A whining sound came from the gaping mouth, and an instant later blood sprayed out; and ran from nose and ears and eyes as well, like black tears. Another of the shamans jerked forward and then slumped with a limpness that Graber knew well—it was the sort that a man showed when he'd had his spine cut, or an arrow through the eye into the brain. Dalan held out his arms, as if embracing the shamans.

"*I . . . see . . . you,*" he said.

The shamans blinked. It took an instant before Graber realized that they'd done it in unison, and even then he could not be sure. When they spoke it was a rustling whisper, in a synchronicity as complete as a Temple choir:

"*I . . . see . . . you.*"

They rose. When they had sat it had been one by one; now they came to their feet like drilled soldiers. They turned to face the war chiefs, and blinked once more . . . at the same instant, every pair of eyes obscured and then open. And *something* looked out from behind those eyes, those faces blank and fixed as if they were formed from dough.

"*Guerr!*" they cried in unison.

Dalan threw his hands skyward in triumph.

"*War!*" he shouted.

"*Guerr di' Dyu!*"

"*God says war!*"

Dalan staggered towards him, face blazing with exultation. "They will fight, Major," he said.

"Good. Though even so . . . it's a big country."

"More than them, Major. More things than the tribesmen will make *war.*"

* * *

"Now, this is something of a sport!" Rudi Mackenzie said. "And a very good way to travel in a hurry, so."

He let his skis plow to a stop with the points angled in, and stabbed his poles into the snow. He'd skied before he came east, but only downhill; mostly at Timberline Lodge on Mt. Hood, a Portlander Crown preserve kept for hunting and sport under forest law. That was a fine swooping wonder he'd seldom tired of when the Regent's Court paid a visit during his annual stays in the north. This type of skiing—cross-country, they called it, which was more sensible than most names—was almost as enjoyable, and new to him. The snow didn't lie long enough in the Willamette lowlands to make it practical and the mountains weren't flat enough.

This gear was different, too; the skis were longer and more narrow, with an arch under the foot, and a fish-scale pattern pointing backward in that section to give you a grip when you pushed off. And the foot wasn't fastened hard to it either, just a loop for the toe and a band.

Ingolf Vogeler came up the low slope with a skating motion and slid to a halt beside him under the shelter of a stretch of white pine. He pushed the goggles up on his face and blinked into the wind that was—again—starting to flick snow at them. It came harder and harder out of the northeast, out of the darkness growing there as the short day died. The cold with it was bitter, the sort that would turn the tip of your nose numb before you noticed it. They'd had a few cases of mild frostbite already, and only stringent checks and careful training had kept the party from worse.

Both men wore loose parkas with quilted linings and

hoods trimmed in wolf fur; beneath them were what the Richlanders called long johns against the skin, scratchy and itchy but blessedly warm, double-thickness pants, knit socks and flannel shirts, sweaters and balaclavas that covered all of their faces but the eyes.

Sure, and the brigandine and its padding are lost in the swaddling of it all! Rudi thought.

With all that and the warmth of effort he was merely a little chilly, but the temperature was dropping fast from the hard cold of day to something that frightened him a little. It was four hours past noon, or a little more, and getting dark even without the thickening clouds. The stretching boughs above them swayed back and forth with a whirring, soughing moan.

"Well, at least none of our bunch are falling over regular anymore," Ingolf said. "We're actually starting to make decent time."

They both looked down at the line of sleds toiling northward over the riverside roadway. The river there wasn't exactly small, but the humped white expanse of ice was already halfway out from each shore, leaving only a narrowing strip of dark moving water in the middle. Slushy lumps of snow-ice floated in it.

Four of the sleds were pulled by a double hitch of horses each, and even with the burden of walking through snow it was less draught-power than pulling a similar weight on summer roads would require. A smaller sleigh hissed ahead with eight pairs of dogs drawing it, something Rudi hadn't seen before. Pierre Walks Quiet managed that, breaking trail with a skill that could have left the rest behind any time he chose. He rode the rear of the sled half the time, then ran tirelessly beside it for a space. His voice was a barking yelp as he commanded the dogs, and they obeyed it like extensions of his will.

The party had slimmed down to a manageable thirty-odd, now; the Readstown forester, the ten questers, and the rest the pick of the Southside Freedom Fighters. Most of them were between the vehicles, gliding forward with the swooping push their hosts in Ingolf's birthplace had taught them. As if to give Ingolf the lie, one of them tangled his skis and pitched sideways; it was just barely visible a quarter-mile away, with the snow thickening between them by the minute. Two of his fellows stopped on either side and heaved him upright, dusting off the snow in a process that was half an exasperated drubbing as well.

"Surprised they all learned how to handle skis this quickly," Ingolf said, unconcerned.

Rudi shrugged. "We're all in hard condition and supple," he said; every physical skill you learned made the next one easier. "And there's nothing else to do, sunrise to sunset!"

Though even he had ached a bit the first few days. This way of travel used *every* muscle you had, and not in quite the same way as anything else.

"It's easy enough to learn passably, though I'd be saying it's a while before we'll all do it really *well*."

He could tell that Ingolf grinned under the knit mask; bits of icicle condensed from his breath broke off the pale gray of the wool.

"Not as good at it as I once was myself, you betcha," he said.

"Ah," Rudi said with mock consideration. "And you're an old man of thirty the now. Suffering from newlywed's exhaustion, I shouldn't wonder, too, eh?"

Ingolf threw a mock punch at Rudi's head, and the Mackenzie rolled his head aside. He was feeling fairly good himself. They were up to about twice easy walking speed now, making up to forty miles a day and looking to do better; if they could keep that up, they'd reach the eastern ocean *fast*. There was an edge in the other man's voice, though.

"Something the matter?" Rudi said.

Ingolf rubbed at his eyes with the palm of his right glove, squinting into the rising weather.

"This isn't even November yet, not quite, and it's feeling more like February. Yah hey, we got *weather* here in wintertime, but this is earlier than I can ever remember it. Not so much the snow; that can happen, in a bad year. It's the cold. We shouldn't be getting ice yet, not real river-and-lake ice. That's earlier than Pierre Walks Quiet can remember, and he was pushing fifty when the Change came. And lived up here in the North Country all his life till then. He was a guide, too. Spent most of his time in the woods, knew every trick the winter could throw."

"Good luck for us, then, traveling so," Rudi said. "Some of the small rivers are already frozen solid." He nodded downslope: "That'll be solid enough to bear weight in a week. I expected it to take longer, that I did."

"Uff da, so did I! We wanted cold and snow, yah hey, but . . . too much is worse than not enough!"

Rudi nodded. "A man can die of thirst, or drown," he agreed.

Then he pulled his goggles down, and they swooped off towards the others; it wasn't steep enough to glide by gravity alone, but they could build up to something faster than a man could easily run. The rhythm was becoming as natural as walking, after the better part of two weeks; *push*-with-one-foot, *slide* with the other, then switch, always remembering the poles—though you could do it without them if you had to. Ingolf still had to hold back a little to let Rudi keep up; his boyhood was returning to him, and with it a skill that wasted no energy at all. The extra speed drove fingers of cold through every possible crevice in Rudi's armor of cloth and leather and fur, tiny little daggers that only the heat his body generated could hold at bay.

"Hungry!" he said, though they'd eaten well at lunchtime.

Ingolf laughed, pacing it to his breath. "Nothing in the whole world like a trek on skis to give a man an appetite! You go fast, but you have to pay for it."

The sandy plains they'd crossed lately had been going back to scrub woods, with farms and villages here and there like oases; most had been willing enough to swap a little, with harvest close past. Now it had been days since the last sign of human beings, and they were starting to come into real forest; white and red pine, darker green hemlocks, bare-limbed maple and beech and birch and oak. The ground was still flattish but with occasional low hills, and here and there a granite boulder. One loomed ahead, like a red and pink and speckled egg under a cap of white. They swung left and right around it, and came up alongside the dogsled.

"Pete!" Ingolf shouted. "Hold up!"

The old Anishinabe called to his team and rested his mittens on the twin handles of his sled; the dogs laid themselves down, noses tucked under tails, and in seconds their pale fur looked like lumps in the snow. He turned before he pulled down the knit mask that covered most of his face; the wrinkled lips were drawn thin, and his eyes a little sunken. He was nearly seventy now, and though he had the endurance of a fit man a generation younger . . . that still made him the equivalent of middle-aged among a band whose next eldest were not quite thirty.

"I don't like the smell of this *merde*," the Indian said,

nodding his head backward into the building wail. "It's not right, not this early; snow, yah, but not this cold all the time. I think this one's going to be worse. Goin' get cold, too much, you bet. We better look for some place to hole up, and fast."

Rudi nodded; when three experienced men all had the same bad feeling, you were well advised to listen. At need the sleds and dome-tents would take them through even a very bad blow, but he'd prefer something stouter to break the force of the wind if it was available.

"The twins should be reporting in soon," he said. "Matti! Pass the word that we'll be camping."

His half sisters did come in with the wind behind them, but in the interim the storm built from nasty to a low howl through the pines. Rudi felt an impulse to hunch as he faced into it; instead he just leaned a little. When the two Rangers came in sight, they were only twenty yards away.

"Old farmhouse, sheds and barns," Ritva said, slapping snow off her ermine-trimmed hood and white face mask and pointing behind herself.

"The farmhouse is down," Mary continued. "Looks like it was abandoned before the Change and collapsed a couple of years ago. Lots of nice dry wood."

"One barn is still mostly up," Ritva continued. "We didn't check inside, but the roof's on. It's one of those potato barns. No tracks we could see, but that doesn't mean much in *this*. It's about a mile; up past that low rocky hill, right on an old laneway through some hemlocks."

"Good!" Rudi said.

They'd seen many of the potato barns in the sandy district behind them; they were three-quarters sunken in the earth to insulate the root crop for storage over winter.

That would make it relatively snug. He thought for a moment, then:

"Matti, get the train moving. Fred, Virginia, rearguard. Ignatius, you're point for the train with Jake. Mary, Ritva, Ingolf, Edain with me; we'll break trail."

"Me too," Pierre Walks Quiet said.

"All right. Let's be going. Faster we're settled in, the faster we can cook supper!"

The wind was hard enough to make skiing into it a chore now, even with pine and birch closing in around them; he was glad of the dogsled to hang on to sometimes, and they all gave a little collective grunt of relief as they came into the shelter of the hill. The laneway was probably a farm track by origin, invisible dirt taking off from equally invisible broken pavement in the growing white mist. Half the snow was fresh, slanting down from the low clouds, and half whipped off the ground by the snarling wind, hiding his own legs when he looked down. When they came through the hemlocks the impact was enough to snatch his breath away; even Garbh hesitated a little before bounding forward at Edain's side, rising and falling in fresh spurts of snow.

It got a little better when they reached the tumbled ruins; someone had planted windbreaks long ago, sugar maples mostly, and beeches. They were bare now, but they were big, towering eighty feet or better, and there were a lot of them with trunks nearly as thick as a man. The farmhouse had been substantial, and old—its remains didn't have the matchstick look that structures from just before the Change displayed when they went down.

Now it was a pile of board and beam slumped into its cellar, and so were most of the outbuildings; a silo had broken off and left jagged teeth standing upright like a shattered tooth. Nearby the rusted hulk of some machine of the ancient world—the type called *tractor*—stood forlorn, half buried. The potato barn was a low long rectangle, roofed in curved sheet metal and with ventilators rising from the top like pipes crowned with pointed conical hats.

"Seems perfect," he said—or rather, shouted. "Let's take a look."

They did; the boards of the building's sides were mostly intact, and the glass in a couple of windows unsmashed. The entrance was double doors, sagging open, down a ramp that must have been for the passage of wagons. They approached, then kicked out of their skis and set those upright in the snow. It was nearly knee-deep on the humans when they put their feet down.

Garbh stopped just outside the entranceway, and even over the wind's keening he could hear the ratcheting menace of her snarl. Edain and he shouted as one:

"Watch out!"

Warrior's reflex overrode surprise; he could feel it happening, like a surge of fire through the cold sluggishness of his body. A great dark shape came out of the doors like something shot from a catapult; he could hear the dog-sled team going wild in their traces. Garbh leapt for a throat and was batted aside like a rag doll, turning head-over-heels with a whining yelp of surprise. The bear had to rear on its hind legs to do that, though, roaring in gape-jawed rage. That gave Edain his single chance. The longbow spat an arrow, and the roar turned to a coughing gurgle for a moment as the cloth yard shaft transfixed the thick neck.

Rudi had his sword out now, in the two-handed grip; not what he'd have chosen to fight an animal three times his weight, quick as a cat and stronger than a team of plow oxen, but it was a great deal better than nothing or a knife if you didn't have a hunting spear to hand. The bruin hesitated only an instant, and then it was on him. Like a wall of dark fur it reared, and the paws swung like living maces fit to snap necks and spatter brains.

Whippt.

The claws passed half an inch from his face as he drove in and ducked; some part of him cursed the snow for hampering his feet. He twisted and hewed, and the yard of sharp steel raked a great forearm open to the bone and skidded off that. Blood spattered at him, striking his goggles, blinding him. He threw himself backward frantically, landing on his back in snow that hampered and clung as he tore them off. Only an instant, but the bear was looming over him like the shadow of incarnate Death, ready to fall in an avalanche of teeth and claws. Rudi snarled back at it, coming up to one knee and tensing for the last effort.

A chain snaked out of the night and whipped around the bear's forepaw. The sickle-blade at the end sank in as Mary set her feet and pulled. The bear's stroke was thrown off, but at the end of her fighting iron the hundred and fifty-odd pounds of Dúnedain woman and her gear traced an arc through the gathering darkness almost as spectacular as Garbh's a moment earlier. She'd wrapped the end around her waist for leverage, and now it worked the other way.

There was a wail of: "Oh, *rrrrrhaich!*" and a thump.

"*Firo, pen ú-celeg!*" Ritva screamed, and loosed an arrow from her recurve. "*Firo, brôg!*"

There was a wet *thunk* as it hammered into the beast's hip bone.

That wasn't going to fulfill the cry of: "*Die, foul beast! Die, bear!*" But it would help.

Rudi surged up while it was distracted, his whole body twisting into the two-handed drawing slash across its belly. Impact shocked up his wrists and arms, more like hitting an oak pell than a man. Fur and thick hide and fat and muscle parted under the desperate power of the blow, and intestines spilled out like writhing pink eels as he followed through. Something hit him, stunning-hard, and sent him through the air; he tasted blood and felt his face tingle and stars shoot through his vision.

Rudi rolled through the snow, blinded by it. Someone landed across him as he did—Ingolf, he realized, as he heard the flat vowels of his curses. They struggled to get up without cutting each other open on longsword or shete, and then an arrow hissed between their heads.

"Be sodding careful!" he bellowed.

Back on his feet he could barely see the beast through the horizontal wail of the snow, though its moaning bellow was loud. Pierre Walks Quiet had an actual hunting spear with him, lashed to the dogsled. Now he'd gotten it free, and he dashed in and thrust. The long point went home in the bear's chest, but it charged even with its staggering feet tripping in its own guts. He ran backward through the snow, half falling, until the butt-cap of the spear rang on the side of the buried tractor. The machine rocked backward, but the impact drove the weapon deep into the charging animal as well.

Rudi and Ingolf hobbled forward. Edain was already there; even Garbh was, limping but game. Her master shot twice, Ritva once, and then Rudi and Ingolf each slammed the edge of their long blades into its spine.

The bear sank forward; Pete's thin form wriggled out from beneath it, the arms and chest of his parka wet with its blood and fluids. The animal gave a last whimper, pawed at its neck, and went limp.

"Back! Let Brother Bear die!" Rudi snapped. "Is everyone all right? Sound off!"

His folk did. Ritva returned with Mary's arm over her shoulder; the one-eyed Ranger staggered over to Ingolf.

"Are you all right, honey? *Bar melindo*," he added.

"I'm . . . just . . . thumped . . ." she wheezed, half collapsing against him. "Nothing . . . broken."

She grinned, though a little painfully. "I feel like I've been hit by a bear!"

Rudi wiped the blood from his sword, feeling his pulse slow and the sweat that soaked his underclothing turn gelid. Controlling his breathing turned it deep and slow and took the tremor out of his hands. There were knocks that would be painful bruises, but that was no novelty.

"Now, that was more like a matter of excitement, anxiety and dread than I prefer before dinner!" he said lightly.

He bent to touch the bear's blood to his forehead and murmur the rite of passing; it had been a brave beast, and deserved honor.

"Why did it go for us?" Pierre Walks Quiet said. "They usually don't, unless they're real hungry, or you push them into a corner, or it's a mother with cubs. We hadn't gone in to its den . . . and it's early for a bear to den up for the winter, even with the weather like this."

Ingolf bent to examine it; snow was collecting on its open eyes and on its mouth and nostrils, which meant it wasn't going to get up again. He spoke thoughtfully, if you could when you had to shout:

"It wasn't mean-sick either. Big healthy four-year-old male, I'd say. And see, nice und fat for winter. That makes them more peaceable, most times."

Mary nodded, shrugged, and then winced a little. "Bears are unpredictable," she said. "Even black bears."

Rudi went on: "I don't know. Perhaps we should have a rite for the Father of Bears. I *do* know one thing, though."

"What?" Edain said.

He was looking around for a place to haul the carcass up to drain, and testing the edge of his knife.

Rudi grinned. "I know what we'll be havin' for dinner!"

Epona whickered at him, raising her head from a heap of feed pellets made of compressed alfalfa and cracked oats and sugar-beet molasses. Rudi whickered back in the horse-tongue; a sound that meant, *Yes, I'm here, relax,* as near as he could tell. The smell of bear was not calculated to make horses easy, even one as brave as Epona. Nor that of blood.

"Oft evil will will evil mar," Mary muttered, leaning back against Ingolf's chest.

She was a little tiddly with the applejack they'd brought from Readstown. They had fires down the length of the potato barn, and it had heated up to the point where you were reasonably comfortable without your parka—provided you kept everything else on. The body heat of the people and that from the horses down near the entrance helped, and the quick patches they'd made on holes in the walls, and the way the snow was piling up outside. It made good insulation.

Bear meat roasted over the coals, sending up little fragrant spurts as drops of fat fell from the richly marbled flesh; a slight blue haze hung under the ceiling, until it drifted out the unblocked ventilators. The air smelled of cooking, and the dryish earth beneath them with its residues of old crops long rotted away to nothing, and less nameable things. They'd found human bones here too, but very old, and much scattered by small scavengers except for the skulls. He'd judged them to be a man, a woman and a young child by the size, and victims of the Change. You still found the like anywhere protected from quick decay, and not near living settlements.

There had been a message in shaky hand scratched on the wall: *Two weeks out of Green Bay. We're all sick. I think from bad water. Please, God, someone, help us.*

I hope they've found peace in the Summerlands, Rudi thought. *And better luck next time.*

They'd buried what remained. Father Ignatius had said the words and planted a cross, it being most likely that they were Christians.

"I said, *oft evil will will evil mar,*" Mary repeated a little louder.

Her half brother raised a brow, sitting cross-legged with the small of his back against his rolled sleeping bag, gnawing mouthfuls off a rib; it was good if a little strong tasting, and much like pork.

Much like wild boar, he thought. *Gamy but not too much so.*

The rich taste of the meat and crisp fat filled his mouth pleasantly; the bear had been eating beechnuts and roots and berries that gave its flesh an aromatic tang. Garbh was lying on her back near Edain in an ecstatic daze, her belly rounded out to tautness and her tongue dangling over her fangs.

"And what would you be meanin' by *that* cryptic remark?" he asked Mary, a teasing light in his eyes. "And yes, I realize it's from the Histories. You needn't give chapter and verse."

Then he took a bite of roast potato—they'd traded for some spuds several days ago at the last farmstead they passed—and a sip of hot spruce-tip tea.

"I mean that loathsome *morn-curuni*, that black wizard in the red robe," she said owlishly. "Sending us storms like Saruman did to the Fellowship on Caradhras."

Ingolf looked over her head—she was leaning back against his chest with his thick arms wrapped around her—and said:

"Yah hey, that's more sensible than I'd like to admit," he said reluctantly.

"And maybe the bear," Ritva said thoughtfully. "That would be canonical, too. Well, nearly. Sending wargs and crebain was."

"Same thing," Mary said.

"Is not."

"Is! Well, yes, it was a *clean* bear. Anyway, the storms made it easier for us to move by ski and sled earlier, and now this bear has helped with our food supplies; so the evil will is marring evil. Pass me another skewer of the liver, would you?"

"Bad medicine, either way," Pierre Walks Quiet said.

He took some of the meat between his teeth, sliced it off near his lips with his curved skinning knife, then went on after he'd chewed and swallowed:

"I'm not happy about this place." Just then the whole metal roof of it, that had survived a quarter-century of winters since the Change, thuttered as if the wind outside would rip it off. The sound had been growing more muffled as the snow built up; now it came louder again, and the south wall creaked a bit as much of the load above fell there with a muffled grumbling like distant thunder. One of the horses threw up its head and tried to pull its tether free. Epona mooched over to the gelding and shoved at it until it subsided, then stood leaning her head on its withers reassuringly.

Virginia Kane shuddered. "You mean, that bear was . . . was *sent* to get us? Like some sort of hex?"

She made a sign against sorcery that Rudi had seen used among the Lakota. Fred Thurston waited a moment and signed the Hammer with his fist, a bit self-consciously, as if reminding himself.

"Father Ignatius?" Mathilda said from beside Rudi.

His hand rubbed her back companionably; she was sitting with her sleeping bag around her shoulders like a blanket, and her arms wrapped around her knees.

"It's a matter of dispute how much actual power the Adversary can give those who serve him," the monk said soberly. "And why God permits it."

He finished wiping down his sword with an oily rag and sheathed it before winding the belt around the scabbard and setting it aside . . . where he could draw instantly. Then he gazed into the fire for a moment before signing himself and going on:

"I think the empirical evidence indicates that the answer to the first question is *quite a bit*, in this case. As for the other, He moves in mysterious ways, to make even evil serve His plan in the end. We can pray for protection, and the intercession of the Blessed Virgin and the Saints."

"Please do!" Rudi said, and heaved himself upright. "The expedition," he added to Matti as she looked a question at him.

That was Portlander dialect for *need to piss.* He *did* make use of the area where they'd dug a pit and screened off with sections of board; that privacy was a luxury, of course. They'd put it by the entrance, on the other side of the horses, which meant he had to spend a few minutes with Epona as well, resting his head on her neck while she nibbled at his hair. The strong earthy-grassy smell of her was reassuring; he'd spend a lot of time as a boy with her, just drifting about and thinking in the meadows below Dun Juniper. That had been perfectly safe; for him, at least, if not for anyone or anything that tried to harm him while she was there.

The doors had been roughly repaired and strongly braced, but they rattled and sent sprays of snow and cold at him through the slits and gaps and the blanket-covered gap where sentries went in and out.

The sleds were arranged to shelter the ramp and tightly lashed together; the dogs were staked out on a line, sleeping easily beneath the snow but ready to wake at clues a human could never sense. Most of the gear was inside, along with as much firewood as all thirty-odd of them had been able to drag before the weather got too thick. On the other side of the entranceway to the building was a dark nook where they'd put the head of the bear, and buried the rent hide and such of the body as hadn't gone to feed the folk or the sled dogs. Though Edain had kept the claws, to give to friends of his whose sept totem was Bear, when he got home.

Rudi paused there on his way back and made reverence, clapping his palms twice and then pressing them together with his thumbs on his chin and fingers touching brow as he bowed from the waist. For a long moment he went down on one knee and stared into the dead eyes; shadows from the fires made them seem almost alive, coals in a mask of snarling ferocity.

Then he spoke softly: "Horned Lord of the Beasts, witness that we killed from need, not wantonness; to protect ourselves and for food. This we do knowing that for us also the Hour of the Huntsman will come; for Earth must be fed and our bodies are but borrowed from Her for a little while. Brother Bear, fellow warrior, we praise the brave fight you made, and we thank you for your gift of life. Go in peace to the honey-meads beyond the Western Gate, where no evil comes and all hurts are healed. Speak well of us to the Guardians, and be reborn through Her who is Mother-of-All."

He thought for a moment, then drew the Invoking Pentacle and continued: "And You strong spirit of the forest, Father of Bears, if wrong was done to Your child, know that we are guiltless of it. We have given Your son his honor and seemly rites. My blood father was called the Bear Lord, and though my totem is Raven, we are kin, You and I. Let Your just wrath fall on those who broke the laws laid on humankind in their dealings with the other kindreds. So mote it be!"

When he came back to the main fire the frozen blueberry turnovers were ready and sending out a toasty-sweet smell. He bit into one, relishing the buttery taste of the envelope and the tang of the filling. It took several before he felt replete, despite pounds of bears' flesh and potatoes and hard twice-baked rye bread. He'd always been a hearty eater; he was a big man, and his lean height was active beyond the common run even when he didn't have to be, but this style of winter voyaging and the demands it made were something new to him.

"Wendigo weather," Pierre Walks Quiet said, after they'd all spent a little time in song and tale-telling. "The colder it is, the more they walk."

Rudi nodded. It made sense that a spirit of hunger would grow stronger in this season when the body's demands were so great.

They'd agreed that the ones who'd fought the bear would be spared guard-watch duty for the night; the sled dogs helped with that, too. Sleeping out in the snow was no hardship for them, though they preferred a spot by the fire when they could get it. Matti finished her evening devotions, slipped off her boots and eeled into her sleeping bag. Rudi did the same, making sure his boots and sword belt were ready to hand. She cuddled against his back, a pleasant solidity even through the double thickness of bags and clothes.

"Nice," she murmured sleepily.

"That it is," he replied.

And I'm being entirely *truthful the now, which shows just how tired I am,* mo chroi!

The fire died down, skillfully banked. He let himself fall into the soft dark . . .

. . . and the cave was deep and darker still. Red eyes moved within it, and a gathering wrath that prickled his skin like a summer thunderstorm, and a rank harsh scent and carnivore breath. An earthquake-deep growl spoke to him. A black wet nose explored his face; it was his own height or more, a bear but not quite a bear, longer-limbed and shorter of face and much, much larger than any he knew. The hairy bulk pushed past him, and he heard its feet falling heavy on the rocky floor . . .

He woke with a little start. Something told him it was hours later, deep night, the hours when the blood ran sluggish. The dream faded, becoming fragments that spun into drowsy nothingness. Somewhere a little ways away a woman's voice spoke, gasping softly:

"Garo nin, bar melindo, garo nin!"

Rudi grinned in the dark. Somehow he didn't think

the Histories included quite that use of the Elvish words for *have me, darling!* but he supposed it marked it as a living language once more. And you couldn't begrudge newlyweds.

Let them have what pleasure they can. I suspect this is going to be a grim journey, and no mistake.

Major Graber looked down grimly at the rent and bloody carcass of the Bekwa sentry. Teeth grinned back at him where the face had been stripped away, and even in the cold there was a slight rusty-iron smell of death, and something musky beneath it.

"Tiger or bear," he said. "Possibly a catamount. Not much eaten."

Though there was a great deal *spattered*, bits of flesh and hair up ten or twelve feet on the neighboring red spruces. One of his lieutenants bent over a patch of snow, fingers moving with steady delicacy. More was sifting down, but you could separate layers if you were skillful.

"Bear, Major," he said.

"That's the third one this week," Graber said. "It's delaying us. We're not going to catch them at this rate. Especially if it keeps *snowing*."

He glared at the High Seeker for an instant, before self-control reasserted itself. The Bekwa dogsleds were far faster than he'd thought they would be, but snow-shoes just weren't as good as skis when you tried to make speed, and their scavenged horses were losing what condition they'd had. Soon they'd have to start eating them, which would slow them further.

Dalan looked at him, then up at the low clouds, then to the north and east. Two of the savages' shamans were behind him. Their movements followed his exactly, as if they and his shadow were all linked by invisible cords. One of them was weeping from an expressionless face, tears freezing on the skin.

"We can gain on them if we go *that* way," he said, and pointed. "We cut the cord of their arc. And . . . if we miss them there, another Seeker was sent this way last year. He will await us with supplies and help. On the river the ancients called *Lawrence*, near the ruined city of Royal Mount."

Graber nodded; he was well schooled in mathematics, which were one of the languages of the Ascended Masters, and useful besides, and in maps.

"As you command, High Seeker," he said.

The wind howled counterpoint as he gave his orders. He shivered a little; not with the cold, but with the gray sameness of it. Had there ever been anything but pursuit and fight and endless trudging? Had he ever ridden in the flower fields of spring, with the wind blowing keen pine-scented sweetness from the slopes of the Tetons? Or sat of an evening after dinner and watched his son take his first steps, laughing as he waved chubby arms?

No weakness! he told himself sternly. *The Prophet gave you this task himself, and you knew death in a foreign land was the most likely outcome.*

"Bad, Chief," Edain said succinctly. "They got hit less than a week ago, I'd say. More than a day. Hard to tell closer, in this icebox of a land."

Rudi looked over the little steading. Four or five families had dwelt there, in two long houses. They'd had a fishing boat for use on the northernmost of the great inland seas. That stretched northwards, frozen now, towards a little rocky islet half a mile away. The only remarkable thing in sight was the bow of a broken ship of the ancient world, towering in crumbling rust-eaten majesty where some storm had driven it on the rocks and broken its back.

The shore bore some scratched-out fields in the rocky earth, with low pine and birch and aspen elsewhere. Shaggy stretches of bush marked ground which would be bog in the warm season, rich in berries and grass. The dwellers had probably hunted a good deal—the travelers had taken several deer they found in a winter yard not long ago themselves—and mined the wreck for metal to work up and trade elsewhere. A modest rectangular barn hinted at livestock, and a substantial smithy near it had two fieldstone chimneys. From the look of things he'd have guessed that the whole had been put up after the Change, but mostly of old-world materials salvaged from nearby.

There was no smell of woodsmoke, and the cold was bitter. It had more moisture in it than usual, too, and that made it cut harder and sap the strength more.

"All dead," Pete said, and spat. "I knew these people here. They were clean. My folks lived a bit east and south, and we traded with 'em. Whoever hit here, they call the Wendigo to themselves on purpose."

Edain nodded. "Parts of them are . . . gone. Like it was a rite."

He looked indignant at that, at the profanation of sacred things as much as the cruelty.

"They're pinned to the walls, what's left of them. It went hard for them, even the little ones."

The younger Mackenzie spat, to show what an honorable warrior thought of such dealings. He also held out a broken bit of arrow, just enough to show the black fletching and neatly made horn nock.

"This was in one of the bodies outside, where they tried to fight."

Rudi rolled it between his fingers, then made a gesture that brought the core of his questers gathered around him.

"Any fodder left?" he asked.

"No grain," Edain said. "That was cleared out—oats and rye, it was, from the few kernels left, and spuds. Plenty of hay still, to be sure. No clover in it, looks like marsh grass, but lots of it and well cured."

"Good. We'll let the horses gorge; and we'll have shelter."

Edain shook his head violently. "I'll not be sleeping under *that* roof, Chief."

Rudi smiled mirthlessly. "I wouldn't either. No, the houses we'll burn, to make Earth clean of it. The barn will do for us and our beasts as well."

"That'll draw them," Ritva warned. "It'll tell them exactly where we are."

"Sister of mine, I'm counting on it. Pete, what's the ice like out there?"

"Thicker than it should be. More like Christmas, or even *Janvier*, maybe. But it's spotty and don't go too far out. Still too thin to carry any weight in some places, foot or better thick in others, so you could drive a sled or even ride horses over it."

Ingolf nodded. "Some places hard as rock, and then you hear a crackle. Seemed to me it's thicker eastwards. Piled up by the current, maybe. Snow's wind-packed on the surface, not too deep except drifts here and there. Like Pete says, it's way, way ahead of time."

Rudi looked out over the lake, out to where white ice faded into the white-gray sky without a perceptible horizon. The surface wasn't table smooth, as he'd imagined it would be; it was more as if waves themselves had frozen, with lumps like congealed porridge here and there, and it was covered with hard-packed snow driven by the wind into rippled patterns. The rocky islet was visible on the edge of sight, topped by a few twisted pines; only the shipwreck made it easy to spot now. Wisps of snow or ice crystal scudded over the surface, gusting up man-high now and then, ankle deep most of the time.

He thought for a moment longer, then held up the stub of arrow: "I think this was done by our un-friends," he said. "Not just the Sword of the Prophet—say what you like of the Cutters, they aren't Eaters. They've picked up local allies, such as our friend Walks Quiet warned they might have."

Everyone nodded. The Indian's hand fell unconsciously to the hilt of his bowie knife with its beaded sheath.

"And it's also my thought that they've gotten ahead of us and are planning on an ambush, the creatures."

Jake sunna Jake grunted. "Bad," he said succinctly. "Don't like trap-inside." Then he grinned. "Like when you and the Archer see us first, eh, Rudi-man?"

Everyone nodded. Fred said thoughtfully:

"Dad always said that you should force a fight when the enemy's got the jump on you and can make you give battle anyway. Force it on your own terms."

Victoria pursed her lips thoughtfully. "*My* Dad always said if you know it's a trap, it's still a trap—for the other guy. You can bust it from the inside. He wrecked the Cutters good a couple of times that way, 'fore they wore us Powder River folks down."

Rudi nodded respectfully. "That's my thought exactly. The enemy will outnumber us, so we need to seize advantage. This will require careful scouting, but we have that heavy little surprise in the last sled of the four—"

The pillar of smoke on the horizon turned to a tiny thread as Major Graber lowered his binoculars.

"That is the hamlet the Bekwa destroyed," he said, his voice freighted with disgust. "Allowing that was . . . unwise. Bad tactics."

"They are savages," Dalan said, with a shrug. "Besides, it matters little what happens to the bodies of the soulless. They are as animals anyway."

Graber grunted noncommittally. That was perilously close to making apologies for abomination; the Dictations were clear that the *form* of humanity was sacred, even among the merely physical who lacked true men's *atman* and who it was fully lawful to *kill*. In any case . . .

"It gave us away," he said.

What was that ancient saying? Worse than a crime, a mistake.

"We cannot wait for them, then, if they are likely to be too wary," Dalan said. "There are less than forty of them in all. Your troopers of the Sword of the Prophet alone outnumber them, and we have more than a hundred of the Bekwa and their allies."

Reluctantly, Graber nodded.

I do not like to give battle when an enemy invites it, he thought. *Even when I have the advantage of numbers. Especially with this enemy. Still, we do have the numbers, and there are no extraneous factors here. It's a flat plain, in effect; hell for quartermasters, but a tactician's paradise. I need only hit them with a hammer heavier than any they can lift.*

A brief brightness: *And then . . . home?*

*   *   *

"They're coming in straight from the east," Ritva panted. "About forty mounted men, the rest on foot."

"How many of those?"

"Better than one hundred of them, less than two."

"Ready, then," Rudi said; he ignored the arrow standing in the cantle of her saddle, as did she. "Fall in."

Now, let's either all get killed, or do something I'd be calling truly spectacular, he thought with a taut grin. *Lady Morrigú, cover me with Your wings. Lugh of the Many Skills, be with me now!*

The little island and its wreck were not far to their rear; the shore was a line of gray and dark green off to the left. It had begun to snow again, a slow light drift of large fluffy flakes. He suppressed an impulse to catch one on his tongue, as he'd liked to do as a child. He'd been praying for a little extra snow, not too much, just enough to cover everything better than careful brushwork could do. And there were worse things to do than catch a snowflake, on what might be your last day in this turn of the Wheel of Life . . .

Instead he looked behind himself and made sure that the guide marks were plainly visible but inconspicuous; he'd made himself unpopular by taking everyone through it over and over again. Even though they'd all known that more likely than not the plan would go south, or change unpredictably. A few crows went by overhead from the shore woods to the island, or perhaps ravens. Somehow they always knew when men were about to lay a feast for them.

"Forward, my friends," he said quietly. "The Lord and Lady keep Their hand over you."

The seven of them sent their horses to the east; besides

Rudi, there were Ignatius, Odard, Fred, Victoria and the twins. Most of the rest of their party were spread out on the rear slope of a long low dune, standing in scooped-out firing positions that left only head and shoulders visible, with spare arrows sticking in the hard snow point down by their hands. It all looked like the best possible disposition of an inferior force.

The dune disappeared quickly behind them; it was hard to see features in this world of white-on-white. His mount's coal silk blackness was the most vivid thing in sight.

Like being inside that snow globe of mother's, he thought. *But one the size of the world.*

Epona was feeling better after a couple of days with all the hay she could stuff down, as well as their hoarded feed pellets. Her knees came up proudly as she advanced at a canter, throwing little rooster tails of light snow up and forward as she paced; it would have glittered if the sun had been out. The older layer beneath creaked and gritted under the ironshod hooves of their warhorses; now and then it creaked a little more with a different, brittle note, that put his teeth on edge like biting down on copper foil.

Epona weighed a bit over a half ton. Add in him, his weapons and armor, and the war-saddle—they'd left off the steel-faced horse-barding today—and it was a third again more. All of that came down on those dancing hooves she seemed to place so lightly and delicately, but he'd seen them punch through a prone man as if he were made of wrapping paper. The water beneath him wasn't far away, it was extremely deep and very, very cold, and in this gear he'd sink like a rock . . . only rocks didn't need to breathe air.

And to be sure, I do. Drowning was supposed to be a

comparatively painless way to die, but so stuffy . . . *Yet a man lives just as long as he lives, and not a day more,* he reminded himself.

The snow picked up a little more, but not enough to be called a storm; he was becoming a judge of those, in this land and in this fimbul winter of a season. After a moment he saw a line of black dots ahead. In another, they were men, tiny but distant. He unshipped his binoculars and adjusted the focusing screw with his thumb.

"Ah, as I thought," he said.

"Your Majesty?" Ignatius said.

"They replaced their horses coming north from wherever they beached their ship on the Ohio, but what they've got are crowbait and badly trained, a lot like the ones I suffered with bringing back Ingolf's wagons. And they've lost more condition than ours, besides starting lower."

"Good," the warrior-priest said. "We can control the distance of our engagement."

"Exactly. For a while, at least."

The fringe of troopers of the Sword of the Prophet were in a formation more ragged than any he'd seen them using before. He nodded again and recased his field glasses. Horse soldiers were only half of what made up a troop of cavalry of any sort. The other half was the horse, and its training and condition were every bit as important as the rider's.

"Bows!" he said.

They all pulled out their saddle recurves and set arrows to the string. All his companions save Edain were good horse-archers; Virginia was among the best he'd ever met, though she didn't draw a very heavy stave. The troopers of the Sword were fine shots too . . . but to use bow and arrow well from a horse's back you needed one you could guide with knees and balance alone.

And I'm counting on that. Otherwise I'd not have dared take us within range of better than twenty bows. Other things being equal, numbers count . . . except to be sure when things aren't equal and hence they don't.

Closer now. He could see one of the Cutters belaboring his mount with a quirt; it turned its neck and tried to bite him on the knee, before he popped it on the nose. That was a sensitive spot for a horse; then it bolted back the way they'd come with the trooper sawing at the reins. Rudi smiled the special smile of a man seeing an enemy's discomfiture, but there were still an unpleasant lot of the Cutters. Closer, three hundred yards, a little less . . .

"*Now!*"

He stood in the stirrups and drew. The recurve bent into a deep C-shape as he drew to the ear. He let the string fall off his gloved fingers, and the rest of his band did likewise. Arrows arched out from the enemy, seemed to rise slowly and then come faster and faster as they went *chunk* into the hard-packed snow and the ice below, or *whipppt* as they flew past.

A Cutter toppled from the saddle, and another; he thought several more were wounded despite their armor. Closer still . . .

"*Retreat!*" he called.

They turned their mounts; there was a *crunch* as Epona turned, and black water leaked out of star-shaped cracks where her left rear had pivoted. He ignored it and shot again, Parthian-style, backward.

"Keep it at this range!" he said, as the group spread out into a line.

Bang.

A shaft struck the long triangular shield slung over his back. The heavy bit of knight's gear turned it, though he felt like he'd been hit with a diffuse hammer. Another shot of his own arched up into the pale gray haze above at forty-five degrees, and an enemy horseman ducked as it went just over his spiked helmet. The companions were rocking along at a slow canter, instinctively focusing their arrows on any of the Cutters who came out of the pack, slowing when the enemy did to keep in touch with the dun mass of Bekwa on foot who swarmed along to their northwards.

Victoria sped a shaft to the east over her horse's rump and whooped: "Yippie-kye-ey! Hoo'ay! We got the sweet spot, you motherfuckers!"

Fred shot next, with that grim businesslike air his father's realm of Boise taught, then Odard and Ignatius, then the twins and Rudi together. They were all shooting as fast as they could get a good target, but at nearly two hundred yards from a moving horse against moving targets that was guess and luck as much as skill. One more hit . . . no, two. Excellent practice at this range and with the snow and white background making it hard to judge distance, and the pursuer's shafts were all over the map. Sooner or later they'd make damaging hits by sheer volume and chance, though.

And I had a perfectly good excuse for keeping Matti out of this one. Even she *thought so. Sweet Brigid, but that makes me worry less! Except about winning, the which we need for any of us to survive.*

It was almost a surprise when Epona snorted, and he noticed they were about back where they'd started. They crested the low dune they'd built and pulled up. A Southsider dashed over with bundles of arrows for their quivers, and then they were waiting with only their heads and shoulders showing over the crest. A few last enemy arrows dropped near them, and then the Sword troopers reined in to a barked command—some of them with considerable difficulty; those must have been the ones with the most recently stolen horses.

Rudi pulled back another arrow; closer this time, say eighty yards, just raise the point *so*.

Whihhht.

The shaft flew out in a sweet shallow curve that had a *rightness* to it. A man threw up his hands to claw at his face and slid backward over the crupper of his saddle. The horse bolted towards shore at a hammering gallop. Halfway there it went through the ice in a billowing gout of water and sheets of broken crystal levering up in angular patterns. A terrible shrill scream rose as it went under the surface and came up again to paw at the edge with its forehooves. That broke off more; it floundered again, and the current swept it below the surface for good and all.

"Bad for the poor beast, but good for us," Rudi said. "Let them watch us *carefully* for the safest routes! And abandon all thought of swinging around our flank."

A trumpet sounded, and the Sword men drew out of easy range. He didn't envy their commander even the obvious chance he had of charging straight into the teeth of seven good bows whose wielders had cover.

"Now he'll try sending in his footmen," he judged, and looked over to his left, northward.

Pierre Walks Quiet and Edain were there, with Jake and most of the Southsiders; call it twenty-eight bows. He waited, enduring the growing cold that seeped in under his armor and gambeson, working his fingers now and then to keep them from stiffening in his gloves. The Cutters' savage allies grew from a dun mass to something larger, until he could see their standards of skull and horns and rayed sun, see them leap and brandish their weapons, hear the yelping nasal war cries:

"Jemesowiens!"

Whatever that meant; and raw shrieks of hatred and menace. They walked forward, gradually building up speed, snow misting up around their feet, looming larger and larger through the gray-white landscape.

"They'll hit a full run just at maximum bow range," Ingolf said meditatively. "That's smarter than any Eaters *I* ever ran into. They're going to eat their losses and charge home. Glad I never came this far north."

"Three hundred fifty yards," Fred muttered.

He didn't have to estimate it, though he was good at that; they'd marked the range inconspicuously. The Cutters began to move again too, *walking* their horses so they could shoot more effectively.

"Three hundred. Two seventy-five. Two fifty . . ."

The savages were moving at full pelt now, a mass six or seven deep and broad enough to overlap the archers on both sides.

"Now!" Rudi muttered to himself.

He wasn't giving the order; Edain could do that just as well. In the same instant Rudi heard him shout:

"Let the gray geese fly—wholly together—*shoot*!"

Snap.

The arrows rose in a cloud; then again, and again. The heads didn't sparkle on this sunless day, but the honed metal had a cold glitter. And from the island—

Tunnnggg.

"Pump! Pump!" Mathilda Arminger shouted.

The vast wreck's bow loomed over them, looking tattered by decay and men's tools, a stretch of letters just visible: —*mund Fitz*—

The two Southsiders worked their cranks, grinning through their frizzy beards, dark faces running with sweat even in the hard chill. This Richlandermade engine was worked with mechanical cocking devices through high-aspect geared winches and bicycle-chain sprocket drives, rather than the hydraulic bottle jacks the Association armies used for their murder-machines. There wasn't much difference in the speed with which it compressed the sets of heavy truck coil springs that powered the throwing arms; whoever had made the design had known their business.

Click, a heavy soft sound as the trigger mechanism engaged.

Mathilda slapped the bundle of darts down in the throwing trough. They were eight inches from base to point, heavy elongated steel pyramids drawn out into fins at the rear, all bound together with a wicker band carefully weakened to last just long enough. She craned her neck to see over the line of bowmen a hundred yards away, spun the elevating wheel to the next spot, and shouted:

"Clear!"

The two crewmen jumped aside, and she jerked the lanyard.

Tunnnggg the second time, ten seconds after the first.

"Pump! Pump!"

Twenty-four darts arched out eastwards and up, towards the massed enemy, spreading as they reached the top of their trajectory and plunged downward. The savages looked up and screamed. The results of the first round, and the continuous rain of arrows, were all about them.

Click.

"Clear!"

She spun the traversing wheel and turned the trough towards the block of troopers from the Sword of the

Prophet; they were better disciplined, and hence more tightly bunched . . . and their horses were bigger targets. A firm jerk on the lanyard . . .

Tunnnggg.

"By God, I think we could break them!" Odard shouted. "With that scorpion. *Face Gervais, face death!*"

"No. We might be able to knock them back a bit, but they'd just go around. Shoot!"

Rudi drew and loosed; he was sweating again now. Drawing a hundred-and-twenty-pound saddle bow was as much heavy labor as throwing sacks of grain onto a wagon, with all the muscles of your torso and gut working. The savages were wavering—the scorpion could throw six times a minute, and that meant a hundred and forty-four of those deadly little darts, and as many arrows again from Edain and his band. A volley of the darts slashed into the Sword troopers as he watched, and horses exploded outward in pain and panic, bugling shrilly.

"They'll come at us now!" he said. "Wait . . . wait . . ."

The enemy trumpet screamed *charge.* The Cutters cased their bows, drew shetes or leveled their lances, booted their skinny garrons into motion. Rudi shot, again, again—the range was closing, and nobody was shooting *back* right now.

"The which is a great aid to concentration. Wait . . . Wait . . ."

Even a bad horse could cover ground very fast indeed. *"Now!"*

Every one of them wheeled their mounts and set them going. Rudi focused on the markers; *left* and then *straight* and then *right* and *straight*—Epona's great muscles bunched beneath him, her body an extension of his own as it had been since his boyhood, as if their thoughts meshed through the same fire of nerve and balance. The seventeen-hand warmblood *danced*.

He heard a sudden scream to his right. Mary's horse had broken through; she catapulted out of the saddle, landed rolling and spraying arrows from her quiver.

"Rochael!" she shrieked.

The dappled Arab mare's forehooves hammered at the broken, floating ice before her. Mary started to run back to help her, but Ingolf swung inward on her blind side. He leaned out of the saddle with skill that made Rudi blink and snatched with a huge and desperate strength at his wife's quiver, throwing her across the saddle in front of him. Boy's rear hooves slipped and the surface cracked beneath them, but he scrambled free and onto the un-weakened section of the ice. Tears ran down Mary's face as she slipped free, but she reached over her shoulder for one of the remaining arrows.

"Clear!" Mathilda shouted.

Tunnnggg.

"Pump! Pump!"

Round shot this time, the six-pound cast-iron sphere arching up like a blurred black dot. It landed behind the oncoming figures that marked Edain and his archers . . . right among the pursuers. Water gouted skyward, and men slid down tilting slabs of ice. Suspiciously regular slabs in part, where they'd patiently drilled holes to be covered with snow. More and more of the weakened ice broke, away from the jagged paths the retreating archers trod, carefully calculated to look like panic-stricken men dashing about witless. The forest-runners' shrieks turned from triumphant to terrified in an instant.

She could see a war chief with bars painted across his face throw his arms out in a frantic *halt!* gesture, but it was too late. Three men tumbled into him, and they all rolled together towards a stretch of black water where ice bobbed and men thrashed. To their left the horse soldiers of Corwin were in a worse state; a galloping horse *couldn't* stop quickly. One went right into the spot where Mary's horse had broken through, and the slim mare started to *climb* it, hammering the rider under her hooves. Another went through, and another.

Click.

"Clear!"

Tunngggg.

A lumpy, gritty stuff was packed around the frame of the scorpion. Thermite ignited easily, and they wouldn't be leaving the engine intact.

"Pump! Pump!"

"She's just limping!" Mary said, joy shining in her one eye as she looked back at her Rochael.

"Mary," Ingolf said, a little reproof in the tone.

Rudi frowned at them, and Mary dropped her eyes as his flicked to the limp burdens the other horses bore. Pierre Walks Quiet's face had fallen in on itself a little in death; the stiff red ice on his parka hid the wound that had killed him in five seconds of startled agony. Jake sunna Jake simply looked surprised, his hands still clutching at the stump of the javelin that had taken him in the throat. Bodies stiffened quickly in this cold.

"Pierre Walks Quiet was your friend, Ingolf," Rudi said. "What words would have pleased him?"

"Pete wasn't Catholic . . . or anything, that I knew of," Ingolf said. "Said he could talk to God out in the woods with the animals, better than in any church. I don't think he'd mind anyone he liked saying words over him, though."

"Now he walks beneath the forever trees," Rudi said quietly.

Ingolf nodded, lost in his own thoughts. Rudi looked at Jake's body.

What will I tell his woman? he thought. *Or how explain to his children what their father was?*

He helped the others bear them into the barn; Father Ignatius murmured the service for the dead beneath his breath. There was still a heap of loose hay; the bodies were laid in it, a faint scent of summers past rising amid the iron smell of blood.

"Ingolf?" Rudi asked.

The big Richlander swallowed, then spoke: "I knew Pete . . . Pierre Walks Quiet all my life, from the Change. It's hard to realize the old man's dead. He was like . . . like one of the *manitou* he used to tell me about. Taught me two-thirds of what I know about woodcraft and beasts and I wouldn't have learned the rest without the start he gave me. Taught me to love it, too. Good-bye, Pete. Damn and *hell*, I'll miss you."

He turned aside, as his voice went thick. Rudi nodded and stepped forward.

"I knew Jake sunna Jake for a far shorter time, but in that time we fought side by side, and saved each other's lives. He was called a savage, but I never saw him kill without need, or heard of it. He was untaught, but he learned more quickly than many I've met who are called great scholars. He saw the beauty in the world the Lord and Lady have given us, though nobody had given him

the words to tell of what his heart said. And everything
he did, he did first for his people. There were the seeds
of greatness in this man, and now all that he might have
done and been is sacrificed for us, his friends. Let us remember him, and be worthy of it!"

Rudi's voice rose: *"Lords of the Watchtowers of the West,
ye Lords of Death and Resurrection.* We light the torch for
Jake sunna Jake, brave warrior who fell for his kin and
friends, face to the foe; and for Pierre Walks Quiet of the
Anishinabe folk, who left comfort and safety to aid in the
world's need. Aradia and Cernnunos, accept Jake's spirit
in the Land of Youth. *Manitou,* bring Pierre's spirit to
the council fires of his people in their long home—"

The fire flared up, and they retreated through the
doors; the barn was tinder-dry wood and beam, and it
would go up like kindling. Already the fire was beginning
to roar. Rudi paused for a moment to lay his hands on
the shoulders of Tuk and Samul, Jake's half brothers.

"He's a good one, us'n bro Jake," Tuk whispered, his
hands tight on his bow. "Done good for Southside."

Rudi nodded. "He was a man I was proud to call
brother-in-arms," he said soberly. "I will help raise his
children as my own. Dun Jake will bear his name. Now
let's go! Mounted until we're well clear, then back to skis;
the horses can't keep going fast with burdens in this."

Ingolf swung into the saddle and drew in beside Rudi.
"Think we should have tried to finish them off?" he said.

Rudi shook his head, looking out through the thickening
snow. "Too risky. There were still more of them, if they
rallied. Now their spirits will be . . . dampened, I think."

Major Graber looked down at the body of the High
Seeker. The shaven-skulled face was blue with cold, and

a slow trickle of water oozed out of its mouth, glittering in the torchlight that drove back the night a little. Snow hissed into the burning wood. Somewhere a man sobbed and then shrieked as their surviving field medic went to work.

"We could try resuscitation," his lieutenant said.

"After more than an hour in this water? No, the Ascended Masters have welcomed his lifestream—"

High Seeker Dalan opened his eyes with a jerk, as if they were pulled up by fishhooks. Then turned his head to vomit out a stream of water. His breath rasped in, then out, and then he coughed—a curiously mechanical sound, like a forbidden engine was working in some mill of the unbelievers.

"I—see—you," he said, and smiled.

CHAPTER SIXTEEN

"Stop the sled," the old woman said, peering out from under her wolfskin hood.

The bricks under her booted feet were cold again now and so was she, even beneath her winter gear and the thick bearskin traveling rug. The wind was rising, hard as the teeth of Hella, full of a hard mealy scent. It flicked kernels of dry sharp snow through the laden branches of the pines, and the bare fingers of the sugar maples and birch writhed. At least it was at her back and the arched cover of the sled broke most of it.

"Are you sure, Heidhveig?" Thorlind said, speaking a little loudly to be heard over the storm.

"Of course not!"

She regretted the snap even as the words left her lips; but she felt the cold in her bones, more every year, an ache that never quite went away. The sun and warmth of her girlhood suddenly came before her, for the first time in years.

The Berkeley hills would be green now, after the first rains. The wind chilly but just enough to make a coat welcome, and the Bay blue, with gulls over Alcatraz, and the smell of eucalyptus . . .

For a moment her eyes teared with longing for a world as legendary now as any hero tale; then she blinked and with the discipline of long practice shut those memories away.

"Sorry," she said. "Just . . . a feeling."

"You don't just have feelings," Thorlind said. "Not *you*, and not *just*."

The girl's no fool, she thought. Then: *Girl! I am getting old! She's a grandmother this year!*

Thorlind pulled on the reins with a *whoa!* The two shaggy horses slowed and stopped as she threw the drag lever and the claw dug into the hard-packed snow, and the outriders drew rein and swung down from their mounts.

Heidhveig let them help her down; Thorlind handed her the staff, and one of the guards brought the lantern from its hook at the rear over the baggage compartment. It shone for a moment on the silver cat's heads on the front corners of the sled, the jet glitter of the raven's heads behind, and the intricate carving that laced the wooden panels of its sides with intertwined figures of elongated gripping beasts, wolves and dragons and birds. In a sudden moment of doubled vision she saw the Oseberg wagon in one of the books she had pored over so diligently when she was young—probably one of H.R. Ellis Davidson's. And now she *was* the seeress in the wagon . . .

It was the kind of dizzying juxtaposition she used to experience often when they were building Norrheim, after the Change.

Why should it happen now? I thought I'd become more like the youngsters, living the legends and not thinking about them.

The winter's afternoon was already growing dark, and

the gathering snowstorm gusted, sometimes clearing for an instant and then cutting visibility to barely beyond arm's length. The woods ended here—the solid forest, at least—giving way to rolling fields and scattered shaws, hidden now in the storm but letting the wind run free. She could just see the high white bulk of the barrow. Before it was an upright slab of granite, roughly shaped, a carved tangle of gripping beasts bordering the runes. The light was too dim to read them, but she didn't need to. She murmured them aloud:

"Bjarni Eriksson raised this stone to the memory of his father Erik Waltersson, called Erik the Strong, he who led his people north through the great dying and got this land for them through his luck and craft and drighten might. Here he lies, to watch over the land he won for his blood and folk. Thor hallow these runes."

"Hello again, Erik, my old friend," she added softly. "You built well. Watch over us all indeed."

In the first years after the Change they had expected Ragnarök every winter, and looked to see the gods themselves come riding down the sky, for surely trolls and etins walked among men. But the heroes they had were men like Erik, the *godhi* of an Asatru kindred who had tried to get closer to the old Gods by studying the old ways. He had the skills they needed for survival and the will to inspire or bully others into using them. Folk had followed him, growing like a snowball rolling downhill around that first core until Norrheim stretched mighty across leagues of field and forest, an island of life in a sea of wilderness and death.

Skis hissed in the dimness, and three bulky figures appeared on the edge of the light cast through the lantern's bull's-eye lens. They were muffled in fur and quilted wool until nothing of them showed save their eyes, but they moved with easy unconcern in the gathering storm. All of them kicked the toes of their boots out of the ski loops as they stopped and jumped to their feet, agile as cats. One had a long bow in his hand, one a great bearded war-ax with a straight four-foot helve, and one a spear; all had double-edged swords and seaxes at their belts, and round shields slung over their backs.

"Who comes to the steading of *Godhi* Bjarni Eriksson on the sacred eve?" one said importantly, hardly even waiting to halt before he spoke; his voice was a young man's. "All who come in peace and fellowship are welcome to share the Gods' feast, but reivers and evildoers and trollmen stay wide of our land, if they're wise. If not, they get a warm welcome and an everlasting bed to lie in."

The guards bristled and fingered the shafts of their broad-bladed spears. Heidhveig braced herself upright on her staff and Thorlind let the light shine on her, so the Eriksgarth men could see clearly even with the storm in their faces.

"*One comes* who saw you all in your cradles, and crawling and squalling butt-naked beneath the benches," Heidhveig said tartly. "You, Roderic Karlsson, and you, Thorolf Pierresson, and you too, Olaf Davesson!"

"Ah . . . sorry," Roderic said, and sounded as if he was, or at least embarrassed. "Ah . . . welcome, welcome, holy *seidhkona*. The Chief will be pleased and honored; we didn't think you'd be here this Yule!"

"If I've made it every Yule Eve for twenty-four years, I can do it once more," she said. "This is the godwoman Thorlind Williamsdottir. And these are men of Kalk the Shipwright's garth, Sven Jacobsson and Ingmar Marcellesson, who swore to see me safe here for the festival."

"Come, come, lady Heidhveig," Roderic said. "And

all of you. Let's get you inside, and a guest cup inside you, and your beasts fed and stabled!"

She started to nod—right now a cup of hot cider or mead sounded *very* attractive—when she felt a sudden sense of pressure, no, of *Presence*. They stopped, staring, as she flung out her hand to silence them. The wind blew louder, the low throbbing rising to a screech, and for an instant it tugged at her cloak until the ends flew forward like wings. The cold cut like a knife, a white pain that seemed to light the land around her. She could see every flake of snow and dead leaf and pine needle, hear the very thoughts of the martins and mink and the bears curled sleeping in their dens.

No, not sleeping—they too were stirring, waking to awareness of a power greater than the storm. Snow muffled all sound but the wind's scream now, yet she could hear hoofbeats, or perhaps it was the thudding of her heart.

"Can't you hear *them*?" she heard herself say. "Can't you *feel* them?"

She twitched as energy surged through her, the old familiar thrill of ecstasy that had won her allegiance long before the Change made all the old stories real.

"What?" Roderic said; Thorlind stepped forward silently and took her arm, lending her strength.

Her eyes sought to pierce the swirling darkness. "The Hunt rides tonight," she whispered, feeling her voice alter cadence as if she were already in trance. "*He* rides the wind, and the dead thunder behind Him over the rainbow bridge. The foam that flies from their horses' bits will bless the land. I feel *His* eye upon us, I hear the crying of His hounds."

Old Man, she continued silently. *What are you up to*

now? What hero will you invite this night to join that ride?

Roderic took a step back. One of his companions clutched at his chest, probably at an amulet; the other drew the Hammer. Heidhveig took a deep breath, feeling the intensity of that awareness fade, and her mouth quirked. Her folk gave the Allfather His due . . . and most of them were just as pleased not to attract His particular attention; Thor was a lot more popular.

The one-eyed Wanderer, the God of wolf and raven, the Terrible One who sent the madness of battle and the mead of poetry to men . . . had his own purposes. She believed those purposes served the ultimate good of the world and of humankind, but she knew that to achieve them He would spare neither Himself nor His chosen ones.

After that she saw little of the garth and its buildings except a blur of lighted windows and folk greeting her. The shock of warmth as they left their outer clothing in the vestibule brought her fully back to herself, and to her aches and pains as that warmth gradually eased them.

The chieftain's hall of Eriksgarth was L-shaped, the shorter end a large frame house built long before the Change as the core of a farm; the longer wing was the hall proper, added afterwards as time and resources permitted. Bjarni and his wife Harberga Janetsdottir greeted her, friendly as always—she'd been an unofficial grandmother to them both from their childhoods—but with a trace of tension that told her Roderic had repeated her words.

"You shouldn't travel in weather like this!" Harberga scolded. "What if you'd been caught in a real storm, coming up from the coast?"

She was tall and fair, her braided hair up beneath a

kerchief, and a six-month belly stretching out the blue wool of her hanging skirt and the embroidered linen panel of her apron, held by silver brooches at her shoulders.

"You'll catch your death!" she went on.

"When you're past eighty that's not something that can be avoided," she said.

But she let them fuss her into a deep chair beside one of the two stone hearths on either side of the hall; the area before it was the honor seat, where the chief and his lady and important guests were placed. Some purists had wanted to use a firepit down the center, and she remembered Erik roaring out what he thought of *that* with an epic vocabulary that he *hadn't* gotten from the Eddas.

More like the 82nd Airborne, she thought reminiscently as she sank into the cushions with a sigh. It had started with *you shit-for-brains dickweeds, do you think the Gods* want *morons for followers* and finished with *freeze your* own *balls off,* you *don't have any use for them*!

Fire boomed amid a sweet scent of burning pine in the fireplace of rough granite, on andirons whose ends rose into wrought dragons; the slanted iron plate at the rear helped cast the heat into the long room. Tapestries fluttered on the walls; the bare logs between were carved in sinuous patterns, hung with round painted shields and racked spears, bow and sword and ax, and mail byrnies that glittered darkly in the wavering light. More carvings ran on the railed gallery that ran around it at second-story height. Two rows of pillars made from the trunks of whole white pines and wrought into figures of gods and heroes ran the length of the stone-flagged floor, reaching up into the dimness of the rafters; some carried rings of lanterns at twice head-height on iron wheels.

Bjarni poured her cider with his own hands, into a big

ceramic mug with *New Sweden Midsomar Festival 1997* printed on it. He was only a little taller than his wife, but broad-shouldered and barrel-chested, his cropped beard and shoulder-length hair as brick red as his father's had been, his eyes blue and steady. The drink hissed and steamed as he plunged a glowing poker into it.

"Ahhh, that's good!" she said, cradling the mug in knotted hands and breathing in fragrant steam like a memory of blossom time. As the heat eased aching joints she lifted it, murmuring softly:

"Hail the hall and the master of this hall,
Hail the mistress and the household she rules,
Hail the wight that wards the holy hearth,
And the spirits that bring life to the land."

By the time she had finished the blessing, the cider was cool enough for drinking. She let the hot sweet liquid run down her throat and get to work on the last of the chill.

The hall was thronged with scores of people, burly bearded men in tunic and breeks, women in long gowns— or sometimes practical traveling trousers themselves; the cloth a mixture of carefully preserved pre-Change brightness brought out for the festival and the more subtle colors of modern vegetable dyes. Either sex might wear an arm ring of gold or silver or steel. Her host had two pushed up on his thick biceps over the cloth of his tunic, the one that bore witness to his deeds and the oath ring he wore when leading rituals. Long weapons were left in the cloakroom or hung on the wall, but nearly every belt bore a fighting knife of the kind called a seax.

Most of the faces were folk she knew, or at least recognized and could place, like the two Micmac envoys in their embroidered tick coats and leggings. Voices sounded like surf, in the Norse-salted English of the Bjornings, or now and then in the nasal French dialect that was the second-most common tongue in Norrheim.

Which is appropriate; plenty of Norman and Frank there too.

Children added their mite, running and playing with the big rough-coated dogs, or sucking on maple candy. There were friendly nods to her in plenty, but the folk left her in peace to talk with the chief.

"Quite a crowd," she said to Bjarni.

He and his wife drew up chairs beside her; a three-year-old girl came and crawled up into his lap and went to sleep with a kitten's limp finality.

"Half the *wapentake* is here!" the Bjorning chieftain said, settling his daughter against him with a father's skill.

The tables and benches were set, running down both sides of the hall and centered on the dais that held the east-wall hearth; good cooking smells drifted in from the house where the feast was in preparation, but some of the guests were already eating slices of dark coarse barley-bread spread with liver paste or smoked salmon or cheese or butter and thick blueberry jam, or munching on apples from the bowls set out. Bjarni's younger sister Gudrun oversaw a team of household women who were filling cups and carrying trays, proud in her new-budded womanhood and grave with the responsibility of helping her sister-in-law, a maiden's long loose hair flowing auburn under a silver headband.

The guests would do justice to the feast as well. They'd come from many miles around, and traveling in this weather needed fuel!

Bjarni's strong callused hand caressed his sleeping daughter's white mane as he went on:

"A lot of the householders wanted to talk things over, and see the divination. Even with a good harvest, there's been trouble—more quarrels than usual among ourselves, troll-man raids in the northern reaches, and the south-mark. Rumors of trouble from the outlands. Folk are nervous and it's a long time until the *Althing* meets."

His hand touched his beard, and his voice fell. "And what's this young Roderic tells me about the Hunt?"

Heidhveig sighed again, letting her head fall back and her eyes close. "He heard everything I *saw*," she said. "But it always means something when—"

Then Roderic was there again; he hadn't bothered to take off his parka, and snow melted on in thick patches on the wolverine fur. His hazel eyes were wide.

"*Godhi*, lady—travelers!"

"Well, show them in!" Bjarni said, irritated. "You *are* on watch, boy!"

"No, *strangers*. Maybe thirty of them! Travelers from the far west, they say, and their leader not like any man I've ever seen before!"

He *was* a young man; his voice shook with excitement. Heidhveig set down the cup, staring towards the door.

Old Man, she thought. *Have you set me to work* seidh *for a hero this holy eve?*

The vestibule door opened, and the lights fluttered in the draught. Strangers crowded it, in the sort of warm wool tunics and pants the sensible wore beneath their outer gear for winter travel, but different from local style in a dozen subtle ways.

Her eyes went to their leader, drawn like iron to a magnet.

I can smell *Orlög on him; a fate like tears and flowers and blood. What does Wyrd weave now?*

He was a tall man, two fingers or so above six feet,

broad-shouldered and narrow-hipped and long-limbed; young, too, well into manhood but younger than her host's thirty. He moved with the supple economy of a tiger, as if even his stillness was always complicit of motion, a thing of dynamic balance that held the promise of sudden blinding speed. When he shook his head slightly damp red-gold hair fell to his shoulders, framing a straight-nosed, high-cheeked, cleft-chinned face that might have been called beautiful save for the thin scar along his jaw and up nearly to the left cheek. There were more on his large shapely hands, but she could see from the look of his blue-green eyes that he would be more likely to smile than frown, on an occasion less solemn.

"It's in peace and goodwill that we come," he said; his voice was a resonant baritone.

It was also full of a pleasant lilting accent she hadn't heard since the old world fell, the soft west-Irish brogue of the Gaeltacht; and she recognized a trained singer's control and pitch as he went on, filling the hall without strain or shout:

"Merry met to the Mistress of this Hearth and to the Lord of this Hall, and to all beneath their roof. We ask guesting if we are welcome, and only leave to pass on if we are not."

The Bjorning chieftain stood, handed little Swanhild to his wife despite a sleepy protest and faced the tall stranger; silence was thick through the hall, and beneath it a humming curiosity. The newcomers were a worn, tough-looking crew, including the women among them— one even had an eye patch—but they had politely racked whatever long arms they carried in the cloakroom. None of the Eriksgarth dwellers were very alarmed, though a few men drifted to stand with arms crossed on their chests behind their leader . . . just in case, which also put them within grabbing range of the arms hung on the walls.

One of the Norrheimer proverbs was to trust no ice until you'd walked on it.

"I hight Bjarni Eriksson, *godhi*—Chieftain—here. Who comes to Eriksgarth on the holy eve?" he said, his voice rumbling deep.

The stranger inclined his head politely to the master of the hall, and then again a little more deeply to Harberga . . . or perhaps to her and Heidhveig both, and touched the back of his right fist to his forehead for a moment. She noticed a small white scar between his brows then.

"Rudi Mackenzie am I, of the Clan Mackenzie; the totem of my sept is Raven. In my own land, I am son to our Chief, and our folk have hailed me as Tanist—as heir. These are my sworn men and followers and kin. We have traveled for near two years from the sunset ocean, over mountain and plain, forest and river and lake, and our goal is to find a ship to bear us on the eastern sea."

A buzz of wonder rose from the crowd, then died away. Bjarni stepped forward and held out his hand; the two men gripped wrists, each taking the measure of the other, and each gave a very slight nod, as if liking what they saw.

"*Come heil* to you, Rudi Mackenzie," the Bjorning chieftain said formally; the phrase meant "come in good health and be welcome." "*Come heil* to your followers also."

Then he added without looking away: "Bring drink to all our guests!"

His sister Gudrun came with a great polished ox horn carved with runes and bound and rimmed and tipped with braided silver, rather than the more usual mugs her assistants bore to the others.

"Welc—" she stammered a little, flushing as Rudi looked at her, then took a breath and began again as he smiled encouragingly:

"Welcome I give
The wanderer here
With bright and blessed draught
Greeted art thou
With grith and frith
Hail in holy hall!"

The man who'd called himself Rudi Mackenzie took the horn with a grip that showed he'd held one before, the point kept down and a little to one side. He drew a sign over the hot mead, touched a finger to it and flicked a drop aside, then raised it:

"Sláinte chugat!" he said. "To your health! I drink thanks to the high Gods of this land, thanks to the spirits of place which ward hearth and home and field, and thanks to my hosts, the Lord and Lady of this hall. And to all beneath their roof, goodwill and welcome. May there always be peace and guest friendship and never a feud between us."

He took another draught, and gave a long apprecia-tive:

"Ahhhhh! And *many* thanks, Bjarni Eriksson. We've come a long cold way from a cold camp this day, and weeks over the ice before that. If ever you journey to our land of Montival in the High West, my house is your house as long as you please to visit. So witness sun-bright Lugh of the Long Spear and Brigid Sheaf-mistress, and

the Dagda and the threefold Morrigú and all the Gods of my people."

"That's well said, Rudi Mackenzie of the Clan Mackenzie," Bjarni answered. "So a chieftain speaks. You're welcome to share our feast, and there's room for all, and warm beds. Or straw, at least! My carles will see to your beasts and gear."

Harberga made a determined sound and levered herself upright, setting her daughter Swanhild down in her chair; for the honor of the house it was her duty to see that her husband's words about food and beds were true, even when the number of guests suddenly went up by a quarter. The girl-child blinked open eyes cornflower blue and looked around; Rudi Mackenzie smiled at her in an unguarded instant of tender delight, and an answering smile lit the toddler's chubby face as she waved.

Then he turned to one of his followers—a thick-armed younger man with a mop of curly hair the brown of old oakwood and a stubborn-looking square face—and took a long bundle handed to him.

"Forgive a stranger's ignorance of your ways," he said, facing back to Bjarni. "In our land, the custom is that a visitor at Yuletide brings his host a guesting gift."

He unwrapped the coarse cloth from the bundle and presented it across the palms of his hands.

"We Mackenzies are a people of the bow, and Aylward the Archer here is not the least of our master bowyers."

Heidhveig's brows rose, and a man behind Bjarni whistled softly in knowledgeable appreciation. The weapon was six inches over six feet, with a long subtle in-and-out curve to the hickory stave; a central riser of burnished curly maple was worked and slanted to give a sure handgrip, and a cutout through the centerline for the shaft was lined with a tuft of wolf fur. The nocks at either end were polished antler, glittering amber-color in the firelight, and the back was covered in a strip of deer sinew, pale beneath the smooth varnish.

The whole had an indefinable *rightness*, a beauty of pure function like the light on the edge of a knife. With it was a baldric and quiver of brown leather tooled with vines; wrought buttons of carved bone sealed little pouches for an arrow hone and spare bowstrings and beeswax. Within the quiver itself were two score of gray-fletched shafts, bodkins and broadheads.

Bjarni smiled despite himself, holding the weapon out at arm's length, running his fingers down its length and then rolling one of the arrows across his thumbnail. Few gifts from all the world's wealth could have been more welcome.

"This is fine work! Ullr himself would not be ashamed to use it; your man knows his craft!" he said. "My thanks to you, and to him. Come, the feast's nearly ready, but you've time for the steam bath and the rocks are still hot. Then we'll eat, and talk."

He hesitated. "We hold a rite after. A divination. You're welcome to attend, or not as it pleases you."

Heidhveig spoke: "I will sit in the *seidhjallr* and speak this Yule," she said. "I think that questions of weight will be asked. But not today. Tomorrow, when Thorlind and I are fully rested and we have sought out the land-wights."

Rudi Mackenzie inclined his head respectfully; Bjarni murmured in his ear. Heidhveig sometimes wondered if the young man realized *her* ears hadn't lost much sharpness, unlike the way it had gone with his own father in the days of his age. She heard clearly, however softly he spoke:

"She does you honor. Heidhveig is the greatest of our

wisewomen; my father was her friend from the land-taking and had good redes of her many a time. She came here from someplace far to the west just before the Change and taught us the old magic. She speaks to spirits, journeys between the worlds. We always have a *seidh* session at Yule—it's a good time for divination, but Heidhveig doesn't sit in the *seidhjallr* herself often these days."

"My thanks, lady!" Rudi exclaimed. "Wisdom is the greatest of all gifts!"

He smiled again, and Heidhveig's mouth turned up in response.

How this one must charm the women! she thought wryly, looking into the sparkling gaze and hearing a few sighs from around her.

Then something moved in her mind, uncoiling from the depths.

Yes, she thought—and knew with a sharp weight of certainty. *Yes. This is the one sent to me.*

"*Par dieu,* by Mary Mother and the merciful Saints, I thought I'd never be warm again," Odard Liu said.

Rudi grinned at him through the drifting mist of steam. The men of the party were all seated on the pine-board benches that made a half circle around the hearth; occasionally a little door would open, and the attendant would stretch in tongs to drop a new heated rock, *clack* on the pile. The hot wet scent of the wood was an aromatic blessing in his lungs; he could feel the sweat carrying all impurity out of his body, and the memory of the ice floes' white grinding death with it.

"I've noticed, my lord Gervais, that you complain and complain . . . but sure, you keep going just the same!"

Odard cocked one black brow without opening his eyes, leaning back with his arms along the front of the bench above. The wintertide journey had thinned him down to muscle and gristle and bone, as it had all of them, and he hadn't had much spare flesh to start with.

"And what else can I do, your Majesty?" he said. "*Stop?* Around *here?* If I ever get back, wild horses hitched to triple reduction gearing won't get me out of Barony Gervais."

"You'd be bored silly in six months," Rudi said.

Odard's voice grew dreamy: "Bored? I'll spend my time lying in a hammock under blossoming peach trees or a pergola of roses, looking out over the vineyards, and giving my loyal peasants an encouraging twiddle of my fingers now and then. And eating pineapple pyonnade and composing poetry about my heroic deeds. Pretty girls will fan me in the summer heat and drop peeled grapes in my mouth and sing for me. When winter comes, I'll go on a fearless quest—as far as the castle solar, where I will read stories about *other people's* adventures and sip real coffee with good brandy in it, as a fire crackles in the hearth and the radiator gurgles."

Ingolf took up the bundle of birch twigs, dipped it into the bucket and flicked water onto the stones. Steam billowed up with a sharp *hssssss*, and someone on the upper tier groaned in pleasure—Rudi thought it was Father Ignatius, and nobody could say *he* wasn't a hardy man. He'd certainly done a full share of the work, and more than his share of scouting on the long rearguard.

"We've got saunas like this in Richland, too," Ingolf said. With a grin at Odard: "After you boil for a while and feel just like a ham, you run out and roll in the snow, or jump into a hole cut in the ice over the river."

The baron of Gervais shuddered theatrically. "Saints have mercy! Even the Bearkillers don't do *that*."

"No, really, it feels good," Ingolf said. "You just don't stay out long enough for your body to lose the heat that's soaked in."

"That's what *you* do, perhaps," Odard said. "*I* do *not*. I'm saving up the heat to hoard like a Corvallis money-lender's gold in a vault."

Fred Thurston had been sitting silent, like a statue of old bronze sheening with a thin film of oil. Now he stirred:

"These people are *Asatruar*, aren't they?" he said

Mary and Ritva could tell him what they'd learned in their mother's household, and they'd been able to find him a few books along the way, but he was anxious for the reality of the tales that spoke to his heart. You couldn't learn much of a faith until you saw how it shaped the souls of those who followed it.

"Yes," Rudi said.

Someone sighed; definitely Father Ignatius this time. Since Fred had been a nominal Methodist originally, the Mackenzie didn't think the priest had much ground for complaint, and went on:

"So I'd judge from what we've seen and heard. Probably it spread here the way the Old Religion did from Dun Juniper, because the ones who brought them through the Change followed it."

Which to be sure is also why nearly everyone around Mt. Angel is a Christian of the Roman rite, he thought. *Or why most are in the lands the Association rules. Sigh as you will, Father, but turn about is fair play.* Aloud he went on:

"And hospitality is sacred to them as well, of which I'm glad. I was worried to death about Epona, that I was.

She's a little old for travel like this, which would be hard on a horse of half her years. But they're treating our beasts right royally, as they are us; nice tight barn, blankets, warm mash, clean water and straw, fodder of the best."

Fred nodded agreement. "They seem like . . . solid people," he said.

"Indeed, the which is what I'd expect. What those Gods they follow value in a man is courage and loyalty, and above all the hardihood of soul to stand and endure and strive, never flinching. Nor would they have come so well through such years—and in a hard place like this—unless they had those things in truth."

Odard shuddered. "Oh, the ancestral virtues! Next you'll say they venerate clean living and hard work."

"As a matter of fact . . ." Rudi replied.

Fred snorted, and said: "How long do you think we'll stay? I'd like to . . . learn a bit."

"A week or two at least. We have to learn the lay of the land here, and the road to the coast, and where we can hope to find a vessel, one willing to carry us in this bleak season. And to tell the truth I'd like to leave our horses and a couple of our wounded here, if we can arrange that. Then a dash to the sea, a dash to Nantucket, and back. Though how by the brazen gates of Anwyn we're to return through that mess we left behind us . . ."

"These folk keep the twelve days of Yule, don't they?" Edain said. "Twelve days of feasting . . . after the trip we've had, that would be just about what I could use, so! And we'd not lose much time. We were slowing that last week or so because we were worn, ourselves and our beasts both."

"It's lucky we ran into someplace that *could* put us all

up in midwinter," Ingolf said thoughtfully. "As well as being well disposed, I mean. We've had to move quick a lot to keep from eating people bare. Of course, we're *supposed* to be moving quickly."

They all laughed; quickly was for short trips. When you had a three-thousand-mile journey one way and the prospect of three thousand miles back, haste lost all meaning. Even for a small picked band a journey of that distance could only be made at walking speed, fifteen miles a day averaged out over the whole, and you'd count yourself lucky to maintain that. They *had* been lucky, since their stay at the Valley of the Sun had been the only time they'd been stuck in one spot for many months by illness, wounds or weather.

Rudi shook his head and poured a dipperful of water over it, enjoying the cool shock.

"Not just luck; it's little we've found on this journey of either good or bad that's mere chance in the way most use the term. And we're moving as quickly as we can while doing what we're supposed to be doing, of which collecting the Sword is an essential part, but only a part. What did Tsewang Dorje say to me, back at Chenrezi Monastery . . ."

He thought, and the wise wrinkled face appeared in his mind's eye, amid the pleasant austerity of his chamber:

"Can light exist without shadow?" he quoted. *"So, I tell you that when you seek to do the will of the gods, and help men rise through the cycles, your very inmost thoughts awaken hosts of enemies that otherwise had slept. As sound awakens echoes, so the pursuit of Wisdom awakens the devil's guard."*

"I would not put it in just those words, my son, yet the good Abbot is a very wise man, in his way," Ignatius said thoughtfully. "But I would guess that he told you more."

"That he did. This: *But I do say that if you are in league with Gods to learn life and to live it you shall not only find enemies. You shall find help unexpectedly, from strangers who, it may be, know not why.*"

"A very wise man indeed," Ignatius said, swinging his feet down and sitting upright on the bench, his whipcord body dim in the gloom. "And a holy man, I think. I learned things of great value in the Valley of the Sun; we all did."

"Even though his is the Way of the Buddha?" Rudi said, his voice slightly teasing.

The priest spoke with a chuckle in his voice, his narrow dark eyes ironic and a finger tapping the air in mild reproof:

"You know the answer to that, my son; you rolled in enough logic at Mt. Angel for *some* to rub off. When men differ from the *magisterium* of Holy Mother Church, they are in error. But when they agree with it . . . why, that simply shows that all truth proceeds from God. We of the Church have it in fullness by revelation in Scripture and from the holy Saints and the Fathers, as well as by reason and moral intuition. But all men can discover some of it, if they truly seek virtue and wisdom, wherever they start the journey. How not? These things come from only one source and it speaks to every heart that listens. So yes, the *Rimpoche* is a holy man, and so, in my view, was the Buddha—or Plato, for that matter. But how much better would they have been, if only they had the fullness of the Divine Logos to guide them!"

"Well, now, *there's* a circular argument, if I ever heard one!"

The priest laughed aloud. "You can't win this one, you

know . . . your Majesty. Though I'll have it with you as often as you please."

"It's you Christians who think you can *argue* your way to truth," Rudi said, with a grin. "Right now, to be sure, I'd rather *eat*. Let's go sluice off!"

CHAPTER SEVENTEEN

Next afternoon Rudi grinned again as he watched Edain collecting his bets after a round of shooting with the bow—and then handing the winnings out as gifts, each to a different man than the one who'd wagered it.

Sure, and there's a wisdom of hand and eye, too, he thought.

There was plenty of room for play in the big enclosure that Eriksgarth made—the hall and house of the *godhi*, smaller dwellings for his carles and their families and the youngsters fostered here to learn, barns and sheds and workshops, all around a court paved with river-smoothed cobbles mostly hidden beneath hard-packed snow. The sky was bright, with traces of high cloud like a white mare's tail. The air was no more than *cold*, without the frigid cutting blast that made your face ache; the fresh drifts sparkled like soft-curved masses of diamond dust in the light.

And Epona is looking better, he thought happily. *Still a bit of that dry wheeze, but her eyes aren't as dull. Some quiet and rest and she'll be fine.*

For shooting with the bow they used the bank of a distant potato barn as a target, a curious structure like a long rectangle three-quarters sunken in the ground and with earth berms heaped up against its walls. There were clear fields beyond that, for a quarter-mile of open fenced pastureland until a holy shaw's trees stood bare-branched around the steep roof-on-roof height of a *stave-hof*, a temple. A bright glitter caught his eye there, paint on one of the riot of carvings.

The locals were good enough archers in their way, but not up to Mackenzie standards, and certainly not to be set against a champion of the Lughnasadh Games like Edain. The young men he'd defeated laughed and slapped him on the back; then three of them looked at each other, nodded, and each picked up one of the plate-sized wooden targets.

With a shout they threw them high, in a spread that opened like the spines of a fan. Edain's movements seemed steady, almost leisurely, but the flat *snap* of the bow sounded three times so quickly that the sound was lost in the hard *crack-crack-crack* of the points striking home in wood. The last of the targets was still man-height above the ground when the arrow punched it away.

"Fetch, Garbh!" the younger Mackenzie said.

The big shaggy half mastiff had been sitting in aristocratic indifference, ignoring the stiff-legged wariness of the local beasts as they stalked closer. Now she trotted off, to return and lay the disks at her master's feet.

"Did you *miss*?" one of the Bjornings said; no arrows stood in the wooden circles. "I thought I heard the strike!"

Edain tossed him one of the disks, skimming it through the air; they were like flat miniature shields a foot across, made from two layers of birch strips glued crossways and rimmed in iron. The Norrheim man held his up and whistled between his teeth, showing the neat round hole punched through near the center of it.

"This is not a little boy who's come among us!" he said.

"Ah, it's the cold steel that wins a battle," one of the others grumbled.

Garbh returned with the arrows held gently between her long yellow teeth, lips curled daintily back. The fletching of each had been stripped off as they made passage through the wood, but they were otherwise intact.

"Not with one of those through your eye," his friend said thoughtfully. "And through your shield first. I'd guess you could punch through a byrnie, too, eh?"

"A mail shirt? Yes, with anything like a straight hit, and a nice bodkin. But a solid steel breastplate or lames, now . . . no, not always through that. The surface may glance the point; you need a closer range and a little luck. Enough shafts in the air at once—an arrow storm, we call it—will do the job right enough."

Edain finshed checking the arrows and slid them over his shoulder into the quiver. He spoke with a little slyness in it:

"You were speakin' of the cold steel? Well, my Chief there, himself, is a very fair shot, enough to keep me exercised, as it were, but a man of the sword first and foremost. Better at that than I am with a bow, if truth be told, and I've fought by his side more than once, in ambuscades, onsets, raids and pitched battles."

He reached out and took an apple that one of the local men had halfway raised to his mouth, twitching it out of his fingers, tossing it up and catching it. Then he threw it with a sudden hard snap, the plump red fruit a blurred streak through the air.

"Chief!" he called as it left his hand.

Rudi had been waiting for something of the sort; the contests had all been friendly, but he didn't think the men of Eriksgarth would have spent this much time with their weapons on the day of a feast if the strangers hadn't arrived. Though they seemed to love games and tests of skill of all sorts, from chess to wrestling and swordplay, and this gathering was a chance for trials between many from isolated steadings.

The apple was aimed more than arm's length to Rudi's left, past what was now his sword hand. That hand flashed across his body and he turned in the packed snow of the yard, granules flying up in arcs from his boots with the speed of the movement. Steel glittered in the cold winter light as he extended in a long lunge, the point an extension of his arm in a play of motion and angle.

Tock.

The point went through the firm flesh of the apple with a surgeon's delicacy, the edge parallel to the ground so that it stopped the motion without splitting the fruit. He held the lunge for an instant, with a background of amazed oaths, then flicked the longsword's point upward and twitched his wrist to send the steel in a shimmering arc.

Tock.

This time the apple tumbled towards the ground in two neat halves. Rudi caught them with his other hand, moving like a frog's tongue after a fly, then wiped the tip of his sword on his sleeve and slid it home. He tossed one half to a grinning Edain as the broad-shouldered bowman sauntered up.

"You almost wasted a good apple, there, boyo," he said mildly. "The which the Goddess of the Blossom-time would not like."

His half was tart and sweet at the same time as he crunched it; a little harder and more grainy than the breeds they grew back home in the Mackenzie duns or the Yakima lands, but palatable. Edain ate his in three bites, his cheeks bulging for a moment, and his gray eyes taking in the awestruck expressions scattered across the open expanse. Some were frankly goggling; everyone here trained to the blade, which meant they had a fair idea of just what combination of speed and control the little demonstration had required.

Now that was more than a bit flashy, Rudi half chided himself. *But then, Edain's only a bit past twenty. And I'm no graybeard yet either! And we wouldn't have done it before those who weren't warriors themselves, sure.*

"I think it's the custom here to push a man a bit. To see what's in him, as it were," Edain said.

"The which Mackenzies would *never* do," Rudi said, and they both laughed.

Edain went on: "They're a bit doomful here, but for the rest it's homelike enough; and they get something more lively with some beer in them."

"That they do!"

"Has it struck you, Chief, that men are not at all unlike dogs . . . especially in the way they greet a stranger?"

As if on cue there was a sudden chorus of snarls; Garbh had one of the Eriksgarth hounds on its back, with her teeth holding its neck ruff. She shook it a little and then stepped back, tense and wary.

"Well, at least we're not expected to engage in arse-sniffing contests," Rudi pointed out, which the dogs were doing at that moment, their tails wagging.

Not far away, Mary Havel—Mary Vogeler, now, Rudi reminded himself—was talking to a big young Bjorning with a battle-ax in his hands. The weapon was a bit unusual; the rear of it was drawn out into the rectangular serrated head of a war hammer. The ax-man looked over at Ingolf, who with Fred Thurston was helping some newcomers unload a roughly butchered moose carcass from their sled, a contribution to the feast and a gift to their chieftain.

The tall Richlander hefted a hindquarter over his back, with no more than a grunt at a weight greater than his whole body.

"Friend, you'll find that Mary can take care of herself well enough, you betcha," he said mildly, and then strode over to where Harberga waited at the door of her kitchen's cold store. Fred sniggered wordlessly as he scooped up two burlap sacks of rye flour and followed Ingolf with one over each shoulder.

The Bjorning flushed, leaned his dreadful polearm against a wall and picked up the practice equivalent—a four-foot helve with a mock blade of light pine, wrapped in felt and rags; no matter how shielded, the seven-pound head of the original would smash bone like kindling if driven hard. Then he took stance, the ax slanted across his body with his hands wide-spaced near butt and helve—an expert's grip. The man was about halfway between Rudi and John Hordle in size, and from the look of him he had the shoulders to move the massive weapon quickly. When he struck the air hummed, but Rudi thought he was pulling the blow.

Mary leapt straight upward over the swing, her own chest-height from a standing start. The Bjorning had expected to strike, or at least to have the blow blocked by the longsword she wore across her back with the hilt over the right shoulder. Instead as it met only air the momentum of the strike pulled his body around irresistibly. The Ranger's hand darted out and tweaked his nose painfully;

then she went into a series of backflips that left her half a dozen yards away.

Tsk, tsk, Rudi thought.

He was a fine gymnast himself, but that sort of thing had little place in actual fighting to his way of thinking. In a fight you should move precisely as much as needed to attack or defend, neither more nor less. The Dúnedain tended to be a bit showy, though.

Some of the onlookers cheered her. Others hooted in wholehearted mirth, bending over and clutching themselves or slapping hands on their thighs—as Edain had said, the two clansmen found the dwellers here a bit *doomful* by Mackenzie standards, but this was a joke after their own hearts. A few of the women watching called comments to the ax-bearer that would have had Rudi's ears flushing, and made the man bellow with anger in his mouse-colored braided beard. He brought the weapon up to guard and began a rush, then halted in wariness.

Now Mary had the chain unwound from her waist, both ends crisscrossing in glittering arcs as she whirled them clockwise and counterclockwise; one held a sickle-shaped blade, the other a steel ball. That was a weapon she'd taken up during their stay in Chenrezi Monastery, in the Valley of the Sun. The monks taught it, and Master Hao said she was a natural for it—it was a *yin* weapon anyway, suitable to her changeful nature.

The Bjorning decided to treat it as if it was a quarterstaff, and struck at the middle spot where her hands turned wrist-over-wrist to keep the chain moving. Mary dropped promptly to one knee, and let the steel links slide through her gloved palms. There was a rattling *chunk* as one end of the chain whipped around the ax helve, and a muffled curse as it bound hand to ashwood. The sickle struck his forearm in a way that would have laid it open to the bone if the sharp blade hadn't been encased in its leather sheath.

He pulled back, trying to free the haft and throwing his far greater weight and raw strength against hers through the metal link. Mary came with the pull and at the same instant the other end of the chain wrapped around the man's knees, whirling itself into a tangle with the steel ball thudding into his thigh muscle with paralyzing force. He began to buckle forward; Mary's booted feet struck him neatly in the stomach, her back hit the ground, and she used his own momentum to throw him roaring over her head with an arching twist and pivot.

There was a heavy, meaty *thud* as he landed in a patch of last night's snow not yet trampled or stained. It puffed up around him in a cloud of glittering crystal, and through it Mary pounced with a cat-screech of Sindarin that Rudi translated without effort:

"So long, sucker!"

She landed astraddle the man, her long narrow dagger out and hovering above his eye. He glared at her for a moment and then his lips quirked up in a smile. That turned into a roar of laughter, and he threw his arms wide in a theatrical gesture of surrender.

"Hrolf Homersson gives you best, shield-maiden! I give you best. What a pity you're wedded already!"

Mary simply snorted as she rose and helped him untangle himself. Ritva sauntered over and put her hands on her hips as she watched.

"I'm not," she pointed out with cheerful helpfulness. "Are you, Hrolf Homersson? Not that I'm proposing, you understand."

Ingolf came back from his task, working his shoulders. He spoke to Mary in the elven tongue, slowly and a bit clumsily:

"Herves"—wife—*"you can throw me on my back and leap upon me when you will, but I may grow resentful if you do it to other men . . . unless there's a dagger in your hand."*

"Herven"—husband—*"with you I will use not the dagger of war for your eye, but the feather-duster of tickling for your man parts!"*

Virginia Kane was demonstrating what you could do with a lariat from horseback; seeing one of their dodging, running number caught and dragged a few yards was another way to tickle the Bjorning funny bone, evidently.

"Their sense of a jest is something . . . robust, here," Rudi observed.

"I like it well enough," Edain said.

"*That's* no surprise. You near killed yourself laughing that time the cow I was milking caught me in the face with a well-beshatted tail."

Edain snickered at the memory. "Chief, a man in his eightieth summer would have thought that funny, and him dead also, much less a boy! The expression on you! *And* you rubbed dung in my hair, as I remember, and we were both covered head to foot by the time we'd stopped scuffling like a pair of puppies."

Rudi sighed reminiscently. "And then your da came out and took us by the ears and pitched us both into the pond," he said. "Lucky it was that was a warm day and we weren't wearing anything but old kilts."

Edain shuddered. "Lucky indeed, Chief. *You* ran back up the hill to Dun Juniper. *I* had to face me mother!"

Just then Harberga came back out the door and called, smiling:

"If the children are finished their play, the meal is ready!"

A herald more formal came out of the main doors of

the hall and blew the summoning horn, a long harsh *huuuuuuuuuu* through the cold air.

The twin doors were twice man-height, thick oak slabs strapped with iron on either side of a framework of beams, and at the end of the long rectangular structure. The roof above towered high and steep-pitched; the gable beams crossed in snarling dragonheads above the snowy shingles, and a steady trickle of smoke came from the mortared fieldstone chimneys. Pillars on either side of the entranceway were carved in a strong stylized style.

The shapes were a red-bearded man who bore a hammer and a woman with a distaff and hair of bright gold; gold covered the elk antlers above. Within was a square stone-flagged chamber ringed with benches, trunks, pegs and racks where outer clothes and weapons could be left. Rudi was wearing his good kilt and plaid beneath his winter gear today—a kilt wasn't as warm as trousers, but it was more than enough for a while, if you had drawers on beneath.

He offered his arm to Mathilda as they went through the inner doors to the hall proper, and she took it.

"Father Ignatius is going to duck out later," she said.

"And you're not, my heart?"

"No. I . . . want to see. It isn't like *participating*, after all."

Is it not? he thought, but kept his silence. *Well, that's between him and you at your next confession.*

Bjarni had seated Rudi at his right, and Mathilda at the Mackenzie's side; those were positions of honor, and let him talk to the Bjorning chieftain. Evergreen boughs in wreaths on walls and rafters scented the air, and a decorated fir tree stood tall in the center. The feast was to be long and leisurely. Rudi enjoyed it—potato soup, roast pork, braised red cabbage, more potatoes prepared in half a dozen ways, a meat pie not quite like anything he'd tasted before—

"Now that's not beef, nor venison either, I think," he said thoughtfully after he'd chewed and swallowed; the ground meat was mixed with minced onion and some herbs, and it had a musky undertone, not exactly rank but strong. "Though it's more *like* venison or elk than any tame beast I've had."

He plied his fork again: "Tasty!"

"Moosemeat tortiere," Harberga said, smiling at his enthusiasm. "Most households here take a moose in the fall, when the frosts set in; we make all the pies then and freeze them in the cold pantry for use all winter. There's near half a ton of meat on a big moose, and the bones and sinew and hide are all useful too, but they take a good deal of killing."

Bjarni's eyes lit and went to one of the spears on the wall; it was a long hunter's weapon, with wings forged into the base of the head to prevent an irate beast from running up it to express one last opinion of the human who'd stuck it.

"Yes, that's fine sport," he said enthusiastically. "None better, except bear or tiger—and the stripe-cats are still rare here. There weren't any at all in this country when my father founded Norrheim; they came up later from the troll-lands."

A scowl: "And too many of them are man-eaters by choice. Bears leave humans alone, usually, and so do wolves—though they'll both eat our stock, ayuh! But the tigers are a menace, and there are more every year."

"They're common in Montival, unpleasantly so some-times," Rudi replied.

Mathilda leaned across and touched the tip of Rudi's nose; there was a tiny, barely visible fleck of scar there.

"I was there when a tiger did that to Rudi with the very end of one claw," she said proudly. "He held it away on a spear until it died."

"It was already wounded," Rudi said lightly.

Then a faraway look came into his eyes. "Remember those lions we came across in the Sioux country?"

"Lions?" Bjarni asked, intrigued. "I've heard of them, but there are none here. Too cold in winter, I suppose."

"Probably too many trees, as well; the beasts don't like close forest. They're spreading north from the desert countries, from the Rio Grande. We were being chased at the time, and sort of ran into them, and through them, at a gallop. It was lucky, in the event—they'd just had time to get good and angry when our foemen arrived expecting to cut our throats and found the lions instead . . ."

Bjarni and his wife chuckled, and so did the rest of the Bjornings within hearing; evidently *that* appealed to the Norrheimer sense of humor too.

"What's an angry lion like?" he asked.

"Every bit as nasty as an angered tiger, and they run in packs like wolves. You"—he pointed his fork at Mathilda—"wanted to keep that cub as a pet!"

"It was *cute*," Mathilda said.

"It was *young*. I've had many a shrewd scratch from ordinary moggies who meant no real harm. One that weighed three hundred pounds, with claws like knives . . ."

They spoke more and pleasantly, of hunting and then local lore; evidently Norrheim was a loose federation of quasi-independent chieftainships, each heading a tribe comprised of *bondar*—yeomen—who pledged allegiance to a *godhi* of their choice, who lead them in war and sacrifice and presided at assembly. The farmers changed the allegiance if it suited them; Mathilda looked faintly scandalized at that, but held her peace about it. Local folkmoots called *things* met each spring to hear cases and vote on laws, and an *Althing* in the summer did the same for the whole. Eriksgarth was the senior chieftainship, its master head of the Bjornings, and home of the *Althing's* meeting ground.

They didn't take a census here, but Rudi estimated from what his host said that the Norrheim folk were about as numerous as the Clan Mackenzie; threescore thousand or a little more, and growing fast, more by births now than by outsiders joining.

"My father made us a people," Bjarni said proudly. "He knew what must be done—when to speak, when to show an example, and when to break heads. Folk who were cast adrift in a world made strange saw it. Others of his Bjorning kindred who came north with him became *godhi* of their own tribes too, as he set them here or there to help put the land in order. I remember a little of the beginning of it; I was six when the Change came, and we left Springfield. That was a thorpe near Boston."

"Boston!" Ingolf said, from the other side of the chieftain. "I've been to Boston . . . if your father made his escape from *there*, and took his people with him, then.he was some sort of a man."

The lamps were lit on their iron wheels and hoisted up the pillars as the evening proceeded; there was unstinted food, drink, song—Rudi came to keenest attention as a harper performed—stories sad or merry or moving— and chanted ancestral epic:

"There was a man named Orm the Strong, a son of Ketil

Asmundsson who was a yeoman in the north of Jutland; and this was before the Dane-lands were one kingdom. The folk of Ketil had dwelt there as long as men remembered, and held broad acres. The wife of Ketil was Asgerd, who was a leman-child of Ragnar Lothbrok. Thus Orm came of good stock on both spear and distaff sides, but as he was the fifth living son of his father he could look for no great inheritance. So Orm was a seafarer, and from his youth spent most of his summers in viking—"

The ways and arts here didn't have Dun Juniper's quick bright shifting glitter, with its ever-present tang of the Otherworld. But there was a deep steady sonorous music to it all, one that had its own harsh magic and strong-boned beauty and spoke to his blood.

Eventually, Bjarni rose—for the first time since the feast started, except once when he'd darted over to quiet two half-drunken brawlers by the simple expedient of grabbing their necks and banging their heads together hard enough to make Rudi wince. Their friends had laid them out under the tables, and the rest had gone on unconcerned with the fallen serving as footstools. Now he hammered the hilt of his seax on the table, and silence fell, more or less; he spoke into it.

"Bjornings, and guests come from far lands! Tonight our luck is strong. The *seidhkona* Heidhveig has come to Eriksgarth and will take the High Seat of prophecy and speak. Let all here behave in seemly wise, as do true men and true women."

Men moved the table before them, and placed a high carved chair with arms on the dais before the hearth. Heidhveig entered from the door that led to the house; Rudi had seen little of her until now, and his hosts had merely said that she rested and felt out the wights—which was what the Norrheim folk called the spirits of place.

Now she paced slowly through the hall, an old woman in a midnight-blue cloak and gown with a cap of black lambskin. Her wrought staff went *thunk . . . thunk . . .* as she walked down the row of pillars, helped by a stern-faced middle-aged woman and several others who were younger but nearly as serious.

"Who's the other woman with a staff?" Rudi murmured.

"Thorlind Williamsdottir—she really runs the *seidh* group these days. She was one of the first ones Heidhveig trained as a *gydhja*, a godwoman."

Mathilda started to cross herself, then refrained; it would be impolite, under the circumstances. Instead she touched the place on her tunic where the crucifix rested below. The helpers set another box on the dais so that the old woman could climb onto the elevated seat; it had a cushion embroidered with ravens, and two carved from wood stood on the seat back. The younger *gydhja* sat on a low stool next to the tall *seidhjallr*, the Chair of Magic. Heidhveig held her staff between her knees, gripping it with both gnarled hands as if it were an anchor planted in the ground.

Bjarni's sister Gudrun took a basin of water and moved around the great room, sprinkling each one with drops flicked from a twig and murmuring:

> *"With water from the Well of Wyrd*
> *All ill that has been;*
> *All ill now becoming;*
> *All ill that shall be;*
> *I banish away."*

The younger godwoman took a drum and began to beat it; a walrus-ivory ring skittered across the taut surface, making the beat throb with a burring tone that filled the hall. She spoke from her stool, her voice low and hieratic:

> *"This hall is hallowed for Heimdall's children,*
> *Safe we sit at the sacred center.*
> *Who will dare the waiting darkness?*
> *Who will walk the way of wisdom?"*

"I will," Heidhveig said.

The seeress' voice was hoarse but strong. Rudi felt the skin prickle on his neck and between his shoulders as she pulled the thin veil draped around her shoulders over her head, so that it hid her face. When Thorlind spoke again, her words seemed to come from a depth—from a cave, perhaps, or a wildwood, or simply from the deeps of time:

"Sink down, then, and be at ease. You know the road well, the way through the Wood between the Worlds, and the plain of Midgard that lies within. Fare onward, wise one, down and around beneath the root of the Tree . . ."

Rudi found his own eyes closing, images forming behind them as the woman went on, leading them from world to world and depth to depth, to the very walls of Hella's kingdom, that he had never expected to see as a living man.

"Down and around we fare, until we come to the Eastern Gate. Here we must wait. For one and one only the gate will open . . ."

Rudi sighed, resisting the unexpected attraction of that passage to the Otherworld. He could feel Matti sitting stiff beside him, and squeezed her hand, as much to keep himself firmly grounded as to comfort her.

Thorlind spoke again:

*"The gate to knowledge gapes before us.
Seeress, is it your will to go through?"*

"It is," the seeress said.

Thorlind began to sing; one by one the rest of the Bjornings joined in. The tune was strange, full of odd sharps. It had a feel of ancientry to it, like old stone still strong but covered in moss and worn with the rains and frost of countless years:

*"Seeress, thy way through the worlds thou must win,
Farther and faster and deeper within,
Fare onward, ever onward, ever on."*

Then she spoke sharply: "Tell us what thou dost see?"
Heidhveig's voice was distant, as if she told of a dream:

*"I see the dark lake and on it the black swan swim-
ming.
On the shore many fires are burning.
The ancestors are awake and waiting.
What would you know?"*

Thorlind chanted:

*"The spell is spoken, the Seeress waits—
Is there one here who would ask a question?"*

For a long moment Rudi thought nobody would; the tension in the hall was palpable, almost like a taste of something sharp and acrid at the back of the mouth. Eyes gleamed in the shadows about.

Then the *godhi* stood. He cleared his throat and spoke in a voice that carried through the hall:

"I've a dispute with the men of the Hrossings. Both tribes have used the land between the Old West Road and Blood Creek for pasture in the summer and for hunting, but our numbers grow and we need to clear and till land there. Bjorning steadings are closer and the empty land should be ours alone, at least as far as the river. How shall we end this quarrel? Will *Godhi* Syfrid see reason, or shall we take it to the *Althing* and the law-speakers? Or must swords be drawn?"

The *gydhja* spoke:

> *"Cease not, seeress, till said thou hast,*
> *Answer the asker till all he knows."*

"I see the autumn woods," Heidhveig said, her voice distant. "The stags are fighting. They clash their antlers, tear up the soil, grunting and heaving. The does are watching. Oh . . . there are wolves in the woods. They circle and leap, carry off some of the does . . ."

There was a sharp intake of breath in the Hall, and a moment of silence before the seeress went on. Her voice was less distant now, as if she had come halfway back to the world of men:

"I see now the meaning. You and Syfrid are so busy butting heads you don't see what's going on around you."

The tension broke in laughter; Bjarni flushed but flung up a hand for silence, and the seeress went on:

"Watch out, or the human wolves will destroy what you're fighting over."

There was a ripple of comment in the hall; Rudi thought he heard approval.

"Ask for a meeting. You may have to give up something to make peace, but that's better than losing all. It's an ill time for good Norrheim men to draw blades on each other. This you know, would you know more?"

"Thank you, seeress," Bjarni said dryly. "I think I understand . . ."

The *gydhja* spoke, her tone formal: "Well hast thou asked and well been answered. Is there another who has a question?"

A woman stood, young enough that some of the awkwardness of girlhood still clung about her. Rudi would have judged her to be two years short of Edain's twenty. Loose hair of a dark yellow color like old honey fell past her shoulders, confined by a headband, which probably meant by the custom of these folk that she was unwedded; at least, most of the women older than she wore theirs braided and bound. Her hands knotted in front of her until she forced them still, licked her lips and stood proudly erect, ignoring the eyes upon her and the murmur of surprise. When she spoke her voice was firm and clear, though light:

"Sigurd Jeansson, called the Bold, my betrothed, has been gone since the fall harvest. He went north in viking with the men of Westmanland-thorpe to seek tools and trade goods in the dead cities, so that we might take up land and make our own homestead this spring at snowmelt, and be wed. When will he return to me?"

The *gydhja* chanted:

"Cease not, seeress, till said thou hast,
Answer the asker till all she knows."

Heidhveig sighed and bent her head beneath the veil. "I call the raven to my aid and take her form. Together

we wing northward over mountain and forest and lake. I
see a mighty river, and on its banks bare-branched trees
beneath a sky like steel; ice floats in the water. A great
bridge of the old world spans the broad flood, half fallen,
and the current foams beneath it. Tall fire-scorched ruins
rise on an island to the west. Was it to the Royal Mountain that he was to have gone?"

"Yes."

"I can see boats on the river, a long canoe heavy with
cargo, the Hammer painted on it and eight paddlers
within. One is tall and ruddy, with black hair and a war
sark of dark leather sewn with steel rings; he has a scar
that turns a streak in his beard white. Is this your man?"

The girl nodded, and the *seidhkona* continued:

"The other boats pursue it. They are many and fierce,
some with their faces painted, some with strings of fin-
gerbones about their necks. A man in a red robe with a
rayed sun upon his breast leads them."

Rudi's breath hissed between his teeth. *I know your
mark, ill-wreaker!* he thought savagely.

The voice of the seeress went on:

"They are shooting arrows—"

The girl gasped and stretched out a hand to the table
to support herself. Her fair skin went chalk white, and her
eyes very wide.

"Men fall in the canoe that flees; it slows, it cannot
escape. It turns and drives towards the boats that pursue.
More arrows fly, and then spears and hatchets. The man
in the ring-sark takes up a great ax and leaps into the
boats of those that harry him, into the midst of many
foes. He is laughing as he strikes, he calls on the Allfather
to receive him—"

The old woman fell silent again, then went on with a
curious gentleness:

"If this is the boat your man was in, I fear he will not return to you. I am sorry. There is no more."

The girl shook. Her voice choked as she spoke:

"All men are born fey. My Sigurd met his fate unflinching and feasts this Yule with the *einherjar* in Vallhol—"

The words stumbled into a moan, and her face twisted as she struggled and then gave way to thick tears, and her knees buckled. Two older women caught her, and helped her from the room amid a murmur of sympathy.

The *gydhja* spoke, her words formal but with concern in her tone: "How fares the seeress?"

"Well enough to continue. I sense there is need in this room, questions that must be asked and answered. Go on!"

"Is there another who has a question?"

A man rose; he was in his thirties, weather-beaten and thick-bodied. "I've cleared old scrubland for a new field on my steading, land not planted since the Change; I've grubbed up and burned the brush and spread the ashes and plowed them under. It lies fallow beneath the snow. Should I seed it with barley when spring comes?"

Rudi suppressed a wry smile. It seemed a little odd, after the last . . .

But it isn't. That man has put his own sweat into the work, and his family's well-being depends upon the results.

Thorlinda chanted:

"Cease not, seeress, till said thou hast,
Answer the asker till all he knows."

The *seidhkona* spoke in a cooler voice:

"Hmm. I can see a field where a crowd of green-clad folk are dancing, but as they circle, others clad in black attack them and most of them fall. I think this means that if you plant there, a blight will get most of your crop. Would you know more?"

The thickset man swallowed, but answered calmly: "Is there anything I can do?"

"I am looking at the barley wights . . . I am asking . . . He says to make offerings to the landwights there. Ask their help, sing to them, and they will tell you what the field needs. This you know. For now there is no more."

"Thank you, seeress."

Thorlind spoke: "Well hast thou asked and well been answered. Is there another who has a question?

Others asked, and were answered. Rudi took a long breath when silence fell, then stood. He was uneasily aware of how the attention of all focused on him.

But this is a true seeing. I must know!

"My friends and I are on a . . . quest. Will we reach our goal safely, and find what we are seeking when we get there?"

"Cease not, seeress, till said thou hast,
Answer the asker till all he knows."

The *seidhkona* was silent for a long moment, then sighed. The sound made the back of Rudi's neck bristle; this was not a rite of his folk, but there was a power here, like a weight greater than the world could bear. As if it would tear *through* at any moment. And more coming; he could feel it gathering in the air, like the stretched tension before a thunderstorm.

"Ah . . . *This* is the one for whose question I was waiting, the one whose wyrd is wound with the fate of the world. At the foot of the Tree the Norns are weaving, but your choices are the thread. Need has bound you together, need impels you. Stay true to one another and you will find your island . . . I see an island, and something that shimmers."

The veiled figure gasped: "*I see a Sword!* Shining brightness! Might is locked within it! Is that where you are going? This is very strange . . . Would you know more?"

"Yes, Lady, if you will."

"Deeper I fare and farther I see . . . A darkness that opposes you there, a troll in the shape of a man. Beware, Son of the Raven! There is a Power behind him, more foul than any Jotun. If you fail, I see the doom of Midgard. You have questioned whether this was the Wolf Age—if this quest fails, Ragnarök will come!"

Her knotted hands clenched, and he could hear her labored breathing: "Would you know more?!"

"How fares—" Thorlinda began.

The *seidhkona* shook her head, a stir through the fabric of the veil.

"No—there is more to be said. This is a war of Powers. The wings of the raven swirl around me . . . oh . . . the Lord of the Ravens is near, near . . ."

Rudi heard his own heart pound, took a deep breath and let it out slowly. He was not ill and dreaming in a mountain cave now, and it was a fearful thing to meet that One.

"Does He have a word for me?" he said steadily.

The *seidhkona* twitched several times, straightened, and then leaned forward, resting one elbow on the arm of the chair.

A rustling stirred through the room, almost a moan. Rudi stood calmly, his hands by his sides, but he knew why that sound had been wrung from this hardy folk—and felt his hand twitch in turn, as if it reached for the hilt of a blade that was not there and would be no use even if it was. The Bjorning seeress was a woman of eighty years and more, never tall and now a little bent, stocky like an ancient oak stump, her body still obedient to a fierce and driving will but failing nonetheless.

Yet now it was as if a man sat there—a tall man, whose movements were fluid strength, and whose face was hidden by a hood, not a veil. He laughed, and the deep sound made the hair stir on Rudi's arms, a long low chuckle rolling inhuman in the nighted Hall. Shadows gathered, moving on the walls with the dance of the flames.

"So, Son of the Bear," the voice said. "I see that you remember our last meeting, on the mountainside where you walked the blade-narrow bridge. I have counseled many a chieftain. What would you ask of me?"

Rudi licked his lips and met that gaze. The Old Man was no enemy to him . . . but he was perilous even to his friends.

"If I gain the Sword of the Lady, will I defeat this enemy?" he asked boldly.

"To gain the Sword will not bring certain victory, but defeat is certain if you fail. Yet victory for your cause may be your own bane, Artos, King to be."

Ah. When speaking with a God, don't ask things you already know!

"I understand that choice, lord. I have accepted it. I will do what must be done, and pay the price of it gladly, for my folk's sake, and for this fair world that the Gods have given humankind to be our cherished home."

A rustle, and Mathilda stood beside him. Rudi started a little, taken from the diamond focus of his concentration; her fists were clenched at her sides, and her breast heaved, but her voice was controlled and he knew the courage that must have demanded. The more so as her faith held such suspicion of all spirits save their own.

"And does Rudi get nothing? If there is . . . if there must be . . . does he get no mercy, no reward for his courage?"

The hooded face turned towards her, and Rudi thought he heard a tinge of kindness in its stern tone.

For boldness is something this One loves, he thought. *And there is no braver heart than my Matti!*

"Mercy is not in my gift, Frigga-of-battle," the Power that had possessed the Bjorning wisewoman said. "Neither for myself nor for those who call on me for victory. I can give a little time, but within that time only you can grant this man the reward he desires, the reward the *man* desires, and not the King. Be brave, be true, and you shall lay his son in his arms!"

"King!" Rudi heard someone mutter, as Mathilda staggered back and sat, stunned. *"The Wanderer grants the stranger kingship from his own hand!"*

The voice of the one on the high seat went on:

"The Bear's Son is not my man, though one of those who rides with him is—and worthy of me he shall be, and worthy of his warrior sire, when he avenges his father's death!"

Frederick Thurston bowed; his dark face glowed, as if seeing beyond the walls of Eriksgarth to a path that led upward. Upward across a bridge sparkling with color, beneath gigantic stars, towards roofs thatched with spears of glittering gold where auroras crackled. Beside him Virginia grasped his arm, glaring at the speaker as if she would spring to protect her man even from *this*, and the voice chuckled again before it continued.

"But though he does not make offering to me, the man

called Artos comes of blood that bears much might; the blood of the Juniper Lady in which runs wisdom from beyond the world of men, the blood his father shed willingly to stand between his folk and their foes, dying and yet in death winning the victory that brought them peace. The Son of the Bear shall add to that might, for he is fated to great deeds. If he wins his victory, his shall be a line of Kings that lives long in glory and forever in the tales of men. If he fails, all fail with him; and then comes the doom of Midgard."

The speaker's head turned, and the folk in the hall bore it as they could, meeting it or turning their heads aside or covering their eyes.

"All of you! If you would stand with the Gods, then I bid you help him. The sword he seeks is more potent than Tyrfing, forged for the hand of a King!"

Only breath disturbed the stillness. "So, Son of Bear, Son of Raven, High King of a realm called Montival that is yet to be and may never be—is that what you wanted to know?"

Rudi shook his head. "The Crow Goddess gives me battle fury, but even the gift of the Dark Mother may not be enough against this foe. Will you, lord, give me battle craft to face him?"

The laugh rumbled again, more gently this time:

"Wise is he who asks for wisdom! That gift, at least, is within my power. Watch for the ravens. They will show you the way."

Rudi bowed for a moment. "Thank you, lord. And when my victory is won and I sit on the throne of the *Ard Rí* in Montival, always shall you and yours have welcome and honor in my lands."

Thorlind the godwoman spoke; her voice wavered between fright and firmness:

"Allfather, we thank you also, but be kind to the seeress, who loves you. Please let her go now, gently, without harm—"

She rose and stood before the chair as the *seidhkona* first straightened and then sagged, and caught her as she slumped forward. Love and terror and pride warred in her voice as she spoke:

"Heidhveig, Heidhveig, my teacher, come back to us, please. That's right—"

The limp form of the old woman stirred, and a hoarse sound came from beneath what was once more a veil. Thorlind's words grew stronger:

"The vision fades, the voice grows silent. Return now, wise one, where we wait to welcome . . . Can you see the Gate? Raven will lead you towards it. Good, now you're through—Let's just get you out of this chair . . . "

Bjarni Eriksson moved forward to help her. They eased the seeress out of the *seidhjallr* and into an ordinary chair. Harberga brought a glass of water and held it to Heidhveig's mouth. The *gydhja* picked up the drum again struck it, the taut hide thuttering:

> *"Now it is time to return. Arise,*
> *Move swiftly and easily, pass around the wall*
> *From the east to the north, from gate to bridge.*
> *Now it is before you, broad and fair.*
> *Cross and ascend the road*
> *Up and around, past Modhgudh's tower . . ."*

Swiftly the journey was completed. Thorlind and the men who'd come with them helped their mistress down from the dais and away to her bed in the house. A rising babble of voices rang out with an edge of hysteria in them, until Bjarni leaped up to the dais and roared:

"Quiet!"

The redbeard's chin thrust out as his eyes went back and forth over his folk, cold and blue. When silence fell he put his hands on his sword belt and spoke bitingly:

"We've heard the words of the High One, through the holy *seidhkona*. He spoke of great deeds—of war and maybe even Ragnarök. Whatever happens, we will meet it—meet it like Bjornings, like free men and women of Norrheim, not like chattering magpies or frightened children! All men die; in the end, even the Gods shall die. The *seidhkona* is old and deserves rest, but she went under death's shadow to bring us this word. Honor her courage with courage of your own!"

The hall fell quiet again, but there was less tension in it.

"Now go and sleep, and think about what we've heard."

He jumped down and walked to Rudi before he spoke again, quietly:

"And you and I, my friend, will think and then we will talk. There are things I must know, if I am to steer wisely . . . and mine is the hand on the tiller here."

"And I will tell them gladly, Bjarni," Rudi said.

Then he smiled. "You can see that there's more than one spoon in this stewpot, and some of them of an exceeding longness!"

Talk they did, and after a night's sleep they spoke into the next day, when Heidhveig joined them; she looked better than Rudi had expected in body, and less nerve-wracked than many others in Eriksgarth by the foreseeing.

"You're well, I hope, Lady?" he said, rising and bowing as her pupil helped her towards the hearth.

She grinned at him, indomitable. "At my age, you're either well or dead. I'm not dead yet. This is just an act to get a handsome young man like you to give me an arm."

He stepped forward and put an arm beneath her hand; it gripped him like a handful of walnuts. He guided her into the cushioned armchair nearest the fire, with Thorlind on the other side. Despite the light words, he could hear her breath whistle a little between clenched teeth as she sank down into the seat. Thorlind fussed with a rug she tucked around. The old woman pushed her hands aside with a good-natured chiding:

"We're in front of the *fireplace*!"

"We were telling my story," Rudi said, as he took seat again across from her. "And trying not to let it go back to the beginning of the world, so! Well, you'll need to know a little of how the Change took us, in the High West—though I was born about this season of the first Change Year. Born on a battlefield, near enough—"

He sketched it in. The details were unfamiliar to them, and what tales had crossed the continent were hopelessly garbled, but the gist of it seemed easy enough to grasp; it was not altogether different from what they or their parents had experienced.

"Lady Juniper!" the seeress said, at one point. "Juniper Mackenzie . . . Tell me, boy—she's short and slight, is she, and with hair brighter red than a fox, green eyes, and a voice like water flowing by moonlight? With a County Mayo brogue she could put on when she wished, that she learned from *her* mother, and you learned from her?"

"You know my mother?" Rudi said, stopping in an astonishment shared by the others. "You've *met* her?"

Then he smiled and slapped his forehead. "Oh! From before the Change?"

"Yes. She used to play with the consort Siobhan ni hEodhusa put together for the Principality of the Mists. It was a great loss to the Kingdom of the West when she moved north again. If anyone lived, she would. But you say that nothing is left in California?" she added wistfully.

"I fear not, except in the most remote mountain parts of the north and east," Rudi said gently. "It was . . . very bad there, from what the Dúnedain explorers have found of late."

"So Kalk saw in *his* vision, before the Change. So my heart said," she said. "That's why I and my family moved here, and just in time."

Then she shook her head and looked shrewdly at Mathilda.

"And your father was Norman Arminger, and your mother Sandra, girl?"

Mathilda nodded warily; her parents had collected enemies, and though they hadn't spoken often of the old world she'd heard rumors enough.

Heidhveig laughed shortly. "And Norman ended up cutting himself out a kingdom from the chaos at the sword's edge? *Why* am I not surprised."

"He was Lord Protector," Mathilda said. "He died in battle . . . well, to tell you the truth, he and Rudi's father killed each other in single combat . . . when I was ten."

"Your sires killed each other?" Bjarni said, a brow going up.

Rudi spread his hands: "But not before we'd sworn the oath of *anamchara* . . . which made us as soul brother and soul sister."

"Ah," the Bjorning said. "Yes, sometimes one duty has more might than another. Also, a fair fight that men chose freely . . . well, that may end a feud, not start one."

Mathilda nodded and went on: "My mother . . . Sandra is Lady Regent now, until I'm of age . . . twenty-six that is. A few months less than two years from now. She held things together in Portland after he died."

"Why am I even *less* surprised at that?" Heidhveig said dryly.

"You, ah, knew them, Lady? You were in the Society?"

"You might say that . . ." she said wryly. "But that was another world—literally. I had another name then. I was another *person* then, and not just because I was a lot younger."

Then, softly for a moment: "That world went down in ice and fire and terror, before you two were born. Let all the old feuds die with it. From what you say, Norman and Sandra did great things, deeds terrible and grand, that few others could have accomplished. For good and ill both."

Farther down the hall, Odard Liu and Ritva Havel were playing their lutes, a crowd of appreciative Bjornings surrounding them—they knew the guitar here, and the harp, but didn't seem to have many lutists. The baron's voice rose in a song he'd composed some time ago, but with altered words. Mathilda flushed a little to hear it:

"The ones who rule over our fair land of Montival
They reign just and wisely, without favor or fear
And no truer lady trod on this good earth
So let the hall ring for the Light of the North!
Let the hall ring for the Princess of Montival—
Let the hall ring for the Light of the North!

"She matches in honor the Prince of our Montival
To all of her subjects she lends a kind ear

Lady by grace, and Princess by birth!
So let the hall ring for the Light of the North!
So let the hall ring for the Princess Mathilda—
So let the hall ring for the Light of the North!

"She carries a sword for the honor of Montival
Before her in battle our foes flee in fear
With her inspiration our knights will charge forth
So let the hall ring for the Light of the North!
So let the hall ring for the Princess of Montival—
So let the hall ring for the Light of the North!"

"He thinks he's a troubadour," she said apologetically, as cheers greeted the song.

"Well, then he probably is," Heidhveig said. "I've heard far, far worse."

She reached across with the staff and prodded Rudi's bare knee below the kilt. "Go on, lad, go on."

Rudi cleared his throat; more than any women he'd met besides his mother and Matti's, Heidhveig seemed able to make him feel like a boy again without even trying.

"Well, two years ago—two years and a month, it was Samhain Eve, and that an omen in itself—Ingolf here rode into Sutterdown, the Clan's only town, having as he thought shaken off the Prophet's men in the passes of the Cascades. They were waiting for him instead, disguised as harmless travelers, and—"

"That's a wild tale," Bjarni said when it was finished, shaking his head. "I wouldn't credit half of it, if it weren't for the *seidhkona*. Even so, it'll take a while to settle my mind around it. How large the world is! How little our share of it seems now, that was so broad yesterday!"

She looked at Rudi: "The Church Universal and Triumphant, eh? I knew a little about them before the Change. They were . . . strange . . . and obnoxious sometimes . . . but they didn't traffic with malevolence or try to turn men into less than beasts. They've been corrupted, to serve the enemies of humankind . . . and of the Gods."

"Corrupted by who?" Rudi asked.

Bjarni shivered a little, and his wife laid a hand on her belly over the child.

"Asa-Loki, 'neath the mountain, chained and raging . . ." Harberga quoted softly.

Heidhveig nodded. "As good a name as any. And unless they're stopped, even one as old as I may yet live long enough to see that One riding with a face of poison to Vigrid Plain, on the last morning of the world."

Father Ignatius nodded crisply and signed himself. "Good *will* triumph over evil in the end," he said. "But it doesn't happen without us working and, yes, fighting for it. Nor is any victory certain until the last days."

Rudi shivered slightly, staring into the fire where white flames danced over the red glow of the coals.

"I've had . . . visions. Some, I think, of what the world might have been if the Change had not come. Some of what might yet be, if the CUT triumphs. Both . . . bad. Very bad indeed. And their common feature that *men* no longer walk the earth, though in some of them things in our shape do. In others, the very soil and air are dead."

"I've seen those too," Ingolf said, his battered hands clenching on his knees. "Only on Nantucket, though. God . . . Gods . . . that was weird! But I saw things in Corwin while I was a prisoner there that were enough to turn your stomach; and things that would make your hair crawl, things that just shouldn't *be*. They've got plans for the world and I wouldn't want them to come true. Those breeding pits—" He shuddered.

"Then we must see that they don't come true," Mathilda put in.

Bjarni's big capable hands gripped the arms of his chair.

"I know that the *seidhkona's* vision was the truth. Thor's Hammer, I *heard* it! I'm a true man; I'll stand with the Gods—which means with you, Rudi—with all my main and my might. But I can't call on every fighting man in Norrheim to march a thousand miles and more to battle an enemy they've never heard of. They'd hoot me off the Thingstone! And—"

He looked at his wife again; love and pain were at war in the glance they shared.

Rudi nodded. "You can't leave your steadings and families unguarded. I wouldn't expect you to."

Bjarni's mouth quirked. "The Wanderer is at home everywhere and nowhere; he has all the world of Midgard to ward and all the sons and daughters of Ash and Embla to guide, and more besides. But this"—his gesture took in the hall, and the lands beyond—"is *my* world, my tribe and folk, the world my father built, the one I want to hand on to my children when I lay my bones beneath the howe. Yes, and watch over afterwards."

His fist pounded the arm of his chair. "But what does it matter if I guard the borders of Norrheim now, and in a generation or two or three etin-craft and troll-men flood over us like a tide!"

Rudi tapped a finger on his chin: "I think there was more than one message in the seeing you made, lady Heidhveig; and more than one meaning to every message. A certain One we've both met is crafty and subtle. You may not have noticed, Bjarni, but the . . . Old Man's . . . word was not the only part of the vision you need to ponder."

At Bjarni's surprised look he went on: "That unfortunate honey-haired lass who lost her man north of here? Well, that's the way we've come, and the Cutters have been at work there too; hence the man in the red robe with the sun sign on it. That was an adept, an evil magus . . ."

"A *trollkjerring*, we would say," Heidhveig said.

Rudi nodded: "Stirring up the wild bands, those you deem troll-men, so. They'll move those against you, I would guess. What other dwellers there are in that country are few and weak, and the Prophet's ambitions are not limited to Montival. Corwin aims to bring all of humankind under their sway in the end."

Bjarni had looked . . . not fearful, but apprehensive, before. Now his face firmed into a thing of slabs and angles; that was a threat he could understand in gut and bone.

"You see as clearly as Heimdall! *That* I can tell the *Althing,* and be believed!"

"And that will serve our common cause," Rudi said. "Otherwise those men will fall on allies of ours, and enemies of the Enemy, farther west."

"But as for *us*, we need to get to Nantucket," Mathilda said. "Your, ah, High One himself said it. Without the Sword of the Lady, we'll surely lose. Mary, intercede for us!"

"The old tales have a number of such swords in them," Ignatius said, half as if to himself. "Many were born by paladins of the Light. Arthur's Excalibur, of course. Durendal, that Roland bore at Roncevalles against the infidel. Perhaps they were less metaphorical and more substantial than my teachers thought. I don't think the pagan elements matter, in the end."

"Tyrfing," Harberga said. "Though I'm glad it's not *that* blade."

"Getting to Nantucket . . . there *I* can help you," Heidhveig said. "I came out here with my family before the Change because of a . . . feeling you might say; and because Kalk told me he foresaw a great troubling of the world while I was dickering with him over a harp."

Rudi couldn't quite hold back a blink of surprise. Heidhveig smiled and stroked one knotted hand over another.

"Yes, I made music once. I stayed with Kalk and his people at the coast through the first month after the Change, before Erik Waltersson arrived; Kalk was pagan too, and a student of the old crafts, and I put them in touch with each other when I heard the Bjornings had come."

"From which meeting many deeds came in turn," Bjarni said.

Heidhveig nodded. "I stay there still when I'm not traveling between garths working *seidh* . . . or just visiting the great-grandchildren, nowadays."

"He's called Kalk the Shipwright," Bjarni said. "He makes ships and much else, at the garth he built by the sea after the Change."

His hand indicated the carved pillars of the hall, and the grim magnificence on the walls; by implication, the dragonheads that reared proud from rafter and roof-tree outside.

"All the finest woodworkers in Norrheim trained with him and his folk. They've cunning smiths and fine weavers there too, and wise in many other arts. Kalk collects craft skill, as some men do gold or horses or fine weapons; and his sons and grandsons are the same."

Heidhveig took up the tale. "The Shipwright's men are great traders and fishermen, and often in viking . . ."

Rudi's eyebrows went up, and she chuckled.

"Oh, that's changed meaning here. They go to the dead cities and hunt for goods they can use or barter. As far as New York, sometimes."

"Hmmm." Ingolf rubbed his short-cropped beard. "I was in the same trade, though overland; I think we were the only Midwesterners to reach the east coast and survive. So far, at least. Vikings? You'd need something like that. Salvage work's . . . well, there are treasures, right enough, but yah, they're hard to get at. I can see why you used that word."

Bjarni shrugged. "We trade in peace with the Isle of the Prince, and with the English Empire and the Norrlanders. And the Icelander folk. Those of them who stayed there and didn't go back to the ancient homelands—to Norrland, it's called now—or to England, offer to the Aesir now too. Not much trade in any one year, but it's welcome."

He scowled. "And besides the troll-men who haunt the ruins, our folk fight with the *blaumenn* sometimes, southward, over salvage rights."

"Blue-men?" Rudi said.

"The English call them Moors," Heidhveig said. "They're from Senegal, really. They're numerous but their lands are metal poor, not having as many cities from before the Change for mining and salvage."

"My foster father, Sir Nigel Loring, helped keep the Isle of Wight alive through the Change, and was a leader in the resettlement of England before he had to flee from Mad King Charles," Rudi said thoughtfully. "He mentioned trouble with them."

"No, they're not friendly to outsiders at all, though I suppose they have their own reasons which seem good to them," Heidhveig said.

Bjarni inclined his head towards Fred Thurston, sitting

astraddle a bench among the group around Odard. He was laughing, his head thrown back, with a mug of the dark Bjorning ale in his hand, and Virgina stood with her arm around his shoulders and his around her waist.

"I thought he might be one, from his looks, but he seems a fine young fellow, and I'd judge him a good man of his hands already."

"Few better, none braver," Rudi said crisply. "No lord could want a better . . . *gesith*, you say?"

"*Gesith*—companion? Yes, or *hirdman*."

"And no warrior a better comrade," Rudi finished.

"He'd better be a strong man, to keep up with *that* she-cat," Harberga said. "She's a wild one, if I've ever seen any."

"She has reason to face the world like a drawn blade," Rudi said soberly. "They're well matched; Virginia's shrewder than you might think from her manner, and Fred uses his head for more than a helmet rest, too. And doesn't lose it when the steel's out."

Bjarni nodded. "Of course, he's an Odinsman. Why, the High One claimed him in person! That's a great honor, though not one I envy; I'll stick with my old friend Thor."

"And if he's good enough for Odin, he's good enough for me," Heidhveig said, with an odd half-chanting tone in her voice.

When they looked at her she shrugged. "Classical reference. Now, we were speaking of Kalk Shipwright . . . Kalk's stubborn—more now than ever, he's even older than me!—and he won't want to risk a ship. Most are laid up this time of year. But I think he'll listen to *me*. And if not to me, then to the High One. Though he offers mostly to Njord and Freyr, himself."

They spent some time thrashing out the details; when

Rudi's party would leave, how Bjarni would help with the journey to the coast, and how to send out messages warning the rest of the Norrheim tribes that trouble was foreseen. The conversation wound up as the celebrations began again in earnest.

Rudi joined in the laughter and applause as thirteen masked youths in gaudy-raggedy costumes entered and cut capers, tumbling and playing pranks.

Then the children in the hall called out their names, seeking to chase them down and tag them:

"Stiff-Legs!" one cried, and clutched the sleeve of a figure who had stilts under his too-long breeks.

The others were caught one by one, some trying to climb the pillars until they dropped back into the shrieking crowd: Gully Gawk, Shorty, Ladle Licker, Pot Scraper, Bowl Licker, Door Slammer, Skyr Gobbler, Sausage Snatcher, Window Peeper, Sniffer, Meat Hook and Candle Beggar.

When they were captured the tumblers handed out shoes stuffed with toys and candied nuts and other treats. Harberga carried a broom around the hall and beat them forth with it, the youngsters following in a chain dance, before relenting and announcing:

"Come, those who wish to come; stay, those who wish to stay; and farewell, those who wish to fare away, harmless to me and mine!"

That brought the rest of the grown folk in for the evening meal—which for a Yule feast started in midafternoon.

"We drink *sumbel* this evening," Bjarni said to Rudi when it was well under way and his wife was away putting their daughter to bed. "You know that custom?"

Rudi nodded. "My half sisters' mother, Signe, is a follower of your Gods and so are many of her folk," he said.

"I've been at *sumbel* in Larsdalen, and the other Bear-killer holds. Perhaps you do it a bit differently, though." He grinned. "For a start, they like to drink it with wine; they've many fine vineyards there. The western side of the Willamette is better for the grape."

Bjarni sighed. "I've never drunk wine, except a few bottles found by Vikings . . . salvagers. They sound like an interesting lot, these Bearkillers of yours. With a fine fair land."

Then Bjarni's smile grew crooked: "Perhaps they're more interesting in a tale of far away than as neighbors!"

"They're not *my* Bearkillers, as Lady Signe would be the first to tell you! Though I've many friends among them, my uncle Eric for one, and my blood father's young namesake by Signe is a very likely lad. And they are a war-like lot," Rudi admitted. "But only in a cause they think righteous."

Bjarni snorted. "I've seen a fair number of fights, Rudi Mikesson, over matters great and small. But never *one* yet where both sides didn't think they'd rightful cause to bash the other."

"A point, a very palpable point," Rudi agreed. "But I'm certain and sure they were always wrong if they fought against you, my friend!"

Bjarni bellowed laughter. "True!"

Harberga returned. "Swanhild's sleeping hard," she said. "They do, at that age," she added to Rudi.

"That they do!"

"You don't have children yet, surely?" she asked, her eyes flicking to Mathilda.

"No, but the little lass reminds me of my youngest sister at that age. Fiorbhinn will be turning ten now; it's a grief to me to miss so much of her life in the swift-changing years. Her hair and eyes are just that shade, and she was always active as a squirrel, until she drops in her tracks."

"*Fiorbhinn*," Harberga said, as if tasting it. "A pretty name. What does it mean?"

"*True-Sweet*, in the old tongue," Rudi replied. "After a famous harp, you see. And well named, for she could sing true almost as soon as she could talk at all. And Swanhild?"

"Swan-battle. Also well named, especially since she learned the word *no!*"

The last remains of pies and pastries were cleared away, the last children not quite old enough for the ceremony shepherded off to their beds, and horns and horn rests were set out—like Bearkillers, the Bjornings considered that the proper vessel for solemn toasts, oaths and boasts. Four youths and four maidens brought in a litter; on it was a gold-sheathed wooden image of a boar done life-size, with the tusks of a real one and a wrought golden ring in its mouth. They carried it around the inside of the long rectangle of the tables, and folk did it reverence.

When the golden boar was set before the chieftain's seat, Rudi noticed that it stood in a wooden tray of dirt.

"That's earth from the first *hof*"—which meant *temple*, more or less—"of the Bjorning kindred, that my father brought north and mixed with the soil here at the land-taking," Bjarni said. "We swear all the greater oaths on this boar, the Oath-Swine of the Bjornings."

"That's a strong rite," Rudi agreed.

"Yes, it's the holiest we have; and this the season for the most powerful oaths."

Out of the corner of his eye he saw Father Ignatius politely taking his leave, and frowning a little when Mathilda and Odard shook their heads and stayed. Rudi wasn't too concerned; he'd gathered that there were still some Christians around here, and that they came to this type of ceremony, if not the *blòt*-sacrifices. It would be difficult to be a member of the community if you didn't.

Bjarni rose and spoke:

"Bjornings and guests! Now we drink *sumbel*; to the Gods, in memory of the ancestors, and to make boast and oath. Take care when you do, for to make oath before all is to lay your words in the well of Wyrd, binding the fate of all. My uncle Ranulf Waltersson shall be *thul* of this *sumbel*"—

An older warrior in his forties nodded, with his arms crossed across his tunic; he was darker and leaner than his nephew, but had a family look of him.

—"and none shall dispute his judgments. Let the Valkyries fill the horns!"

Harberga and Gudrun led a group of women—kin of the chief, for this was a duty of honor and high regard—to pour mead from the pitchers they carried. Most of the drinking so far had been ale, and usually not very strong ale at that; this mead was heady, smelling of flowering meadows gone, and itself a boast of sorts—being made from honey it was expensive in this land where life lay sparely, and only a great chief could bestow it so lavishly.

Bjarni's horn was bound and tipped with rune-graven gold, and bore a carving of a woman carrying a horn to a man who rode a chariot pulled by goats. He held it high:

"I drink to Odin, to Freyr and Freyja, to Njord, to almighty Thor, and to all the Gods and Goddesses. Hail, Aesir, hail Ásynjur!"

"Wassail!"

Rudi raised his horn and drank; the mead was dry and

strong, and left a slight catch at the back of his throat. There was nothing in *his* faith that forbade it. Some of the dwellers signed the Hammer over their horns before they lifted them; a few used the Cross. Some touched the mead with a finger and then their foreheads rather than drinking; Harberga did, he noticed, probably for the un-born babe's sake.

Bjarni lifed his horn again: "I drink to our ancestors, who made Norrheim with their might, their main, their craft and luck. Most of all, I drink to my father, Erik Waltersson, Erik the Strong. Drink hail!"

"Wassail!"

The Bjorning chieftain paused and took a deep breath. When he spoke his voice was matter-of-fact.

"Most of you were here when the *seidhkona* took the high seat last night. Through her the Allfather spoke, and laid a duty on all those who would stand with the Gods to aid our guest, Rudi Mikesson of the Mackenzies, called Artos, Son of Bear and Raven."

He stepped down from the dais and laid his free hand on the golden ring clenched in the jaws of the gilt boar; there was a tense hush, for that was the oath-ring of their folk. Swearing on it bound doubly.

"As first *bragarfull*, I swear to make Rudi Mackenzie my blood brother; to have the same friends and the same enemies, to give each other sanctuary without stint, to share our goods, to foster each other's children at need, and each to avenge the other's death on any foe and give him his rites if he falls on foreign soil. This I swear by almighty Thor."

His uncle Ranulf stood; the *thul* could object to an oath. "You swear more than you can perform, Bjarni Er-iksson, for blood brotherhood needs the will of two. Will our guest support your oath?"

Rudi nodded. "I will," he said, calmly but forcefully.

He rose as well, and they stood facing one another across the golden boar. He drew the *sgian dubh* from his sock-hose and nicked the flesh at the base of his right thumb. Bjarni did the same with his seax. They clasped hands, letting the blood mingle, then raised them to allow a drop to fall on the holy earth; then each ran a drop into his mead horn and offered it to the other to drink through linked arms.

"Drink hail!"

"Wassail!"

A murmur ran through the hall as the two resumed their seats; the oath bound the Bjornings as a whole, through their chief. Rudi thought most of them were satisfied; he was himself. Bjarni was a man you could trust to have your back; their acquaintance had been brief, but intense.

A young woman stood and raised her horn. The looks and exclamations and a few gasps told him that this was *not* expected.

"I drink to Odin, Lord of Ravens," she said. "And I ask him to witness the oath I shall make."

It was as if the room held its breath. Rudi recognized the girl who'd asked after her man Sigurd at the divination, though she looked to have aged a decade in a day.

But the long amber-blond hair was shorter now— roughly hacked off below the ears, a man's style among the Bjornings. And she was wearing a belted tunic and breeks and boots, not the gown and long apron; all her clothing was in black or dark blue. These folk didn't make as much of the differences between men's dress and women's as Mathilda's did but from what he'd seen they were more particular about it than Mackenzies, especially on formal occasions like this.

The clothes had some significance here, something

that he wasn't quite grasping. Bjarni's mouth had closed in a grim line, and Harberga was frowning. An older man and woman seemed caught between anger and tears; probably her parents.

The tall young woman walked down and crossed to the Oath-Swine; as she did the lamplight glittered on a pendant she wore, a *valknut*, a set of three interlaced equal-sided triangles with the points upright.

Now that I know. It is Odin's mark. I think—

She laid her hand on the ring and spoke: "This I swear and promise: that I will have vengeance for my betrothed, Sigurd Jeansson; I will be a shield-maid until I have taken a wergild of lives tenfold for his, taken them by my own hand—"

The *thul* stood, and more quickly than before. "Asgerd Karlsdottir! To speak these words in *sumbel* is to link our fates to yours in the well of Wyrd! If you fail, all of us bear the ill luck that falls on the foresworn. What sith, what recompense, can you pay if fulfilling this oath is beyond your might?"

The ravaged face lifted. "If it is beyond my might, it is not beyond my main, my soul strength. If I fail in this oath, the price I offer is this: my life. I will fulfill my oath, or I will die with my face to the foe."

Rudi hissed slightly between his teeth. *If ever I saw someone in most desperate earnest, this is she*, he thought.

"This is a dreadful oath," the *thul* said. "By it you deprive your kindred of strength, not only yours but that of your children who might be."

Proudly, she replied: "I am a free woman of Norrheim, and of the Bjorning folk, and of age. I have said what sith I will pay to support my oath. May I swear, or not?"

"All men are born fey. All women, too," Ranulf said heavily. "You may swear; your oath is accepted."

"So I swear, by Victory-Father. Drink hail!"

She did more than take a draught; she drank steadily, until the horn shed only a drop when she held it upside down. The *Wassail* was ragged; when it died down, Asgerd turned and looked Rudi in the eye. The mead had put red in her cheeks, but her voice was still cold:

"Since the High One commanded us to aid Rudi Mikesson of the Mackenzies, and his foes are those who slew my man, I will fulfill my oath in his service if he will have me. I am trained to arms, I can use sword and spear, and I am better than most with the bow. I've hunted and trapped and know the ways of land and water. There are deer and wolves who could testify to it, if they lived! But if he will not, I will follow nonetheless."

Hmmm. That *I didn't expect either*, he thought, a little dismayed.

Then his gaze turned professional. She was tall for a woman—a hair less than his half sisters, perhaps the slightest touch taller than Mathilda—and looked fit.

She moves well. And there's nothing wrong with her nerve, I'd judge. Apart from that—

He looked over to Ranulf; he'd gathered that the brother of the Bjorning founder was an arms master and one of his nephew's right-hand men.

"All our folk *are* trained to weapons play," Ranulf said.

It was a little grudging, but with the air of a man who wouldn't bend the truth about the trade he loved. The same judicious appraisal went through the rest.

"Though women usually put it aside when they wed, and few ever fight except at greatest need, when their home garths are attacked. Asgerd isn't as strong as a man with her inches, of course, but she's strong for her weight, and quick, and more skilled than most girls her age. Sigurd Jeansson was a fine fighting man, often in Viking, and he sparred with her much. Nor have I seen her flinch from a blow on the practice field, even the hardest."

Asgerd nodded. "My Sigurd said he would have no coward, no weakling, to be mother of his sons or to guard his steading when he was away."

Unexpectedly, Edain spoke as well. "I saw her shooting at the range earlier," he said. "She's got a good eye. The archer's eye. Not the heaviest bow, but she's sure, and fast; she'd pass trial for the First Levy at home. Though there's room for improvement, of course."

She shot him a look of startled gratitude; there was even the hint of a smile in it. Rudi nodded; that settled the question of her skill with the bow. Archery was something an Aylward took *very* seriously.

"I will accept your service, Asgerd Karlsdottir," he said. "But I will tolerate nothing reckless or heedless. So, before we leave Eriksgarth you must swear to me by my own people's oath. I give you fair warning: that oath will bind you tightly. My war band has but one will, and that one is *mine*."

"I will swear that oath."

Asgerd walked slowly back to her seat and sat; Rudi judged her stunned by success . . . and not the least regretful.

That brought a clamor of young Bjornings wanting to enlist with the questers. Rudi picked carefully, just enough to replace the Southsiders killed or too badly wounded to continue, six men and another woman.

Looking for adventure, I think, he decided. *Or for a trip away from troubles; or perhaps for gain, rising with a King newcome to power and willing to risk all for it. Or such reasons mixed together. Not a bad start. I've been questing for the Sword; but once I have it, I must build a host.*

"And that is all for now," he said firmly; he thought Bjarni looked a little relieved. "When I return with the Sword, we shall see what we shall see. I fear that my blood brother will need all the strong sword arms he can muster before then, and need them here."

There were pleased nods from the yeoman landholders at that. Several heads of household rose and pledged to take in their wounded or horses; others swore to provide gear or goods to those who'd joined him, even costly items like mail shirts. Which was welcome; they hadn't brought along all the gear of their fallen, there being no space in the sleds to spare. Bjarni caught Rudi's eye and nodded.

Rudi stood. *Ogma of the honey-tongue, be with me now,* he thought, then pitched his voice to carry:

"Folk of Eriksgarth, of the Bjornings, of Norrheim, by now you know somewhat of my story. Hear also what my mother said when she held me over the altar in our *nemed*, our sacred wood, when she gave me my name and made prophecy:

"Sad winter's child, in this leafless shaw—
Yet be Son, and Lover, and Hornèd Lord!
Guardian of my sacred Wood, and Law—
His people's strength—and the Lady's sword!

"This was the fate laid upon me at my birth; *Orløg*, you say. Here I swear to take up this destiny, and the Sword. I will defeat the black evil of Corwin, and free those it holds in thrall. I will be *Ard Rí* in Montival; I will

be High King. To my own people I will be land father
and give good lordship and fair judgment; in my lands
each shall hold his own, and each folk shall follow their
own customs and Gods and laws, subject only to the
common good. To foreign friends—such as yourselves—I
will offer the open hand of welcome and alliance, and see
that none trouble any who come to trade or visit. Only
to the reiver, the evildoer, the oppressor and the invader
shall I show the edge of the Sword, but to them it shall
be a sword of fire indeed. So I swear, by the Gods of my
people, by the Maker of Stars, by the Lady of the Ravens
who has held me under Her wings; and also I swear by
great Odin, Victory-Father, who has given me of his
strength and wisdom here and elsewhere."

He took the oath-ring in his hand. "So I swear; so
shall I do. And if there comes a day when the King must
die for the people, then I will go consenting, with open
eyes. *Drink hail!*"

"*Wassail!*"

Mathilda smiled at him over her horn, but tears trem-
bled in her eyes. She rose:

"I have sworn service as vassal with Artos the High
King already. Here I swear that I will take him for my
man, for my war captain, for my King, and keep faith with
him in all ways so long as life is in me. Drink hail!"

"*Wassail!*"

Edain stood in his turn. "I started on this quest a boy,
following a friend. Along the way I've found a King to
follow, who's still the best friend and comrade a man
could have. I swear I'll stand by him as best I can, all my
life long. Drink hail!"

"*Wassail!*"

The others followed; the twins swore their pledge in

liquid Sindarin, causing a little confusion. Odard went last, and stood silent for an instant. When he spoke his voice was low at first:

"When I started this journey, I came because of the Princess more than Rudi. There was bad blood between my family and his . . . A man's mind is never all of one thing, nor does he know himself or all his reasons beneath the masks he wears. They deceive even the wearer. But by following Rudi, I've found enemies worth fighting, and a man . . . a King . . . *worth* following. I will follow him, and raise my sons to follow his. Drink hail!"

"*Wassail!*"

CHAPTER EIGHTEEN

"You attack this time," Ritva Havel said to Asgerd Karlsdottir. "On the count—one—"

The Ranger had her parka off, and wore only the down-quilted vest, wool undershirt, wool tunic, padded gambeson and mail-lined leather jerkin. That was miserably chilly but exercise would help, though there was a hint of moisture in the air today that made the cold sink right into bone and joint. For some reason the same quilted padding that turned a mail shirt hellish in summertime did nothing for you in weather like this. At least the cold muted the harsh rank smell of old sweat and rancid oil inseparable from armor, leaving the clean scent of spruce and pine the strongest odor around them.

"Two . . ."

The edge of her shield snapped down the visor of the sallet she was wearing, and the steely gray light of the winter's day shrank to a line of tarnished brightness across her eyes through the vision slit. Her shield came up under her chin, and her feet felt for the balance—the mealy snow moved beneath her boots, as bad as sand for leeching away speed. Sword up, point up . . .

"*Three!*"

"*Ho La, Odhinn!*" Asgerd hawk-screamed.

She moved like a swift slender metal statue in her mail byrnie and nose-guarded conical helm and cut with the cry. The hilt-forward position of her sword turned into a sweeping circle that came down towards Ritva's head as her feet moved her forward like a stooping hawk. The Norrheimer-style round shield was held by a single grip beneath the boss, and she kept it always between them, ready to strike with it as the sword hammered down. Ritva brought her own shield up in a flash of motion— and around, so that it didn't block her vision, and arrived slanted at an angle.

Crack.

The hard birchwood lath of the practice blade bounced away from the curved surface of the shield. Ritva grunted as the blow rocked the convex circle of plywood and bull-hide and painted sheet metal against her shoulder and shocked through her arm where it ran between the el-bow-loop and the rim-grip.

Strong! she thought approvingly.

The same impact helped her swing aside and out of the path of the Bjorning's rush. Her left foot moved forward and her right followed it in a skipping crabwise step, blurring-fast. The blunt point of her wooden sword drove home and Asgerd gave a cry that was half frustration and half stifled pain as it took her on the back of the knee below the edge of the byrnie.

That sent her off-balance as the leg buckled; Ritva struck with her weight behind it in the same instant, shield punching into shield. The younger woman went over on her back with a hard *thud* only slightly muffled by the deep snow under a leafless maple, and an *ooof!* as the impact knocked the wind out of her lungs. The

Ranger skipped forward to tap her lath-sword at the base of the Bjorning's throat.

"Ah, I think I see your problem," Ritva said, sliding the smooth curve of the visor up the forehead of the sallet.

Asgerd slowly levered herself out of the snow, blowing and shaking her head, snatching off her helm by the nasal bar to strike at the snow that had packed up under it and into her hair.

"You're better with the sword than me!" she snarled, her breath puffing white in winter air. "And you're more experienced. That's my problem! You've killed me four times and I've only wounded you once."

"Yes, but that's not your *problem*," Ritva went on. "You've been well taught, but your problem is that you're fighting like a man."

"Well, if I'm to fight, it probably won't be against women!"

"No. But . . ."

She turned to Mary. "Let's show her the Parable of the Door. You do the sounds."

Mary grinned, a remarkably piratical expression with the eye patch; they'd played this game as instructors at Mithrilwood ever since they graduated to *ohtar* rank, and had missed it on the trip. Aunt Astrid and her *anamchara* Lady Eilir had come up with it, back when they first brought the Dúnedain together.

Running off the unsuitable and training the teachable, she thought. *Both good fun.*

A *lot* of discontented teenage girls had turned up at Stardell Hall over the years, drawn by the lure of the Dúnedain name and the glitter of the Histories . . . and weary of the endless routine of churn and hoe and loom. Or the damp hands of pimply-faced local swains, as opposed to dreams of some Elven Prince. Or in the case of Mary and Ritva Havel, tired and bored with being spare heirs.

Which is about as useful as being a wagon's fifth wheel.

Ritva turned back to the Bjorning, who was dusting more snow off her byrnie and the seat of her breeks. If you let it melt into your clothing, the dampness could linger for days on the trail. There wasn't much chance to get *people* warm and dry, much less their clothing.

"Fighting is like opening a door. Now, imagine there's a door here," the Ranger said.

She stuck the practice longsword in the snow and sketched a portal with her finger, and pointed out the features:

"Nice solid door. Here's the hinges. Here's the handle and the latch. Now, imagine a man trying to open the door. Here's how he'd probably do it."

"Belch," Mary put in, with an alarmingly realistic accompaniment.

"Urrgghhh!" Ritva said.

Her hands went up and gripped the sides of the imaginary door. Then she whipped her head forward.

"Bong!" Mary shouted.

Again.

"Bong!"

Again and then she stopped, scrunched one eye closed while rubbing her head and scratching her backside, then reversing the process.

"Belch," Mary put in. *"Fart."*

"Me smash! Arrrggghh! *Me smash! Me smash!"* Ritva bellowed, mock-guttural.

She mimed head-butting the door over and over, her features contorted into a mask of cross-eyed rage and lips slack as if she was drooling; then the eyes rolled up in her head and she fell backward into the snow.

"Now!" she said, bouncing back up again and clapping her hands together. "Here's how a *woman* does it."

Ritva reached out, lifted the invisible latch—Mary supplied the *click*—turned the knob, stepped through, and closed the door behind her, with a final *clunk* from her sister.

"You see?"

Asgerd looked at them both. Her face had been grim almost all the time since they left Eriksgarth; now it lightened a little. The smile had to struggle up like a fish broaching from the depths, but she managed it. Then— Ritva's eyebrows went up—she started to giggle. After a moment she spoke:

"I think I see a little of what you mean. We have a saying, that when your only tool is a hammer all your problems start to look like nails."

"We have the same proverb," Ritva said.

Though if it's John Hordle or even Rudi, they just walk through *the door without noticing it's there. But that would undermine the lesson, so . . .*

She went on: "The Gods have made men and women differently. They have hammers. We have needles. If you want to fight well, you have to fight like a first-rate woman, not like a bad imitation of a man."

She took up the lath practice sword again. "Rudi can break a shield's frame with a straight flourish cut like the one you used, if he hits full-on; and break the arm underneath it, sometimes."

Asgerd blinked. "With a one-handed blow from a *sword?*" she said incredulously. "With a battle-ax or war hammer, perhaps . . ."

"I've seen him do it. Or slash right through ring-mail."

"So can Ingolf," Mary said. A little reluctantly: "Rudi's faster, though."

Ritva nodded. "For you or me, trying to do that's just a waste of effort and leaves you open to the counterstrike. Or . . . you're about my height. Or Odard's or Edain's. But getting into a shield-to-shield shoving match with either of them is a bad idea—they've a third again our weight. More muscle, heavier bones. Let's try something a little different—"

Edain came up on skis, then slid to a halt to watch for a while. Garbh sat beside him, her tail curled around her feet and black nose going back and forth, tongue dangling behind white puffs of breath.

"Not bad," the young clansman said, after a flurry of blows. "But it's time for lunch, and then to get moving again."

He grinned at Asgerd. "They beat me all the soddin' time too," he added. "Sure, and it's like trying to hit a ghost."

She snorted, too winded to speak for a moment. Edain politely didn't look at her too closely, or in too nonprofessional a way, as she shrugged into her loose parka with its mottled cover of white and off-white and brown, and buckled on her sword belt and the baldric for her bow and quiver that she'd hung on a branch. The shield rattled as she slung it over her back as well; a cover of bleached canvas hid the colorful black-and-red painting of a fylfot. Garbh came over and butted a friendly nose beneath a hand and the Bjorning paused to ruffle the big beast's fur, which seemed to soften her mood a little.

"Do they beat you at shooting?" she said, tossing

down her skis from where she'd leaned them against a birch and stepping into the toe-loops.

"No. They're better than fair shots, but not nearly as good as me," he said straightforwardly.

"But better than me?" Asgerd asked, with just a touch of belligerence in her tone.

"For now, yes. Rangers train hard and long. They're not farmers; they fight and hunt for a living. You could be as good, but it'll take a year at least, or more depending on how much time you put into it."

Asgerd nodded, her face calm but approval in her eyes.

She'd have scented flattery, Ritva thought, and hid her grin.

"Now, they're both a total failure at milking a cow, mind," Edain said. "More of a moo and a kick they'd get if they tried than aught in the pail."

The two Rangers snorted, and Asgerd chuckled. They all slid south and east—and slightly downhill—towards the valley where the main caravan lay with its sleds. Or bounded easily in a series of puffs of snow, in Garbh's case.

Edain's not quite the bluff simple Mackenzie crofter he puts on. That was quite clever.

Asgerd seemed like a nice girl, if grim—which was understandable, given what had happened to her betrothed—and far less likely to meet a bad end than that Mormon woman back in Idaho. Ritva wished him all success, as she might a younger brother.

As I might a considerably *younger brother, though we're with a year of the same age. Still . . . he's always felt younger than us. Men grow up more slowly.*

And there wouldn't be as many religious problems if

things went well, which wouldn't be soon anyway. Those faiths of the Book with their exclusive claims to truth were a complete nuisance; look at the bother it had caused for Rudi and Mathilda.

"You live by the sword too?" the Bjorning girl asked Edain. "Or the bow," she added.

"Not all the time, no, not until this trip. Mostly I help me da on the farm, and in the bowyer's workshop we have; that's what Mackenzies do, work the land and follow crafts. My mother's a weaver of some note, and well known for that and her cheeses—people come from as far away as Corvallis to buy 'em both. To be sure, Da was First Armsman of the Mackenzies for years and years— war leader of the Clan, under the Chief. But everyone who can fights when it's needful, among Mackenzies. Only a few are warriors all the time."

"As with us," Asgerd nodded. "Only the *hirdmen* of a *godhi* . . . the guards of a chief . . . make a trade of war. We haven't had a big war for a long time; not since the years after the land-taking, when they say whole bands of reivers were abroad, desperate and hungry. Just scuffles and skirmishes since then, and—"

Her voice broke for a second; then she cleared her throat and went on doggedly:

"—and those who go in viking to the dead cities must fight often against the troll-men."

They talked, stumbling over terms occasionally; Ritva and her sister helped when they were at a loss for words, or used them differently. Rangers traveled widely and had to be good at picking up how meanings had drifted in the last generation, and she could speak Spanish and some French as well as English and Sindarin. It was harder with Asgerd, because her speech was speckled with words from old languages Ritva knew only as names, or with French.

Not the ancient tongue that Portland's nobility liked to affect now and then, either, but a quacking nasal local dialect like nothing she'd ever heard before.

Asgerd nodded when she was satisfied. "You're a *bondar*, a yeoman's child, like me, then," she said to Edain. "Neither rich nor poor, eh?"

It seemed to make her easier in her mind if she could place someone by station and kindred. Edain shrugged.

"Right. We've got a good farm and we're well thought of in Dun Fairfax . . ."

"*Dun* means *village*, more or less. Thorpe, you might say," Ritva put in.

Edain nodded. "In our village. But not great chiefs, no."

Asgerd sighed. "It seems a rich *land* though, this Montival. Gardens yielding into November! Stock grazing outside *all winter*? We have to feed ours hay and turnips and grain five months of the year! And I've never tasted those fruits you talked about, grapes and peaches and cherries and apricots and hazelnuts, they're only old words here."

"The Willamette's fine country, and that's a fact," Edain said. "Better than aught I've seen on this trip— Iowa was very rich indeed in grain and swine and cattle, sure and it was, but cold in the winter too from the looks of it, and no vineyards to speak of, and not nearly the fruit orchards we have. And flat! *And* short of timber, the which we are not. The Lord and Lady have blessed us."

She bristled a little, and he added: "It's not bad soil here. Those were fine spuds at Eriksgarth, and the stock was good."

Then he looked around; they were traveling down a small river valley now, narrow between low steep densely forested hills, mostly pine and spruce with an occasional stand of taller white pine, and broadleaf trees along the water. Naked rock showed here and there, through snow and the thin soil beneath.

"Or at least that bit about Eriksgarth wasn't bad. This here would break a farmer's heart, it would! And any plow he tried to use on it. Fine timber trees, I grant, but ours stand taller."

"They say the folk of the old world cut so many here in Norrheim . . . they called it Maine then . . . that few grow as tall as they might," Asgerd said. "Or as tall as they will grow by my grandchildren's time. That's hard to imagine, but . . ."

The three westerners nodded at her shrug; they'd all grown up on tales of a world of marvels vanished before they were born. You never knew exactly which were true, and which mere fable, either. Not even the old people agreed on that!

"It would be a good place for a Ranger steading," Ritva said. "We don't farm. We keep to the woods and wilderness, mostly, and live by the hunt and what the forest yields. And what we're given to *protect* farmers from bandits and beasts," she added virtuously. "That buys us grain and wine, and cloth and weapons . . . whatever we can't make or grow for ourselves."

Edain snorted. "That, or what *merchants* pay you for protection of their caravans," he pointed out.

"They don't *have* to hire us," Mary said.

"No. You just loudly announce that so-and-so isn't under your protection. The which is to pin a great sodding sign on their backs: Rob This One, eh?"

Mary sniffed as her skis hissed rhythmically. "If we didn't announce it, that would be like cheating the honest ones who pay. Overcharging them, you know? And

there's what we get from the other realms by treaty for
bandit hunting and patrolling."

Edain grinned, enjoying the teasing game: "And what
you get by *exploring* for the good of all, the which so
often leads to stores of gold and silver and jewels and
other treasure from the old times falling into your hands,
somehow, and isn't that a curious thing, the wonder and
the joyous surprise of it!"

Ritva frowned. "It's traditional," she said, in a slightly
huffy tone. "Dúnedain have *always* done those things.
Except for that bit just before the Change when the world
got so weird and crowded."

Edain snickered when her nose went up, and she
didn't go into detail.

Mostly because I don't think I could go into detail, she
thought.

When you were the child and niece of rulers, you grew
up knowing how much effort and planning had to go
into provisions and equipment, and what a disaster it
could be if you didn't have something essential when and
where it was needed. The Histories painted Gondor as
normal enough, if a bit seedy and run-down, but they
were irritatingly vague on how the original Dúnedain had
made their livings after the fall of the North Kingdom,
much less on how they outfitted their warriors. Supposedly the Rangers of old hadn't even *told* people how their
labors in the wilderness kept settled folk safe, much less
demanded dead-or-alive rewards and head prices for outlaws and a yearly stipend as they did now.

*How did they get the price of a meal and a night's sleep
at the Prancing Pony in the Third Age? Barliman But-
terbur didn't strike me as the sort who'd let you run up a
big tab.*

Where had the Dúnedain children and old people lived? Armor was expensive and needed skilled specialists to make and keep up, as well—did they have weapons smiths of their own? For that matter, how had they gotten pipeweed from the Shire? It wasn't as if the hobbits would give it to you.

They couldn't all have sponged off Elrond in Imladris, like hairy smelly short-lived poor cousins, she thought. *Or hocked ancestral treasures to the dwarves whenever they ran short. Aunt Astrid has enough trouble making the people who owe us money pay up even* with *a contract! It's a puzzlement.*

Edain's hiss brought her up; she angled the points of her skis together, snowplowing to a halt and focusing outward. Garbh was standing at point, her body lowered and muzzle locked forward like a compass needle; the cold muffled scent to a human nose, but hers was almost infinitely keener. They all kicked their toes out of the loops and stooped low, motionless, listening.

"Gruck! Gruck!"

That was a raven; a deeper cry than a crow. A black shape flogged itself into the air a little ahead, where a lone spruce leaned over a boulder, then drifted stiff-winged back to its perch, cocking an inquisitive and hopeful eye downward.

Something dead, she thought, as she reached over her shoulder for an arrow. *Someone, rather. Garbh wouldn't act that way for ordinary carrion.*

Mary held up two fingers and then tapped them to the left. Edain nodded and ghosted off to the right, with Garbh swinging wide to cover his flank. Asgerd followed man and dog with blade in hand, creditably quiet, the gray steel of the Norrheimer broadsword at one with the brown and white and green of the winter woods. The two

Rangers traced a course like drifting mist by drilled habit, from bush to boulder to tree, until they looked through a tangle of reddish wild blueberry canes. Ritva relaxed and let her breathing slow, let her gaze drift a little out of focus for an instant—that was how you could see patterns best, if nothing was moving.

Her eyes met Mary's single one, and they nodded slightly. The man curled in the shadow of the rock was unmoving, and snow had collected on his thin sparse beard. Edain came in from the other direction, and waved them forward.

"Garbh found his back track," he said. "Only one, and hours old. Blood spoor, too." He looked down at the corpse and pointed a toe.

"Arrow," he said succinctly.

The fletching had broken off, and a stub of it stood from the body's ribs, two hands down from the left armpit and a third of the way in towards his spine.

Ritva nodded. "Someone got him while he ran. And he kept going longer than I'd have expected, with that in him."

People did, sometimes, when great need or a very strong will drove them. She and Mary dragged the man into the light. The body was slight, less than their own weight; a very young man, just old enough to raise a brown peach fuzz of beard, and long in the legs. Even beneath the winter gear his gawky coltishness was obvious. The open eyes were hazel. Ritva paused to close them, before she continued her examination.

Poor lad, she thought, with the slightly abstract pity you felt towards an unlucky stranger. *You didn't get many years, did you? But Earth must be fed, soon or late. Dread Lord, be kind; Lady Mother-of-All, comfort him. Return him from the Halls of Mandos to a better fate.*

"He's been here a while, but he only *died* a little while ago," she said. "See, he's not very stiff yet. Blood on his face and under this leather armor—"

Ritva rubbed some between thumb and finger, before she scrubbed with snow and put her glove back on:

"Some has dried, but some of it's still tacky. The arrow nicked a lung, I'd say."

Asgerd spoke, alarmed: "That's a war sark of the kind they make at Kalksthorpe! He's a Norrheimer, but not a Bjorning. He must be one of Kalk's folk. But I've never seen an arrow like that. It's some sort of cane, not ash or cedar."

"The unfortunate fellow was headed *out* of Kalksthorpe, and kept going as long as he could though he must have known he was dying, the sorrow and black pity of it," Edain said thoughtfully.

Asgerd pointed north and west. "There's a steading that way. About ten miles. We didn't go near it but anyone coming inland without supplies would head there first. Or if he bore a word of war for others to spread."

"Rudi needs to know about this," Ritva said with conviction. *"Now."*

"Yes, yes, I'm ready," Heidhveig said. "But—"

Rudi looked at her with concern; the journey had been hard on her, despite taking it by easy stages and the well-made sled, and her getting the indoor bed when they stopped at some lonely farmstead. Her wrinkled face was a little gray, though she'd made no complaints.

Sure, and I've gotten well used to traveling only with those young and very strong, he thought. *Even armies would have trouble matching the pace we've often set. And I need her to talk to this Kalk.*

"But it's odd . . . someone should have met us by now," she went on. "There are always hunters out, and winter is the best time for traveling."

His glance turned keen, but she shrugged beneath the bearskin rug. "No, no, nothing definite. Just a feeling."

Thorlind paused: "She doesn't *just* have feelings!"

"My thoughts exactly, good lady," Rudi said.

She's a fussbudget, is Thorlind, he thought silently, while most of his mind mulled distances and numbers. *But a fussbudget of considerable wit.* And *no mean worker of her craft, either.*

Thorlind pulled a precious pre-Change thermos out of a box beneath the driver's seat of the sled and poured steaming hot rosehip tea into a cup. Heidhveig took it meekly, which made him a little more worried about the old Norrheimer seeress, but there was a prickle down his spine that hinted at more immediate problems.

I haven't seen my unfriend Graber of late, nor the red-robe. Too much to hope for that they both drowned when the ice broke. I don't see how they could know where I was heading, much less get there first . . . but then, they've done things I don't understand before.

Rudi's head went up and down the trail of sleds. The little portable stove on one was smoking beneath a cauldron. The Bjornings made endless pots of stew in early winter, boiling it thick and then freezing it in blocks to store in their cold pantries. The travelers had brought a good many of those bricks along from Ericksgarth; it meant a great saving in time and effort since you need only throw in some snow for extra water and put the pot over the fire until it was hot enough to be served.

Virginia oversaw the distribution of the results today. Rudi accepted a bowl, a spoon and a slab of rye bread, stale but with some sharp hard yellow cheese melted onto it. The stew was ground moosemeat again, with potatoes and peas and onions and carrots and turnip in it too, plain food but good fuel for the furnace. He'd put far worse things past his lips at need.

"I'll be glad to get out of these trees," the woman from Wyoming said, and looked around with a slight shiver. "Gol-durn, but it's bleak country here!"

Rudi nodded gravely, though he had a flash of what it had been like in the Valley of the Sun amidst the Tetons last winter. It would be worse out on the High Plains, in the Powder River country where the Skywater Ranch of the Kane family had been before the armies of the Prophet overran them. There a wind could travel a thousand miles without a wood to break the hard teeth of it; they called that a lazy wind, too idle to go around a man—so it went right through like a spear instead. Riding after herds in a blizzard *there* . . . the very thought was enough to make a man's stones ache and his nose feel frostbite. Not to mention that the commonest fuel in those parts was dried cowpats.

It's all where you're raised, I suppose, he thought. *I don't think it's the cold that oppresses you, Virginia, but the strangeness.*

Then he looked around at dark pines, pale snow, leafless maple and birch, low clouds the color of frosted lead. And remembered blossoming orchards below Mt. Hood, with drifts of cherry pink and apple-blossom white flying free amid a scent to make a man drunk; or lying in a clover mead near Dun Juniper with the bees humming beneath a sky of cloudless blue so deep a man could lose his soul in it and the High Cascades hovering on the horizon like banners of green topped with silver; or riding across the Horse Heaven Hills with the sun on his back and mustang herds running with the wind in their manes . . .

No doubt this place had its own loveliness; even now there was a stern majesty to it. He'd never seen it in the short bright nights of its summertime, or the quick flowering spring, or the gold and scarlet beauty of its fall plumage. Still and all—

"I'm *tired* of this," Mathilda said quietly from beside him. "I want to go home. I want to *be* home. I want to be at a garden masque in Castle Todenangst and *bored* out of my mind."

Rudi's mouth quirked. "And it's precisely my thought you've just given voice," he said. "Though I might call it sitting in judgment at Dun Juniper, listening to a pair of stubborn crofters quarreling over a cow until I yearned to smack their thick skulls together. Yet then again, *a chuisle mo chroi*, darling treasure of my heart, where you are, home is. For there my heart dwells."

A brilliant smile rewarded him, the smile that turned her strong face beautiful for an instant.

Heidhveig gave a slight snort, and Rudi pulled out a map Bjarni Eriksson had given him and spread it before her, a new one on fine white calfskin parchment, but based on an ancient guide for wayfarers called *Rand McNally*. He thought the blue and scarlet and golden border of writhing dragons and curl-tusked trolls was probably modern work, along with the bearded faces puffing wind from the corners. The trail they were following came down from a lake—frozen now—and debouched onto the shore where Kalksthorpe stood, its little harbor sheltered by a nook of land.

"Robbinston," he murmured, reading the other name in brackets below *Kalksthorpe*.

Heidhveig nodded, revived by the drink and hot food. "That was the name before Kalk's folk came . . . myself among them. Right after the Change; we knew we had to leave Houlton. All my family and friends I'd talked into coming east, and Kalk's followers, and a bunch of others who thought we knew what we were doing. There was this barge full of canned goods—"

It's natural for the old to dwell on the past, Rudi thought.

Her finger traced their path. The low hills gave way to flat land along the water's edge; it was where the St. Croix—what the Norrheim folk called the Greyflood— gave out onto the ocean; sheltered still, but easy of access, and with islands and a rugged coast of fiords to the southward.

"The land is mostly cleared back a mile from the palisade," the seeress said. "There are mills outside, here and here, and timber yards. Not much farmed land, just enough for summer pasture and truck gardens. The thorpe's food mostly comes from the sea, and in trade down the river and from inland."

Rudi was about to reply when one of the sentries sounded an alarm. They all looked up as the twins came gliding in on their skis, with Asgerd and Edain behind. His teeth showed a little at the sight of a man's body slung over the younger Mackenzie's back.

"We found him in the woods. Not long dead, and from his back trail, he came up from the place we're going," Edain said, laying the man down. "Arrow in the lung; he kept going until he couldn't, then lay down and died."

"He was trying to make Erling Jimsson's steading, I think," Asgerd put in. "It's the closest."

Thorlind made a sound.

"Olaf!"

She went to her knees beside the young man as she came up and saw his face. She took the stiffening body in her arms, holding the boy's head against her shoulder, rocking him. Her voice was naked:

"Oh, Olaf, Olaf!"

Heidhveig pushed herself erect, leaning on her staff.

"I know him," she said quietly to Rudi, underneath the muted sounds of her pupil's grief. "He's her nephew Olaf Knutsson, her younger sister's son and Kalk's oldest great-grandson, just fourteen. Something terrible must be happening at Kalksthorpe. He is . . . was . . . a very swift runner, for a boy. They sent him for help, but someone shot him on the way."

Rudi nodded. "I'm sorry if we've brought ill luck upon your folk," he said.

Thorlind looked up. "You haven't. Whoever's attacked us has. If you owe me anything—"

"That I do, Lady, and freely I acknowledge it."

"Then give me blood for my blood! I will raise a *nithing*-staff and curse whoever did this, but I need a sword to do the work."

"I will that," Rudi said gently. "By the Morrigú I swear, and by Macha and Badb Catha, and by the greater One that the Three make."

Then his voice went hard and brisk. "We need a scouting mission. I'll lead it."

Ingolf cocked a brow. "That's grunt's work," he said bluntly. "Your more-balls-than-brains Majesty," he added, with a dry tinge to his voice. "Grunts can be idiots. They mostly just get themselves killed. Bossmen . . . Kings . . . can't afford to be stupid. Your life isn't your own to throw away anymore."

Rudi looked at him. It was on the tip of his tongue to say *if I'm the King, I give the orders.* But . . .

But nobody is less able to indulge a whim than a ruler, if he wants to be a good one. Ingolf has the right of it.

He sighed. "You've talked me into letting someone else do the work, you silver-tongued bastard of a man. I can deny you nothin'."

Then he looked about. "Mary, Ritva, you're going. And Edain. Are any of you Bjornings familiar with the land here? Fighters only," he added.

The Norrheimers looked at each other. A few raised hands uncertainly. Asgerd cleared her throat.

"I've come here six times . . . no, seven, but I was a little girl the first time. My father brings hides and wool and butter after the first hard snow to trade for cloth and tools and stockfish. We stay a week or two, and I know the neighborhood a little."

Rudi flicked his eyes quickly to Edain and his half sisters. They all nodded, quick slight jerks of the chin.

"Good, you're the fourth," he said aloud. "You're also the youngest and least, and don't forget it. Get me what I need to know, Edain, then get back, and quickly. The rest of us will move forward, but slow and cautious. We'll sprint the last bit, I expect."

"I wish we had our destriers," Odard said.

Rudi grinned. "I doubt there's room for a charge of knights here, my lord Gervais. Now, Asgerd, show me on the map how we can approach. I'm thinking the main trail is a *bad* idea the now, until we know exactly who it is has come calling at Kalksthorpe."

"Be patient with them, Jawara," Abdou said.

He hunched his shoulders against the cold wind off the sea, and even more against the itching feeling of being immobilized here ashore while his ships swung at anchor. The sea was his element; this continent was alien and hostile. He liked feeling that way. It kept you alive.

"Supposedly they're some sort of Muslims," he went on.

Abdou al-Naari was a tall lean man in his thirties, with skin the color of old saddle leather, part-owner and captain for his kin-corporation of the corsair schooner *Bou el-Mogdad*, named after a fabulous ship of the ancient world. His subordinate Jawara was shorter, a little younger than his thirty-six, thicker-built and ebony black, with three scars like chevrons on each cheek; he had named her sister ship *Gisandu*—Shark.

Jawara looked over at the men they were now allied with, the core of disciplined ones in the reddish-brown armor with the rayed sun sign on their chests and the rabble of savages around them. When he spat, it was for the benefit of both groups; and perhaps also for the man in the green robe and turban who was standing and talking with them. In the old days that dress would have meant he was a hadji, one who'd made the pilgrimage to Mecca. A few men bold enough or mad enough or lucky enough or all three had made the journey across the length of the Sahel and the Red Sea since the Change and found nothing human left in the Holy City except dry gnawed bones. Now the green cloth merely meant a pilgrimage to Touba, where Cheik Bamba of the Mouride Brotherhood had dwelt.

Jawara's voice held a sneer as eloquent as the gobbet of spittle:

"If they're Muslims, I'm the Emir—and I'm not freezing my balls off here. I'm sitting in my palace at Dakar, sipping coffee and smoking good khif this very moment under a screen grown with jasmine, while pretty girls bring me plates of *cheb-ou-jen* with *yète*."

Abdou spat himself, and shivered as it froze on the ground with a slight audible crackle. The thought of good hot coffee and some decent food was enough to make him want to howl. They were both bundled in furs and wool over their armor, and the wind off the estuary was still enough to make a man feel as if he was walking about while three days dead. Gray sky, gray water, dun-colored patches of rock, dark green pine, pale snow; it was all calculated to convince you that you'd become a ghost without noticing it.

The memory of mangroves alive with brightly colored birds beneath cerulean skies, of blue, blue breakers turning to white foam as they went crashing on silver sands beneath rustling palms seemed infinitely distant. He was hungry for it, the sights and the warmth and the very *smell* of smoked fish and onions and tomatoes cooking in peanut oil.

"The Marabout says they are believers," Abdou said. "And *he's* supposed to be a very holy man."

"If he's a holy man, I'm not the Emir. I'm his third wife," Jawara said.

Abdou grinned. "I thought you were his catamite with a bottom sweet as a ripe mango?" he said innocently.

Jawara made an obscene gesture at him, and they both laughed. Abdou did have his own doubts about the Marabout. Supposedly he was in favor with the new Grand Khalif of the Mourides, and the captain had welcomed him along on this venture when he turned up asking for a place—it reassured the men and made them feel God's blessing to have a cleric around.

He himself wasn't so sure. His own family were of the older Tidjiane brotherhood anyway, not the Mouride. And he was an educated man, literate in Wolof and in his native Hassaniya dialect and in the classical Arabic of the Holy Book, and even a little in *Française*, the dead *kufr* language of the sciences; also he spoke enough English for trade and war. He'd spent time at the Emir's court, as well, and he inclined to orthodoxy. The brotherhood founded by Cheik Bamba had been powerful in his land for a very long time and more so since the Change, but the reverence the Mourides paid to their hereditary religious leaders struck him as little short of *sherk*, idolatry.

What need of intermediaries? There is the word of God, and God; that is enough for a believer. But you had better not say that where one of the Mourides can hear you, especially if it's a Baye Fall madman.

There were two of them always with the Marabout, wild-looking men with their hair in plaits and great brass-bound ebony clubs in their hands. Both loomed like giants, and Abdou was not a small man.

And . . . how did he know where to find these so-called Muslims? It was as if they were waiting for him here on this begotten-of-Shaitan wilderness shore.

"Well, at least the plunder should be good," Jawara said, working his hands in his gloves; one dropped caressingly to the pearl-encrusted hilt of his scimitar. "This nest of pagans has been scouring the God-smitten cities on these coasts longer than we have. And they make some very clever things themselves."

"And they're a nuisance when they clash with our people," Abdou said. "Yes, we'll probably get a richer cargo than we could scavenging the ruins ourselves. But I hate losing good men getting it. This will cost us more than fighting a few ignorant cannibal savages in the dead lands. These Norrheimers may be pagans, but they know too cursed much how to make good armor and war engines and fight in ranks, for instance. Bad as fighting the Ashanti."

Jawara brightened. "There'll be women, at least, when we take the place. That warms a man up!"

.

Abdou shrugged. The dwellers here were polytheists and so legitimate prey by sharia, the holy law, but experience had shown these northern peoples were useless as slaves. If you took them back to a civilized climate they just sickened and died of the fevers. On balance it was a good thing, because it made it impossible for the English Nazarenes to invade the House of Peace rather than just make punitive raids. Besides, he found the fishbelly skins and skeletal faces of whites repulsive; even after so long at sea, he'd wait until he got home to Fatima.

"Get your mind out from between these hypothetical womens' thighs, Jawara: first we have to break their wall and beat their fighting men," he said sourly. "*And* hope no English ships come by before we can. This is far too close to the *Gezira-al-Said*, the Isle of the Prince; may God sink it."

The coast of the river estuary ran northwest-southeast here, with a hook of land protecting the site of the town. On the landward side was a wall of tree trunks, squared and sunk deep, bolted together with heavy steel rods and wound each to the next with metal cable. A little in from that was another wall, and the space between was tight-packed with rock and rubble to make a bulwark of solid strength. Blockhouses of large tight-fitted logs laid horizontally studded the wall, with two by each of the gates. The seaward approach was protected by more logs—but those were sunk in the seabed, angled outward, their ends tipped with vicious metal blades like the heads of giant spears. He could see some of them from here, frosted and menacing and bearded with icy tendrils of weed, but some were always underwater even at low tide. Only the dwellers knew the paths through them.

His own ships were anchored safely out of range offshore, their rigging half blocked from here by the rearing complexity of the pagan temple's shingle roofs. Both were two-masters built in the Saloum delta of sapele and iroko, low fast snakelike craft designed for speed at sea and handiness around shallow coasts. The pagan war boats were formidable where they had room to move, but they couldn't thread their way out through their own obstacles, not when they had to come slowly and in the face of catapults throwing globes of stick flame.

He'd come in out of the dawn three days ago and caught them tied up. That blockade duty pinned his ships down as long as he stayed here, though. Which also meant he couldn't dismount more than a pair of light engines for besieging the town, not nearly enough to do significant damage.

The Marabout—Cheik Ibra, he was called—was in conversation with one of the strangers. They were too far away for Abdou to follow the talk, but close enough for him to hear that it was in English. That made his mouth tighten. How *had* Ibra learned that tongue? In the lands of the Emirate of Dakar only seafarers did, and of them only a few.

"Ahmed," Abdou said, raising his voice slightly.

His son trotted over, proud in his fifteen years, a slim young man who already bid fair to be taller than his tall father someday. He was prouder still of being on his first foreign voyage.

"My father? I mean, Captain?"

"Fetch the learned Cheik for us."

The boy walked over to the strangers with self-conscious dignity. He transferred his spear to the left hand that also held the grip of his shield, so that his right could touch brow and lips and breast as he bowed and murmured a polite formula. The perhaps-holy man nodded and walked over to the two corsair captains.

"I have good news, God willing," he said cheerfully; he didn't even seem to mind the vile weather here.

"God willing indeed," Abdou said. "What could be good about this place except seeing the last of it, when that is His will?"

"Confounding the pagans and plundering their goods?" the Marabout asked dryly. "And *then* seeing the last of it?"

Jawara nodded. "Yes, but how? Charging those walls would leave nothing but heaped corpses—and if I'm to be a martyr, I want to be a victorious one. And we can't sit here long. Too likely a warship of the accursed English Nazarenes will come by, may God confound *them*. Their merchants put in here to trade every now and then, too."

All three men nodded. In theory the Emir of Dakar had agreed to forbid these waters to ships from his realm after the defeat he suffered at the Canaries from the united *kufr* fleets a decade ago. Abdou and Jawara had both been there, fighting beside their fathers in their first real war, and had been among the lucky minority who escaped alive from the arrows and flamethrowers and the waiting sharks.

In practice the Emir had neither the power nor the wish to control the ships that sailed from the tangled swamps and creeks of the Saloum delta, looking for revenge as well as wealth. Their folk *needed* the salvage of the ruined cities, not just metals but gears and springs and glass and a hundred other things; and the English charged usurer's rates for such. But the treaty allowed their navy to attack vessels in the exclusion zone on sight, which they did with ghastly efficiency.

The Mouride cleric went on: "These men—who are veritably followers of the Prophet—"

Abdou caught a glimpse of *something* he didn't like in

the man's eyes then; something like mockery. He gritted his teeth and ignored it. There was work to do.

"—say they can build a trebuchet. There's plenty of timber in the barns and outbuildings, and their savages to do the rough work. They need some help with tools, and our ship's carpenters and smith, but they have an engineer who has erected one before and knows the proportions."

The corsair leader rubbed his chin beard, shuddering a little as bits of ice condensed from his breath fell off it. The strangers had already built mantlets, thick sloped wooden shields on wheels that would stop arrows and bolts. The corsairs had brought two light pieces of deck artillery ashore; a rover ship was built for that sort of flexibility. But the six-pounders wouldn't knock that wall down, not if they threw roundshot from now until the Day of Judgment or until the ships' ammunition ballast was all gone.

We might be able to set it on fire. Or the town. But charred ruins yield little plunder. A trebuchet could break down the timbers and spill the rubble core.

A trebuchet was the most powerful of war engines, and the simplest; a giant lever pivoting between uprights, with a box of rock fastened to the short end and a throwing sling to the long one. Given one of those and enough time they could batter their way through walls of well-fitted stone blocks, or even ferroconcrete, much less timber with rubble fill. A big trebuchet could throw a half-ton rock the better part of a mile, but they weren't naval weapons—more a matter of fortress and siege warfare—and none of his carpenters and metalworkers were familiar with them.

But given time *is the word to remember here. Risky! Still . . .*

The plunder *was* tempting, and the chance to show the Norrheimer pagans that interfering with his people wasn't a good idea even for battle-drunken madmen. If he had been a timid man, he wouldn't have become a corsair. Growing peanuts and rice was much safer than being the skipper of a Saloum rover, and trading in cotton and indigo was *almost* as lucrative.

A big trebuchet can make a ramp out of that wall. By God and His Prophet, though, I know who's going to lead the assault, when it comes—and it isn't going to be my *men.*

The thoughts took only an instant. "We'll do it. And let us not give the infidels the precious gift of time."

"So, tell me about your betrothed," Edain said quietly when the scouting party had stopped for the night.

Ritva gave him a look and slipped away to take the first watch. They'd made a cold camp here; no fire, of course, just rearranging some snow below an overhang and bringing in some spruce boughs for insulation between their bedrolls and the ground—as long as you were out of the wind it was the earth below you that sucked away the body's heat. All that they had to do was unroll the sleeping bags, arrange their weapons close to hand, and huddle close while they gnawed on sausage and cheese and crackerlike rye flatbread. And kept their canteens in with them, to keep the water from freezing.

The air was clear above for a change, with coldly glittering stars shining in glimpses through the needles of the spruce and pine. Air soughed through the branches, sending an occasional mist of snow like powdered silver down towards the ground.

He thought Mary's single eye gave him an ironic look too over the fur-trimmed edge of her bag. They all used the same type, greased leather lined with fur and down-stuffed quilting, with catches that could be loosed with a single movement. The two Dúnedain had had their own from the beginning—Rangers went places where it usually got this cold—and he'd gotten his in Readstown. The Bjorning girl had something almost identical.

Sure, and these things are an amazement, Edain thought. *With one of them and all your clothes, you can get all the way from* frozen to death *to just* miserable *in only an hour or two! Ah, but wouldn't it be nicer with two?*

You could join two of them together; Mary and Ritva often laced theirs into one. Asgerd wasn't interested in being that close with *him.* Yet. Not that you could do anything *but* huddle in weather like this. Freezing to death was no joke when it got this cold.

"Sigurd was a hero!" she said. Then: "His father was one of Erik the Strong's handfast men. He came north with his bride and won land, but Sigurd was the third son, and—"

Edain made approving noises. Asgerd was hotly devoted to this Sigurd's memory and he had *no* objection. The man was dead, after all; also it proved she had a loyal heart. When she'd run down and made herself depressed—he winced slightly as the eagerness in her voice turned to the sort of sadness that made you feel core-chilled even on a warm summer's day—she said with obvious effort:

"And what will you do when your chief . . . your King Artos . . . has this Sword?"

"Like something out of an old tale, isn't it?" Edain said dreamily.

"Like Anduril, the Flame of the West," Mary said; there was no irony in her voice this time. "When the sword is ready, the King returns."

"We'll take it back home, and the worst of luck to anyone who tries to stop us," Edain said. "And Rudi . . . Artos . . . will raise armies, beat the Cutters, and everyone will hail him High King."

"Everyone?" Asgerd said, her voice a little pawky. "You have no disputes or feuds, out there in the West?"

"Everyone who knows what's good for them will," Edain said. "And for the rest—"

He had his bow with him in the bag, to keep it that little bit more supple; he stuck the tip of it out and wiggled it a little. Mary gave a grim sound of assent.

"And when he's King, what will *you* do?" Asgerd asked.

Edain frowned. "Fight for him when he needs me to ward his back," he said. "Help Da on the farm between times. Take over the holding when he's gone to the Summerlands, and sure, I hope that's many years yet."

Asgerd laughed, with an edge of iron to it. "From the sagas, that's not what happens to the right-hand men of new-made Kings."

Mary chuckled too, the sound just as grim. "She's got you there, Edain. We don't know everything of what being High King will mean, exactly. But I give you any odds you're not going to see much plow-and-pitchfork work. Boyo," she added with malice aforethought.

"Teeth of Anwyn's hounds!" Edain said, dismayed; he *liked* tending the land. "Da did, and he was First Armsman!"

"Of the Mackenzies. Rudi's going to be *High King of Montival*, though. Rudi said he wouldn't spare himself, or us, to see the work of the King done right. Did you think he was joking?"

"No. It's not the sort of thing he'd jest on," Edain said unhappily. "I just thought he meant he'd put us in harm's way in battle if it was needful . . . how different could High King be from being Chief?"

"Times have changed," Mary said. "The world's not as simple as it was."

He could see Asgerd nodding. "Here too," she said. "There's been talk of choosing a king of Erik's line. There's more people now, for one thing. The realm needs more steering."

Not just a pretty girl who's middling good with a sword, Edain thought. Then: *I was looking forward to going home. Maybe I can't, even when we're home again!*

Then Mary's head went up; he felt a prickling himself an instant later . . . as if he was listening to an absence of sound rather than a noise in itself. Asgerd's head went back and forth between them, puzzled.

Smart, but she hasn't spent as much time as we on the trail with lunatics and boogeymen after her, that she has not, Edain thought grimly, and pulled the toggle that opened his bag.

Ritva made a twittering sound before she came into sight, to avoid hasty arrows. She was wearing a winter version of the war-cloak, white, mostly, with less vegetation and more broad strips of pale cloth that made you look like a lump of snow when you stopped.

"We're a bit closer than we thought. I spent half an hour right under one of *their* sentries," she said. "Come look."

CHAPTER NINETEEN

Rudi could see the throwing arm of the trebuchet move despite the bright morning sun rising behind it. The great wooden baulk was tiny as a matchstick in the distance even through the binoculars he held in his left hand; his right was around the tree trunk, hugging the rough resin-smelling wood. The picture swayed as the big pine did. The two of them were high enough up that their weight made that sway worse, like a rock at the end of a stick, but the snow-clad branches all around should still hide them as long as he was careful not to let light flash off the lenses.

The war engine was of the simplest, a thick upright beam on either side braced with shorter logs fore and aft like a double inverted V. The throwing arm was another tree trunk swinging between them, roughly smoothed and pivoting on a metal axle a third of the way along. The stone in its sling lay loosely on the trampled snow for an instant, as the arm stood pointing downward. Then the ropes were released. For an instant the great box of rocks on the shorter end stayed poised aloft; then it began to fall, slowly for an instant, gathering speed until the air whirred. The long arm moved even faster, dragging the sling along the packed snow in a shower of shavings and lumps, then soaring aloft. The cradle of woven rope whipped upward at its end, and at the height of the curve the eye that held it closed slid off the carefully shaped hook at the end of the beam.

A dull *whunk* and heavy creaking sounded as the weighted end of the throwing arm rocked back and forth at the bottom of its trajectory, the longer tapering part upright like a mast swaying in a storm, with the loosened sling for a pennant. All the while a two-hundred-pound boulder flew free. It spun lazily through the hazy air, seeming slow even though he knew it was traveling faster than a galloping horse, if more slowly than an arrow. Then there was a *crunch* that made him wince slightly even at this distance. The field glasses showed man-thick logs snapping like twigs. A section of wall wavered and sagged outward, its frame of rod and cable shattered by the repeated blows. Rubble poured out as the logs tumbled, and now the inner row of timbers was exposed.

Captured oxen were brought up to hitch to the winch that would haul the machine back to its ready position, and men began to roll another rock forward.

Edain showed teeth in what was not quite a smile. "I thought the Cutters were against machinery?" he said quietly.

He wasn't using glasses, but his unaided vision was the keenest the Mackenzie heir had ever met.

"They are; complex ones. Not levers," Rudi said grimly. "And to be sure, that's as simple an application of leverage as you can get, short of a club like the Dagda's for the bashing of heads. They've bashed well at the blockhouses on either side of the stretch they're knocking down, you notice?"

He'd brought Edain up for a reason. The young man was more than bright enough to learn more of war than what you needed to lead a few archers.

And I'm going to need him. *For all that I've got so many capable commanders-in-the-making in this band.* "Engines there?" Edain said.

"There were. And enough well-protected archers shooting through slits to make an assault like sticking your rod into a meat-grinder with a madman turning the crank. Whoever's in charge there knows his business. It's how I'd take the place myself, if I was in too much of a hurry to starve them out. Now quiet for a second."

He turned his attention to the rest of his enemies' efforts. There were the two ships anchored offshore, keeping the water approach covered with their deck engines. He estimated them as a bit more than two hundred tons' burden each, substantial but not large. Probably with large crews, but there was no way to tell for sure how much of their space held men and how much food and water—they were far from home and from secure supplies.

And a camp ashore at twice bowshot from Kalksthorpe's defenses, of tents and brushwood huts surrounded by an abatis of tree trunks with their branches sharpened to act as obstacles. He rough-counted the men there, and the ones behind a row of mantlets before the breech. There were archers, stepping aside from the cover of the wheeled shields to shoot now and then, dueling with those on the wall. Two light throwing machines as well. One bucked and spat as he watched; what the western world called *scorpions*, more or less. The roundshot smashed chips off the pointed edges of the logs along the fighting platform, and he thought he saw a man fall, though he couldn't be certain. There was a haze of smoke over the town, but no great black plumes. The attackers weren't using incendiaries.

Still, overshot rounds will smack through roofs and into kitchens or forges. Fire's always a threat in a wood-built town.

"Twenty-five or thirty of our old comrade Graber's Sword of the Prophet," he said.

"Sure, and they're as hardy as cockroaches!" Edain said.

"They're good fighting men, and no mistake," Rudi said. "Nor is there any giving up in them, at all. They're worthy of a better cause. Three times that number of those Bekwa savages; maybe four."

Edain grunted thoughtfully. Rudi could read his thought: fierce men, fearless and deadly on their own ground, but lightly armed and not trained for a stand-up fight.

"And as many again from those ships, the Moorish pirates. They look well armed and most malignantly expert in their trade, the grievous sadness and pitiful misfortune of it, *ochone*."

"Two hundred inside the wall, less any they've lost, from what our friends of this land say," Edain said. "Counting every booger and arsewipe, as me da would put it."

"And just thirty-six of us here," Rudi said. "Call it two hundred, two hundred and thirty on either side."

He cased the binoculars and tapped his knuckles thoughtfully on his chin for an instant.

"This is going to require the most careful timing," he said. "We're enough to pull it off . . . but only just, do y'see."

"With luck, and the Lugh's own favor."

They slid down the tree, dropping from branch to

branch and springing the last ten feet or so. His companions gathered around him.

"It can be done," Rudi said. "To boil it down, we wait until they're all engaged, then attack them from the rear. But it's possible only if we have some advantage of surprise. Take them at just the right moment, and it will work. Otherwise, bloody failure. The problem there is that the Cutter magus has what I'd be calling a most unpleasant habit; he knows things he should not. Not with just his five senses."

Thorlind was gray-faced but determined. "He will not."

"Not this time," Heidhveig said. "I can . . . feel him. Like putting down your hand and having it push into a rotten corpse seething with maggots. He's very strong. But we can blind him. For a little while."

"A little while is all we'll need. We must also take out their sentries, as many as possible. Delay the alarm as long as we can."

"When will you attack?" Thorlind said.

"Not until they've made their breach in the wall. Not until they've launched *their* attack, and are fighting in the town itself, tangled up amongst the buildings with no way to run."

Thorlind's face was grim, and Heidhveig's like an age-worn stone.

"So long?" she said. "You must wait until they've entered our home?"

"Yes," he said with calm firmness. "We aren't enough to count on driving them off if we attack sooner. A blow struck when your enemy's off-balance is the one that knocks him down so that you can put the boot into him. And even if we did put them to flight earlier . . . we would not reap and savage them as we must. Pushing an enemy back isn't enough, nor even making them run; too much chance of their returning the favor, manyfold, some other day. I want to catch them between my hammer and the anvil of the town and *crush* them. And the price of that must be paid, for it is the price of victory."

"Paid by my people," Thorlind said.

Rudi met her eyes and nodded. "For the most part, yes. The cost of defeat would be much higher."

Heidhveig gathered her bearskin robe around her shoulders. "I'm glad I don't have to make decisions like that," she said softly.

"And I'd be glad never to make them either," Rudi said. "But if I'm to make them, make them I will, and properly."

He raised his head from the map. "Ingolf, you're in charge of the main body; Father Ignatius, you're second in command."

Then his finger went over the parchment. "As for their sentries . . . Mary and Ritva, you take the ones here. Edain, Asgerd, here. Fred and Virginia, here. Matti and I will see to the removal of the ones here in the center, and them causing such a blockage and obstruction, the spalpeens."

That was a legitimate use of his own talents; he was much more likely to succeed than anyone else they had.

I'm a general with an army of about platoon size, right now. And one with a round half score of followers fit for the command.

"Ingolf, you come forward with the main body, and we'll rejoin as you do. Then we cross the open ground and hit them before they can disengage. Keep ranks; no quarter until I command, or they all throw down their arms. Lady Heidhveig, Lady Thorlind, you'll remain here. Is everyone clear? Then let's *go*."

* * *

The enemy sentries should be here, Rudi thought, twenty minutes later, baffled. *They had perches in the trees.*

Instead everything looked just as it had; the last fringe of pines, towering over hummocky ground covered in thick soft snow . . . and no sentries waiting concealed in their branches, as Edain and the others had reported.

That snow exploded upward right at his feet. A man came after it, the long knife in his hand flashing upward. The point struck him in the pit of the stomach, and breath gusted out of him with a grunting *ufffff!*

Shock and fear happened, but distantly; as distantly as pain. Will forced air back into his lungs in a whooping gasp. He could see his own shock reflected in the other man's dark face, exaggerated by the bar of white paint across his eyes, as the knife tip stopped on a plate of the brigandine beneath the Mackenzie's parka. The knife kept prodding, reflexively, as if the man couldn't believe it hadn't sunk hilt-deep and ripped upward.

"Merd'!" the Bekwa blurted.

Rudi snarled, an utterly unconsidered guttural sound that sprang from the back of his throat. His long-fingered hands flashed out, weaponless, and clamped on the man's chin and the back of his head, *twisted* and pushed in one sharp ninety-degree turn to the left. There was a brief fibrous resistance and a sharp sound like green willow sticks breaking. He released the body instantly, and it fell limp as a banker's charity as Rudi whirled.

His sword hissed out, but the knee-deep snow leeched agility. Two men had come out of the same sort of deep hide as his attacker, snow allowed to drift over loosely woven spruce branches. Rudi's mind calculated without prompting, and his arm swept forward in a smooth arc.

The long hilt left his fingers with a feeling of inevitability like the sensation when you leap from a height into water. The yard-long blade turned twice in a blurring twinkle.

Thunk.

A heavy wet sound with a crackling beneath it, incongruous somehow in the cold air. The Bekwa who'd been about to stab at Mathilda's back looked down, goggling at two feet of longsword sticking out from his chest just below the breastbone. Blood steamed on the steel, and as it leaked out of his mouth and nose. Rudi stalked forward as the third man attacked Mathilda; she had her kite-shaped shield up, and the smooth curved visor of her sallet down. The long parka concealed her coat of titanium-alloy mail, but not the vambraces or greaves or gauntlets, and the metal had a gray glint in the bleak morning sunlight.

The Bekwa was bulky in his furs, but no taller than she, with a four-foot spear tipped with a spike of ground-down steel strip in his right hand and a knife in his left. Snow fountained out from under his feet, the moccasins throwing up trails like arcs of powdered diamond. The same snow was more than knee-deep on Mathilda; she waited in the perfect knightly form her instructors had taught, left foot forward and sword ready over her head. He could see d'Ath's instruction in it.

The savage came in with desperate speed. He leapt the last few feet, just as Rudi reached his dead comrade and wrenched his longsword free; the hilt and blade stood up like a mast from a ship. Then he was close enough to hear Mathilda grunt as the weight of the Bekwa struck her shield, the point of the spear grating across her helmet as she flicked her face and the vision-slit away. But she was already crouched and ready for the impact; the broad curved surface of the shield turned the swift thrust of the knife. The man reeled back, and her sword moved in an

economical overhand chop that ended with a crack of
steel in bone, then a low stab under the ribs. He sat
down, staring at the nearly severed forearm that jetted
blood onto the snow, clutched it to his chest and sank
backward to die.

There was only the panting of their breath in the cold
silence, and a murmur of something like *melleur place*
from the wounded savage. The face beneath the crude
paint was young, thin with bad feeding and rather sad as
the ferocity leeched out of it. His eyes wandered for a
moment, blinking and glazing with a look Rudi recognized; blood loss starving the brain. The Dread Lord's
wing had passed over his face, and it would be only seconds now.

"Maman?" he whispered.

Then he smiled uncertainly for an instant, and the expression fell away as he went limp. Mathilda closed his
eyes, drew the Cross on his forehead, then rose and
leaned against Rudi's shoulder.

"He said *we were going to a better place*," she said quietly as he squeezed her for a moment with his free arm.

"I don't doubt he has," he said. Then: "Earth must
be fed."

Rudi touched a finger to the blood on his steel and
then marked his forehead, murmuring the salute to the
departed. After that he whistled a fluting trill like a
bird's—not any particular type, but with a generic avian
sound. A few minutes later the same call came from the
woods about. Edain appeared with Asgerd trailing him;
she looked a little wobbly. Garbh trotted at his heels,
massive head low and licking her hairy chops, with a little
congealed blood from a slight cut on her right
shoulder.

"All right?" Rudi said; he couldn't see any wounds on

the Bjorning girl, though there was a spatter of red drops drying on the mottled white of her coat.

"In the event, Chief," the young clansman said. "They'd come down from their perches, though, and weren't where we expected, and there was an extra one. I had to shoot a bit fast—the last one was only winged. Asgerd took care of him, though. Might have been right nasty, if she hadn't."

"My first." She swallowed and added. "It . . . wasn't like practice. More like pig-butchering time. And as if I was watching myself kill him."

Edain put a hand on her shoulder for a moment. "He chose to come onto your land uninvited with a weapon in his hand," he said. "When a man does that, he consents to his fate and makes you clean of his blood."

She took a pair of deep breaths and nodded. "That's true. And . . . that's one towards my oath," she said, her voice growing stronger.

Then she looked at Garbh. "That dog is a man-killer."

Edain grinned. "To be sure, when she needs to be, or when I tell her, she *is* a man-killer. So am I. And so are you, now."

Asgerd nodded, but there was a dubious expression on her face, as if she was trying to frame an objection but couldn't quite think of the words.

"And we've both hunted wolves, eh?" She nodded again. "The Gods have made the world so that sometimes we must kill to live; not just us, but our brother wolf and tiger and bear too. In the end, the Hunter comes for us all. Earth must be fed."

Mary and Ritva were silent when they came ghosting up; the one-eyed Ranger was wiping the sickle blade on the end of her fighting chain, which was comment enough.

Fred and Virginia appeared next; the girl from Wyoming had a fresh scalp at her belt, and the dark young man was limping very slightly. Rudi went forward with slow care, then down on one knee behind a screen of leafless brush at the edge of the woods—where forest met open country there was always a screen of it. Through his binoculars he could see past the besieger's camp, which looked empty now except for a few threads of smoke that were probably cookfires, or heating water for healers to use.

Beyond that the town wall was even more battered than it had been from his treetop lookout earlier; they were getting a boulder into the air every fifteen minutes or so, good practice with a hastily built weapon and un-trained crew. Shattered timber and rock made a rough low slope through the gap the trebuchet had pounded. The two scorpions bucked again, and the loads they threw trailed smoke. They *were* using incendiaries now, the best possible way to knock back any defenders massing to hold the breach. Thick volleys of arrows hissed up from behind the mantlets, not individually aimed but falling in a steel-tipped rain where any defenders would be.

Graber knows his business, to be sure. And I'd be betting that the pirate captains do so, too.

Crackling and muffled footfalls came from behind him; you couldn't move two-score warriors through the forest silently at a trot, even if they were all woodsmen individually.

"Ready," Ingolf said, slightly breathless; running in armor did that, no matter how fit you were.

"Their outposts didn't give any alarm," Rudi said; which was a stroke of luck, even with experts in what the Dúnedain called *sentry removal* at work.

He raised his voice: "Form on me. Archers to the front, and then on the flanks when we charge. Edain, the usual for an assault. Now wait for the word . . . and when I give it, a steady trot keeping good order, no more. It's useless a man is when he's too winded to fight."

Even as he spoke figures spilled out from behind the mantlets, running forward towards the ruined wall of Kalksthorpe under the cover of the arrowstorm and the globes of napalm. Those lifted as they swarmed screeching up the rough slope, arching higher to fall safely behind the first rank of the defenders. The crest seemed to sprout armed men as the survivors of the bombardment rose to meet them. Faint with distance he could hear the screams of the Bekwa, and a deeper chant:

"Cut! Cut! *Cut!*"

The Moorish pirates had slung their bows; they formed up in two solid blocks behind the sloped siege shields, waiting and still. Tall poles or spear shafts held green flags over their heads, with a squiggle of some unfamiliar script in silver on them, visible as the sea wind streamed them out. The bleak light glinted on their spearheads, above the dun mass of their tall almond-shaped hide shields. Here and there ostrich-feather plumes danced on a helmet or jewels glittered, oddly cheerless in the light of northern winter.

Odard hissed between his teeth. "I suspect that they're not all blood brothers out there," he said. "It's *after you, my friends. No, no, I* insist, *after* you!"

"You are a cynic, my lord Gervais," Father Ignatius said; he was on the other side of Mathilda from Rudi. "I fear you are right this time, as well. Your Majesty?"

"Wait. Wait," Rudi said, even as another long guttural shout rang out, this time from the corsairs:

"Alllaahuuu Akbaaaar!"

"Wait . . . not quite yet . . ."

The green flags waved and the rover crews ran forward

towards the thump and clatter and screams of combat beyond the broken wall.

"God is Great," the priest murmured. "So He is indeed. But men, alas . . . Father, forgive us for what we are about to do, and forgive us that we can see no better way. Lord who blessed the centurion, bless us also this day. But Thy will alone be done, for Thy judgments are just and righteous altogether."

"Holy Mary, Lady pierced with sorrows, Queen of Heaven, intercede for us, now and at the hour of our deaths," Mathilda added soberly; she held up her sword for an instant by the blade, kissed the cross the hilt and guard made, then tossed it up and caught it ready. "For us and for our foes."

"Amen," the Christians said.

Tension grew, with a taste like hot copper and salt at the back of his throat. For a moment Rudi thought the wings beating above were in his mind. Then he realized they were two real ravens, launching themselves from a tall spruce. They soared upward, circling above the town. He felt a chill worse than the sweat congealing on his flanks under the armor and padding. Then a great calm, and under it a lifting current of hot anger.

"Yes," he said. "It's time, Victory-Father." Louder: "For Montival! Follow me!"

"Artos and Montival!" his companions called.

The wedge of them trotted out into the open ground, snow floating up around them like dust to the pounding of booted feet.

"No!" Abdou al-Naari snarled, cuffing a man over the head with a gloved fist. "I'll castrate the first man who plunders before the battle ends!"

The crewman staggered, dropped the golden necklace he'd been pulling off a body and picked up his shield again. An arrow struck quivering in it a moment later with a hard dry *thunk* and the man's eyes rolled in shock.

Abdou coughed; the whole town wasn't burning, but there was enough smoke to lie thick. And it was a maze of lanes and log houses with steel shutters over their doors and lower windows; from the upper ones came arrows and spears, rocks and jars of burning lamp oil. Bodies of pagans and corsairs and their allies littered the trampled mud and dirty snow of the street, in a mess of blood and broken weapons and men who shrieked or whimpered or tried to crawl aside and bandage themselves.

Spears and axes waited behind a rough barricade of carts and furniture a little farther down; he could see the tiered roofs and gilt and painted dragonheads of the pagan temple beyond. If they took that, only the boat sheds and docks remained.

"Shields!" he called.

The *Bou el-Mogdad*'s crew rallied, raising a wall of wood and leather ahead and overhead as well. Under that tent he looked around for his bosun, shouting the man's name:

"Falilu!"

The man looked up, and Abdou pointed to a well-placed house larger than the others with his sword.

"That one. Clear it and get us some covering fire while we storm the barricade."

The man nodded, grabbed a dozen hands who were all archers. They slung their bows, lifted a thick timber and began beating in a door; it gave off a thudding *bang* like a huge drum as they rammed their way through.

Then it fell inward, and they drew their blades and charged in; screams came out then, but only a few clashes of steel on steel.

"The rest of you, with me. *God is great!*"

They charged the barricade with their tall shields locked together against missiles. Those rattled and thunked and banged off the protection until the moment they had to climb the obstacle; here and there a man fell, silent or screaming or cursing, but the others closed ranks and kept up the rush. Steel probed for his life as the wild corsair charge struck. He knocked the spearhead aside, slicing up it at the wielder's fingers; a snarling face loomed out of the corner of his eye and a huge two-handed ax swung towards his head. Another man's shield put itself in the way; Abdou could hear it crack beneath the force of the blow.

He slashed at the pagan's face and he fell backward in a spray of blood as the ugly yielding feel of thin bones breaking flowed up wrist and arm. Grown men and boys and elders and even shrieking women were in the crowd facing the corsairs in a heaving, stabbing, shoving mass. Then they turned and pulled back as a shower of black cane arrows came slashing down from the house, driven by powerful whalebone-backed bows.

Abdou braced the point of his scimitar on a broken cart and his weight on the pommel for a moment to sob for breath, waving his free hand to Falilu, who grinned from the second-story window before he loosed another shaft.

Then a choked-off cry of pain drew his notice. Ahmed was crumpled at his feet, trying to get the broken shield off his arm. Abdou helped his son, and though the youngster was silent his teeth brought blood from his own lips.

"Not broken, dislocated," the father said. Then, in a sharp bark: *"What's that?"*

The boy's head jerked aside to see what had brought the cry of alarm. In the same instant his father grabbed the arm, pulled and twisted. The joint went back into its socket with a *click* audible as much by feel as through the noise of combat. Ahmed made a stifled sound, but the rough treatment was over before he could shift his attention back to it.

"And you saved my life." Abdou grinned into the pain-sweating face. After a moment the younger man grinned back. "Now stay close. That arm will be too sore to hold a shield for days."

They pushed on over the ruins of the barricade, and the houses drew back on either side. The triangular open space before the silver-worked and gilded doors of the idolater's temple—even then a brief *what a place to sack!* went through his mind—was crowded, but the fight was shaking itself out into lines after the chaotic scramble through the streets. His crew linked up with that of the *Shark*, and Jawara was there, grinning like the predator itself.

"We have them, I think," he yelled.

Abdou nodded and let the battle surge past him; his head went back and forth. The pagans were still fighting, but they were outnumbered now . . . and most of the casualties on his side had been the weird allies the Marabout had found, not his own folk. Which was *just* as he'd planned.

A cry came from behind him; in Wolof, and not just the sort of screaming—usually for their mothers—that men in unendurable pain made. He turned, and his eyes went wide in alarm. It was one of the men held left as a rearguard at the broken wall. Two gray-fletched arrows stood in the back of his steel-strapped cuirass of doubled hippo hide, and his left forearm and hand were a dripping mass of ruin through which bone showed pink-white. His right held the broken stub of a sword.

The man fell forward into Abdou's arms, and the captain turned and laid him down gently on his side. Blood bubbled out across his broad dark face, and his eyes were blind as they hunted about. It was a younger cousin of his, not much older than Ahmed.

"What is it, Dia?" he asked.

"Too many," the man mumbled. "Couldn't stop them. They come. Warn the skipper! *Hurts!*"

"You have warned me," Abdou said.

He spoke loudly, to cut through the haze of agony and fear. The other did hear, and understand for an instant.

"You die with honor. Go with God, ghazi of the Faith. The gates of Paradise open for you."

The man forced a smile, shuddered, jerked, died. Abdou rose and met Jawara's eyes.

"We're fucked," the other man said. "So much for our allies' *sentries* who were *experienced woodsmen.*"

"They met someone more experienced," Abdou said. "We couldn't divide our forces and we didn't know the country. Probably some force from inland."

Which was any corsair's nightmare on a longshore raid; you had to strike swiftly and then *go*. He drew a deep breath. A rover captain had to be able to think quickly in an emergency—even a disaster, as this had suddenly become. He went on urgently:

"Your men are closer to that southern gate and it's probably not held anymore. Chances are any of the pagans there hurried back into the street fighting when we came over the wall. Get going. Cut your way through anything you meet and stop for nothing. It can't be helped. *Inshallah*, we can break contact and follow you."

Jawara started to protest, and Abdou grabbed him by the shoulder and shoved him backward hard.

"Go! Now! We'll hold them as long as we can and then retreat. You can cover us from the water with your ship's catapults. *Go!*"

What in Shaitan's name happened at the wall?

"Volley! Forward six paces. Volley! Forward six paces! Volley! Forward six paces—*pick your man.* Volley! Volley! Wholly together! *Volley!* Forward six paces!"

Edain had the bowmen well under control. Two dozen longbows bent and spat at the sparse line of corsairs opposing them in the gap of the shattered wall. A third of them fell, and the rest wavered as the heavy-armed band around Rudi came up behind the thin line of archers. He knocked down his visor with a hard *snick-clack*!

"Morrigú!" he shrieked, as the world shrank to a slit. *"Charge!"*

They ran forward in a wedge with him at the point; the archers slung their bows, drew blades or axes or mallets, and followed. A curved sword swung at his head as he leapt up the body-littered slope of the broken wall, agile as a great steel-skinned cat, screaming like a panther in battle heat. He ducked beneath the stroke and stabbed up at the man above him. The point of the western longsword went in behind the chin and punched through the thin bone that shielded the brainpan. Rudi wrenched it free; Matti's shield knocked aside a spearpoint probing for his face, unseen until the last instant. His own shield blocked a slash and he cut the man's legs out from under him with a chop that severed a thighbone.

Cries rang out, battle slogans where they weren't just raw shrieks of rage or of pain:

"Morrigú! *Morrigú!*"

"Allahu Akbar!"

"Jesu-Maria!"

"*Haro*, Portland! Holy Mary for Portland!"

"Ho La, Odhinn!"

"Face Gervais, face death!"

"Artos and Montival!"

There was a long moment of slipping, scrambling fighting on the uncertain footing of the broken wall. Rudi felt an arrow hammer into his knight-style shield; six inches of it showed through the inner felt lining just beside his forearm until he broke it off with the hilt of his sword. The Moors' bows hit hard. The man was behind a balk of timber, fumbling another shaft onto the string when Rudi's lunge punched the point of the longsword into his throat.

It didn't sink deeply—the lunge had also slammed Rudi's shield and chest against the pinewood—but it was enough to send him back, both hands scrabbling at the wound. Rudi vaulted over into the place he'd occupied, landing with a grunt under the weight of his armor and dodging a stroke from a curved slashing sword in the same instant. A big Bjorning named Hrolf followed Rudi, roaring, one of their newcomers from Eriksgarth. His blow met and snapped the sword in a shower of sparks, then crushed the Moor's shield hand right through the thick leather with a swing of the hammer side of his ax.

"Edain. *That one!*"

Rudi pointed with his sword as the wounded man dodged beneath a return stroke that would have taken his head off, turned and sprinted into the town; you could tell when a man was running *to* something, as opposed to just *away*.

The younger clansman sprang up on the balk of timber behind him. The pirate staggered as two shafts thudded into his leather armor, then ran on and vanished behind the corner of a building. His comrades ducked and backed, wavering on the edge of panic as Rudi stood ready with dripping sword and shield up under his visor's beak. Arrows showered down on them as more and more of the attackers came over the ridge and put their bows to work. Garbh paced the rubble at Edain's feet and barred blood-dripping red teeth.

"There they go!" Mathilda said breathlessly, as she scrabbled over to join him.

The last few pirates broke and ran, down into the smoke-fogged streets. Rudi looked over the town, recalled what the descriptions and maps had said, made a quick decision.

We need to put a lid on the kettle, he thought. *Otherwise they'll squeeze out, if they've their wits about them. But I wish I had more men to spare.*

"Odard!" he called.

The Portlander noble looked at him, mouth a grim line beneath his visor and sword dripping crimson-dark.

"Take six men and block that road there, the one to the south gate. Hold if anyone comes at you, push on to the square in front of the temple if nobody does."

"Your Majesty!"

That's actually starting to sound more natural, and less like a joke, some corner of Rudi's brain noted.

Odard dashed off. Rudi led the rest down the ruined wall and into the town—there was a clear strip inside the defenses, and then houses.

"Come out!" he shouted. "Kalksthorpe folk, come out and fight!"

There were probably a lot of dwellers still inside, waiting to sell their lives hard when their doors were beaten in. He filled his lungs and shouted again, a great bass sound like a trumpet in the fouled street, overriding the sound of boots and the growing clamor of combat.

"Come out and fight!"

The folk of Kalksthorpe came out of their homes to join them as they loped down the street, with sword or ax, spear or smith's hammer in their hands.

We're not going to make it to the south gate, Abdou al-Naari knew. *Maybe we should have tried for the water and the boats . . . No, it was fated. I shouldn't have listened to that so-called holy man!*

He could have been content with what he'd found in Miami and Baltimore and been halfway back to home by now with a good if unspectacular cargo; the knowledge was as bitter on his tongue as the wormwood tea the hakims brewed for fever.

The last knot of his crew formed up around him, their backs to the blank log wall of a warehouse or workshop. The newcomers surrounded them, in wildly mixed gear that didn't look like Norrheimer equipment at all. The leader of the strangers came at him, leading the rush. He was a tall young man in full armor that showed through the rents in his winter coat; a crescent moon cradled between antlers showed on his shield.

But he moved like moonlight on water under the weight of steel and wood and leather, his long straight sword trailing red drops as he whipped it in an effortless figure eight. A taut grin showed beneath the beaked visor of the odd-looking helmet, with light stubble the color of sunset along the jaw; behind the vision-slit were eyes as blue-green as tropic seas.

This one is trouble, the pirate captain's experience told

him. Then: *No. He is the shadow of Azrael's wings. He is death.*

Abdou called on God—or croaked—and cut at the unbeliever's knee. The kite-shaped shield twitched into the path of the slash and glanced the blow, leaving him off-balance. The corsair twisted desperately and tried to get his own tattered hippo-hide shield up as the return thrust came for his throat, driving like the strike of a cobra, faster than any man had a right to move. He succeeded just enough to keep his windpipe unslit. Instead it plowed into his shoulder like the kick of a horse focused behind a narrow point of steel, breaking the mail links and tough leather, nearly breaking the bone. Agony ran through his body like rays of sunlight.

His sword fell from nerveless fingers, and the captain of the *Bou el-Mogdad* looked death in the face as the blade rose again. He dropped his own shield and grabbed for his enemy's, snarling as he tried to wrestle it away while his hand scrabbled for his dagger. The effort sent ice spikes into his wounded shoulder. Another, slighter figure attacked beside him.

"Ahmed, no!" he cried.

The straight longsword beat the boy's scimitar out of his hand with a snapping backhand slash and plowed on to cut flesh. In the same instant the green-and-silver shield smashed into Abdou like a collapsing wall in an earthquake, hammering him back against the logs behind him; the impact of his helmeted head on the wood had him seeing flashes of light for a second. There was no more room to retreat and his sword arm hung useless.

"Surrender!" the man who'd wounded him shouted, his blade poised to pin the rover captain to the logs. "Surrender, and sure, we'll spare you all!"

There was a brief pause, as men panted and glared hate

at each other from arm's reach. Ahmed was alive, rolling on the dirty snow and clutching at his twice-hurt arm. His father looked to either side; a dozen men were all that were left on their feet, though more of the fallen might live if they got help soon.

"I surrender," he growled thickly in the English tongue, and threw down his dagger and raised his hands. "We not fight more. No kill."

Or at least he raised his left, which still worked. The weakness and nausea of blood loss made his vision swim, and his lungs sucked at the cold air. His men did the same, all except one gone battle mad, who charged instead. A spear cut off his war cry, and an ax came down on his neck; Abdou kept his hand up, but for a moment he thought it would do him no good, as the killer's weapon went up for another smashing strike.

Then the stranger flicked his sword out. Even awaiting death, Abdou blinked at the casual speed and precision of it, faster than a shrike and more delicate than an artisan's graver tapping patterns into a silver dish. The sharp point rested in the bushy thicket of the ax-man's brown beard, and the Norrheimer froze motionless, his eyes rolling down to look at the length of blood-running steel. Behind him was a ring of his friends and kin and neighbors, looking on with interest; a Norrheimer even bigger than most barred their way with a gruesome hammer-ax weapon held parallel to the ground, leaving him isolated among the odd-looking company.

He had courage, though. "Who are you to stop me avenging my folk?" he asked.

The man with the sword at the ax-man's throat used his shield to push up his visor. That revealed a face that was beautiful in an alien way, though red and running with sweat. His breath puffed white in the chill air.

When he spoke the harsh English language held a lilting music, but the words might have been hammered from iron:

"I'm Rudi Mackenzie of the Clan Mackenzie, and High King of Montival, the which you couldn't know by looking at me. I'm the man the Gods have chosen to save the world, the creatures—the which you couldn't know either. But I'm also the man who saved your pisspot town, boyo, the which you *should* know by the evidence of your own eyes."

He prodded, very slightly, and the Kalksthorpe man swallowed.

"But be telling me now. Do I look, do I look in the *least little bit*, like a man who'd let you break his oath for him?"

"No," the Kalksthorpe man whispered.

His eyes locked on Rudi's like those of a rabbit on the very last wolf it ever saw.

"I promised these men quarter if they'd throw down, and throw down they did."

"Sorry," the Norrheimer muttered, as the sword withdrew.

"See to their wounds as you would those of your own folk, and then lock them up. Swear to it!"

"I swear. By Forsetti who hears oaths, and by my own honor in the sight of my kin."

"Give them food and water too . . ." He turned to Abdou: "Wait, pork is *geasa* for you, am I right?"

Abdou nodded, dazed as the pain started to push through the fading blaze of urgency; he bent to lift his son.

"*Haraam*, unclean, yes," he said.

"Then give them something they *can* eat." To his own followers: "Move! We have work to do yet!"

*   *   *

"Are you sure they won't harm those prisoners?" Father Ignatius said as they trotted southward.

"Reasonably, yes," Rudi said grimly. "And I have a use for them, I think, too."

Mathilda snorted something that was almost a chuckle. The Kalksthorpe folk were getting themselves organized with surprising speed, tending the hurt and putting out fires and scouring for enemy stragglers. He didn't think any such left within the walls would survive the next quarter hour however hard they tried to surrender, except the ones he'd given quarter.

"You!" he called.

The man was in late middle age with dark silver-shot hair receding from a high forehead and even darker eyes; he threw another bucketful of water on a smoldering wall and turned.

"Yah?" he said, nodding in friendly wise.

"Is anyone down by your boats? If you can get men out, they might be able to seize those enemy ships, or at least one of them, before they're crewed and away."

"I'm Thorleif Heidhveigsson," the man said, picking up a spear. "I'll see to it. Odinleif! Thorvin! Freyjadis! With me!"

Bodies lay thicker as they approached the gate. Thick enough to be worrisome; he'd sent Odard to do some flanking, not fight a major battle. Rudi hissed softly as he saw two of the Southsiders he'd sent with the young baron. They were the only ones still on their feet, and they were both badly wounded.

The hiss turned into a curse as he saw what they stood about. The most senior of them looked up, and went almost limp with relief.

"Rudi-man! Chief! They hits us hard. Too many!"

Mathilda gave a little sound, like a cat's, then clamped her lips shut. She didn't dash forward, but they all stopped around the figures on the ground, scattered where they'd fallen in the melee. Two near the end were in the armor of the Sword of the Prophet; another pair were the dark-faced corsairs. One of those was a near-giant, with his wiry black hair in long knotted locks and a great brass-bound club lying by his hand. His dark eyes were still open in a stare of astonishment, and one leg was slashed to the bone just below the hip with all his life's blood spilled from the huge wound.

The fifth was Baron Odard Liu de Gervais. He lay limp, his head propped up against a sack of something someone had dropped, with two trails of blood leaking out of the corners of his mouth. Battered shield and broken sword were near his limp hands. He opened his slanted blue eyes as they approached and smiled slightly.

Father Ignatius went down on his knees beside the fallen man; Rudi signed quickly, and the others dragged the bodies aside and helped the Southsiders. For a moment he was chiefly aware of relief; he'd nearly sent Edain on this errand. That brought a stab of shame, and he moved forward to kneel.

"I need you, Father, but not for that," Odard said, in a breathy whisper as the cleric started to reach for the latches of his armor.

The priest examined him through the gear instead; the injured man bit back a gasp at one gentle touch. Ignatius looked up at Rudi and Mathilda, and shook his head very slightly. Odard saw it and nodded a little.

"I can . . . feel the bones grating. The big one . . . caught me full-on. Please. Things to say . . . first. Taking off the hauberk would . . . do it quick. Got to . . . keep still."

"No," Mathilda whispered. "Not after we've come so far!"

"Dice . . . don't fall sixes . . . forever. Had to be . . . someone," Odard said. "Mathilda . . . I do love you. Didn't at first. Then I really did. Sorry I ever lied . . . to you."

She took one of his hands. Tears fell on it, but she raised it to her lips. "I love you like a brother, Odard. Like the brother I never had. I always will."

Rudi could see how hard Odard tried not to laugh, and felt a sudden upwelling of emotion in himself he recognized as close to love indeed.

May I face the Huntsman as boldly, he thought. *And to be sure I've never yet met a woman who understood why saying that drives men crazed.*

Odard's voice was light: "I don't even feel mad at hearing that bit about being a . . . brother, Your High . . . Mathilda. So I must be . . . dying. Look . . . after my family."

This one is not a perfect man, Rudi thought. *Who is? Not myself! But he's a man indeed.*

She nodded and clasped the hand in both of hers. "I will. I'll try my best for your mother. And I'll take your brother and sister in ward myself; they'll always have my protection and my favor. I promise it before God."

"Tell them . . . I died . . . well?"

Then she leaned closer and kissed him, very gently, on the lips.

"You are my knight, Sir Odard Liu, valiant and true as steel, with honor as golden as your spurs."

"I . . . think I am, at last."

His eyes turned to Mary and Ritva and Rudi. "Mother . . . wanted you dead. Because of my . . . dad. I . . . didn't, not ever, really. Took a while to . . . see it."

Rudi leaned forward and—very lightly—touched Odard's shoulder.

"You've been a true friend, brother," he said. "I'll miss you. For yourself, and because you'd have been a right-hand man to me. One I could trust with my back."

"To quote . . . your father . . . this . . . sucks," Odard sighed, and then a sudden effort not to cough made sweat spring out on his face.

When he spoke again, there was a gurgle to it. "I would have followed you, Rudi. And I just get my . . . head straightened out and I die. Shit! Good-bye to . . . all of you. It's been . . . fun."

He moved one hand; Mathilda helped wrap his fingers around the hilt of his sword and move it, so that he could kiss the cross made by that and the stub of blade.

"Father?" he said, weak and breathy now. "We'd better get . . . started. There's . . . a lot to . . . confess."

They all moved back, and the priest leaned forward, opening the boiled-leather box across his back, taking out a long strip of cloth, kissing it and draping it about his neck. Rudi took another step backward when he heard Odard struggle to say:

"I confess to Almighty God, to blessed Mary ever Virgin . . . and to you, Father, that I have sinned exceedingly—"

Some things should be private. They all turned, making a wall between their friend and the world for a long set of moments. Nobody spoke as the murmured words sounded behind them. The twins looked the most stunned; they'd known Odard as long as he had, if not so well, and had always played a half-serious game of verbal feud with him. But even Virginia had been with him for most of a year now, and a damned intense one at that. Ingolf leaned close to Rudi and said very softly:

"I never liked him all that much. But by God, he's game."

Rudi nodded and murmured: "I thought the same."

The priest's voice rang a little louder behind them:

"*—Paradisi portas aperiat, et ad gaudia sempiterna perducat. Amen.*"

Odard's *Amen* was thready, barely perceptible.

"*Benedicat te omnipotens Deus, Pater, et Filius, et Spiritus Sanctus. Amen.*"

"Amen."

"Quickly, now, my friends," Ignatius said. "The Death Angel comes."

Odard's face was very pale now; the oil gleamed on his eyelids as they fluttered. The eyes moved as those he'd known best knelt around him, a greeting and farewell. After a few labored breaths he smiled; it should have looked grotesque, with the blood on his teeth, but it didn't. His face lit, looking *past* them somehow.

"*So . . . beautiful!*" he said, coughed blood and died.

CHAPTER TWENTY

"You are the man Abdou?" Rudi asked, leaning back in the chair.

That put his back to the window, which would make him an outline against the daylight and his face less readable, always an advantage. Mathilda sat at his right hand and Father Ignatius on the other; the *seidh-kona*'s sprawling household had found Matti Norrheimer woman's garb while their own was repaired and cleaned, a dark blue wool dress, head scarf and long apron of embroidered white linen and shoulder brooches of silver and jet. The pale winter light shone through the broad stretch windows and on his captive; this was an upper chamber, with a loom pushed up against the wall.

The Moor wasn't bound, but Edain stood behind him with his bow slung and his hand on the hilt of his sword, his square face wary and grim.

"I Abdou. And I commander of fighting men, just same like you."

The pirate captain was a tall man, as tall as Rudi himself, though more slender. Stripped of armor and outerwear he had a long robelike blue tunic embroidered at the shoulders and loose white pantaloons, both filthy and stained. There was stubble on his cheeks apart from the tuft of chin beard, and straws in his wiry hair beneath his skullcap; he smelled of sweat and dried blood and general misery, but he stood like a prince, his dark brown hawk-face calm despite the bruises and scabs. His injured right arm was in a sling.

"Why did you come to make war here?" Rudi probed.

"Because I think I win . . . just same like you."

Rudi laughed; the least shadow of a smile touched the corners of the prisoner's mouth for an instant. The clansman spoke:

"I am Rudi Mackenzie of the Clan Mackenzie; also called Artos, High King of Montival."

"I Abdou al-Naari al-Kaolacki, lord," the man said. "You say with English . . . Abdou the Moor from Kaolack."

"You're not all Moors?" Rudi asked, curious.

"No, lord. The peoples of north to the . . . Senegal River, you call it . . . are Moor. Beni Hassan. Many comed to south after the Change; my father be . . . one Moor. Comed Kaolack, comed sailor. Most there, they Wolof, Serer tribes."

The world is so wide; its folk and their Gods and ways so many! Rudi thought. Wistfully: *And one man's life is not enough to learn them all, even if he had no other business.*

The corsair's English was understandable, as long as he spoke slowly. Besides the thick accent, Rudi thought he'd learned from someone who spoke an English dialect unlike any used in Montival; now and then it reminded him a little of the way Sam Aylward sounded. Occasionally he spoke first in a liquid, pleasant-sounding tongue that was probably his own, and then translated.

"You are well?" Rudi went on.

Again the slightest smile turned up the corners of the man's mouth; he moved the fingers of his hand in the sling, and touched his temple with the other.

"*Suma bop dey meti*," he said. "I a headache, wounds pain little bit. My father is . . . fighter for Emir. Myself too. Captain of the *Bouel-Mogdad*. Hurt not . . . not big new thing."

"You *were* a captain," Rudi said sternly. "You are pirates, who came here to plunder; and you were taken in arms. So your lives are forfeit, and by right of battle you and your ship and your men belong to me, who spared you and took your surrender. You are mine to deal with as I will. Is this not so, Abdou al-Naari?"

"*Inshallah,*" Abdou said. "All things as God wills. No God except God; Muhammed is Prophet of God. What you do to me, that is will of God too. If you kill me, I am martyr for Faith and go to Paradise, sins forgiven."

That little speech was partly a bargaining gambit, he thought. *And partly what the man actually believes.*

It wasn't that a brave man was impossible to threaten. You just had to do it carefully.

"Who spoke of killing?" he said, spreading his hands. "Have you been treated well? Do you have what you need?"

"There food and straw and blankets and fire, medicine for our hurt. Two die, maybe one more soon. Others heal; my son Ahmed heal." He shrugged. "*Inshallah.* Need more water to wash, and how say, soap."

"You shall have it. And now, why did you come here, Abdou al-Naari? This place in particular, I mean."

"Marabout . . . Holy Man . . . say he have . . . how you say English . . . see in head thing far away."

"A vision."

"Yes, vision from God. Say followers of Prophet need

help, Muslim like us. Also rich plunder. And worshippers of many false gods . . ."

"Pagans," Mathilda said helpfully.

Abdou nodded without deigning to look at her. "Pagans, Norrheim men . . . fight our people, many time. Fight on sea, fight in dead cities. We teach lesson."

"The men with the sun sign on their chests met you near here? Led by one in a red robe?" Rudi asked.

"Yes. Marabout say, them men believers in Prophet."

His voice sounded dryly skeptical. Father Ignatius leaned forward from Rudi's other side.

"Followers of *a* Prophet, Abdou al-Naari. Not of *your* Prophet; of a living man who claims that title."

Rudi could see shock on the corsair leader's face, and for the first time there was heat in his voice:

"Muhammed is last of prophets, peace upon him! Some before—Issa, Jesus you *nasrani* call him, and Ibrahim before Issa. They prophets with message from God. No more after Muhammed! Is *haraam* . . . unclean thing, from Shaitan!"

"Blasphemy," Ignatius said helpfully.

Abdou nodded vigorously, winced and repeated the gesture despite the pain.

"Blasphemy," he agreed. "Is that word."

And he believes it, Rudi noted with interest. *This one is no fool. Even a short acquaintance with the Cutters would have shown him they weren't really of his faith. And this Holy Man . . . he must be also a servant of whatever Power the Cutters follow.*

"The folk here would kill you," Rudi said. "For vengeance, the which you have earned by falling on them without cause or warning. And they don't keep slaves. But I have a use for you and your ship."

Abdou's spine stiffened a little further. "Will not aid

you against believers, my friends," he said. "Kill us all first."

Rudi shook his head. "I wouldn't ask you to fight your own folk," he said, and added to himself: *Nor would I trust you if you said you would. Loyalty to clan and tribe and one's own blood isn't the* only *call on a man. But it's the foundation of all else.* He believed *that* with all his heart. There weren't many people alive a generation after the Change who didn't. Aloud he went on:

"I need a ship to take me and my followers to an island—"

They talked back and forth for a few minutes; Abdou had never heard the word *Nantucket*, or seen it except on old maps. His eyes went wide as he realized what his captor meant.

"Isle of the Accursed!" he said. "There magic there! Sorcery, strong magic."

"And to be sure, there is," Rudi said implacably. "Yet there I need to go; and my hosts here can spare neither crew nor ship, after the damage you did them. So it is to there I require your service. There, and back again."

The Moor thought for a moment. "You give back ship of my, I do this thing for you?"

Rudi threw back his head and laughed; the man might be a shameless saltwater bandit, but he had courage, to bargain so, alone amongst angry strangers and with a sword hung over his neck.

"You don't lack for stones, that's plain, Abdou al-Naari!" he said. "No. What you get for this service is your lives and the clothes you wear, no more. The ship and its cargo and gear goes to the folk of Kalksthorpe, as compensation for their losses."

"As wergild," Heidhveig said sternly. "Blood price. Count yourself lucky that our friend Rudi Mikesson needs you. And that he's a man of honor, and that we honor his wishes because of our debt to him."

The Moor looked at *her*. She sat like the spirit of the soil itself; the orange tabby-cat in her lap added its golden stare. The pirate captain blinked and nodded silently with wary respect, making a furtive sign with his good hand. Rudi went on:

"Once we're back you and your men will be held until an English ship puts in—and the Norrheimers have agreed to *not* ask them to hang you as pirates and enemies of humankind. They'll say you were shipwrecked here, which in a way is true enough."

Abdou winced slightly. "Big money English make our families pay," he said.

"Ransom."

"Ransom, yes." Then he shrugged. "Money come, money go, maybe come again, *inshallah*. Dead man dead always. We do. Go to Sorcerer's Island, take you."

He looked down at his arm. "I can navigate, another day, three, four, arm strong enough to hold sextant. Not enough my men able to work ship goodly. Only ten, not hurt bad too much. Wait, more ready with more days, crew big to sail ship with you."

This time Rudi's smile was thin; he didn't think Abdou al-Naari was stupid . . . and the Moor probably didn't think Rudi was stupid enough to entrust himself to a crew composed wholly of his corsairs, though he also probably thought there was no harm trying. And while Rudi couldn't navigate, he did know enough to keep an eye on the compass and the stars, so al-Naari wouldn't be sailing them off to Dakar or the Saloum delta.

"I have some men who've sailed," he said. "I have sailed myself, a little. More who can pull on a rope at need. I'll be bringing all my war band along; thirty-two of us. With your ten, that should do nicely for a short voyage of no great difficulty in a schooner. The others can stay here and heal from their wounds."

Al-Naari made that almost-smile again. *And be hostages, especially your son*, went silently between them.

It was good when men understood each other. The dark aquiline face was wholly grave when the book they'd found in his cabin was borne in, unwrapped and placed before him.

"And you will swear on your own holy things," Rudi said. "Let your own God hear your oath."

A week later two ravens swirled around the masts in Kalksthorpe's little harbor, on a day that dawned with bleak brightness in the east and a brittle cold in the wind out of the west. Rudi cocked an eye up at the dark forms. This was a natural place for the birds to congregate; the Norrheimer were a cleanly folk, but a fishing haven always had something for the birds. That tang of fish and fish guts was there, and silt, cold seawater, a faint reek of smoke even this long after the raid. There were plenty of gulls, too, though the great black birds ignored those. They perched for a moment on the foremast, and then took off southward along the coast.

The *Bouel-Mogdad* rose and fell slightly at her mooring at the end of the long T-shaped pier; she was a bit bigger than any of the Kalksthorpe ships. Kalk Shipwright himself prodded at her railing near the wheel and binnacle with his carved staff.

"I don't like this squared stern," he sniffed. "Weakens the stem, to my way of thinking. But the wood's sound. We don't have timber like this! The way it's worked . . . some is good. Some's strange."

Rudi nodded gravely. Kalk was old—nearly bald save for a fringe of white hair, stooped, his scalp and gnarled hands liver-spotted. His face reminded the Mackenzie of a turtle's, ready to snap out from beneath its shell. But his pale eyes were still keen, and so was the mind behind them.

As far as the Mackenzie could see the *Bouel-Mogdad*—it was bad luck to rename a ship—was in fine condition; he'd seen ships often enough in Astoria and Newport, sailed up and down the coast and studied the art of their making a little in shipyards he'd visited. The corsair vessel was a two-master and rigged all fore and aft, which made her a schooner, technically; about a hundred and ten feet long and thirty at its widest a third back from the sharply raked bow. The poop deck was about four feet above the level of the main; the fantail at the rear held one turntable-mounted war engine, crouching like a dragon of coils and angles behind its sloped steel shield. Another like it was placed in the bows—those two had been dismounted for the siege, and were now back in place—and three more sat on each broadside on limited-traverse mounts.

He could appraise the murder-machines with a true expert's eye, if not the ship. They differed from the ones made in Montival-to-be in a hundred details, but the laws of the mechanic arts knew no boundaries. They had about the same performance as a six-pounder scorpion, though they were marked for *three kilos* instead.

A net full of barrels swung by overhead, with one of the ship's spars used as a crane, then dropped smoothly into the hold. That was stores for the voyage, though mostly they'd added rock ballast to keep the lightened vessel stable. Folk swarmed about, working at the last touches to make her seaworthy; even the dark grained wood of the deck shone. Ashore a gang were singing as they dragged a long bundled sail down the pier, like a great beige snake with many legs.

The tune was a good one to work to, and it had a fine stormy rhythm:

"North to the coast of Iceland
South past the shores of Maine
Out with the whaling fleet
And north to the pole again
Over the world of waters
Seventeen seas I've strayed
Now to the north I'm sailing back
Back to the trawling trade!"

"And there's more mortise-and-tenon work in the hull framing than I like. Bolts hold better with a sheering strain," Kalk went on, after a pause that made Rudi think the elderly Norrheimer might have dozed. "Easier to replace."

Abdou al-Naari had his right arm out of the sling, though it would be a while before it regained full strength. He touched brow and lips and heart, and bowed to Kalk as one craftsman to another.

"You make good ship here," he said; his English had improved perceptibly in his brief time as a prisoner. "But we Kaolack men, first in Emir's country make more than big-big-big canoe after Change. We know skill of hands. I help build this ship, draw plans, see all make. Pick trees for her, too."

The master of Kalksthorpe glared at him, then nodded unwillingly.

"She's yare," he said. "Good work is good work."

"What is word, *yare*?" Abdou asked.

More barrels and bales swung on board. There was

plenty of room. They'd sent ashore the cargo picked up as the Moors cruised north along the coast, carefully selected metals, alloy steel, copper and brass and aluminum, lenses and telescopes and binoculars and microscopes, glassware, fine pre-Change cloth preserved as if new in sealed packages, wrought gold and silver and jewels, ball bearings, surgical instruments, springs and gears and light machine tools, circular saw blades and medicines and chemicals.

"Yare is . . . eager. Ready. Fit," the old man said.

Wealth couldn't bring the dead back, but the gold and gear would mean the Kalksthorpe folk wouldn't have to risk any voyages of their own southward in the coming year or two. That would save lives in itself.

"I glad you like ship," Abdou said quietly, and with obvious pride. "She good, fast, ride storm like bird. *Yare*, like you say."

Kalk gave him a hard smile from under tufted white brows. "So by Njordh, we'll get good use out of her, now that she's ours, *blaumann*."

Abdou winced; he'd seemed to grow an inch when he trod his ship's deck again. The song grew louder as the work gang approached, mounting the forward gangplank and feeding their burden down into the hold:

"Back to the midnight landings
Back to the fish-dock smell
Back to the frozen winds
As hard as the teeth of Hell!
Back to the strangest game
That ever a man has played
Follow the stormy rollers, back
Back to the trawling trade!"

Kalk looked around nodded once more, then headed down the gangplank himself, his staff going *thunk . . . thunk . . .* , a hollow sound on the boards.

And I do think he's envious of us, Rudi thought. He sniffed the air, with its scents of pine and pitch and salt. *Not that I blame him! I've done deeds of some weight, but this will be the strangest of all my farings.*

Rudi and Mathilda followed. The *seidhkona* and a small group of her townsfolk waited on the dock. The rest had said their farewells, and the day's work didn't wait with repair and rebuilding added to the usual labors. Thorlind looked at Rudi:

"You haven't taken all my vengeance yet, Artos King."

"I will, Lady," he said soberly, with a slight bow. "It's not a peaceful voyage I'm sailing on. Earth must be fed— and the sea, too, is always hungry. If I come back hale, you'll know the tale of it."

As if to comment on that, the last of the chanty came from the hold:

"And it's home with the harvest wind
And back to the Greyflood tides
Run to the starboard rail
And leap to the water's side—"

Heidhveig raised a hand in blessing; Rudi bowed in acknowledgment, and they went back on the waiting ship. The others waited for them; most on the main deck, which was a few feet down from the low poop that held the wheel, binnacle and compass. Rudi took his stance by the wheel, watching carefully. Two of Abdou's corsairs held it; that was skilled work. The Norrheimer skipper acting as harbor pilot was ready there too, arms crossed on his chest and dark hair flowing free in the cold breeze.

Other Moors stood ready on the deck, each with three of Rudi's folk close by, ready to help and under orders to learn all that they could. The pirate bosun looked up to his commander.

Abdou spoke, in his own language and then English: "Cast off!"

Townsfolk unlooped the hawsers from the bollards on the pier and the sailors pulled them back on deck, coiling them neatly. A Kalksthorpe boat was already secured to a towing hitch forward; the upright oars swung down, ten on a side, and dug into the blue-gray water. A deep chant echoed to time the stroke:

> *"Tyr hold us!*
> *Ye Tyr, ye Odhinn—*
> *Tyr hold us!*
> *Ye Tyr, ye Odhinn—"*

The pilot pointed silently as way came on the ship with a jerk that made some stagger. The two helmsmen spun the wheel to keep the ship in the tugboat's wake; the underwater obstacles were intended to keep hostile ships out, but they'd do just as well to rip the bottom out of a ship that was leaving. Beyond the last of them the movement of the *Bouel-Mogdad* changed, longer and harder as her bow turned into the swells. The little galley came alongside after it cast off the towrope, and Rudi shook hands with the pilot; it was Thorleif Heidhveigsson, he who'd captured her on Rudi's urging, and he grinned at the younger man.

"Now we'll have to rearrange some of them," he said.

He nodded overside to where one of the outsize spear-heads was just below the surface.

"Cold work," Rudi said. "But a warm greeting for rovers. I'll see you again, Thorleif, and the Lord and Lady willing it won't be long."

"Don't count any man lucky until he's dead," Thorleif said, and touched the silver Hammer that lay beneath his jacket. "Thor ward you with his might, Rudi Mackenzie."

"And yourself, my friend. Merry met, and merry part, and merry meet again!"

The wind was out of the west; it contributed to the hard pitch and roll as the waves took the ship under the quarter. Abdou looked at the sky with its high lines of mare's-tail cloud, at the compass, and then ordered in two languages:

"Make sail all! Up, up!"

His bosun shoved teams into position; Ingolf followed him, watching closely. A high screech brought both ready, and then they heaved, hauling the lines in hand-over-hand. Pulleys squealed. The long gaff-sails slid up the masts and then swung out as the booms turned. A thuttering like snapping branches and then the canvas snapped taut, swelling out into a series of curves and tri-angles, and the ship heeled to port until the dark planks sloped like the roof of a house. A fore-and-aft ship like this was economical of men, and the sails could be man-aged from the deck for the most part.

The bowsprit dug in, then broke free in a burst of crystal spray that shot back along the deck to sting Rudi's cheeks with an icy salt benediction. The motion turned

to a long lunging swoop, and waves of white curled back
from the sharp prow. Gray and white and blue, Mother
Sea stretched ahead of them, the manes of her snowy
horses running to the very horizon. A whale spouted in
the middle distance, twin plumes rising from the water
before its slate-colored length slid back below, and the
flukes slapped foam into the air.

"Glad to be back at sea, Abdou al-Naari?" he asked.

The Moor looked at him; he was bundled in wool and
felt until only his face showed. He snorted:

"In Dakar my lord the Emir have . . . has powerful
machine, his hakims make. Wind turns, much thump.
Pistons. Makes ice come. Put in drink juice on hot day.
Ice is very good *there*."

Rudi felt his legs flex and turn to take the rocking motion of the deck; it was easier than a trick like standing in
the saddle of a galloping horse. Mathilda smiled at him a
little shakily, her face pale, but she faced into the breeze
and breathed deeply and grew steadier. Edain smiled as
well—and then rushed for the leeward rail. Asgerd followed him and waited politely until the first racking
heaves were over, then offered him a cup of water from
one of the butts. When he'd spat and cleared his mouth,
she asked sweetly:

"Feeling better, master bowman? Hunger weakens a
man, they say. What you need is food."

"Please—errrrk—"

"Why not have some fried fat salt pork, nearly fresh?
Or cod cooked in cream with onions—"

Edain gave a wordless cry and dashed back to the rail.
Half the watchers laughed, except for a few hanging over
it themselves. The rest mostly grinned; even Matti did, and
she was usually tenderhearted and liked Edain well. Virginia Kane—Virginia Thurston now, since Lady Heidhveig

laid the Hammer in her lap at the handfasting ceremony two days ago—fairly staggered about hooting with mirth. Fred Thurston was looking a little queasy himself, but not enough to join the fish-feeding chorus line.

Seasickness was one of those things everyone found humorous except the sufferer, who wished for death and wasn't granted it. The only one wholly sympathetic was Garbh, who curled against Edain with whines and nuzzles and ears laid back above anxious eyes.

But it can be no joke, if it goes on long enough, for weeks of sweating misery. I don't think any here will. Edain always runs to the rail and always recovers quickly, if I remember our boating trips rightly.

"We keep this tack," Abdou said to Rudi, after he'd cocked a tolerant eye at the sufferers and their audience. "Long tack, as long as wind is steady. Like . . . *so.*"

He pointed southeast. "Clear Cape Cod. Then turn for Sorcerer's Isle. Maybe have to beat up into Sound; that take more time, more work."

And to be sure, his English is much *better when it comes to nautical matters.*

"How long?" Rudi asked.

He could feel his skin itching with the need, now. The Sword glowed in his mind, brighter than the winter dawn.

"Seven days, maybe. Winds . . . might come on storm; then have to run for open ocean get sea room. *Inshallah.*"

Rudi sighed. *Every man has a right to his faith. But I could come to* hate *that word, sure and I could.*

In the meantime . . .

"All of you!" he called. "Those who aren't tending the rigging. We'll drill with these deck engines; there's plenty of ammunition—"

Or at least plenty of roundshot beautifully worked from heavy granite, which the corsairs used for ballast. The four-foot javelins and globes of napalm the engines could also throw were far too valuable to use here where they couldn't be recovered.

"—and it's my thought the work will do us no harm."

Edain and the other sufferers mostly staggered erect at that; something to distract them from their miseries would be good . . . and somehow he doubted it would be a simple matter of sailing, this last league of his quest. Mathilda came to his side after the exercise was over. Most were set to sparring with individual weapons, but the two of them had done more than their share of the artillery practice.

Sparring on crowded, shifting ship timber required learning new reflexes. Once again he noticed how Abdou and his folk ignored her and the other women; he wasn't sure if that was courtesy, scorn, or a mixture of both. Mathilda was beginning to notice it too, and in no kindly spirit.

"What do you think of our Norrheimers, *acushla*?" he asked her.

Quickly appraising people and how to get the best from them was the most basic of the ruler's arts, or a commander's. She turned to the matter seriously at once; the daughter of Sandra and Norman Arminger would always take the trade of kingcraft seriously. He felt a sudden rush of warmth as he watched her frown and wind a lock of seal-brown hair around one forefinger. If he was to be High King, there would always be someone by his side he could share all his mind with. And their strengths and weaknesses complemented each other; he was a better field commander, though she was far from bad at it, but she excelled him equally on the administrative side.

"Most of them were . . . good enough," she said thoughtfully.

They'd sworn in seven new recruits in Eriksgarth; one had died in the street fighting against the Cutters and their pirate allies, and another had been too badly wounded to come along afterwards. They'd both been fair-to-middling youngsters, and too little-known for him to feel any great personal grief beyond the regret a lord had for any follower who fell. Still, leading men into battle meant accepting that some would die. That was a cost of doing business, and he didn't ask anyone to risk what he would not. Three of the remainder were promising beginners, luckier than their fallen friends rather than more skillful. Two . . .

"Hrolf Homersson is the best of them," Mathilda said, watching the exercise. "Remarkable, in fact."

Rudi nodded; the man gave a guttural shout as he leapt to the rail and back and again, swinging his great ax against a target dancing on the end of a pole and turning the massive weapon as if it were a willow switch. The light on the honed edge made sparkling patterns, cold as the wind that keened and whipped bits of ice from the rigging.

"He's as strong as I," Rudi said. "Maybe a bit more, in fact."

He was about three inches taller than the Mackenzie, and considerably heavier too. Not as fast, but not a lumbering ox either. More of a "swift enough," and thoroughly agile too, which wasn't quite the same thing. He had a mouse-brown beard that he wore in a braid that reached halfway down his chest, and his long ax bore a war hammer's serrated head opposite the curved blade.

"Though I wouldn't have thought even a man that size could use that . . . that *thing* . . . effectively," Mathilda said. "He can, though. Blasted right through a lot of parries and he never had to hit the same man twice."

She winced slightly; some of the wounds it had dealt had been grisly even among the usual butcher's-shop horrors of a battlefield ruled by edged metal driven with desperate strength and savagery. Speed let you dodge or block a blow. Weight and strength could make it count even so, crush a shield or brush aside or snap a parrying blade.

"I wouldn't care to stand and take a blow from it, even in a suit of plate," Rudi agreed. "Ulfhild the Black there is next on that list, I think."

She was not actually very dark; black of hair and eye and with skin of a medium olive. Back home he'd have thought she was Hispano with a fair dash of Indian and nothing remarkable, but those looks were much rarer here—and the Norrheimers thought beauty in a woman meant fairness. All their songs and legends spoke of women who looked like Asgerd, or Rudi's half sisters, or their mother, Signe, and aunt Astrid. That must have been a burden to her, that and the small-eyed, heavy-jawed looks that were three notches down from Mathilda's pretty-plain features even in the flush of youth. She was about Mathilda's five-eight-and-a-bit, too, but thirty or forty pounds heavier; not fat but solid and . . .

Meaty, he thought.

Ingolf stumbled back with a yell as her blunt, padded lath practice blade slammed painfully under his mail-clad ribs in a wicked rising stroke before he could get his shield in the way. The narrow edge of a live steel sword might well have broken bone there, could possibly have severed the rings and would certainly have hurt badly.

"Fast as a viper," Rudi said approvingly.

Not as fast as he, but he'd only met two warriors in all the world who were. Both were women, oddly enough: Tiphaine d'Ath and Lady Astrid of the Rangers. Though perhaps not so very oddly. Fighting women were less common than men even among Mackenzies or Dúnedain and still more so elsewhere, but the ones who stuck with it as a trade and survived any length of time tended to be exceptional. They had to be, and the way for a woman to excel at weapon play was to be very quick indeed.

"Perfect balance, too, even on a pitching deck and this the first time for her at that," Rudi continued. "Good technique, though there's room for improvement there. And plenty of fire in the belly. Ulfhild will be valuable, I'm thinking."

"Yes, you're right," Matti said, while her lips made a moue. "But I don't like her. She's . . . disagreeable."

Rudi nodded; that was true too. Sour, in fact; short-spoken to the point of rudeness, and sullen. Folk like that could be formidable fighters, but they could also breed trouble in a war band. Rudi thought there was a little more in Mathilda's expression of distaste. He wasn't vain of his looks, and the other sex were less affected by sheer eye-comeliness than men anyway, but he could tell total disinterest when it flicked across him in a woman's gaze.

He kept his thoughts there to a raised eyebrow and did *not* say: *the Grand Constable and Lady Delia don't make you frown that way, now!*

Saving things like incest or oaths of fidelity Mackenzies just didn't care who lay with who or how, as long as all parties were of age and consenting. The Goddess Herself had said *All acts of love and pleasure are My rituals.* Catholics had more things that were *geasa*, forbidden. Sins, in their terms. In his experience they also broke their taboos more often than his clansfolk did, and were more likely to practice hypocrisy, and also to wrack themselves with guilt.

Indeed, sometimes they're happier to wallow in guilt at a sin than to avoid it in the first place! I don't know exactly how the Norrheimers arrange such matters, but they're more straitlaced than we, I think. How most tribes of humankind do make tangles for themselves!

A snort told him Mathilda had been following his thoughts with uncomfortable precision. That had been happening more and more; they'd always been close, but now they'd been so long in each other's sporrans it was becoming a little eerie at times.

"It just struck me," he said casually, "that if I'm to be High King of all Montival, it won't do to be saying: *Well, and how simple it would be, if only you poor deluded fools would do things sensibly, as Mackenzies do!*"

"I can remember how much doing that made *everyone* love you in Association territory," she said dryly, and nudged him in the ribs. "A couple of times."

"Well, I get on well enough with Father Ignatius," he said. "And Abbot Dmwoski at Mt. Angel."

"That's not going to help you with *all* the Catholics," Mathilda said. "I like the Order of the Shield myself— they're mostly very holy men, and to tell you the truth I think Father Ignatius is a saint—but a lot of the secular clergy and some of the other Orders really dislike them, so you can't show them too much favor. You'll have to watch that."

"I'll have you to watch it for me, praise the Gods!"

She shook her head vehemently. "No, Rudi. Artos! You'll need to handle the Church directly, and not just in Portland's territory. I can be Lady Protector there, but you'll have to deal with the Archbishop-Cardinal; he'll be Rome's man to head the Church in the whole realm. That's not just . . . preaching and the sacraments . . . that's land, that's wealth and influence, that's *power*. It's the only two universities in Montival apart from Corvallis, too."

Rudi mock-groaned. "Next you'll be saying I need to think about taxes!"

"You do," Mathilda said bluntly. "A King needs his own revenues, that nobody else can interrupt, so—"

"So he can reward his supporters, yes, and buy weapons and make gifts and give aid in times of disaster. Matti, I'm not *altogether* gormless!"

She flashed a smile. "Sorry, darling. You'll have the Lord Protector's lands and dues and tithes through me, and so will our heir—"

He winked at her, and she blushed and continued doggedly: "But that will make its own problems."

"Portland already weighs heavier in the realms of the Meeting than many like, true. But there's Fred."

They both looked over to where the son of the first President of Boise was testing his long saber against Asgerd's sword and shield.

"When he's President there, he's promised me that the US of Boise shall be part of Montival. It was his father's dream to reunite the lands . . . and if this is a bit of a different way to do it, he's content with that."

"And he doesn't insist on being the one ruling the whole, unlike his elder brother," she said. "I'm glad. I like him, but I wouldn't risk our children's inheritance just on that. Fred keeps his oaths, though; he'll be a good vassal."

"There is that. He hasn't decided how to settle the succession there—"

Mathilda smiled grimly; for a moment she looked very much like her mother, though in face and form she took more after Norman Arminger. When she spoke her voice was definite:

"I've come to know Virginia. Unless she's childless, it's settled. He just doesn't know it quite yet."

Rudi shrugged; it wasn't all that important. Fred was a young man yet, younger than Rudi. Any reasonable length of reign would make things solid.

"And Boise is smaller than the Association lands, but it has more than twice the population and wealth," he said. "That'll keep things in balance; that and bringing Pendleton and the rest of the eastern plains into the kingdom. For the future . . . there's all the lands to the south of Ashland, empty."

She chuckled. "Mom's Westria Project."

They shared the joke, and Rudi went on airily: "There's just the little matter of beating the Prophet and Martin Thurston of Boise, the creatures, before we set all in order."

She nodded and took his arm. "No great problem."

He looked out to sea to hide the bleakness that rested in his eyes for a moment.

I calculate our odds as about even, when *we have the Sword. And even then . . . how many will live to see the victory? How many will lie for the scald crows? There are victories that leave you with wounds that cannot fully heal. And not just in the Histories of the Dúnedain.*

"Well, then, that's the fate of the High West settled," Rudi said. "Now let's keep our fearless followers from recalling their stomachs by working them a bit more. You take one half, I the other, and we'll play at storming and defending the poop deck by turns, eh?"

He leapt lightly down to the main deck; despite his

two-hundred-odd pounds of bone and muscle and armor he landed lightly as a cat.

"All of you! We have to learn to fight with a ship as a battlefield. We'll divide into two teams and each into three squads. Hrolf Blood-ax and Ulfhild Swift-sword, you'll be with me . . ."

The big Bjorning grinned, setting aside his murderous weapon for the practice version. Ulfhild nodded silently, but her face flushed with pleasure at the new use-name.

CHAPTER TWENTY-ONE

Dawn made shadows across the moving deck. Rudi stretched and drew his sword, saluted the glow where the rising sun was about to break over the horizon and began a slow routine that gradually quickened. There was enough space on the main deck just behind the foremast to work out, if you were careful—and being careful was part of the training. A longsword and a tall man's arm had a great deal of reach, but endless practice had given him a reflexive grasp of where every bit of edge and point would go. It wasn't quite as certain on the pitching deck of a ship, and he needed to do better with that.

A little like horseback, but not entirely. It's fortunate indeed that I enjoy the sword, he thought. *For I'd have to spend just as much time at it if I didn't. Also, I wouldn't be as good at it, and would die . . . die sooner, at least.*

When he finished he was sweating despite the cold that bit at his nose and ears and made the inside of his nostrils stick occasionally. He steamed a little, in fact, and not just the deep puffs of white breath. That warmth wouldn't last more than a few seconds if he stayed still, with this wind out of the northeast that lashed his shoulder-length mane backward from his face beneath the headband. He sheathed the sword on the belt hung from a belaying pin in the collar around the mast, put his waterproof parka back on and buckled on the belt over it. Nobody else but the deck watch was up yet. This was the day they expected to make landfall, and the hold was stuffy and crowded, but the others preferred it to early rising.

Or most did. Someone was standing on the fantail by the war engine; he recognized a Bjorning voice, and a woman's—not Asgerd, but deeper and rougher. Ulfhild Swift-sword, then. And she was chanting softly, facing northwards along the white track of the schooner's wake, with arms raised at either side and palms upward. There was a dreamy yearning in her tone that made him blink in surprise.

> "Skadhi, shining goddess
> Hear me, ice-bright beauty
> Your winter white wards Midgard
> As Ulfhild sails the whale's-bath
> To drighten lord is oath-bound
> Ring-giver fares to Utgard
> And Skadhi's shield-maid follows
> Yare am I for battle
> So Skadhi, stand by Ulfhild
> She-wolf fights 'gainst trollcraft
> Holy huntress, help me!"

"People will *always* surprise you," Rudi murmured very softly to himself. "For their minds turn upon themselves in coil and counter-coil. We do not ever know ourselves completely. How can we know another?"

He waited until she was finished to walk up the short ladder staircase to the poop. The two men at the wheel nodded to him—one was a Southsider, the other a corsair. Ulfhild had already turned; she gave him a short dignified inclination of the head and then met his eyes, standing proudly with her left hand on the hilt of her sword. He liked that. Norrheimers didn't truckle to their Gods or to their chieftains either.

"Good morning, Ulfhild Swift-sword," he said. "Today we make landfall."

"Good morning, lord," she said. "I am ready."

Which was about as many words as they'd exchanged since the oath she'd sworn, apart from orders. She hesitated, and he waited patiently, withdrawing the edge of his self. There was a trick to that, almost like hunting, which drew folk out.

"The others are awake," she said.

They'd turned the captain's cabin over to the womenfolk of the party; a little inconvenient for the two wedded couples, but on balance the best way to handle the crowding of the ship as a whole.

"May I ask you a question?" He nodded, and she went on: "Why did you arrange the quarters that way, lord?"

"Princess Mathilda's folk have different ways from mine. They're . . ."

He hesitated; *modest* wasn't exactly what he meant. "Much more shamefast about their skins, I think you would say. You can't always take account of that when men and women are together on a campaign, but there's no harm in doing so when you can."

"I understand," she said. Then more hesitantly: "I don't think your betrothed . . . the Princess Mathilda . . . likes me, lord. Have I offended her?"

"No," Rudi said.

Or not by doing *anything in particular*, he thought, which was what she'd actually meant. Aloud he went on:

"Some people just don't take to each other. I have no ill to say of you; you fought well at Kalksthorpe, and you've worked hard and obeyed orders without complaint since. And you are sworn to me, not her. Tell the Princess that we'll be having a conference in there as soon as it's clear; her, myself, the Moorish captain, Ingolf and Father Ignatius."

She hurried off, with an air of relief.

"We just nearly there," Abdou al-Naari said twenty minutes later.

The captain's cabin of the *Bou el-Mogdad* had touches of lavishness; inlaid wood, mother-of-pearl in traceries of alien script, thick cushions of butter-soft red leather, hanging lanterns of intricate metal fretwork wrought in brass and silver. Rudi admired the workmanship—there were few things Mackenzies valued more highly—and the neatly compact folding tables, chart case and cupboards for instruments, racks for weapons and armor. There was also a shelf of books, mostly older works on navigation and geography in French, pre-Change guidebooks for travelers giving details of cities on the western side of the Atlantic, and several volumes of poetry in languages he didn't recognize. Besides leather and cloth and lamp oil the room smelled surprisingly of some faint flowery scent.

Right now, five tightly bound bedrolls rested against the walls, or against the cushioned couch below the slanting stern windows. Rudi and Edain had the little cabin to the port, Ignatius and Ingolf the one to starboard, and the rest of the crew had the hold and forecastle, carefully arranged so that the corsairs were always shadowed by at least one of his war band.

The lanterns glowed, dispelling the last of the dawn twilight, and Rudi's closest stood around the table and looked at the map, with the dividers and set square atop it. More and more cold bright sun spilled through the skylight as the night died, flowing clear as diamond.

They all held bowls in their hands and plied spoons as they thought. The *Bou el-Mogdad* had a well-fitted galley but she'd been down to dried dates, dried salt fish, a little rice and weevily sorghum by the time the corsairs reached Kalksthorpe. Rudi had restocked before they sailed, and this was steel-milled oats cooked with dried blueberries and honey, welcome for stoking the fires. Nowhere on a wooden ship was completely dry, or less than cold on these seas in this season. He hadn't grudged the Moorish captain a monopoly of his coffee set and beans; it was a rarity for the very wealthy in Montival, but the man came from a land where it was common and he was used to it. Abdou sipped at a cup as he indicated the map. Rudi had to admit the scent was intoxicating, though the Moors brewed it thick and strong enough to melt a spoon.

"We sight Sorcerer's Isle today, if this wind holds," the rover captain said.

He traced their course; southeast down to just below the hook of Cape Cod, and then across the wind west and south towards Nantucket. That had been a little more tricky, a shorter leg but needing more time; these were shoal waters, and the shallows had shifted unpredictably since the charts were made.

"And that fast sail. No troubles," Abdou said.

There had been one ship flying the White Ensign of Greater Britain, but it had simply come close enough for King-Emperor William's men to hail them and check that they weren't Moors. That conversation had taken place with the Imperials' twenty-four-pounder catapults pointing at them out of open firing ports in the steel hull, and a team at the pump handles of a flamethrower. Rudi had prudently sent all the hostage seamen below before the warcraft reached speaking distance.

"Really, should give me ship back, for such goodish sail working," the corsair went on, his voice elaborately reasonable.

"And then you awaken from the pleasant dream, Abdou, weeping for the fading beauty of it in the cold light of dawn," Rudi said dryly.

We'll never be friends, he thought. *If I hadn't needed him I wouldn't have sworn him safety, and then the Kalksthorpe folk could have hanged him and dedicated the sacrifice to the High One for all I cared.*

It was a King's duty to see pirates dead without excessive formality, and a very needful one. What was a King for, if not to see that his folk could sleep sound in their beds and know they'd be able to keep what they grew and made? Still . . .

But he's a brave man and no fool, and a likeable rascal. Though doubtless I'd feel a wee bit less charitable if it was my coasts and folk he and his kind threatened.

"Best to approach from the north," he said aloud, with an uncomfortable feeling that Abdou had followed the thought. His finger showed where the harbor entrance opened between its breakwaters.

"Though from what the guidebook says it may have silted up," he added. "We may have to go in with the longboat."

"It's not just more ruins from before the Change," Ingolf said. "I don't know . . . but I don't think we'll just . . . walk in."

He set his bowl aside and wiped his mouth with the back of one big hand, elaborately unconcerned, but his battered features were tight-held. One thick finger rested a little to the west of the town's hatch of streets.

"This is where I landed, back . . . uff da, four years ago! There's a village there. Partly refugees from the mainland who came after the Change, a couple of families . . . but Injuns, too. Injuns who'd never heard of white men, or seen iron or corn. We walked through the woods to what the maps said should be the center of Nantucket Town, on the harbor there and . . . that's where it all happened. But it wasn't anything like what the books say. No houses, no open fields or recent scrub—forest, old, old forest. Oak trees that had been growing two or three hundred years. And chestnuts . . . the books say all the chestnuts in this part of the world died of a blight nearly a century before the Change."

Abdou nodded impassively, but Rudi could see his Adam's apple move. The Moor's voice was calm when he spoke; like anyone who dealt with extreme danger routinely, he knew that the best way to tame fear was simply to ignore it, refuse to admit it even, so that it couldn't build on itself. If you kept the body calm, it calmed the mind.

"You to understand, we would have use for island there. Good safe place within range of dead cities to water ship, take on wood, not be possible many savages . . . Eaters, you say . . . like are in dead cities, near dead cities."

"It would make a good base, you mean."

"Yes, base. But we not try many year from now, ah, you say, for many years now? Only one harbor, and . . . when ships get close, crews say many things. Lights, head hurting. Sometimes just find they far away again and—"

He reached out to his chronometer where it hung on the wall and slid one finger across the glass, as if moving the hour hand ahead.

—"time is . . . gone. Maybe rest of island better. Maybe not. Not try."

"I've reason to believe we'll be allowed in," Rudi said. "And—"

A cry came, and the ringing of a bell: *"Sail ho!"*

Abdou almost jostled him in the doorway; they all leapt up the stairway to the poop. The ocean reached crisp blue to the horizon, with a wind out of the north that chopped icy spray from the running whitecaps. The lookout was Edain, long since past his illness. He scrambled down the rigging—harder than on a square-rigger's ratlines—and pointed westward.

"Two-master, Chief. Looks a lot like this ship."

Rudi's brows went up. "All hands on deck," he called. "Battle stations."

He noticed how the corsair's bosun—Falilu, the man's name was—gave a quick glance at his skipper and received a nod before obeying. Whistles and bells called the crew. Metal shields went into prepared slots in the rails, giving the defenders a rampart against boarders. Nets were rigged above that; folk helped each other into their armor, and set out garlands of stone shot for the catapults, sheaves of arrows and javelins for humans. Long boarding pikes were ready to hand. The rover crew weren't armed, but they helped with the labor.

He turned his head to Abdou al-Naari as the rushing drumbeat of feet and cries subsided. The last sound to cease was the *crink . . . crink . . .* as the war engines were cranked to full compression, and the multiple *click . . . click . . .* sounds as their triggers engaged. Abdou had been allowed to keep his binoculars, if not his sword; they were needful for his work conning the ship. He leveled them now, and breath hissed between his teeth.

"Is ship *Gisandu*," he said, when the oncoming vessel was still doll-tiny. "*Shark*, English word. Jawara captain."

"Why would he be here?" Rudi asked.

"I do not *know*," Abdou said, and then hid his distress under an iron calm. "How know we come here? *I* did not until you say! Jawara know-think me dead. No Kaolaki captain come here. And *Gisandu* short supplies, have cargo, not want to meet Empire ship. Makes no . . . no sense . . . not go home."

"Would your Jawara try to rescue you?"

"Yes, yes—my wife his sister. We be like brother, sail, fight side by side years. But how rescue me, even if he knows? Sea fight, most likely everyone die. Better pay ransom. That right fashion of doing. Dead man not bring back good thing for children, family, town, tribe. Not . . . not *responsible*, is the word?"

Rudi nodded. When both ships could throw globes of napalm at wooden hulls, death *was* the most likely outcome of a slugging match with no restraints. He knew these corsairs were proud and brave, good fighting men, but they were in business to make a profit and not to die. Salvaging was a dangerous trade but a trade still; so was outright piracy, in a way.

"Then from what you say, I think it most likely that your friend does not command that ship," Rudi said. "The false Marabout does, or the High Seeker, or both. And Graber should still have twenty or so of his men; and some of his Bekwa. If they escaped to the *Gisandu* with your friend's crew and struck without warning—"

Abdou hissed again, and raised the binoculars. "Maybe. If those two evil sorcerers like you say. Now *I* want rescue *Jawara*. Will talk to him."

The *Gisandu* came closer with shocking speed; both vessels were sailing with the wind on their beams, a good angle for their rigs. She looked much like her sister-ship, save that someone had painted a toothy mouth on her bow at the waterline. He leveled his own glasses. Most of the crew tending the sails were corsairs, but he could also see the reddish armor of the Sword of the Prophet, and Bekwa. More might well be waiting belowdecks.

"Land," Abdou said. "Nantucket."

Rudi started slightly; he'd put it out of his mind. When he looked over his left shoulder it was there, a long low bluish-green line, marked with white where surf pounded. Just as Ingolf had said, the high bluffs were marked with a tangle of low thick forest. None of the trees were over fifty feet or so, between the sandy soil and the salt sea breeze, but it was plainly old-established.

"Jawara at wheel," Abdou said. "Shields up. Catapults ready. They closing us, want come alongside."

"Don't come too close," Rudi warned.

He didn't put his hand to his sword. Abdou had had personal experience of what Rudi Mackenzie could do with a blade, and confirmation watching him practice since. Strain showed on his face, graving the lines beside his dark eyes that a lifetime of squinting over water had produced. The deck was silent now; Rudi looked behind him for an instant, and Mathilda gave him a cheerful-seeming smile and a thumbs-up from beside the murder-machine on its turntable.

For one mad instant he imagined telling the corsair *turn back*. And sailing, sailing away over the horizon, ignoring the place he could feel calling him as northward drew a compass needle. Going somewhere peaceful, and . . .

Just saying "No, thank you very much, O Powers, you

never asked me *what I thought of the idea of being the fore-doomed Hero, now, did you?"*

His mouth quirked upward. He could imagine that; he could imagine strolling barefoot over the waves and into Nantucket. And both were about as likely. A spire showed there now, white and beautiful, like a Christian church. A squat lighthouse, beside the narrow entrance to the harbor. No wrecks or obvious impediments in the channel. He blinked. *Was* that a spire? Or buildings? Or was there a ship, a metal ship of oddly towering squared-off shape in the channel itself? When he blinked again the water was empty of all but a few wildfowl and a curious seal that reared its forequarters out of the water to watch. But there seemed to be a shuddering in the air. His mouth felt dry, and he swallowed several times.

"Let's get by this man, so inconvenient and obstructive as he is, first," he muttered.

"Close," Abdou said. "They on starboard. Safer for us."

The *Gisandu* was heeled over against the same norther that was making the *Bou el-Mogdad* bound forward at a good twelve knots. That put the rail the *Shark* had towards its sister-ship sloping down, and its counterpart on Rudi's own ship point *up*. Which meant that the *Bou el-Mogdad*'s war engines would bear on the other corsair vessel while the enemy weapons were pointing down into the water.

He glanced out of the corner of his eye at Abdou. Just opening fire was not going to be a good idea, if he wanted this man's cooperation. And he'd promised not to try to force him to fight his own people. Onrushing speed; the *Shark*'s bow was dark with men. Soon he'd be able to see their faces. Closer, well within range, closer still . . .

Abdou had a speaking trumpet. He used it to shout

across the diminishing distance, through the whine of wind in rigging and the endless slapping white-noise *shsrrshshrrsh* of water along the hulls of the ships:

"*Jamm ga fanan!*"

Rudi had learned that much Wolof in the last few days; it was a greeting.

"*Nanga def, Jawara?*"

The thickset black man at the wheel of the other vessel didn't reply. Not in words; instead he screamed, a long desolate sound like a prisoner's cry from deep within some dungeon. Almost at the same instant—

Tunnggg!

A globe flew towards them from the bow engine of the other ship. It trailed smoke in a low flat arc. There was a *crack* as it struck near the *Bou el-Mogdad*'s own prow, and the onrushing bow wave scrubbed its load of liquid fire off to float oily orange-red on the ice-blue waters.

"Shoot!" Rudi shouted.

He hardly needed to. Arrows lifted in a rushing cloud from the *Bou el-Mogdad* at Edain's bark of *wholly together!* A like volley came back, and every one of the broadside engines on the other ship cut loose. Most of their loads struck the water harmlessly—even at maximum elevation their angle was bad. The arrows were another matter. Rudi swept his knight's shield up, giving the corsair shelter as well. Three shafts stuck quivering in it, and one banged off his left greave and skittered off across the deck. More rattled like metal hail on the sloped shield of the engine Mathilda commanded.

The *tunggg* of its discharge sounded very loud, and all the starboard broadside machines and the bow-chaser shot in the next half second. Sheet-metal shields rang and distorted and collapsed as the heavy granite balls struck; some of them went over the barricade or through it, plowing gruesomely through flesh and sending snapped rigging and wood splinters flying.

Abdou was screaming orders at the crew on the rigging lines and at the helm; the men there crouched and spun the wheel. The schooner paid off suddenly and heeled southward; booms swung out as it turned to run before the wind, and Rudi ducked as the thick timber swept by overhead. The *Gisandu* turned behind them; the world swung with disconcerting speed, and suddenly he could look over his shoulder and see the other vessel appallingly close. Another globe of napalm snapped out. There was a crash below as of glass and shutters, and a wisp of smoke billowed up.

"Falilu!" Abdou barked.

The bosun led a rush of men with buckets of sand and water. Then the slim Moorish captain shook his head in amazement.

"He not talk! Just try to kill me, his brother!"

"He's not his own man, Abdou al-Naari," Rudi said grimly. "His mind and soul are not his own."

"Now I believe," the corsair said grimly. "Not before. But now, yes."

Mathilda jerked the lanyard as the stern rose. Rudi could feel the deck quiver a little beneath his feet as the force of the throwing arms was transmitted through the turntable. The stone ball skipped twice, plunked through the very top of a wave and then caught the *Gisandu*'s bowsprit at its base. There was a cracking sound loud enough to hear, and Abdou winced even then; he must love these ships like his own children.

Falilu came back upside; there were scorchmarks on his clothing. He spoke in rapid Wolof, moving his hands in a fashion that left no doubt as to what he was saying.

"Old pagan dog not get use of *Bou el-Mogdad* after

all," Abdou said with grim amusement. "Falilu make fire slow, not able put out. Ship burn to waterline. Soon now, soon."

Tunnngg.

They both ducked, but the bolt from the *Gisandu*'s bow-catapult hit the steel protection of their stern-chaser and pinwheeled away and up in fragments. Shields were raised and men ducked across the deck against that hail. Father Ignatius came to the wheel, wiping off hands bloody from field surgery.

"Two dead, five wounded," he said.

Rudi thought swiftly and spoke to Abdou. "Take her straight in and to the dock."

"Dock?"

"*That* dock!" Rudi said.

Abdou blinked as if he were only then aware of the tangle of quays ahead. Rudi realized with a chill in some distant part of his mind that the Moor *hadn't* seen them until that moment.

"Ram it. We'll leap off—the ship is doomed anyway. Ignatius, see that the wounded all have someone to carry them."

Unexpectedly, Abdou spoke: "I, my men not fight. We carry hurt, though."

Rudi nodded grateful acknowledgment as the corsair called orders in his own language.

"Ingolf?" he went on.

The Richlander swallowed. Rudi didn't think that was the dangers of battle that brought the sheen of sweat to his face despite the cold.

"I came in the other way. But . . . right up that street from the harbor, the one the maps call *Center*, and then left where it forks. The house with the pillars on your right. I think. It was . . . mixed up, there, at the end."

"That's what we'll do, then. You lead and—"

Ignatius shook his head. "You and the Princess must go first, Your Majesty," he said. "I will hold the rearguard with the rest."

He smiled when Rudi started to object. "What have we made this journey for if not to get *you* to the Sword? And the Princess is my charge. If you would save us, accomplish your mission swiftly."

The smile grew broader as he patted his own hilt. "Gain your Lady's Sword, your Majesty. I also have a sword blessed by a Lady, and a mission laid upon me. I *will* fulfill it."

"Right," Rudi said tightly.

More smoke was coming out of the stern windows, trailing along on either side of them as the wind that pushed the ship took it. It gave a little cover, and the *Gisandu* had to turn slightly every time she fired; the bow-chaser couldn't shoot directly over her own bowsprit. The stern-chaser on their own ship could, but . . .

"The deck's starting to get very hot here!" Mathilda called; not alarmed, just reporting.

She jerked the lanyard. *Tunnnggg.* This time there was a splintering *crack* almost immediately, as the shot caught the other vessel at the waterline. They were gliding southeast through a narrow passage now. A broadside of incendiaries came flying at them as they came about to head directly south and the harbor opened out around them, a broad shallow lagoon. Two globes smashed against the steel shields and hissing fire ran down. Their own replied, and a sail came rattling down on the *Gisandu* as a stay was severed. Corsairs worked frantically at a deck pump to wash the napalm down and into the sea before it started another fire.

Edain and his picked archers crowded onto the poop

deck. He was firing like a machine across the hundred-yard gap, draw-aim-loose-nock-draw, chanting under his breath:

"*We are the darts that*—got you bad, bastard!—*Hecate cast!*"

Rudi made himself turn. As he did he realized that *something* had been inhibiting him, something besides his natural desire to keep his eyes on the men trying to kill them all. He blinked and shook his head, but there was nothing wrong with his eyes. It was as if he saw multiple images laid one upon another, like paintings on layers of glass. A festival where men and women danced through snow. Tall-masted ships tied at the docks. Something smooth and silvery and massive that *floated* above the water, then turned its nose skyward and rose with impossible speed . . .

Then a very solid dock and roadway, wharfs on barnacle-encrusted tree trunks, what looked like a street of low brick buildings, interspersed with white-trimmed gray shingle shops and leafless winter trees, with church steeples rearing beyond. No dwellers . . . or was that a band in oilskins with duffel bags over their shoulders? No, they were gone. And the dock was *there*.

"Brace for impact!" he shouted, as it loomed before their bowsprit, and looped his elbow around a line.

Crack. His feet skidded out from beneath him. A long crunching, grinding sound, and the bow reared up as the huge momentum of the two-hundred-ton vessel ground into timber and stone. Nearly everyone else fell too; Mathilda went sliding past him as the impact pitched her off the gunner's seat of the weapon, and he snagged her with a leg. She clung to his sword belt as the long echoing crash continued and the deck canted more and more steeply beneath them. Their helmets rang together as the foremast broke with a sound like thunder and came down on the shattered dock.

Silence except for snapping wood and the growing burr of the fire beneath them.

"Go, go, go!" Ignatius shouted.

Rudi hauled Mathilda upright as if her solid weight and the armor were nothing. They ran along the side to the buckled rail, up to it, down onto the crazy-quilt mess of the dock where the schooner's weight had struck. His leg went through a broken board and he wrenched it free. Then they were running, up past a dry fountain and onto a stretch of cobbles. His weight pounded down through his boots, but the sound was too *deep*, as if he were walking on a drumhead. An arrow went past them . . . but it *floated* past. His run turned to steps in a dream, one where you floated. He floated, past primeval forests, past a rough hamlet hacked from the woods where folk in rust-colored coats and high-steepled hats and long dresses gaped at him, past the street he'd first seen, but dense with the cars and trucks of the ancient world, past the same with ox carts heaped with fish . . .

"Here. We'll hold them here!" Ignatius shouted; the stone basin of the fountain blocked part of the street.

Shields locked on either side, and the archers fanned out in two forward-slanting wings from side to side of the roadway. The *Bou el-Mogdad* was burning like a pillar of fire now, delaying the men the *Gisandu* carried and making it impossible for her deck engines to shoot. They came staggering out of the smoke anyway, and first was a man in a tattered red robe the color of dried blood. His hands were held out before him like claws, and his eyes were windows into negation.

"Noooooooo!"

The endless wail was as much shriek as word, and less a protest than a single long scream of what he *was*, or what the thing that wore the man like a glove was. Ignatius raised his sword and brought up his shield, but behind the visor of his helm he shouted for joy as his gaze met those wells of night without end.

"Yes!" he cried. "Eternally, *yes!*"

Behind him Edain barked: "Let the gray geese fly. Wholly together—*Shoot!*"

The bows snapped, and men went down in the ragged mob of Bekwa and Sword troopers and corsairs who rushed forward as the arrows sleeted into them, but there were too many, far too many. Three punched into the High Seeker, but his body simply flexed and came on.

"Noooooooo!"

"You shall not pass, Hollow Man!" Ignatius cried.

And then—

Knight-brother Ignatius snatched at his sword. It wasn't there, nor was his armor and gear. Instead he wore the simple Benedictine robe and cowl; after an instant he was conscious that he sat on a bench. Before him was a cloister, slender white stone columns supporting arches on three sides of a garden and fountain where water played before an image of the Virgin. The shadows within the walk hid tall doors; behind them was a hint of bookcases full of leather-bound volumes. Within the court the sun ran dappled on the water that lifted and fell in its basin, shifting in spots of brightness through the leaves of tall beeches; a few flower beds stood in troughs between walkways of worn brick, shimmering in gold and silver and hyacinth blue.

The day was mild and dry and warm, with scents of rock and wet and warm dust, and somewhere a hint of incense. It was very quiet; the sound of the plashing fountain, a few *cu-currrus* from doves that stalked past, perhaps very faintly a hint of chanted plainsong in the distance. He smiled. It wasn't Mt. Angel, but it was as if . . .

As if it is the distilled essence of everything I loved about the abbey, he thought. *Peace, beauty, wisdom. God.*

Beside him another monk sat; the man threw back his cowl and smiled. Ignatius' eyes went a little wide. It was Abbot-Bishop Dmwoski, but as he'd first seen him as a postulant, the square hard face amused at his earnestness but in a way that was kindly, not mocking.

"Am I . . . is this . . ."

"No, you are not, my son," the abbot answered.

"Then, you—"

Dmwoski laughed; it had been a rare thing on Mt. Angel, but it lit the warrior-cleric's sternness like a candle through the glass shutter of a lantern.

"Not yet, as your life thread is drawn; *there* I am currently fighting the sin of despair, and grappling with a sea of troubles. Time is different here. Or rather, we're not entirely in time as men understand it."

"I always thought you would be a saint," Ignatius blurted.

Dmwoski frowned. "All human souls are, potentially. I . . . have been allowed to progress."

"And this is—"

Another chuckle: "And yes, this *is* where you think it is. Or as much of this . . . one of the many mansions . . . as you can currently understand. Think of it as a metaphor, but a true one."

"Such peace," Ignatius breathed, wondering.

He drew the air into his lungs, and then glanced behind him. A long table reached into dimness; someone was turning the pages of a text, and the bright colors drew him even through the glass and across the distance.

"Yet . . ." he said. "It does not feel in the least static."

"Never. More like an endless high adventure; or rather, what an adventure *should* be. We cannot fully know Him, yet we can know ever *more* of Him; and in that is the completion of our natures. Come, walk with me, my son."

They rose and folded their hands in the sleeves of their robes. A bell rang somewhere as they paced through the cloister and out the gateway, a great bronze throb that seemed to scatter brightness through the air.

"Why am I here, then, Father?"

"Partly as a reward. I flatter myself that I was a good judge of men, and choosing you for the mission to the east was perhaps the best decision I ever made. And you met one who is a far, far better judge; one who laid a charge upon you. Both of us are very pleased with you."

Outside they walked on a country lane. Land rolled around them, green field and wood and orchard. It was like and unlike the land of little farms around his birthplace, like the summers of his remembered boyhood when the chores were done and he lay watching the clouds and dreaming vast formless dreams until his mother called him in for dinner. Far distant mountains climbed steep and blue, their peaks floating like ghosts of white. He thought the silver towers of a city rose in their foothills, tall and slender and crowned with banners.

"And partly you are here to give you heart for what is to come. Much depends on you."

"Then . . ." He looked around. "Victory is not assured? Even though we have reached our goal?"

Dmwoski shook an admonishing finger. "*This* is our common goal, my son. And no victory is ever assured until the very last. We are made in His image; and so we have freedom, which must necessarily include the freedom to fail. Adam and Eve walked with Him in unimaginable closeness when time itself was young, and *they* failed their test. Yet even their failure was redeemed, for mercy is infinite and grace fills all creation."

"But . . . forgive me, Father, but if *you* are here, don't you *know* whether we succeeded or failed?"

"No. That *I* am here is . . . sealed in Eternity, as it were. But *how* I arrived at this is still—from your point of view—contingent, because it is in Time, not in the eternal Now. Did I die defending the altar at the last, against a tide of triumphant darkness? Did I die of old age, in bed, with you among the watchers, contented and tired and longing for this with hope and confidence? That, my son, is up to *you*."

"And where are my companions?"

"They also are being told as much Truth as they can bear, in the words that will mean most to them."

"As am I?" Ignatius ventured.

Dmwoski laughed again. "There is one God, maker of Heaven and Earth," he said. "Start with that, my son, for it is absolutely true. But you must build your own faith. That is something only you and God can do together."

A bird flew from the hedgerow by them, caroling and trailing colorful feathers. Their sandaled feet scuffed through the thick white dust of the road; insects chirped. Beyond the hawthorn barrier apricots glowed like little golden suns in their world of green leaves.

Ignatius shook his head in rueful acknowledgment.

"You still reward work accomplished with yet more work, Father!"

They laughed together. He stooped and picked up an acorn:

"I remember, Father, how once you lectured my class of novices and used a seed like this as a simile for the soul. How every stage of the tree's long life was implicit in it, yet never guaranteed before it came to pass?"

"I'm glad you remember. I taught you as best I could . . . and what I taught you is true. *Very* true, I find. But not . . . complete."

"How could it be?" Ignatius said. "Didn't you tell me also that Truth is a ladder of many rungs, and that from each we gain a new perspective?"

The abbot rested a hand on his shoulder; it was a light touch, but the younger monk felt a sudden shock at the *depth* of the contact. As if he was a ghost, a figment, and the contact had revealed him as unreal, a dream within a dream that strove to wake itself from illusion.

"I tried my best," Dmwoski said. "I sinned as all men do, and sought forgiveness, and sinned again despite my wishes. Yet perhaps the most important thing I accomplished in my life was my part in forming *you*, my son."

"That . . . is a humbling thought."

Dmwoski snorted. "It should be! I merely had to be the best possible version of myself. For every day of your life, you must strive to be the chosen Knight of the Immaculata!"

"Yes," Ignatius said, and was elsewhere.

Rudi Mackenzie made another step, and another. Arrows drifted past him, and he could see them turn as the fletching caught the air. He cast away the world-huge weight of his shield and knocked the sallet helm off his head. Their clatter on the cobbles was distant, like the beating of surf on beaches a world away. Mathilda staggered beside him, then slid to the ground and *crawled*, dogged and brave, and her love like a force behind him, pushing him forward into a world of resistant amber. A building loomed, handsome and simple, three stories of red brick with white pillars beside the door.

The door swung open, and light blazed from it. His hand went up before his eyes, but the light shone through it, through *him*, as if it were real and he a shadow. Within it was a shape, straight sweep of tapering blade, crescent guard, long double-lobed hilt, pommel of moon opal grasped in antlers. Pain keened into his ears, his eyes, his mind. A lifetime of it passed in each step. His foot touched the first step, the second, the threshold—

"Mother?" Rudi Mackenzie said, walking forward.

The three figures around the campfire looked up at him. His eyes flicked back and forth. The fire killed some of his night vision; he could sense huge trees rearing skyward, like the Douglas fir in the Cascades above Dun Juniper but grander still and with more deeply furrowed reddish bark. Scents like spice and thyme and flowers drifted on air just cool enough to make him glad of his plaid.

He glanced down for an instant. He *was* in shirt and kilt and plaid. The short slight redheaded figure in the middle wore a shift and arsaid, and leaned on a rowan staff topped by a silver raven's head. On her left was a tall thin woman with black skin and broad features scored by age, her cropped cap of white hair tight-kinked, wearing unfamiliar clothes that had the look of a uniform. On her right was a not-quite-girl of a little less than his own age, long-limbed and blond and comely, in a strange outfit of string skirt, knit tunic, feathers and a necklace of amber-centered gold disks.

"Mother?" he asked again.

Then the wholeness of what he was seeing caught him. *Three* women, youthful and matronly and aged . . .

"Yes," the one who bore the countenance of Juniper Mackenzie said. "I am."

"Are you—" He hesitated. "Are you *my* mother? Or . . . *Her?*"

His hand moved in a sign. She answered it. "And the answer to that, my lad, is . . . yes!"

Impish amusement glinted in her green eyes for a second. The black woman snorted; there was something about her that reminded him of Sam Aylward, though there was no physical resemblance at all. When she spoke there was a soft drawl to her words:

"Call *me* a Crone, and you're toast, *bukra* boy."

Rudi didn't know what a *bukra* was, but he suspected the word—she prounced it as *bookra*—wasn't a compliment.

He brought the back of his right hand to his brows.

"As you wish, Wise One," he said—which was just another name for the eldest of the Three.

"Damn, but it's annoying to be just a person again when you're used to being an archetype. Or vice versa. I suppose we had to. I feel like someone has squeezed me down into a can of Coke."

She looked at her own hands, flexing the fingers as if the sensation were unfamiliar.

"Marian, how long have we known each other?" the blond girl said, a soft purling lilt in her tones.

"Forty-seven years, or untold billions, depending on how you define *we* and *know*."

"And either way you're *still* a grouch."

She smiled at Rudi. "And they called me Deer Dancer, in my day. I died three thousand years before your birth, on another turn of the Wheel. I was the Maiden sacrifice, and I was the Mother who loves, and in my age I tossed silver hair to dance down the Moon. Now I wear this face of Her once more, for a little while."

Two ravens soared down from the branches and landed on one of the logs that flanked the fire, preening and grooming themselves. Somewhere a wolf howled. Sparks drifted upward, into boughs underlit by the flames, towards stars larger and brighter-colored than any he'd seen before; yet that paled beside the shining glory of a full moon. Despite the darkness, what he could see was hard-edged, somehow more *definite* than any vision by the light of common day.

If the trees had spoken, he would not have been surprised. He did not feel as if he dreamed; rather that he had *woken*, as if he had been drifting beneath the sea all his life and now had plunged upward like a leaping dolphin into the shock of air and light.

Rudi made reverence; then he stood erect, his arms crossed on his chest.

"Why am I here, Ladies?" he asked bluntly. "When last I remember I was on a task of some urgency."

"You are here to understand, a little," the Mother said. "We have to come towards you in forms you can grasp so that we can talk at all; but that limits Us."

"Of course," he said. "How can a man tell all his mind to a child, or a God to a man? What *can* you tell me?"

"What did I tell you about magic, child of my heart?"

Many things, he thought. *But . . .*

"That it doesn't stop being magic when you understand it?"

She nodded. "Then *see*."

Darkness; a nothingness in which he floated, nothingness so complete that even *emptiness* was absent and duration itself had not yet begun. A point of light, and existence twisting as it expanded and the arrow of time sprang from the string, soaring upward. Darkness that swelled, dense and hot and pregnant with Being, and then a flash of light as suns fell in upon themselves and lit. They burned with a glow that illuminated curtains of red and yellow fire, structures so vast that worlds would be less than grains of sand amongst them. Stars and galaxies flying apart from each other. Darkness again, as they dwindled into distance. Suns turned swollen and red and guttered out, or exploded in cataclysmic violence that faded into cankered knots of twisted space. Those boiled away in turn. Darkness more absolute than imagination could encompass, as the stuff of matter itself decayed into absence. Darkness without end, for nothing was different from nothing and nowhere was anyplace and everywhere.

"What does that remind you of?" his mother's voice asked.

He blinked back to something *like* the waking world, where light flickered ruddy on tree bark.

"It's . . . it's like the way Sandra Arminger sees the world. From what I picked up over the years in what you might be callin' her unguarded moments. Dead, in a way. Everything moving on its own, without spirit. Grand and glorious and wonderful, but . . . empty. And we gone like a candle flame when we die."

He blinked alarm. "You're not saying that's *true*, are you now?"

She smiled gently at him, and indicated their surroundings. He nodded, taking the point, and she spoke:

"No. But once it was, until it was *made* to be different. What did"—she looked up at the ravens—"a certain old gentleman tell you once about history and time?"

He blinked again; that night on the mountainside was far distant in miles and months, but it wasn't the sort of thing you forgot. Even if you'd been dreaming a vision while your wasted body lay on the edge of death. He repeated what those deep tones had so cryptically revealed:

"Fact becomes history; history becomes legend; legend becomes myth. Myth turns again to the beginning and creates itself. The figure for time isn't an arrow; that is illusion, just as the straight line is. Time is a serpent."

After a moment he went on: "Was *that* truth? The whole truth?"

"Yes. No."

The figure who bore his mother's semblance smiled sympathetically as she denied him certainty. The blond maiden spoke: "It's so hard to say this in words—"

"But hey, you'll give it a try, 'dapa," the black woman said sardonically.

The Maiden tossed her fair head and said: "Then *see* again."

His body dropped away, and once again he floated in nothingness. The point of light, and the same eon-upon-eon passage from light to dark. But this time a light was born in the last darkness, and it *looked* at him.

"That is Mind," the Mother whispered. "Wisdom. Wisdom itself, that brought together all knowledge of all that ever was."

"Hope," the blond Maiden added. "Love."

"That's *us*," the black figure of the Wise One said.

"Including you. Many times removed. Mo' removed than you can imagine. More than we can say in words—"

"You keep *saying* that, but you speak in words none-theless!" Rudi said, exasperated. "And it's more ignorant I am afterwards than ever I was before!"

"Then *see*," the Three said together.

This time the perspective was different. More abstract; he strained to see pattern, and meaning, but for a long moment all was chaos. Then order appeared. Instead of the point of light, there were two great sheets of . . . Being. Rippling through spaces in which whole universes of stars would be less than one kernel of barley in an ocean, like the banners of divinity flying on the ramparts of the Western Gate. The sheets drifted towards each other, and in that contact was born the light he had seen at the Beginning of his twin visions.

But there was a difference. Something passed from one cycle to the next. Something tiny, yet containing *every-thing*, and from that all changed as existence spread out again.

"Mind," his mother, all Mothers, said. "The universe births life. Life creates Mind. Mind encompasses that which bore it blindly, spreads through all the stuff of matter and makes a new Heaven and a new Earth. One in which from its beginnings through all time life is no accident, and is not doomed to death forever, but instead is transformed. To return upon itself once more and give Itself birth."

"And *now* there is a God," the Wise One said.

He fell through singing veils of light, struggling with awe and anger at himself, that he could not grasp the concepts roaring by him like dragons. Then he stood be-fore the fire again.

"Is Godhood many, or one?" the Mother said.

"Both," Rudi replied. "Both at once."

"She is all things." The Maiden nodded. A sigh. "And so, He is divided."

"Your friend the padre would say there was war in Heaven," the Wise One added. "He's not wrong, either. Don't mistake this you're seeing for the *only* truth."

"The Cutters!" he said suddenly. "As above, so below. Sure, and if there's war here, there must be so above."

The three nodded. The Mother spoke:

"Not exactly. In the stuff of Mind, there is . . . it's more like arguing with yourself than a fight between Good and Evil. Would you say a tilled tamed field is best, or a wilderness unbound and unguarded, living only by its own law?"

Rudi blinked. "Why . . . both, of course. How could either be *best*? Both are needed for the wholeness of things. Humankind is there to be the guardians of it; to tend, to take what they need, but not to take all."

"Yet some long for order; for the hedged garth, for the tame-bred kine, for the richness of the grafted fruit. Some long for the wolf's howl. Some would have the universe unfold as it will, and run to its ending as matter itself decrees; others would take matter up into the stuff of Mind."

"Submission against structure," the Maiden said.

"Not a fight for us, unless you mean inner conflict and that happy therapeutic horseshit," the Wise One snorted. "But it's sure enough a fight at *your* level, boy! One between Good and Evil, or Us and Them, which is close enough for government work."

"You need have no doubt I'll fight," Rudi said grimly. "Whether I may win or no. The Cutters . . . the Cutters and the Power behind them claim all humankind and the world as well, and say none of us may breathe or believe save as they permit. If a *God* said that to me, a God with the sun in His left hand and the moon in His right, I would dispute it by the sword. Or my fingernails, if they were all I had."

"Good man! And it's a fight you'd better win, 'cause we can't do it for you. Not without undoing ourselves and more worlds than this."

Rudi nodded his head, a single brief jerk. He wasn't sure of much, but he was suddenly certain that the *person* whose appearance that Power bore had also been a warrior once.

"You've shown me matters great and terrible, Ladies," he said. "But . . . one thing I *do* know, and always did. This Earth of ours, however bright and dear and grand to us, is but the smallest fleck in all that is; and you've shown me that that All is vaster by far than I knew. Yet here the Powers are contending for our allegiance as if we were the sum of things. Why *us?*"

The Three looked at him. The Maiden spoke gently:

"Because here is where Mind begins. There has to be a one first place . . . and this is that one. From it, all else springs."

"Fermi," the Wise One added. "Not to be too paradoxical."

The Mother cast an exasperated sidelong glance. "Don't stray from the issue just because you're limited enough again that you *can* be distracted, Marian."

To Rudi: "It *nearly* didn't happen here either. Mind is a weapon as well as a blessing, and its power is terrible even when newborn."

"The Wanderer spoke of a child with a knife, or with fire."

She nodded. "Terrible *especially* when newborn."

They faded before his eyes. For a moment he saw the

island, but with no cover save a few crumbled ruins of brick and stone, a bank of sand that *glowed* with heat. Hills of salt lay where the ocean should have been, save for pools in the distance that seethed in a bubbling roil that would end only when they were gone forever. The air lay thick, hazy, hot, and motionless.

"A thousand times ten thousand times that was the end," the Maiden said. "Or others that were worse."

"What could be worse than *that?*"

The same landscape, but the very air was gone somehow; the sea had turned to ice, that sublimed outward into the outer dark beneath a sky that crawled with steely energies and strange, powerful engines. Then another vision, where water still curled on the sandy beach beneath a clear blue sky where birds flew, but their patterns were mathematics precise beyond his comprehension. A man walked between buildings that were perfect, and empty. He turned to look at Rudi for an instant, and where his eyes should have been were silvery tendrils that waved and sought.

"We could agree on stopping *those* histories," the Mother said, as the campfire returned. "Edging them out, cycle upon cycle, until they vanish in implausibility."

"Yet the Others would not let us do much more," the Maiden said, sadness in her voice. "What we did . . . was something so terrible that only a greater terror made it possible to think it."

The Mother nodded. "All we could do while Mind was divided . . . was take this island out of its year, so that it could then reach across the spiral and make the Change. The Change gives you time, no more, as the island was given time. Time to learn, so that when you regain the powers taken from you they'll be used properly. How the future of this turn on the Wheel is shaped . . . what *we* become . . . that is up to you. You youngsters. You are the *seed* of God. We can turn through time—we have traveled the endless coil—but we cannot do more than help, and open possibilities."

The Maiden scowled. "The Others can. They *take*, because they care less for the damage they do, they who serve entropy. So we have made the Sword for you, to sever their power and show humankind the truth of things. That much *we* can do in this turn of the Wheel, without breaking reality asunder with our contentions. All the rest is your burden."

Rudi took a deep breath. "I will bear it."

There was a glint of tears in the Mother's eyes as she spoke with a trembling tenderness:

"Then bear what you must, O my child, my child."

The Maiden's warmth, a scented flower meadow in spring:

"Do what you must, beloved."

The Wise One's sternness, like rock and iron:

"*Become* what you must, to serve the world's need."

And he was . . . *elsewhere*.

The others saw him as he stumbled down the stairs, bleeding from nose and ears and eyes and mouth. The sheathed form of the Sword lay across his palms. He met their eyes, and choked out:

"Remember. Remember, all of you. Most of all you, Matti, *anamchara*, beloved."

Mathilda's voice was infinitely gentle: "Remember what, my darling?"

"That I was a man, before I was King. Remember for me, when I forget."

His hand closed on the black double-lobed hilt, and

the moonfire in the opal glowed. He drew the Sword, thrust it high.

And screamed as pain beyond all bearing ripped through him like white fire, turning his body to a thing of ash and smoke.

He screamed, and *knew*.

EPILOGUE

BD breathed out, and in, and out, and in, her chest vibrating with the deep-toned sounds of the power raising, breath steaming in the chilly air. That was full of the mountainside forest scents, the musty smell of damp earth and the spice of fir resin, wet wool and the sputtering torches. Every one of her sixty-odd years ached in her joints, from today and from the hard travel south from the Kyklos villages. Mist drifted across the steep forests and the outthrust knee that held the *nemed*, merging into the clouds above.

This Imbolc ritual had given her no peace. As many as could make the journey to the *nemed* had come, and it was crowded, almost enough to jostle her; she was far from the only non-Mackenzie. The dim late-afternoon sunlight slanted through the circle of great bare-limbed oak trees in shafts, picking out people in hooded robes of many colors, though white and yellow dominated. It was Imbolc and the rising of the sun, the lengthening of the days that started the Wheel of the Year anew.

Beginnings, she thought. *Start of term for Moon Schools, babes brought for wiccaning, apprenticeships started. But not this time.*

On the roughly chiseled altar a large sheep's milk feta perched on top of the huge round of braided bread. This was the only time of the year when sheep's milk was used to make cheese, for the ewes went dry when the lambs were weaned. The crackle of the *teine eigin*, the need fire in the bowl-shaped stone hearth, gave a little warmth.

Sternly BD brought her mind back to the chant and the purpose of the power raising. It was possible to lose oneself in the chant, but once concentration was lost, so was power. And power was their need. The strength of the CUT to influence people who were in any way corrupt had left every realm in the countries of the Meeting—

Montival, she reminded herself

—in Montival exposed. Castles were falling through treachery. The CUT's ability to defile was like tentacles of poison stretching into minds, like threads of mold in spoiled bread.

Thank you, Athena, that some can detect their High Seekers. And fight them. Gray-eyed One, Maiden of the Spear, Defender of the Polis, aid!

In her mind's eye she could see the spiral, the cone of power rising. It wobbled, dangerously. She shook her head and took a deep breath, projecting the *ahhhh* in deeper tones than the people around her. The lower sound caught, spread, humming through bone and blood until her very teeth vibrated with it. Folk focused on the task at hand. She hadn't been the only one distracted by fear.

We are losing this war.

Juniper was in the center. She held her rowan staff overhead, turning deosil, the staff—the distaff—taking up the power, revolving widdershins above her head. BD focused on the silver raven, perched on the head of the staff; inwardly she felt a sudden spurt of homely laughter at what a real bird would do, held horizontal like that.

Flap his great wings and go: crawk! she thought.

In her mind's eye the power was stabilizing, the buildup almost complete. The air felt heavy with it, like the tension before a thunderstorm; she could smell the tingle in the air, feel it prickling the little hairs along her forearms and on her neck. From her usual position in the East, as Apollon's Pythia, she shot a glance across at Judy, who also was watching. Judy caught her glance and nodded. They signaled the other two guardians and raised their hands. Voices soared from the deep tone of the *ahhhh*, rising to a banshee shriek as the Mackenzies followed their lead.

Birds and small animals broke from cover, flew and ran, rustling the branches and tall grass around. Juniper twisted the staff in a complicated figure-eight pattern, raising it high and then bringing the heel to the ground with a thump that dug it in several inches through the yielding turf and soft earth beneath. She ran her hands up the staff gathering the melded power and flung them up, palms to the sky.

"Light!" she cried. "Gods most high! Lugh of the Sun! Brigid of the Healing Flame! Give us Light! Lugh, help us *see*! Lugh, help us see into hearts! Lugh, God of *Light*!"

And Juniper's palms glowed, two shafts of light cutting upward through the wan afternoon. They rose and merged in a twisting column. The dim gray turned bright—just on the edge of pain, but turning every twig and blade of grass into a maze of glittering diamond for an instant. Not since the old world fell had she seen such brightness, but it surpassed those ancient wonders. A moan went through the crowd, and as one they dropped to a knee. A few went on their bellies and beat their heads on the turf.

She *could* see, into the hearts of trees, into the roots of the mountains, into herself. But nothing was dream-like. It was more *real* than that, hard, sharp-edged, definite, each mote and lingering sere yellow leaf and fir needle so intensely itself that she could have wept for wonder.

That's not a vision! her mind gibbered, and she felt her body shake, commanded it to be still and her throat to let breath pass.

The light was within her, but it was also without.

Not just *a vision. It's not a metaphor. I'm not just seeing it with the Inner Eye. That's* photons, *by the Gods, as real as sunlight or a burning torch! Apollon Helios, Lord of Light, be with us now!*

The light soared and spun, broadening into a wall that stretched into the clouds and moved eastward, fading as it went. Instant by instant it swelled, and then was gone— gone from the body's eyes, at least.

Juniper's head was tipped back, her mouth fallen open, her eyes black with the dilated pupils. Before BD could react pain hit, a pain she had only felt once before, on the day of the Change. And a voice echoed, like the wind in crags, like the growth of flowers, roaring like a lion and as silent as the fall of windless snow:

Artos holds the Sword of the Lady! The Sun Lord comes, the son of Bear and Raven! The High King comes, as foretold! Guardian of my sacred Wood, and Law! His people's strength, and the Lady's sword!

Fast and sharp, the pain was gone. Juniper brought trembling hands down to her chest level and looked at them, swaying and beginning to buckle at the knees. BD and Judy and the other High Priestesses moved forward. Nigel was faster; his fox mask pushed up on his head, he snatched her into his arms, looking at the tears flowing down her cheeks. The staff cracked across his cheekbone, unnoticed.

"Did . . . you see that?" she whispered. "Did anyone else see *that*, or am I mad?"

"I saw. And I'm a confirmed skeptic, remember? Or I was. You're not in the least mad. It's far stranger than that."

She raised her hands to him, quivering as they touched his face. "They're just my own worn hands. That's all they are!"

"That's what they were, my dear," he said with tender denial. "But that's not *all* they are. Not anymore."

NEW IN HARDCOVER
from

New York Times bestselling author
S.M. Stirling

THE HIGH KING
OF MONTIVAL

With *The Sword of the Lady*, Rudi Mackenzie's destiny was determined. Now he returns to Montival in the Pacific Northwest, where he will face the legions of the Prophet. To achieve victory, Rudi must assemble a coalition of those who had been his enemies a few months before and forge them into an army that will rescue his homeland.

Only then will Rudi be able to come to terms with how the Sword has changed him, as well as the world, and assume his place as Artos, High King of Montival...

R0049

New York Times bestselling author

S. M. Stirling

First in a brand-new series

A TAINT IN
THE BLOOD

A Novel of the Shadowspawn

Eons ago, Homo Lupens ruled the earth. Possessing extraordinary powers, they were the source of all of the myths and legends of the uncanny. And though their numbers have been greatly reduced, they exist still—though not as purebreds.

Adrian Breze is one such being. Wealthy and reclusive, he is more Shadowspawn than human. But he rebelled against his own kind, choosing to live as an ordinary man. Now, to save humanity, he must battle the dark forces of the world—including those in his own blood...

**Available wherever books are sold or at
penguin.com**